Nemo Deum Vidit
—The Inhabitants

Nemo Deum Vidit —The Inhabitants

First Edition Published: April 23, 2025

Author: Choi Ji-heui
Publisher: Lee Kil-an
Publisher Location: Sejong Publishing Company

Address: 12, Heukgyo-ro 71beon-gil, Jung-gu, Busan, South Korea
(Bosudong 2-ga)
Phone: 463-5898, 253-2213~5
Fax: 248-4880
Email: sjpl5898@daum.net
Publication Registration Number: No. 02-01-96

ISBN: 979-11-5979-761-3 03810

Price: 35,000 KRW / 24.9 USD

All rights reserved. No part of this book may be copied, reproduced, transmitted, or distributed in any form or by any means without the prior written permission of the author, except as permitted by the terms of purchase or applicable copyright law. Any unauthorized use or distribution of this text constitutes a violation of the author's rights and may result in legal consequences.

Nemo Deum Vidit
—The Inhabitants

The Novel Based on Real Stories

Choi Ji-heui

Translated Korean by Jeon Young-ook
Edited by the author with assistance of ChatGPT

SEJONG

Introduction

We are all *inhabitants* scattered upon this earth!

The main title of this book, *Nemo Deum Vidit*, is a phrase from the Gospel of John. It means, "No one has ever seen God." Humans, as mere inhabitants of the Earth, must live meaningfully and do their best to thrive. What is the meaning of all life on Earth? Where does the will of God reveal itself in our lives?

This book seeks to portray a journey of searching for God through the traces left behind by those who lived before the author.

What lingers in the place where a life was lived and passed? How will future generations sense the struggles and joys of those who came before them as time flows on? Where have the brilliance and vitality of life vanished? Is it all, in the end, just a fleeting moment in the vastness of time, leaving behind only a trace of dust?

The suffering in human life often stems from societal conventions rooted in one's environment and from conflicts within the family. In their homeland—the "boneland" where their roots run deep—individuals strive to find meaning along the ever-shifting currents of time and society. Amid this struggle, some look to God, yearning for a glimmer of hope.

This story is based on the real-life experiences of the Gyeongju Choi family, spanning four generations (1926 - 2001) in Sancheong, Gyeongsangnam-do, South Korea. This book explores where true personal value lies within family dynamics that reflect Korean cultural identity and the painful transformation of social customs.

The story spans 31 chapters, beginning with the sorrows of a family with four sons and three daughters, born to one father and three mothers. Even as they endure the loss of their children, the parents cling to God's promise of new life, persevering through an endless cycle of pain. They, too—like all other living creatures—knew that they were merely transient beings, inhabitants passing through this earth.

Choi Hong-seon, born in 1881, was the 28th eldest grandson of the Sangseo-gong branch of the Gyeongju Choi clan. A devoted father, he championed equal access to wealth and education for all his children, regardless of gender. With a profound love for humanity, he rose above social divisions, believing that just as time is naturally accepted, so too should be the existence of God.

Il-seop, proud and sensitive, could not endure a moment of humiliation and took his own life before his father, Hong-seon. Yet his wife, Bok-hee, carried on with quiet strength, embracing her roles as a wife, matriarch, and mother of seven. The story begins with Bok-hee's marriage in 1926 and unfolds primarily through her memories.

Hong-seon's first daughter, Ki-soon, born to his second wife, Lady Hwang, excelled in her studies at a prestigious Japanese medical college but was unable to graduate. Upon returning to Korea, she endured the pain of a broken engagement and struggled with mental illness. Yet she resisted both societal and familial constraints, determined to survive as a woman of her time.

Se-joon, Hong-seon's great-grandson—a gentle poet and, for a time, a psychiatrist—lived with deep devotion to protecting his mother, Jong-hee, until his untimely death.

In the latter half of the story, beginning with Chapter 20, the narrative reaches its core, focusing on the theme *Nemo Deum Vidit* ("No one has ever seen God" - John 1:18). It shifts to the trials of Soo-gon, Bok-hee's nephew, and his family. Despite immense suffering—the disappearance of their second daughter, the sudden death of their son Yo-han, and their youngest daughter's decade-long coma—Soo-gon and his wife, Hye-young, devout Christians, hold firmly to their belief that God has always watched over them. The arrival of new life in their family brings renewal and salvation, reaffirming their faith that, even in the midst of pain, they have always been in God's care.

The flow of a family's bloodline and surname is never merely a coincidence. When coincidences repeat, they become a destiny to be fulfilled.—The Author.

Contents

01 Earth, Water, Fire, and Wind 15
Autumn 1952: The New House∗—The Story Carried by the Wind

02 The Head House of Choi Clan 31
1956: The Big House—Birth: The Continuation of Karma?

03 *Gakseoli* 51
1957: The Big House—The Bright and Dark Sides

04 Bok-hee, a New Mistress of the Estate 69
1926: The Big House—Three Mothers-in-Law

05 The Choi Household 87
From the 1920s Onward: The Big House, the New House, and the Saemmy House in Sancheong—Surnames and Characters

06 Hong-seon, His Fate and Fortune 111
1943–1945: The Big House—The Family Motto

07 A Child Chasing After Birds 131
Until 1944: The New House—My Father's Legal Wife

08 The Posthumous Child 153
1945: The Big House—Those Left Behind

09 Ki-soon's Marriage 169
Summer 1945: The New House—The Unconcealable Nature

10 A New Beginning Brought by Pain 187
1945–1947: The New House—Struggling to Mend

11 The Korean War I 205
1950–1956: Seoul, Sancheong, and Busan
—Ki-hoon's Pain and Marriage

| 12 | The Korean War II | 229 |

1950: The Big House—Lee-seop's family

| 13 | The Korean War III | 251 |

1950: Seoul and the Regions Near Sancheong
—A Fragile Man and a Shameless Woman

| 14 | The Footprints of Destiny | 271 |

1950−1952: Seoul and Sancheong—Children of the New House

| 15 | Ki-soon's Return to Hometown | 299 |

June 1952: Tokyo and Sancheong—The Fading Memories

| 16 | Freeloading | 317 |

Autumn 1952: Busan and Sancheong—The Family of Min-ja

| 17 | *Salpuri* — Exorcism | 339 |

Winter 1952: The Gyeongho River—Plunging

| 18 | Blood and Bone I | 355 |

1954: The New House—Degeneration

| 19 | Blood and Bone II | 369 |

1955: The Big House and the New House—Instinct and Habit

| 20 | The Child in Silk Beoseon | 387 |

1960: The Big House
—A Web of Thoughts Weighing on the Scale of Time

| 21 | The Shadow of the Past | 409 |

1961: The New House—The Wind of Convention

| 22 | The Death of the Lady Hwang | 435 |

1963: The New House—The Edge of Time

23	Ki-soon, Flying as a Bird 1968: The New House—Shards of a Mirror	447
24	Bok-hee's 60th Birthday Party 1970: The House of Ki-hoon in Busan—Blessing and Ill Fate	465
25	The Eldest Grandson of the Family, Bone or Entrusted? Since 1971: Busan—The Sons of Ki-hoon	487
26	Missing of the Mi-young 1975: Masan, Busan, and Sancheong—Soo-gon and Hye-young's Hardships	509
27	An Unreachable Hand Since 1978: Busan and Seoul—First Love	527
28	Those Who Erect Their Own Tombstones 1979–1981: Seoul, Busan, and Masan—Ignition of Desire	549
29	The Man and the Woman 1980–1982: Busan and Seoul—False Expectations	565
30	True Betrayal 1983: Busan, Seoul, and Masan—Greed and Emptiness	585
31	*Nemo Deum Vidit* — No One Has Ever Seen God 1990–2001: Busan, Seoul, and Masan—Hope and Conviction	611

The appearance of Choi Hong-seon in his late 60s

Choi Hong-seon (Family Tree)

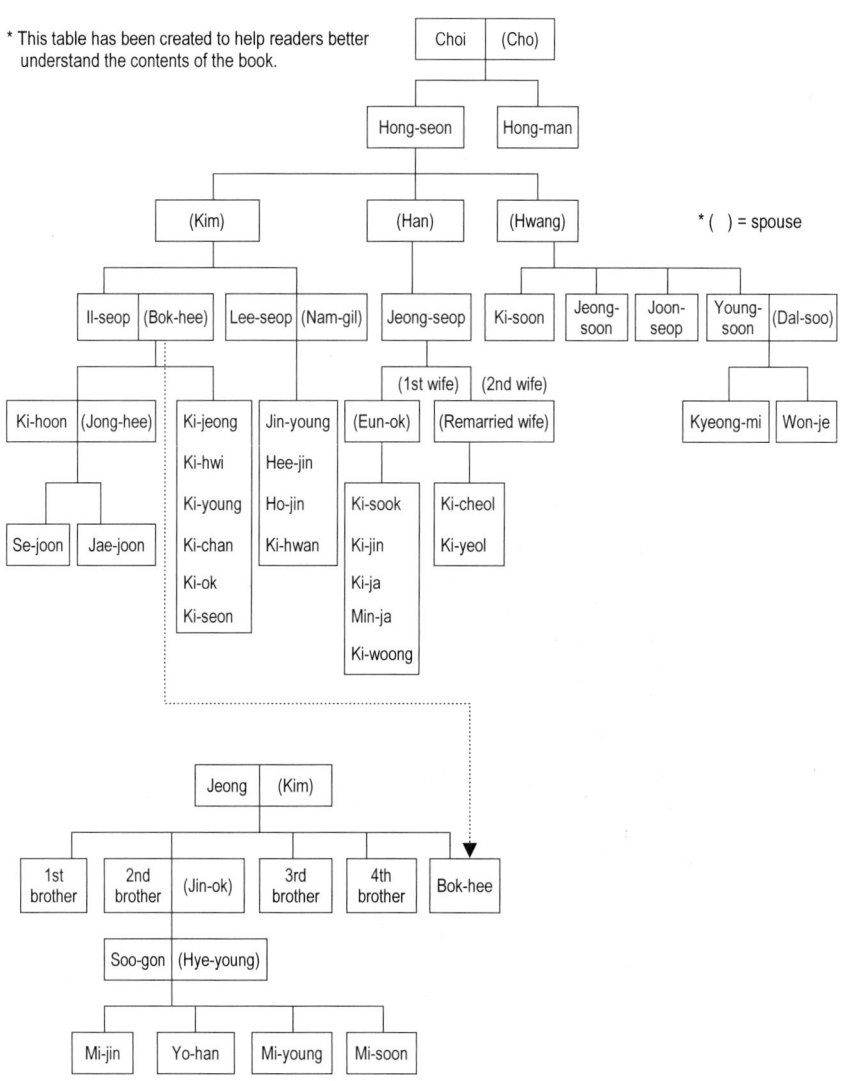

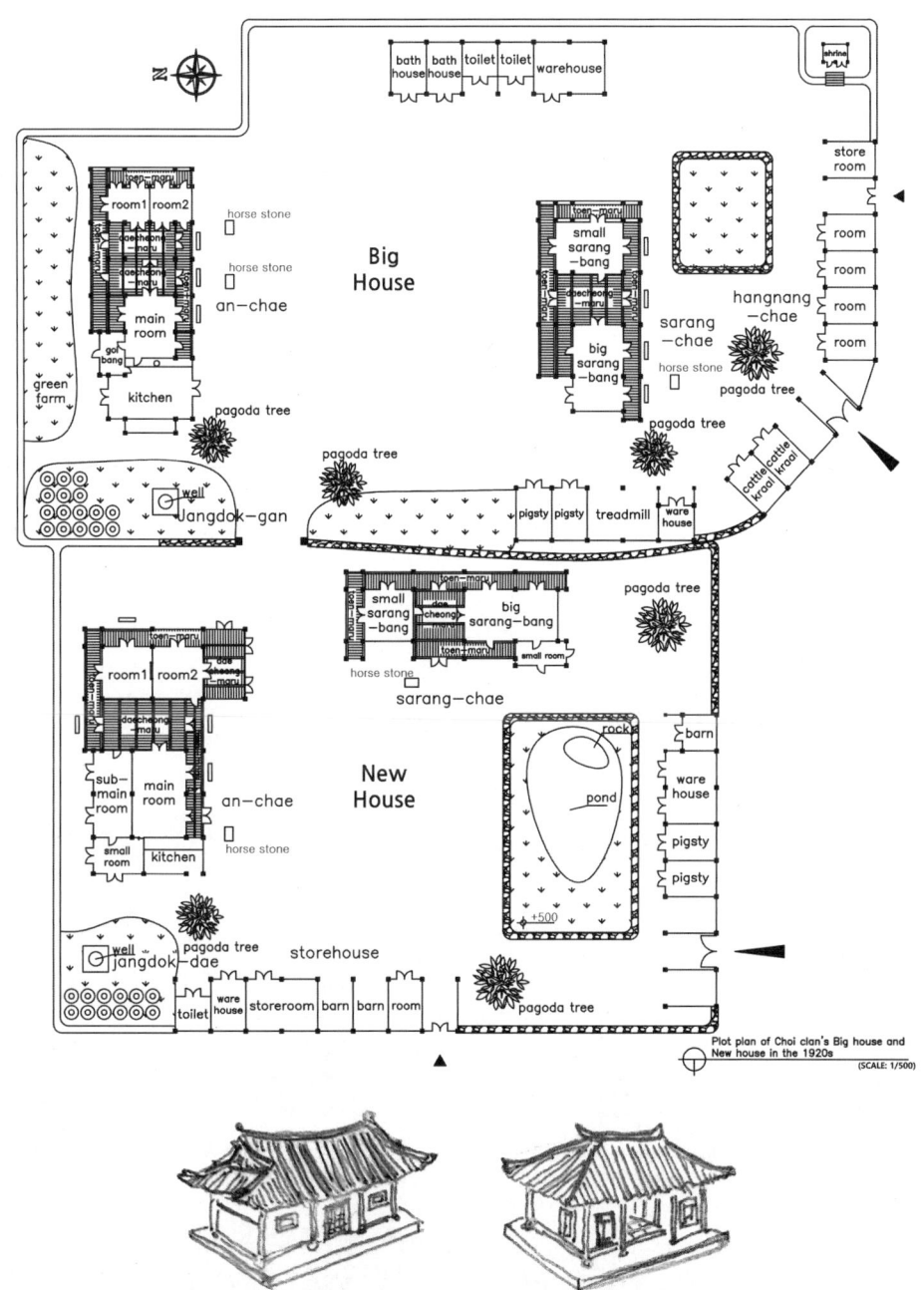

Hipped and Gabled Roof *(Paljak)* and Hipped Roof *(Ujingak)*

01
Earth, Water, Fire, and Wind

Autumn 1952: The New House*
—The Story Carried by the Wind

Earth·Water·Fire·Wind (Oil Painting on Canvas, No. 20)

In a small room with a low wooden desk, a woman was crouching in front of the desk, spreading colored paper onto the floor and carefully selecting pieces. She folded square sheets of colored paper diagonally and then cut along two-thirds of the diagonal with scissors. The corners of the paper were folded inward, leaving a hole in the center, and the red paper was attached to an L-shaped stick. Another stick had blue paper attached to it, and in the same way, sticks with yellow, green, and white paper were made. They were pinwheels.

She gazed at them intently, with a hint of uncertainty in her eyes. To ensure the pinwheels spun freely, she created a small gap between the stick and the paper, securing it with *changhoji*[1]. This gave the paper enough room to catch the wind and spin effortlessly.

Remnants of her work lay scattered beneath the desk and across the floor in the small room. Wooden chopsticks, repurposed as L-shaped sticks, mingled with squares of vivid red, orange, yellow, green, blue, navy blue, and purple paper. Pieces of resilient Joseon *changhoji*, which were used to secure the sticks and paper, along with a paste pot made of flour, completed the scene of creative chaos.

After some time, the woman rose and carefully placed the newly crafted pinwheels into a small, round bamboo tray. Grasping several in her hand, she stepped out into the yard. She paused before the garden—a mound of earth and stones stacked high between the *an-chae* (the women's quarters of the *Hanok*, the main living quarters) and the *sarang-chae* (the men's quarters of the *Hanok*). It stood like a sentinel in the yard.

Though referred to as a garden, it was more like a mound of soil, with

---

1) Changhoji: Changhoji is a Korean traditional paper, also known as hanji, made by boiling and refining the bark of the karinaki tree.— Based on Naver's Korean dictionary.

small stones carefully stacked to about the height of an average person's waist, which rose from the courtyard. At its center lay a small pool, nestled within the soil—a humble pond. Originally, in the 1920s, it was once a proper pond and garden, but after the Korean War, some parts of it collapsed.

The woman circled the garden, looking for patches of bare ground where no flowers or shrubs were planted. After carefully choosing her locations, like a child exploring the garden for the first time, she positioned the pinwheels, one by one. After placing each pinwheel, she gently and reverently placed the flat of her hand on the ground as she whispered to herself, "*Earth.*" Eventually, all the pinwheels in the tray stood like vibrant flowers along the garden's edge. As the *wind* stirred, the pinwheels whirled, filling the air with a soft, enchanting hum.

The woman, hearing the gentle spinning sound, knelt and scratched the soil around the base of each wooden chopstick pinwheel with a small trowel she had held earlier in her left hand. She gathered the loose earth, pressing it firmly with her palms to secure the pinwheels. Murmuring to herself, "You have to step on the soil several times to make it firm ground," she repeatedly patted the soil with her palms, ensuring the pinwheels stood firmly. Her hands moved rhythmically in a tender, persistent effort to anchor her delicate creations in the earth.

But upon closer inspection, as she planted the pinwheels in the garden, her feet, still wrapped in white *beoseon*—traditional Korean padded socks—but without shoes, moved quietly across the soil.

Perhaps she had stepped directly from the room into the courtyard.

And then, as if having accomplished some grand endeavor, she lifted her foot in the garden and proceeded to softly tiptoe with her heels slightly raised, as though treading upon a plush carpet. It was the season when winter's breath began to touch the earth. The island-like garden, adorned with clusters of low shrubs, chrysanthemums, and scattered wildflowers, resembled a patchwork of nature's splendor.

She moved away from the trees and made her way towards a small pond, its edges meticulously crafted from upright stones, nestled at the garden's heart, where a serene pool surrounded by carefully placed stones awaited her.

Meanwhile, the pinwheels she had made and positioned so carefully around the edges of the garden flapped their little paper sails in a colorful display, still producing a whirring sound as they spun. She cupped her left hand around her ear, as if trying to amplify the sound of the spinning pinwheels. Then Ki-soon said,

"The pinwheels spin with the force of the *wind*. They are like *storytellers, bringing me news of those who have already died but who remain invisible to me now.*"

She strained her ears against the keening wind, trying to discern words and their meaning from the sound of the spinning, whirring pinwheels.

However, with her attention so focused on the sound of the little pinwheels, the woman lost her balance and fell face-first into the small pond at the centre of the garden. The *beoseon* she wore, already wet, offered little grip on the gravel surrounding the pond. A light drizzle had been falling intermittently for some time now, but she might not have noticed. She seemed unaware that her beoseon-clad feet were damp, absorbed entirely by the sound of the spinning pinwheels, oblivious to everything else.

The shallow pond, dug into the earth at the very heart of the garden, was slightly longer than twice the height of an average person. Though it was barely knee-deep, it was still deep enough to be called a pond. Small pebbles lined the edge and bottom of the pond, and a few goldfish could be seen hiding among the aquatic plants, their heads tucked away in the greenery.

As she slipped, her face, shoulders, and chest became drenched, and she instinctively reached out, desperately grasping for something to grab. It was sheer survival instinct. The bottom of the pond was covered with a layer of small pebbles, and some of these had also been scattered around the edges and were coated with a slippery green sludge.

Yet, even in the midst of such a crisis, the woman did something that felt strangely out of place. When she saw the shimmering goldfish darting away from her, hiding among the aquatic plants and weeds, she reached out as if to catch them with her hands, like a child chasing after scattered objects.

She barely managed to grasp the large rock in the middle of the pond, which had somehow remained intact even during the bombing. Luckily, the rock, which was more than a meter high, had a curved, protruding section. She clung to it with all her strength. With a sigh of relief, she adjusted her position and tried to lean against the broad surface of the rock.

As she rested against it, her face was reflected in the water of the pond. As she peered into the water, she suddenly cried out in surprise—a small, urgent sound filled with alarm and fear. Ki-soon said,

"Who is that? Who's looking at me?"

With a look of fear etched on her face, she cast her gaze around, but there was no one in sight. Only the sporadic whispers of the turning pinwheels reached her ears. Some of them, drenched by the relentless rain, had wilted, no longer spinning even when the wind stirred, and instead emitted a faint, trembling murmur as the dampened paper fluttered weakly.

She listened intently, as if trying to clutch at the elusive sound of the pinwheels, but suddenly, a profound emptiness swept over her, and her head drooped, as if weighed down by the heavy stillness around her. She stood there for a few moments with her back against the rock. The weeds whispered around her as she folded her knees and slowly descended into the relatively shallow water once more, her gaze fixed upon her reflection in the pond.

She sank into the pool as gently as blades of grass falling to the earth, and a quiet realization dawned upon her. Her eyes widened, and a smile slowly formed on her lips. She said,

"Oh! It was you. Yutaka!"

Gradually, she let her gaze soften, no longer fixed below the surface, and sank into the water, utterly spent. Though the changing season should have made the pond's water cold, she only smiled, seemingly immune to its touch. With a serene expression, she gently submerged her face and head into the shallow embrace of the pond, seeming to seek a moment of quiet immersion. Ki-soon said,

"Yutaka, do you remember? Aomori, the ryokan[2]. I tried to go with you..."

Or at least, it seemed as if she had said that.

Before she knew it, she had sunk even deeper into the water. She extended her legs, pressing her shoulders against the pond's bottom, and rested her head against the rock's submerged base, surrendering herself completely to the tranquil depths.

The gentle drizzle soon ceased, and a soft breeze began to stir once more. With her eyes closed and her body immersed, she could distinctly hear the pinwheels spinning—a sound akin to a whirling whistle.

As she moved her head in the water, following the steady currents, the sound rose and fell, varying with the direction of the *wind* and the movement of her hair. The woman opened her eyes, wide and childlike in the water, and muttered to herself, "Hey, watch this! It's the *wind*! You remain still and lifeless until the *wind* comes and brings you back to life! Isn't that right?"

She opened her mouth wide and stretched out her arms to the sides like wings, drawing in a deep breath. It was as if she were inhaling all the air around her, taking deep, powerful breaths. Then, Ki-soon said,

"See how the pinwheel comes to life only when the *wind* blows? Must I perish to resurrect those who died before me? The truth is, I feel nothing

---

[2] A traditional Japanese inn: Usually with a communal bath and other public areas.—This information was written by the author.

for them — they are already gone. All around me, in my sight, within my being..."

Saying so, she soon closed her eyes. There was little movement. About twenty minutes later, the sound of a woman muttering was heard again.

"Sweetheart! Are you alive? It felt so natural, I had forgotten. Who are you? Mhm, I am..., it's me.

It's you too... like the air. The air has always been part of nature. I have always been too. As a member of this household, as a daughter, at least as a student, as a woman... yet no one believes I am alive now. No one speaks to me. Am I dead?

Then, whose voice is it that I hear when the pinwheel turns in the *wind*? Only the *wind* speaks to me... Is it only the souls of the dead riding the *wind* that talk to me? They would never lie!

But what the paper wings whisper as they spin obeys *the law of the wind*, and *once it goes, it never returns. They never say the same thing twice.*"

While Ki-soon was muttering to herself after having fallen into the pond, the sound of footsteps came from somewhere.

Yoo-sang[3], a man carrying a load of wood on his back, made his way from the servants' quarters of the New House* to the main building. Spotting her, he shouted in alarm, hastily dropped his load of wood, and rushed into the pond. He said,

"Oh, Big Mistress! What happened to you? You've fallen into the pond on a day like this! Why did you, who aren't even that strong, end up like this? Hurry, get on my back. It's starting to drizzle, and the east wind has been blowing since morning. Luckily, I came to bring you more

---

[3] Yoo-sang: Yoo is the family name of the senior manservant. During the Japanese Colonial Period (1910-1945), Koreans were required to adopt Japanese conventions regarding their forms of address and nomenclature. Mr. Yoo was addressed by the staff and residents of the estate—"Sang" meaning "Mister."—This information was written by the author.

firewood, or who knows what might have happened if I hadn't come here? What's going on here?"

Yoo-sang carried her on his back, treating her with the gentleness one might show to a child. He made his way to the main room of the main house (*an-chae*), gently guiding her inside. Then he shouted again, his voice booming loudly enough to be heard in the Big House* across from the New House*. Then, he shouted abruptly.

"Look! Look! Is anyone here? Hey, Jeom-rye in the Big House*! Lady Hwang! Where on earth is everyone? Why is this house so empty? If you can hear me, please come to the main room! We're in serious trouble!"

Then, he turned to Ki-soon, who lay on his back with her eyes closed. 'Your *beoseon* and clothes are drenched... You can't stay out here like this without anyone knowing. Where on earth has everyone in this house gone? How long have you been alone, Big Mistress? Oh no, this is really bad. Are we going to have to deal with another string of funerals?' He muttered these words to himself, anxiety evident in his voice.

As no one responded from either the Big House* or the New House*, he gently laid Ki-soon on the floor of the main room, treating her like a precious treasure, dripping wet. He then opened the closet, spreading a blanket and mattress on the floor. However, he couldn't lay her down there immediately; her clothes were soaked through. He needed to remove her wet garments first.

Despite the urgency, he hesitated to undress her, as she was a grown woman. Regardless of how the world had changed, "The distinction between the sexes" had to be maintained. In his haste, Yoo-sang placed his hand on Ki-soon's forehead and then on her chest, feeling a faint warmth beneath his fingers. Yoo-sang spoke to himself in a quiet voice, as if someone were around him.

"Oh my! In the midst of this bloody Korean War, where life itself teeters on the edge of preciousness and peril, why should the distinctions between the sexes matter? Should I not first save the one who has faced such horror? Removing the soaked clothes and warming her body should be my immediate concern. If we value life above all and time slips by, survival will give us the strength to carry on... Now, let me tend to the drenched garments of this Mistress"

After removing her outer skirt and jacket, and just as he was delicately taking off her underwear, he felt an inexplicable tremor in his hands. At that precise moment, the door to the main room was stealthily pushed open, and someone slipped inside. Yoo-sang, though he had done nothing wrong, leapt up in surprise.

When he lifted his gaze, he saw Jeom-rye, the young errand girl from the Big House*. She was a 14-year-old with braids on either side of her head, dressed in a black cotton skirt that reached her knees and a white cotton *jeogori*, the traditional Korean jacket. She said to Yoo-sang casually, as if without much thought.

"Hey, uncle Yoo, why are you staring at me with such wide eyes, looking so startled? How did Ki-soon, the Big Mistress of the New House*, come to this?"

As Jeom-rye's eyes wandered to the floor, she noticed Ki-soon's outer jacket already discarded, leaving only a damp undershirt clinging to her moist skin. The contours of her small, plump breasts were faintly visible through the sheer fabric. She could also see Yoo-sang's hands trembling ever so slightly.

Yoo-sang quickly covered Ki-soon's body with a thin blanket that was nearby. He said in a feeble tone.

"Jeom-rye! You startled me! Why are you only coming now? I carried the Big Mistress on my back after she fell into the pond, and I shouted so loudly for help. Why did you come so late? I was in such a hurry to get her out of these wet clothes.

But ... women's clothes, once soaked, are so difficult to remove. It took more effort than I expected. Now that I've caught my breath, please take over. Remove her clothes properly and warm her up. She seems to be alive ... I'll be going now."

Jeom-rye, as if trying to flee from the sudden event, quickly spoke to hide her startled reaction. "*Aje*[4])! I'm not strong enough to take off my Big lady's wet clothes. There's no one in this house or the neighboring one. Lady Hwang from the main room went to Jinju today to visit her aunt. Young-soon, the younger lady, might have gone to the house down the road to play, and I haven't seen her all morning. So you don't need to worry about anything strange—there's no one around to see. Please, save the Big Mistress, Ki-soon."

After catching sight of Jeom-rye's indifferent face, Yoo-sang steadied his trembling hands and slipped them under the blanket to remove Ki-soon's inner skirt. Though he anticipated that the inner skirt, being thinner, would be more difficult to take off than the outer one, it slid down surprisingly easily with a few firm tugs.

Leaving the task of removing her underwear to Jeom-rye, Yoo-sang then directed his attention to Ki-soon's *beoseon*. *Beoseon*, the Korean socks tightly fitted to her feet, seemed too challenging for the young Jeom-rye to handle, so Yoo-sang took it upon himself to remove them. Although he had already confirmed that she was breathing, Ki-soon remained collapsed, her eyes shut. Once more, Yoo-sang reassured himself by observing the gentle rise and fall of her slender chest.

The *beoseon* worn by Koreans were distinguished by their pointed, nose-like front. Despite being soaked, they maintained their proud shape, the curve of the *beoseon's nose* protruding visibly beneath the blanket. As Yoo-sang's eyes caught sight of this, his heart trembled, and tears welled up. Gently, he began to remove the muddy, wet *beoseon* from Ki-soon's small feet, his hands shaking with emotion.

Two years ago, during the winter when the Korean War erupted,

---

4) Aje: An alternative word for "Uncle" in the dialect of the Gyeongnam Province. It is generally used in place of "Mister" when the relationship is familiar.—This information was written by the author.

Yoo-sang's wife was found dead at the bottom of the Gyeongho River. Initially, he felt a fleeting sense of relief upon discovering her body, but the sight that greeted him in his yard was devastating. There, beneath a straw mat, lay his wife's bloated, waterlogged corpse, her body stiff and frozen from days spent submerged. Yet, her feet remained unchanged. Like Ki-soon, the Big Mistress, Yoo-sang's wife had worn white *beoseon* on her unusually small and delicate feet.

As Yoo-sang painstakingly removed the wet *beoseon* from Ki-soon's feet, she stirred, her body trembling. She muttered incoherently, her eyes fluttering open for a brief moment before closing again. Her lips moved as if in conversation with an unseen presence, her eyelids twitching with effort. She frowned, her forehead creasing, and she tossed and turned restlessly.

Before Ki-soon could awaken, Yoo-sang was eager to leave the room. After asking Jeom-rye to finish up, he quickly piled the wood he had brought beside the kitchen of the New House.* Then, he hurried toward the *Jangdok-gan*[5], the area for jars at the Big House*, taking a shortcut often used by the Choi family members.[6] Some people in the main house, like the master the great Big Elder, Choi Hong-seon, frequently used that path. Among the workers, Yoo-sang and Jeom-rye were the only ones who, like the Hong-seon, were allowed to use the shortcut.

As Yoo-sang walked away, almost fleeing, his mind wandered back to the image of Ki-soon's skin, as pale and smooth as white jade. He couldn't shake the scent of her hair from his nose, a fragrance he had inhaled as he

---

5) Jangdok-gan: A traditional Korean space for storing fermented condiments like soy sauce, soybean paste, and red chili paste. It typically consists of large clay jars (*jangdok*) placed in a sunny, well-ventilated area, often in the courtyard of a home. This space reflects Korea's fermentation culture and is key to preserving traditional flavors. The jars are still in use today, the number of jars and quality of food they contained were an important signifier of a family's wealth and status since very ancient times in the Koreas. In particular, in this book, this space(~*gan*) is used to signify the area on the side of the Big House, serving as a connection between the Big House and the New House.

6) Refer to the Choi family's Plot plan at the beginning of this book.

laid her head on a dry pillow. Despite having wiped her hair with Jeom-rye using a cotton towel, it had not been combed for some time, and a faint, lingering odor of old salted-seafood soup clung to it. Yet, strangely, it reminded him of the scent of his deceased wife's hair, evoking a flood of memories as he walked briskly away.

As Yoo-sang removed Ki-soon's wet *beoseon* and gently tried to dry her water-swollen toes with a towel, Ki-soon let out a startled cry, "Ar~argh," her voice trembling with fear. Sensing her distress, Yoo-sang turned to Jeom-rye and softly instructed, "Please wipe the Big Mistress's feet with warm water and put on fresh *beoseon*. It's important to keep her feet warm. I don't know how long she was in that pond." With that, he quietly left the room, leaving Jeom-rye to tend to Ki-soon.

As Yoo-sang left the main room, Ki-soon felt a lingering warmth where somebody had been — a fleeting sensation that passed over her as she lay on the floor. As she opened her eyes, staring at the ceiling, the warmth seemed to dissipate with someone's departure, replaced by an overwhelming cold that enveloped her entire body.

Ki-soon pulled the dry towels and blankets tightly around her head and chest, but still, her teeth chattered uncontrollably. She felt as though a chilling wind was seeping through every joint in her bones. Her tangled hair and body exuded a damp smell. Closing her eyes again, she thought to herself, *If I hold my breath like this, I could last over three minutes... I could have died. I could have gone back to the wind....*

Jeom-rye went to the kitchen of the Big House* and then returned to the main room of the New House*. Ki-soon had emerged from under the blanket and was now sitting on the floor, her eyes unfocused as she stared at the wall. She was muttering to herself. Jeom-rye listened intently, holding her breath, and heard Ki-soon say,

"Don't forget to breathe! You need to breathe! I ... must live!"

Then, abruptly, her tone shifted to panic. "You must never go outside the room! Never go outside! I ... I'm scared!"

Understanding her distress, Jeom-rye approached Ki-soon with the gentle assurance of someone much older. She opened her arms and embraced Ki-soon, holding her close, like a mother animal cradling her young. Then Jeom-rye said softly, as if soothing a child.

"Big Mistress, didn't I tell you again this morning not to go outside the room under any circumstances? You must not go outside; it's a serious matter. There's no one in the New House* today. Lady Hwang is gone, and so is the Big Elder. And as for the youngest lady, Young-soon, I wonder if she's returned yet. But she's no help; she's always holed up in her room.

Big Mistress! you must stay inside.

Please, take a deep breath! You need to breathe properly to survive, to endure the *wind*, right?

And... why are there a glue pot and pieces of colored paper under that desk? I cleaned everything up this morning. I'm the only one who gets scolded by Lady Hwang. If you keep making those things like pinwheels and creating a mess in the room or yard, I'll be in trouble.

... If you light a candle like before ... it's a huge problem. I could be kicked out of this house. The girl who worked here before me, she was always sneaking around with a neighbor's servant, and I don't know if she played with fire whenever she had the chance. People in the neighborhood keep saying, 'It's playing with *fire*. It's playing with *fire*.'

So, you must never play with *fire*. And..."

Before Jeom-rye could finish her sentence, Ki-soon, who had been leaning against Jeom-rye's chest, suddenly remembered something. She opened her pale, delicate hand and struck her own chest. Then, with that same hand, she repeatedly slapped the wall of the room. Ki-soon said in a slightly clearer voice, as if addressing someone with emphasis.

Ki-soon:

"Don't degenerate into a human being! Don't degenerate into a human being!"

The flames flickering in her eyes seemed so alive that they looked as if they might move like *fire*.

However, Jeom-rye appeared completely unfazed by Ki-soon's actions and mutterings. Holding towels and a tin bucket she had brought from the Big House kitchen, she hummed softly to herself. She wandered around the yard, heading toward the wall of the *Jangdok-gan*, which connected to the side wall of the New House* and the kitchen of the Big House*[7].

---

7) To aid in understanding the contents of this book, asterisks (*) have been attached to clarify important place names. The terms Big House and New House follow the names used by the villagers at that time. The owner of these houses is called Big Elder, and his name is Choi Hong-seon. Due to certain circumstances, he ended up with three wives.
—The Big House is where Lady Kim resides. In Korea, the term Big House does not refer to a large building but signifies the main house or the original house where the legal first wife or the primary wife lives, making Original House a more fitting term. The villagers referred to the house where the first legal wife, Lady Kim, lived as the Big House-First Wife's House. In Korea, when there are multiple wives and children, the children born to subsequent wives are taught to call the first wife, who was married in a legal ceremony, Big Mother, following a similar custom.
—The New House is where Lady Hwang, whom Hong-seon married later, resides. It is not simply a new building but rather signifies the house where he lives with his second legal wife, hence the term New (Wife's) House.
—The Saemmy House (which does not appear in Chapter 1) will be introduced in later chapters. This house is where Hong-seon lived before formally marrying his second wife after his first legal wife. It has a very deep and large well, hence the villagers called it the Well House or Saemmy House. In Korean, "well" is pronounced as "saem" or "saemmy."
Moving forward, the asterisk (*) symbol will be omitted.
—According to the Encyclopedia of Korean Culture (https://encykorea.aks.kr>Article), the term Big House refers to the house that continues through the eldest son in a clan. The Great Ancestral House refers to the house of the great-grandfather, and the Small Ancestral House refers to the house of ancestors below the great-grandfather, which is also called the Big House. The concept of collective homogeneity within the paternal kin group remains nearly the same.-The above interpretation is based on the author's references to testimonies and materials from remaining relatives.
—The Korean words that have deep meaning in this text are written in italics.

02

The Head House of Choi Clan

1956: The Big House
　　—Birth: The Continuation of Karma?

—The father had a son, and the son had another son. There are also sons who are very distressed and sad because their sons resemble their fathers. However, a certain person was overjoyed that his grandson resembled his grandfather.

The beginning of all karmas comes from me(myself), that is, the stubbornness and obsession of "me". — Author.

Some of the women were busy moving back and forth, in and out between the small room and the kitchen in the main house. At that time, the woman from the servants' quarters, who was escaping from the main room of the main building to the *daecheong-maru*, was saying something to Jeom-rye, who was following behind her, mumbling. Kim's wife from the servants' quarters called out,

"Hey, Jeom-rye! Hurry up and bring a raw egg as the midwife instructed and put it in the pregnant woman's mouth. You also need to speak with Lady Jeong, the madam of the main room in this house, who has been sitting in front of the well since the crack of dawn, rubbing her hands after setting the table.

I mean, the pregnant woman has already been bleeding for six hours—it's pitiful. Only the baby's head has come out, and then it stopped... Oh man! I'm out of breath just watching. What should we do? If this goes on, the mother will keep losing strength and won't be able to push! She's completely exhausted. Hurry up! Tell her and come back, okay?"

Jeom-rye, as if she had already given up, stared at the ground and spoke in a small voice.

"Oh, ma'am, I've already told her more than three times. Lady Jeong, the madam of the main room, sat at the table for her late master's birthday next to the *Jangdok-gan* and has remained there ever since. She didn't say a word after hearing what I said. Is it really such a big deal—just an egg? Can't we just take one from the basket in the chicken coop and put it in the pregnant woman's mouth?"

Kim's wife shook her head to the side, as if denying Jeom-rye's words. Then, as if she had suddenly remembered something she had forgotten, she moved toward the barn where the cows were kept.

In the barn next to the *haengnang-chae* (the servants' quarters of a *Hanok*), cows poked their heads out toward the food trough, waiting for breakfast. Looking for a large gourd bowl used for cattle feed, she tapped it against the wall of the *haengnang-chae*, emptied the bowl, and murmured to herself.

"Living in this huge house ... if I look closely, I see that the well-to-do *yangban* (*Joseon* aristocrats) often fare worse. The frail mother lies there like a lifeless body, her lower half exposed for half a day ... where the baby should be coming out.

And what about the baby? The poor thing's head is just barely sticking out, staying there as it is. Isn't it only a matter of time before the rest of the body follows if she keeps bleeding like that?

It's almost certain that this baby, like the first one, will be weak and sickly all the time. The baby is going to be born long past the due date. How could that happen? It's so difficult to be born healthy and strong in such circumstances. Tsk ... what if this baby, like the last one, has a pale face? This time, it seems like he's already dead.

Oh, I must be crazy! I can't believe I'm saying these things. I've spoken words that could cause big trouble..."

Then, after glancing around, she approached the steaming cow porridge pot as if nothing had happened. She stirred the porridge with the gourd bowl she had previously emptied by tapping it against the wall. She then scooped the porridge into the food trough, where the cows eagerly stretched their heads out. Moving their heads up and down, they ate the porridge hungrily, flicking their tongues as if they had been about to stick their heads directly into the steaming porridge at first. Afterward, she set off straight for the pigsty.

That day, as usual, the woman had risen around 4 a.m. to prepare a birthday table for her husband, who had passed away 11 years earlier. And, as she had done every day since coming to her husband's home, she did not forget to offer a bowl of clear water to the ancestors. She was the matriarch of the Choi family, known as the "Head House" by the villagers, and the eldest daughter-in-law, Jeong Bok-hee. Usually, at around 4:30 in the morning, she would place a bowl of clear water—drawn first from the well in front of the kitchen—and rub her hands together. It was a greeting offered to the ancestors of the Choi family and the guardian spirit who protected the land of the Choi household.

In a corner of her mind, she firmly believed that the reason she and her seven children had survived the absurd and bloody conflicts of the Korean War was due to the "Sincere prayer" she offered every day.

Bok-hee had little time to dress herself up, as she was always busy with housework. However, every year, she bathed and dressed neatly in a white *hanbok*[8], carefully groomed, as she stood before her husband's birthday table. This was because, to her, it was a time to meet her husband. Usually, when she was busy rushing around doing housework, she would hike up her long *chima* and tie it tightly around her waist so it wouldn't drag on the ground and get dirty. But this time, she left the long *chima* flowing freely, not wanting to lose the elegance of her *hanbok*. It was as if her deceased husband were right in front of her, watching her.

The first thing she did on her late husband's birthday was visit the

---

[8] Hanbok: The traditional Korean attire, consisting of a jacket (*jeogori*) and a skirt (*chima*) for women, and a jacket and pants (*baji*) for men, known for its elegant and flowing silhouette.

shrine, built at the highest place in the house, where the ancestral tablet was enshrined. She bowed to them. Inside the shrine, up to four generations of ancestors were enshrined, arranged to be prominently displayed, similar to the ancestral shrines found in the homes of ordinary middle-and upper-class families during the *Joseon* Dynasty. She bowed three times in front of her husband's ancestral tablet, placed at the far end.

After that, she returned to the main building. In front of the kitchen, she sat before the two *soban*s[9] that she had set up in advance. She placed a bowl of clear water on the first small *soban* and offered her sincerity. Once this was done, she moved the *soban* aside. Next, she made a deep bow before a medium-sized *soban* prepared for the birthday ritual and the ancestral tablet, on which her husband's name was written in black ink on white paper and attached to a wooden frame.

A moment later, as if convinced that the prayers to the ancestors and the ceremony commemorating her late husband's birthday were complete, she struck a match and lit the white paper bearing the inscription of the ancestral tablet. The paper read: "Gyeongju Choi's student husband, Choi Il-seop." As she watched the paper burn and turn to ashes, she spoke in a small voice, unheard by anyone.

Bok-hee:

"Look at this, Master! At the age of 35, you left behind seven children, and yet ... no words? I wish you would visit me in my dreams.

No matter how much property remains, do you have any idea how hard I must work to keep it secure in my hands? A single misstep, and it could vanish in a day.

Because of that accursed 6·25 War, our family's property is nothing like it once was. With so few hands to help, I have to tend even to the smallest tasks to keep the house running. Trustworthy people are nearly impossible to find. It's just Yoo-sang and Seok sen[10], only those two.

---

9) Soban: A traditional small Korean table, often used for individual dining or serving meals.

Though the war is said to be over, every day of our lives feels like a battlefield. It seems impossible for this country to return to the way it was before the war — I mean, in terms of the human heart.

Shortly after the war, our house was taken and dubbed the "People's Army Accommodation." When the U.S. military "Big noses" and South Korean soldiers arrived, the People's Army fled. But that's a tale from the daylight hours. Things change at night. Though years have passed since the war ended, those who survived still linger.

Perhaps the poor souls hiding in the valleys of *Jiri Mountain* ... maybe they are the partisans[11] the townspeople talk about. I'm not sure if that's who they are ... but it seems the war hasn't ended in everyone's minds.

Life, truly, is the hardest struggle. Though their visits are less frequent now, like owls, they emerge at night, seizing whatever food they can find. Even now that the war is over, I wonder if our household will ever return to its former state...

By the way, my Master ... the youngest child born the year you passed away, a posthumous child, Ki-seon, will enter the third grade of elementary school this year. Whenever Ki-seon, who doesn't even know your face, asks about her father, my heart sinks.

Yeo-bo[12], My master, today is your birthday. Even though you are no longer with us ... I'm sorry, I shouldn't have said that.

Something else about the house ... oh, your stepmother's birthday

---

10) Seok-sen: Seok means a person with the surname Seok. Sen, meaning Mr, is a remnant of Japanese. "Sen"means "Sen-sei" in Japanese language, which has a slight honorific meaning for the tenant farmer. (Author's note.)
11) Partisan: This term refers to non-regular military guerrilla fighters. It is officially recognized as a "Russian loanword" in the National Book Dictionary. The etymology traces back to the Russian word Partizan. In English, "Partisan" originated from the French word parti, which initially meant party members, comrades, and partisans. By the 17th century, it had come to signify local warlords. Today, it refers to a guerrilla or an irregular combatant and is used similarly to the term "Guerrilla."— Author's summary, referring to Naver Dictionary.
12) Yeo-bo: A term of endearment between married couples in Korean, like "Honey" or "Darling."—Referenced by the author from the Naver Korean Dictionary.

party, held last month, was a modest affair. My sister-in-law, Young-soon, the third daughter of the New House, is supposed to attend secondary school this year, but her mind is not well. There's a fear she might lose it, like her eldest sister. A few years ago, they invited a renowned monk and held a grand memorial service, which cost a lot of money ... but things are still the same.

It's no wonder your father seems out of his mind these days. His health is deteriorating little by little, but he still lives with your stepmother, doesn't he?

Oh, my ... you... After you died, I thought the sky had fallen, and I feared that your father, grieving the loss of his golden eldest son, wouldn't be able to go on. But life continues for those who are still living—for him and for me, too. I made up my mind countless times with a hardened heart, but just thinking about my children made it impossible to go through with it.

You shouldn't have clashed with your father from the start. I tried to dissuade you ... but now you've been gone for more than a decade.

My old man, my dear! You won't even appear in my dreams. How could it be?..."

She, who had been muttering to herself as if delivering a private speech for a long time, suddenly stopped talking and stood up, sensing someone's presence.

Then, after clearing her throat a few times, she took the ancestral tablet inscription bearing her husband's name, which had turned to gray ash, and placed the burnt paper on her right palm, blowing it away with her breath. The burnt paper scattered into ashes with a "Who~o" sound, though some fell to the ground. She rubbed the ashes with the rubber shoes she was wearing and buried them by pressing them into the ground with the front end of her shoe.

After adjusting her clothes once, she took a piece of fish from the plate and a tri-colored pancake from the small tray in front of her. The remaining liquor from the bottle used in the ritual was poured to one side of the *Jangdok-gan*—an offering for the cats and birds snooping around the yard. Even the small glass of alcohol on the table was sprinkled onto the ground.

This concluded this morning's ceremony—her daily hand-rubbing and annual birthday ritual for her husband. But today, something felt uneasy, not as comfortable as before. Bok-hee thought it might be because of her daughter-in-law's impending delivery.

That morning, one pair of eyes watched her especially carefully.

After the ceremony, it was time for her to take a deep breath before stepping out to look around the house, leaving an empty *soban* at the entrance of the *Jangdok-gan*. At that moment, Min-ja, who was temporarily staying in the New House, quietly walked toward the front veranda of the main room in the Big House and had been observing Bok-hee's profile for some time.

Min-ja didn't intend to spy, but she was envious and amazed that Bok-hee began her day by setting a table and rubbing her hands in prayer for her ancestors. She kept watching. After Bok-hee slipped out of the yard and returned, Min-ja murmured to herself, 'Bok-hee *Eonni*[13], sister-in-law, is truly a remarkable woman. They say she begins each day with prayers for the ancestors and meticulously oversees the entire household, without fail, every single day…'

The inner quarters of the house (*an-chae*), where Bok-hee placed the *soban* and offered her bows, had a central wooden floor (*daecheong-maru*) with

---

13) Eonni: Eonni or Unnie is a Korean term used by a girl or woman to refer to an older female sibling. However, it is not limited to family relationships; it can also be used to address an older woman in a friendly or affectionate manner. In English, there is no direct equivalent, but it is usually translated as "older sister" for a biological sibling or "older female friend" for a close acquaintance.—Interpreted by ChatGPT

rooms facing each other on either side.[14] Bok-hee surveyed the house before entering the main building. From the kitchen entrance, Eun-sook's mother from the back house and several neighborhood women were peering into the room through the holes they had made in the window paper, moistening their fingers with saliva to do so. Even a burly wandering manservant had joined them, drawn by the spectacle. Instead of heading to the rice fields where he should have been working, he conspired with the women, listening intently to the pregnant woman's moans.

Bok-hee felt a surge of anger at the thought of her eldest daughter-in-law, now lying in agony with labor pains. While the birth of a healthy grandson would bring great joy, Bok-hee couldn't help but feel a pang of discomfort at the thought of her daughter-in-law eventually being treated as the new madam of the main room in this house.

Then, without realizing it, Bok-hee bit her lips tightly and murmured again in her mind, 'I have lived here for nearly thirty years... and my young children, my six unmarried children, are all looking up to me, their mother, with wide-open eyes... I must keep holding this house together and take care of it. Yes, that's right.'

Once again, she murmured to herself in a small voice, as if lamenting.

'Ki-hoon, my son, has no worries, but his wife—that daughter-in-law of mine—is too weak and knows nothing about housekeeping. Tsk, tsk ... she isn't fit to be my eldest son Ki-hoon's spouse. She seemed so brave the day we met to discuss the marriage, but it appears I was seeing a phantom.

She became so frail after she got married. There's nothing she can do right. ... She doesn't do anything properly. Even when she's pregnant, she won't eat a single meal unless Jeom-rye, whom she brought from her parents' home, prepares it for her. It's really worrisome. How will she manage the household when she takes over? Tsk, tsk...'

As she said this, she spoke more loudly, as if she didn't care who

---

[14] Refer to the Choi family's Plot plan at the beginning of this book.

heard her. It was also a remark meant for those gathered outside the pregnant woman's room to hear.

Bok-hee:

"Oh dear! What's all this commotion? None of you workers are at your posts, and instead, you're all gathered here? Really? Get to work!

And have you ever seen such a frustrating person? Who in the world doesn't have a baby? Why is it taking her so long?

... Did you think everything would be fine just because you married my precious son? You should know how to give birth easily, just like everyone else, and hand the child over to the elders.

What's the big deal about having another baby that you're causing such a commotion in the neighborhood for hours, as if you're doing something grand? Tsk, tsk, tsk... But now, you seem too weak to even give birth to a single child.

... And the eldest grandson is sick almost every day, so his maternal grandmother in Jinju is raising him. If this baby is weak too, who will you leave it with this time?

I can never raise it. Do I have the time in this busy life? You certainly need to pay attention.

Got it, daughter-in-law?"

After finishing her words, she forcefully pushed open the door to the room where her daughter-in-law, Kim (Jong-hee), lay. Muttering in her mind, she continued,

'No matter how hard you try... You, a weakling, a chick neither physically nor mentally strong, will never bear two robust sons! Of course, you can't. With your fair skin and your attempts to live life as easily as a plant in a greenhouse, you can't survive properly.

Three years ago, and now too — even if a woman like you were to rise from the dead — you may never have a son as strong and splendid as my great son. Only if the gods of heaven and earth favor you ... I don't know...'

She was about to open the door and step inside, muttering to herself, when suddenly, a burst of applause erupted from the people watching the room. The woman next door, a midwife, saw Bok-hee trying to enter and, in high spirits, as if she had accomplished something significant, said.

Hadong-ddigi[15] (Midwife):

"Oh, Lady Jeong, madam of the main room! Finally, the baby has arrived. It's a boy—a young master! As everyone knows, I'm not trying to boast, but your daughter-in-law almost passed away. She was utterly exhausted, with the baby's head out of the womb for hours while still losing blood. Perhaps because he was born a month overdue, the umbilical cord was wrapped around his neck, and his face was dark, likely from swallowing too much meconium. Fortunately, both mother and child seem to be all right. Don't worry. It looks like we won't have to face a tragedy today."

Bok-hee inwardly flinched at the midwife's words. *Damn it! A woman like you—why do you boast as if delivering a baby for money is such a grand achievement?* But Bok-hee maintained a completely expressionless face as she spoke. Bok-hee said,

"Oh my! Hadong-ddigi, thank you for your hard work. Who else could have saved the mother of such a frail child without any trouble but an experienced midwife like you? It's all thanks to you, Hadong-ddigi. I'll pay you handsomely, so please continue to take good care of her.

I mean ... even the baby's bath is left to you. Such a tiny newborn is not familiar with my hands; it's too small.

And ... as he surely resembles his mother in some ways, he might be frail too. Please do me this favor. The eldest grandson took after his weak mother, and this one might be the same. '*The apple doesn't fall far from the tree,*' after all."

Bok-hee concealed her true feelings, not wanting to handle the blood

---

[15] ~ddigi: The ending of words usually used to indicate where married women's hometown is in Korea, that is, the word "~ddigi" is interpreted as referring to the hometown where the person was born, which is a certain color or emotion.—Based on Naver's Korean dictionary.

of a newborn if she could avoid it. A grandson would bring her more joy than a granddaughter. However, if her usually reticent mother-in-law suddenly changed her attitude towards her daughter-in-law just because of a grandson, it would seem unsightly.

As people often said, *'When a person is nearing death, their heart changes,'* but Bok-hee disliked even more the idea of treating her daughter-in-law, who had just given birth, any differently from how she had before. If she were to start taking care of her weak daughter-in-law and treating her warmly, it would make her look like a mercurial mother-in-law in the eyes of the neighbors.

No matter how much she tried to hide her disdain for her daughter-in-law's every action, it could still be sensed in some subtle way. She didn't want to say anything more that might expose the tension in their relationship. She didn't feel very good, but above all, nothing untoward should happen after this birth. The blame couldn't lie with either the young life that had arrived long past the due date or the mother. And any behavior that was indecent or unbecoming of a dignified mother-in-law should not be known to anyone.

It was especially significant since today was the birthday of her late husband, whom she revered as if he were heaven. Bok-hee grasped the midwife's hands as if nothing had happened and said,

"I leave the child and the mother to you," before stepping out of the room. Bok-hee was surprised at herself, realizing she was acting completely differently from before. She then murmured,

'Usually, when daughters-in-law give birth to a son, they take it as an opportunity to assert themselves over their mothers-in-law. What should I do in the future if she tries to rise above me? That daughter-in-law pretends to be weak, but she has given birth to two grandsons.

She's not going to treat me roughly, is she?...'

However, in one corner of her heart, she was also a little curious about what her young grandson looked like and whether he was healthy. Even though she didn't like her daughter-in-law, Jong-hee, at all, she felt conflicting emotions—pity for Jong-hee's frail health and a reluctance to openly take care of her.

What the hell were these thoughts? Bok-hee clicked her tongue softly. 'So, I'm a mother-in-law now. Tut tut...' she murmured, lost in thought.

Who doesn't want a son? Whether in rural or urban areas, it's clear that every household is short of hands and that sons, who bring other people's families, are treated better than daughters.

Bok-hee had given birth to her first son, Ki-hoon, but in between, she had four daughters among her sons. There was a time when she felt a little ashamed to face Hong-seon, the Big Elder and the Head of the Choi household, who was also her father-in-law. After all, following Ki-hoon's birth, the great Big Elder never explicitly said he was disappointed that Bok-hee had more daughters than sons.

Rather, it was what Lady Kim, the madam of the main room of the Big House and Bok-hee's mother-in-law, always said that troubled her mind. Lady Kim would say,

"Oh my gosh, my daughter-in-law, you're stronger than your husband, so you keep giving birth to daughters. Take better care of your husband. I heard that if a woman is strong, she gives birth to daughters." Bok-hee had grown tired of hearing it.

The desire for a son, the hope for that son—however, when the grandson was safely born, Bok-hee, the baby's paternal grandmother, said, "I don't want to give the baby his first bath." Upon hearing this, the midwife and those around her began to whisper among themselves.

Nevertheless, Hadong-ddigi, the midwife, had been helping out at the Choi household for over thirty years, so she quickly understood Bok-hee's request and remained respectful as always.

Bok-hee was about to leave the room after making that comment, without looking at the child's face at all. As she turned around, the midwife quietly said to her. Hadong-ddigi said,

"Lady Jeong, I understand. But somehow, that grandchild has something familiar about him in my eyes. I don't know yet ... but I think it's a face I've seen somewhere in this house. If not today, then at least tomorrow, why don't you meet him first, even just briefly? After all, people are watching."

However, Bok-hee did not even pretend to hear the midwife's words. When Bok-hee quickly left the room, the mother, Jong-hee, felt a heavier and hotter pain in her chest than the pain of a difficult delivery. She clasped her chest with her hands and unknowingly bit her teeth tightly.

As she left the room, Bok-hee said, as if Jong-hee could hear,

"For the next few days, I will not come to the front room of the main house where my grandson is lying. From now on, I will stay in the empty small room of the *sarang-chae*." Jong-hee was also told this. Bok-hee added, "I don't want to smell the blood of a newborn baby because I've become weaker than before, and I don't want to see a mother who's feeble." Jong-hee could hear the last part, too.

In this way, Choi Ki-hoon, the 30th-generation descendant of the small Head Family of the Gyeongju Choi clan, had his first son, Se-joon, followed by his second son, Jae-joon. Se-joon was born on July 8, 1953, and Jae-joon on May 14, 1956. Jong-hee was 25 years old at the time of Jae-joon's birth. Fortunately, she gave birth to a son for the second time, which was more celebrated than having a daughter. The village women who were taking care of her said that it would be difficult for her to regain her energy quickly after childbirth.

Jong-hee had a difficult labor when she gave birth to her first son, Se-joon, and the delivery of her second son was just as hard. Se-joon, the eldest son, had to be sent to Jinju, where Jong-hee's mother lived, due to a high fever and persistent diarrhea. After Se-joon was sent to her parents' house, Jong-hee worried that she would be hated by Bok-hee as well. Everyone working in the Choi household was wary of the hawk-like, piercing eyes of her mother-in-law, Bok-hee.

Jong-hee repeatedly wished in her heart to join her husband in Busan by any means, especially since she had to endure Bok-hee's scrutiny even while pregnant with Jae-joon. It would be fair to say that she was unprepared for pregnancy, childbirth, and the harsh realities of a countryside marriage. Her mother-in-law, Bok-hee, frequently said, "If you're so weak, you can't live a country life like this, especially not in this Head Family home! You have to be determined." To be honest, Jong-hee had no idea what kind of place the Head Family was until she got married.

Since the second great-grandson was born into the household, when the great Big Elder Hong-seon, who had gone to another region for work, returns home, he will call for his daughter-in-law, Bok-hee. He will then ask, "Who does the young great-grandson resemble?"

In addition, under the watchful eyes of the neighbors, Bok-hee finally decided to enter the room where her daughter-in-law, the mother, was lying. It was the tenth day since she had given birth. When Bok-hee entered the room, as expected, her daughter-in-law's whole body was swollen, and she looked frail, as if she were on the verge of death. Bok-hee hated seeing her bedridden daughter-in-law but also felt sorry for her.

Bok-hee decided to turn her eyes away from where Jong-hee was lying, a frown forming in the middle of her forehead. Jong-hee also heard the door open and, as if she were asleep, lay on her side, turning her back to face the wall. Bok-hee focused only on the small life wriggling next to Jong-hee, wanting to see the face of her young grandson, the baby who was ten days old.

The smell of childbirth blood had faded, but the whole room still felt somewhat damp. Bok-hee didn't care whether her daughter-in-law, Jong-hee, who was lying with only her back visible, was really asleep or just pretending. She had entered the room merely to fulfill her role as a mother-in-law.

Determined to focus solely on her little grandchild, Bok-hee carefully examined the tiny toe that peeked out from the baby blanket. Somehow, the shape of the toe felt familiar. She pulled back the small blanket to reveal the baby's feet. The baby frowned slightly, opened his eyes wider, and placed his hands in front of his stomach, fiddling with them as if he were hungry, but he didn't cry.

The blood in the baby's umbilical cord had almost hardened. The baby had exceptionally large and plump fists, with the thumb being particularly thick and large, resembling the shape of Bok-hee's own thumb. As a woman, she had often heard the saying, "She bereaves her husband—She becomes a widow." *Her thumb was shaped like a king snake's head, a supposed omen of widowhood.* But this baby was a boy. He wouldn't become a widow like her. *You can be a man with skillful hands*, Bok-hee thought to herself.

As Bok-hee looked at her grandson's toes, she suddenly felt a sharp pull from the back of her neck to the top of her head, and her heart began to race uncontrollably. Although the toes of a ten-day-old baby can be said to be almost the same for everyone, they still vary slightly from person to person. The baby's toes were nearly identical in length, just like those of her late husband, Il-seop. Il-seop's toes were almost the same length as his last two toes, and the overall shape of his foot resembled the toes of a stone statue from the *Silla* Dynasty, which could be seen in any temple in *Joseon*.

It is said that a ten-day-old baby cannot see anything, yet her grandson opened his eyes as if he were looking at something intently. The baby's eyes moved as if closely examining the ceiling of the room. It was as though he wanted to see Bok-hee, turning his face toward her.

Bok-hee leaned in closer and made eye contact with the child. The baby sniffed, his nose twitching as if trying to catch the scent of Bok-hee's body while facing her. Bok-hee gently held the baby's unusually thick palms and toes, then screamed involuntarily.

Bok-hee exclaimed, "Oh, my handsome grandson! Do you recognize this old lady? By the way, where did this grandson come from? Who do you think you look like?" She then flung open the door of the main building and called out loudly. Bok-hee shouted,

"Oh, my! People of the neighborhood! Come over here. Congratulations! I think my old man has come back to life. He looks exactly like my old man!

Even his testicles look the same—like black sesame dregs! My old man is alive and has been *reincarnated*! How can I not be happy? My old man has returned to me alive again as my second grandchild!"

In the end, the day Jae-joon was born turned out to be the same as his grandfather Choi Il-seop's birthday. From that day on, ten days after the delivery, Bok-hee moved into her daughter-in-law's room and practically lived there. She never let go of her grandson, Jae-joon, keeping him in her arms constantly. After about 15 days, Hong-seon[16], her father-in-law, returned to the Big House after touring various provinces, disposing of the items he had received, and finishing his business. Bok-hee took Jae-joon into Hong-seon's room to greet him. She said,

"Father, have you returned from work? The second great-grandson and I greet you. My baby is healthier and stronger than when he was born. Would you like to take a look?"

Hong-seon said,

"Okay, eldest daughter-in-law, Sori-ddigi[17](a variation of Hyori-ddigi for easier pronunciation), you've had a hard time taking care of the housework and managing the family while I've been away. Because you're reliable, I can still go out to do business, knowing you're keeping everything in order.

---

16) Hong-seon: Bok-hee's father-in-law, everyone calls him great Big Elder.
17) Sori-ddigi: Since her parents' house was called Hamyang Hyori, people around her sometimes pronounced "Hyori" as "Sori," a Gyeongsang-do dialect.

Well, is this the second great-grandson who was born this time? So, when is his exact birthday?"

Bok-hee replied,

"Father, it is the 14th of May."

Hong-seon was inwardly startled, but he deliberately pretended to remain calm on the outside. "What? May 14th? That day ... isn't it your husband's birthday? Is it true that this great-grandchild was born on the same day as your husband's birthday? Let's take a closer look at this child's face again." Bok-hee replied,

"Yes, Father. But there's something I really could not imagine. This baby was born about a month later than the usual due date. Normally, if a baby stays in the mother's womb for that long, the baby either dies or has some complications. So at first, I said I wouldn't even hold him in my arms. Just like last time, I was worried that the baby might black out or be in poor condition.

But this baby stayed in his mother's womb for close to 35 extra days, right up until his grandfather's birthday. Everything about this amazes me. According to the midwife, when he first came into the world, the baby had black skin and seemed lifeless, with the umbilical cord tightly wound around his neck. But he's becoming clearer and healthier every day.

Isn't that really strange? Father, what do you think of it? His face and toes look exactly like his grandfather's."

Hong-seon was very surprised to hear Bok-hee's remarks, but he did not show it outwardly. Bok-hee could see that Hong-seon held the second great-grandson in his arms, carefully examining the young baby's facial features. Soon, his expression grew dark.

In reality, how could a child who is only about a month old look unusual? As we know, people change with age. So if we have a unique feeling about a living being just a month after birth, it's likely that our thoughts and perceptions are being projected onto them. Hong-seon said,

"Sori-ddigi, looking at this boy's face and his entire appearance, I think he looks just like my father. You might say he resembles your husband, Il-seop, but I don't see it that way. Look at his glossy and thick hair! He was born late, likely because he wasn't nourished well in his mother's womb. How common is it for a month-old baby to have such glossy hair?

A life that entered the world with so much difficulty ... I heard he was born in distress, with the umbilical cord wrapped around his neck. Ahem, um, um...

So, is your daughter-in-law recovering well? No matter how busy you are, as her mother-in-law, please take good care of her. Above all, caring for the mother's health ensures that the baby will grow up healthy. After all, Jong-hee grew up like a plant in a greenhouse. I want you to take extra care of her."

Bok-hee replied,

"I hadn't even noticed how glossy and thick the baby's hair is. I've heard stories about how Grandfather's beard was just as thick and shiny... As the baby gets healthier, his mother is also improving little by little each day. I will make sure to take good care of them both ... though the baby's mother is quite a picky eater.

And Father, no matter who this child resembles, shouldn't we ensure that he lives a long and healthy life? I am so happy about this, no matter what anyone says. Is it okay to name this baby, your great-grandson, Jae-joon, as you suggested before?"

Hong-seon replied,

"Yes, make sure you like the name. When I have time, I will write it down in Chinese characters and have Yoo-sang put it on the family register."

And in his heart, Hong-seon mused,

Sori-ddigi, you must think that this child looks a lot like your husband, Il-seop. Does that mean Il-seop has returned as my great-grandchild because of some unresolved grievance? Perhaps not. Even if someone is born into a new body, I believe that human nature does not change just because they have lived another life. How could you speak of reincarnation? Even in the next life, one can only attain the same level as in this life. The very essence of a person doesn't change.

In my heart, Sori-ddigi ... if your husband has indeed returned to us like this, we must ensure that he does not make the same rash decisions that once led him to take his own life. Anyway, let's place our trust in this child.

Shall we trust this child, just this once?

So that he can fulfill all his desires and live a long, prosperous life.

With that, Hong-seon lifted baby Jae-joon, wrapped in his blanket, and pressed his forehead to the baby's. His eyes filled with tears for no apparent reason. Smiling, he held his forehead to Jae-joon's once more, then quietly closed the door and left without another word.

As Hong-seon passed through the men's quarters of the Big House and headed to the New House, he felt his legs trembling unknowingly.

03
Gakseoli[18]

1957: The Big House
—The Bright and Dark Sides

---

18) Gakseoli: A derogatory term used to refer to "*Jang-taryeong* singers." These individuals wander around marketplaces or streets, dressed like beggars, singing songs while begging.
—Referenced by the author from the Naver Korean Dictionary.

There was a rumor that a first birthday celebration would be held for Choi Jae-joon, the great-grandson of Choi Hong-seon, from the wealthy Choi family in Ok-dong, Sancheong, Gyeongsangnam-do. As Jae-joon grew healthier every day after his birth, by his first birthday, he had become a chubby, healthy baby that everyone could recognize.

In contrast, during the time of his elder great-grandson, Se-joon, who was particularly frail, no one had heard about a first birthday celebration. One reason was that, in those days, many children struggled to survive past their first year due to poor medical and environmental conditions. However, even at the age of four, Se-joon's health remained weak. The townspeople heard that Se-joon was still being cared for at his mother Jong-hee's family home in Jinju.

The Sangseogong branch, tracing its lineage back to Choi Chi-won, the founder of the Gyeongju Choi family, and down to Choi Hong-seon, the 28th descendant, was abuzz with preparations. They were planning a grand first birthday celebration for the second great-grandchild, Jae-joon, seemingly setting aside the frail first great-grandson, Se-joon, who represented the 31st generation.

To the people in the neighborhood, it didn't matter whether the celebration was for the first great-grandson, Se-joon, or the second great-grandson, Jae-joon. What mattered was the festivity itself. Rumors spread that the esteemed Big Elder, Hong-seon, had decided to host a lavish first birthday party for his great-grandson, bringing joy and excitement to the Choi family and their neighbors alike. The townspeople eagerly anticipated the celebration, longing for such a neighborhood gathering after a long time.

Why did they decide to hold a first birthday party for Jae-joon, the second great-grandson, when the same celebration had been skipped for

Se-joon, the first great-grandson and 31st-generation descendant? The villagers speculated that it was probably due to the pleas of Bok-hee, Jae-joon's paternal grandmother.

As previously mentioned, when Se-joon, the eldest great-grandson, was born, hosting a feast for a young child would have been heavily criticized, given the lingering aftermath of the Korean War. It was unimaginable to cook food and celebrate for a young child when people were starving right before their eyes. Regretting that a first birthday party had not been held for her eldest grandson, Bok-hee hurriedly informed the villagers of this feast, as if to make amends.

On the morning of the first birthday, May 14, 1957, the *Sadang-pae*, a troupe of strolling actors, was called upon for the celebration after a long hiatus. Upon their arrival, the members of the *Sadang-pae* donned tattered garments, blending seamlessly with the appearance of genuine beggars. From the break of dawn, even before the festivities began, they roamed around the house, indistinguishable from actual beggars.

Amid the yard, real beggars, dressed in similarly ragged attire, mingled with the actors. The difference between the real beggars and the *Sadang-pae* impersonators could only be discerned by smell. Genuine beggars exuded a pervasive, musty odor—an unmistakable scent that emanated from their very being.

As Jeom-rye walked through the courtyard of the main house, she encountered one such individual dressed in beggar's clothes. Holding her nose with one hand to fend off the stench, she hurried into the kitchen, navigating the peculiar blend of reality and performance that marked the day's unusual festivities.

"Wow! The stench is overwhelming. It's as if he has never bathed in his entire life. And those *Sadang-pae* actors? How do they manage to perform in such a state? Unbelievable," Jeom-rye spoke in a low voice, wiping her nose with the back of her hand through her sleeve.

Of course, amids the chaos of war, disabled veterans who had lost limbs gathered in groups—some with iron hooks attached to their severed wrists, others limping on prosthetic legs—crouching near the house. Early in the day, they huddled together, concealing their growling stomachs as they sat in a corner of the yard, basking in the sunlight and waiting for the feast to begin.

Most disabled veterans of that time primarily collected scrap paper or junk, using crude bamboo baskets slung over their backs and iron hooks to gather and sell what they found. When that wasn't feasible, they resorted to threatening children with their hooks or begging for food with pitiful gestures. Those with amputated legs usually worked as shoeshiners in the cities. But here in Sancheong, their options dwindled to gambling, drinking, and the accompanying rowdy behavior.

Even four years after the ceasefire, men with hook hands and beggars were still a common sight throughout Korea. The war's aftermath lingered, its misery not easily dispelled. Sancheong, a more generous countryside compared to Busan or Seoul, attracted many disabled people and beggars. Yet, living hand to mouth remained a struggle. They would emerge whenever a feast was anticipated or whenever people gathered with food, begging for sustenance and drink, hoping to partake in rare moments of abundance.

For those who arrived that day, the first birthday party of the great-grandson of the wealthy Choi family in Sancheong was not something to be closely scrutinized. Most people came quietly, drawn by the mere mention of a "Party house." Many of them were also villagers and longtime inhabitants of Sancheong.

Hong-seon instructed Bok-hee and his family to serve a hearty meal to everyone who came. After preparing all the food, Bok-hee brought a chair near the main house to sit with the esteemed Big Elder, Hong-seon. Jae-joon, dressed in a *hanbok*, sat on his grandmother Bok-hee's lap.

A large table was set up on one side of the yard, adorned with layers of *baekseolgi* (white rice cakes), fruits, and snacks. Also, on the table, a bamboo tray held various *doljabi*(the traditional first birthday ritual)items used to predict Jae-joon's future, including a package of coins, jujubes, a pencil, and thread.

In front of the kitchen and beside the bathroom yard, where a large cast-iron cauldron always stood, firewood was stacked to create a substantial fire. Two pots of beef soup simmered, sending up clouds of hot steam. Neighboring wives coiled boiled noodles into towering shapes, piling them so high that they nearly toppled from a bamboo basket. After cutting the noodles into small pieces for garnish, they stir-fried beef in soy sauce, made egg pancakes, and arranged them in wicker trays on the food shelf, ready to top the noodles.

The women in charge of the food beckoned their children, who were wandering around the yard, and urged them, "Eat quickly until you are full!" The children who were called over, despite receiving playful noogies, eagerly slurped up the noodles, happy that their bellies were getting full.

As the crowd grew, the beef soup in front of the kitchen quickly ran out, and the pot from the bathhouse was soon brought to the front of the kitchen. Meanwhile, in the pot next to the bathhouse, pork rice soup simmered, filled with various cuts of pork intestines and *seonji* (clotted blood), bubbling away. Of course, *makgeolli* (traditional Korean rice wine) flowed freely, accompanied by an abundance of spicy pepper and potato pancakes. Five large jars of *makgeolli* and two boxes of particularly salty herring had been prepared for the relatives. The fish were baked just in time for the newly arrived guests, placed on a large tray, and set on the table.

The children ran around laughing, noodles dangling from their mouths. The adults bustled about, ensuring plates were piled high and glasses were never empty. The air danced with the delicious aroma of sizzling soups and crispy pancakes, blending perfectly with the lively hum of laughter, cheerful banter, and the occasional clink of glasses. As the feast carried on, bellies filled to the brim, and the laughter grew louder, conversations flowed freely in a way that hadn't happened in ages. It felt like a celebration of life itself, bursting with warmth and joy.

Usually, at a first birthday party, the parents would sit holding the child. However, Ki-hoon couldn't come down to Sancheong that day due to an urgent matter at his senior's house. Naturally, Jong-hee, Jae-joon's mother, would have taken his place, but she gave up her seat to Bok-hee, her mother-in-law. Bok-hee sat with Jae-joon tightly on her lap.

At the end of the birthday party, *doljabi*, the guests who came to congratulate them said, "Baby, pick it up, the good thing..." Jae-joon picked up a thread and a package of coins from the birthday table that had been set up.

Bok-hee clapped her hands loudly and exclaimed, "Oh my, look at this! My grandson is gripping that bundle of coins so tightly—he's surely going to make a lot of money in the future! And just look at how he's holding that long thread with his little fingers, it means he'll live a long life too... How wonderful this is!" Her face lit up with a beaming smile, overflowing with joy.

Jong-hee, pushed behind Bok-hee, watched Jae-joon and Bok-hee's actions with an emotionless face. Soon after Jae-joon's first birthday commemorative photograph was taken, Jong-hee quietly left the gathering and returned to her room, sensing that a performance by the *Sadang-pae* would soon begin. Her expression remained vacant, leaving only an empty, desolate look in its place.

Immediately, the *Sadang-pae* performance was ready to take place in the yard. They laid out long straw mats as compactly as possible. People began to sit in rows. The *Sadang-pae* invited to Hong-seon's house was a small troupe gathered by Yoo-sang, not a large one with many members. Yoo-sang explained to Hong-seon that it was difficult to find large troupes anymore, as they had gradually scattered after the liberation from Japanese colonial rule and the Korean War.

When the troupe appeared on the straw mat, the crowd erupted with shouts of "Wow! It's a *Gakseoli*!" The performers were dressed like the beggars seen on any street, their attire reminiscent of the *Gakseoli*—the singing beggars or Korean gypsies. They wore bands of yellow and red cloth, intertwined with straw strings, tightly tied around their foreheads. Their tattered clothes, patched with black fabric over gray cloth, looked like a quilt of rags. Loose, worn-out pants completed their beggar disguise.

Their songs and dances, performed in the guise of *Gakseoli*, captivated the audience in the courtyard of the Big House. Children gathered at the front of the straw mat stage, sitting on the ground for a better view, huddling together as closely as possible. When the front seats filled up, they brought additional straw bags to shield themselves from the cold ground. Some children were seen munching on *jijimi* (fried pancakes) hanging from wooden sticks.

The gate of the Choi house was wide open, welcoming an audience of over 200 to 300 people, including locals and passersby. People stood or sat not only in the yard but also in various other spots. Bok-hee, sitting proudly with Jae-joon on her lap on a chair placed high on the *daecheong-maru* (large wooden floor), was the centerpiece of the gathering. She was pleased with herself for contributing to the further prosperity of the household.

My three sons, four daughters, and two grandchildren from my eldest son, Ki-hoon... I, Jeong Bok-hee, married into this Choi family, and even though my husband passed away early, I raised so many children and cultivated both the land and the people. Yes, indeed. As the eldest daughter-in-law of this Head Family, as the Mistress of the Big House, I have done well, she muttered to herself with satisfaction.

Bok-hee had been shopping for groceries and preparing food for ten days straight to welcome the guests to the feast. She had barely slept, making three buckets of *sikhye* (sweet rice drink). She had asked her sister-in-law to bring millet taffy in two large bamboo baskets, but it had already run out. Yet, she felt no fatigue.

Sitting with Jae-joon on her lap, she felt reassured and rejuvenated. It was as if she had returned to her youth, raising Ki-hoon, and as if Jae-joon were her own son. She was on cloud nine, buoyed by the joy of the celebration and the pride in her family's legacy.

At one end of the mat, a person beat a drum and called out sounds somewhere between "Yippee!" and "Great!" in rhythm with the performers on the mat. There were about five people dressed as *Gakseoli*, and as soon as they arrived that morning, they asked Yoo-sang various questions about the house. Yoo-sang was hesitant to answer. One of the performers was a relative of Yoo-sang, and noticing Yoo-sang's uneasy expression, the relative spoke to him.

Sang-cheol, casually inspecting the back of his hand, spoke to Yoo-sang as if in passing.

"Uncle, you might forget how you answered because the head of our troupe thinks he's somebody, dragging us around needlessly. He's not that smart. There were times he didn't even know where to get the money. Ha-ha... Listening and then forgetting as soon as he turns around—that's his specialty. Maybe it's because he drinks every day."

Yoo-sang provided only basic answers to their questions—mostly information that everyone in the neighborhood already knew. He reasoned that they were asking in order to incorporate it into their performance. After all, it was unlikely that the local people were unaware of the happenings within Choi Hong-seon's family. These days, owning a lot of land wasn't a crime, unlike during the Korean War, and he felt there was little to conceal. He decided to view their inquiries as part of their craft—a means to enrich their play with local color and authenticity.

The *Gakseoli* sang their lively tune.

Gakseoli Gap (2 persons) and Gakseoli Eul (2 persons):

"Oh~ hooray, hooray, hooray, here we go,

Oh~ hooray, hooray, here we go!

The *Gakseoli* from last year didn't die; they've returned again.

Wow~, this guy was the son of a dignitary,

But he shunned the ruler of eight provinces and became a *Gakseoli*."

Gakseoli Gap:

"Yippee~, it's going in. Whoopee~, it's going in.

Hey, look!

Friends!

Where the hell am I?"

Gakseoli Eul:

"Pshaw, I'm no friend. I'm a big yellow snake, gramps,

who's lived here for 100 years."

Gakseoli Gap:

"Gosh, damn it! The Japanese have already eaten all those yellow snakes because they're good for rejuvenation.

The rest—those wham-ditty,

To protect the husbands who died in the war,

To volunteer for women who are enduring hardships,

All the stupid, rude bastards who know their faces

and names have eaten them up.

Right,

They ate all the snakes that protected every house.

Now, to protect the house, should we bow to *Jo Wang Sin*,

the kitchen god, in the wood-burning stove of every home?

You must eke out a meager living at the right time to survive!

So, dear friends, listen quietly. Now, is that big yellow snake, the old man who acts like a rude bastard, still alive?

Was he eaten?

Seeing that there are no words, he must have already been cut with a snap [*Gakseoli* sticks out his tongue, pretending to cut his neck with his hand], hasn't he?

You, rotten guy! Then it was a dead big snake.

Whoa~ it's a ghost! It's a ghost!"

[Woo-dda-da-da-da, he kept beating the drum.]

Gakseoli Gap, Eul:

"Oh~ hooray, hooray, hooray, here we go,

Oh~ hooray, hooray, here we go!

So where am I ~~~

This is the granary of this mountainous and pristine land,

Where the hills fold and curve like the skirts of a resplendent woman.

This place, once known as San-Eum, is now called Sancheong,

Where mountain gods gather from near and far!"

Gakseoli Gap:

"Then ... whose house is this, by the way?

That's what I'm talking about."

Gakseoli Eul:

"Since ancient times, there have been two kinds of houses:

One refers to the house itself, whether it is covered

with roof tiles or straw.

The other refers to the people who live in the house.

What's that beggar asking about?

The house itself?

Or the owner and his family who live there?"

Gakseoli Gap:

"You dolt!

The owner of this house is named Choi,

Hong, and Seon.

He owns one-third of all the land in Sancheong..."

Gakseoli Eul:

"Hey, even a passing dog knows that, you dolts!
Now that the great-grandson of this household has been born,
Isn't everyone here ready to celebrate and have some fun?
Didn't the great-grandfather himself set this day aside for all of us to enjoy?
Am I right, or are you right?
Now, let's all say hello to the esteemed Elder Choi,
the owner of this house,
His second great-grandchild and Lady Jeong.
[Gakseoli Gap and Eul bowed.]
"Let's shout together!
Yippee~ it's going in! Whoopee~ it's going in!"

In the midst of their performance, they coaxed villagers to join them on the straw mat, making them laugh by dancing the *gopchu* (hunchback) dance and the dog-leg dance. Bok-hee noticed that Jae-joon had fallen asleep on her lap. To make him comfortable, she removed his *hanbok* and carried him to the main room of the house, laying him down gently.

Meanwhile, as the cheers grew louder, it became evident that one of the performers was walking on a tightrope outside. Balancing with a long pole in both hands, he hopped along the single line, mesmerizing the crowd. People gawked in amazement, their mouths agape, and clapped their hands in awe.

"Wow! That's really thrilling and awesome! How on earth do they jump so high?"

Gakseoli Gap:
It's a bit warm right now, but before long, the day when you
eat warm red bean porridge on the winter solstice will come.
You all know the sound of making red bean porridge, right?"
[Flapping sound in boiling porridge, giggling.]
As the crowd burst into laughter,
Gakseoli Eul:

"What? What? What's wrong?

Does it sound familiar?

Giggling...

[Eolssu!~].

Is it like the sound when your mom and dad did milling every night?

Mom holds the bat in dad's center tightly in her hand

and asks him to do more,

So dad does the milling again...

Until his stomach sinks in and becomes slim.

Again and again,

Flapping, flapping...

doing the milling bustling.

All night, the night never ends."

Gakseoli Gap:

"The eldest daughter of the house, upon hearing it, said,

'Oh man, you're going to have another younger sibling?

We already have five younger siblings!'

Why is this night of the winter solstice so long?

Come on, right? Right?"

The crowd giggled and laughed. Jeom-rye looked through the onlookers as she walked back and forth between the kitchen and the yard. Her eyes met those of Yong-sik, the new farmhand, who was sitting in the second row of the straw mat. Her face turned red as she felt her heart warm without realizing it. Min-ja, who was watching Jeom-rye from the side, smiled and poked Jeom-rye's side for no reason.

The feast didn't end until five in the evening. In a little while, the busy farming season would be upon them, but on that day, they ate their fill and laughed for the first time in a long while. The villagers and relatives, who had gathered from near and far, greeted Hong-seon and Bok-hee before returning to their homes. The house returned to its usual quiet.

Bok-hee arranged the leftover food to prevent it from spoiling. The soup was boiled once more, and the *jijimi* was fried again to serve as side dishes for the family the next day. It was a day when Jae-joon, a newborn baby just one year old, neither cried nor fussed and spent his time with dignity.

Bok-hee felt proud and confident in Jae-joon for such small things. Jong-hee followed Bok-hee into the kitchen, pretending to arrange the side dishes, but with a tired face, she retired to her room early in the evening and lay down. As Jong-hee entered her room, she murmured, "Oh, when I gave birth to my eldest son, I couldn't even get him a bowl of warm honey water, but this time, my second child is sitting on a flower cushion before the eldest one."

As evening deepened, mugwort was gathered in the yard and burned to drive away the bugs. The weather was still chilly. Hong-seon sat cross-legged on a bamboo flat bench placed in front of the detached house. Sang-cheol, one of the performers that day, was Yoo-sang's only maternal nephew. What Sang-cheol said as he received payment for the performance weighed heavily on Hong-seon's mind.

Sang-cheol said,

"It has been a long time since we last met, Big Elder! It's already been almost seven years since you took refuge at my grandmother's house. They say the war is over, but isn't it frustrating to live like this? My head always feels like it's floating in the air ... I feel like I'm losing my mind. I don't know if I'm the only one who feels this way or not.

[Looking closely at Hong-seon's face].

By the way, are you okay these days, Big Elder? It's only been two years, but you don't look well.

Whenever I come to this house ... I think of Joon-seop. Joon-seop and I are friends. Whenever I came to Sancheong, we used to hang out together for a few days. I don't know much about other things, but ... Joon-seop must have waited and waited for you, Big Elder, to reach out to him.

[At this moment, Sang-cheol glanced at the play group behind him].

You must be very tired today, so we're going to leave now.

Thank you for inviting us. Goodbye.

Thank you for paying generously.

May you live long and stay healthy."

Perhaps because Sang-cheol had lived a wandering life when he was young, his accent did not fit any particular region. However, Hong-seon knew that his character was not so rough. Otherwise, in the summer of 1950, he would not have been able to hide in Imchon and would probably have been shot straight away by the North Korean People's Army. Many landowners who lived in Sancheong, Jinju, Hapcheon, and other areas died in such a manner, as they were considered the mortal enemies of the people.

No one in Sang-cheol's family reported Hong-seon's family. Sang-cheol's aunt, who was Yoo-sang's wife, and Hong-seon, Ki-hoon, and Jeong-seop were able to survive thanks to hiding there during the fiercest period of the war. No matter how careful Sang-cheol's father was with his words, if someone had really said just one word, they would have been found and killed quickly.

Yoo-sang's brother-in-law, in other words, Sang-cheol's father, was one of the district heads who received red armbands from the People's Army in charge of Sancheong. He was a tenant of Hong-seon, managing the mountains and fields over the hills, and a faithful man who took care of this house. Yoo-sang and Sang-cheol's father were people who truly cared about Hong-seon. In August 1950, landlords and their families were all shot dead as soon as they were discovered. At that time, Sang-cheol's father gave his house to Hong-seon so he could escape. It was Sang-cheol's maternal grandmother's house.

And Joon-seop, whom Sang-cheol said was his friend, was the only son of Hong-seon and his wife, Lady Hwang. He was still officially listed as "Missing" on paper. However, Hong-seon no longer believed he was alive. Joon-seop must have died. Joon-seop disappeared in front of the gate of the New House, just as Il-seop had died in the *sarang-chae* of the Big House. Since no one had seen the body or confirmed anything, the entire family kept their mouths shut.

Without realizing it, Hong-seon recalled the faces of the children he had buried deep in his heart. As a father, Hong-seon did what he could for his children: Il-seop, Lee-seop, Joon-seop, and Jeong-soon.
However, what was the result?
But Hong-seon was asking himself what the result was. It is not common for children to die before their parents. In the event of war or a major disease, one cannot help but die. But how does a child, who leaves his parents to witness his death with their own eyes, live on in their memory?

How can someone who has not experienced it firsthand understand his pain? The wound, which settled deep in his heart, left more than just a scar of sadness over time. An old Korean proverb says, '*They don't see where the affection comes in, but there is a place where it goes out.*' A father's love for his child cannot be described in words.

However, if one's child dies first, the parent will see themselves as a sinner. Parents blame themselves for everything. Even if others don't say such things, it is very difficult for most parents to escape that guilt. Sometimes, they say, "It's all destiny. What can we do about life and death?" Yet, even as they utter those words, the outcome remains unchanged. Is this what becomes of a fractured bond between parent and child in the end?

The deaths of his children happened in this order: Il-seop was the first, dying in front of Hong-seon in 1945. Second, Joon-seop disappeared on a summer day during the Korean War in 1950. Joon-seop had come home early for summer vacation from Seoul. At that very moment, a bombing occurred after he left the gate, and nothing else was known. Third, his beloved daughter, Jeong-soon, died of cholera. Jeong-soon's body was able to be properly laid to rest, even though she had almost become just another patient lost on the road in Seoul, where they had no connections.

What about Il-seop's twin, Lee-seop? There was no news of him. He had already disappeared before liberation and left no trace. We didn't know where he was, where he had gone, or whether he was alive or dead. In that case, it was almost certain that Lee-seop was dead.

The only son who survived was Jeong-seop, born to Lady Han of Saemmyjip. (Saemmy is the local dialect for *saem* in the Gyeongnam province, meaning spring or well. *jip* means house in Korean.)

Hong-seon wanted to be kind to everyone, including his sons and daughters—his own children. That was all he had in mind. War and infectious diseases could, in some ways, be seen as natural causes of death. But among his children, who was it that Hong-seon truly wanted to treat the best?

That was it.

"A guy named Il-seop, Choi Il-seop. Oh, that guy. I really wanted to be nice to him, but that was all..."

Hong-seon muttered, lowering his head in solitude.

It's said that all children are the same, but why? Why does the mere mention of Il-seop's name pierce Hong-seon with such pain?

Hong-seon muttered,

"Bad guy, you lived only that long and then left..."

He didn't know who he was talking to.

And what about Joon-seop? He was one year younger than Hong-seon's grandson, Ki-hoon. Always overshadowed by Ki-hoon, Joon-seop could never speak his mind properly in front of his father, Hong-seon. Exceptionally feminine and shy, Joon-seop's news reached Hong-seon after he fled to Imchon and later returned home.

At that time, Hong-seon had experienced sudden blindness, unable to see anything for a while. So naturally, just as when Il-seop died, he didn't venture outside the gate—for a while.

Who could Hong-seon possibly confide in and reveal his heart to? Throughout his life, he had never done anything shameful enough to be pointed at by others, nor had he ever caused harm. How had he lived so wrongly to deserve this?

After the deaths of his children, Hong-seon tried to remain as confident as before. No matter how hard he tried, the words, "Among the descendants of Hong-seon Choi's family, the sons were short-lived," haunted him. These words sapped his strength and dulled his desire for life. His attachment to life grew faint. The anchor that should have secured him gradually slipped from his grasp. The ship carrying him and his family had turned into a drifting wreck, aimlessly wandering the open sea.

Is this the nature of the relationship between parents and children? If a child thrives, the parents are happy; if a child suffers or dies young, the parents are heartbroken, feeling that all the responsibility lies with them. Is that it?

Hong-seon murmured to himself, "I was once confident and had a strong will to live, stronger than anyone else. I had children whom I could teach through my actions and words... Were they listening to me? What does a child's long or short life have to do with obeying their parents?"

Hong-seon answered himself, "Maybe not. I don't think so." He had long since reached that conclusion. There was something he had learned alone, only after his children had disappeared.

Hong-seon thought,

Parents only play the roles of father and mother for a very brief moment in time. Their children come into this world through them, mere conduits. These children, bearing the titles "my child" or "our child," temporarily borrow the bodies and minds of their parents. Some children closely resemble one parent or the other, while others do not at all...

Il-seop! Joon-seop! Lee-seop! Jeong-soon!

You lived believing that the visible bodies and the minds you borrowed for a while were yours forever. But they were never truly yours, nor were they ours. The true you will remain as you are, even if you are reborn in a different form in the next life...

Hong-seon sat on the flat bench, then suddenly stood up to shake off the delusions rising like smoke from the mugwort fire. "Oh! I'm captivated by delusions again. The past can't be returned..." As he spoke, he felt his chest tighten and a hot ball of fire rise up his throat.

He stepped off the bench and slowly moved toward the *Jangdok-gan* (the place for gathering jars) of the Big House, following the path leading from the yard of the Big House to the inner yard of the New House.

In the *Jangdok-gan*, a short cherry tree had burst into bloom right next to the well, its petals now fallen, while green shoots sprouted between them. The young cherry leaves, shaking in the wind, were bathed in the moonlight. The delicate leaves, with their deep black-green hue, would soon fade here and there, touched by the damp droplets from the deep stone stair of the well. This cherry blossom tree had been planted the year after Il-seop left.

04

Bok-hee, a New Mistress of the Estate

1926: The Big House
　—Three Mothers-in-Law

At the end of April, as spring arrived, azaleas bloomed splendidly on the mountains, and the cries of cuckoos echoed from one peak to another. Eight palanquin (*gama* in Korean) bearers, carrying a wedding palanquin, departed from Hyori, Hamyang-gun. From there, they climbed an uphill mountain path along a small ridge leading to Sancheong.

The palanquin, beautifully decorated on the outside, was clearly intended for a wedding. Typically, four bearers carry a palanquin on their shoulders, but this one had eight. Passersby could infer from this that either the bride's family was of high status or the bride herself was of considerable weight.

The palanquin departed from the bride's house in the morning, but it was not until evening that it arrived at the groom's house, located in the middle of Sancheong. The wedding palanquin stopped at the entrance of the servants' quarters by the gate. About twenty people were waiting in line for the palanquin, stretching from the servants' quarters to the front yard of the main building. Several kerosene lamps had been prepared in case it arrived late.

The bride stepped out of the palanquin, wearing a traditional *Joseon*-era wedding gown with a *jokduri* (Korean bridal crown) on her head. The bride, who was to be married the next day, was Jeong Bok-hee, born in 1910. She was sixteen years old, 170 centimeters tall, and had a round face with a slightly angled chin and large, bright eyes that tilted up slightly at the sides.

As the bride got out of the palanquin, two women quickly approached and whispered in her ear. One of them promptly took her hands and rejoiced. Tae-jeong (the groom's aunt) said,

"Welcome, *Jong-boo* (the wife of the eldest grandson of the Head Family in Korea). Thank you for coming all this way through such rugged roads. The wedding ceremony is prepared for tomorrow morning, so please go to the main house first and have something to eat. I've heated up some soup and rice."

After the bride entered the main house, the women and male servants who had been waiting in the yard went back to their rooms. The servants living in the house returned to the servants' quarters, and the tenant farmers who worked near the house went back to their own homes. The servants who had returned to the servants' quarters whispered among themselves.

Jong-sik (a servant) said, "Did you see the new bride, the New Mistress of this house? Few of the men here can match her height. And those eyes... Whether you look at her from the side or the front, her eyes are immense, and the sharp corners behind them are quite intimidating. Yet, it takes someone like that to become the Mistress of such a grand family. She truly carries the presence of a New Mistress. I wonder if Lady Kim, who sits quietly in the *gol-bang*, will find some comfort and relief thanks to her formidable daughter-in-law."

Cheon-seung (a servant) said, "What are you talking about? It is said that the eldest madam of the main building searched all over Hamyang and Geochang but couldn't find anyone like her, so she eventually accepted her. I'm sure she found someone who could offer her a little protection.

First of all, she saw the bride's appearance and how well the elder brothers in the family are doing, so she could reclaim a place that had been taken from this house. But now that she has been pushed out of the family register, she has been completely erased. Don't you think so?"

The servants who heard this walked quietly to the side of the wall near the servants' quarters where they were staying, instinctively covering their mouths with their hands as they whispered among themselves.

By morning, many people had gathered between the main building and the *sarang-chae*. The main gate of the Big House was wide open, creating an air of excitement. Beggars and the *pungmulnori* (Korean farming music play) group, who always rushed to find weddings where they could perform, paced around eagerly, eyeing the seats on one side of the yard that they seemed poised to occupy once the feast was set up.

The groom, Choi Il-seop, born in 1907, was slightly shorter than the bride, who wore a *jokduri* (the official bridal hat). He wore a *samo* (the official groom's hat). He was nineteen years old, about 165 centimeters tall, and of a small build—slightly thin, like an ordinary Asian man. His face was slender, with a slightly pointed chin, and he had rather fair skin. A distinctive feature was that the bridge of his nose was higher at the middle of his forehead than that of most ordinary Asians, and he had delicate eyes with single eyelids.

The groom looked once more with a smile at the bride, who stood on the other side of him, her head slightly bowed as she adjusted to the timing of the wedding ceremony. Il-seop thought about the previous night and had only a faint memory of how his first night in Hyori had passed.

After the first ceremony, he drank, and Bok-hee's four elder brothers and friends playfully hit the soles of his feet for fun. As they encouraged him to drink more, Il-seop barely remembered anything afterward. By the time he returned to the newly prepared room, it was already very late at night. Under the dim lamplight, the first thing he did was remove Bok-hee's *jokduri*, which looked uncomfortable—without even taking a close look at her face.

Then, he simply fell asleep in the room with the lights off. However, he did recall saying to the bride, "Did you eat dinner before bed? Thank you for waiting for me all day."

He guessed that the bride, who was three years younger than him, might not have eaten anything all day, dressed in uncomfortable clothing and wearing a *jokduri*. Bok-hee had been a little nervous all day yesterday. Her shoulders were stiff as she struggled to wear an uncomfortable wedding suit after putting on a *jokduri* and applying makeup called *yeonji* (rouge on the cheeks) and *gonji*[19] (rouge on the forehead).

It seemed that she had hardly touched the food at the table where the groom had eaten first. However, the groom had intentionally left two delicious side dishes on the table for the bride, so Bok-hee could eat them as much as she wanted.

In her heart, she thought, *He will be a man who always cares for me as his bride.*

As soon as dawn broke, the groom left the bridal room. It was customary at that time for the groom not to stay in the bridal room until late in the morning. Because of this, she didn't get to see Il-seop, as she was busy preparing to leave for Sancheong early.

Bok-hee felt more at ease after seeing the groom's disciplined and calm demeanor last night when she arrived in Sancheong. There were already rumors that she had three mothers-in-law.

She thought, *I won't return to Hyori, my parents' house, from now on. This is the house-in-law where I will live for the rest of my life, but I'm worried because I haven't heard much about my mothers-in-law...*

However, at the same time, she felt much more reassured when she steeled her mind with the thought, *I will face whatever comes my way, and this house will be my home anyway.*

Today, during the wedding ceremony, she caught a glimpse of Il-seop's expression. The groom standing before her had a more serious look than when she had seen him yesterday at her house in Hyori. He spoke only a few words to his aunt Tae-jeong, who was busy preparing for the wedding ceremony, then kept his mouth shut and remained silent. He observed the movements of those around him, concentrating intently.

---

19) Yeonji and Gonji: A traditional Korean cosmetic used to decorate the cheeks and lips in red hues, made from safflower or cinnabar. Painting a bride's forehead with a circular mark using *yeonji* is called *gonji*. The two are often mentioned together as *yeonji gonji*. This practice is believed to have originated from Shamanistic culture, where red was thought to ward off evil spirits. —The above explanation is adapted from the author's entry on Naver Namu Wiki.

As a commemorative photo of the wedding ceremony was being taken, a large crowd gathered inside the yard—including the main building's yard and the *sarang-chae*—as well as outside the gate. Among the crowd, a child murmured softly, "Wow! The bride with the *jokduri* is as tall as a pole. She also has broad shoulders, but the groom is small and pretty." Indeed, the bride stood beside the groom like a sturdy pillar, her large, wide skirt enveloping the groom, who was noticeably shorter than her.

After the wedding at the groom's house, preparations for *Pyebaek* [20] were underway on the large wooden floor of the main house. The groom's parents, along with about twenty to thirty close relatives, sat around the main area. The bride and groom changed into their *Pyebaek* robes. Bok-hee was informed that they would bow to the relatives in succession, starting with four bows to her parents-in-law.

The bride and groom first bowed to her father-in-law, Hong-seon, and mother-in-law, Lady Kim of the main room. Bok-hee then presented beef jerky to Lady Kim, which had been prepared in advance. Tae-jeong assisted with all the procedures. Lady Kim threw jujubes and chestnuts onto the new bride's skirt. These items symbolized the wish for many descendants and a prosperous family, a hidden meaning that Bok-hee fully understood.

The couple then bowed to the relatives and neighbors one by one. Finally, they bowed to all the relatives gathered in the yard for the ceremony. Everyone said, "Bless you. May your offspring flourish and bring prosperity." These warm words of blessing were directed at the bride and groom.

After her marriage, Bok-hee barely remembered the faces of the Choi

---

20) Pyebaek: *Pyebaek* (Hyeongugorye) refers to the bride greeting her parents-in-law and the groom's family, a ceremony known as *Pyebaek*. This traditional wedding ritual was established when *Joseon* adopted Confucianism as a political ideology and incorporated Chinese customs.— In reference to Naver Folk Museum materials.

clansmen, aside from the brief meeting on that day. Nevertheless, they lived nearby and encountered one another several times a year, just a few steps from home. Now, the most important people in her life were her parents-in-law, whom she would care for as a daughter-in-law for the rest of her life. She briefly reflected on her first impressions of them.

The parents-in-law sat opposite the bride and groom, who stood with their hands clasped together. Choi Hong-seon, her father-in-law, was born in 1881 and was the Elder and Head of the Family. Everyone called him "The Big Elder" or "Beard Grandfather." The Big Elder sat in the center, with Lady Hwang and Lady Kim on either side of him, and Lady Han seated next to Lady Kim.

In the village and surrounding areas, people said that he owned so much land and property that "It was impossible to pass through Sancheong and its neighboring areas without stepping on the land of the Big Elder, Choi Hong-seon."

Choi Hong-seon's ancestor was *Sobeoldori*[21]. His middle ancestor came from the *Sangseogong* branch, which descended from Choi Yeon, the 10th-generation descendant of Choi Chi-won. Hong-seon was the 28th-generation Eldest Grandson of the Choi family, the small Head Family in Okdong-ri, Sancheong-myeon, Sancheong-gun. His nickname (Aho) was "*Jayu*" (In Chinese characters, the name means "a little child," and in Korean, "Jayu" translates to "Freedom" in English.), and his pen name (Ho) was "Heomjae."

How important is it now to know the size of the land he owned, the

---

21) Sobeoldori: A foundational figure from the *Silla* period and a key contributor to its founding. Before *Silla* was officially established, he was the village head of Dolsan Gohechon, one of the six villages in Gyeongju-si. "*Sobeol*" is believed to mean "*Soibeol*," similar to *Seorabeol*, the old name for *Silla*. It is said that Choi Chi-won, the 25th-generation descendant of his son Choi Daebeoli, became the founder of the Gyeongju Choi Clan.—The above is summarized by the author from Naver Namu Wiki.

number of livestock he had, or the number of tenant farmers?

As people go through life, events unfold, and naturally, property and wealth are consumed. Even today, his great-grandchild is listed as the owner of a considerable amount of land. It seems that Hong-seon's property has been maintained for over 100 years since his time.

In 1979, Sancheong-myeon became Sancheong-eup. Bok-hee married into the Choi family in Okdong-ri, Sancheong-gun, in 1926. By 2022, Sancheong consisted of one eup and ten myeon. Originally, when Bok-hee got married, the Choi Head Family belonged to Ok-dong, Saengnim-myeon. Later, when the area was reorganized under the eup system and became Saek-dong, it became part of Sancheong-eup. This is how she remembered it.

The property owned by this family, which had existed since before the Japanese occupation, covered more than one-third of the area and its neighboring regions in 1926, when Bok-hee married into the family. Although the exact boundaries could be determined by examining the addresses from that time, most of the current younger descendants are unaware of them.

Lady Hwang, the lawful wife at the time, sat closest to the left of Bok-hee's father-in-law, Hong-seon, the Big Elder. Hwang had married three years before Bok-hee, bringing a substantial amount of farmland and dowry. At the time of her marriage to Hong-seon, Hwang, who was 16—the same age as Bok-hee when she married—was strikingly beautiful, with a round face and large, clear, pretty eyes.

Next to Hong-seon, the Big Elder, sat the groom's biological mother, Lady Kim. Anyone could see that the groom, Il-seop, closely resembled his mother. It was difficult to determine exactly what Lady Kim had looked like in her younger years. By the time of Bok-hee's marriage, she had a thin, long face with a slightly elongated chin, similar to her husband's, and narrow eyes. The most distinctive feature of Lady Kim's face was her pointed nose, which stood out between her cheeks. Her eyes were narrow and delicate, but her nose had a high bridge with a sharp, pointed tip.

That day was a joyful one, as it marked the marriage of her eldest son. Lady Kim sat with her eyes slightly narrowed, her hands clasped tightly in her lap. Her shoulders were drawn inward, giving her a somewhat stiff posture. However, she did not exude an intimidating presence as a mother-in-law toward Bok-hee.

In retrospect, Bok-hee recalled that Lady Kim had been quieter that day than at any other time in their entire life together. This made Bok-hee briefly wonder whether living together in the future might prove difficult.

Next to Lady Kim sat Lady Han, known as "Lady Saemmyjip." She had a round face, large eyes, and a gentle, feminine figure, but her most distinctive feature was the deep, eight-shaped furrows around her mouth. Rather than focusing on Il-seop and Bok-hee, who were getting married, she was watching her son, Jeong-seop, intently. However, Jeong-seop deliberately avoided making eye contact with his biological mother.

Lady Han's voice was unique—a low, raspy tone that was unforgettable once heard. She rarely appeared in public, attending only the *Pyebaek* ceremony and not reappearing afterward. During the ceremony, Bok-hee sensed that Lady Han was staring at her intensely, even though Bok-hee's vision was slightly obscured by her *jokduri*. When their eyes met as Bok-hee bowed and raised her head, she even felt a sting in Han's gaze.

Reflecting on why Han had looked at her so intently, Bok-hee realized it was because Han was worried about her son, Jeong-seop. Just a few months after Il-seop's marriage, Jeong-seop also rushed into marriage under Lady Han's strong insistence.

These were Bok-hee's first impressions of her in-laws after joining her new family. Behind the Big Elder sat two women and one man. The two women were the Big Elder's younger sisters, making them Bok-hee's aunts-in-law. Among them, Hong-seon's cousin, Tae-jeong, was always by Bok-hee's side, assisting with the wedding. The one man was Choi Hong-man, the Big Elder's younger brother.

What words of blessing did the mothers-in-law offer to Bok-hee, their new daughter-in-law, during the *Pyebaek* ceremony?

Lady Kim said, "Have a good life on good terms."

Lady Hwang said, "You're in charge of a big household, so please keep it healthy."

Lady Han said, "Be wise even when difficulties arise."

In retrospect, Bok-hee realized that those words were actually reflections of their own hopes and lessons learned through their married lives. Rather than offering conventional blessings, they shared wisdom shaped by their experiences in their husband's household.

Even a casual word revealed their personal thoughts. Unlike the customary and formulaic phrases often spoken by the elders of the family, they expressed personal experiences from their own lives as women. As mothers-in-law, they felt the need to set an example for Bok-hee, a new member in their intricate web of relationships. Regardless of their individual relationships with Hong-seon, to them, Bok-hee was now their daughter-in-law.

Then again, when recalling her father-in-law, who oversaw and governed all household affairs, and his relationship with the family members, this is what Bok-hee remembered.

The Big Elder, Choi Hong-seon, had such a distinctive appearance that once you saw him, you couldn't forget him. His voice was large, resonant, and clear. Unlike most Asians, he had a high nose bridge that started where his eyes met, giving him a striking look. The thickness and shape of his nose were well-proportioned to his face.

Bok-hee had been told that he had started growing his beard in his mid-twenties. Because of this, the villagers also called him "The Elder with the Big Beard." Even in his late twenties, his beard sometimes grew so long that it reached down to his chest.

The most distinctive feature of Hong-seon's appearance was that he had a double eyelid on only one side—his right eye had a prominent double eyelid, while his left did not. However, as he aged and his eyelids drooped, this difference became less noticeable.

The overall shape of his face was a rounded oval without angular jaws. Yet, perhaps due to his large eyes and high nose bridge, his appearance was far from that of a typical East Asian. In many ways, he resembled a Westerner.

Due to his commanding presence and his firm, clear, low, and deep voice, anyone standing before him was likely to feel intimidated. What unsettled others the most, however, was his unwavering self-confidence.

In his younger years—during the time when Bok-hee married into the family and for a long period afterward—Hong-seon was always like that. Only with the passage of time did he begin to change. Bok-hee recalled that his self-confidence started to diminish after experiencing the Korean War, which occurred ten years before his death.

Hong-seon was the kind of person who had unwavering faith in himself. He always had the mindset to accept any outcome, regardless of his own judgments and decisions. He never blamed others for any unfavorable results.

Bok-hee's husband, Il-seop, always referred to Hong-seon as "Father," but Jeong-seop from Saemmyjip, like others, called him "Big Elder." Occasionally, Jeong-seop would also call him "Father," but Bok-hee recalled hearing this only a couple of times after she got married.

Jeong-seop, who was a year older than her husband, always seemed to lack a certain sense of confidence. This was likely related to the circumstances surrounding his mother, Lady Han. It could have been one reason, or it might have simply been part of Jeong-seop's inherent personality. He was someone who put all his effort into following whatever Hong-seon instructed him to do.

Joon-seop, the son of the Big Elder and Lady Hwang, was about 20 years younger than his two older brothers. Naturally, he was not present on the day Bok-hee married. Bok-hee remembered that Joon-seop also called his father "Big Elder." The Big Elder had his son, Choi Joon-seop, with his wife, Lady Hwang, when he was 49 years old.

If anyone had to say who most resembled Hong-seon in appearance, it would be Jeong-seop of the Saemmyjip family. It could also be said that the groom, Il-seop, bore a stronger resemblance to his father than his twin brother, Lee-seop. However, Il-seop primarily took after his mother, Lady Kim. Il-seop often said to Bok-hee, "I may not resemble my father much in appearance, but I feel there's something similar in the overall atmosphere that my face exudes."

In terms of appearance, Joon-seop closely resembled his mother, Lady Hwang, but he rarely showed stubbornness regarding his own matters, which was entirely different from his mother's nature. In her younger days, Lady Hwang had been very stubborn. Joon-seop did not inherit this trait from her.

A person's minor speech habits or physical characteristics can often reveal a lot about them.

Bok-hee's parents' home, Hyori in Hamyang-gun, was where the Jeong family lived together, alongside Confucian scholars from places such as Cheonggye *Seowon* and Namgye *Seowon*[22]. However, Bok-hee's mother had married into Hamyang from near Imsil in Jeonbuk Province. When Bok-hee visited her mother's house as a child, she noticed a skeletal structure with a face that had double eyelids and a high, Western-like nose—features similar to those of her father-in-law, the Big Elder, Hong-seon, whom she met after getting married. Bok-hee was also taller and had a

---

22) Seowon: These were the most common educational institutions in Korea during the *Joseon* Dynasty. They were private academies that combined the functions of a Confucian shrine and a Confucian school.—In reference to the Naver Korean Dictionary.

larger build than most women of her time. Her elder brothers were over 180 centimeters tall, had exceptionally white skin, and thick, curly hair.

People in some parts of Sancheong and near Imsil occasionally encountered individuals with unusual, exotic features, distinct from the indigenous people who lived there. It was believed that the Dutchman Weltevree[23]—known in Korea as Park Yeon (1378 - 1458)—who entered the country at the end of the *Goryeo*[24] Dynasty, had descendants in the region. Local people believed that Imsil was an area where the descendants of Park Yeon, who had become naturalized Koreans, lived together.

Bok-hee and Il-seop's marriage was arranged through an agreement between her father-in-law, Hong-seon, and her father. While traveling to western Gyeongsang Province on business, Hong-seon stayed in Soodong-myeon, Hamyang. There, he met Bok-hee's father, who lived nearby, and they developed a close relationship. The two men shared a deep interest in herbal medicine and treating the sick or wounded. They were known for helping sick people in their neighborhood, either by visiting their homes or by having them come over for herbal medicine and acupuncture. They provided their services free of charge to those in need and charged only those who could afford it.

In the early 1800s, most medical knowledge in Korea, known as Korean medicine (Oriental medicine), was passed down orally. Good medical books were rare, especially in the countryside. The knowledge originally came from China, with significant contributions from figures like Pyeon-jak[25], a famous doctor from the Warring States Period of China,

---

23) Weltevree: A Dutch seaman and teacher, he is said to have been the first Westerner to settle permanently in Korea.—In reference to Naver Folk Museum materials.
24) Goryeo: A powerful Korean kingdom founded in 918 CE during a period of national division known as the Later Three Kingdoms period. It unified and ruled the Korean Peninsula until 1392 CE.—In reference to the Naver Korean Dictionary.
25) Pyeon-jak (401-310 BCE): A physician from *Balhae,* in what is now Hebei and Shandong

and from the Ming Dynasty's *Bonchogangmok*[26]. During the *Joseon* Dynasty, reliable knowledge of Oriental medicine spread to the private sector in Korea, particularly through Heo Joon.

Hong-seon and Bok-hee's father were not professional doctors, but they were dedicated to classifying diseases and finding suitable treatments. They meticulously recorded the illnesses and wounds of the patients they treated. Using acupuncture and moxibustion, they applied treatments to the hands and feet based on the location of pain. They also classified the effects of medicinal plants by season, carefully collecting and drying them for future use.

In particular, Hong-seon was well-versed in the proper use of herbal ingredients. Most of his knowledge was based on Heo Joon's *Donguibogam*[27]. Whenever he had time, Hong-seon practiced on himself, often asking Bok-hee to boil or grind herbs to experiment with their efficacy. For all medicinal ingredients, *Bonchogangmok* remained his foundational text.

Fortunately, Sancheong had a longstanding reputation for its association with Yu Ui-tae[28], a famous Korean doctor of the 18th century. Perhaps for this reason, people eager to learn about Oriental medicine and

---

Provinces of mainland China.—In reference to the Naver Korean Encyclopedia.

26) Bonchogangmok: A pharmacological text compiling medicinal knowledge from various regions of China, published by Li Shizhen (1518–1593 CE) during the Ming Dynasty.—In reference to the Naver Korean Encyclopedia.

27) Donguibogam: Completed around 1610 and published by Heo Joon (1539–1615), a physician appointed to the Royal Court. Written in Classical Chinese, the scholarly language of the time, the text was commissioned by King Seonjo of the *Joseon* Dynasty (1392–1897 CE). It was later translated into Korean, ensuring its widespread accessibility. —In reference to the Naver Korean Encyclopedia.

28) Yu Ui-tae (also known as Yu I-ta): A prominent physician who lived during the reign of King Sukjong in the late 18th century. He was renowned as a miracle doctor (Shinui) for saving many people from the agony of diseases in regions such as Sancheong, Jinju, Hapcheon, and Geochang. Particularly notable is Yu Ui-tae's *Majin Pyeon*, a medical book closely related to the development of treatments for measles and smallpox in the late Joseon period. This work was published earlier than Jeong Yak-yong's *Magwae Tong*.—These facts were summarized by the author with reference to Naver Encyclopedia.

medicinal herbs often gathered in Sancheong. It was said that groups of learners would come from all eight provinces of *Joseon* to Sancheong. Hong-seon was well-acquainted with various herbal medicines and possessed considerable skill in acupuncture.

In 1926, when Bok-hee entered the Choi household, there were many servants. It was a bustling estate, much like any landowner's house in *Joseon*, with people constantly coming and going. In front of the *sarang-chae* and *haengnang-chae*, three to four horse stones stood near the yard, where horses could be tied.

After her marriage, Bok-hee saw Hong-seon riding a magnificent horse with a glossy black mane to a horse ranch at the base of *Jiri Mountain,* accompanied by his servants. They would stay there for a few days and return with their prey.

Bok-hee never asked anyone exactly how large Hong-seon's horse ranch was. She only inquired briefly with Yoo-sang, the reliable butler who was almost always by Hong-seon's side. Yoo-sang, responsible for nearly all of the estate's external affairs, was Hong-seon's most trusted confidant. Yoo-sang explained, "Since this is a mountainous area, there is no need to manage it as a structured ranch. The size isn't very large, but it is sufficient for fifty horses to run and play."

However, the only person who accompanied Hong-seon to the horse ranch was Jeong-seop, Lady Han's son from Saemmyjip.

Lady Kim, the lady of the Big House, moved to a small room (*gol-bang*[29] in Korean) behind the main room two days before Bok-hee married into the family. As the first mistress of the Choi household, Lady Kim was born in 1879, making her two years older than her husband, Hong-seon. She married at the age of twenty-one and moved into this

---

29) Gol-bang: A small, enclosed room located between larger rooms, often used for storage or as a private space in traditional Korean houses. It is typically situated between main rooms, such as between a bedroom and the kitchen, and can be somewhat isolated or hidden from view.—This information was written by the author.

house, which was considered quite late for marriage at the time.

Lady Kim had never shown any disappointing behavior toward Bok-hee, as everyone in the neighborhood knew. However, she may never have felt truly proud of living in the main room until she met her daughter-in-law. Like all women of that time, she believed that *"Once a woman marries and moves into her husband's house, she stays there until death."*

Behind the main room, connected to the kitchen in the dining space, there was a small *gol-bang* with an *ondol* (hot stone floor—Korean traditional floor heating system). It was hidden behind sliding Japanese-style paper doors, giving the impression of being concealed behind the main room. From there, one could get a good view of the kitchen. Since the doors were sliding, they could be quietly opened, allowing someone to exit discreetly if no one was present outside the main room.

Lady Kim could sit in the *gol-bang* and hear everything happening in the kitchen—the movement of food and all the women's conversations. It was a very small room, but its *ondol* floor remained warm throughout the year, thanks to the heat from the kitchen.

People in the neighborhood referred to the house where Lady Kim lived as the "Big House" because she was Hong-seon's first wife. This was after the Big Elder, Hong-seon, had a formal wedding ceremony with his second wife, Lady Hwang.

When Bok-hee married Il-seop, she wasn't just entering a world that belonged to her husband alone; she was stepping into a life intertwined with his blood relatives. After completing the *Pyebaek* ritual and returning to the main room, she felt a surge of determination rise within her like a swelling tide:

"From now on, I must fight to the end in this Choi family and protect what matters most!"

After paying another round of respects to the Choi ancestors at the family shrine, her resolve became even stronger. The adversary Bok-hee envisioned was not a specific person. From the moment she stepped into her new home, her life was dedicated solely to her husband, Il-seop, their future children, and herself. Unconsciously clenching her fists, she resolved to face each day with wide-open eyes and to live her life fully and fiercely.

To Bok-hee, Sancheong became as familiar as Hamyang, a place she had known well since childhood. She strove to embrace the scents of this land and this house. A home is a place that only the strong can claim. On this land of survival of the fittest, she resolved to remain as the tenacious "*inhabitant*" who endures to the very end.

05
The Choi Household

From the 1920s Onward: The Big House,
 the New House, and the Saemmy House
 in Sancheong
  —Surnames and Characters

A Neighbor's House in Hometown (Watercoloring on Kent paper, 364x515mm)

According to data from 2021, Sancheong County (Gun) is located in the midwestern part of Gyeongsangnam-do, South Korea. The county office is situated in Sancheong-eup. The area covers 794.61 km², with 19,600 households and a total population of 34,360. Originally known as Saneum, it consisted of the two towns of Sancheong and Danseong. In 1767, the name was changed to Sancheong. In the third year of King Gojong's reign (1895), its status was changed from a hyeon (prefecture) to a gun (county), and in 1914, Danseong was merged into Sancheong. (Source: Wikipedia—Referenced by the author.)

In 1966, the total population was 115,728. In the 1920s, when Bok-hee got married, Ok-dong, where the Choi family lived, was part of Saengnim-myeon. At that time, according to Japanese statistics, there were 265 Korean households in Saengnim, with a total Korean population of 1,309. (Source: theme.archives.go.kr.)

According to Bok-hee's recollection, in 1926, not only Saengnim-myeon but also the neighboring villages had an estimated total population of about 1,500 people. Therefore, considering that around 250 people attended Bok-hee's *Pyebaek* ceremony that day, it is reasonable to assume that approximately one-sixth of the population participated.

Hong-seon's house was not a high-class residence from the late *Joseon* period in terms of area or scale, but it was a large house equipped with everything necessary. When Bok-hee got married, the total area was about 1,400 *pyeong*. One *pyeong* is equivalent to 3.3 square meters.

This area was sometimes seen in farming-oriented households, as it was quite a large piece of land. The house was built in the mid-1910s and featured a hipped roof. (For roof types of Korean tiled houses, refer to the illustration at the beginning of this book.)

If it had been a high-class residence in Seoul or the Gyeonggi region, it would have had a *paljak* (gabled) roof with gable ends. Compared to such houses, this house had a lower (*ujingak*) and more modest hip-and-gable roof, typical of Korean tiled houses. Under the roof, it had simple eaves without decorative extensions, which was not characteristic of luxurious upper-class residences.

The house was divided into three main sections: the *sarang-chae* (men's quarters), *an-chae* (women's quarters), and *haengnang-chae* (servants' quarters). The living quarters included the *an-chae* and *sarang-chae*, where the Choi family resided, and the *haengnang-chae*, where wandering laborers or permanent young workers lived. In addition, there were workspaces such as a mill powered by an ox, a family bathhouse, and a grain storage area of about 20 *pyeong*.

Compared to the economic scale of the Choi family, the somewhat modest hipped roofs of the *an-chae* and *sarang-chae* were attributed to Hong-seon's wisdom by the villagers. During the *Japanese colonial period*[30], the design of the house, built during this time, resulted in a modest, middle-class appearance. When the house was built in the mid-1910s, at the very beginning of the Japanese colonial period, all assets had to be monitored by the Japanese. People said that Hong-seon deliberately chose a slightly lower roof design. It was built relatively modestly to avoid drawing attention and to reduce economic exploitation by the Japanese, demonstrating meticulous calculation.

For example, Hong-seon's ancestral home, built around the 1860s, had a *paljak* (gabled) roof, a style typical of upper-class residences during the *Joseon* Dynasty. The *sarang-chae*, *an-chae*, and *haengnang-chae* together covered about 600 *pyeong* and featured high gable roofs. It was a properly

---

[30] The Japanese colonial period: Which lasted approximately 35 years from the annexation of Korea on September 29, 1910, to the liberation on August 15, 1945 (often rounded to 36 years).—According to the Encyclopedia of Korean Culture by the author.

equipped upper-class house. The roof style symbolized the house's dignity.

As mentioned earlier, the layout of the *an-chae* followed the straight-line shape typical of houses in the southern regions of the Korean Peninsula, complete with a *toen-maru* (a narrow wooden porch running along the outside of a room, similar to a veranda).

On the family's "Bath day," it became a communal event, with Seok-sen and Yoo-sang instructing the servants to diligently carry firewood and branches. These were used as kindling for the large iron cauldron in the bathhouse, situated a short distance from the *an-chae*. The bathhouse's iron cauldron was large enough to comfortably accommodate about four people. A large cotton cloth was laid at the bottom of the cauldron to prevent slipping and to protect feet from the hot metal surface.

The bathing order started with Hong-seon, followed by Il-seop. Among the younger generation, Ki-hoon went first. The men soaked their bodies in the iron cauldron and then finished washing on the bathhouse floor. After the men of the house finished bathing, the women took their turn. Next to the *an-chae* and beneath the wall behind the kitchen, jars for storing kimchi and grains were buried. In the vegetable garden attached to the wall, they grew lettuce and various vegetables that could be used as side dishes.

In front of the *daecheong-maru* (large wooden floor) of the *an-chae* (inner quarters and main house) was the *sarang-chae* (outer quarters). In the large room of the *sarang-chae*, the Big Elder primarily resided, while Il-seop lived in the lower room. Similarly, there were rooms on both sides of the *daecheong-maru*. The doors of these rooms were located at both the front and the back, allowing for good ventilation and visibility of passersby when opened during summer days.

Even after Bok-hee got married and moved in, literary guests who wrote poetry or painted would often stay in the *sarang-chae* for several days. However, in the year of Korea's liberation from Japan—yes, from that year (1945) onwards—such visitors were rarely seen in this house.

That was the year Il-seop passed away.

In the lower room of the *sarang-chae*...

There were two gates, and when you entered through the main gate, an old, tall pagoda tree stood in the yard to the left, towering well above the gate. To enter the gate from the wide alleyway, you would see a row of animal feeding troughs lined up along the house's wall. Every morning and evening, the livestock ate feed made from leftover food and barley husks that had been boiled together. After eating, the troughs were washed and lined up again along the wall. Leftover side dishes and food from the house were gathered in the feeding troughs. The next morning, they were taken from the troughs, mixed with grain husks, boiled, and then fed to the animals. Sometimes, when it rained, the rainwater running down the tiled roof of the *haengnang-chae* would wash the troughs clean.

Upon entering through the main gate, the yard was covered with gravel and coarse sand. Inside the wall were the *haengnang-chae* and storage rooms, where half-pounded grain, sacks of beans, and other grains waiting to be processed were stored together in the mill.

Later, in the 1970s, part of the house's wall was torn down. The *haengnang-chae*, the cow shed, the pigsty, and the storage rooms were removed to make way for a new road. The remaining land in front was divided and sold to others, leaving only the *sarang-chae* and *an-chae*.

Where the small gate originally stood, a wide new road for cars was built right in front, and a large new gate was created in front of the *sarang-chae*. Instead, part of the large old gate was removed, and a new wall was built to create another small gate. This small gate along the narrow alleyway became the main entrance for women carrying goods from the market. Of course, the cows, pigs, and feeding troughs disappeared as well.

As you know, the *an-chae* was where the women managed household affairs. The *sarang-chae* was primarily where the men resided, and it had shelves with stationery and books for painting and writing. When guests arrived, drinks and meals were served in the *sarang-chae*.

From the 1910s, when the house was built, until Korea's liberation in 1945, renowned painters and calligraphers visited and left their works, which were kept in Hong-seon's closet. Most of these works were lost during the Korean War in 1950 and amidst the comings and goings of people. Some of them were said to have been distributed among family members and passed down.

The house, referred to as "The Big House," had nearly identical floor plans to two other houses called "Saemmy House" and "The New House."

Starting with Saemmyjip (as previously mentioned, "*jip*" is the Korean word for "house" in English), it was the residence of Lady Han, the second wife of Hong-seon. Choi Jeong-seop, the son born to Lady Han, was a year older than the twins Il-seop and Lee-seop. The total area of Saemmyjip was about 800 *pyeong* (approximately 2,645 square meters), and it was located a bit away from the Big House. To reach it from there, one had to walk slowly for over 20 minutes, passing through several intersections. This house was completely destroyed by a bombing during the height of the Korean War. Naturally, the large well was buried as well. The site and its surroundings are now occupied by the Sancheong Office of Education.

Next, the New House, from a distance, appeared to be connected to the Big House. This New House was approximately 900 *pyeong* (about 2,975 square meters) in size. It was the residence of Lady Hwang, the third wife of Hong-seon, and her family. The gate of the New House was situated in the opposite direction from the Big House's gate. To enter the New House's gate, one had to take a different alleyway than the one leading to the Big House. Thus, the inhabitants of the New House and the Big House rarely met directly.

However, Hong-seon, being the head of both houses, had an access passage connecting the two houses for his convenience. There was an open area that allowed passage between the *Jangdok-gan* (platform for crocks of sauces and condiments) in front of the Big House's kitchen and the yard of the New House's inner quarters. This was *the only part where there was no dividing wall* between the Big House and the New House.

The partial space of the *Jangdok-gan* at the Big House served as a *shortcut* to the New House. Thus, if viewed from above, the Big House and the New House would appear to be attached like twins.

As mentioned earlier, *the open wall* between the *Jangdok-gan* of the Big House and the New House was used only for special matters by familiar servants and close family members of both houses. For example, although Hong-seon resided in the New House, he often received lunch and dinner from the Big House and ate them at the New House. Sometimes, he would eat the food prepared by Bok-hee from the Big House in the *sarang-chae* of the Big House. This arrangement was likely because both houses belonged to Hong-seon and functioned as an economic community.

In fact, when Bok-hee married into the family, most of the land and wealth had already been significantly expanded and developed by Hong-seon himself. Hong-seon, Bok-hee's father-in-law and the master of the house, would introduce himself everywhere as, "I am a merchant."

If you search for the names of notable figures from Sancheong County in 2020 online, you will mostly find a few individuals from the Choi family who held local government positions, as well as a person from a related family who served as a Supreme Court Justice. However, it is difficult to find information about those who worked in education or other professions.

The omission of Hong-seon's name from such records cannot be attributed solely to the passage of time. However, the historical records of that village are traces of the lives of the people who lived there. This raises questions about how well local figures were recognized when the information was posted online.

Even if the researchers were not familiar with the Sancheong area, it is questionable how much they inquired of elderly residents who might have heard of Hong-seon, as it was only about a hundred years ago. Typically, young civil servants tasked with such record-keeping are satisfied with listing individuals who held political office or had notable achievements in government. Although Hong-seon called himself a merchant, it is unfortunate that a figure like him was overlooked.

Hong-seon's father was once appointed to an official position. However, Hong-seon himself identified as a businessman, and since he never revealed even his small deeds to the outside world, this might be the reason why his achievements were not widely known. Hong-seon also contributed to the Korean independence funds on several occasions.

More than his public deeds, what I want to highlight about the esteemed Elder Hong-seon is something else. During those difficult times, Hong-seon became *a model Elder whom the local people followed and respected.*

There was a certain individual who had considerable wealth and silently helped those around him who were in need. More importantly, he treated everyone equally, regardless of social status, and lived harmoniously with them. He willingly helped and taught the uneducated and struggling people around him to live righteously.

Even after his own children passed away before him, he never blamed anyone and continued to care for many descendants. Despite the pain caused by the loss of his children, he maintained his purity and innocence. Living righteously while enduring pain is a difficult and valuable way of life.

However, assessments of such a life may vary, for values ebb and flow with the tides of time.

So, how did Hong-seon, who built and managed these three houses and their families, come to possess such immense wealth?

I investigated the formation of the family's wealth, primarily based on Bok-hee's recollections. Hong-seon's father was awarded the rank of *Uigumbu Dosa*, a fifth-rank official, during the reign of King Gojong (the

26th king of *Joseon*, 1852 - 1919) in the late *Joseon* period. Typically, a fifth-rank official would have been required to reside in Hanyang (now Seoul). However, after *Joseon* became a colony of Japan in 1910, regional governance by the *Joseon* king would not have been effective. Considering accounts from neighboring people, it is likely that this position was granted during King Gojong's reign and that it was a temporary post extending to the provinces.

Given the circumstances of that time, it can be inferred from the title *Uigumbu Dosa* that Hong-seon's father was assigned a role overseeing Gyeongsang Province on behalf of the central government in Hanyang. For example, he would stay in his region, receive the king's policies through various channels, gather local representatives to communicate and make decisions, and then relay the results back to the king. This seems to have been the extent of his duties.

The father of Hong-seon's pen name was "Heukyang," which translates to "Black Goat" in Korean. A pen name, or *aho*, is akin to a nickname, often chosen by oneself or given by friends. His nickname was briefly mentioned in Hong-seon's earlier words. Due to his unusually thick and glossy black beard, he chose this pen name himself. His other pen name was "Gongyeo," meaning "Shared."

Of course, Hong-seon's family had always owned about 500 *majigi*[31] of rice fields. However, it was said that Hong-seon's substantial wealth in the 1920s was largely due to his mother, Lady Haman Jo. At that time, women's names were not recorded, so her full name is unknown. Her surname is listed as Haman Jo, with *Haman* referring to the *Bon-gwan* mentioned later.

---

31) Majigi: Originally, one *majigi* referred to the amount of land that could be sown with one mal (ten doe, approximately 18 liters) of seed. The size varied by region, ranging from about 150 *pyeong* to 300 *pyeong*. Typically, a rice field *majigi* was considered to be around 200 *pyeong* (661 m^2), while a field *majigi* ranged from 100 *pyeong* (331 m^2) to 300 *pyeong* (992 m^2), depending on the region.—This information is summarized by the author from factin.tistory.com.

Lady Jo, Hong-seon's mother, came from Milyang in Gyeongnam. She was the only daughter of a large landowner in Milyang and brought with her one-third of her family's wealth when she married. This indicates that even in the early 1870s, it was not uncommon for women to bring their family's wealth into their marriage.

She sold most of this wealth and bought many cows. Around the time her son, Hong-seon, was born, these cows were moved to neighboring areas to engage in "Cow leasing[32]." By the time Hong-seon was 15 or 16 years old, the profits from this venture had grown enormously, and they owned over 1,000 cows. At that time, one cow was worth enough to buy a typical thatched house, making it a significant household asset.

From a young age, Hong-seon began pursuing what he believed to be his talent—trading. He traveled to various regions, immersing himself in business. Although he was active during the late *Joseon* period, it is likely that his activities were connected to the tradition of peddlers[33] and merchants. These peddlers, known as *Bobusang*, carried out extensive trade activities and played a significant role, especially in times of national crisis, by procuring and supplying food and other essentials.

Using the wealth amassed by his mother as capital, Hong-seon engaged in what would now be called the logistics and distribution industry. He primarily operated in the western Gyeongnam region, as well as in Busan, Gimhae, and Miryang, from the late Joseon period. He occasionally handled goods produced in Japan and China, receiving them

---

[32] Cow leasing involved borrowing cows, raising them, and then selling them after they matured or bore calves, sharing the profits with the cow owner.—According to the Naver Korean Dictionary.

[33] Peddlers: A term encompassing both "bottled merchants" and "pack merchants." Pack merchants (*Busang*) existed before the Three Kingdoms period, while bottled merchants (*Bosang*) began during the *Silla* period. It is said that they had strong principles of discipline, etiquette, and mutual assistance among themselves. From the *Joseon* period onwards, they were actively involved in various activities, such as procuring and supplying food during national emergencies.—This summary is referenced by the author from the Standard Korean Dictionary.

in the Incheon or Busan areas and trading them within his main operating area in western Gyeongnam.

His extensive knowledge of traditional Korean medicine was partly due to dealing with medicinal herbs as commodities, but also because such knowledge was necessary for his business. He often had to transport goods over long distances on poor roads, far from home. In such work, he needed to be prepared for injuries or acute indigestion among his workers.

In the past, when clean water was scarce, people frequently suffered from stomach aches due to drinking contaminated water or eating unclean food. In other words, transporting goods along narrow, winding roads mainly involved carrying them on people's backs or using devices like *jige* (a traditional Korean A-frame carrier) wooden carriers. During such transportation, bruises and joint injuries were common. These incidents could also occur in remote, sparsely populated areas. Therefore, having a general knowledge of medical care was essential.

Hong-seon purchased almost every book related to emergency medical knowledge that he came across. This is why his *sarang-chae* in the Big House was filled with various books on traditional Korean medicine and basic medical texts. He made an effort to expand on what he learned from these books. Every time he climbed the mountains, he meticulously recorded information about the small flowers, roots, and stems that bloomed according to the region and season in his notebook, studying them thoroughly.

As a result, neighbors often ran to Hong-seon's house for help whenever they suffered from stomach issues or injuries. Bok-hee mentioned that the smell of medicinal tea brewing never ceased in the Big House.

In addition, from the mid-1930s, Hong-seon sold some of the rice paddies and fields he had purchased to buy Japanese stocks. The route through which he acquired these stocks was through Yang Gon, a relatively close relative living in Japan. Gon was the son of a cousin on Hong-seon's mother's side and had been living in Japan since the early 1930s.

Gon had a tumultuous childhood. His mother married three times because her first two husbands died early. He was beaten daily by his third stepfather for no reason and eventually left that house, moving between various relatives' homes. Gon's mother could no longer bear to see her son in such a pitiable condition, so she sent him to another relative with the last name Yang as an adopted son. Following his adoptive father's surname, Gon became Yang Gon.

After growing up to some extent, he told his family, "I will go to Japan to earn money," and boarded a smuggling ship to Japan.

Gon started from the bottom in Shimonoseki, Japan. Initially, he worked on a fishing boat but gradually made his way to the northern regions close to Russia, including Hokkaido. After 1940, he settled in Hokkaido, where he married a Japanese woman. Her father was a well-known yakuza (Japanese gangster) in the area.

Hong-seon got in touch with Gon and began exchanging letters with him in the mid-1930s, learning about the situation in Japan. Following Gon's advice, he initially bought stocks related to the fishing industry in places like Otaru, Hokkaido. Later, through Gon's introduction, he also bought other types of stocks in Osaka and Kumamoto.

When Japan was defeated in 1945, the Japanese money and stocks Hong-seon owned became worthless. However, due to the 1965 Korea-Japan Agreement, Bok-hee knew that some of the remaining stocks were partially compensated by Japan. By that time, Hong-seon had already passed away, so Bok-hee's eldest son, Ki-hoon, handled all the assets.

Nonetheless, even in the 1940s, Choi Hong-seon, the esteemed Big Elder, maintained a solid economic foundation without any issues.

What kind of people were the members of the Choi family?

When talking about people, what best describes a person? Is it their age, blood type, hometown, or physiognomy? Among these, which best reflects an individual's temperament and disposition? Do their hometown and physiognomy offer the most comprehensive answers? Most might agree with this, but there is a more definitive answer.

The author first considers that foreigners living in Korea may want to know what Koreans are like. Even among Koreans themselves, if they want to gain a rough understanding of the people they are dealing with, it is important to know their surname.

What significance does a surname hold for Koreans?

If Korea differs from other countries in some way, it is in how clans have historically gathered to form villages and maintained clan-based communal living for a long time. This was due to the difficulty of transportation and the ability to live self-sufficiently without much need for external interaction.

Typically, a clan-based society refers to a stage before the establishment of a class-based society. It is said that during the *Joseon* Dynasty, Korea developed a certain level of class hierarchy with the *yangban* (civil and military officials) system and a structured social order of scholars, farmers, artisans, and merchants.

However, even in the 2020s, it is common for Koreans to ask, "What is your surname? Where is your hometown?" when meeting someone for the first time. This may be because they believe that knowing a person's surname and hometown can give them some insight into the person's character and disposition. It is also a way of trying to understand where the person they are communicating with has lived and what they have learned from their ancestors.

Is this a reasonable assumption? Whether one believes it or not, and while it is unlikely to be universally proven or certain, Koreans generally perceive it this way. Of course, it is difficult to generalize the overall characteristics of a surname, regardless of whether a person received it from their father, mother, or through adoption.

This practice of asking about one's hometown and surname first is similar to using physiognomy as statistical predictive data. But how can physiognomy reveal a person's disposition or future?

Literally speaking, physiognomy is mostly used for conjecture. For example, by looking at a person with a certain type of physiognomy, people generally try to guess what kinds of hardships and sufferings they might be experiencing in their daily life, how they might overcome those difficulties, or how they might live in the future. They look for small pieces of evidence that correspond with the person's current situation through their physiognomy in order to predict the plausibility of that person's life.

In Korea, due to its small territory, clan villages have been maintained for a relatively long time. Regional affiliation has influenced residents and inhabitants in certain aspects of their collective or individual temperament. Sometimes, these surnames are also used as tools to categorize people.

For instance, consider the Gyeongju Choi clan, to which Il-seop, the husband of Bok-hee, belongs. They are often described as being stubborn and highly competitive, yet also having drive, responsibility, and consideration.

When meeting someone for the first time, if their surname is Choi, one might have the preconception—Ah, since they are a Choi, they are probably somewhat competitive and driven, so they should be capable of handling this task. This bias can be either positive or negative, whether used by those trying to include someone in their group or by those deliberately trying to exclude them.

Surnames, even if they appear to use the same Chinese character "Choi," are divided into different "*Bon-gwan*[34]." For instance, Gyeongju,

---

34) The term "*Bon-gwan*" refers to the origin of a clan, based on the birthplace of the clan's founder (*sijo*) or middle founder, or the ancestral seat of the clan. *Bon-gwan* is also known as "*Hyangjeok*," which means the hometown of the clan's progenitor or ancestors. In other

Jeonju, and Haeju are examples of different *Bon-gwan* for the Choi surname. Thus, generalizing about all Choi individuals is difficult.[35]. For example, Choi Il-seop is a Choi from Gyeongju, and his given name is Il-seop. Here, Gyeongju is the *Bon-gwan*, and the surname is Choi.

In other words, Korean surnames must include the regional name, bon-gwan, before the surname. Through *Bon-gwan*, one can know the place where the clan's progenitor lived and understand their lineage and status. As seen in the previous example with Yang Gon, a person's surname plays a significant role, especially in forming their identity.

The *Bon-gwan* should not be regarded as merely the birthplace or hometown listed in modern personal documents. Nowadays, administrative computerization allows for the easy change of birthplaces in records. Although the name in documents can be changed, the hometown is the place where an individual was born and raised. If the hometown is seen as the cradle of a person's personal unconsciousness, then the *Bon-gwan* might be considered the cradle of the collective unconscious within the individual.

Therefore, revealing one's surname in Korea implies sharing this deeper context.

As a Choi with roots in a specific region, one's life would reflect this lineage. However, in the present day, even though Korea is a small country, its population has grown. With more frequent intermarriages with other ethnicities and foreigners, it is impossible to define a person solely by their surname. Focusing only on a surname to understand a person can be seen as

---

words, it refers to the place that represents the origin or ancestral homeland of the clan. Source: Naver Knowledge Encyclopedia and Korean dictionaries.—Summarized by the author.

35) According to the 2015 census by the Korea National Statistical Office, there are 2,333,927 people with the surname Choi, making it the fourth most common surname after Kim, Lee, Park. The Choi surname has 387 recorded bon-gwan, but only 43 bon-gwan with verified progenitors and lineage, including Gyeongju, Jeonju, Haeju, Gangneung, Tamjin, Suseong, Saknyeong, and Hwasun.—This summary was extracted from Naver Wiki Dictionary by the author.

foolish. Therefore, some people rely more on one's *saju*[36], or even their zodiac sign.

However, to understand Koreans a bit better, it is important to acknowledge such factors. It shows how powerful and formidable local customs can be and serves as evidence of their influence. The deeply ingrained characteristics of the local soil must be remembered for their tenacity. *Only those who learn and adapt to the habits of their habitat can survive more robustly in that environment.*

The mentions of surnames in this book should be regarded as general secular evaluations, and they may not necessarily apply to every individual. After all, is there anything as harmful as prejudice when meeting people?

In contrast, no other country outside of Korea distinguishes a person's character or disposition based on their surname. Thus, discussing surnames in this way can be considered a uniquely Korean approach.

In other words, when people in England talk about those with surnames like Adams, Allen, Anderson, Baker, or Ball, they do not say that Adamses generally behave in a certain way or that Andersons typically handle things in a particular manner.

However, in Korea, such factors carry some weight. Local surnames derived from regional characteristics can be significant. This means that *Bon-gwan* (the origin of the clan) associated with a surname, as well as the habits of ancestors in that regional *habitat*, are not entirely unrelated to a person's characteristics. This also reflects that Korea, with its relatively small territory and close-knit regions, is quite distinct from other countries. While we're on the topic, there is another unique aspect of surnames in Korea compared to other countries.

Since we are on the topic, there is another point about surnames that

---

36) *Saju* (Four Pillars of Destiny): The four components of a person's birth year, month, day, and time, each represented by a stem and branch. This system is used to predict a person's fortune and destiny based on these elements.—Referenced from Naver Korean Dictionary by the author.

makes Korea different from other countries.

In most other countries, when a woman gets married, the possessive term "Mrs." is often added, implying "belonging to that person." Depending on the country, the woman may even abandon her maiden name and take on her husband's surname after marriage.

In Korea, however, this is not the case. Traditionally, women retain their maiden surname even after marriage. For instance, although Bok-hee married into the Choi family, she continued to use her surname, Jeong, throughout her life. This can be seen as a form of respect for a woman's original surname in Korean culture, or it might indicate that the inherent nature of the surname is considered independent of marriage.

Talking about surnames might be seen as clinging to outdated practices. However, the author wants to point out that the characteristics of surnames subtly manifest in an individual's thinking, which cannot be ignored, at least in Korea.

While living her married life, Bok-hee, raising her children who carried Il-seop's Choi surname, often said, "Like a pestle in a mortar, shooting up sky-high and then quickly subsiding, *ppulttagui*"[37] From Bok-hee's perspective as a Jeong, Il-seop and his children had remarkably similar temperaments. Choi individuals tended to lose their temper quickly and without thinking, showing impulsive and hot-headed traits. Literally, Il-seop often exploded in anger like fire but soon calmed down.

Therefore, the people living in the Choi household knew that if anyone in the family got furious over something, they just needed to endure for a bit, as the anger would soon pass. It seemed that Il-seop couldn't wait

---

37) According to the Naver Korean Dictionary, "*ppulttagui*" is a colloquial term for a person who gets angry or loses their temper. It can also be referred to as "*ppul*" or "*ppulttagu*" in dialects. The term "*ppulttuk-ppulttuk*" describes someone who suddenly and repeatedly loses their temper.—Referenced from the Naver Korean Dictionary.

even for a moment, and his fiery temper was so uncontrollable that it might have led to his own demise. Bok-hee wondered if he had regretted his actions immediately before his death, though no one would ever know.

There is also a saying that many people often hear: "In a certain village, a person with the Choi surname was so stubborn and stingy that not even a single blade of grass could grow where they sat." This indicates that Chois are known for their stubbornness and their tendency to dominate those around them, to the extent that "Even weeds cannot sprout where their presence has suppressed them."

Because of such circulating remarks, regardless of their actual *Bon-gwan*, Chois often face prejudice. In first encounters between people, it is common to hear, half-jokingly and half-seriously, "Oh, you're a Choi? I've heard that not even a single blade of grass grows where a Choi sits."

During his life, Il-seop lived quite grandly, always conscious of others' opinions. He was often described as a stubborn and obstinate Choi, but all his actions had a clear principle behind them. Bok-hee remembered this as Il-seop having a unique affection and pride in his Choi surname, even more than in his roles as a father or husband. Il-seop lived as a Choi until the end.

He was the son of Hong-seon, who, unable to control his fiery temper, threw himself into the flames, leaving behind words of regret.

The people of Sancheong lived with a mix of various surnames, such as Changnyeong Jo, Gimhae Kim, Gwak, Hwang, and Lee. While their children moved to different regions, some eventually returned to their hometown.

How, then, could one describe Il-seop's biological mother, Lady Kim of the Big House?

She was from the Gwangsan Kim clan, one of the most numerous surnames in Korea, with one in five Koreans bearing it. The Kim clan is broadly divided into the *Silla* and *Gaya* lines.38) It is generally said that Kims are determined and affectionate. Despite being abandoned by Hong-seon, as Il-seop's mother, she remained steadfast and maintained her position. Due to the sheer number of Kims, they can be divided into many subgroups. However, most Kims are known to be quick-witted and capable of adapting their behavior to suit others. This can be seen as a rough characterization of Lady Kim.

Next, how about Lady Hwang of the New House?

The Hwang surname has several *Bon-gwan*, but the main ones are Changwon, Jangsu, and Pyeonghae. The progenitor was Hwang Rak from the Later Han dynasty in China, who, while en route to Vietnam as an envoy during Emperor Guangwu's reign, was shipwrecked and arrived in Pyeonghae of *Silla*, where he naturalized and became the ancestor of the Korean Hwangs.39)

Lady Hwang of the New House was from the Deoksan Hwang clan. The Hwangs are known for their distinct personalities and strong sense of pride. While living in the Big House, Bok-hee rarely heard anything offensive from Lady Hwang. This showed that she was meticulous in guarding her own affairs. Some relatives of the Choi clan believed that the Hwangs were particularly stubborn—almost childishly so.

Bok-hee thought that Lady Hwang's assertiveness stemmed from her tendency to express her thoughts openly rather than keeping them hidden. It

---

38) The *Silla* Kim line, starting from Kim Alji, is divided into the Gyeongju Kim line from King Gyeongsun and other non-Gyeongsun lines like Gwangsan Kim, Gwangneung Kim, and Seonsan Kim. Over 70% of *Silla* Kims belong to the Gyeongsun line, including Gyeongju, Gimnyeong, Andong, and Uiseong Kims. The non-Gyeongsun line includes Gwangsan, Gwangneung, and Seonsan Kims. Additionally, there are nine other surnames derived from the Silla Kim clan, including Gamcheon Mun, Gangneung Kim, Goksan Kim, Gwangju Lee, Suseong Choi, Andong Kwon, Yeongyang Nam, Cheorwon Gung, and Taean Sa.
— Summarized from Naver and blog.naver.com by the author.

39) According to the 1985 census conducted by the Economic Planning Board, there were 134,347 households and 564,265 individuals, ranking 16th out of 274 surnames.
— Summarized from www.hwang.ne.kr > jokbo by the author.

seemed that her stubbornness was mostly directed toward her husband, Hong-seon, and their children.

How about Lady Han, the lady of the main room at Saemmy House?

Lady Han of Saemmy House was from the Han clan[40]. People say that members of the Han clan are free-spirited, dislike being tied down, are quick-witted, and prefer their own work. Bok-hee did not interact much with Lady Han, who was from the Cheongju Han clan.

The general opinion about Lady Han's nephew, a chief judge, was that he was very kind to others and exceptionally meticulous about his work. Lady Han attended Bok-hee's wedding ceremony but soon returned to her own home. When Jeong-seop was around ten years old, she remarried and moved to another house. Although Bok-hee didn't see her often, they did meet a few times.

With this, the author has outlined the story of surnames surrounding the Choi family members, illustrating their general characteristics.

Now, let's delve into the story of how the Eldest Patriarch, Hong-seon, distributed his substantial wealth. Each son was given nearly the same amount of property when starting a new family—that is, upon getting married.

About ten years after Bok-hee's marriage, around the late 1930s, Hong-seon began to organize some of his assets, including stocks and land that had yielded returns. He called together his younger brother, Choi Hong-man, along with Jeong-seop, the son of Saemmy House, as well as Il-seop and Lee-seop. Lee-seop, Il-seop's younger brother, had received a larger share, including a brewery, when he got married. Hong-seon

---

40) The Han surname ranked 11th in population among Korean surnames, with 773,404 individuals recorded in the 2015 Population Census by Statistics Korea. This clan has 10 bon-gwan: Cheongju, Danju, Pyeongsan, Hanyang, Anbyeon, Yangju, Goksan, Hongsan, and others.—Summarized from Naver Wiki by the author.

redistributed a total of 320 *majigi*, allotting 80 *majigi* each to these three sons and Hong-man.[41]

Receiving the same amount did not mean that the land or economic conditions became equal. The clear fact was that initially, everyone received an equal share from Hong-seon. Hong-seon believed that "The descendants of the Choi family should be educated without worrying about tuition if they want to study." Initially, the children lived well together, based on the nearly equal property distributed by Hong-seon.

However, as time passed, new lives were born, bringing with them the responsibility of raising and educating them. There was no end to the unexpected challenges, both big and small. Such is life.

Although it was a *Jongga* (The Head Family of a Clan), it was a small branch descending from the progenitor Choi Chi-won, so there was no need to count every member of the Head Family.

Hong-seon's direct descendants, spanning three generations, numbered 27. By the time he passed away in 1960, the total number of descendants he had seen in his lifetime had grown to over 170. It is often said that the Head Family's House (*Jonggat-jip*) performs ancestral rites for four generations. These four generations refer to the boundary where grandchildren can still meet their great-great-grandfather face-to-face.

From the fifth generation onward, the rites transition to the twice-yearly ancestral rituals (*sije-sa*). This means that approximately 170 people within the four generations from Hong-seon either saw him directly or at least grew up hearing stories about him.

By the time a family reaches four generations, most descendants are old, sick, or have passed away. Yet, the hearts of the remaining descendants stay rooted in the place of their childhood. That place is called "Home and Habitat." Now, the land and houses from those times look sad and shabby. However, a hundred years ago, it was a bustling and lively

---

41) Refer to footnote 32) on page 31 of this book.

place, home to the residents of the Sancheong Choi family.

For some, it was sorrowful; for others, glorious; and for some, it brought tears of blood. But they lived well there.

There was a time when it was like that.

Sancheong Choi Hong-seon and his descendants.

People become stronger and find it easier to survive and obtain food by living together rather than alone. To secure more food and take possession of it more easily, they create regional boundaries and claim their own territories. These territories are sometimes divided through invasions and attacks, and at other times defended through conflicts.

The Sancheong region of *Mountain Jiri* in the southern part of the Korean Peninsula has been home to various families with different surnames, continuously inhabiting and maintaining their lineages.

However, due to genetic concerns, exogamous marriages[42] occurred between different communities, and bloodlines gradually mixed. With the collapse of the clan society, the significance of surnames has become nearly obsolete. Even so, in the 2020s and beyond, the power of regional traits associated with surnames and *Bon-gwan* still plays a role, to some extent, in the minds of most Koreans. As long as surnames continue to be maintained, this will likely remain true.

---

42) Clan Intermarriage Issue: According to the Geography section of the Annals of King Sejong (*Sejong Sillok Jiriji*), the family names Jeong, Ha, Kang, and So are recorded as the prominent families in Jinju-mok, Gyeongsang Province.—*Sejong Sillok*, Volume 150, Geography of Jinju-mok, Gyeongsang Province. Due to the high frequency of intermarriage within the same village, members of the clan association avoided intermarrying with the Ha, Kang, and So families, considering them as part of their own family. —Summarized by the author with reference to Naver Wiki Encyclopedia.

06
Hong-seon's Fate and Fortune

1943 – 1945: The Big House
—The Family Motto

It is undeniably challenging to build a legacy, yet even more arduous is the task of preserving it and wielding it wisely. While I do not mean to elevate Hong-seon merely for amassing his fortune, I seek to illuminate the way he lived his life—as an inhabitant of Sancheong, as a Choi, and as a father.

In the grand ancestral home of Sancheong, within the main building of the Big House, there is a long, revered piece that hangs at the highest point, connected to the ceiling of the *daecheong-maru*, the large wooden floor. This artifact is a wooden signboard, inscribed with "the family's guiding principles,"—a sight common in many Korean households. Since the *Joseon* period, it has been customary for Korean homes to display such family mottos.

The Choi family's motto in Ok-dong reads: "*Geungeomsega*"— Diligent, Thrifty House. This motto encapsulates the essence of a household committed to a life of diligence and frugality. It is a testament to the values Hong-seon instilled in himself and his descendants:

"Be diligent and thrifty, and shun arrogance."

Hong-seon, above all, practiced what he preached. However, it is only natural that while some people readily embrace such teachings, there are also descendants who do the opposite. If what was inherited from the previous generation is squandered here and there, there may eventually be little left to practice in terms of "frugality."

Choi Hong-seon, the landowner who personally penned and carved this maxim, sought to lead by example through the smallest of actions, particularly valuing change and seemingly trivial deeds. In many ways, he epitomized the frugality typical of the Choi family, a trait well known to all his children.

No matter how profound a teaching may be, understanding it is one thing, practicing it is another. There will always be those who deviate from such principles. Bok-hee smiled at the thought of her second son, Ki-hwi, who, despite growing up hearing these teachings, could never fully embrace them. Hong-seon, the venerable Elder and Ki-hwi's grandfather, emphasized the importance of saving and avoiding bravado. Yet, Ki-hwi did the exact opposite. His life, more than that of any of Hong-seon's children, seemed to embody the very antithesis of these values:

"Act pompous with more bravado."

Furthermore, even after growing up, he used his mother, Bok-hee, as a front to seize a considerable amount of land that Hong-seon had left to his younger sisters, taking it all for himself. Despite this, he never lived well or comfortably. Ki-hwi was a person whose vanity drove him to inflate his image in front of others, interpreting Hong-seon's teachings in the exact opposite way they were intended.

Hong-seon often said, "In this small country where even a piece of paper is scarce, do not waste a single sheet." He would dry and reuse the paper that the children had blown their noses on, repurposing it for the toilet. Similarly, he lived by the motto, "If you want to save big money, value small change," and practiced these words throughout his life.

The village children called him the "Big-bearded Grandfather" because of the beard he had grown since his mid-twenties. He was often seen carrying Yoo-sang and some servants, checking the ancestral rites table at home, or working on local market days.

On such market days, he would sternly scold those who were drunk and addicted to gambling, his voice thundering like a rebuke. The villagers recalled that such people, upon spotting even the tip of his beard from a distance, would immediately flee.

For a few households with outstanding individuals who could not continue their studies due to difficult family circumstances, he secretly sent someone to offer support out of kindness. Although no evidence remains, Yoo-sang once told Bok-hee that Hong-seon had also discreetly contributed to the Korean independence fund several times through intermediaries.

One might wonder how a man who held himself and others to such high standards could have three wives. This, however, can be seen as a relic of the *Joseon* era, where concubinage among the wealthy was deeply ingrained in society's fabric.

But one cannot judge him solely by that. Hong-seon devoted himself wholeheartedly to his children and family, adhering rigorously to his principles. This commitment was likely one of the things he most cherished and sought to protect.

Il-seop's birth mother, Lady Kim, married Hong-seon in 1900, at the behest of Hong-seon's mother, Lady Jo. Lady Kim, two years older than Hong-seon, married later than most women of her time. Official records, however, listed her birth year as 1881, making her appear the same age as Hong-seon. Even after five years of marriage, they remained childless. This caused concern among those around them. If asked about the relationship between Hong-seon and Lady Kim, relatives would likely attribute their difficulties to differences in personality.

Lady Kim, a member of the Gwangsan Kim clan, had a long face and fair skin, standing about 150 cm tall. Her sharp, sarcastic tone was often cited as a potential cause of friction with Hong-seon. Yet, Hong-seon never openly discussed their relationship, although his descendants were familiar with his metaphor comparing people to food.

Bok-hee recalled Hong-seon saying:

"People are not like other things or food. You can leave food you don't want to eat and take it out again when you're hungry, but no matter how long you avoid someone you don't want to see, it never becomes any easier to face them."

Hong-seon often worked tirelessly, with few days off, traveling across the eight provinces of *Joseon* to conduct business. During this time, Lady Kim heard from her neighbor, Lady Han, that Hong-seon's child was going to be born. On January 23, 1906, Choi Jeong-seop was born. A few months before Jeong-seop's birth, Hong-seon arranged for Lady Han to receive a house. This house, spanning approximately 800 *pyeong* of land, included both an *an-chae* and a *sarang-chae*. Lady Han, a childhood friend and neighbor of Hong-seon, was Jeong-seop's mother.

Han's family home was located at the entrance of the Big House. The relationship between Hong-seon and Lady Han was not widely known, but their families were close, and her brothers were well acquainted with Hong-seon. The house where Jeong-seop was born had a large well, earning Lady Han the title of "Madam of *Saemmyjip*".

About a year after Jeong-seop's birth, Lady Kim gave birth to twin sons. The firstborn was Il-seop, Bok-hee's husband, followed by his twin brother, Lee-seop. Despite having these two reliable sons, Lady Kim's relationship with Hong-seon remained unchanged. Due to his mother's influence, Hong-seon spent only one night a month in the main house where Lady Kim resided. To ensure the welfare of his first son, Jeong-seop, as well as Lady Han, Hong-seon granted them 160 *majigi*.

Jeong-seop, who became more charming by the day, was adored by Hong-seon, as were Il-seop and Lee-seop, who brought him immense joy and pride.

Hong-seon referred to Lady Kim, the mistress of the main room, as "Lady Co-nalaemi" (a nickname derived from the local dialect, implying a long and sharp nose). The depth of affection between the couple was not visible to others. Although Hong-seon did not visit Lady Kim's quarters after the birth of Il-seop and Lee-seop, he never failed to send restorative herbal medicine to her through Bok-hee twice a year, ensuring her vitality.

Il-seop completed his studies at the renowned Dongnae High School in Busan. He never addressed Jeong-seop, who was a year older, as "brother." Even when Jeong-seop won a silver medal in national table tennis (representing Japan due to the occupation) and secured a job at a bank in Busan, Il-seop offered no congratulations. Few people understood Il-seop. With his refined eyes, curly hair, and prominent nose, he had the appearance of a scholarly gentleman. Yet, his love for the arts, combined with his timid and narrow-minded nature, made him appear somewhat aloof and reserved.

No further explanation was needed. He couldn't bear to see Jeong-seop surpass him. Even among brothers who shared the same womb, differences arose, and jealousy festered. There was no need to elaborate on the emotions that existed between half-siblings born of different mothers.

Moreover, Il-seop was undoubtedly burdened by his father Hong-seon's expectations. Yet, like any ordinary son, he longed for that gaze more than anyone else. Though blunt with other family members, Il-seop was deeply affectionate toward his wife, Bok-hee. He had a romantic and innocent side, enjoying horseback riding and the guitar from a young age. His antics, such as doing handstands and acting playful in front of his mother, Lady Kim, often brought laughter to others.

However, Il-seop's environment undoubtedly contributed to his seemingly harsh disposition. It all began, perhaps, when Hong-seon married his third wife, Lady Hwang, who, like Il-seop, was sixteen at the time. It was said that from the moment Hong-seon married her, Il-seop's smile vanished.

When Hong-seon sent Lady Han from Saemmyjip back to her family without explanation, both Jeong-seop and Il-seop questioned his decision. Was it because their father never explained his choices to his sons?

Their father's lack of communication, even in significant matters, may have been the root of their confusion and discontent. But from Hong-seon's perspective, explaining his reasons to his sons might have been uncomfortable. Jeong-seop and Il-seop were simply not the kind of sons who would be made aware of such details. Five or six years after separating from Lady Han, Hong-seon married Lady Hwang. However, these transitions were undoubtedly difficult for Jeong-seop and Il-seop to accept.

The important point is that these events made Il-seop, a sensitive and introverted man with blood type A, feel even more sorrowful. Despite his inner turmoil, Il-seop never once defied his father, Hong-seon.

Why did Hong-seon part ways with Lady Han, who had given birth to his first son?

As Jeong-seop grew older, Hong-seon privately resolved to marry Lady Han formally. He adored his son Jeong-seop, who, in turn, followed his father closely...

Yet, discovering a spouse's infidelity inflicts immense pain. Hong-seon stumbled upon Lady Han's affair, leaving him with a deep sense of loss. Nevertheless, he couldn't dismiss her based solely on suspicion, given that she had given birth to his son. He needed solid evidence. Thus, Hong-seon needed to plan carefully. To understand this, we must first discuss the routine business procedures Hong-seon followed.

Even while establishing a household with Lady Han, Hong-seon worked tirelessly. Typically, any task Hong-seon undertook required considerable time to complete. When he left home, he estimated the total amount of goods needed and brought four to five, sometimes as many as eight, able-bodied men with him.

His business trips typically lasted from a fortnight to a month. He traveled with several horses, along with porters and errand boys to assist him. Although inns and restaurants were available, they were not always reliable, so he made sure his men carried enough food and sleeping mats to camp out if necessary. Having started this business in his mid-teens, Hong-seon was already a well-known figure in the surrounding region. He possessed an exceptional talent for managing and leading people. Both his employees and business associates knew him as a trustworthy and excellent merchant.

The incident involving Lady Han unfolded as follows:

When Jeong-seop was about ten years old, Hong-seon unexpectedly returned early from a business trip and decided to go to Saemmyjip. Usually, upon approaching Saemmyjip, he would send a messenger ahead to inform Lady Han, with a message such as, "I am currently at such-and-such place and will arrive at Saemmyjip around this time."

However, that day, exhausted, Hong-seon did not send any advance notice. After finishing his business, he headed straight to Saemmyjip and entered Lady Han's room unannounced. Startled and disoriented, Lady Han hesitated to acknowledge him. Instead, in the dark room, she fumbled, her hands brushing against Hong-seon's feet several times. This behavior struck Hong-seon as peculiar, as if she were trying to confirm the identity of the man in her bed.

From that moment on, Hong-seon began investigating Lady Han's activities while he was away. It turned out that she had known a man for several years. After Hong-seon left for business, this man regularly came to Saemmyjip and spent the night with her. Hong-seon inquired about the man's identity. He discovered that Lady Han had been involved with a young Confucian scholar from the neighborhood. This scholar, still adhering to traditional ways, wore *Joseon-style beoseon* (traditional socks), whereas Hong-seon had switched to modern ones.

Late that night, when Hong-seon slipped into Lady Han's bed, she hesitantly felt his feet multiple times before recognizing him and saying, "Is that you, Big Elder? I was surprised you came without warning." Her hesitant reaction confirmed Hong-seon's suspicions. Nevertheless, it was not easy for Hong-seon to part ways with Lady Han, who had given birth to his son, Jeong-seop, based only on her interactions with the scholar. Lady Han could easily deny the accusations.

This incident ultimately led Hong-seon to make a decision. He devised a scheme to verify his suspicions. Feigning a business trip, he informed Lady Han of his expected return date and then departed. Hong-seon planned to return earlier than stated and catch Lady Han and her lover in the act. The scheme worked flawlessly, leaving Lady Han with no choice but to accept Hong-seon's judgment.

In intimate relationships, an unspoken intuition exists that only the involved parties can perceive. Given Hong-seon's extensive experience dealing with people, he might have sensed the truth more quickly than most. This heightened intuition, or "sixth sense," can be so acute that it operates even in complete darkness, relying solely on instinct. It's often said that some warriors blindfold themselves to sharpen their senses of hearing and movement.

Hong-seon quickly discerned the intentions behind Lady Han's actions. When she felt his feet and recognized the Japanese socks, she then nestled into his arms. This behavior aroused his suspicions, prompting him to catch her in the act.

Was this the end of Hong-seon and Lady Han's relationship?

Even after dismissing Han, Hong-seon could not leave Jeong-seop solely in her care. Han did not desire this outcome either. From her perspective, unspoken disappointments about Hong-seon might have lingered. Every individual harbors justifications for his or her actions, whether right or wrong.

Jeong-seop remained with Hong-seon after Han remarried. This experience with Lady Han prompted Hong-seon to reflect deeply on what truly matters in a life partner beyond mere affection. He pondered, "What is more important than just saying, I like you. I love you?" This introspection led him to adopt a more discerning approach to choosing a life partner, shaping his future decisions about marriage. Overwhelmed by anxiety, Hong-seon confided in his mother.

"Mother, what should I do? I married at 19, but no matter how much time passes, I cannot find peace when I see Il-seop's mother or hear her voice. Must I return to Il-seop's mother simply because I separated from Jeong-seop's mother? I cannot bring myself to enter Lady Kim's room."

His mother, speaking from the wisdom of her years, responded,

Lady Jo said,

"No one will truly understand what you are going through. You have some wealth, so some people suggest you remarry. As a woman, I'm not sure whether that would be the right thing to do. However, we only live once, so don't do anything you're unwilling to do. No one truly knows the intricacies of a couple's life except the couple. Follow your own judgment."

Seven years had passed since Han left, and Hong-seon found himself with a new wife. His conclusion was that a suitable marriage partner should be a woman with minimal interaction with men to minimize the risk of marital failure. Consequently, he sought a young woman from a struggling family, someone who saw marriage as a means to restore her family's fortune. Such a woman would be willing to marry an older man and follow her husband's lead. If this young bride requested a condition for marriage, the older groom would comply, ensuring both his peace of mind and her satisfaction.

When Hong-seon's mother saw his new bride, Hwang, she closed her eyes, perhaps in resignation and relief.

When Il-seop turned 16, seeing his father marry Hwang—a girl the same age as him—filled his heart with bitterness and grief. His mother, Lady Kim, sat in silence, looking more despondent than ever.

Il-seop had originally planned to attend high school in Pyongyang, but Hong-seon persuaded him otherwise, and he ended up in Busan instead. The farther he could be from his father, the better. When Il-seop heard of Ki-soon's birth, he vowed, "When I grow up and have my own family, I will leave Sancheong and the house where I grew up."

Yet, breaking away from Hong-seon was not immediately feasible. To the villagers, Il-seop was still the eldest grandson of the Choi family. Il-seop half-heartedly attended school with the money Hong-seon sent. He even wasted his tuition money at a *gisaeng-bang* (a house of Korean courtesans) in Dongnae, skipping school and squandering it, all the while hoping that his father, Hong-seon, would call for him directly.

He deliberately misbehaved several times. However, Hong-seon never came himself; instead, Yoo-sang visited the boarding house in Busan multiple times, delivering the message: "Your father is worried and says you should either return to Sancheong or stay in Busan and finish school." Hong-seon could not entirely dismiss the thought that he understood the reasons behind Il-seop's wayward behavior. However, what mattered more to Hong-seon was securing Hwang's devotion. From the time of their marriage, Lady Hwang had made several clear demands of Hong-seon.

As Lady Hwang requested, Hong-seon officially registered her as his wife. He also purchased a 300 *pyeong* house for her family. In addition, he provided land and financial support to ensure that her two younger sisters could receive the best possible education. After Lady Hwang gave birth to two daughters in succession, she insisted, "Any future children we have, whether daughters or sons, must receive the best education available."

Hong-seon promised to honor her every demand. He believed, "Il-seop may have strayed a bit due to my remarriage, but he will find his way once he starts his own family." Consequently, as soon as Il-seop graduated from high school, Hong-seon arranged his marriage to Bok-hee. Similarly, Jeong-seop married Eun-ok, a graduate of Ilshin Girls' High School in Jinju, as per Han's request.

When Il-seop graduated from high school, Hong-seon told him, "Follow me around and learn the business," but Il-seop just blinked in response. Lee-seop was the one who accompanied Hong-seon several times. Il-seop ventured out just once to learn the silk and goods distribution business in Japan and China but never did so again. This was his first and last foray into his father's world.

In the New House in Sancheong, Lady Hwang gave birth to daughters, and Il-seop had several children as well. Of course, Jeong-seop and Lee-seop also experienced significant events of their own.

By the time Hong-seon was in his fifties, the number of family members he had to care for had increased dramatically. Until the early

1940s, managing his vast property was never a problem for Hong-seon.

However, one summer day in 1944, while at the market, Hong-seon encountered his clansman, Choi Gil-joon. They talked for a while, and then Gil-joon cautiously asked Hong-seon, Gil-joon said,

"Hong-seon, the Eldest Son, I heard that Il-seop recently sold the land in Shindeung. Do you know anything about it?"

Although Hong-seon was shocked, he pretended to stay calm to learn more about the situation.

"Oh ... that land? I told Il-seop to sell it and bring me the money because I needed it. But I'm not sure about the details... Uncle, do you know how much it sold for?"

Gil-joon frowned slightly and said, "... Well, it's a bit strange. ... I heard that even though everyone knows that land is fertile and valuable, he didn't get a fair price for it. Not only that, but he also sought help in selling another piece of land. He wanted it sold to someone familiar with the land.

Could it be that something serious has happened in the household of the Eldest Grandson? Is there a way for me to know if something is going on? The person who told me this hinted that Il-seop appeared to be in a hurry."

Hong-seon laughed, feigning nonchalance as he spoke, "Uncle, Il-seop started a small business a few years ago, which has probably required a lot of money. There may be things he hasn't discussed with me due to his busy schedule. I should ask him soon. By the way, Uncle, when you have time, would you like to come over for a game of *janggi* (Korean chess)?"

Gil-joon replied, "Sure, I'll do that."

But as Hong-seon turned away after speaking with him, his heart pounded, and a wave of nausea washed over him. Gil-joon's revelation shook him to the core. Struggling to think clearly, he barely registered

Gil-joon's reply and quickly left the market. The land Hong-seon had given to Il-seop consisted of five plots, all renowned as *munjeon okdap* — fertile rice fields located right in front of the house.

Reflecting on the situation, Hong-seon realized that he hadn't seen Il-seop much at home in the past two months. Upon returning to the Big House, he asked Bok-hee to fetch a bottle of *jeongjong* (refined rice wine) for him.

Sitting alone in the *sarang-chae*, he reflected on the matter.

Il-seop already has six children, and Sori-ddigi is pregnant again, he mused, feeling a growing unease. *From the moment my sons were born, they grew up without ever lacking money. While I gave them money, I never taught them how essential money is in life, nor that earning it always requires some form of effort or cost, whether through labor or something else,* he recalled.

This realization weighed heavily on him as he contemplated what lay ahead. He spoke in a quiet voice,

"I didn't realize I needed to teach my grown sons how to earn and save money. I thought that if I just sent them to school, their minds would expand and they could take care of themselves ... I trusted them too much. There is still plenty of land left, so they won't starve immediately, but ... if, as fathers, they don't have money in hand, how can they support all these children?

What will happen if they can't even afford to educate their children, let alone manage the inherited land properly? There's nothing more degrading than having to beg for food ... I raised my sons so they would never have to depend on others for money.

Oh! Hunger can strip a person of their dignity, and I raised Il-seop without even making him understand the shame of it!

I'm the fool here! What should I do now?

If he doesn't uphold his responsibilities, his family will starve as well..."

That night, Hong-seon stayed in the *sarang-chae* of the Big House, but he did not hear Il-seop return home. At dawn, he visited Gil-joon again. From him, he learned who Il-seop had dealt with and the sums involved. They spent the whole day gathering information, and by evening, they had uncovered the full details.

Il-seop had sold all but one of the lands entrusted to him by Hong-seon or had used them as collateral to borrow money.

That night, Hong-seon planned to stay in the *sarang-chae*, but Lady Hwang sent a messenger, saying she had something urgent to discuss. He went to the New House to sleep. However, sleep eluded him, weighed down by worry. As it turned out, Hwang had no urgent matters to discuss. She had only sent the message to lure Hong-seon away from the Big House, unaware of his turmoil.

In recent days, news about Jeong-seop had dwindled. After graduating from high school in Busan, he quit his banking job, where he had worked for three years, and returned to Sancheong. Despite being offered a public official position in Sancheong-eup due to his strong academic reputation in Busan, Jeong-seop refused the offer, as Hong-seon learned from an acquaintance.

 Hong-seon's heart was weighed down with worry over his two sons. He felt suffocated, and phlegm constantly rose in his throat. With no other choice, he decided to summon his two sons for a conversation. But whose issue should he address first?

He decided to summon his younger brother, Hong-man, first.

Hong-man ran a small store in front of Hong-seon's original main house and lived off the land and rice paddies he had received from his brother. Unlike Hong-seon, Hong-man had a distinctly unique appearance. He had delicate features, small eyes, a fair face with double eyelids, and a thin, straight nose. His appearance resembled that of the "beautiful women" often depicted in paintings of *gisaeng* from Kaeseong during the *Joseon* Dynasty. The only difference was that he had a topknot instead of a *gisaeng*'s hairpin. He stood at about 165 centimeters with a slender build. Even if someone claimed he was a woman in disguise, it would have been believable, as his appearance, voice, and movements were remarkably feminine.

Hong-seon and Hong-man were so different in temperament that the villagers often questioned whether they were truly brothers. Fortunately, he was quite good at running errands for his older brother, Hong-seon, and occasionally served as a confidant to him. Other than that, Hong-man had little else to do.

When summoning Hong-man, Hong-seon also decided to call Jeong-seop from Saemmyjip, since Jeong-seop was a year older than Il-seop. He wanted to ask them about the various rumors circulating in the neighborhood concerning Il-seop and whether there was anything else he might not know.

Hong-seon asked, "Jeong-seop, have you heard anything about Il-seop? How is he faring these days?"

Jeong-seop replied,

"Big Elder, I haven't heard much. But a high school colleague mentioned that Il-seop often frequents the Jinju *Gisaengjip* and meets with Japanese bankers there. What's troubling you? If he's visiting a *gisaeng* house, it's akin to gambling, whether he realizes it or not... [Waving a hand] Not that Il-seop is gambling—it's just that the Big Elder despises it the most. A *gisaeng* house is often associated with such behavior, isn't it? So, I was worried. I didn't know whether I should tell you..."

Hong-seon gave a slight nod. Just because someone was seen entering a *gisaeng* house in Jinju didn't necessarily mean he was gambling there—it was impossible to know for sure. However, merely frequenting such places was certainly not appropriate for a man with a family.

If Jeong-seop's words were accurate, Il-seop's actions could not be overlooked. What Hong-seon detested most was a family man visiting a *gisaeng* house, especially for gambling, which was a surefire path to ruin.

Hong-seon couldn't shake the uneasy feeling that Il-seop might still be frequenting such places, unable to let go of the behavior he had indulged in during high school.

Upon hearing Jeong-seop's words, Hong-man chimed in.

Hong-man said, "Brother, summon Il-seop immediately. As they say, '*Strike the iron while it's hot.*' Let's confront him and get his decision."

However, Hong-seon hesitated. Meeting Il-seop and discovering his involvement in such misconduct would deeply upset him. To Hong-seon, Il-seop was like a piece of precious *Goryeo* celadon, a treasured jewel.

Despite Jeong-seop's achievements in table tennis and his good nature, Hong-seon's heart was more invested in Il-seop, whom he saw as fragile and easily hurt. Although Il-seop bore a striking resemblance to Lady Kim, he undeniably suffered the most when Hong-seon married Lady Hwang. He shut himself in his room for two days, unable to face the new reality. His anguish stemmed not just from his father's remarriage but also from the erasure of his biological mother, Lady Kim, from the family register. Having to place Il-seop and all his brothers under Lady Hwang's authority was undoubtedly the primary reason for his distress.

In stark contrast, Jeong-seop observed the situation with calm, wide eyes, like a docile ox, merely blinking at the unfolding events. Il-seop, however, was noticeably absent, retreating into his room and refusing to come out.

Hong-seon vividly remembered that day. When Ki-soon was born to Lady Hwang and they later celebrated her first birthday, Il-seop did not attend, his absence a poignant reminder of his silent rebellion. The more Hong-seon tried to reach Il-seop's heart, the farther Il-seop withdrew. Despite his efforts, Hong-seon failed to bridge the gap between them. With a heavy heart, he often thought, *Il-seop, you rascal, will you understand my feelings when you have sons of your own?* Over time, Il-seop had three sons, including the intelligent Ki-hoon, who was younger than Ki-soon. Still, Il-seop remained distant from his father.

After sending Jeong-seop and Hong-man away, Hong-seon ensured that they kept their meeting a secret from Il-seop. Alone in the *sarang-chae* of the Big House, he sank deep into contemplation. Closing his eyes, he was consumed by the furnace of his thoughts.

In the silence, a vision of Il-seop as a newborn baby, wearing a swaddling jacket and smiling brightly, appeared, his face fair and delicate. A moment later, that fair face darkened, as if tormented by something, and twisted into an expression of agony.

"It was just a dream ... I must have imagined it," Hong-seon murmured.

He realized that this vision was likely a reflection of his troubled mind, his concern for Il-seop manifesting as a terrible bout of sleep paralysis. Hong-seon could not share his anguish with Il-seop's mother, Lady Kim, or his wife, Bok-hee. The more he kept his suffering to himself, the more his heart ached for Il-seop. He found himself unable to focus on how Hong-man, Jeong-seop, or Il-seop's twin, Lee-seop, were managing their inherited properties. Though he had heard snippets about their affairs, nothing seemed as urgent as Il-seop's situation.

After that incident, when Jeong-seop met with Hong-seon again and expressed concern about Il-seop a few times, Hong-seon would always reply, "He'll be fine. Don't worry too much. Just take care of your own family."

Despite these reassurances, Jeong-seop couldn't help but show subtle disappointment.

The more Hong-seon focused on Il-seop's handling of his property, the more freely Jeong-seop and Lee-seop began managing their own shares, buying and selling as they pleased. Hong-seon seemed indifferent to their financial dealings, neither questioning them nor showing any interest. Although Jeong-seop appreciated the freedom to use his assets as he wished, he also felt a pang of resentment toward his father. As a son seeking validation, Jeong-seop did everything he could to stay within the boundaries set by his father and earn his approval.

The complex dynamics between father and sons, and the varied attention given to each, reflected Hong-seon's struggles in balancing his legacy and affections.

But it seemed that Hong-seon's mind was elsewhere. Perhaps it was because Il-seop had three sons, while Jeong-seop had no sons—only four daughters—and Lee-seop also had three daughters at that time.

Jeong-seop comforted himself with the thought: *Since I don't have a son yet, the Big Elder, Hong-seon, is more interested in Il-seop, who has many sons.* He resigned himself to his situation. He could not forget what Hong-seon had once said:

"Il-seop has three sons, so he needs money to provide for them properly. A father bestows upon his children both his surname and his social status. That identity gives them confidence. They need confidence to act courageously in all they do. Therefore, I must manage Il-seop's property more carefully!"

Reflecting on these words, Jeong-seop wondered what social status, confidence, and courage he truly had. He clearly understood that Hong-seon was most concerned about Il-seop, who had many sons to inherit these attributes.

One day, following Hong-seon's instructions, Jeong-seop and Hong-man summoned Il-seop. Jeong-seop could see that Il-seop was in poor condition. With a heavy heart, Jeong-seop was the first to speak.

Jeong-seop said, "Younger brother! The Big Elder, Hong-seon, is very worried about you. Can't you handle things more properly?"

Feeling accused, Il-seop retorted, "Who are you to push me around? Mind your own business."

At those words, Jeong-seop instinctively threw two punches at Il-seop's face. Hong-man later recalled that he had to separate them.

When Hong-man recounted this incident, Hong-seon dismissed it as a minor quarrel. Though he thought to himself, *Jeong-seop has done enough, so Il-seop will come to his senses,* he still spent his days with lingering worry. A week later, however, Il-seop passed away. Hong-seon was the most heartbroken. He never imagined that such a trivial action would affect Il-seop so deeply.

Who was there to blame? At a loss for what to do, he could only stare out at the world beyond the door from the *sarang-chae* of the Big House. The day Il-seop took his last breath, as Hong-seon watched him die, the thought suddenly crossed his mind: *Ah, so this is the vision that has tormented me every time I closed my eyes.* Hong-seon held Il-seop on his lap as his life faded and sobbed.

"Il-seop, you fool. It's your father. Open your eyes."

The hallucinations that tormented Hong-seon grew stronger. Visions of strangulation and death engulfed him, transforming a once bright and youthful life into murky blackness.

Even after Il-seop's death, the hallucinations persisted, haunting him whether his eyes were open or closed. The more he tried to forget, the more vivid they became. What was once a vibrant life had become nothing more than a small, gray heap of ash in his mind. For months, Hong-seon secluded himself, spending all his time in the *sarang-chae*.

Observing his father's state, Jeong-seop muttered to himself, *I'm just a shell. I don't even have a son to care for yet... I wish I could experience the sweat and anxiety of a father trying to protect his child...*

He lowered his head, burdened by the weight of his father's silent grief.

07
A Child Chasing After Birds

Until 1944: The New House
—My Father's Legal Wife

Ki-soon was about three years old. On a sunny spring day, when the world brimmed with the excitement of blooming flowers, tender green shoots, and the joyous chirping of birds, little Ki-soon, the cherished daughter of the Choi family, was drawn to the enchanting melodies of the birds and wandered out of the house.

One day, with the unsteady steps of a toddler, three-year-old Ki-soon ventured beyond the familiar confines of her home. She found herself in an alley and sat blankly under the electric pole at the intersection of the neighborhood. It was Sook-jin's mother, a vegetable peddler passing through the alley, who noticed young Ki-soon and gently led her back to her worried family.

Born in 1925, Ki-soon was followed into the world by her younger sister, Jeong-soon, the very next year. As they began to toddle, their mother constantly admonished them, "No matter what happens, do not leave the house." The stern warning rang in their ears, shaping their childhood. By the time they could roam the yard freely, they had deeply ingrained their mother's words within themselves.

Ki-soon, who had once strayed from home at the tender age of three, understood this as a manifestation of her mother's heartfelt fear for her safety. That solitary adventure, guided by the elusive song of birds, remained an exception in her otherwise sheltered life. From then on, Ki-soon played contentedly at home alongside her younger sister, Jeong-soon. When Jeong-soon turned four, both sisters wore the handkerchiefs embroidered with yellow and purple violets that Hong-seon had gifted them the previous winter. They delighted in playing house in the yard, gathering unused side-dish bowls for their make-believe games. With each passing day, as their steps grew steadier, their world expanded from the confines of their room to the open spaces of the yard, where their imaginations could flourish.

When they received the white poplin handkerchiefs embroidered with small flowers as a gift from Hong-seon, Ki-soon nestled into Hong-seon's lap while sitting on the wooden floor. "Father, thank you. Am I pretty?" she said, her tiny arms wrapping around his neck. Jeong-soon also ran over and hugged Hong-seon in the same way. Their father seemed to possess an uncanny understanding of their hearts' desires.

When Ki-soon turned six, he arranged for a Japanese teacher to come to their home so that they could learn the violin. Jeong-soon diligently practiced simple Japanese children's songs and Mozart's *Twinkle, Twinkle, Little Star*, mastering the bow's movement. Ki-soon, though uninterested in music, watched her sister with admiration.

Ki-soon's passions lay elsewhere; she loved to draw flowers and birds and enjoyed writing. At the age of five, she proudly inscribed her mother's name on the first page of her notebook: "My Mother—Hwang Pil-hye." Her mother, touched by the gesture, stroked Ki-soon's head, their eyes meeting in a tender moment. Ki-soon and Jeong-soon believed they were the only children in the world blessed with such a father as Hong-seon.

Yet, a day would come when their sheltered world expanded, revealing the world beyond. Their days were spent playing house, practicing the violin, and playing the small reed organ on the *daecheong-maru*, until one day, the loud, heavy sound of footsteps disrupted their routine.

They were around six or seven years old, preparing to enter elementary school. They needed to learn the Japanese characters used in school but also studied *Hangul* in secret, obeying their mother's instructions. On a hot and humid day, Ki-soon and Jeong-soon lay face down on the *daecheong-maru*, their notebooks spread out before them as they practiced writing, fiddling with their pencils.

The sound of the footsteps felt heavy, perhaps because they vaguely sensed something brutal and frightening in it. The "thud, thud" sound came to a stop right in the middle of the yard at Ki-soon and Jeong-soon's house. Before the heavy footsteps trudged onto the *daecheong-maru* of the New House, a cacophony of crashing noises, like jars shattering under the assault of stones, pierced the air from somewhere nearby. This disturbance, emanating from a neighboring house, seemed unrelated to them, yet was unsettling.

Soon, the thunderous footsteps, laden with ominous energy, were accompanied by the murmur of unfamiliar voices, converging on the house they had always known as their own. It was then that Ki-soon first beheld the face of Il-seop from the Big House.

Ki-soon, startled, lifted her gaze from her notebook. The owner of the heavy footsteps was clutching a sizable stone. With alarming swiftness, he charged towards the *jangdok-dae* beside the main house of the New House and began smashing the jars. The girls, startled, scrambled to sit up, their hearts pounding. The man, now consumed with anger, stormed back towards them, his expression even fiercer than before.

As Ki-soon's mother locked eyes with him, Ki-soon noticed her hands trembling, her mouth slightly agape. Ki-soon and Jeong-soon, sensing danger, dashed across the floor to the safety of their room. They shut the door behind them, clung to each other, and wept, though they did not fully understand why. Inside the room, baby Joon-seop lay under a thin blanket, undisturbed by the commotion. From outside, their mother's voice rose in a mix of fear and confusion.

Lady Hwang: "Il-seop, what brings you here?"

Il-seop: "Why? Do you want to hear me call you 'stepmother'? Isn't it enough that you married a man twenty-six years your senior, had children, and now live here? Do you have to meddle in my affairs too? You might appear virtuous on the outside, but I know you're the one spreading those rumors. Didn't those words come from your mouth? Did you worry about my future?

A passing cow would laugh at that! Do you think everything will go your way just because you say so? But I won't let it slide. What are you going to tell my father about what happened today? Tell him everything, every single detail!"

Lady Hwang: "No, I don't know why you're doing this, but I have never spoken ill of the Big House members to Big Elder. I have certainly never mentioned anything about the eldest son. Please, explain what's going on so I can understand."

The tension in the air was palpable as Ki-soon and Jeong-soon clung to each other, their tears flowing freely, sensing that their world was on the brink of a seismic shift.

Il-seop sneered, "Now that you have a son, you think everything will go your way. But that's never going to happen. I'll keep my eyes wide open to see how well he ... grows."

With that, he stormed off, his heavy breaths matching the weight of his anger. As he crossed the yard, he kicked several of Ki-soon's toys, sending them skittering away. He then turned the corner of the house and vanished from sight. The few people who had followed him trailed behind, disappearing with him.

After he left, Mother remained seated on the floor, her gaze fixed downward, lost in thought. Ki-soon's curiosity was piqued. How had they vanished without entering or leaving through the gate of the house?

The very next day, she took a few cautious steps along the wall at the corner of the yard, determined to uncover the path taken by the man with the heavy footsteps.

To her astonishment, she discovered a gap in the wall next to their house. It was through this breach that Il-seop and his entourage had made their exit. Ki-soon marveled at how oblivious she had been to the fact that the wall of their home had a hole, allowing strangers to come and go unnoticed by her family!

As she raised her eyes, she noticed an array of jars neatly arranged in the adjoining yard. There were more jars than in her own family's *jangdok-dae*. These jars likely held soy sauce, soybean paste, and red pepper paste, as well as pots of salt storing dried fish and other provisions, all meticulously organized. To young Ki-soon, the rows of jars resembled a congregation of tall and small stone Buddha statues standing in solemn meditation. Polished to a gleaming finish, the jars sparkled like teeth in the sunlight, their surfaces as smooth and clean as the bellies and heads of monks.

In a single day, at the tender age of seven, Ki-soon had seen and learned so much. She could not forget the fury in Il-seop's eyes. The man who made the heavy footsteps was a son born to the father of the so-called "Big House," making him Ki-soon's eldest half-brother. She also came to learn that his name was Choi Il-seop.

After the incident, Ki-soon witnessed her mother endure several more humiliations at the hands of Il-seop. Ki-soon and Jeong-soon went to Jinju for middle school. Whenever Ki-soon and Jeong-soon thought of Sancheong, their hearts were always enveloped in a sense of unease and foreboding.

When they returned home during vacations, they heard from Joon-seop about the events that had transpired in their absence. Until the youngest child, Young-soon, who was born in 1941, took her first steps, such incidents continued to occur. Joon-seop had no choice but to witness them. He recounted how, on one occasion, Il-seop stormed in and slapped their mother twice across the face, glaring at her fiercely before leaving without explanation.

Their mother gradually fell silent. Even when she saw Ki-soon or Joon-seop, she rarely smiled. On such days, they would rush to her, burying their faces in the folds of her skirt as she stood there, lost in thought. Ki-soon later realized that her mother trembled more than they did. She secluded herself in her room, shutting out the world, closing her ears and eyes to its harshness.

Sometimes, when Ki-soon came home, she stood outside the main room, straining to hear any sound from her mother's chamber. There was no crying, no noise at all. Instead, she noticed that the handkerchief tucked inside the sleeve of her mother's *jeogori* (*hanbok*) was often soaked, the wet fabric staining the sleeve. Her silence did not signify the absence of tears; the damp handkerchief bore witness to her silent weeping.

The mother did not say anything about the Big House to Ki-soon, nor to Joon-seop or Young-soon. Instead, she seemed to cling tightly to something within, immersing herself in her sewing. Whether it was a needle, an iron, or scissors, her hands were never idle.

In one corner of her room stood a large, square needle box woven from smooth, tall sedges, dyed yellow or red. In the center of the box, the Chinese character for "luck" was woven in thick red sedge. Their mother made and mended their *hanbok*s, her fingers deftly working with the materials from the sedge box. Through her fingertips, she channeled her unbearable pain into the meticulous work of her needles, scissors, iron, and threads.

Once you come to know something, everything that has ever caused even the slightest doubt starts to make sense little by little. As for what Il-seop had done to her mother, Ki-soon wanted to tell Hong-seon in her mother's place. That was what Ki-soon thought when she was about ten years old. However, she knew she would surely be scolded by her mother.

It was as if her mother already knew what was on Ki-soon's mind, for one day she sat Ki-soon down. Lady Hwang gently took Ki-soon's hands and spoke softly.

Lady Hwang:

"Ki-soon, my dear, you are a bright and articulate girl, able to speak well in front of others. But, Ki-soon, remember this: there are secrets one must carry to the grave."

Ki-soon, puzzled, asked, "Mother, what is this secret I must carry with me until I die?"

Lady Hwang continued, "You see, my dear, if I were to say something that would bring pain to others, what good would that do? What I mean is, always be mindful of what you say, especially to those closest to you. For instance, if someone came to our house and something happened, you mustn't tell anyone in the family about it."

Ki-soon, still confused, asked, "Mother, who are the closest people to me?"

Lady Hwang explained, "The closest people to you, my dear Ki-soon, could be me, your father, your elder sister Bok-hee in the Big House, your younger siblings, or even our neighbors."

Ki-soon, contemplating, replied, "But, Mother, the closest people are... family, and we see them every day. How can I keep secrets from them? For instance, the other day, Ki-hwi from the Big House teased me, saying, 'Auntie, sis, auntie! There's a caterpillar on your head. Ew, it's so gross.' He then yanked one of my braids and ran off. That kid is always doing something annoying. He calls me 'auntie' or 'sis' and plays all sorts of weird pranks. The little rascal acts as if I'm his younger sibling.

So, does this mean that, just as Mom said, I shouldn't tell anyone about what I've been through, not even kids like Ki-hwi or anyone else? Is that what you mean?

But sometimes, I really want to talk, and if I don't, my mouth feels itchy. I need someone to talk to, like Jeong-soon or you. And I should be able to tell Father too, right?"

Lady Hwang, her voice firm, said, "No, never. Not to your father."

After a pause, she added, "Ki-soon, my dear, what I mean is, never tell your father, especially not him. Even he is just a man, and if he shares it with someone in the family, things will get more complicated. Whatever you see or hear, it's best to keep it to yourself."

From that day on, instead of speaking out, Ki-soon began to observe the Choi family members more closely. She gradually understood that her father, Hong-seon, had many responsibilities and was often called "Big Elder" by others. As the eldest son of the Choi family, he was the source of the family's wealth, which he distributed to the other family members. Everyone depended on him, watching his every move. Ki-soon realized that while her father might be the strongest person in the family, he also bore the heaviest burdens.

After finishing the third grade, Ki-soon began to understand more deeply. She often pondered, *What would have happened if I had told Father that Il-seop had come to our house, slapped Mother, and cursed her? Mother would have suffered even more humiliation from Il-seop. That's why she told me to stay silent. But in some ways, Il-seop* oppa (one's older brother in Korean) *is a coward. He only showed his true colors when Father, Hong-seon, was not at home.*

In Ki-soon's memory, this was the essence of Il-seop.

From the first time Il-seop visited, Ki-soon frequently lingered around the *Jangdok-gan*, the boundary between the New House and the Big House. Occasionally, she saw her father suddenly appear in the yard, almost like a magician materializing through the *Jangdok-gan*.

As usual, Father would come to the main building of the New House, sharing fascinating stories with Ki-soon and Jeong-soon. He would ask Jeong-soon to play the violin melody she had been learning. Knowing Ki-soon's love for birds, he made two birdhouses and hung them under the rafters of the *daecheong-maru* in the main room. He placed a pair of yellow parakeets in one of the wooden houses and said to Ki-soon:

"Ki-soon, these parakeets must live together as a close pair, like mandarin ducks. A male and female must be together. When you get married, these birds will be embroidered on the pillowcase you prepare for your marriage. Aren't parakeets and mandarin ducks beautiful?"

Ki-soon envied the wooden house where only one male and one

female bird lived together. She often dreamed and hoped that Hong-seon could be solely their father, envisioning an ideal family with one father, one mother, herself, and her siblings. Many times, she thought such a family was the true definition of family.

When Ki-soon became a middle school student and went to Jinju, the parakeets, once nestled under the rafters of the *daecheong-maru*, were moved to her boarding house. However, during her absence, the owner of the boarding house failed to secure the cage door properly, and the birds flew away. After this incident, Ki-soon resolved never to raise birds again, especially parakeets. She could not bear the sight of a pair of birds kissing each other every morning and preening their feathers.

Upon returning to her home in Sancheong, she expressed her feelings to Hong-seon. Ki-soon:

"Father, I won't keep birds anymore, especially not parakeets. They remind me too much of what I long for but cannot have. It hurts me too much after they left."

Hong-seon gently responded, "Sweetheart, *becoming too attached to any one thing can lead to heartache*. Sometimes, even the best things must be let go, like water flowing until it finds its place. The parakeets were loved by you, and that's what matters."

His words were meant to comfort her.

In 1943, during the summer vacation of her third year at Jinju Girls' High School, Ki-soon returned home. She was reading a Japanese-translated novel, *Wuthering Heights*[43]. She was reading it on the *daecheong-maru* of

---

43) Wuthering Heights: Emily Brontë's novel, set against a desolate natural background, portrays a love and hate relationship that can be described as wild and demonic, with lyrical yet powerful prose. It is noted for its deep exploration of human nature, which is mixed with contradictions and chaos. —Summarized with reference to Naver Encyclopedia by the author.

her house when Il-seop approached, his footsteps heavy and deliberate. Il-seop's face was dark and gaunt, a clear sign of his hardships.

He asked Ki-soon, "Where did your mother go?"

Ki-soon replied, "Il-seop brother, my mother went to the market."

Il-seop scoffed, "Brother? Do you think it's appropriate to call me that, given our circumstances? Just because the family is registered a certain way doesn't mean we share the same status. Titles are for those on the same level!"

When Ki-soon first saw Il-seop at the age of seven, his attitude had remained unchanged even when Ki-soon was in her senior year of high school. That kind of small habitual phrase—the words "*seochul*" (born out of wedlock) and "*jeokchul*" (born in wedlock)—his condescending words, and references to their illegitimacy filled Ki-soon, Jeong-soon, and Joon-seop with resentment.

With the power of those words, Il-seop's disdainful attitude towards Ki-soon and their mother, Hwang, had remained unaltered over the years.

... *Born in and out of wedlock!* Ki-soon thought bitterly.

Ki-soon and Jeong-soon carried Joon-seop on their backs and took care of him until they left for Jinju Girls' Middle and High School. When Ki-soon was in the upper grades of elementary school, she mingled with the children from the Big House and Saemmyjip. Ki-hwi, in particular, often came to the New House, pestering them with various antics. Though younger than Joon-seop, Ki-hwi tried to bully him every time they met.

One day, Il-seop noticed Joon-seop and Jeong-soon playing with Bok-hee's children. Il-seop called the Big House children over and scolded them. No matter what, Il-seop was still Hong-seon's son. Even if he was the same age as their mother, Hwang, Il-seop was undeniably Ki-soon and Jeong-soon's older brother, and Joon-seop was indeed Ki-hwi's uncle—at least according to the family register.

However, to Ki-soon, it seemed that such notions meant nothing to Il-seop. Ki-soon, reflecting on these moments, dimly realized *how the complexity of family ties and societal expectations had shaped their lives, leaving her to navigate a world where love and hatred intertwined like the threads of fate.* And whenever Ki-soon witnessed Il-seop's attitude, she couldn't help but feel that there was a stark disconnect between Hong-seon's family motto and the descendants who were supposed to uphold it.

Her father, Hong-seon, had instilled in them two core principles: "*Geungeom-sega*," which meant thrift and saving through generations, and "*Yeokji-saji*," which urged them to put themselves in others' shoes.

Though Ki-soon endeavored to understand Il-seop, she realized it was a one-sided effort. To Il-seop, these teachings were mere words, devoid of meaning. Whenever she saw Il-seop or even heard his name, an unspeakable heat rose within her—a simmering rage that she knew could become a consuming fire.

This feeling intensified when she turned fourteen.

The children of the New House, including Ki-soon and Jeong-soon, often bore the brunt of the mischief caused by Bok-hee's children from the Big House. The pain of these small cruelties lingered, unaffected by the passage of time. For example, Bok-hee's second son, Ki-hwi, frequently bullied Joon-seop. When Ki-soon and Jeong-soon were in elementary school and Joon-seop was seven, Ki-hwi would call out to them, saying, "Aunt, aunt, come see this! I have something for you." They would step out of the room only to have a can thrown at their feet. Upon opening it, they would find wriggling worms inside.

Jeong-soon, startled, would spill the can, and the worms would burrow into the ground. It seemed Ki-hwi had collected earthworms that surfaced after the rain just to frighten them. Joon-seop, compassionate even towards the worms, would gather them into a corner of the yard. These incidents were numerous, but Ki-soon never spoke of them individually. Everyone in the village and at school knew the dynamics of the Choi family's the Big House, the New House, and the Saemmy House.

Ki-soon, being a few years older than Ki-hoon, found herself in an unacknowledged competition. Despite her academic excellence and honors, she received no praise. Ki-hoon of the Big House, on the other hand, was celebrated for his every action. The villagers called him "the Eldest Grandson of the Choi family, a Small Genius," and never compared him to Ki-soon or Jeong-soon. Ki-hwi pretended to play with her younger brother, Joon-seop, only to tease him in the end.

Young-soon, the youngest, remained secluded in her room. And whenever Ki-soon happened to pass by the *sarang-chae* of the Big House and ran into Il-seop, he would ignore her greeting. Instead, he would say something like this:

"What's this? This damned brat of a girl, looking all cheeky... Just because the houses are stuck together, you come and go as you please. How annoying!"

After hearing this, Ki-soon stood there, frozen like a statue, before slowly turning away. Il-seop's demeanor was so intimidating that neither Ki-soon nor Jeong-soon dared to argue with him. When such encounters occurred, she retreated to her room, shutting the door and avoiding the outside world as much as possible—much like Young-soon. Jeong-soon did the same.

Joon-seop, however, continued to hang out with Bok-hee's children despite being teased. When Ki-soon and Jeong-soon returned home for vacations from Jinju, they still rarely ventured outside.

It had become a habit.

The confines of the room seemed to be the entire world for Ki-soon, Jeong-soon, and their mother, Hwang. Outside, the beautiful chirping of birds, whose names they did not know, brought some pleasure to their ears, but Ki-soon's appetite remained dull. Whether it was summer or winter, Ki-soon only felt happy on the first day of her return home. By the next day, she felt as if her head was burning, her heart pounding, and strange, unfamiliar sounds echoed in her ears. The herbal medicine brought by her mother only made her feel nauseous.

Starting from her first year of high school, Ki-soon noticed that she often suffered from such ailments during vacations. She pondered, *If this illness stems from the heart, what about Mother, who has to endure everything even more than I do?* Ki-soon chastised herself for her belated understanding.

Jeong-soon also desperately say this, "Sister, I want to grow up and leave this house soon." However, whenever they thought about leaving, they couldn't help but wonder, *How will our mother live on her own?* No matter how they considered it, the two daughters felt powerless to help their mother. Ultimately, they decided to focus solely on their own problems—to cover up their mother's plight, avoid it, and pretend not to know.

This decision was both a means of survival and a source of deep, lingering guilt.

Ki-soon found herself lost in thought.

My mother, known as "Lady Hwang," might be seen as an "ambitious woman" who came at the age of sixteen to manage the household. Perhaps that's why Il-seop harbored such resentment toward her. Was it the distribution of Father's wealth among us, her children, that fueled his hatred? That could be part of it.

And ... when the youngest, Young-soon, was born, Father was already sixty years old. He refused to have a traditional 60th birthday celebration. In 1941, after Young-soon's birth, our mother took me, Jeong-soon, Joon-seop, and the baby to the Sancheong Catholic Church for baptism. My mother had been baptized when she was young. Her baptismal name was Maria. My maternal family had already embraced Catholicism.

Then my mother said, 'We should follow the will of the One in heaven. When I die, make sure to cremate me and completely forget about any ancestral rites.' With these words, she pierced our hearts. My baptismal name was Rosa, Jeong-soon's was Cecilia, Joon-seop's was Peter, and baby Young-soon was baptized as Anna.

And she said, 'Don't hold memorial services for me. Please cremate my body and scatter the ashes in the Kyungho River.'

I was sixteen when I heard my mother's words. I had returned from Jinju in high spirits for Christmas, only to have my mother's words weigh heavily on my heart. They became the fulcrum, pressing down on the very core of my suffering.

Talking to herself like this, she realized, *Ah, from that time on, I began saying, 'I have a headache,' more often to my mother and siblings.* With that, she placed her hand on her forehead.

Catholicism in Korea permits ancestral rites, but it doesn't require Confucian-style bows or elaborate food preparations. After giving birth to Young-soon, why did Lady Hwang make such a resolute statement to her children? Did she intend to prepare them for her departure in advance? Her insistence on not having a memorial service seemed to reject the life she had lived as their mother. Lady Hwang was certain that her body would never lie next to her husband, Hong-seon, in the Choi family's gravesite.

At some point, Ki-soon began to see her mother, Lady Hwang, in this light.

'Lady Hwang, my mother—before she was my mother—came to this place, the Choi family house in *Sancheong*, this *habitat*, through marriage, to spend the rest of her life. Just as she did back then, with the same courage she had at the beginning, couldn't she have grown stronger?

Perhaps, if she had known nothing, she might have. But she understood the concepts of the Head Family and the Eldest Son's duty, and the fact that there was a legitimate wife whom she had displaced. Did she become weak because she grasped the extent of the jealousy, envy, and danger surrounding her? It seemed she could not regain her strength and was oppressed by some unseen authority.

In truth, my mother, Lady Hwang, took us to the cathedral, but I saw that beneath her pillow, there were Buddhist scriptures like *The Heart Sutra*, *The Hymn of Dharma Nature*, and several other Buddhist books that had occupied that space for a long time. My mother, in some ways, was also a young girl of *Joseon*. This process shows that she had been internally struggling between the long-standing customs she had lived by before marriage and the life she wanted to build after marriage.

Those books were so worn from being read over and over that every page was marked with her touch, the pages soft and delicate from wear. Was she diligently studying these Buddhist texts to find answers to her present life—a life filled with different sorrows and stigma, so unlike the life she had imagined when she first married and came to this place?

Or perhaps, through the meditation and wisdom contained in those texts, she reflected on her own past greed and ignorance of others' hearts? Did she come to understand the profound wisdom of letting go only after enduring heartache and pain? Even so, her actual marriage required an immense amount of sacrifice and courage, especially with her children depending on her.

People's customs do not change easily. While books spoke of human equality and free marriage as if they were a given, real life was entirely different. One might expand their knowledge through scriptures, but true wisdom is acquired only through suffering and criticism. For most people...

Or perhaps it was something else. My mother had no economic power, no financial independence. Naturally, not only her children but even her own place in the future seemed uncertain. The money that came through her husband was not solely hers. Simply being his wife did not guarantee her a share of his wealth. Moreover, living as the second wife of a man twenty-six years her senior was not a secure position. What posed the greatest threat to her security?

It was the sons of the first wife and the watchful eyes of those around her. Marriage, in its many forms and contexts, differed in process and outcome for millions. The greatest threat came from humans themselves—

the sons of his first wife and their descendants. They scrutinized my mother, my siblings, and me, ever vigilant in protecting their own interests and their mother's legacy.'

Ki-soon realized that these complexities intertwined and twisted like threads... Then Ki-soon suddenly saw her face reflected in the wardrobe, which had one side made of glass, designed to display the bedding. She mumbled to herself.

'I, Choi Ki-soon, do not hate being a Choi. The continuity of our ancestors and descendants, inheriting the same family name — is that a coincidence? A Choi begets a Choi, and another Choi begets another Choi. Even if marriage, as an event, might seem coincidental, that coincidence repeats and gradually creates inevitability. Eventually, a definite law forms. No one knows what results this inevitable law will bring over time.

My mother always had a small handkerchief. On that handkerchief, finely embroidered with silk thread, were the characters "Cause and Condition." '

Ki-soon found the following information about "Cause and Condition" in the school library. In the seventh chapter of the third volume of the *Lotus Sutra*, it is written: When one marries (sensation), love arises (craving), and with love, one desires to possess (clinging). This leads to the birth and life (becoming and birth) of a being, during which aging and death, anxiety and sadness, bitterness, and suffering occur. After death, during the process of rebirth, one passes through a state of darkness and nothingness (ignorance), then, due to certain actions, begins to think and develop a sense of self. Through the six sense bases (eyes, ears, nose, tongue, body, and mind), one interacts with external objects (contact), and through this interaction, sensations are formed, repeating the cycle. This is known as the Twelve Links of Dependent Origination (ignorance, volitional actions, consciousness, name and form, six sense bases, contact, sensation, craving, clinging, becoming, birth, aging, and death).

And when she was sixteen, her mother once said to her softly.

"Ki-soon, my dear, remember that '*in* (cause)' is the direct power that brings about a result, and '*yeon* (condition)' is the external, indirect force that assists '*in*.' Everything that happens is a blend of these forces. Our lives, intertwined with joy and suffering, are a testament to this delicate balance.

... My dear, you are already sixteen. Your mother married into this house at that same age. After your great-grandfather passed away, I found these words in his personal notes: 'A person's life and death are shaped by the repeated processes of chance, which stem from inevitability.' I read it when I was thirteen and didn't understand it then. Even now, its full meaning eludes me. But I have come to realize that everything is governed by '*in-yeon*,' the interplay of cause and connection.

Your father and I must have shared a deep bond in a past life, which led to our marriage and to you. My wish for you, Ki-soon, is to pursue your studies and contribute to this country—like your aunt, the principal of Jinju Girls' High School, who has established herself as a female educator.

Life is challenging and dark now, but even if you find yourself in a shadowed corner, you must stand strong. You must become a pioneer for all women. To do this, you must confidently and firmly carve your own path and raise your children with the money you earn."

Her words were long and seemed almost impossible to achieve, but something resonated with Ki-soon. Her mother was looking ahead, trying to foresee the future for herself and her daughters, and was asking them to do the same. She didn't want to be marginalized in this family, but her power and confidence were gradually waning. Ki-soon also didn't want to be pushed aside like her mother. She vowed to protect herself, her mother, and her younger siblings with greater strength. Yet, she couldn't help but feel a dark cloud looming ahead.

Despite the challenges, there were moments of happiness, however fleeting. Sancheong, with its harsh climate, was both hot and cold, making life difficult. In 1944, Ki-soon was admitted to S Women's University in Seoul. On a cold winter day before the announcement of her entrance exam results, she took out "Persimmon Kimchi, salty persimmons fermented well in salt water" from a large jar in the Big House yard. She enjoyed them with Jeong-soon and Joon-seop, sharing laughter and stories.

Joon-seop said, "Even when the ice was frozen solid, just taking out a few pieces of persimmon kimchi from the big saltwater jar and eating them would make you feel so refreshed!

Especially that salty yet sweet taste, with the crispy texture of the persimmon — once you tried it, whether you were an adult or a child, you would never forget it! It was the best winter snack you could enjoy all season long! Bok-hee, the sister-in-law from the Big House, is truly talented!"

Jeong-soon went on and on, saying that she, like her older sister Ki-soon, would go to that S Women's University in Seoul next year. She kept talking late into the night, saying, "The cold noodles that Bok-hee *Eonni* (older sister) from the Big House made were incredibly delicious, but I've only had them twice." Stories always come to life when there's something to eat. It was a cherished time with her beloved younger siblings.

In those moments of joy, Ki-soon couldn't help but recall Il-seop's angry face when Jeong-soon mentioned Bok-hee. Surely, if Il-seop had seen Ki-soon chatting pleasantly with her younger siblings like this, he would have said:

"While you sit here chatting and giggling, your sister, Bok-hee, makes snacks for the workers, feeds the family, and works until her hands blister and turn red. Shame on you! Do you think food just appears on your plate? Even the delicious salty persimmon kimchi you enjoy is made from discarded scraps, pressed down with a stone, and left to ferment over time. You should be ashamed! How can you eat so thoughtlessly, without a shred of guilt?"

His harsh words echoed in Ki-soon's mind, a stark reminder of the complex dynamics and expectations within their family. Ki-soon muttered to herself in a low voice:

"Shameful? To whom? Should I be ashamed?

The neighborhood children also took persimmon kimchi from the jar at the Big House. Who on earth should I be ashamed of?

Myself? Is my existence, my family's existence, shameful?

Did I choose to be born?

Does he begrudge me and my younger siblings even the rice we eat? The rice that comes from Hong-seon, my father..."

Il-seop always called the New House family "Shameful things!" It was a habitual saying. The sea of habits! It had become a sea hardened by ingrained hatred. Habits, habits—it was those habits that were the problem. The habit of giving up in advance, the habit of certain words and phrases. Even those habits were not originally there.

Perhaps when Il-seop called the children of the New House "Shameful creatures!" it was because that was what he valued most. And Ki-soon, certain of this, cried out in her heart:

Because he ended up being registered as an illegitimate man?

Yes! That's what brings the greatest shame, doesn't it?

He resented being illegitimate and having to share his father Hong-seon's attention and love with others. It was our presence—our mother and us, the children of the New House—that made Il-seop feel ashamed.

I hate him. I hate him, and I hate him even more. I hate Il-seop.

But here ... you are again, complaining about illegitimacy and legitimacy?

Ki-soon, Choi Ki-soon, that's another of your own bad habits!

Muttering to herself in self-reproach, Ki-soon let out a bitter laugh.

Determined not to be consumed by her own thoughts any longer, she shook her head vigorously. Just then, she noticed the "University Admission Notice" lying on her desk. As she looked at it, her mother's voice echoed in her heart like a hook:

"... Don't ask questions, just cremate me and scatter my ashes!"

As long as Il-seop, who always called them mere rice-consuming humans, was around, her mother would live each day holding her breath in this Choi household.

Ki-soon took a deep breath and exhaled slowly. *Even if I can't share in this house's property, I will become a school teacher after college,* she resolved. The quickest and most certain path for a woman to secure her independence was to become a teacher.

As she drifted to sleep, she envisioned a large blue bird with expansive wings, soaring freely wherever it desired.

08
The Posthumous Child

1945: The Big House
—Those Left Behind

Outside the gate, a white flower bier adorned with numerous large blooms stood solemnly. A lantern hung before the gate, signaling that this was a house of mourning. Though marked by sorrow, the house's distinction lay in the hushed demeanor of its visitors. Most departed silently after a quiet drink, speaking little.

Indeed, when news of the funeral spread, beggars and neighborhood children gathered and loitered in front of the main gate. A few family members from the same clan were eating slices of boiled pork as a side dish, mixing hot broth with rice inside the tent set up in the yard of the Big House. The people coming and going from the mourning place whispered unusually quietly. After bowing in respect at the funeral table set up in the *sarang-chae's* main hall, they placed their envelopes next to the incense holder and promptly left the house.

A group of mourners came and went only as evening approached. As the chief mourner, Ki-hoon wore a white *durumagi* (a traditional outer garment worn during the *Joseon* Dynasty), draped over his right shoulder without his arm in the sleeve. On his head, he wore an unhemmed *gulgeon* made of coarse hemp cloth, and in his hand, he held a bamboo *sangjang* (mourning staff). He was dressed in the traditional *gulgeonjaebok*.[44] Bok-hee, with her hair let down, wore a mourning robe made of coarse hemp cloth and a hemp towel on her head, topped with a *turdure* made of straw rope.

Ki-hoon, in his mid-teens and clad in mourning clothes, along with his young siblings similarly dressed, guarded the funeral hall with wide, blinking eyes. Despite being in mourning attire, Bok-hee occasionally went

---

44) Gulgeon and jaebok refer to the traditional white clothes and headpiece worn by Koreans during mourning rituals.—Referenced from the Naver Korean Dictionary.

to the kitchen, concerned about the food for the visitors.

Lady Kang, wife of Saemmyjip Jeong-seop, was among the first to visit, accompanied by her three-year-old daughter Min-ja and her elder sisters. Nam-gil, Lee-seop's wife, also moved between the kitchen and Lady Kim's room. As daughters-in-law of the Choi family, they claimed responsibility for the reception, but their efforts left much to be desired. A neighbor, Sangdong-ddiggi (a woman from Sangdong), was the only one who assisted Bok-hee, managing and serving food, alcohol, rice, boiled pork slices, and salted shrimp to the visitors.

Three white tents were erected in the yard between the main building and the men's quarters, laid with straw mats. Several large *soban* (small tables) were set for visitors to sit and eat. Some visitors seemed prepared to stay the night, anticipating the body being placed in a coffin the next morning. They were mainly Choi clan relatives, sitting on straw mats and quietly drinking.

At that moment, a man cautiously entered the main gate, glancing around. Instead of heading to the tent set up in the yard, he went straight into the kitchen of the inner quarters. It was Cheol-jin, who owned a photography studio. Peeking in, he cautiously poked his head into the kitchen, his eyes darting about nervously. He said,

"Hey, ma'am Sangdong, could I have a bowl of water? Why is it so quiet here? The eldest son of this family passed away so young, and now the house is eerily silent. It's not bustling with visitors like you'd expect from the house of Mr. Choi, the Big Elder."

Sangdong-ddiggi, the cook from the house just below, sized him up briefly before raising a large tray of pork and placing it near his nose. She had a fair idea of why Cheol-jin, a relative of the Choi family, had come straight to the kitchen instead of joining the others in the yard. Known for his talkativeness, Cheol-jin couldn't help but share what he knew. He seemed eager to unearth any scrap of information and liked to portray himself as well-versed in the affairs of the Choi household.

Cheol-jin had borrowed substantial sums from Hong-seon and often turned to him for help during tough times. To others, he would boast, "Mr. Choi, the Big Elder, listens to me. If you need anything from the house, tell me first. I'll hear you out and decide." His pretense of friendship with Hong-seon stemmed from the fact that Cheol-jin's father had died in another province, leaving him without close kin. As a result, Cheol-jin's mother had raised her two teenage sons alone until she was nearly forty. Hong-seon was well aware of their struggles. Despite her poverty, Cheol-jin's mother never failed each year to greet Hong-seon with a basket of millet taffy.

Cheol-jin's mother often ran errands for Bok-hee. The reason she was not seen at the house on a day like this was that she had gone to Hapcheon a few days earlier to take care of a patient for pay, as Cheol-jin later told Bok-hee. Even now, Cheol-jin did not seem to fully understand his mother's difficult circumstances. The fact that a woman over sixty years old had gone to nurse a patient showed how difficult their life was. Cheol-jin called out loudly enough for Lady Kim in the small room next to the kitchen to hear him.

Cheol-jin approached, his voice raised,

"Madam of the main room in the Big House, this is Cheol-jin, the photographer from the store at the intersection. Oh, dear, your son passed away so suddenly. I'm at a loss for words. By family ties, he was like a nephew to me. But tell me, when exactly did he pass away? I mean no disrespect, but as a member of this clan, I'm deeply curious about the circumstances of his sudden passing."

No response came from *gol-bang*, the small room. Instead, the creaking of doors opening and closing, followed by the faint rustling of movement, filled the air. The door to the main room, which faced the front yard, opened. With no answer forthcoming, humbled, Cheol-jin retreated to the yard tent, accepting the pork tray from the cook and settling down.

Lady Kim, the mistress of the main room, had spent the night propped against the wall of the *gol-bang*. She blamed herself for not having sensed that something was wrong when Il-seop had visited three nights ago, just after dusk, and had bowed deeply twice. No matter how much she thought about it, the idea that Il-seop had taken his own life that night still felt utterly unreal. She couldn't fathom why she had failed to notice the signs—signs that, with just a little more thought, might have been clear.

As these thoughts rose to the surface, Lady Kim felt as though her heart might burst. Her chest heaved violently, and her breath grew increasingly labored, as if weighed down by unbearable grief and a crushing sense of injustice.

She threw open the door to the *gol-bang* and then the one to the main chamber, flinging them wide with a trembling resolve, as if desperate to let the biting cold air rush in. But as she stood there, shivering in the frigid breeze, the crushing weight of her failure overwhelmed her. Her voice seemed to carry the scent of despair from days of starvation.

"Ah! What a pitiful, wretched fool I am. This useless, cursed mother of his is still alive, gasping for breath, struggling to stay alive. This pathetic excuse of a mother!"

The words spilled from her lips, venomous and laden with self-loathing, as though each syllable might wash away even a fragment of her unbearable guilt. An old saying goes, '*When a child dies before their parents, the parents' hearts ache so deeply that their very insides feel as if they are melting away.*' Yet here she was, breathing painfully, as if her body remained unbroken. Her long life had now become a burden.

Unbidden, she spoke aloud, "Il-seop, you heartless man, leaving behind six children as you ended your own life. If someone had to go, it should have been me."

Until now, Il-seop and Lee-seop's existence had allowed her to endure her diminished status as a woman and withstand Hong-seon's indifferent gaze. Unlike the old woman in the back room who had been cast aside long ago, Lady Kim had her two sons, sustaining her fragile dignity. She tried to convince herself, whispering, 'I can bear it. I must bear it.'

When she couldn't sleep at night, nausea overwhelmed her. She was unable to eat or drink. Initially, she felt an indescribable hatred toward Hong-seon. After all, he was Il-seop's father. Seeing Hong-seon's entire body turn as blue and broken as Il-seop's softened her hatred, if only slightly.

Who could understand the loss of a son better than his father? The father who had lost his own child would understand best.

Kim then rebuked herself, *Oh, you foolish woman, for blaming his father for your son's death!* For three days, she spoke to no one. She neither ate nor drank. Forcing herself to stand, she stumbled to the kitchen stove and grabbed half a kettle of *makgeolli* (Korean traditional rice wine). She decided to drink it, close her eyes, and get some sleep.

Il-seop, now cold and stiff in death, remained silent and left no words for his mother. Since Il-seop's passing, Lady Kim's eating habits have changed drastically. She had already been eating little since Bok-hee's marriage, but now she consumed even less, often subsisting on nothing more than half a kettle of *makgeolli* for an entire day.

Bok-hee managed the household even after her husband's funeral, ensuring everything ran smoothly except when latecomer mourners arrived to pay their respects. The neighbors and relatives praised her, saying, "The eldest daughter-in-law, Hyori-ddigi, is remarkable. She handles everything with such grace and strength, stronger and more capable than any man." Yet, behind her back, they whispered, "She's destined to be a young widow; she's just too strong for her own good."

Bok-hee was aware of their gossip. Gazing at her unusually large and thick thumb, she pondered, *Is this finger, like the head of a king snake, the reason I couldn't escape becoming a young widow?*

Bok-hee endured with such strength not only because of her six children, but also because of the life inside her that felt as if it would tear through her belly at any moment. Though it felt as if her throat were lined with sharp thorns, making it impossible to swallow anything, her stomach growled constantly. When the time came, she forced herself to eat and worked tirelessly, all for the sake of a safe delivery.

Resentment toward Il-seop grew within her. 'Life is stubborn and relentless, yet he ended it so abruptly,' she thought bitterly. Fifteen days after Il-seop's death, Bok-hee drank a glass of *makgeolli* left in the kitchen —her first drink ever. The cook, Sangdong-ddigi, watched with concern.

Sangdong-ddigi said, "Madam Sori-ddigi, your belly is about to burst, and it looks like you'll have a healthy son. And now you're drinking — something you've never done before... Are you all right? Take it slow."

The *makgeolli* slid down her throat with a sharp, tingling sensation, burning as it went down. Tears streamed down her cheeks—tears she had never shown to anyone before. To others, she had always seemed too tough to cry, but now those tears flowed relentlessly. People always said her pronounced cheekbones made her look tough. As she sat on the kitchen hearth, staring at her reflection in the small mirror hanging in the corner of the dining room, she found her face even more unappealing. She pushed the dining room door shut, hiding the mirror from view. *A widow's fate ... they say it's self-made, and you live as you look ... a fate is a fate*, she thought, allowing the tears she had held back all this time to pour out at once.

After a moment, Bok-hee, determined to face whatever came next, tensed her legs and sprang to her feet. Bok-hee muttered,

"Hey, Jeong Bok-hee, remember who you are! You came from Sudong, Hamyang, to Sancheong. Who am I? The Choi family's eldest daughter-in-law. If I crumble now, this family will be doomed.

Hong-seon, as a father, is weakened by this tragedy, and so is the child in my womb. Who would find joy in seeing me fall apart? Everyone who once envied our prosperity would mock us, claiming we had only been pretending. They'd whisper about how I couldn't manage my husband or children, as if I had caused the very pillars of this house to collapse.

I must gather my strength.

I am the eldest daughter-in-law of the Choi family!

The eldest daughter-in-law!"

She shouted these words, setting the *makgeolli* bottle down on the wood-burning stove. She wiped her tears with her palm, clutching the warehouse key tightly in her right hand, and headed briskly toward the mill to check the grain.

As Bok-hee exited the kitchen, she heard the distinct sound of a door closing in Lady Kim's *gol-bang* next to the kitchen. The sound sharpened Bok-hee's attention; Lady Kim would often push her sliding door shut with a resounding "ta-ak" or "kwa-ak." The sound of the door reminded Bok-hee of Lady Kim's dry, dark brown hands, hardened from years of labor.

She realized that no matter how long she waited, she would never again hear Il-seop's cheerful greeting as he returned from Jinju, riding his horse with his cape fluttering. This thought steeled her resolve.

'I need to be stronger now, more than ever,' she told herself, gritting her teeth.

Bok-hee recalled past moments with Il-seop.

Il-seop would lovingly tease her, "When people are young, they show off their figures; when old, their clothes. But you, my wife, will age slowly because of your strong constitution. Even if you don't change your clothes often, you'll always be fine. I'm so at ease with someone as strong and healthy as you," he would say, patting her prominent cheekbones and cheeks.

Il-seop was a loving son to Lady Kim. Whenever he arrived home late and couldn't greet Lady Kim, he always made sure to greet her the next day. When he went to see her, he always brought a tray with a warm cup of sake(*jeongjong* in Korean) and snacks like dried pollack or seaweed chips. Il-seop followed Hong-seon's teachings: "*Chulpilgo Banpilmyeon*—When leaving the house, one must inform, and upon returning home, one must greet."

Il-seop said,

"Mother, even if you skip breakfast, have some of this sake and these snacks later. Bok-hee put great care into making the perilla flower clusters as delicious as possible. She carefully selected only the young flower stems, and each delicate petal was brimming with the nutty flavor of perilla, resembling a cluster of grapes. She thoroughly washed them in salt water, dried them, and then coated each one with a mixture of glutinous rice paste, chili powder, salt, and sesame seeds. After that, she hung each piece on a clothesline, allowing it to dry completely under the sun.

When fried in oil, it produces a crisp, satisfying sound—much like Bok-hee's prickly personality: crunchy, flavorful, and nutty. The coating, mixed with a bit of chili powder, adds a spicy kick with a sharp, tangy flavor. Food reflects the cook's touch and character, doesn't it? Just try some. Don't skip meals. This snack embodies Bok-hee's character.

Who else would have spent more than three years traveling between Sancheong and Jinju, diligently learning the art of brewing liquor and mastering seasonal dishes from Jinju's most renowned restaurants and *gisaeng* houses, all to fulfill the role of the head family's daughter-in-law? It is a true testament to Bok-hee's relentless effort and perseverance. Though I was the one who encouraged her, still..."

Il-seop must have been Lady Kim's only source of comfort. After Bok-hee married into the family, Lady Kim voluntarily moved into the small side room attached to the main bedroom. Although there were other rooms in the main house, she chose to stay in the small room (*gol-bang*) from that point on. Claiming that she had trouble digesting food, she often replaced lunch with half a jar of *makgeolli*.

Bok-hee's daughters teased their grandmother by calling her "'Kim

Jusa, Kim Dosa." The term *"Dosa"* refers to those who practice an ascetic life. Since they often forget to eat and drink alcohol instead of meals while practicing day and night, they become *"Jusa"*—a play on words for a drinker. However, Bok-hee's eldest son, Ki-hoon, insisted that his younger siblings address their grandmother, Lady Kim, as "Grandmother, like a bodhisattva," as she was a compassionate person. Ki-hoon was particularly careful to ensure that his siblings treated her with proper respect.

Bok-hee knew that Lady Kim had likely been confined to her small, stuffy room for days. She was aware of the judgmental eyes of Lady Hwang from the New House and the neighbors' gossip about Il-seop's death. Despite Hong-seon's insistence on silence, the doctor and a few others had seen Il-seop when he died, and rumors had spread. Hong-seon, like Bok-hee, never shed tears publicly. She understood that his seemingly straightforward and easygoing personality masked deeper struggles. His efforts to cope were evident. Since Il-seop's death, three of Hong-seon's teeth had fallen out, and he had needed dental treatment just the day before.

For the past few months, Bok-hee had known that Hong-seon had been keenly aware of where Il-seop was spending his money. About two years ago, Il-seop had struggled financially because of the "Hwashin General Store" he had opened in the heart of Jinju. The store mainly sold rare items imported from Japan, making them very expensive. Passersby would often remark, "Wow! That's really amazing. It looks great!" showing their considerable interest in the well-stocked and displayed items. However, maintaining such a store came with significant expenses. Since last year, Il-seop had been borrowing money by mortgaging rice paddies and fields in various places.

As rumors spread, Hong-seon's concern and curiosity about Il-seop's endeavors grew more intense. Il-seop was well aware of his father's watchful eye. Bok-hee deeply understood the extent of Il-seop's efforts to prove his ability to succeed on his own, without relying on his father's support. He yearned for Hong-seon's approval. Much like his father, who had amassed wealth through the logistics and distribution trade, Il-seop aspired to manage his general store with equal success. As the eldest son and rightful heir of the Choi family, he was determined to prove to everyone that he could stand tall and prosper financially on his own.

However, business proved to be exceptionally challenging. Though Bok-hee managed to provide some covert assistance through her siblings, it was far from sufficient. Il-seop visibly lost weight, and his struggles were evident to Bok-hee. She tried to persuade him, saying, "How about scaling it down a bit?" But her efforts were in vain.

Il-seop harbored a fervent desire for a grander store filled with even more exquisite items. Understanding his ambition, Bok-hee found herself unable to firmly support downsizing the store. She was acutely aware of Il-seop's towering pride and his unwavering determination not to be outdone by anyone. Thus, when a man who took his role as family head seriously made an unusual remark to Bok-hee, she should have recognized that it foreshadowed a significant event.

The night before he decided to end his life, Il-seop called her to the *sarang-bang*. Il-seop said, "*Yeobo* (a term of endearment between married couples), you've endured countless hardships since marrying me. You've followed my wishes faithfully, but now I have a sincere request. Place your hand on my chest."

Gently, Bok-hee placed her hand on Il-seop's chest, feeling his heart pounding beneath her palm. His once robust body had become frail, his chest painfully thin and fragile.

Il-seop said,

"My dear, from now on, I must entrust you with the household duties even more. It seems I will soon need to embark on a long journey. With six children to care for, you will barely have a moment to rest. In my absence, you will bear even greater burdens. But I have faith in you. I believe you will manage well, remembering that I am always with you in spirit..."

Bok-hee asked in a trembling voice, trying to steady her startled heart,

"*Seobangnim* (a respectful term for a husband), why are you saying this? Are you planning to go somewhere far away? I'm due to give birth in about fifteen days. Where could you possibly be going? Are you thinking of going to Manchuria as we discussed? I am heavily pregnant. How long do you plan to stay if you go? If you're heading to such a distant place, what about travel expenses and the Hwashin store in Jinju? Are you planning to close it? It's a store that has required such a large investment over the years. Will you abandon it without seeing it through?

Seobangnim, have you prepared for all that? Travel expenses, a clear plan, and..."

Her words trailed off, laden with concern and confusion, as she grappled with the gravity of his intentions. Il-seop had no answer. Instead, he pressed his lips together tightly as if he had made a firm resolution. The light in the room was exceptionally dim that day, obscuring Il-seop's features. Reflecting on it later, she realized he had likely darkened the room on purpose. After Il-seop's death, bruises, both large and small, were revealed on his cheeks and forehead. When he met Bok-hee the night before, she had not noticed these bruises due to the poor lighting.

On the surface, Il-seop might have appeared strong and unyielding, but perhaps he was more fragile than anyone realized. Deep down, he was a man who constantly carried the weight of his father Hong-seon's other family members from the *Saejip* (the New House) household and his half-brother Jeong-seop from the *Saemmyjip* household. These were the people with whom Il-seop and his father had to share their attention and concern.

And though she seemed to be a victim of Il-seop, Lady Hwang of the New House was, in fact, the woman who had usurped the place of Il-seop's mother, Lady Kim. Behind every decision Hong-seon made sat Lady Hwang, always wanting to know every detail. During the busy farming season, only Hong-seon and Il-seop appreciated the immense work Bok-hee undertook. Others simply accepted the sacrifices made by Bok-hee and Il-seop as something expected, without a word of gratitude.

As they harvested crops and collected rent from tenant farmers, the management of these processes varied from household to household, but people still flocked to this grand house (Big House) every day. Consequently, there was a constant need for more rice and food.

Why did it have to be this way?

Il-seop knew his wife was doing all the work, and even though there were no overt complaints about the property that had already been divided, people compared their shares, always feeling that theirs was insufficient. In reality, Il-seop's Big House had few remaining assets compared to the large number of family members. However, because Bok-hee meticulously saved and managed resources carefully, the household ran smoothly. Hong-seon knew this best, and so did Il-seop. However, Lee-seop's wife complained the most...

Anything related to Bok-hee was a thorn in Lee-seop's wife's side. "If I were the eldest daughter-in-law of this family, I wouldn't be living like this ... tsk tsk..." The last "tsk tsk" was particularly unpleasant to Bok-hee's ears. However, fighting was only worthwhile when the opponent was of equal standing. Lee-seop's wife pretended not to understand her own character, even though everyone knew what she was like. No one acknowledged her.

Furthermore, Bok-hee was her senior. As Hong-seon said, "The senior should endure," so Bok-hee did not get angry when she heard complaints from Lee-seop's wife. Instead, Bok-hee responded,

"Sister, the eldest son is naturally supposed to be born first. So, I became your senior by fate. If you don't stay in your place, you should not speak recklessly. They say money and wealth have eyes, and they go to those who protect and manage them well. Being a senior is more difficult. It's not as easy as it seems. There's much work to be done."

Nam-gil jutted out her lips in a pout but quickly concealed her expression and responded half-heartedly, as if trying to brush off Bok-hee's words. Nam-gil said,

"I understand, elder sister, but when you think about it, isn't your household also living off father's property? I'm saying this because your husband is the eldest son and has received more than I did. If I were you, I wouldn't just do housework diligently like you. I would lend money at high interest with that large sum of money and seek opportunities to increase our wealth by going outside. I know that money has eyes. Of course."

The villagers remarked that Il-seop's wife, with her masculine name and extravagant ways, always seemed dissatisfied with even the smallest matters in the Choi family. Nonetheless, Bok-hee never lost her position as the eldest daughter-in-law and never quarreled with Nam-gil.

However, after Il-seop's death, Nam-gil gradually became more audacious and assertive. Bok-hee had a general idea of what kind of *simbo* (deep inner feelings in Korean) Nam-gil harbored. Although her actions were unpredictable, they were somewhat transparent. Pursing her lips, Nam-gil often made a big fuss, frequenting Lady Hwang of the New House rather than Lady Kim of the Big House.

According to Sindeung-ddigi, the wife of a tenant farmer:

Nam-gil said, "Since Il-seop, the eldest son, passed away, if my husband, Lee-seop, is alive, he will become the eldest son of this family. Though I haven't heard from him yet, if he shows up even if tomorrow, the hierarchy in this house will change, and he'll naturally assume the role of the eldest son. Then my position ... will be different from what it is now."

Nam-gil was making a fuss with such preposterous ideas. Bok-hee couldn't fathom why Nam-gil was making such absurd claims, but she decided to scoff and ignore it. She chose to ignore Nam-gil, who was as shrewd as a mouse and always sought her own interests, regardless of her masculine name. Bok-hee knew that Hong-seon understood Nam-gil's true nature and how deeply she cherished Il-seop.

Il-seop had a strong artistic sensitivity and a knack for making witty remarks, but his self-esteem was stronger than anyone else's. Even after marrying Bok-hee and having children, he still sought the attention and recognition of his father, Hong-seon. He wanted to be the most outstanding of Hong-seon's sons. Everyone has weaknesses and a natural instinct to avoid hardship. However, some people, when their self-esteem is damaged, conceal their vulnerabilities even more.

When Il-seop died, Hong-seon said,

"Il-seop, my boy, no matter what anyone says, you were the most important treasure to me. I should have understood your high self-esteem better ... you foolish boy."

Hong-seon had always believed, '*The stupid child needs to be scolded and pressured, while the smart one needs gentle persuasion to understand what the father wants.*' He never dreamed that Il-seop would leave his side so soon. If Hong-seon had persuaded Il-seop, who was more sensitive and intelligent than anyone else, and had been honest with him about the situation... would Il-seop have changed his mind? If Il-seop hadn't disappeared so quickly, would Hong-seon's heart have broken like this?

After Il-seop left, Hong-seon often went to *Jegak*, a building near the tomb used for ancestral rites, in Deokwooji, a secluded place, and cried bitterly.

Being born a man could also be a weakness.

'*A man must not cry in front of others.*' Who had said this?

He was a person before he was a man. Tears flowed freely.

Hong-seon had numerous nightmares of falling into a deep, empty hole, unable to move his arms or legs. He grew increasingly weak, both in body and mind.

Only Bok-hee knew the full extent of Hong-seon's suffering.

Was it because of her sharp intuition, inherited from her father-in-law, Hong-seon?

About twenty days after Il-seop's passing, the youngest daughter, Ki-seon, was born on February 23, 1945—a posthumous child.

09
Ki-soon's Marriage

Summer 1945: The New House
—The Unconcealable Nature

In 1945, *Joseon* (Korea) was liberated from Japanese rule. As World War II ended in Japan's defeat, this land also became free from colonialism. Il-seop had also passed away. During this time, women began to embrace the concept of the "New Woman."[45] Having lived through this transformative period, the women of this country became more assertive.

However, the world was not a place where women could easily achieve their ambitions. Ki-soon frequently engaged in discussions with Jeong-soon about how to navigate life with confidence. Through their childhood observations, they found an answer. It stemmed from the life of their aunt in Jinju, Principal Hwang, whose way of living served as an inspiration. No matter how enlightened the country had become, they understood that to overcome their circumstances and stand with confidence, they needed to secure respectable professions.

Thus, for a woman to be recognized and respected, she had to become a teacher, a doctor, or a pharmacist. Achieving such a position required a significant investment of time and effort in education and dedication. This led them to ponder: what was more important in a woman's life, a career or marriage?

They decided to postpone thinking about it for now. Although Ki-soon had been admitted to college, she had only completed her education at a public high school for girls. Jeong-soon, too, was set to graduate from the

---

45) New Woman: Originating in Britain, where women first demanded the right to vote, this term traveled from Britain to Korea via Japan and became a popular phrase in the 1920s. According to the Encyclopedia of Korean National Culture, the New Woman referred to educated women during the colonial period who pursued new values and attitudes, often causing social controversy. These women, first appearing in Victorian England and soon becoming a global phenomenon, sought economic independence, questioned the traditional marriage system, and asserted their independence. In Japan, the New Woman emerged in 1920, and in Korea, it was introduced by Korean women who had studied in Tokyo.
— Summarized by the author.

same institution next year. Could this be because, like Jeong-soon, Ki-soon also had little understanding of what society was really like?

They, as young women, had little notion of how harsh the world beyond their home could be, a world shaped by the interplay between men and women. They were merely country girls, naive and sheltered, who had only known the confines of their schools and homes in Sancheong and Jinju. They were like frogs in a well, unaware of the vastness beyond.

In any society or household, until something significant happened, they had no inkling of the extent of the influence men could wield just by virtue of being men.

Lady Hwang always starched the fabric stiffly before ironing and would place her iron on the floor near the entrance to her room. The iron required hot coals and patience for the task. Once imbued with the heat of the coals, it would glide over the starched fabric, smoothing out every crease and fold. When it came to ironing large quilt covers, at least two or three people were needed. Two would hold the fabric on either side while one skillfully maneuvered the hot iron over the wrinkled cloth. Hong-seon's garments, once pressed by Lady Hwang on a sturdy base with the hot iron, would regain their crispness. She lived with her sewing basket and the container for storing the iron always by her side, her constant companions in her meticulous craft.

The iron, clutching its searing heat, relied on the heat of the charcoal fire to serve its purpose. Similarly, women confined to the household might need to endure many more trials to understand the world beyond their homes. Marriage and childbirth, societal rites of passage that came with age, were akin to traversing these metaphorical furnaces. For Ki-soon and Jeong-soon, it was nearly impossible to envision how their evolving bodies and minds would navigate these changes. The mere contemplation of it brought a vague yet palpable sense of unease.

They never discussed these matters with each other. The deep, unknown fear was something they dreaded discovering or even acknowledging within themselves until they faced it firsthand.

As Ki-soon stepped out onto the *daecheong-maru*, she noticed the door to her mother's room slightly ajar. The house was silent except for the faint sound of sniffles and a slight cough. Ki-soon paused in front of her own room, directly across from her mother's, and listened intently. This had become a habit of hers for some time now.

Her mother was sewing. Upon closer inspection, Ki-soon saw that it was a piece of light yellow silk, though the part her mother held was a murkier shade of yellow, as if soaked with water. When Ki-soon opened the door and entered, Lady Hwang looked up in surprise. As she had seen in childhood, her mother's tears had stained the fabric.

As if nothing had happened, Lady Hwang spoke to Ki-soon. Lady Hwang said,

"Ki-soon! It's your first vacation since you started college, and I'm delighted to have you home. However ... there's something on my mind that troubles me. It's just that ... your father has been talking about your marriage and seems to be making preparations for it.

You're of age now, so what do you think? Are you ready to get married? Weddings can always be arranged ... but I'm curious about how you feel about marriage."

And Lady Hwang spoke cautiously while observing Ki-soon's expression. "So, how are you enjoying your studies at university?
I still can't decide which is better, continuing your education or getting married. What matters most is your own feelings."

Ki-soon replied in a childlike, curious voice.

"Mother, there's something I realized when I went to university. These days, I believe that women can live well and take care of themselves if they have their own careers. But despite saying this, the girls around me don't seem to make a strong effort to find jobs. I don't understand their way of thinking.

There are so many things I don't know about the world, especially since moving to Seoul... Personally, I want to study more. As for marriage, I'm not ready. I don't want to follow the mindset of other girls blindly. I will speak to my father first. These are my thoughts."

Lady Hwang said,

"Sweetheart, when I was sixteen, I thought I had fulfilled my duty if I had enough to eat and could help my younger siblings study. I believed it was enough to live cleanly and decently. My marriage enabled me to do these things, but I never imagined it would bring such pain to my children. But you will live a different life than I did..."

Ki-soon said, "Mother, please stop saying that now."

Upon hearing Ki-soon's words, Hwang acted as she did during mass at the Catholic church every Sunday. She struck the left side of her chest with her right hand, saying, "It's my fault. It's my fault. It's my great fault."

When Ki-soon saw her mother behave that way, she could hear no sound of sobbing. However, she could feel the hot tears welling up within her mother. She could even sense the echoes of tears that had long since dried. Even though her mother had long learned to conceal the sounds of her suffering, and those sounds had faded over time, the pain remained deeply embedded within her.

Lady Hwang lowered her head and spoke in a trembling voice.

"Forgive me. I brought you into this world as my child... But let's not think of death. Instead, think about marriage. This is your mother's wish."

At that moment, Ki-soon felt as if she could see into her mother's heart. Although her mother had never expressed her thoughts in words to Ki-soon...

Ki-soon,

"The Innocence of Guilt—With a heart so proud and unyielding, my mother stood tall in all aspects of her life, never bending, never compromising. When her own lofty and noble heart, once placed upon a pedestal, became the subject of others' scorn, she could not understand why she was being condemned.

She believed herself to be so pure and immaculate, beyond reproach, unable to accept any accusation against her. My mother could neither accept nor acknowledge the hushed whispers about Il-seop and the others. For in the depths of Mother's heart, there was no shadow of guilt.

The Innocence of Guilt! Those who point fingers, their own flaws hidden and distorted, yet remain blind to them in their own reflections, carry the shadow of a desire to commit the same sins.

Thus, they scorn. They accuse.

Is that why they do it?

The shadows of the heart, the shadows within my mother's heart?

I could grasp only fragments... The space between a child and a mother—so familiar, yet so unreachable—remained."

The following evening, Hong-seon summoned Ki-soon to the *sarang-chae*. After some preliminary remarks, he finally broached the subject: "How would you feel about hastening the marriage arrangements? This is your father's wish."

Ki-soon, unable to respond, lowered her head and silently left the room. This was a new side of her father. She sensed that Hong-seon was emotionally vulnerable. However, he had always said, "Even a daughter should be supported in pursuing her studies; that is a father's foremost duty."

Perhaps the void left in his heart by Il-seop's departure made him yearn for solace through his eldest daughter, Ki-soon, even if it meant marrying her off before she could complete her studies. The mere thought of marriage, though vague, filled Ki-soon with anxiety. In her first year of college, she had only gone on two blind dates with students from H University and other colleges in Seoul. She had met no one who stirred even the slightest interest in her. Her resolve to marry only after securing a job remained unchanged.

The day after Hong-seon's summons, Ki-soon decided to speak her mind. As she sat with her father and mother, she resolved to say, "Please give me more time." She then decided to leave Sancheong hastily, fearing that if she stayed longer, she would be coerced into a marriage she did not want.

However, as Ki-soon was packing her bag, her mother entered the room, sensing her daughter's unease.

Lady Hwang asked,

"Sweetheart, is there someone you care about or have made a commitment to?"

Ki-soon replied,

"No, mother. There's no one like that yet. I just want to get a job after finishing my studies and then think about marriage."

Lady Hwang said,

"I have hesitated a lot, as you know. But now, in this family, with your brother Il-seop gone and Joon-seop still in middle school, I hope you can understand your father's feelings.

If we see you meet a good man, make him your husband, and live happily with him, I believe your father and I will find peace, which will help alleviate his emptiness and pain. So, I hope you can change your mind and respect our wishes."

Ki-soon tossed and turned for three days, contemplating her mother's words. She wrestled with her desire to return to Seoul and sought to understand what she truly wanted. On the fourth day, she decided to express her thoughts to her parents. Ki-soon said,

"Father, Mother, if you truly wish for me to marry, I will accept it, but

I have a condition. May I speak?"

Hong-seon and Hwang were grateful that Ki-soon, who had always been strong-willed, was now willing to listen to her parents. In fact, Hong-seon had already started searching for a suitable groom a month ago, engaging well-known matchmakers from the Gyeongsangnam-do area. He had planned to arrange meetings with three potential suitors during Ki-soon's vacation.

Looking back, this was only possible because of Hong-man. Hong-man, Hong-seon's younger brother, had taken the initiative in this task, speeding up the process. Hong-seon's only wish was for his daughter, Ki-soon, to marry a man from a respectable family.

However, deep down, he thought that Hong-man's advice wasn't entirely wrong when he had suggested, "... Since we have enough money, wouldn't it be better to choose a marriage partner who can elevate the Choi family's name?" Hong-seon, finding some merit in his brother's words, agreed that it was not a completely bad idea.

Ki-soon said,

"Father, Mother, even if I get married, I want to marry into a family that will allow me to finish my studies. In the future, women must have their own careers not only to be self-reliant but also to be better role models for their children. If such a family cannot be found, please give me more time to finish my second year before deciding on a marriage.

I will consider what is best for our family."

Hong-seon said,

"I understand what you're saying, but finding a family like that might be difficult. If you insist on continuing your studies, people might label you a 'new woman' or a 'progressive woman.' I don't know if there is a family in this region of stubborn Western Gyeongnam. I'm not sure if there's a respectable family that would accept such an idea.

However, I will keep your wishes in mind and search for someone suitable. So, to clarify, are you agreeing to marriage under these conditions? Is that what you mean? I'll start looking for such a match."

Bowing her head, Ki-soon added softly, "Yes, but only if my wishes are respected." She returned to her room and gazed at the ceiling. *If I marry, the day I leave this room might not be far off,* she murmured to herself. *I wish I had more time...*

Just then, Joon-seop and Jeong-soon burst into her room, seeking her attention when all she wanted was quiet. Joon-seop, with a childish whine, begged, "Big sister, please make us some delicious chive pancakes."

About ten days passed.

Hong-man was frequently seen conversing with Hong-seon as he walked in and out of the *sarang-chae* of the New House. The family of the Big House began to catch wind of the situation. Jeong-soon returned to high school in Jinju after a brief stay in Sancheong to catch up on her studies. Joon-seop, who was in his early teens, and Young-soon, the youngest of the four, came to Ki-soon's room, eventually falling asleep after playing and whining. As Ki-soon looked at their sleeping faces, tears welled up, as if they were not just her younger siblings but her own children.

Uncle Hong-man, who had been diligently arranging Ki-soon's marriage, had not been seen for a while.

After the initial discussions about the marriage, there had been little news for nearly a month. Ki-soon silently hoped, *Marriage is already undesirable for me. I should continue studying. I dearly wish my marriage story would just fade away like this.* Determined to prepare for her second semester, Ki-soon hastily gathered her belongings and packed her bag, ready to head back to Seoul with a sigh of relief.

However, that afternoon, Hong-seon called Ki-soon to join him and Hwang. Hong-seon said,

"Ki-soon, I just discussed this with your mother. You should delay your trip to Seoul. A family has emerged that accepts your conditions. They are willing to take you as their daughter-in-law and have agreed to let you continue your studies after the wedding. So, I think it's best to have the wedding ceremony first. Your mother and I have set the date, and it is set for five days from now."

Ki-soon looked at Hwang, who nodded. She was flustered. *But how much better it would be if I could finish this semester,* she thought. She also realized she needed to know what the man she was going to marry looked like. Hwang spoke to Ki-soon, trying to persuade her.

"Honey, for now, let's trust in your uncle Hong-man. He said that the groom is handsome. His family is refined and well-mannered; his father is currently the county governor. If you marry before returning to school, you may be able to continue your studies while living at your husband's house starting this second semester."

Ki-soon found herself unable to make a decision. She had never seriously contemplated marriage, always considering it a distant concern. However, the prospect of being allowed to continue her studies even after marriage made the idea less daunting. When she looked at her parents' faces, it was clear they had already made up their minds.

At the women's university she attended, many female students were rumored to have married almost as soon as they enrolled. Such sentiments were commonly accepted: "If a woman has a pretty face and comes from a good family, getting married quickly is the most advantageous thing she can do. Becoming the daughter-in-law of a respected family or the wife of a well-regarded son is the pinnacle of a woman's life."

Her classmates often echoed a cynical belief: "A female student who completes her entire university course must either be unattractive or come from a poor family. Only a woman who has been deeply hurt would remain unmarried and finish college." These words, which she often heard, underscored the societal pressures and expectations that weighed heavily on Ki-soon.

At first, Ki-soon was astonished by what she heard.

"What kind of strange notions are these? Is marriage truly the most important thing? Is a woman who marries quickly deemed a respectable woman, and is marrying quickly for any reason seen as a mark of high status? What is this nonsense, as if a woman is a commodity in a market?" Married women often viewed unmarried women not as choosing to remain single, but as being unable to marry. Ki-soon was even more shocked to realize that, despite being in the 1940s and receiving a university education, these women's way of thinking seemed stuck in the *Joseon* Dynasty.

Her classmates said, "What are you talking about? A woman is a product, a display item, and the beautiful and desirable women are sold first. Why did I study so hard? I wanted to get into a better college. In short, *marriage is business!*"

A woman's abilities include her appearance and academic achievements, but her family's background is also a significant factor. This is true for both men and women. This is because the choice of a spouse affects how a family's status rises or falls after the spouse joins it. While love is said to be the most important factor, in reality, it may not carry as much weight. Thus, an individual's social ranking is often perceived as being determined by the combination of the individual and the family they marry into.

However, such views are rarely found in esteemed philosophical texts, which are read by either the highly rational or the slightly mad. These texts often proclaim that the act of loving another person is the noblest pursuit, and that marriage should reflect and stimulate that noble spirit, transcending socio-economic barriers.

Children born outside of marriage are often labeled as illegitimate and remain outsiders in society throughout their lives, both professionally and socially. Some argue that marriage should be approached with careful consideration and viewed as a sublime union. But is this truly right?

Ki-soon desired to shape her own destiny, but such ideals seemed confined to the textbooks in her school. The influence of the new women's movement still lingered among them. The societal shift that had opened doors for many women to pursue higher education—an opportunity largely unavailable to previous generations—had yet to fully take root.

When *Joseon's* E School first opened in the late 1890s, many respectable families in *Joseon* were reluctant to send their daughters to a school that enrolled women of uncertain backgrounds. They had heard that most of the students were orphans or maids. Only the most progressive families considered sending their daughters to such an institution for education.

Graduates of E School ventured into society and took up jobs; some even married into reputable, affluent families. Eventually, the school experienced an influx of students from wealthy and prominent families. An increasing number of students began traveling to Japan and the United States for further studies, a testament to the transformative power of education. Today, E Women's University is recognized as a prestigious institution in Korea.

Ki-soon and her sister felt very fortunate whenever Hong-seon habitually said, "As long as the family has the financial means and the will, everyone, regardless of gender, should receive the best education." Their aunt, who served as their role model, epitomized this belief despite remaining single. Ki-soon and Jeong-soon recognized that their circumstances differed slightly from those of their aunt's generation. Nonetheless, they harbored a vague hope of securing stable careers after graduating from college. For Ki-soon, getting married quickly during a break from her studies was never her primary goal.

Yet, Ki-soon found herself unable to resist the anxious, expectant gazes of her parents, who scrutinized her every expression closely. It was even more challenging for her to ignore the emptiness in her father, Hong-seon's heart—a void left by the loss of Il-seop.

Ki-soon sat in her room, wearing a *jokduri* on her head, with *yeonji* and *gonji* dotting her face. She wore several heavy layers of bridal clothing. She had barely eaten anything the day before, busy preparing for various tasks. Hwang was restless and unable to focus on anything. Her face was tense, and she often seemed absent-minded.

In her haste, Hwang called in some neighboring women to assist with the wedding preparations. They murmured among themselves about Hwang's sluggish condition, speculating, "Ever since she was slapped and collapsed after an encounter with the eldest grandson, Il-seop, last year, something seems to be amiss. She should just get through this wedding safely..."

Ki-soon understood that there must be a reason why her mother was so insistent on proceeding with the marriage. Dressed in her bridal attire, she stared at the wall. Suddenly, she felt Il-seop's angry eyes glaring at her from somewhere on the wall where her gaze had settled. Ki-soon quickly closed her eyes, thinking that if she could just get through the wedding ceremony, it might bring some solace to her mother's troubled heart.

She closed her eyes, trying to endure Il-seop's haunting presence. It was bewildering—to see her brother Il-seop's face at a moment like this... She silently chastised herself. Struggling to suppress her thoughts, she endeavored to focus solely on waiting for the groom in quiet anticipation.

Eventually, the groom arrived, greeted her family, and had a drink. As the chaos unfolded, Ki-soon thought, 'I guess this is what a traditional wedding ceremony is like.' She waited for the commotion to subside, musing, 'They say marriage is the most important event in life, but it feels like one of the most surreal experiences.'

Ki-soon remained still, waiting in her room. She understood the sequence of events that followed after the groom entered her house and endured the entire wedding process. It was a time of considerable distress, but she tried to concentrate only on waiting for the groom without saying a word.

The sounds of Jeong-seop, the half-brother from Saemmyjip, drinking and greeting the groom along with his relatives, grew louder. As the evening passed, the groom-to-be, visibly drunk, sat at the dining table, the sound of his movements echoing through the room. His *samo-kwandae* [46] was slightly askew.

Ki-soon couldn't shake the thought: 'Why does he have to be so drunk on this important first night, to the point of not being able to stand straight? There are so many bizarre wedding rituals that I just don't understand.'

In fact, since the morning — or rather, since lunch the previous day — Ki-soon had barely eaten anything while waiting, which was probably why she was starting to feel hungry. No matter how long she waited, the groom did not enter the room. Growing impatient, Ki-soon wondered what was happening on the wooden porch (*daecheong-maru*) and peeked through a crack in the door to see what the groom was doing.

Before entering the bridal room, where the bride was still waiting without even removing her ceremonial headpiece, the groom had eaten every last bit of food on the table set on the porch. There were clearly two sets of utensils placed there, but he had eaten everything.

Seeing the groom like that, Ki-soon, unable to contain herself, burst out in frustration to Bok-hee, who had also been sitting next to her, waiting.

Ki-soon said,

"No! He must be a fool! The bride has been waiting for him, unfed for nearly two days, still wearing a *jokduri* and cumbersome clothing... Yet, he's eating all the food on that table. I will have nothing to eat!

Oh my! He knows nothing about first-night etiquette or the respect a husband should have for his wife. He only cares about filling his own

---

[46] Samo: A hat made of silk. Gwandae: A traditional Korean official's hat and belt. Originally, the *samo* and *gwandae* were formal attire worn when one obtained an official position, but they later became customary attire for weddings.—Referenced by the author from Naver Korean Dictionary.

stomach!

Ah! I have ended up with such a greedy, foolish man as my husband! I'm doomed. I'm doomed! Oh, I should never have married!

I cannot share a bed with such a fool. He will eat too much, stumble into my room, snore, and pass out.

He's a man who only thinks about himself and has no consideration for his wife! That much is certain!

He's already lying there like that, so I'll put an end to this right now, making sure he never comes in! Damn it!"

Ki-soon tore off her *jokduri* and wedding garments, quickly changing into casual attire. She sat down, facing the wall, resolutely refusing to turn toward the *daecheong-maru*. Bok-hee relayed the news to Hwang, and even Hong-seon came to console her, but Ki-soon's resolve remained unshaken.

That night, the groom, Jo Jong-cheol, fully sated and heavily intoxicated, fell asleep on the *daecheong-maru*. Unable to be roused, he was carried to the men's quarters, completely missing the newlywed room. The household, which had anticipated a lively celebration on the first night of the honeymoon, fell into dead silence.

The groom awoke very late the next day, nearly at ten in the morning. Realizing that he hadn't even spent the night with his bride, he felt the sting of rejection keenly. It was quite literally a case of the groom being "*naeso-bak*."[47] The groom had waited in the *sarang-bang* for over half a day. Yet, the response from the bride's house remained the same: "We couldn't break the bride's stubbornness." Outraged and seething over what had happened to him, he lashed out as he left the New House.

Jo Jong-cheol spoke in a loud, furious voice, his anger seething.

"No! Do you have any idea who I am? How dare you do this to me?

---

[47] Naeso-bak: A term that means being neglected by his wife, in contrast to "*oeso-bak*," where a husband neglects his wife.—Referenced from Naver Chinese Character Dictionary by the author.

Does everything depend on the bride's will? So, am I not a man?

Until now, whenever I showed up in Jinju or the *Dongnae Gisaeng-bang* in Busan, all kinds of women flocked to me, showering me with praise. And now, I'm not good enough?

How dare you desert me? Huh? Really?

I'll never let this go! I'll never tolerate that arrogant girl!

I'll tell my father about all the humiliation I've suffered in this house.

Do you think you're the only woman studying in Seoul?"

He stormed out of the room, shouting loudly so that Ki-soon could hear. She stood all night, facing the wall in the main room, unfazed by his tirade.

Jong-cheol screamed angrily, shouting at the top of his lungs.

"You're just the daughter of a concubine.

Don't think I don't know that! How dare you, you outrageous bitch!

I don't know what kind of guy you've been hanging around with in Seoul, but I will never forgive you!

You're a girl who doesn't know her place.

You're the daughter of a concubine, and you should live like one!"

Just as Jong-cheol was about to turn around after speaking, something suddenly flew toward him. The moment Ki-soon heard Jong-cheol's words, she was unable to contain her anger and threw a brass water bowl at him. Though she hadn't thrown it with much force, it unfortunately struck him on the back of his head. Letting out a cry of "Ouch!", he collapsed on the spot, weakened.

All of this happened in the courtyard of the inner quarters.

At that moment, Ki-soon was mortified, and Jong-cheol seemed quite shocked. Perhaps it was also due to excessive drinking the previous day. Like a large, rotting tree trunk, he tumbled forward, landing in the middle of the yard with a loud thud.

All the neighboring women who had come to help with the wedding preparations screamed, "Oh my gosh!" covering their mouths with their hands as they ran into the kitchen in shock. The entire house suddenly erupted into chaos.

After a moment, Ki-soon, who had been watching from inside the room, ran out barefoot, her expression slightly calmer, and tried to help the fallen man. About twenty minutes later, Jong-cheol opened his eyes to find dozens of strangers staring at him as if he were a spectacle.

10
A New Beginning Brought by Pain

1945 – 1947: The New House
—Struggling to Mend

At a Buddhist Temple (Watercoloring on Kent paper, 364x515mm)

Ki-soon examined Jong-cheol's head, finding no visible trauma. Some people carried Jong-cheol to the *sarang-chae* and laid him down. About two hours later, Jong-cheol, who had been lying motionless, suddenly got up as if nothing had happened.

The traditional Korean doctor, who had been observing Jong-cheol from the *sarang-chae*, attempted to examine him once more. Unaware of Jong-cheol's condition, the doctor had been summoned earlier, prepared to administer acupuncture or any necessary treatment. Jong-cheol, however, brusquely brushed off the doctor's touch and stepped out of the room. Feeling humiliated and profoundly upset by the events in this house, Jong-cheol stood in stunned silence. He gathered his servants and household members, who had been waiting outside, and stormed out, grumbling at the gate of the New House.

Ki-soon thought it was finally over. She retreated to her room, locking the door behind her, and spent the rest of the day there.

The next morning, she went to her mother's room early in the day. She wasn't sure when her mother had woken up, but she found her working on a white cloth, sewing a *jeogori*. It seemed she had stayed up all night. Her mother was cutting something that looked like a sleeve, and Ki-soon noticed that the fabric was wet with her tears. Her mother spoke, her voice heavy with sorrow.

Lady Hwang:

"Ki-soon, what do you think is the fairest thing in the world?"

Ki-soon:

"I don't know. I've pondered that question at times. It seems to me that nothing in this world is truly fair, nothing at all."

Lady Hwang:

"Really? I've always thought that life itself is the fairest thing because it is evident that all living creatures, all beings, exist in worry and anxiety. Consider it for a moment. Isn't it fair that we live in a world where everyone experiences pain? Some suffer from one thing, others from another. But imagine, this suffering might be an intrinsic part of being alive.

The fairest thing is that we all die eventually. In death, we no longer feel this pain, so it isn't so bad, considering we endure it while alive.

Ki-soon, let's live our days ... until they come to their natural end. Tears keep falling because I am alive, aren't they?"

Ki-soon:

"Mother, no matter how much we wish to live, we will all die someday. But is there really such a significant difference between living and dying? While we are alive, we stand and walk because of Earth's gravity. Later, when we lose the strength to stand and walk, we lie down and close our eyes for the last time. We lose the ability to open our eyes, to speak, to move. Life has fulfilled its purpose.

We are bound by Earth's gravity, whether alive or dead.

So, I think what is fair is gravity. Earth's gravity. It is the one constant in this world. But even that doesn't seem entirely right. The gravitational pull on a hawk soaring high in the sky and an earthworm crawling at the bottom of the world can differ slightly."

Lady Hwang,

"My dear, I don't know much about things like gravity, but what I'm saying is that being alive itself is fair. We strive to live... Think of your siblings, especially the youngest, Young-soon. It is crucial for me to sustain this household and to continue living within it. In other words, let's not give up. Let's endure until our last day.

By the way ... the groom's father is the county governor. He won't stay idle. What are you thinking? Wouldn't it be wiser to take refuge somewhere else? Why don't you pack up and leave right away? Alright?

I think it would be best. I'm scared. Even a small amount of power, if wielded recklessly, can be dangerous..."

Before the conversation could end, a loud noise erupted outside the room in the main house. Yoo-sang stood outside the room, urgently calling out to Lady Hwang and Ki-soon.

Yoo-sang,

"Big Mistress, please leave the kitchen at once and escape over the wall. It's best to avoid any confrontation. Early this morning, people from the groom's house arrived, demanding, 'Where is the Big Mistress?' They're causing a commotion!

Oh my! The burly men, enormous in size, pounded on the gate of the main house, demanding that it be opened. The new servant, who had just started yesterday, let them in. Now, they're running around wildly, asking where the young lady is—dashing here and there throughout the house.

We need to gather all the villagers, but it's so early in the morning... Most people have already gone to the fields to work, and there are no strong men at home to help. It seems they'll be here any moment now."

And then, in a small, barely audible voice, he added, "At present, the Big Elder went to Master Jeong-seop's house early this morning. He mentioned having something to discuss..."

Ki-soon:

"No, let it be, Uncle. What's the worst that could happen? That I might die? I haven't committed a crime worthy of death, so what can they do? Just tell them I'm here."

Soon, three large men stood at the door of the main room in the New House. The men:

"Madam! Big Mistress, are you there? We've heard you're here, and we've come on behalf of Mr. Jo, the governor of Sacheon-gun. Whatever we do next, it's by his orders, so don't hold us accountable. We don't see any men around to stop us, which is good. That makes things less awkward for us."

The men drove the cows, pigs, and chickens out of the barn. They poured cow porridge into the yard and smashed the soy sauce jars in the *jangdok-dae*, filling the air with the sharp scent of fermented soy sauce.

They must have seen Hong-seon leave early in the morning, which is when they decided to strike. One of the men muttered, "Hey, let's finish up quickly and get out of here. If the Elder who left earlier comes back, we'll be in trouble. The young master will be in trouble with the governor if we stick around. Let's call it a day, all right?"

With that, they disappeared shortly after causing the disturbance.

The previous night, Hong-seon had confided in Hwang, "Now that the marriage is off, I plan to appease the county governor, Jo, and clean up this mess. Apparently, he's a money-grubber. I didn't realize that before... Anyway, his obsession with money might help us now. At dawn, I'll ask Hong-man and Jeong-seop to visit Governor Jo."

Perhaps Hong-seon went with Jeong-seop to see someone who knew Jong-cheol's father well, hoping to smooth things over. And Hong-seon had said,

"The easiest way to deal with difficulties is to use money to resolve them. Money is convenient ... but if they don't get paid, things could get more difficult. Worse still, they might take the money and not handle the situation properly. Pretending to value reputation over money ... it complicates things for everyone. And what if, after paying them, it becomes even harder to get the work done?"

These words lingered in Hwang's mind.

Although the men had left the New House and were no longer visible, Hwang's anxiety remained. She felt an unshakable premonition that something dire would befall the family due to Ki-soon's broken engagement. To soothe her troubled heart, she had been holding onto her sewing kit jar—*dangsaegi* (a sewing box in the dialect of Hamyang and Sancheong, Gyeongsang-do)—since last night. She had long believed that concentrating on something was an easy way to relieve worries when anxiety struck.

Earlier, when the men had caused a commotion at the house, she had been so anxious that now she could feel her whole body trembling again from clenching her fists so tightly. Lady Hwang noticed that from that time on, her hands and legs occasionally went numb, preventing her from moving quickly. It had started after she was slapped and knocked down by Il-seop last year. Even Hong-seon eventually discovered her condition, but there was little he could do because she refused to take herbal medicine or get acupuncture. Hwang had resigned herself to her fate, choosing not to take any action for her own well-being.

Moreover, during the recent uproar at home, she had clung to Ki-soon with all her might, fearful that her young daughter might act rashly against the unruly men. Lady Hwang was unaware of just how tightly she had embraced Ki-soon until her daughter gasped, "Mother, I'm suffocating." Only then did Hwang loosen her grip and release Ki-soon from her desperate hold.

About thirty minutes after the men had caused a ruckus and left, Jong-cheol's voice echoed through the yard of the New House.

Jong-cheol:

"Pshaw! I thought the rich Choi family of Sancheong would be impressive, but it's nothing special! Hey! Choi Ki-soon! You're nothing! Your family, too, is insignificant! All that wealth is just a bit of land! Even if a third of Sancheong's land belongs to the Elder in this house, it's still nothing more than a countryside as small as a crab shell. What's so great about that compared to the wealthy people of Hanyang? And you're not even a legitimate child..."

Unable to contain her anger upon hearing this, Ki-soon sprang up from her crouched position and ran out to the *daecheong-maru* of the main room. Ki-soon:

"Yes, Mr. Jong-cheol! A thug who wastes time with *gisaeng* and idles away under his pompous father's name, nearing thirty without any accomplishments! Even if I'm the child of a concubine, you are hardly worthy of marrying a decent woman like me! You lazy, worthless scoundrel! I'm never going to marry a fool like you! So what if your family is wealthy? Do all three brothers even share the same mother? At least I know who my parents are; you don't even know your own mother! You miserable wretch! You don't even understand your own situation. If you have no further business here, leave before I call the police!"

Enraged by her words, Jong-cheol charged at Ki-soon. He swiftly climbed up to the main hall and grabbed Ki-soon's long tresses of hair. In her desperation, Ki-soon, falling with her hair caught, struck Jong-cheol's face with an iron rod from her mother's sewing *dangsaegi*, which was placed by the threshold of the main room. As Jong-cheol rolled around in the yard, clutching his forehead, everyone gathered around. Realizing what she had done, Ki-soon was overwhelmed with fear. Her heart pounded like a drum, and she collapsed, trembling all over.

A week later, Ki-soon was taken to the police station because of Governor Jo's lawsuit. The police determined that Jong-cheol's injury was just a slight scratch on his forehead from the iron rod.

To prevent the situation from escalating, Hong-seon acted quickly. He sold off gold pieces, rice paddies, and fields, converting them into a large sum of cash. Hong-seon then went to the yard of Governor Jo's house and knelt there for about half an hour. Governor Jo, feigning reluctance, finally conceded, acknowledging that he knew his son was a troublemaker.

In the end, Hong-seon paid a large sum to Governor Jo, and they agreed to drop the lawsuit, allowing Ki-soon to return to the New House. After her return, Hong-seon said nothing to Ki-soon. She was filled with remorse and shame, unable to voice her apologies or seek forgiveness, berating herself for her rashness.

The incident underscored Ki-soon's realization that she indeed possessed the infamous *"hot-tempered Choi disposition."* Bok-hee remarked to Ki-soon, "Oh, blood can't be deceived! That quick and fiery Choi temper! Why couldn't you endure a bit more?" She cast a sidelong glance at Ki-soon, fully aware of the sacrifices Hong-seon had made. To quickly gather the required cash, he had to sell off land and goods for less than half their original value.

When Hong-seon returned home, Hwang went to the *sarang-chae* yard, her hair unpinned and loose. She knelt in her *beoseon* and sought forgiveness. But Hong-seon simply said, "You don't have to." He gently held her hand and patted her back, sending her back to the main building. After returning to her room, Ki-soon did not emerge for about fifteen days.

One day, Jeong-seop came to comfort both Ki-soon and Hwang, bringing with him Sancheong's renowned native honey.

Jeong-seop:

"Stepmother, don't be too harsh on Ki-soon. How can a young girl who has only known her family be expected to accept such an outrageous man as her groom? Men like him are unheard of in our family. Stepmother, please encourage Ki-soon while keeping in mind the Big Elder's concerns. I brought some fine native Sancheong honey. Drink warm honey water to soothe your spirits and warm your hearts."

Then he added one more thing...

Jeong-seop said,

"I'll find a better man for Ki-soon. A wound inflicted by a man should be healed by another man. This whole marriage debacle happened because Uncle Hong-man rushed into it without a proper investigation. Had we looked into it more carefully, this wouldn't have happened."

After Jeong-seop left, Ki-soon retreated to her room, her mother's words echoing in her mind—words she had first heard when she was just thirteen. Lady Hwang:

"Ki-soon, Jeong-soon, how will you survive these harsh years? A woman's life is often worse than that of an earthworm writhing in the dirt..."

At that young age, Ki-soon had no grasp of what *"tough"* truly meant. Her mother's frequent lament — '*A woman is worse off than an earthworm, wriggling on its belly in the lowest place just to survive*' — had seemed absurd to her. Comparing the grotesque earthworm to so many pretty and beautiful women seemed ludicrous. It took years of experience to slowly understand her mother's words.

Whenever Ki-soon heard the word "tough," she thought of the old pagoda tree standing in the yard of the Big House. Did that tree know what it meant to endure harsh and tough times?

Were the people living in the Big House, next to that ancient pagoda tree, happier than her family in the New House?

The Big House, where Hong-seon first lived with Lady Kim, was known as "Pagoda Tree House." A pagoda tree stood in front of the *sarang-chae*, and another in front of the *Jangdok-gan* of the *an-chae*. The year Il-seop left, a tiny cherry tree was planted next to the well. No one knew when it would bloom.

Even in the New House where Ki-soon lived, there was a pagoda tree next to the *sarang-chae* of the main building. It was younger than the tree in the Big House, but it did not thrive; its leaves yellowed from illness. It was a mystery. Only the pagoda tree in the Big House, symbolizing the power to "defeat bad luck," grew well. Since childhood, Ki-soon had envied that tree, believing it held the key to protecting the Big House's inhabitants.

The medium-sized pagoda tree near the entrance of the *Jangdok-gan*, situated between the Big House and the New House, concealed the secret entrance to Ki-soon's home. In summer, its lush leaves shaded the path to the well, scattering like rain on windy days. The young housemaid from the Big House would hum and sing as she gathered the fallen leaves with a bucket of water.

Songs and music have a way of resonating in the mind and clearing the head, no matter the person's station. The housemaid, regardless of how often her name changed, endured her hard work by singing. The necessity of labor songs was well understood, and the pagoda tree near the well in the Big House likely made the task more pleasant.

The pagoda tree at the New House stands at the entrance, leading from the gate to the main building. Although it hasn't grown as tall or robust as the one at the Big House, its presence is better than nothing. Its most significant role is to block the view of passersby, ensuring they can't see what the New House family is doing. It shields the household from prying eyes, making it impossible to see inside from the alley outside the wall.

Moreover, in front of the tree lies a large pond, something the Big House lacks. Though not very deep, the pond always hosts a few elegant koi, gracefully swimming around.

Does my house hold more secrets that others must not know about? Have we ever placed a wooden bench under the shade of the tree and enjoyed carefree moments, humming songs like the family at the Big House? Have I ever looked at that pagoda tree with loving eyes, even once?

Even the trees would rather stand at the Big House. They have more to do there, at least more than at our house.

Our life here is one of hiding. This is not a proper life, Ki-soon muttered to herself. She hadn't realized how many thoughts she had about a single tree.

The Big House held *gijae-sa* (ancestral rites) about fifteen times a year. Around the pagoda tree, they would rub their hands together or pray to their ancestors and the spirit of the house grounds. Food crumbs often fell in offering, attracting street cats, crows, magpies, and other birds. Moreover, the well near the *Jangdok-gan* tree drew the women of neighboring houses and village folk, adding to the bustling life under the tree.

But the pagoda tree in the New House stood next to the main building, beside a small well. Few visitors came, save for Ki-soon's family. It served merely as a childhood playground for Ki-soon and Jeong-soon and stood in a quiet space where their mother checked the soy sauce and *doenjang* (soybean paste) only a few times a year.

No matter how much Ki-soon admired the pagoda tree, with its lush green leaves sprawling grandly at the Big House, the residents there often found it an eyesore. In particular, she often resented her father, who insisted on having lunch brought over nearly every day by Bok-hee from the Big House. The maid working under Bok-hee would balance a tray of food on her head, walk around the *Jangdok-gan*, and bring it into the New House through a gap in the wall.

Then, the housemaid would speak loudly enough for Hong-seon to hear, "Big Elder, I'm bringing the food that Madam Hwang of the New House made. Big sister, Madam of the Big House, Bok-hee just tasted it."

Both Ki-soon and Jeong-soon knew that the food had been crafted by Bok-hee's skill from the start. Ki-soon was aware that the housemaid's words were merely a scripted formality dictated by Bok-hee.

As she glanced at the yard of the Big House near the *Jangdok-gan*, Ki-soon couldn't help but recall Il-seop's angry face, as if he were about to storm in. She remembered how he would push open her mother's door, his face red with fury, standing there with his shoes still on.

Lost in her thoughts, Ki-soon found herself shouting involuntarily.

"Ah, I wish I could forget everything. It seems that time does not flow in the realm of human memory. When it's quiet and no sounds can be heard, the door to the world can shut completely. The dead and the living wish to meet at the intersection of memory and converse. How far can my memory reach? Will I ever be able to venture out into the world again?"

Her thoughts then wandered to her mother, Lady Hwang.

... Perhaps my mother, Hwang Pil-hye, at the tender age of sixteen, eager to escape her impoverished home, had decided to marry quickly and come here. She was someone's daughter ... parents and children each inhabit different worlds. We must acknowledge that first, Ki-soon mused, realizing how her thoughts diverged from her mother's.

Around the age of fourteen, Ki-soon began to notice the changes. Now ... at twenty, she saw that little had changed. Her belief that her mother's memories would merge with her own had faded. Her mother remained an enigma, a person with many facets that Ki-soon couldn't fully understand.

Perhaps due to the trauma she endured from the incident with Governor Jo's family, Ki-soon's daily life came to a standstill. She submitted a letter of withdrawal to her school and spent more time indoors than ever before.

Unable to bear seeing her in such a state, Hong-seon arranged for a night out, sending Bok-hee and Ki-soon on a sightseeing trip to enjoy the fresh air. They visited a temple in Hamyang. In such remote mountain temples, numerous small hermitages were often found in the vicinity.
Here, men stayed to study for civil service exams, pursue scholarly fame, or delve into Buddhist teachings.

When Bok-hee and Ki-soon first arrived at the temple, several young men passed through the courtyard. The chief monk explained, "These are young scholars residing in the hermitage just behind this temple."As they passed Ki-soon, she noticed that they were around her age, about twenty, and that there were three of them. One of them, clad in a black leather jacket—a rarity at the time—had short-cropped hair like a monk.

After the evening offering (dinnertime), Ki-soon and Bok-hee stepped out into the temple yard. The men they had seen earlier were also walking there, along with a few others. In the center of the temple stood a small three-story pagoda, around which people circled, chanting softly what sounded like Buddhist scriptures. Ki-soon guessed that the three young men were clearing their minds before studying through the night.

Though it was dark, Ki-soon recognized the man with short hair. He now wore round glasses and a loose black shirt. As they circled the pagoda several times, Ki-soon found herself locking eyes with him. Embarrassed, he quickly averted his gaze to his companions. Ki-soon thought to herself, 'Oh, these must be the law students from Seoul that the chief monk mentioned earlier when he served us green tea. But they look so young, especially him.'

That night, Ki-soon suddenly woke up, startled from her sleep without knowing why. She had a strange dream. There was no doubt it was a dream, but it was so vivid that it felt real. She dreamt that someone was sucking her nipples hard, and she woke up from the sharp pain. When she opened her eyes, she saw Bok-hee sleeping quietly beside her. Ki-soon vividly recalled that the man in her dream—the one who had bitten her nipples—was the short-haired man she had seen in the temple yard earlier that evening.

'Oh my, all sorts of things happen. I've never had a man on my mind at all, and now I have such a weird dream ... I don't even know his name,' Ki-soon muttered to herself, clutching her chest. As she entered her twenties, Ki-soon realized that her experiences as a woman had been delayed compared to those of others her age. Despite this, she vowed never to give her heart to a man she didn't like. The sexual experiences of other women were entirely foreign to her.

After her visit to the temple, Ki-soon seemed to be gradually stabilizing. Noticing this, Hong-seon asked Lady Hwang if Ki-soon could stay in the hermitage for about three months.

Lady Hwang:

"Honey, Big Elder, it would indeed be good for Ki-soon to spend time in a temple or get some fresh air in the mountains. But ... she has always wanted to study. Why don't you discuss it with Jeong-seop? Ki-soon's aunt is also very worried."

Hong-seon and Hwang called Jeong-seop to discuss Ki-soon's future. This was Jeong-seop's response. Jeong-seop:

"Big Elder, Stepmother, even though Ki-soon is Catholic, it wouldn't be bad for her to study in a temple. I believe studying Buddhism could be beneficial in life. To me, Buddhism seems like a progressive philosophy that systematically addresses human perception and thought. It is a valuable field of study."

Lady Hwang:

"Still ... Ki-soon is a young girl with unhealed wounds from her broken marriage. I think it's better not to send her to a hermitage where there are many men."

Hong-seon:

"I don't know yet. What would be best for Ki-soon?"

Jeong-seop:

"Big Elder, Stepmother, studying Buddhism in a new environment is beneficial, but I'll take more time to consider it. If ... in a moment of youthful impulsiveness, Ki-soon decides to cut her hair and become a Buddhist nun, would there be any way to stop her?

What I suggested earlier can wait. Reflecting on Ki-soon's bright nature since childhood, she has remained a virgin, having never slept with a man despite being married. Why not suggest she pursue a new field of study? Let's call Ki-soon and ask for her thoughts."

Jeong-seop called Ki-soon before Hong-seon and Hwang, encouraging her to express her thoughts freely. After a moment's hesitation, Ki-soon spoke in a small voice. Ki-soon:

"I don't know what to do yet. But staying here is unbearable. Please send me somewhere else, like Japan or ... somewhere."

Jeong-seop:

"Ah! That makes sense. Considering how fluent you are in Japanese, as if it were your native language, you could certainly excel in school there. Yes, Big Elder, Stepmother, let's send Ki-soon to Japan so she can pursue the studies she has always longed for."

Thus, Ki-soon was able to express her determination: "Before my mind grows dull, I need to study something that will secure me a profession. If I'm to study, I want to pursue medicine in Japan, where I can truly make a difference."

Hong-seon nodded in agreement, finding it an unexpectedly good idea. Jeong-seop, the son of the Saemmy House, was friendly and sincere toward the New House family. Although intelligent, Jeong-seop tended to trust others too easily, which had occasionally caused minor setbacks for Hong-seon in business dealings.

The important point was that Jeong-seop was fundamentally good. What he did to Il-seop was never for his own benefit, and it was hard to assert that Il-seop's death was directly caused by Jeong-seop's actions. It was a tangled web of emotions between blood relatives. No matter how Hong-seon tried to rationalize it, he couldn't find peace. At some point, Hong-seon decided not to disregard Jeong-seop's decisions as a way to forget Il-seop.

However, there was something about Jeong-seop that Hong-seon found difficult to understand. Despite Hong-seon's numerous suggestions that Jeong-seop get a job, he was always reluctant. When he asked, "Why don't you get a job?" Jeong-seop replied,

"In this harsh world, few can respect a man who abandons his family to study alone in a temple. The world is not a place where one lives in isolation. Moreover, it's not easy to humble oneself before others, especially when he has enough property at home."

Jeong-seop's unrealistic and dependent mindset constantly troubled Hong-seon. If a son follows his father's instructions without resistance, he might be seen as cowardly or foolish. However, Hong-seon could not comprehend why someone responsible for a family would refuse to work.

Nevertheless, Hong-seon resolved not to repeat with Jeong-seop the mistakes he had made with Il-seop. He chose not to worry or interfere with his son's affairs, deciding to wait and see if Jeong-seop would eventually find his own path. Whenever he worried about Jeong-seop, he consoled himself with this thought:

Yes, I've given you enough property, so how you use it is no longer my concern. That's right. If I try to intervene, I might end up in trouble, just as I did with Il-seop. But when did I become so passive? Is it because of my age?

Hong-seon blamed himself but ultimately decided to trust that Jeong-seop had his own plans. Still, Jeong-seop's complacency and lack of initiative frustrated him. Jeong-seop lacked the drive and courage to embrace new challenges. Hong-seon suppressed his urge to criticize, choosing instead to focus on Jeong-seop's positive traits.

Hwang informed the family in the Big House and her younger sister in Jinju about Ki-soon's plans to go to Japan. Ki-soon's aunt, following suit, exchanged letters with Lady Hwang almost daily, discussing Ki-soon's future. Hwang was delighted at the prospect of Ki-soon becoming a doctor after studying in Japan.

Despite Japan's proximity to Korea, various procedures were necessary for Ki-soon's departure. During the preparation period, Ki-soon immersed herself in Buddhist texts.

Although the legal issues with Jong-cheol were resolved, he still occasionally appeared at Ki-soon's house to torment her. Jong-cheol wasn't interested in Ki-soon's activities. He showed up out of spite, harboring a grudge over his broken engagement to another woman. The story of Jong-cheol's canceled marriage was relayed to Hong-seon by Yoo-sang, who heard it from relatives in Sacheon.

In response to Jong-cheol's harassment and to fortify her daughter's spirit, Lady Hwang packed Ki-soon's belongings and sent her to a boarding house near Jinju Girls' High School. Ki-soon spent her days in the school library, reading everything from the *Heart Sutra* to Eastern philosophy. After school, she meditated at the Catholic church across from the boarding house.

Ki-soon, dressed in a white blouse and a black two-piece suit—popular among female college students—was strikingly beautiful. Her juniors at the boarding house often said, "Ki-soon, the senior from the Sancheong Choi family, looks like a foreign movie star."

In the winter of 1947, Ki-soon finally left for Japan to study. Hong-seon arranged for Jeong-seop to accompany her, ensuring that all preparations were in place so Ki-soon could focus on her studies without difficulty.

11
The Korean War[48] I

1950−1956: Seoul, Sancheong, and Busan
—Ki-hoon's Pain and Marriage

---

48) Korean War: In this book, the conflict is referred to as the 6·25 War (Korean Conflict) or the Korean War. To briefly summarize the situation of the Korean War:
  − June 25, 1950: The sudden invasion of South Korea by North Korea.
  − July 7, 1950: General MacArthur's UN forces halt the advance of North Korean troops.
  − September 15, 1950: The successful Incheon Landing Operation cuts off North Korean forces, leading to the recapture of Seoul on September 28.
  − October 2, 1950: UN forces advance beyond the 38th parallel and capture Pyongyang on October 19, reaching the Yalu River at Hyesanjin and the Tumen River by the end of the month. Kim Il-sung requests aid from the Soviet Union and China.
  − October 25, 1950: The Chinese Communist Party, having established the People's Republic of China in October 1949, decides to intervene in the Korean War. They form the Chinese People's Volunteer Army under the command of Peng Dehuai and create a joint command with North Korean forces.
  − November 29, 1950: The UN forces, pushed back by the Chinese and North Korean armies, retreat south of the Chongchon River.
  − December 4, 1950: Pyongyang is evacuated.
  − December 6, 1950: Pyongyang falls to North Korean forces.
  − December 14, 1950: UN forces begin to assemble at Hungnam for a sea evacuation.
  − By the end of December 1950: UN forces retreat to the 38th parallel.
  − January 4, 1951: UN forces relinquish Seoul to North Korean forces.
  − March 14, 1951: UN forces recapture Seoul.
  − March 24, 1951: UN forces advance north of the 38th parallel.
  The war ended on July 27, 1953, when a truce was signed at Panmunjom between the UN commander and the communist commanders (North Korean and Chinese forces).
  —The above summary was referenced by the author from Naver Encyclopedia and Doosan Encyclopedia.

The theater was teeming with people. Even the narrow spaces between the seats were packed. This was the Myeong-dong Theater in Seoul. On the stage, dozens of individuals dressed as members of the North Korean People's Army were conducting a grim event. They all wore red armbands near their shoulders, and some had bands with inscriptions running diagonally from shoulder to chest. One by one, certain names were called out, and the charges against each person were read aloud. The accused, their hands bound behind their backs, would kneel beneath the stage before being hauled up onto it.

Though the names of the accused varied, their alleged crimes were strikingly similar. "Xxx, from such-and-such region, a wicked landowner, a villain who bled the landless and poor dry." This was the common accusation. It was a so-called summary People's Court, and no other events were scheduled in the theater.

Ki-hoon was determined to witness everything that transpired inside the theater from start to finish. He had many questions and wanted to see for himself how communism, as practiced, compared to the theory he had read about in books.

Early Sunday morning, June 25, 1950, the North Korean People's Army advanced into South Korea, accompanied by the sound of small gongs (*kkwaenggwari*)[49], as trumpets and flutes heralded their arrival. After swiftly capturing Seoul, they moved on to the next phase of their plan.

---

49) The *kkwaenggwari* is a small, handheld gong used in traditional Korean music. The instrument is an essential component of Korean folk music genres like *pungmul* and *samulnori*, which involve percussion ensembles. Beyond musical settings, the *kkwaenggwari* has cultural significance in Korean rituals, festivals, and agricultural celebrations, where it contributes to the energetic and festive atmosphere.—This interpretation was excerpted by the author with the help of ChatGPT.

Several universities in the Seoul area and the remaining city inhabitants were rounded up and brought to the Myeong-dong Theater. From liberation in 1945 until 1947, the South Korean Workers' Party (*Namnodang*) was formed and had solidified its organization. On the surface, the North Korean People's Army labeled the event "A Briefing Session for the Citizens of South Korea on the Construction of the Democratic People's Republic of North Korea..." Such rhetoric was used to rally people around them.

Ki-hoon was somewhat aware of the situation both inside and outside the school. At that time, anyone literate was intrigued by Marxism and the new social class theory, and many were easily deceived. He, too, spent time discussing class theory with his high school alumni and new friends in Seoul. In particular, many students at S University(SNU) Law School, where he studied, were unknowingly veering toward biased perspectives.

However, theory and practice often diverge. Driven by an insatiable curiosity, Ki-hoon decided to witness firsthand the reality of Marxist theory. Thus, he entered the Myeong-dong Theater that day.

One by one, landlords' names were called, and if they were sentenced to "death," they were shot on the spot. The atmosphere inside the theater was electrifying, punctuated by thunderous applause and enthusiastic cheers. The shock and immense fear were palpable. There was no defense or due process for those who were shot. The individuals wearing red armbands wielded the power to take lives at their discretion. The event began with a brief speech, starting with the phrase "To liberate South Korea..." but it quickly transitioned into the People's Court, where executions were carried out immediately. Names were called, shots were fired, and the crowd cheered.

Observing this, Ki-hoon became convinced that escaping the Myeong-dong Theater alive was nearly impossible. Those who were called to the People's Court and executed were not only the ones kneeling beneath the platform. When a name was called, it was shouted aloud, and the individual was located. If the person was in the theater, they were brought before the court.

As time passed, the crowd's excitement intensified. The theater reeked of blood, reminiscent of a slaughterhouse. The atmosphere grew increasingly frenzied, as if everyone had become ghosts—driven mad by a lust for sacrifice, eager to destroy even the last vestiges of their own souls. The entire audience was consumed by a crucible of extreme fervor.

Suddenly, Ki-hoon clutched his belly and crouched down, mingling with the feet of the packed crowd. Despite being covered in dust, he decided to crawl across the theater floor. As he was kicked by the feet of others, he rolled and clutched his stomach tightly with both hands.

By sheer chance, he tumbled to the theater entrance, where a man in a red armband stood guard, glaring at him with fury. Theater guard (a North Korean soldier):

"Comrade, why on earth are you acting this way? Is something wrong?"

Ki-hoon:

"Comrade, I fear my appendix is about to burst. The pain in my abdomen is unbearable, and I feel like I'm losing my mind. Soon, it might turn into peritonitis, and I'll become a burden to everyone here..."

Before he could finish, the theater guard spat at him in disgust and snapped, "Such bad luck! Just get out quickly!" He gestured for him to leave with an air of contempt and annoyance.

Ki-hoon spent nearly 20 minutes crawling through the theater, his entire body covered in dust and grime. He feigned a painful crawl, clutching his stomach and stumbling until he was out of the theater guard's sight. Once out of view, he bolted with all his might. Staying in Seoul seemed impossible, so he resolved to head for the mountains. At that time, all the main roads were already under the control of the North Korean People's Army. He planned to hide during the day and traverse the mountain paths by night.

Relying on his instincts, he walked endlessly until he found a house where he could seek refuge. The residents told him, "If you go down the mountain from here, you'll reach the Daejeon area." Trusting their guidance, he continued along the mountain path.

After walking endlessly, exhausted, he finally reached a spot where he could rest. He leaned against an old, small grave and, unable to fight his fatigue any longer, fell asleep there.

Without realizing that night had fallen into complete darkness, he opened his eyes only when he felt hungry. Upon opening them, the vast and pitch-black stillness of the night, combined with the thought of being alone, sent a chill down his spine. The only food he had was two barley rice balls he had received from the kitchen of a house he had briefly visited the previous day. Trusting his instincts once again, he decided to hurry southward, guided by the stars in the sky.

Human adaptability is remarkable. As he walked, he grew accustomed to the faint moonlight. However, a moment of carelessness caused him to misstep on a jagged stone while descending. Ki-hoon tumbled down a slope, landing with a thud. He had seen a bush covered with leaves and stepped on it, only to find himself slipping into a deep hole. His legs, utterly exhausted, slowly gave way beneath him.

Instinctively struggling to survive, he flailed, trying to grasp anything around him. The fall happened too quickly. Every branch he reached for broke away, leaving his hands empty. He cursed himself for his momentary lapse in vigilance, half-asleep.

The place where Ki-hoon had fallen reeked of rot. The ground beneath him felt mushy and uneven. As his eyes adjusted to the dim moonlight, he realized he was surrounded by dead bodies. It was impossible to tell whether there were dozens or hundreds. He saw only the backs of heads — bodies twisted like shrimp, hair covering their faces — sometimes lying flat, piled in layers, stuck together. There were young children, men and women, the elderly, and the young.

In the moonlight, the bodies appeared as a heap of lifeless figures. Many lay with mouths agape, limbs twisted grotesquely. Those who faced the sky did so with eyes wide open, frozen in their final moments. Ki-hoon reminded himself, "The dead are not scary. Only the living, those who can move, are frightening." Steeling himself against the horror, he struggled to escape.

He clawed at the soil of the pit with his fingernails, creating footholds. With frenzied determination, he climbed step by step until he finally pulled himself out of the pit.

"I was surely leaning against the grave just over there, wasn't I? I only meant to tilt my head back and rest my eyes for a moment, but did I fall into a deep sleep? My eyes were open, and I was walking, but I must have been in a half-dream state. When did this pile of corpses appear? And why couldn't I detect the stench of decay when I was by that grave? Is the nose the quickest organ to tire and adapt? It seems I can't even trust my own senses, my sense of smell, to be precise."

He said, lowering his head.

Ki-hoon had occasionally encountered the scent of rotting human flesh on his way. In war, no matter where one went, there was the stench of blood and the smell of decomposing flesh. The acrid stench of escaping gases was pervasive. However, back then, it had been limited to one person in a specific place, or perhaps just a few.

To survive, Ki-hoon thought, *Perhaps focusing all my attention on the smallest details around me had only dulled my sense of smell more quickly.* No matter how he looked at it, he had no desire to die on the roadside in the midst of this war. Just like anyone else.

Still, the questions did not stop. When and how had the bodies buried there met their deaths and been discarded?

Judging by the condition of the corpses, it was unclear whether they had been killed elsewhere and then brought here or if this pit had been dug in advance, with people shot alive and dumped into it. As if to encourage himself after climbing out of the pit, Ki-hoon wanted to feel that he was alive. He pinched and slapped his arms and legs. He was alive.

But where exactly was this place? As far as he knew, he was somewhat familiar with areas like Sancheong, Jinju, and Seoul. However, he was just a young, inexperienced student who had focused only on his studies. He had no clue where he was.

And even if he knew who had committed this mass murder, what difference would it make?

Still, what was certain at the time was that the North Korean People's Army was sweeping through nearly every part of the South, advancing relentlessly. The dead were likely local inhabitants. 'A large number of people here have died and disappeared so miserably. This place will soon be filled with other life forms,' he thought.

Then, another concern filled his mind. Beyond his own survival, he began to worry about his grandfather, Hong-seon; his mother; and his younger siblings, who remained in Sancheong. Determined, he decided to find his way to Sancheong as soon as possible.

For the first time, he prayed to an almighty God.

"God, I have viewed everything with a narrow mind, seeing You only as the Lord of Israel. No matter where I am or what I do, I believe in You, Jesus Christ, the omniscient and omnipresent Lord. As I live, I seek You. Please allow me to survive and return to my home in Sancheong. From now on, I will live with gratitude for all that is given to me. I won't waste my life or time."

For Ki-hoon, this period of suffering became his greatest lesson, surpassing any book by a great author or any teacher's instruction he had ever received. "Don't take a life needlessly. For the benefit of one group, or because of differences in thought or opinion, don't recklessly harm others."

These words escaped his lips.

As he walked, Ki-hoon contemplated how to shape his future.

'If I return home alive, perhaps I should become a judge and prosecutor in a gold-rimmed hat, as my grandfather, Hong-seon, tacitly suggested. What do judicial officers truly do?' he pondered.

'No matter how well they predict and judge, they are only human. Ultimately, they chase their own interests and eliminate those who pose even a slight threat. They deal with all kinds of people who commit heinous crimes and spend all their efforts trying to evade the law. Going through such experiences would guide him forward, striving to find meaning and purpose in a world marred by chaos and conflict.

Moreover, if one takes on such a role, illicit money will inevitably flow in. At times, one might be compelled to act against one's conscience. There will be moments when turning a blind eye to immense power becomes necessary. It's clear that money and power sit at the top of the food chain. The fact is, no law will prohibit doing anything evil to maintain such a position. And the high status attained in such a manner will never provide true comfort in the end.'

Ki-hoon did not want to fall into a delusional world ruled by an insatiable desire for more and an ambition to climb higher. He lacked confidence. He despised the idea of acting against his conscience before God and suffering the ensuing torment. 'Oh, if only I could live safely and return to my hometown of Sancheong. If I survive, I'll find at least a job I enjoy—one that doesn't violate my conscience,' he resolved.

He also thought of his responsibility to care for his younger siblings and mother in place of his father, who had passed away early, as the eldest son of the Head Family.

By the time Ki-hoon arrived at the house in Sancheong, after roughly 35 days of not washing or eating properly, his 178-centimeter-tall frame weighed a mere 43 kilograms. When it rained, he endured, his body soaked in sweat and covered in soil. As a result, his head and body were swarming with lice.

Bok-hee sighed with relief, hugged her son who had returned alive, and prayed with gratitude to God. After barely getting through two days, Bok-hee said, "Hurry up and prepare to move."

They had heard that the main house in Sancheong was going to become the "North Korean People's Army officers' quarters for the western Gyeongnam region." Yoo-sang brought this news early that morning. The North Korean Army was sweeping down like a tidal wave.

Bok-hee summoned her children to the main room and said,

"North Korean soldiers will be using this house. You will all probably have to sleep together in a small room in the main building. The important thing is that if you are asked anything, you must act as if you know nothing and respond accordingly."

Speech was strictly controlled.

For some time before the North Korean soldiers arrived in Sancheong, the people of the Big House, the neighborhood, and Saemmy House gathered daily in the *sarang-chae* of the Big House. They spent their time there, nervously awaiting what was to come.

After hearing that the North Korean People's Army would soon enter the Sancheong area, Hong-seon left for Sang-cheol's grandmother's house with Ki-hoon, Jeong-seop, and Ki-hwi, in a village called Imchon. Sang-cheol's father was briefly mentioned at the beginning of this book. He was a fairly high-ranking informant for the North Korean People's Army, wearing a red armband in the area when the People's Army soldiers came down to *Jiri Mountain* in the southern part of the country. It was said that he assumed a heavy responsibility because, as a tenant farmer, he was broad-shouldered and led people well. He was appointed as a regional commissar by the communist forces.

He had warned them in advance that Hong-seon's Big House would be used as accommodation for North Korean People's Army officers. In fact, Yoo-sang and Sang-cheol's father had known each other since childhood and considered each other brothers rather than just relatives. The two were on excellent terms. As a result, Sang-cheol's father arranged for his sister to marry Yoo-sang.

Regardless of his actions, Sang-cheol's father was a man who understood the necessity of certain measures. He cleverly evacuated Hong-seon's sons and grandchildren to his wife's house, embodying the saying, *'The darkest place is under the candlestick.'* His idea was that even if they searched all other houses, they would overlook the house of a prominent informant's wife. The reason behind this will be discussed later.

The People's Army occupied the Big House for about forty days. While they were there, rumors spread about the U.S. military's landing operation in Incheon. The North Korean soldiers, feeling increasingly vulnerable, struggled to maintain control. They searched the entire village, capturing all the men and dressing them in North Korean People's Army uniforms. Even young students, aged 13 to 15, were taken. If caught by the North Korean soldiers, they were forced to join their ranks unconditionally —a fate as good as a death sentence.

Sang-cheol's father believed that even if the People's Army searched every corner of Sancheong and its neighboring areas, they would never think to search his in-laws' house—the home where the mother of a People's Army informant's wife lives. Indeed, his plan worked as expected. Hong-seon and his family hid for more than fifty days in the barn next to the backyard. After the People's Army retreated, they returned safely to Sancheong.

But why did Sang-cheol's father and Yoo-sang risk everything to protect Hong-seon and his family?

Sang-cheol's father was one of Hong-seon's tenants. No matter how well Hong-seon treated his tenants, it was unheard of for a tenant to risk his life for his landlord. Yet Yoo-sang and Sang-cheol's father did exactly that. They gambled everything, including the lives of their families, to save

Hong-seon and his kin.

Although it was never confirmed who was responsible for Yoo-sang's wife's death, it was believed that she had been killed by the last remnants of the North Korean army. Thus, they gave their all for Hong-seon, driven by a bond of trust and loyalty stronger than blood ties.

Yoo-sang had been working as a farmhand for Hong-seon since his mid-teens. After his father's death, Yoo-sang's mother had pleaded with Hong-seon to take him in. Growing up in the same village, Yoo-sang and Sang-cheol's father had known each other from an early age. The deep connection between Hong-seon and Yoo-sang's family was rooted in life-saving acts. Sang-cheol's father was a man who, in his quest to protect the lives of his kin, understood the importance of showing respect to others, transcending the confines of his own social class.

Around 1943, Sang-cheol's youngest uncle fell gravely ill while working as a farmhand. He was feverish and grew weaker by the day. Upon learning of this, Yoo-sang, unable to stand by any longer, sought help from the esteemed Elder, Choi Hong-seon. At Yoo-sang's urging, Hong-seon rushed to the thatched house where Sang-cheol's family lived.

The patient lay on his stomach in a small room, and the family had seemingly given up hope. Hong-seon examined him, removed his upper clothing, and found a massive abscess on his back. It was severely infected, swollen with pus, and badly festering. The abscess had grown so large that it was too late for conventional treatments like Japanese plasters or heated herbal medicine. Sang-cheol's youngest uncle had been delirious with a high fever for over a week, teetering on the edge of death.

Hong-seon pulled a tool bag from inside his coat. These were times when the Japanese were frantically waging a war that destabilized and drained resources, leaving Korean (*Joseon*) families with nothing. Every household struggled to find enough food to eat, clothes to keep warm, and basic supplies — all supplies were scarce. The Korean people had been forced to surrender all iron items, including spoons and chopsticks, to

Japan. All the grain was taken. Starving, people resorted to peeling and eating tree bark. Even weeds were not spared. Medicines became even more precious.

Over time, the mountains of Korea became barren, stripped of their resources. People struggled desperately to avoid starvation. Even students scraped pine resin to use as fuel for Japanese planes. They gave up their silver hairpins, as well as the silver spoons and chopsticks they had received at weddings.

Fortunately, Hong-seon's house had a Japanese first aid kit containing several knives, scissors, and disinfectants used for dissecting hunted animals. Hong-seon pulled out two knives from the bag, wrapped them in cloth, and tucked them into his coat. Selecting a sharp-edged knife, he heated the blade over a candle several times. He then thrust the knife into the large abscess on the patient's back. As the pus pocket burst, a mixture of yellowish and reddish liquid flowed onto the floor. He cut the torn skin in a crisscross pattern.

But that was not the end. The challenge was removing the large amount of pus. Even if he pressed around the abscess to squeeze it out or used a cloth to absorb it, there was no telling when it would be fully drained. The young patient, weakened by high fever and malnutrition, was on the brink of death. Completely cleaning the pus from the wound seemed impossible.

Hong-seon then asked Yoo-sang to boil some highly salted *Joseon* soy sauce in a small pot. The abscess on Sang-cheol's uncle's back will only stop coming back if the pus is completely removed. Although young, Sang-cheol's uncle always carried heavy burdens on his back. Whether his tender skin had chafed from various tasks or the wound had simply been neglected, nobody knew. Observing the seemingly endless flow of pus, those around him sighed with regret and a sense of resignation.

At that moment, Hong-seon placed his mouth over the abscess. He took a deep breath and then sucked out the pus. When his mouth was full, he spat it out and continued sucking out more with all his might. Everyone was astonished, watching Hong-seon, who showed no sign of disgust. He instructed them to bring the boiled soy sauce over. He took some into his mouth, swished it around, and spat it out into the yard. He repeated this process until all the pus was removed.

Afterward, he soaked a cotton cloth in the highly salted, blackened soy sauce. The abscess cavity, now free of pus, was exposed, revealing blackened and reddened flesh, with some bone visible. Hong-seon pushed the cloth into the abscess cavity, wiping it several times until no more pus was visible. He then soaked another cloth in the soy sauce and packed it into the wound. He wrapped the patient's back with a fresh cloth and instructed Sang-cheol's family, "Remove this cotton cloth about two hours after I leave."

From that point on, no more pus came from the wound, and new flesh began to grow. The patient, who was 14 years old at the time, gradually began to recover. This act solidified the bond between Yoo-sang, Sang-cheol's father, and Hong-seon. They came to trust and follow Hong-seon implicitly, frequently visiting the Big House in Ok-dong and offering their help without hesitation.

A person's current situation always bears the imprint of their past actions.

The men of the Choi family saved lives in Imchon, thanks to Hong-seon's selfless dedication. His actions not only saved his own life but also those of his descendants, who might have perished at the hands of the People's Army. Their relationship was built on trust and mutual reliance on what was most precious to them. Additionally, neighbors recalled several instances in which Hong-seon had saved lives. He empathized with and cared for the lives of others as if they were his own.

Hong-seon, Ki-hoon, and Jeong-seop returned from Imchon upon hearing that the People's Army had vacated the Big House. However, in early September 1950, U.S. forces launched a surprise attack to expel the remaining North Korean People's Army. Their initial targets were the "headquarters of the People's Army" and the accommodations of high-ranking officers. Day and night, planes bombarded Sancheong and nearby areas, unleashing cannon fire from the skies.

During this turbulent period, Ki-hoon found refuge in a place called Deokwooji *Jegak*, away from the Big House, thanks to the care of Bok-hee and Hong-seon. One day, needing his books, Ki-hoon asked his second sister, Ki-young, to fetch them from the *sarang-bang* of the Big House. While leaving the gate with a bundle of books on her head—works by Hegel, other Western philosophers, and texts on legal philosophy— Ki-young was caught in a U.S. bombing raid.

Ki-young lost her left eye forever in the bombing. After the war, Ki-hoon dedicated himself to caring for his sister throughout her life. Given the limited medical technology of the time, she underwent several arduous eye surgeries. Ten years later, she had to be fitted with an artificial eye. For a woman, losing an eye was a profound wound—not just physically, but also in terms of appearance. The bombing also inflicted damage on other parts of her body.

Remarkably, Ki-young never expressed any resentment towards her elder brother. Despite her injuries, she and her younger siblings continued to treat Ki-hoon with the utmost respect, viewing him as both their eldest brother and a father figure after the death of their father, Il-seop. Ki-hoon, in turn, took great care of his younger siblings and their families, supporting them as much as he could while maintaining significant social influence.

Shall we take a brief look at Ki-hoon's upbringing?

Ki-hoon exhibited exceptional intelligence from an early age, attending elementary school for just three years before skipping ahead to the sixth grade. Neighborhood residents marveled at his ability to learn basic Japanese characters in just 20 minutes at the age of four.

His third-grade teacher, Kimura, recognized his potential and arranged for him to transfer to an elementary school in Japan, believing that studying there would benefit him more than completing the sixth grade in Sancheong. Hong-seon and Bok-hee were delighted and joyfully sent him to Japan.

However, Ki-hoon did not continue his middle school education in Japan. Instead, he returned to *Joseon* and enrolled at Jinju Middle and High School, a prestigious institution in western South Gyeongsang Province. There, Ki-hoon excelled, consistently ranking at the top in all subjects. He remained in contact with Kimura's family throughout their lives.

The reasons behind Ki-hoon's decision not to attend middle school in Japan remain unclear. It was a choice he made independently, and one can only speculate about the experiences he might have had there. Later, Ki-hoon shared his thoughts with his son, Se-joon, who was a high school student at the time. Ki-hoon said,

"I respect Dr. Woo Jang-choon[50] the most, a renowned agricultural

---

50) Dr. Woo Jang-choon(1898~1959): A renowned Korean scholar, botanist, and agricultural scientist active in Korea during the Japanese colonial period and into the late 1940s and early 1950s. Dr. Woo was born into abject poverty to Korean parents living in Japan and overcame severe discrimination in Imperial Japan to become a well-respected teacher and researcher. Dr. Woo's research proved that a completely new plant could be created by crossbreeding plants of the same genus, despite being of different species. His theory astonished the World Breeding Association, challenging the long-standing belief that crossbreeding was only possible within the same species. A new plant created through such crossbreeding is called the "Woo Jang-choon Triangle." After Korea gained independence from Japan, the Korean Promotion Committee was formed, and Dr. Woo Jang-choon arrived in Korea in March 1950. He successfully developed disease-resistant and flavorful cabbages and radishes. He devoted his life as a scientist to helping his hungry and struggling country rebuild after the war until his passing in a hospital. His research included studies on *Sudoyigijak*, which played a key role in imported rice distribution, and recommendations for cultivating tangerines suited to Jeju Island's environment.—This information has been summarized by the author with reference to Naver namu.wiki sources.

scientist from *Joseon*. Most Japanese people rarely support Koreans who surpass them; instead, they go to great lengths to belittle and despise them. I know this all too well. Despite such challenges, Dr. Woo was a true patriot who dedicated his research to alleviating the hunger of the Korean people. I understand that the Japanese pushed him into agriculture to undermine his capabilities, yet he proved himself to be an outstanding scholar in that field. His work aimed to save the starving people, and for that, he has my utmost respect."

Ki-hoon excelled in every aspect, yet he also endured the tumultuous storms of adolescence. During the winter vacation after his first year of high school, he disappeared for several weeks, causing teachers and friends in Jinju and Sancheong to anxiously search for him. During this time, he secretly took the entrance examination for the law school at J University in Seoul, and passed. To everyone's astonishment, he appeared on the Jinju High School campus wearing a college uniform, cap, and cape—riding a horse.

It was later revealed that he and his friend Kim Tae-hong had orchestrated the event. They had met at the school's horseback riding club, and Ki-hoon had passed the exam without officially graduating from high school. His teachers were shocked by his audacity.

Fortunately, Ki-hoon was not punished due to his outstanding academic performance and behavior. Tae-hong, however, had a history of similar behavior and was expelled. Tae-hong's father was a church pastor in Jinju, and friends often joked, "The sons of pastors, judges, prosecutors, and teachers—that is, the children of those whose titles end in '*sa*'—tend to be troublemakers."

After the incident involving his admission to J University, Ki-hoon became more cautious about making friends. However, it seems he was not entirely sure whether making friends and getting married were truly separate matters. This was because he believed it would be best to leave the matter of marriage entirely to Bok-hee. In any case, let's take a closer look at how his marriage unfolded.

Marriage was indeed a different matter from making friends.

While couples should be good friends and sometimes play that role in strong relationships, Ki-hoon did not have a specific type of woman in mind. The main reason was likely his own calculation that, by accepting the wife his mother, Bok-hee, recommended, the family, as the Head Household, and many aspects of their household would remain stable.

Did his experiences of hunger and hardship during the Korean War profoundly change him? The harrowing journey from Seoul and the struggle to survive for more than a month had a significant impact. Above all, he came to prioritize family affairs over his own desires. As the eldest son, Ki-hoon believed that the family's well-being hinged on the health and stability of his mother, Bok-hee, who had become a widow at age 35.

He resolved to leave the matter of his marriage to his mother, Bok-hee, and simply wait and see.

Bok-hee was secretly pleased with Ki-hoon's decision to entrust his marriage to her. If Ki-hoon got married and brought his wife home, she would help relieve his mother's workload and take care of the family. As the eldest in the family, it was inevitable that he would eventually marry. He needed to honor his widowed mother and ensure that his younger siblings also married. Therefore, Bok-hee's approval was paramount.

To Bok-hee, Ki-hoon was the perfect son. In her eyes, Ki-hoon was an exceptional individual admired by everyone, and she depended on him as if he were her late husband. He was the most precious and cherished person in her life. Now that Ki-hoon had grown old enough to have a wife and children, marriage was necessary to continue the family line. To Bok-hee, Ki-hoon was not only her child but also a source of pride and joy—a remarkable and outstanding son, no matter where he was.

Hong-seon also valued Ki-hoon's opinions and often accepted his suggestions. When Ki-hoon's father, Il-seop, passed away, Hong-seon entrusted a significant amount of property to Ki-hoon. This happened when Japan was on the brink of defeat in the war, seizing everything that could support its war efforts from every corner of Korea. Koreans were compelled to surrender these resources without protest. During this period, much of Hong-seon's property was transferred to his grandson Ki-hoon, who had to pay a substantial gift tax. Ki-hoon was in his mid-teens at the time.

Ki-hoon needed to ensure the future marriages of his younger siblings and manage the property handed down by Hong-seon. To uphold the family's continuity and prestige, it was crucial to reinforce his mother Bok-hee's authority. Ki-hoon believed that the family would be properly maintained only if he first submitted to Bok-hee's wishes and followed her guidance. Therefore, Ki-hoon concluded that his wife should be chosen by his mother, Bok-hee. He was not in a position to pursue a marriage based on love. Ki-hoon convinced himself that choosing someone he personally liked would only cause trouble for Bok-hee. Thus, he resolved to marry without even meeting his bride beforehand, trusting Bok-hee's decision completely.

Bok-hee, true to her role, arranged the marriage and proceeded with it without showing Ki-hoon the woman he was to marry. Later, Ki-hoon told his son Se-joon, "I never expected to feel love for the woman who would become my wife. That was my mindset." Thus, in the early summer of 1951, amid the ongoing war, Choi Ki-hoon married Kim Jong-hee, both from Jinju. Due to the war, it was difficult to find a car, so Ki-hoon traveled to Jinju, where the bride resided, for their first night. The next day, they rented a truck and returned to Sancheong, fortunate to have found transportation.

However, Jong-hee turned out to be quite different from what Bok-hee had anticipated. She was a city girl with fair skin, unaccustomed to housework. She enjoyed reading novels and had a passion for embroidery.

With the war still raging, the household bustled with family members, workers, and other residents from the homes of relatives. Jong-hee struggled to manage the household affairs amidst the constant activity.

Bok-hee grew increasingly frustrated with Jong-hee, who contributed little to managing the household. Although neighbors praised Jong-hee for her beauty and regarded her as a fortunate and attractive daughter-in-law, Bok-hee could only feel frustration.

Why did Bok-hee welcome Jong-hee as her daughter-in-law? One might say it was all fate. Jong-hee had never engaged in the rough farming work that required physical labor, and she knew nothing about country life. The sole reason Bok-hee favored Jong-hee was based on a single impression when she went to meet her with the intent of arranging a marriage.

When Bok-hee first visited Jong-hee, she found her wearing Japanese-style pants and chopping firewood with an axe in the corner of the yard. That sight alone made Bok-hee decide to choose Jong-hee, setting aside all other considerations.

But from Jong-hee's perspective, what would it have been like?

The day she was seen doing housework and chopping firewood was both the first and the last time she ever performed such tasks. Bok-hee and the matchmaker had secretly gone to the house without informing anyone, pretending to be guests at the oriental medical clinic run by Jong-hee's father.

On the day Bok-hee came to see Jong-hee, the household was unusually busy from early morning. All the male cousins who lived nearby had left. Jong-hee's mother, feeling unwell, asked her, "It's chilly all over my body, so please chop firewood and light a fire in my room." Unable to refuse her mother's request, Jong-hee chopped firewood with an axe, unaware that her future mother-in-law was watching.

Whether this event was mere coincidence or the result of some intention on Jong-hee's mother's part remains unknown. Jong-hee, slightly irritated at having to chop firewood that day, wore a taciturn expression. Seeing Jong-hee's flushed face, Bok-hee became convinced that she was a healthy and vigorous woman.

Bok-hee thought to herself, *Yes, a young woman who chops firewood is proof that the household is warmed and sustained by her efforts. And her flushed face surely indicates that she is strong and full of vitality. Seeing such a capable woman here today! I must bring her into our family so the Choi household can flourish.*

That impression was the last of its kind. None of the vigor displayed during that initial meeting reappeared in Jong-hee's actions once she began living in Sancheong. Though she was quiet, she was not truly taciturn, and she knew nothing about managing a rural household. The bustling household required hard labor and caring for six young siblings-in-law, including the youngest, Ki-seon, who was only six years old.

The eldest sister-in-law was the same age as Jong-hee. Unlike her other sisters-in-law, she was quite short and had a habit of pouting, never quite able to keep her mouth shut. She carefully observed everything Jong-hee did. Despite this, she was the kindest and most carefree of the sisters-in-law. She got married later that year and left Sancheong.

Jong-hee's father ran an Oriental medicine clinic in downtown Jinju. She knew how to cut and handle herbal medicines from assisting her father and was adept at bookkeeping. However, she had never experienced cooking porridge for cows, farming, or managing tenant farmers and household staff. It was unsurprising that she had never encountered such tasks before her marriage. Managing daily meals for several families proved especially challenging. Before marriage, her household consisted of her father, mother, one brother, and cousins. Although cousins frequently visited, they mostly lived in their own homes and only came when called.

To aid Jong-hee in her new married life, a young girl named Jeom-rye was brought from Jong-hee's family home. Jong-hee only ate meals when a kitchen maid or another worker prepared them. The responsibilities of managing a farming household, with its numerous families, workers, and livestock, were overwhelming for Jong-hee.

During her pregnancy, she developed an aversion to food. The hard barley-mixed rice and coarse side dishes did not suit her palate. As she struggled to eat properly, her first pregnancy ended in a miscarriage. Nevertheless, she became pregnant again, but her health continued to deteriorate. She couldn't bring herself to tell her family in Jinju about her difficulties.

However, food began arriving from Jinju, as if her parents had sensed her hardships. Her mother's worried intuition seemed to have been correct. They likely had an idea of the challenges she faced in a rural Head Family household. Fish packed in wooden boxes and goat meat in tin pots were sent to the house in Sancheong.

Yet, these delicacies rarely reached Jong-hee. Dozens of fish in a carton would be used as side dishes for her brothers-in-law for several days. Goat meat, too, was consumed by her sisters-in-law and brothers-in-law. In their prime, they ate voraciously. As a result, the food intended for Jong-hee, a pregnant woman, rarely reached her.

Jong-hee frequently found herself unable to eat much due to her aversion to greens and vegetables, causing her to feel hungry frequently. She often suffered from stomachaches and dizziness, making it difficult for her to get up and move around. Her body grew weak, and she often staggered while walking. Despite her determination to do her best with housework, she blamed herself for her inability to meet her own expectations due to her physical condition.

Seeing this, Bok-hee grew increasingly frustrated with Jong-hee. Furthermore, Bok-hee worried that if Ki-hoon found out about Jong-hee's deteriorating condition, he might blame her for Jong-hee's hardships.

At the time, Ki-hoon was teaching German at his alma mater, Jinju High School. With the war ongoing, Korea faced a shortage of schoolteachers. Ki-hoon was recognized and invited to teach at his alma mater, and even though he was still a college student, it did not matter. He worked in Jinju and would return to Sancheong on Saturday afternoons. On the days he returned, Bok-hee would pull Jeom-rye aside and caution her.

"Jeom-rye," Bok-hee instructed, "You may have already noticed this, but let me be clear. Do not mention that your lady is unwell or anything of the sort when the eldest master comes home. Even though Jinju is close, I don't want to trouble him with concerns about the household while he is working away. If he asks about his wife, you must reply, 'Yes, she is always well.' Do you understand?"

Jeom-rye lowered her gaze and bowed her head. As mentioned earlier, Jeom-rye was a worker that Jong-hee had brought from Jinju. As a mother-in-law, Bok-hee had chosen a girl she deemed suitable for her son, confident that her daughter-in-law would dutifully follow her wishes. And so, she brought Jong-hee into the family. However, things had not gone as planned, leaving Bok-hee with a lingering sense of dissatisfaction.

Unaware of his mother's true feelings, Ki-hoon, her eldest son, expressed his concern. "Mother, what should I do for Jong-hee since she is so frail? Is there anything I can do to help her?" He seemed genuinely sympathetic to Jong-hee. Bok-hee found it increasingly difficult to endure these moments, as her son's attention and care seemed divided between her and his wife, Jong-hee. Each time Bok-hee heard such words from Ki-hoon, she felt even more uneasy.

To Bok-hee, Jong-hee's delicate and often sickly demeanor seemed insincere, as if it were a ploy to capture Ki-hoon's heart. This perception only deepened Bok-hee's dislike for Jong-hee. She viewed Jong-hee's every action with disdain, interpreting each one as an attempt to usurp her role within the family.

Was it that high expectations had led to deeper disappointment? Or, as the neighbors often speculated, was it the fear of losing her eldest son's affection to his wife that fueled her animosity? Bok-hee often clutched her chest in frustration and lamented her situation.

Bok-hee,

"Oh, this stubborn persimmon taste! When persimmons are bitter, you can grimace all you want, but what am I to do with the bitterness that festers within me?"

Jong-hee had collapsed multiple times due to severe gastric ulcers after suffering a miscarriage. The ulcers had been induced by an overdose of sleeping pills. Despite Ki-hoon's persistent inquiries, he never learned why Jong-hee had taken such a large number of pills, as she remained silent on the matter.

But in Bok-hee's mind—Jong-hee's life in Sancheong was becoming increasingly intolerable with each passing day. Jong-hee would often take to her bed, feigning illness to garner more attention from her husband. She aimed to show Ki-hoon how difficult life was with her in-laws, hoping to elicit his sympathy. Observing her daughter-in-law, Bok-hee interpreted Jong-hee's actions solely with this intention in mind. Bok-hee might not have been entirely wrong.

In fact, Jong-hee genuinely wished to live alone with Ki-hoon, using her frailty as an excuse. Living with him was her greatest wish. Ki-hoon had no choice but to spend a long time deeply torn between his mother and his wife, finding himself in a constant state of worry.

Then, despite concerns over her fragile health, Jong-hee conceived and eventually gave birth to their son, Se-joon, in 1953. However, Se-joon had been frail since birth, suffering from frequent diarrhea and high fevers, which left Jong-hee sleepless and anxious. Eventually, Jong-hee's parents took Se-joon in, and he lived with them for several years.

In 1956, Bok-hee's second grandson, Jae-joon, was born. Since Bok-hee had decided to take on the responsibility of raising Jae-joon, Jong-hee was finally able to join her husband, Ki-hoon, albeit with a heavy heart. When Jae-joon was born in 1956, Ki-hoon had just begun his career as a university professor in Busan(PNU) and was living there alone.

Some time after Jae-joon's birth, when Jong-hee left the house in Sancheong, she cried an unimaginable amount. Perplexed by her tears, Ki-hoon tried to comfort her, saying, "Why are you crying? Please don't be so upset. Even in Busan, my siblings and mother will visit often, and we'll see each other soon."

However, his words only deepened her sorrow, and her tears flowed unchecked. By the time the bus from Sancheong arrived in Busan, Jong-hee's eyes were swollen from crying.

Determined to be independent, Ki-hoon had secured a home for them without any help—not even from Hong-seon. Their new home was a modest two-room shack perched atop a hill in Dongdaeshin-dong, Busan, amidst a densely packed settlement of similar dwellings.

Ki-hoon and Jong-hee lived there for about three years. During this time, Jong-hee gradually let go of her longing for Sancheong. The companionship of neighboring women, who were close to her in age and also young mothers raising small children, brought her solace. They became good friends with Jong-hee, with two in particular standing out: the wife of a math teacher at N Girls' High School and the wife of a post office director. These two were especially close to her and always respectfully addressed her as "Professor Choi's wife."

12
The Korean War II

1950: The Big House
—Lee-seop's family

Ttang-ttamukgi, the Game of Conquering Land (Oil Painting on Canvas, No. 30)

When war breaks out and chaos ensues, is it a natural instinct of the human mind to seek safety in numbers? Do people gather because they find comfort in company, preferring to see with their own eyes how others are faring and to share their fears and hopes in conversation?

If someone becomes an adversary in a certain context, they may want to observe more closely how that person fares in a crisis. For instance, in the chaotic and perilous conditions of war, if an entire household perishes suddenly, what becomes of their home and possessions? Are there people who see such tragedies as opportunities to seize what is left behind?

People took refuge in the Big House of Choi Hong-seon, known as the Pagoda Tree House, carrying their belongings in bundles. Among them were Lee-seop's wife and children—Lee-seop being the twin brother of Il-seop.

Two days into the Korean War, Lee-seop's wife, You Nam-gil, arrived at Choi's house with her children. She first visited Lady Hwang of the New House to pay her respects instead of going to Lady Kim in the main room of the Big House. Perhaps it was because Hong-seon was seated next to Lady Hwang.

Nam-gil spoke in a hushed tone.

"Father, Stepmother, as I reflect on it, five years have passed since my brother-in-law, Il-seop, passed away. But if my husband, Lee-seop, returns, shouldn't I resume the duties of the eldest daughter-in-law?"

Hong-seon responded in a stern tone, "Dear, whether he returns or not, that is for Lee-seop to decide. That changes nothing in this family. Besides, no one knows what has become of Lee-seop. So, hold your tongue."

Upon hearing this from Sangdon-ddigi, Bok-hee mused, "Perhaps Father knows whether Master Lee-seop went to Japan or intentionally disappeared to cut off communication."

After Hong-seon's firm words, Nam-gil quickly bowed to Lady Hwang and Hong-seon, then retreated to a small room in the New House to arrange her belongings. By evening, as if nothing had happened, she emerged to dine on the *daecheong-maru* of the Big House with her three daughters and son.

Nam-gil, Lee-seop's wife, had stopped visiting the Choi family for a while after her husband disappeared. It wasn't so much a disappearance as it was Lee-seop concealing himself. Only Bok-hee and Il-seop knew a bit of the truth. Hong-seon, his father, and even Nam-gil, his wife, might have suspected or known something about Lee-seop's whereabouts, but they chose to feign ignorance, unable to speak of it aloud. Nevertheless, all news of Lee-seop ceased in November 1944.

Lee-seop inherited a substantial amount of property from Hong-seon, nearly equivalent to what his brothers, Il-seop and Jeong-seop, had received. Additionally, when Lee-seop confided in Hong-seon that Nam-gil had been pregnant before their marriage, Hong-seon bestowed an extra brewery upon him. In 1925, when Lee-seop married, the brewery was a lucrative venture. Despite Japanese crackdowns, the people of *Joseon* secretly produced and consumed liquor with fervor, using millet and corn flour when rice was scarce.

However, no matter how profitable a brewery might be, if the money was squandered faster than it was earned, it soon vanished. After their marriage, rumors of Nam-gil's extravagant spending reached Hong-seon. Perhaps this was why he refrained from further augmenting their estate and did not concern himself with their household economy. By the time Lee-seop's third daughter was born, rumors had spread that Lee-seop had sold the brewery to a neighbor at a dirt-cheap price.

Lee-seop had enrolled at Dongnae High School in Busan but failed to graduate. Whether it was due to academic struggles or other interests remained unclear. What is known is that he began learning business from Hong-seon earlier than Il-seop did.

It was during this period that he met You Nam-gil, a girl who had moved to Sancheong with her single mother after living in Masan. As previously mentioned, Nam-gil became pregnant before marriage, prompting Hong-seon to hastily arrange their marriage. Tragically, they lost their first child, but two years later, they welcomed their first daughter, who was the same age as Ki-hoon. Two more daughters followed in quick succession, and about a decade later, they had a son.

Lee-seop, a dizygotic twin and the son of Lady Kim, bore no resemblance to his brother Il-seop, either in appearance or character. Il-seop had fair skin, a high-bridged nose, and features that mirrored their mother's. In contrast, Lee-seop had very dark skin and a low, slightly flattened nose with a round tip. His appearance resembled neither his father, Hong-seon, nor his mother, Lady Kim.

The circumstances surrounding Lee-seop's disappearance are best recalled by remembering the day he visited Bok-hee and Il-seop before Il-seop's death. Bok-hee remembered that day quite vividly.

For a few years after Lee-seop got married, he frequently visited Il-seop's house, and there seemed to be no trouble in his marriage. However, at some point, his visits gradually became less frequent. Il-seop and Bok-hee assumed it was because Lee-seop was busy with work.

An early winter day in 1944, Lee-seop visited and asked Bok-hee to prepare a drinking table. Bok-hee, delighted to see him after a long time, prepared a table and went into the *sarang-bang*. As she entered, Il-seop remarked, "Come here and talk with my brother. It seems he has something on his mind. Ha-ha..."

Since Lee-seop had rarely visited in the past few years and had suddenly shown up, Bok-hee replied, "I will," and took a seat. With a somber expression, Lee-seop began to speak after taking a few sips.

Lee-seop:

"Brother, Sister-in-law, I won't be able to visit this house again. I need to go to Busan late tonight to catch a ship to Japan in the evening the day after tomorrow. And I will never return to Sancheong.

I must shamelessly ask you to look after my children and my wife. I'm not sure if she'll heed your advice. She's stubborn and materialistic, and there's a high chance she won't listen even if you try to guide her..."

Il-seop responded, "You're telling me now that you're leaving tonight? I see. You must have made up your mind long ago. Was it last year or some other time...? Is it exactly because of what you told me back then that you're now leaving for Japan?"

Lee-seop spoke, his voice laden with worry, "Yes, I have four children, all still so young... Especially my fourth child, Ki-hwan, makes me worry even more about his future. Why do you think I've hardened my heart like this? I've heard that this illness tends to appear only after a certain age.

What if ... someday, while he's still young, he's stricken with a disease that covers him in abscesses, forcing him to hide in a corner, shunned by everyone?

How heartbreaking must it be for me as a father?

Isn't that the kind of illness that robs people of their will to live once they have it? Just thinking about it is so painful that I feel like dying. Of course, if things go well in Japan and I make a fortune, I might be able to return and find a cure for my children's illnesses. But that's just a hope. I don't know if money can truly cure such diseases.

And with everyone saying that Japan is going to lose the war, what hope is there? But Japan is the only place I know, so I must go."

Il-seop responded, "Look, Brother. See? I guessed right. If the children catch that illness, there'll be nothing you can do... It was because of that, wasn't it? We now know that terrible illness can never be fully cured. With your meticulous nature, I'm sure you've been silently worrying for a long time, unable to tell anyone.

But now, suddenly, you say you're leaving today, just like that? What can we do? Ah ... I'll gather all the money I have and give it to you. And now, aside from this bag you're holding, do you have nothing else? By the way, did you say anything to your wife that might have made her suspicious?"

Lee-seop shook his head. He hadn't told Nam-gil about his plans. "I told her I am going to Busan to meet a friend. I'll inform her when things go well," he said. Bok-hee, witnessing the exchange between the brothers, felt out of place. She wanted to say something to Lee-seop, but the brothers didn't give her a chance. Il-seop fetched Japanese currency from a bag he kept in the closet and handed it to Lee-seop.

Lee-seop simply said, "Thank you, brother," and took another drink.

The *sarang-bang* in the Big House lacked luxurious or attention-grabbing furniture. The only valuable items were kept in the Hwashin General Store in Jinju, which Il-seop had established. Recently, Il-seop had learned from Yoo-sang that Hong-seon had delivered a considerable amount of money as military funds to the *Joseon* Independence Fighters heading to Manchuria. However, Il-seop couldn't locate the money anywhere. It was clear Hong-seon had hidden it in a secret place known only to him.

When Il-seop suggested informing their father about Lee-seop's departure, Lee-seop firmly objected. The morning after Lee-seop left, Il-seop informed Hong-seon, "Father, Lee-seop visited me late last night. He's going to Japan on business."

Hong-seon nodded and studied Il-seop's face in silence before asking, "When did he say he would return?"

Il-seop replied, "He doesn't know yet."

Hong-seon pondered aloud, then said, "Making money in Japan is becoming more difficult. He should think it over carefully before leaving, or perhaps he could discuss it with me first...

One might say that it's still too early to claim carelessly that Japan will lose the war... People are the same everywhere, but prosperity comes when the country is stable. This isn't the best time.

Still, family stability is maintained when the father of four is at home, standing strong like a pillar, ensuring the family's well-being doesn't falter. Nam-gil's bad habits won't change for the better over time...

Il-seop, please visit your brother's house often to check on them and offer encouragement. You know Nam-gil's nature well. Women can be easily influenced by bad company if they aren't regularly supported."

Words are very convenient tools. They are difficult to grasp until they are spoken. That is merely speculation. How can you know what's on someone's mind if they don't speak?

We, ordinary people, only hear what is said and reflect on it. *The value of words depends on their truthfulness and their impact on the listener.*

Lee-seop said nothing more that evening before leaving for Japan. Only Il-seop, Lee-seop, and Bok-hee gathered around a small drinking table in the dimly lit *sarang-bang*, bowed deeply, and said their goodbyes. It was impossible to know whether they expected to see each other again, but on the surface, that was all.

A few days after Lee-seop's departure, Bok-hee asked Il-seop why he had gone to Japan. "Are you talking about leprosy, the so-called 'bad disease'? Please answer me." But Il-seop remained silent. Instead, he said,

"Darling, I feel so alone. I didn't realize it when Lee-seop was here, but now the thought of not seeing him for a long time weighs on me."

In Bok-hee's view, Jeong-seop of the Saemmy House was also lonely. However, Il-seop disliked Jeong-seop, who was kind and easygoing by nature. Thus, even though Il-seop found himself alone, there was no chance he would confide in Jeong-seop about anything.

Although Lee-seop looked different, his temperament was as direct and urgent as Il-seop's. The brothers shared an intensity. Bok-hee felt frustrated that Il-seop no longer had deep conversations with Lee-seop and didn't confide in her about his business affairs. Whenever Bok-hee tried to discuss business matters, Il-seop would say, "It's all up to me. A woman shouldn't concern herself with such things." And yet, at times, he would say, "You handle the household matters so efficiently that it really puts my mind at ease while I'm working outside." It was strange that he would say such things. But it seemed clear that Il-seop couldn't fully trust Bok-hee simply because she was a woman.

Nevertheless, this was the situation with Lee-seop, as Bok-hee had pieced together from repeatedly pleading with Il-seop.

Lee-seop said that he had visited Masan because his wife, Nam-gil, kept insisting that they visit her hometown. This was in 1943. However, they couldn't find any of Nam-gil's family members who had been living there when she got married. They went around asking people in the area and found out that Nam-gil's family had moved away to an unknown place.

While searching for them, the two ventured to a leprosy village where they found Nam-gil's family living in a mud hut on the beach near Masan. There, Nam-gil's mother, younger brother, and sister were living among other leprosy patients. The sight shocked Lee-seop profoundly. Unable to bear it, he left without spending the night with Nam-gil's family and returned home to Sancheong.

Upon his arrival, he gathered his children. In particular, he paid close attention to his youngest son, Choi Ki-hwan, who resembled him and was a long-awaited child for both Nam-gil and Lee-seop. Lee-seop gazed at his older and younger daughters, who stared back with wide, unblinking eyes. Young Ki-hwan slept on his eldest daughter Jin-young's back. Without a word, he sent them out of his room and closed his eyes, thinking, *At some point, those children will be abandoned and ostracized because of this terrible disease.* He tried to calm his troubled heart.

Worried about his family's future, Lee-seop felt he should consult his older brother, Il-seop, more frequently until he could make a decision. However, he hesitated to disclose everything to Il-seop, as he had noticed that his brother's demeanor had recently darkened. Il-seop seemed overworked and exhausted after opening a general store in Jinju, his face looking even more fatigued than Lee-seop's.

As mentioned earlier, Il-seop and Lee-seop were twins, but they looked quite different, even in appearance. Il-seop's children would often say this: Ki-hwi, Bok-hee's second son, humorously referred to his father, Il-seop, as a "white radish root" and his uncle, Lee-seop, as a "dark cabbage root." Radish roots are white, and cabbage roots are dark on the outside but white inside when scraped. Bok-hee's children laughed among themselves, saying, "Father has a pointed nose and Uncle has a blunt nose, so cabbage it is."

When Lee-seop arrived at their house, Bok-hee's children greeted him excitedly, exclaiming, "Wow! Cabbage Root Uncle is here!" Despite his somber appearance, he was a cheerful, friendly brother-in-law who always smiled and helped with even the smallest household tasks. Like Il-seop, Lee-seop had a kind and timid nature, though he, too, could have a fiery temper on occasion. Although Il-seop and Lee-seop differed slightly in appearance, they both possessed immense pride. They were similarly narrow-minded, disliking open discussions about their affairs with others.

Bok-hee noticed that this trait likely stemmed from their mother, Lady Kim, the matriarch of the main household room.

Lee-seop's wife, Nam-gil, had rounded eyebrows and was a woman who skillfully used her smiling eyes to charm others. In truth, the environment she had grown up in from an early age was far from affluent. Someone had told Bok-hee that Nam-gil had been raised in difficult circumstances by a single mother.

Nam-gil's casual attitude towards money often irritated Bok-hee. "Oh, my gosh, it's just a few pennies. If it were me, it wouldn't even be a handful of money. You're so small-minded, tut tut..." she would say thoughtlessly, irking Bok-hee with her words and actions.

However, Bok-hee had to tolerate this behavior because she was older than Nam-gil. She remembered her mother's teachings: "Fighting is only worthwhile when your opponent is comparable to you. Don't fight with those younger or less fortunate than you; it's not worth it." Bok-hee tried to endure Nam-gil's provocations, keeping her mother's wisdom close to her heart.

Nam-gil never seemed to grasp the gravity of the situation. Whenever she had the chance, she often made a clumsy attempt to assert herself in front of Bok-hee. She lacked the awareness to feel embarrassed or ashamed, even when she mismanaged the household with deceit. She always said, "It's just bad luck this time. Next time, I'll do better and make a lot of money. It's because small things go wrong, and then everything gets tangled up." She never understood her fundamental problem: she was greedy but lacked intelligence and ability. Regarding such people, Koreans would sarcastically say, *'With a short tongue but wanting a long spit.'*

This aptly described Lee-seop and Nam-gil's situation.

Ultimately, it was clear that Lee-seop had disappeared because he feared for his children's future after witnessing leprosy in Nam-gil's family. According to what he had told Nam-gil, going to Japan meant he could never return. In the years since Lee-seop's disappearance, Nam-gil rarely shared news, claiming she was managing well and talking about "her children's tuition and starting a new business" with the property she had received from Hong-seon.

However, it was inevitable that problems would arise for the children and their family as they grew. By the time of the marriage, all the property Nam-gil had received from Hong-seon had been squandered and eventually lost. When things turned out that way, she decided to take her children and use the Korean War as an opportunity to move into the main house. The first time Nam-gil suggested they move into the main house, Bok-hee strongly opposed it, but Lady Kim of the Big House managed to persuade her.

Lady Kim said,

"Sori-ddigi, don't be so upset. There's already a war, and everyone is on edge, so there should be no disturbances in the household. Your father wasn't the type to take advantage of others' misfortunes or run away when life got tough, was he? Hong-seon cared for other families even at the expense of his own well-being.

Nam-gil, though wasteful and sometimes unpleasant, is still your younger sister, after all. So be generous and take her children into this house. I ask this of you."

Lady Kim persuaded Bok-hee to accept Nam-gil and her children into the house with her heartfelt words. Bok-hee, unwilling to continue stewing over the matter, decided to accept the situation for now. She instructed her daughters, saying, "From now on, you will share a room with your cousins. Aunt Nam-gil and her son Ki-hwan will stay in the lower room of the main house in Grandmother Hwang's New House. Keep that in mind."

However, soon after, Ki-hoon returned, and Hong-seon, along with his descendants, fled to Imchon. As Yoo-sang mentioned, the Big House was occupied by the People's Army. Initially intended solely for the officers, the People's Army also took over the *sarang-chae* of the New House, marking the gate with the sign, "Residence of North Korean People's Army Officers in the Western Gyeongnam Region."

After some time, consequently, Nam-gil's daughters vacated their room in the Big House, moved into the small room in the New House, and slept alongside their youngest brother, Ki-hwan.

The entire family gathered only in the main building of the Big House and the main building of the New House, the spaces designated for the women. During the first few days after Nam-gil's family moved in, she rarely participated in meal preparations, often complaining, "I'm tired and not feeling well." Therefore, once the meal was prepared and served, she would bring her daughters and son to the main room's wooden floor (*daecheong-maru*) to eat. Once again, she behaved unpleasantly.

However, once the house became a lodging for North Korean soldiers, Nam-gil changed her behavior. She began rising earlier than Bok-hee, setting the table, and frequently moving in and out of the kitchen.

The side dishes Bok-hee had prepared in advance gradually disappeared, at times leaving her children with only rice. Until now, Bok-hee had been preparing meals for both the officers and the soldiers with the help of two neighboring women. When Nam-gil packed her bags and moved into that house, Bok-hee thought that, as the second daughter-in-law of the Choi family, Nam-gil might at least be of some help.

However, Nam-gil was of no help at all. From the very first day she moved into that house, the most she did was occasionally help deliver meals to Lady Hwang of the New House. Ever since Nam-gil started showing up early in the main house's kitchen, the quantities of delicious radish kimchi, soybean-pickled perilla leaves, rare and highly salted fish like herring, and fermented shrimp noticeably dwindled.

The first person to notice this was Lady Kim, the matriarch of the main house. Lady Kim said to Bok-hee,

"Listen, Sori-ddigi. Early in the morning, I heard a commotion in the main hall, so I looked out. Even though the People's Army soldiers sleep in the *sarang-chae*, they come to the *daecheong-maru* of the main building to eat. I noticed three tables set up there, and on one of them, there was a large amount of roasted laver, more than on the other two. It was placed on a small tray, along with a bowl of salted shrimp.

But when I stepped out of the *gol-bang* after smoking a cigarette, the piled-up table had disappeared. I asked Nam-gil, who had just come back from the *sarang-chae*, 'Where did the table that was set up over there go?'

She replied, 'Ho-ho, Mother, that big pillar clock in this house must have eaten it up. That clock seems to eat rice and seaweed because it's so old. Ho-ho...'

Sori-ddigi, I asked her about the table, but she gave me such an incoherent answer. And saying that the clock ate the roasted laver, what kind of nonsense is that? That wretched woman, Nam-gil, is such a good liar. She's mocking us with her irrelevant words. Claiming a clock eats up food is truly absurd.

Sori-ddigi, what I mean to say is, we can roast the laver again, but don't waste your effort trying to figure out where the side dishes disappear to or where the table goes."

Bok-hee immediately understood what Lady Kim was implying. So Bok-hee began preparing fewer side dishes and serving smaller portions for the North Korean soldiers to ensure her children had enough food. A few days later, Nam-gil exploded in anger, throwing a tantrum and raging furiously. She threw a fit, jumping up and down in outrage. Nam-gil exclaimed,

"Oh, my goodness, I'm furious! It's so unfair to be treated like a widow when I haven't heard whether my husband is dead or alive. Now you're accusing me of being a thief who hoards and steals side dishes? Huh? You didn't say that, did you?

Your youngest child, Ki-seon, said to my daughter Hee-jin, 'Hey, elder sister, where does your family take our side dishes after stealing them? Even when my mom struggled late into the night with Sangdong-ddigi and Hadong-ddigi, your family didn't help at all.

Did you take all the prepared side dishes and eat them separately? Who are they for? My mom is so busy that she's exhausted from preparing food late into the night. Why does she set the table last for us? Why is your mother always so busy and never helping with any housework? Don't steal and eat the fruits of my mother's hard work!'

That's what Ki-seon said. I can't live with this resentment!

Lady Kim! Madam of the main room! Mother! Please listen to the second daughter-in-law's side of the story!"

Bok-hee, though tempted to confront and expose Nam-gil, decided to leave things as they were. She had enough to worry about with Hong-seon and Ki-hoon still in Imchon, wondering whether they were safe and if there was any news of them. She also wanted to avoid becoming the subject of neighborhood gossip. The neighborhood was already in a state of panic due to the People's Army camping everywhere. Every household was struggling to survive, trying to save even a single grain of rice to feed their children.

Despite being family, Nam-gil, with her cunning ways, had moved into the Big House and was secretly taking food intended for Bok-hee's children... Bok-hee was filled with curiosity and a sense of injustice. She wanted to expose the truth quickly but restrained herself, knowing she had to maintain her composure as the eldest daughter-in-law. Her inner turmoil only worsened as she wondered how much longer she would have to endure Nam-gil's deceitful behavior.

However, she knew it was only a matter of time before it became clear who was responsible for the missing side dishes and the dining table from the *sarang-chae*.

Rumors had been circulating that the U.S. and South Korean armies were preparing to begin bombing. As Bok-hee cleared the table, she heard that the North Korean soldiers were retreating quickly. They planned to withdraw to the deeper parts of *Mount Jiri* in southern Korea to avoid the imminent bombing.

The night before their hurried departure, someone tapped on the paper window door of the main room where Bok-hee was sleeping. It was midnight. Bok-hee opened the door slightly and saw the face of Kim Joong-jwa (Lieutenant Colonel), a senior officer in the North Korean People's Army. In terms of the South Korean military, he would have been a lieutenant colonel. Unlike other People's Army officers, he was quieter and made fewer demands. He was relatively decent compared to other North Korean officers.

Kim Joong-jwa said,

"Comrade Bok-hee, you've worked hard to prepare meals for me and my men. We must retreat immediately. I'm in a hurry, but do you know which room Comrade Jin-young is staying in? I have something important to discuss with her."

Bok-hee said that Nam-gil's eldest daughter, Jin-young, was in the lower room of the main quarters in the New House. After saying that, Bok-hee, utterly exhausted, quickly fell into a deep sleep.

The next morning, when she woke up, all the North Korean soldiers had left, and the house was completely empty. Feeling relieved, as if a weight had been lifted, Bok-hee walked through each room, taking her time to inspect the house for the first time in a long while. Cleaning up the mess left behind by the soldiers seemed like a minor task.

She wondered why Kim Joong-jwa had sought out Jin-young the previous night. Strangely, neither Jin-young nor Nam-gil's family were anywhere to be seen. Bok-hee asked her second daughter, Ki-young, to bring a broom and a dustpan. She also enlisted Ki-chan and her daughters to help clean the house. Little Ki-seon returned with a broom and a portrait of the Virgin Mary, which she had found buried in the backyard. She was carefully wiping the dust off the frame.

Despite the family's noisy cleaning efforts, Nam-gil's family was still absent. Just then, Lady Kim, the matriarch of the main room, appeared and spoke from the *gol-bang.* Lady Kim remarked,

"Usually, they prepare a separate table nicely to be 'fed' to the big clock on the *daecheong-maru* and wait, but today, the table didn't appear, and no one came to eat.

Every morning, they stack up such delicious laver... And why isn't Jin-young showing her face? She carries the table in and out, acting charming all the while."

Bok-hee had already noticed something was off. Nam-gil, along with Jin-young, had been frequenting the main house kitchen and was overheard saying to a passing Sangdong-ddigi,

"Tell the eldest mother, Bok-hee, to continue preparing the communal meals for the subordinates as usual. Jin-young and I will take care of setting the table for Kim, the lieutenant colonel and leader of the North Korean officers. After all, we should contribute something if we're eating in this house. And if we win over that leader, won't it make life easier for our family in the future?"

When Bok-hee heard this from Sangdong-ddigi, she found it somewhat convenient. With many family members to care for and the absence of Hong-seon and Ki-hoon, avoiding any disturbance in the household was paramount.

Jin-young, Nam-gil's eldest daughter, was a cute girl with a chubby build, like her mother, and a charming smile. It wasn't until that afternoon, after the North Korean soldiers had disappeared, that Nam-gil showed up at the main house with Jin-young, Ho-jin, Hee-jin, and Ki-hwan in tow.

After skipping two meals, they went straight into the kitchen, set the table, and devoured all the remaining food and rice in one sitting. Meanwhile, Lee-seop's family paid no attention to the circumstances of the New House, the main house, or Saemmy House, focusing solely on feeding themselves day after day.

Ten days after the People's Army left, Bok-hee contacted Imchon. Following this, Hong-seon, Ki-hoon, Ki-hwi, and Jeong-seop returned to Sancheong. Bok-hee prepared a feast with an array of side dishes for them.

Upon their return, they received news of Joon-seop. The bombings in this area, which had begun with Joon-seop's disappearance, showed no signs of abating. The relentless American bombardment continued, aiming to push the retreating North Korean forces further back.

Some neighbors and members of the Choi family gathered again in the Big House, saying, "Let's wait and see how the war unfolds and find a way to survive."

During the bombardment, Saemmy House, where Jeong-seop's family lived, was obliterated. Nearby homes also suffered from the relentless attacks. Directly across from Saemmy House stood an elementary school that had been commandeered as the "Western Gyeongnam North Korean People's Army Headquarters." As a result, Saemmy House, situated opposite the school, was destroyed. The U.S. military's bombing missed its intended target and hit Saemmy House instead. Fortunately, the elementary school remained unscathed.

As a result, Saemmy House, where Jeong-seop and his family had lived for so long, was completely destroyed. They were devastated. As mentioned earlier, Bok-hee's second daughter, who had gone on an errand for Ki-hoon, was injured and bedridden after shrapnel from the bombing struck her eye.

Meanwhile, Nam-gil and her family remained indifferent to the plight of the Saemmy House and the Big House. They huddled together in the lower room of the New House and stayed there for several more months. At some point, Jin-young occasionally began eating alone in the kitchen. Then one day, Jin-young came face to face with the family from the Big House.

Why hadn't they noticed until things reached this point? In the chaos of war, everyone prioritized their own matters. People were too busy to pay attention to others.

It was only then that Bok-hee realized Jin-young's waist had become noticeably thicker, and from the side, her belly appeared slightly rounded. According to Sangdong-ddigi, around that time, Nam-gil and Jin-young often quarreled in their room. The issue was whether to abort the baby. Naturally, their voices rose, and word eventually spread about Jin-young's pregnancy. When people looked closely, they said she appeared to be in the middle stage of pregnancy. Even while eating in the kitchen, Nam-gil tried to soothe Jin-young, and Bok-hee overheard the conversation.

Then one day, Nam-gil suddenly decided to take charge. Her whispering turned into a loud, curt voice. Nam-gil declared,

"Yes, life can be unpredictable. The North Korean army has withdrawn, but who could have foreseen this chaos? They had such power, dragging everyone to the people's court and commanding the entire town. I thought we could manage quite well back then.

It's okay, Jin-young! No one will blame you for being pregnant amidst this mess. But having a child without a father is a greater problem. It's better to listen to your mother and end this pregnancy early. You're only in your early 20s, with a long future ahead. There's no rule that says you can't marry again when you find a good person. What's the big deal about being pregnant during a war, when life and death are so uncertain?"

It was just like Nam-gil to think that way. Nam-gil's pragmatic view seemed to influence Bok-hee's daughters, who acted as if they no longer cared about Jin-young's pregnancy. Once Jin-young and Nam-gil's opinions had somewhat aligned, Nam-gil suddenly became busy outside the house from that day onward. Bok-hee had a slight premonition that she was on the verge of stirring up new trouble.

Despite the war and the bombing, the autumn of 1950 brought a bumper crop. With so few people available to work, the rice paddies that had escaped the bombing waved golden in the breeze. Bok-hee had her sons and daughters take turns keeping watch, and she hired several workers to harvest the grain with sickles.

At night, she had a worker guard the rice fields to prevent theft. Bok-hee had no time to worry about Nam-gil's family. She was deeply concerned about her second daughter, who was now blind in one eye.

However, she couldn't blame Ki-hoon for cherishing his books; he hadn't known the bombing would occur. Bok-hee was busy taking care of her children and managing the remaining fields and paddies.

In the meantime, Nam-gil caused yet another scandal.
She borrowed money from people in Sancheong, Hamyang, and the market, as well as from many acquaintances, and then chose not to repay them. After borrowing money for several days, she and her family fled in the night.

Before their escape, creditors from the Sancheong market came to the New House for the first time. During that time, instead of retreating, Nam-gil raised her voice even louder. Hong-seon remained silent, seemingly resigned to Nam-gil's behavior.

Soon, creditors from Hamyang, where Nam-gil had many connections from running her brewery business, came to the Big House to demand repayment. When the families of the Big House and the New House refused to listen to her any longer, Nam-gil decided to flee. The Sancheong Choi family was left to deal with the bitter aftermath of Nam-gil's debt scandal, compounding the wounds left by the war. The families of the Big House, the New House, and the Saemmy House all suffered.

Lady Hwang did not disclose the amount she had lent to Nam-gil, so Bok-hee was unaware of the sum. However, Jeong-seop suffered significant financial losses in his household.

Until the morning of Nam-gil's escape, she feigned innocence and caused a commotion in the yard of the Big House. At that time, Jeong-seop and his family were staying at the Big House, as their own home had been destroyed. Nam-gil raised her voice to the creditors,

"In this chaos, people's lives matter most. What is truly important?

Don't worry, I'll tell my father-in-law, and he will repay the debts in due time.

It is the law of nature! Some must die, and others must live. My children and I cannot die over money. I have nothing now, so if you want, cut my belly open and take whatever you find!"

Lady Kim retorted,

"Nam-gil, why are you so shameless? Early in the morning, you set the table for the People's Army with a bowl of white rice —hard to come by —along with delicious laver and Korean daisy kimchi.

Where on earth did the rice come from? Oh, tut-tut ... pathetic... You did not even serve me a bowl of rice. Now, using the Choi family's name, you borrow money from people you know and remain silent about it. Is that right?

Where did you come from, Nam-gil? You even adopted a man's name to appear intelligent, yet you lack sense. You spend money recklessly and then pretend ignorance. Lee-seop disappeared without witnessing all this, so in a way, was it for the better? Such misfortune!"

Nam-gil responded,

"Oh, Mother, how heartless you are! I didn't know where Lee-seop was going, so I thought things would improve if I arranged for my daughter to marry an officer of the People's Army. You're always bringing up the past. What a miserable life I have!"

Lady Kim retorted,

"What did you say? Did you prepare that delicious rice for the clock ghost to eat? Why is the ghost so fortunate? And now you can't get in touch with that clever ghost?"

As the mother-in-law and daughter-in-law quarreled, people from the local market threatened to take Nam-gil to the police station, causing a commotion and demanding her arrest. Nam-gil's children cried, their faces pale with fear.

Seeing this, Jeong-seop promised to pay off some of her debts, ensuring that the crowd did not take her to the police station. Despite this, Nam-gil disappeared without a word of thanks to Jeong-seop. In the middle of the night, without informing anyone, she packed her bags in the New House and vanished with her daughters and son, leaving behind only the echo of her absence.

Up until that time, Jeong-seop had some wealth in his possession. He owned a substantial amount of land. Thus, long ago, Jeong-seop advised his maternal cousin, the nephew of his biological mother, Lady Han, to pursue further studies. At the time, this cousin, Mr. Han, was working as an elementary school teacher in places such as Jeonju and at Jinju Normal School. With Jeong-seop's support, he studied for several years and eventually passed the judicial examination in 1942, which was the Japanese Empire's Higher Civil Service Examination in Law. In later years, Mr. Han became a Supreme Court Justice and founded a distinguished family of legal professionals.

In this way, Jeong-seop extended his generosity to others on several occasions, never hesitating to part with his own money. Though he might have received words of gratitude from those he helped, his own children at Saemmy House began to endure financial hardships. Until that point, Jeong-seop could not have foreseen the greater misfortunes that lay ahead in his own life.

13
The Korean War III
1950: Seoul and the Regions Near Sancheong
—A Fragile Man and a Shameless Woman

About two months after the Korean War broke out, Joon-seop of the New House, who had been out of contact until then, finally returned to Sancheong. He had been attending S Agricultural College in Suwon, diligently pursuing his studies. Lady Hwang's tears of joy flowed endlessly when she saw her son return safely from Suwon to Sancheong.

While Hong-seon and Ki-hoon were seeking refuge in Imchon, Lady Hwang's greatest worry was Joon-seop. The silence surrounding his fate had left her in a constant state of anxiety. She had received word about her second daughter, Jeong-soon, through Principal Hwang of Jinju, who had learned of her well-being from a friend in Jeong-soon's department, which provided her with some measure of solace.

At the peak of the war, Joon-seop had taken refuge in a small hermitage nestled deep within a mountain, a short distance from Suwon. For over a month, he remained in this secluded sanctuary. The location was so remote that the sounds of battle were barely audible. There, he managed to sustain himself on one modest meal a day, enough to stave off starvation.

As his stay extended, Joon-seop resolved to return to Sancheong. He began his journey of evacuation later than most. Following the monks' advice, he decided to conceal himself during the day and travel southward under the cover of night. On one such night, he stumbled upon an abandoned private house but found it devoid of people and lacking any food. For nearly a month, he wandered in this manner.

One day, as Joon-seop wandered, starving and gazing up at the sky, he spotted a group of refugees moving along the hillside where he was hiding. Summoning his courage, he emerged from the shelter of the bushes and decided to follow them. The evacuees, dressed in humble garments, carried bundles on their heads, in their hands, and on their backs. Some rode on ox-carts, while others trudged alongside, their possessions weighing them down. They moved in clusters, threading their way down the mountain path. Joon-seop slipped into their ranks, but not a single eye turned his way.

As they trudged along the mountain path, the drone of an airplane filled the air. A voice rose above the murmur of the crowd, instructing, "The plane's coming from the right! Everyone, get to the right side of the mountain and lie down!"

Obediently, the refugees scrambled to the foot of the mountain and lay flat on the ground, their bodies pressed to the earth. It was said that planes flying high had better visibility in the opposite direction and that bomb drops were more accurate.

Among the refugees, the children were the most pitiful. Desperation drove them to eat dirt and stones from the ground, their distended bellies likely teeming with parasites. Their faces, covered in sores from various skin diseases, bore the grimy stains of neglect and suffering.

Joon-seop, indistinguishable among them, walked without a clear destination. All he knew was that they were heading south. In a haze, he moved with them, walking and sleeping in a daze. His emaciated, frail body was jostled within the crowd, his face pale and sallow.

Fortune smiled upon Joon-seop when he came across a passing cargo truck. It carried him to Hamyang, in Gyeongsangnam-do. The presence of civilian cargo trucks suggested that the North Korean soldiers were retreating, falling behind in the war, and that the People's Army had not yet reached the remote corners of the village.

Stepping off the truck, Joon-seop found himself among another scattered group of refugees and joined their ranks once more. In the villages they passed, some kind souls offered rice balls to the weary travelers. With the help of these strangers, Joon-seop managed to find a place on another truck, this time heading toward Sancheong. The truck was overflowing with people, their numbers far exceeding the sparse luggage it carried.

He finally approached the town of Sancheong. After disembarking from the truck and trudging along, Joon-seop noticed an uncanny stillness that blanketed every street. It was well past the depths of night, nearing 4 a.m., when Joon-seop finally slipped through the slightly ajar gate of the New House. Standing before the main room, he gently grasped the handle of his mother's door and gave it a faint tap-tap.

In a barely audible whisper, he called out. "Mother, it's me, Joon-seop." Lady Hwang, who had been awake praying at dawn, was startled by the familiar voice. She hesitated, her heart racing, then rushed out, biting her tongue in her haste. Her prayers had been answered — her son had returned home safely, alleviating the heart-wrenching uncertainty she had endured since the war's outbreak.

Clutching her rosewood rosary, she kissed it fervently and murmured, "Mother, I have lost nothing. I will only do as You wish."

News from Bok-hee revealed that the North Korean military had withdrawn just the day before, but the future remained uncertain and fraught with danger. There was no word from Hong-seon, still in Imchon, and the presence of a grown college student like Joon-seop in the house posed a significant risk. If the remaining People's Army forces discovered him, he would be conscripted into their ranks immediately. It was clear that if they captured him, Joon-seop would be led down a path from which he would never return.

Lady Hwang ushered him into the kitchen, keeping the lights off, and prepared a bath for him. Afterward, she settled him into the small room adjacent to the kitchen in the main house. She decided that at dawn, she would find someone to help escort him to Imchon, where Hong-seon was.

But suddenly, that morning, the staccato bursts of machine-gun fire shattered the silence of the entire village. It was the People's Army's final offensive, their last desperate act. The remaining soldiers fired recklessly down the alleyways, while others looted the houses for food and clothing. Their plan, it seemed, was to gather what they could and flee south, perhaps to the mountains of Jiri or beyond. By approximately 8 a.m., an eerie calm had returned to the village. The alleyways lay deserted, not a soul in sight.

Lady Hwang recalled hearing the distinct North Korean accents just two days earlier. During that time, the People's Army had filled the mornings with their loud chatter, eating and washing, their voices echoing from dawn until late at night, sharp and incessant like machine-gun fire. Accents from Pyeongan-do, Hamgyeong-do, Kaesong, and other unknown regions blended into a cacophony. Even inside her room, these voices startled her.

Since Hong-seon had gone to Imchon, she felt as though she had been left to face this harsh world alone, each day a bitter struggle, like chewing sand. "You haven't heard from Joon-seop, have you? He's such a quiet boy—it makes me worry even more," were Hong-seon's parting words before he went into hiding, leaving her with an anxious heart.

Lady Hwang had no clear plan for sending Joon-seop safely to Imchon, where Hong-seon was. She resolved to discuss it with Bok-hee and decided that, even if they couldn't hide him in Imchon, where Hong-seon was staying, they had to hide him somewhere else to save his life. How many times had she prayed each day for the war to end quickly? Yet now, as if by some magic, the People's Army had vanished, as if sucked into some vast, unknown void in the village.

Lady Hwang decided to summon Bok-hee through the neighbor woman who worked as a kitchen maid, but she doubted whether Bok-hee would come willingly right away. Bok-hee had never been easy for Lady Hwang to deal with. Recently, Bok-hee had endured much heartache over Nam-gil's affairs and had shouldered all the household duties while serving the People's Army. Hwang realized that she had turned a blind eye to Bok-hee's struggles all this time.

Now, wanting to discuss her son Joon-seop in a gentle tone, Lady Hwang found it difficult to find the right words. She hesitated, unsure of how to begin. Yet, despite her reservations, Bok-hee, upon hearing

Hwang's summons, arrived in the late afternoon, stepping into the main room of the New House. Lady Hwang said,

"Hyori-ddigi, you've always handled your duties as the eldest granddaughter-in-law of this family without complaint. I thank you for that... " Lady Hwang began, her voice soft. " But as you know, you and I are the only ones left to manage the main household. I need to discuss something important with you."

When Lady Hwang saw Bok-hee's face, her sharp expression remained unchanged, her large eyes angled upwards in a fierce gaze. Bok-hee had no idea that Joon-seop had returned. At that moment, Joon-seop appeared before them, dressed neatly. He slid open the door of the small room off the kitchen and stepped into the main room.

Lady Hwang's face showed more surprise than Bok-hee's.

"Sweetheart, greet your elder sister-in-law, Bok-hee," Hwang said. Joon-seop bowed to Bok-hee, who reciprocated the gesture. Lady Hwang said softly, "Sweetheart, it must have been very hard traveling down from Suwon to here. And it's not certain that the People's Army has truly left.

It's getting dark. Where do you plan to go? What if you're taken by the remaining soldiers?"

Joon-seop reassured her,

"Mother, don't worry. Last night, I heard that a young woman who traveled on the same truck as I did lives nearby, near the Sancheong intersection. Her home is in Chahwang. I finally managed to get some proper sleep after such a long time, and even if night falls, there's nothing to worry about anymore. This is our home, after all.

I don't know exactly where she lives, but I plan to walk along the ridges between the rice paddies, using the moonlight as my guide, to find her. I want to see how she's doing. The cathedral near our house still stands; I want to find some peace there as well.

She has only her mother and grandmother. Our home may not seem like a single-parent household to others, but it often feels empty and sad. It must be frightening for her to be at home with only women.

When I arrived last night, it was late, and we held hands as we got off the truck. I'm both curious and worried about her. I'll return quickly, even if it's late. Please don't worry and get some rest.

Elder Sister-in-law Bok-hee, I'll visit and greet you properly next time. Take care of yourself."

Joon-seop's earnest plea moved Lady Hwang. He had never spoken of "a woman" before. Hearing him mention one now brought her a sense of joy. Joon-seop had always been shy around people, especially women, often turning red in their presence. He used to say, "If someone wears a skirt, isn't she a woman? Are women really different from men?" He would blush whenever young female workers came to the house.

Lady Hwang nodded and said, "I understand. Be careful," as she watched him walk toward the gate. Joon-seop donned a yellowish jacket and stepped out toward the gate. It was late afternoon, and the sky was beginning to darken.

The sound of a passing plane seemed louder than usual. As Joon-seop left, he raised a hand to cover his ears, as if he were weary of the noise. He waved to his mother and Bok-hee before stepping out. Hwang and Bok-hee were both surprised by how much Joon-seop's attitude had changed. There was no way to stop any of his actions. No, they couldn't ignore the earnest look in Joon-seop's eyes.

The son who spoke so confidently about a woman now looked as if he had become an adult. The timid, overly cautious, and fragile boy, Choi Joon-seop, had changed. As Hwang glanced at Bok-hee's expression, she saw a slight smile. Bok-hee, sensing that Lady Hwang might feel a bit embarrassed, responded with a faint smile of her own.

Just as Joon-seop was presumed to have left the gate, an explosion shook the New House violently. Shells rained down on the village like a storm, filling the air with dust and debris. The explosion was unmistakably close.

Once again, the entire house shook with the force of the blasts, with dust and deafening noise erupting like a tempest from somewhere in the yard and near the front gate, making it feel as if the entire house would be lifted off the ground. When Lady Hwang opened the door to the main room, she saw that the front gate and the entire pigsty had collapsed.

Fortunately, the main part of the New House remained intact, while the *sarang-chae* was only partially destroyed, visible through the thick haze of dust from the bombardment. Dogs from the neighborhood, which had been hiding beneath the floorboards of the Big and New House, darted out in panic. Their pitiful yelps echoed as they fled, some collapsing with final cries. Beyond that, there was nothing but dense smoke and a cloud of earth and dust, obscuring everything from view.

The bombed area was left unrecognizable.

Joon-seop had been standing right there, in that very spot, just a few minutes ago before leaving the room ... but now, there was no trace of him. Lady Hwang, standing beside Bok-hee, clung to her tightly before collapsing right there on the spot. She fainted. Joon-seop had vanished—into the wreckage and dust left by the shell.

Bok-hee moved back and forth between the main room of the Big House and the New House, tending to Lady Hwang until she regained consciousness. She ground the precious pine nuts she had saved to make porridge and placed some rare seaweed beside the bowl.

For the first time, she closely studied Lady Hwang's face as she lay there, unaware of her son's fate. Until now, Bok-hee had always thought of Lady Hwang as an extraordinary person, entirely different from ordinary women like herself, so she had never really looked at her face.

Il-seop had often said, "That woman has a wicked nature, ensnaring my father. She must be different from people like us," and Bok-hee had unconsciously accepted his view. But now, Lady Hwang no longer seemed so strange. 'She's just a regular person too—a mother with a child, an ordinary woman,' Bok-hee murmured to herself.

Upon hearing the news about Joon-seop, Bok-hee's third daughter, Ki-ok, mumbled in confusion, "Uncle Joon-seop must have been so lonely. On the day he died, he went with the villagers. Chun-sik from next door and Yang Dong-sik's father from down the street, they all went with him as well. I heard they were all classmates, seniors, or juniors at the same elementary school as Uncle Joon-seop..." Ki-ok had overheard the adults talking about what happened to Joon-seop and repeated it, not fully grasping its meaning.

The entire village was devastated, with almost no food left.

Yet the Big House, which had been used as lodging for North Korean officials, was nearly untouched. *It's strange,* Bok-hee thought to herself. *Despite the chaotic bombings, all the belongings in the main house remain intact.*

Bok-hee took a small hoe to the patch of earth behind the main house, beneath the corner of the wall, which had been dug deep and leveled. She unearthed the lid of a large earthenware jar hidden there. When she opened it, she found rice, barley, beans, salt, sugar, gold, and money inside. Bok-hee touched the contents thoughtfully. She realized that she would soon need to buy new food supplies and felt overwhelmed by the many tasks ahead.

As Bok-hee fervently wished for Hong-seon and Ki-hoon to return soon, she found herself sniffling despite her resolve never to cry after Il-seop's death. She marveled at her own resilience in managing the household thus far, almost unable to believe it herself. Yet the uncertainty of the future loomed large, filling her with dread. "Oh, how weary I am!" she murmured softly, the words escaping her lips unbiddenly.

The people rose from the ashes of the bombings, clearing the rubble from every home. They prepared to return to their ordinary, pre-war homes, where life had once thrived. While tidying up near the New House, someone found a scrap of yellow cloth and brought it to Lady Hwang. It was the same color and material as the jacket Joon-seop had worn when he stepped out of the front gate.

Lady Hwang could never forget the color of that fabric. The jacket, which had originally belonged to Hong-seon, had been passed down to Joon-seop as he grew. Upon seeing that scrap of cloth, any lingering hope she had clung to of Joon-seop's survival was utterly extinguished. She retreated to her room, immobilized by grief. With no body to bury, she resolved to declare him "Missing."

Yet she wished to discuss and finalize this decision properly when Hong-seon returned home. Joon-seop was not the only one; other villagers who had perished unseen would also be declared missing. In the chaos of war, such a fate had befallen countless individuals. Their existence, reduced to mere names, would gradually fade from memory—an all-too-common consequence of the ravages of war.

Hong-seon and Ki-hoon returned home, thankfully, in good health. Exhausted, Hong-seon listened silently as he was told about Joon-seop's disappearance. He quietly entered Lady Hwang's room, took her hand, and remained wordless for a long time.

Is it even possible to console a mother who has seen her child vanish before her eyes?

After the People's Army retreated from the *sarang-chae* of the Big and New Houses, bombings followed. Rumors spread that American and South Korean troops would soon sweep through the village, inspecting every home. Yet as night fell, figures resembling People's Army soldiers still emerged from the darkness, raiding homes for food and terrorizing the villagers.

Bok-hee, having studied at the village school, knew little about Communism. However, she had witnessed firsthand the actions of the People's Army officers who had occupied her home for over a month. The People's Army often proclaimed, "It's the party's order. Follow the party."

Bok-hee learned that "the party" referred to the Communist Party and its belief in Communism. They claimed, "Our party treats all people equally. We distribute land and status fairly ... so follow us."

Nonetheless, Bok-hee clearly observed how miserably the common soldiers of the People's Army were treated. The high-ranking officer stationed at her house was Comrade Kim Joong-jwa, a man from Pyeongan-do, North Korea, who carried himself with palpable self-confidence. Though she didn't know who had initiated the relationship, it was apparent that he had become involved with Jin-young.

The night before Kim left the house, anticipating the U.S. military's bombing, he hesitated as if waiting for someone. Bok-hee did not dwell on the reason at that time. It was clear he was tormented by something, whether it was a personal matter or the ideology he had faithfully followed. He was still in his early thirties. After all, the People's Army soldiers were men like any other, capable of loving women. It seemed he was the father of the child Jin-young carried in her womb.

Ideology is complex. When a person must choose between personal matters and a deeply held belief, he or she may waver. In theory, one's external actions should align with one's ideology, but internally, one might follow the call of the heart. Communists, however, were expected to choose ideology over everything. They were indoctrinated to make decisions for the party at all times. Their families and even their personal desires became tools for the party's agenda. They promoted gender equality on the surface, yet within the party, women's bodies were seen as communal property for the cause of ideology.

Among the village maidens Bok-hee knew, some had been dragged to the valleys of *Jiri Mountain* and had become victims of this cruel facade. These young women, she imagined, had been forced to surrender their bodies, minds, and entire lives to the People's Army.

Upon returning to Imchon, Jeong-seop found that relentless bombings had obliterated his house, forcing his wife and daughters to take refuge with their neighbors. Consequently, Jeong-seop and his family temporarily sought shelter at the Big House. Meanwhile, because of his gentle demeanor, Jeong-seop was repeatedly harassed by market vendors demanding information about Nam-gil's whereabouts. In the end, as previously mentioned, Jeong-seop decided to sell the land under his name to settle Nam-gil's debts. This seemed to bring the matter of Nam-gil's debts to a close. Some creditors, not having confronted Nam-gil herself, engaged in prolonged disputes with Jeong-seop before finally leaving the Big House late at night.

Yet no matter how far Nam-gil had fled under the cover of night, how long could she endure in a completely unfamiliar place? Amidst this chaotic and perilous turmoil, with three young women and a small son in tow, where could Nam-gil and her family have gone?

Nearly three months had passed since Nam-gil and her family had left, leaving the household in disarray. One day, Bok-hee discovered a suspicious black bundle tucked away in a corner of the *Jangdok-gan* area.

Who could have placed it there? It was certainly not there the day before. Though the bitterly cold winter, with its icicles hanging from the eaves, had passed, the bright days of spring were still distant. Bok-hee hesitated, wondering whether to leave the black bundle alone. However, realizing she could not ignore something left in her own storage area, she decided to open it.

Bok-hee brought the bundle into the kitchen and carefully unwrapped the heavy black cotton cloth. Inside, to her horror, lay the lifeless body of a newborn, its umbilical cord freshly cut. The infant's body was already icy cold from exposure. "Oh my goodness, what on earth is this?" she cried in shock. Startled by her exclamation, Lady Kim, who had been tapping her tobacco pipe in the inner room, called for Bok-hee to come inside.

Lady Kim said,

"Hey, Sori-ddigi. Why are you so surprised? Is something wrong? Come in here and tell me."

Bok-hee showed Lady Kim the gruesome contents of the cloth. Lady Kim glanced briefly before closing one eye tightly. The cloth was wrapped in two layers. Lady Kim spoke in a low voice, as if she knew something. "Sori-ddigi, do you have any idea what this could mean?"

Lady Kim asked, "I haven't seen Nam-gil's family for a while and was curious. But late last night, I saw a shadow creeping around the house. When I peeked out, I thought it looked like Nam-gil.

She hadn't been around for a long time, but she appeared last night, sneaking about with a bundle in her hand. I had a feeling something was off. Just now, when I heard you gasp so loudly, I immediately thought it must be related to that incident. So, what do you think?"

"Oh my," Bok-hee responded. "I knew Nam-gil was a treacherous woman, but why would she commit such a heinous act and bring it to my home? What is she trying to achieve with this? She's been hiding somewhere, not showing her face for some time, and I started to worry about the children she left behind. I even considered searching the entire village for them. Every time I try to forget, the creditors show up at my door and keep harassing Min-ja's father from the Saemmy House.

Considering all the trouble Nam-gil has caused my family, I can't just let this go. Her actions are beyond despicable,"

She trembled, her voice filled with anger and frustration.

Lady Kim sighed, "Oh dear, don't take it that way. Even a kind heart has its limits, but committing evil deeds leads to a bad end, doesn't it? You've endured so much, turning a blind eye to her actions. Remember, she's miserable too. But now ... what should we do with this poor baby?"

Bok-hee ground her teeth in frustration. Yet as Lady Kim, her mother-in-law, implored her to show compassion for Nam-gil, Bok-hee reluctantly replied, "Let's think about it." She then set about preparing the dining table for Hong-seon.

Watching her, Lady Kim murmured to herself. "Isn't a baby a life too? Sori-ddigi carries such a heavy burden. Nam-gil stubbornly insists on someone else dealing with this mess, but that's too much.

Nam-gil, that *mundi* (in this case, a troublemaker or a wicked person. Originally, it was a term used to refer to leprosy patients), keeps dumping her problems on others to clean up what her daughter did...

Truly shameless!

Lee-seop married into such bleak prospects; no wonder he struggled silently. But now, what will be done with this poor baby wrapped in black cloth?"

Bok-hee woke her third daughter, Ki-ok, from her sleep. Ki-seon, stirred by the commotion, also awoke. Ki-seon, a posthumous child who had never known her father's face, usually fell asleep clutching a picture of Jesus to her chest.

Though Bok-hee couldn't quite pinpoint why, she always felt a deep pang of tenderness for Ki-seon. To her, Ki-seon seemed the most trustworthy among the children. Following her mother's instructions, Ki-ok prayed over the tiny corpse wrapped in black cloth. Then, they dug a shallow grave in a field at the base of the village mountain, far from the house. The ground had been parched for some time, and it wasn't until the hard earth had soaked up a considerable amount of water from the hot metal bucket that the hoe could break through. They temporarily buried the newborn's body there.

When Lady Kim saw Bok-hee and her young daughters returning through the gate after completing the task, she motioned for them to come to her.

Lady Kim:

"Good job. But I didn't get a clear look earlier. When you unwrapped the cloth, was the baby a girl or a boy?"

Bok-hee:

"What does it matter if the dead baby was a girl or a boy? It must have been a premature baby, one that came into the world too early. They are such sinful people. But if you're still curious, I'll tell you — it looked like a girl to me. So, isn't the baby's father Kim Joong-jwa of the People's Army, the one who was in charge here? And, of course, Jin-young is the mother."

Lady Kim sighed, "Yes, that's right... The poor thing must have been born too early, couldn't even eat properly, and must have died within a few days. If we confront Nam-gil, she'll just make some absurd excuse. We don't even know where her family is now.

The most brazen and vile thing in the world is a human being. People appear when they need something and vanish when they don't."

In retrospect, it was clear that Nam-gil had ulterior motives from the moment she started frequenting the kitchen, especially after learning that the Big House had become the quarters for the North Korean People's Army officers. Nam-gil had insisted on dressing up her fair-faced, pretty eldest daughter, Jin-young, and sending her to run meal errands for them.

Bok-hee should have sensed something was amiss. Despite her stern appearance, she was completely oblivious when it came to foreseeing such sinister deeds.

Lady Kim continued, "Hey, Sori-ddigi, *truly bad people never realize their own wickedness. They think everyone else is a fool. Every word they speak is a lie or an excuse.* You are the most important woman in this family. The rise and fall of this household rests in your hands. They say you work like an ox and that you're tough. You are the pillar of this family, so be strong and take even better care of us. When Nam-gil shows up, confront her sternly."

However, after dealing with the infant's body, a fleeting thought crossed Bok-hee's mind: Nam-gil might harbor some unfounded resentment toward her for this. Her premonition proved correct.

The next evening, Nam-gil returned to the Big House alone. Feigning sorrow over Joon-seop's tragic death once again, as if it were a new revelation, she first paid her respects to Lady Hwang before approaching

Lady Kim. Spotting Bok-hee, she began speaking about matters that hadn't even been asked about, all the while furtively gauging her reaction.

"*Hyeong-nim* (Big Sister)," Nam-gil started, "I was scared and intimidated by you. I stayed in the lower building of the New House, setting the table for the People's Army to help you and provide some support. My family lived in the Big House and the New House, and I was trying to earn my keep.

But please don't misunderstand my attempt to help as me trying to take over as the mistress of this house, bypassing my sister-in-law, the eldest daughter-in-law of the Head Family.

If anyone tries to blame me for something so unreasonable, I've done enough and I won't stay silent. Uh... Still, if there's something that has upset you, I apologize in advance. Oh dear, I'm sorry if I caused any trouble."

Bok-hee said, "Nam-gil, did you consider what it means to be the daughter-in-law of the Head Family before you acted? How can you so casually claim that title? I've worked so hard until now..."

Nam-gil interrupted, "Oh, no, I said I'm sorry, didn't I?

I thought it would be prestigious to be the eldest daughter-in-law of the Head Family. I imagined that if I became the mistress of this Big House, I would gain some benefits. But is there anything special? Like an ox, I only work hard and take care of customers.

Still, if Lee-seop were to return, since he's a twin, wouldn't I have the same rights after Il-seop passed away? If only I had Lee-seop, wouldn't I be the second daughter-in-law of the Head Family too? That's all I was thinking about."

Though she spoke confidently, Nam-gil's voice faded as she watched Bok-hee's reaction. Bok-hee responded, "Well, I was about to look for you, but thank you for showing up. I think you know why I wanted to see you, don't you?"

Inwardly, Bok-hee held back her anger, thinking, 'You shouldn't make such careless excuses when it comes to human life. No matter how young the life, throwing it into someone else's hands is inexcusable. Do I have to spell it out?'

Before Bok-hee could even start to speak, Nam-gil sharply rolled her eyes upward like a hawk, revealing the whites of her eyes. Her eyes and hands trembled as if something inside her were twisted, showing signs of agitation. Though short in stature, Nam-gil had sharp, hawk-like eyes and a mind that was always quick and calculating. Then, shortly after, Nam-gil seemed to try to avoid Bok-hee's cold gaze. She spoke in a much more subdued voice than before, showing a hint of nervousness.

"*Hyeong-nim*, I know roughly what you want to say to me. But aren't you like an older paternal uncle's wife to my children? I'm not a bad person. Who would have thought my daughter Jin-young would be left alone like an outcast? Kim Joong-jwa was so infatuated with her, always saying, 'You're pretty, you're pretty.' If their side had won, neither Jin-young's situation nor mine would be so dire.

Our family is now staying at my friend's house, but it's not a good situation there either. If you already know everything, just handle it. I'll be anxious if we stay at her house for too long. I'll take my children to my second cousin's house in Busan. If we can get a truck in Sancheong-eup, we have to leave quickly."

For the first time, Nam-gil showed submission to Bok-hee, saying, "I'm sorry, *Hyeong-nim*, please take care of everything. Aren't you the great mother of my children?" This was also the last time she had expressed such sentiments.

The life that had come from Jin-young's body was now just an object to Nam-gil. However, Nam-gil did not wish to stain her hands with blood. Considering this, could it be that the corpse stirred at least a semblance of shame within her? Given that the deceased was someone's grandchild, could it be that it evoked in her some slight pang of guilt, however faint?

Surely not. The child would have been born before even completing its full term in the mother's womb. What is clear is that whoever starved it to death immediately after birth held no sentiment whatsoever toward that fragile life. Especially in this still quite chilly weather—to wrap the tiny body in a thin cloth and leave it atop a jar... At least, Nam-gil was the kind of person Bok-hee knew.

Bok-hee said, "So, you're leaving everything to me? Then don't blame me for anything later. Are you seriously leaving a dead child for me to deal with? And ... how is Jin-young, the child's mother? Is she doing well?"

Nam-gil seemed on the verge of saying something significant but instead shook her head and took Bok-hee's hand. Bok-hee felt no warmth in the gesture. Bok-hee thought it was a hollow attempt to avoid responsibility. Nam-gil quickly excused herself, heading to the kitchen to eat. Not a single word she said was credible. Whether she truly intended to go to Busan or her second cousin's house remained uncertain...

Lady Kim said,

"Sori-ddigi, you must make a firm decision now. Nam-gil might say one thing and then hurt you later with something else. She's not an ordinary woman. Didn't she go through multiple men, even without my son? Only Jin-young is to be pitied, having learned such things from her mother.

But why did Nam-gil carry the baby to term if she didn't want it? Maybe Jin-young was trying to raise the child, but with all this chaos, she couldn't even find a way to get rid of it?

The baby was quite well-developed... Even if it had been born at full term, it's clear she starved it to death. But in this chaos, many babies have died. Even Joon-seop, a grown man, vanished in a fireball right in front of his mother..."

While Bok-hee and Lady Kim were talking, Nam-gil had already left. Lady Kim had likely come to assess how her actions were being dealt with. This was her way of avoiding direct involvement. Nam-gil, a shameless person, had committed ugly and despicable deeds without taking responsibility. As Lady Kim said, "*The meanest and most despicable behavior often comes from within a person's mind.*" Bok-hee sighed, thinking, 'Maybe it happened because I stepped back, being softer-hearted than I appeared. Nam-gil, such a wicked person!'

The instinct to survive can sometimes drive people to harm others, especially in times of war. War often provides a cover for even the most heinous acts. When the hidden atrocities committed during wartime eventually come to light, by what standards will they be judged?

In the war-torn land, countless acts of rape, mass murder, robbery, and theft took place. These crimes were committed both among the inhabitants themselves and, more openly, against those in other areas. The war-ravaged land seemed to serve as a testing ground for all the evil humanity could conceive. Yet, despite the devastation, Korea managed to emerge from the dark tunnel of war. Thanks to aid from many unknown countries, the path to recovery began. Relief efforts and supplies started pouring in.

On the night Nam-gil vanished, young Ki-seon and Ki-ok, barely past toddlerhood, resolved to do something for the infant they had hastily buried earlier that day. They retrieved the small body, still wrapped in cloth, and placed it in a small bamboo basket they had brought from home. Then, they tucked the basket deep into a pine grove on the hillside near the *Gyeongho River* and covered it with small, gentle stones. Kneeling before it, they prayed for the soul of the lost child. At the bottom of the basket that held the body lay a portrait of Jesus.

The North Korean People's Army despised paintings of Jesus and the Virgin Mary, Bibles, and rosaries. They saw these symbols of faith as enemies to be destroyed. When news came that the People's Army would be entering the house, Ki-ok and Ki-seon had preemptively taken down the portrait of Jesus hanging in Bok-hee's room. They carefully wrapped it in paper and buried it in a field. Once the North Korean soldiers retreated, Ki-seon retrieved the frame, but sent it away with the remains of the young life. 'From now on, I will be able to sleep well without that portrait of

Jesus,' she thought to herself.

Nam-gil's family did not go to Busan, as she had said. The following year, news reached Sancheong that Jin-young had married an older doctor from North Korea. Her wedding took place in Seoul. When Ki-seon and Ki-ok heard about Jin-young's marriage from Bok-hee, they remarked with a bitter smile, "Even if a woman's past is a bit complicated, if she has a pretty face, her flaws will be overlooked."

Many years later, during a reunion at Sancheong Elementary School, Bok-hee heard something intriguing from an old friend of Jin-young. That friend had stayed in touch with Jin-young throughout her life, and one day, she asked her, "Jin-young, were you happy in your marriage?"

In response, Jin-young said, "I don't know. If being married or living together for a long time allowed one to have such thoughts, how wonderful that would be... The person I loved the most was a soldier named Kim, who came from the far north. Military uniforms are quite striking."

14

The Footprints of Destiny

1950 – 1952: Seoul, Jinju, and Sancheong
—Children of the New House

Born in 1930, Choi Joon-seop was a son who lingered only on the edge of the barrier erected by his father, Hong-seon. What made him so afraid to step out from under Hong-seon's shadow? Perhaps it was the presence of his three much older brothers, men old enough to be called fathers by his friends.

He deeply envied his *Nuna* (elder sister), who could call Hong-seon "Father" without hesitation. To be honest, Joon-seop never had the courage to call Hong-seon "Father." To him, Hong-seon was always an observer, someone who stood aloof and detached, meticulously scrutinizing his every action and word. Hong-seon was a daunting figure, a towering presence that influenced everything.

Peeling away the layers of his fear, Joon-seop came to understand, albeit slowly, that his trepidation stemmed from his own perceived weakness. It took him fifteen years to come to terms with this frailty. The mere mention of the word "Father" instilled a profound and overwhelming dread in Joon-seop. The powerful often erect impenetrable barriers to maintain their control over those who are keenly aware of their power. Such impenetrability provides a sense of security that prevents others from easily challenging or even perceiving their true might.

As time passes, the children grow older and begin to scrutinize their father's every action and word. They reflect not only on how he treated Joon-seop but also on how he interacted with their brothers, sisters, and mothers. Even his most subtle gestures and facial expressions are dissected in an attempt to uncover some deeper meaning. What is it that the children seek from their father?

Joon-seop had another intimidating presence in his life besides Hong-seon: Ki-hoon of the Big House, who lived with them like family. Ki-hoon, though only a year older than Joon-seop, was a source of great difficulty and discomfort. He revealed no vulnerabilities to anyone in the New Household.

Ki-hoon called Joon-seop "*Aje*" (a dialect of Gyeongnam province for uncle) in front of others. Joon-seop often sensed a hint of irony in Ki-hoon's use of the term. Ki-hoon also referred to Joon-seop's elder sisters, Ki-soon and Jeong-soon, as "Aunt," but the word felt hollow, ringing empty like a vessel. What significance did these terms of address and degrees of kinship hold?

Only Joon-seop felt the heartache. He thought,

Even my father cannot be easily called "Father!" This isn't the Joseon Dynasty, so why do I feel so distant from the man who is my father? And yet, I am not the child of a concubine.

When Joon-seop was in the first year of middle school, Ki-hoon, who attended the same school, was already celebrated as a brilliant student among the upper grades, particularly excelling in math and English. In contrast, Joon-seop only ranked 10th in his class.

During a vacation in Sancheong, Joon-seop had to present his report card to Hong-seon. That day, he hesitated, unable to hand it over immediately. Observing Joon-seop's reluctance, Hong-seon remarked,

"Joon-scop, don't aim too high. Everyone has their own place. You just need to keep up with others."

To Joon-seop, this sounded like, 'Even though you're my son, I don't have high expectations for you. Ki-hoon is enough for me.' It seemed clear that Hong-seon did not expect much from Joon-seop. Or perhaps he meant, 'I already know your limitations, so don't overreach?' It was ambiguous whether these words were meant to console Joon-seop.

Hong-seon used to play joyfully with the neighborhood children until Il-seop passed away, as Bok-hee (his elder brother's wife, *Hyeongsu*) told Joon-seop. Hong-seon would engage in Korean hopscotch

(*Ttang-ttamukgi*), read books, and share old tales with the local children. After playtime, he would distribute honey snacks and large, eyeball-shaped candies. Joon-seop also enjoyed a few delightful moments with Hong-seon, alongside his nephews from the Big House. They would play together and then retreat to Hong-seon's room to savor the delicious treats he offered.

His father, Hong-seon, embodied the spirit of *Jayu* (In Chinese characters, it means "a little child," and in Korean, "Jayu" translates to "Freedom" in English.), which was also his childhood name. He was a man without barriers. In the spring, he ran through fields with children, picking herbs and flowers. In the summer, they caught carp and mandarin fish, sharing them raw in a spicy fish stew. Autumn saw them catching locusts, which, when fried in oil and sprinkled with salt, made a delicious side dish.

Hong-seon valued fairness above all. He disliked measuring how much each person received in comparison to others, trusting instead in his own sense of equitable distribution, which he arrived at through careful consideration. When Hong-seon gave an additional brewery to Lee-seop, it was because Lee-seop's wife's family was struggling financially. It was also said that Hong-seon did so because Nam-gil, who would become Lee-seop's wife, was pregnant before marriage.

Yet, why did Hong-seon place all the family's expectations on Ki-hoon, Il-seop's son, his grandson? Ki-soon, Joon-seop's eldest sister, also had excellent grades, but was that why? And why did he transfer nearly all his wealth to Ki-hoon when Ki-hoon was only in his mid-teens?

Joon-seop often wondered, 'What about me? I am undeniably his son, too. Why doesn't he have any expectations for me?' It was profoundly sad and disheartening, even for a child, to feel that his father had no expectations for him.

It wasn't just about Hong-seon's legacy; it was about the paternal love that Joon-seop felt was not fairly distributed. At least that was how it seemed to Joon-seop. When Joon-seop was consumed by such thoughts, he descended into a miserable abyss, so deep that he sometimes wished to die.

In 1945, was it possible that Hong-seon had placed higher expectations on Ki-hoon due to the pain caused by Il-seop? Il-seop had suddenly stopped breathing right in front of Hong-seon. Was Hong-seon's fatherly guilt driving him to place all his hopes on his grandson Ki-hoon? Or perhaps Hong-seon had already been wounded deeply by Il-seop, and to protect himself from further pain caused by any of his children, he chose to remain a distant observer.

Joon-seop thought, 'Ah, that's it. Hong-seon is merely watching from afar to avoid being hurt again by his children. Even I... So, even Father Hong-seon has a vulnerable side, just like me...' However, one day, something happened that momentarily lifted Joon-seop from his dark and consuming thoughts.

It was during the summer vacation of his second year of middle school when he returned to Sancheong. As he walked past the narrow, winding alleyway of his neighborhood, he saw the local children engrossed in a game of *ttang-ttamukgi*, or land-grabbing. They had marked the ground with faint lines using crumbling stones, delineating their territories. Along these lines, they stood up small boundary stones. Each child, armed with a stick, took turns hitting a solid pebble, aiming to knock down the boundary stones perched along the drawn lines. If a boundary stone was hit and toppled, they measured the distance it moved. The area from the original line to the fallen boundary stone was claimed, and new boundary lines were drawn to expand their territory. This was the essence of *ttang-ttamukgi*, the game of conquering land.

As Joon-seop passed by, unaware, one of the children swung a stick. A pebble and the stick slipped from the child's hand and flew towards him simultaneously. The pebble struck his forehead. The stick, with two pointed nails embedded in it, tore the skin off his brow as it passed by. Blood streamed down his face from the corner of his eye. Fortunately, he did not lose his sight.

When Hong-seon saw Joon-seop entering the house bleeding, he rushed out of the yard in alarm. He quickly carried Joon-seop on his back and ran to the nearby clinic, which was visible from the intersection. This clinic, run by a doctor from Jinju, had been in operation for some time, ever since the Japanese left.

Bursting into the consulting room, Hong-seon carefully laid Joon-seop down on the examination table.

Hong-seon said,

"Hello, Dr. Kim, please take care of my son. He was just passing by some children playing in the alley, and I think a nail embedded in a stick tore the skin around his eye. He hasn't said much, even though he's bleeding heavily... Please examine him carefully. He's a quiet and well-behaved boy."

Hearing these words, Joon-seop was astonished at Hong-seon's assessment, which was entirely different from what he had imagined. He exclaimed to himself, 'Wow! My father called me his quiet and patient son...' Hong-seon held Joon-seop's hand tightly as the doctor stitched the wound and the pain began to subside. Hong-seon's hands were as steady as a warm blanket, enveloping Joon-seop's small hands and gripping them firmly. At that moment, Joon-seop thought with childlike innocence, 'How I wish I could be injured like this every day just to be cared for by Hong-seon!'

That wasn't the only significant event that year.

As the wound on his brow healed, another incident occurred. Toward the end of summer vacation, Joon-seop and his neighborhood friends went to the *Gyeongho River* to catch freshwater fish and swim. The previous day's heavy rain had made the current swift and the conditions unsafe for swimming. Despite this, Joon-seop felt an inexplicable urge to plunge into the river and swim.

As he frolicked in the water with his peers, splashing and playing, Joon-seop's face suddenly flushed, and he began to gasp for breath.

"Oh no! I think someone is pulling my legs! Guys, hold me!" he exclaimed.

In an instant, Joon-seop was floundering, struggling against the pull of the water. Shouts erupted from the children and adults nearby. As Joon-seop was pulled deeper into the swirling current, he drifted farther and farther from the onlookers. He kicked and thrashed with all his might, desperate to stay afloat.

Just then, he heard someone plunge into the river with a resounding splash. Moments later, Hong-seon wrapped his arm tightly around Joon-seop's neck and cut through the current. The person who had dived into the water was Joon-seop's father, Hong-seon.

Earlier that day, Hong-seon had been inspecting the dikes around his fields nearby and had decided to cool off with a swim in the river. Initially, he had no idea who was being swept away, but he instinctively dove into the water to save the person. As he pulled the person to safety, he saw his son's familiar face and hair and realized it was Joon-seop.

People in the neighborhood remarked that Hong-seon seemed even more shocked than Joon-seop himself. Was this the nature of a father-son relationship?

The precise timing of it all! It must have been perfect timing, guided by fate.

After those incidents, Joon-seop decided to let go of his negative thoughts about Hong-seon. That summer, during those two crises, Joon-seop glimpsed the hidden depths of Hong-seon's heart. From then on, he was no longer afraid when passing by Hong-seon's room. 'No matter what my father, Hong-seon, thinks of me, *he is good and understands self-sacrifice. I am truly proud that he is my father*,' Joon-seop thought, clenching his fist in determination.

Joon-seop's heart swelled with pride simply from living with a man like Hong-seon. He felt joy in being Hong-seon's son and no longer envied his nephews in the Big House, where Bok-hee lived. He decided to dedicate himself to becoming a good farmer and to protecting the land of

Sancheong, the land of Choi Hong-seon. This was a decision Joon-seop made at the age of 15.

In both the New House and the Big House, where the children were growing up, small events occurred almost daily. The troublemaker was Ki-hwi, who was one year younger than Joon-seop. Ki-hwi, the second son of Bok-hee, was a handful who never gave his mother a moment's rest.

Ki-hwi was exceptionally tall for his age and received many love letters from girls because of his mature demeanor. By the time he entered middle school, he was already 176 centimeters tall, with a well-defined nose and Western features, making him the envy of local girls.

Joon-seop attended middle school in Jinju while Ki-hwi went to school in Sancheong. During vacations, Ki-hwi would gather local boys to regale them with stories about girls, becoming the center of attention. He was indifferent to the age of the girls he dated, sometimes exchanging love letters with older high school girls, and at other times with younger students.

Despite his flamboyant personality, Ki-hwi understood Joon-seop's shy nature better than anyone else.

Ki-hwi said,

"Joon-seop, *Aje*, do you think that just because these girls are in elementary school, they don't know anything? Some girls might be a bit forward, while others are very innocent. But no matter what, they're all girls, and there's a way to handle each of them. Their age doesn't really matter; you just have to see them all as women.

There's one important rule when dealing with women. If you know this, you're set.

I call it *the law of action and reaction*. If a girl gives me a certain response, I must give a corresponding reaction to move things forward. Girls never say outright whether they like something or not, just like you... So, if a girl happens to brush her hand against mine, I must either grip her hand firmly or gently pinch and twist the back of her hand. That's absolutely necessary.

Aje, have you ever given any kind of reaction like that? That's why girls don't flock to you. When you understand it, it's simple. It's essential to have an exchange of actions and reactions. Like I always say, it doesn't matter if a woman is young or old; she's still a woman."

Joon-seop was vastly different from Ki-hwi. He couldn't keep up. Even in high school, let alone middle school, Joon-seop had never managed to speak to a girl. Occasionally, on the way to school or while passing through the streets, there was a schoolgirl he would encounter and exchange glances with a few times, their faces becoming familiar over time. Yet, Joon-seop never knew what to say or how to approach her. He couldn't even make proper eye contact.

His middle and high school years slipped away as he simply watched and waited, unable to muster the courage to speak.

Women were scarce at S Agricultural College in Suwon, where Joon-seop enrolled. Having only spoken to his sisters, Joon-seop sometimes thought there was something abnormal about him. Despite his efforts, he couldn't find a way to change this. Ki-hwi, seemingly aware of this, continued to tease Joon-seop even through letters.

May 13, 1950
From the Flower Garden of Jinju

Dear Joon-seop,
Aje,
It's Ki-hwi writing to you. Although we're both majoring in agriculture, I'm in Jinju, and you're in Suwon. How have you been? I'm adjusting well here. If you come to Sancheong this summer, I'll tell you all about how many girls I've won over in Jinju.

By the way, I want to remind you of what I've been teaching you. It's a shame you haven't realized how exciting college life is.

Do you remember? The law of action and reaction—such things should be learned as soon as possible! Missing out on this is a shame.

Dating or passion—if you can't do that, you are abnormal without a doubt. Maybe romance just isn't your thing?

I'm just joking. Don't take it too seriously. Life isn't that complicated. Isn't it best to just have fun? Isn't that why men and women exist?

Wishing you joy and fun,
Your ever-cheerful nephew, Ki-hwi

Ki-hwi sent this letter along with a picture of himself and a woman. When Joon-seop saw it, he chuckled and pushed the picture and the letter into his desk drawer. He then thought of his mother. She was much younger than his father, Hong-seon, and very beautiful, but she rarely spoke. Was she always so quiet, even before he was born? Joon-seop could never tell what his mother was thinking. When Joon-seop looked at Hong-seon and his mother, he often thought, 'Women, men, marriage ... such things are meaningless. Just look at my father and mother.' This belief had been with him since he was young.

However, after that summer day in middle school, he began to realize where his own problems lay. It was neither his father, Hong-seon, nor his mother, Hwang, who had no expectations for relationships—it was Joon-seop himself.

Joon-seop discovered that the deeper he dug into himself, the more emptiness he found. 'Yeah, like Ki-hwi said, maybe life isn't such a big deal. I should try to think less. My problem is a life without action and reaction. After this semester, when I go to Sancheong for vacation, I will try to find myself. As a college student, I won't concern myself with kids like my eldest nephew Ki-hoon and Ki-hwi. I'm going to be myself.

I mean ... there's a girl who was in my third-grade class at Sancheong Elementary School. I'll ask her out and take her to a tea shop. I'll try to hold her hand. I'll use the law of action and reaction, too. But ... what if she already has someone she likes? Should I just forget about it? No, I'll find out what's going on...

Wow! Choi Joon-seop, you've improved a lot.'

Joon-seop would sometimes get caught up in his own fantasies. He would say to himself,

"The right girl for me would be someone from my hometown rather than a Seoul girl with her refined speech and appearance."

While Joon-seop was in Suwon, his so-called sleep paralysis dreams became less frequent than in his childhood. When the exams were over at the end of the semester, Joon-seop was determined to return to Sancheong with a new attitude. He especially needed to find a woman for himself. He knew he needed to prepare for navigating relationships, even if it meant reading more novels about dating. Just thinking about it made Joon-seop excited every day.

As the end-of-term exams approached, Joon-seop was about to head home after taking several tests. The commotion outside prompted him to turn on the radio. People running past his boarding house shouted in alarm:

"The Han River bridge in Seoul has collapsed!"

Fearful of what awaited outside, Joon-seop confined himself to his room for several days. It was only after the boarding house had emptied out that he finally mustered the courage to join the mass exodus. Seeking refuge, he remembered a temple in the mountains on the outskirts of Suwon, a place he had visited a few times with friends from his department. There, he spent nearly a month in seclusion.

On his journey from the temple to Sancheong, Joon-seop experienced hunger and hardship like never before. Still, Joon-seop was lucky to blend in with other refugees as he walked from Suwon toward his home in Sancheong. Although he lost his way at times, he managed to hitch a ride on a truck twice and eventually made it back home. As soon as he arrived, Joon-seop buried his face in Lady Hwang's chest and wept for a long time. In his mother's arms, he felt the warmth and comfort of a mother's embrace.

When the day dawned, Joon-seop resolved to find the woman he had seen on the rattling truck the night before. Though she wasn't in his third-grade class, she seemed receptive to him. Despite the heat and dust, she maintained her elegance. 'Now, I, Choi Joon-seop, will go to Chahwang to find that woman,' Joon-seop muttered to himself.

He remembered that when Joon-seop got motion sickness from the long truck ride, she comforted him. He had barely eaten for days, and when he vomited bile onto her skirt, she didn't flinch. If no one else had been there, Joon-seop might have buried his face in the folds of her skirt. She didn't show any discomfort; among the crowded passengers, she simply looked at him with pity. Joon-seop thought her expression was very similar to that of his mother, Hwang.

Joon-seop came home, washed up, and took care of a few things, realizing it was already past lunchtime. He couldn't wait any longer. He just wanted to see her face, to know she was okay. He noticed Lady Hwang and Bok-hee discussing something, but his desire to visit her before nightfall was overwhelming.

Joon-seop felt an unusual buoyancy in his heart and body. He bid a brief farewell to his mother and Bok-hee, his sister-in-law, and hurried toward the gate, his steps unusually brisk. For days, airplanes had been soaring overhead with a shrill whine, and sporadic bursts of loud explosions sent plumes of smoke skyward. The drone of the planes, which he had heard incessantly while fleeing, seemed especially grating today.

As Joon-seop crossed the yard and approached the gate, a deafening roar erupted above, and the earth and buildings around him trembled with a tremendous crash. His body, as light as a feather, was hurled skyward.

It was a late summer day in 1950.

When Jeong-soon was around four years old, she noticed something while sitting on her father's lap: her father looked much older than her mother, a very beautiful woman. Her mother, calling Hong-seon "*Yeobo,*" would say to them, "Hey, Jeong-soon, Ki-soon, you should say hello to your father. Now, say, 'Father, did you sleep well? Good morning.'" From the age of two, when Ki-soon and Jeong-soon took their first steps, they would come out to the *daecheong-maru* in the morning and greet Hong-seon, who was already seated there.

When their youngest sister, Young-soon, was born, Hong-seon was 60 years old. Young-soon started talking and doing everything later than her peers. Like her brother Joon-seop, Young-soon constantly felt intimidated and uneasy around her nieces and nephews, Bok-hee's children. She was always careful, watching their every move.

At that time, Hong-seon bought expensive Japanese toy tea sets, beautiful Western-style dresses adorned with lace, and leather sandals for Ki-soon and Jeong-soon. Hong-seon would laugh heartily as he lifted his eldest daughter, Ki-soon, over his head, making her perform cute antics. He adored her older sister, Ki-soon, immensely and wore the same affectionate expression for Jeong-soon as well. For a time, Ki-soon and Jeong-soon believed that the only inhabitants of their world were they, their father Hong-seon, and their mother.

One day, however, they discovered that their father had another family. Despite this revelation, they never felt a change in Hong-seon's affection for them. He would often say things like:

"Ki-soon, Jeong-soon, if girls are capable, they can go out into society, work, and become anything. However, nothing is more valuable than a woman marrying well. Look at the *Joseon* Dynasty. When a virtuous woman becomes a queen, she supports her family for generations. Still, I often think about how difficult it must have been for a woman to be a queen. Of course, nowadays, even if you wanted to be a queen, you couldn't.

A woman is happiest when she is loved by her husband. Even if you become judges or prosecutors, the work will be difficult and demanding. When can a woman in such a position properly care for her children and greet her husband warmly?

So, you should focus on your studies first. I'll pay for your tuition, so don't worry about what you will do in the future."

Everyone in the Choi family knew that Hong-seon had lost much of his vigor after the death of Il-seop, the eldest son of the Big House. It may have been to avoid disappointing their mother, Hwang, that Hong-seon said such things to his daughters. He paid for his daughters' tuition but did not seem to have high expectations for them. After Il-seop's death, it was quite evident that he tried to marry off his older daughter, Ki-soon, to the son of the county governor, perhaps to fill the void in his heart.

Jeong-soon knew that Ki-soon had never been interested in marriage. Her attempt to comfort Hong-seon may have worked to some extent. It was painful to think of the humiliation Ki-soon had suffered after breaking off her engagement with the seemingly handsome and idle son of the county governor. No one could have predicted that Jong-cheol would continually harass Ki-soon.

Perhaps it was because of Ki-soon's situation, but Hong-seon had yet to mention anything about marriage to Jeong-soon. Or perhaps he was still undecided. It remained to be seen whether, after finishing her final semester and returning home for summer break, Jeong-soon would hear anything about marriage from Hong-seon.

'Oh, I can't believe I've already finished my two-year college course,' Jeong-soon thought, thinking about how time had passed. In fact, Jeong-soon had only told her mother, Hwang, that she had taken a leave of absence from school twice.

Jeong-soon was 22 years old, but when she closed her eyes, her childhood memories were vivid.

How much Hong-seon had loved and cherished Jeong-soon and Ki-soon! However, discovering that Hong-seon had another family was like a bolt of lightning out of the blue. Ki-soon pretended to be more surprised, but Jeong-soon believed Ki-soon had known all along. Ki-soon was at least more sensitive and intelligent than she was.

Their goal was not only to leave the Big House family but also to leave Sancheong naturally. When Jeong-soon went to Jinju, Bok-hee's daughters pouted and said, "Thanks to the care and interest of her aunt, the principal, Aunt Jeong-soon was able to enter Jinju Girls' High School just like that."

However, Principal Hwang, their aunt, was not the type of person to show favoritism. Jeong-soon and Ki-soon had taken the entrance exam on their own merit, and there was nothing improper about their admission. Jeong-soon had wanted to stay at her aunt's house while attending school, but her aunt opposed it, saying it might give other students a bad impression. Jeong-soon knew her aunt was being considerate, helping her find a boarding house and securing a good teacher for her at the start of a new school year. Bok-hee's daughters completed middle school in Sacheon or in Sancheong. Ki-jeong, the eldest daughter, seemed eager to get married. She had a fondness for her elementary school teacher, or so it seemed.

Jeong-soon took after her father, Hong-seon, with large Western-like eyes and a slightly prominent nose. While she didn't dislike her figure or appearance, she wasn't entirely satisfied with it either. By contrast, her elder sister, Ki-soon, took after their mother, Hwang, with her classic round face, a delicate and feminine nose, and large, expressive eyes.

All of Hong-seon's children inherited his curly hair. Among them, Joon-seop had the curliest locks, while Jeong-soon often despised her own curls for their untidy appearance. Ki-soon, on the other hand, had the least noticeable curls. Jeong-soon always felt that her eldest sister, Ki-soon, had a unique beauty that was rare.

Since entering high school, Jeong-soon had wanted to resume her childhood piano lessons. However, she kept postponing it until, upon entering university, she resolved to use her own earnings to pursue her passion. The University she attended was affectionately dubbed "The Field of Reeds" by her friends, but it was actually a well-regarded women's college in Korea.

Fortunately, she befriended a music major who also resided in the same boarding house. This acquaintance proved invaluable, as Jeong-soon was able to advance to an intermediate level of piano under her tutelage, and the lessons were quite affordable. Though their relationship began as a teacher-student relationship, it quickly evolved, and they became inseparable companions, spending nearly every day together.

Jeong-soon initially sought piano lessons to find a sense of inner calm. The act of synchronizing melody and rhythm offered her a small but significant solace, helping her momentarily forget her loneliness. As Jeong-soon spent more time with her piano tutor, she found herself increasingly reluctant to return home to Sancheong. The looming prospect of marriage discussions filled her with dread. To buy herself more time, she wrote a month before graduation to her father, Hong-seon, and her mother, expressing her desire to see more of the world and remain in Seoul until she received her teaching assignment.

"Until I am appointed a schoolteacher, I wish to see more of the world and stay longer in Seoul before returning to Sancheong," she wrote.

Thus, after completing her studies, Jeong-soon remained in Seoul, her heart lightened by the newfound freedom. Jeong-soon's close friend, a piano major named Shin Soo-jeong, had become her inseparable companion. Though they didn't do anything particularly productive, they spent their days idly wandering with other girls, reveling in their youth.

One day, Soo-jeong arranged a meeting with some men she knew, setting it for June 25, 1950. It was the day the national military lifted its emergency alert, allowing over a third of the troops to leave their barracks.

Filled with excitement, the girls stayed up late into the night, their conversations blooming like flowers. They spoke passionately about Korean literature and the fascinating yet tragic lives of contemporary female artists. Their hearts raced with anticipation, and sleep eluded them.

However, at dawn, chaos erupted throughout Seoul, shattering the serenity of their plans. The sounds of gunfire, cannons, and blaring horns grew louder, piercing the early morning stillness. People poured out of their homes in a frenzy, moving from house to house in a state of panic. Radios were switched on, but they offered little solace, repeating the same plea: "Fellow citizens, remain calm and stay indoors..."

After spending a night of uncertainty, Jeong-soon and Soo-jeong faced a crucial decision: should they stay in Seoul or flee together? They chose the latter, realizing that delay could be perilous.

Embarking on their harrowing journey, Jeong-soon followed Soo-jeong's advice and smeared black shoe polish on her face. Despite the oppressive summer heat, she dressed in multiple layers and wrapped her head in a black cloth. The peculiarity of Soo-jeong's plan astonished Jeong-soon, but she complied. They traveled primarily by night, navigating mountain paths in their shabby, dark attire.

Fortune favored them as they joined a procession of refugees.

Soo-jeong, demonstrating remarkable leadership, led the way and kept the children close. Initially, Jeong-soon perceived Soo-jeong merely as a piano major, but she soon realized her friend possessed a multitude of talents. Trusting Soo-jeong's instincts, Jeong-soon followed her lead. Soo-jeong was no ordinary woman.

They encountered several other groups of refugees along the way, yet managed to continue their journey. About 25 days after leaving Seoul, they finally reached Yongam-ri in the Jinju region, Soo-jeong's hometown. Their timely arrival in the mountain village, so early in the war, seemed either a stroke of luck or divine intervention.

It turned out that Soo-jeong's father was one of the resilient mountain men who roamed all over Korea during the Japanese occupation. As soon as Korea was liberated from Japan, Soo-jeong's father became one of the mountain men who wandered tirelessly in search of the iron stakes that the Japanese had driven into Korea's land in an attempt to sever its spiritual energy. Had Soo-jeong inherited this legacy of resilience and defiance?

From an early age, Soo-jeong's father regularly took her with him on his mountain expeditions, determined to raise his only daughter to be strong and resilient. This upbringing endowed Soo-jeong with survival skills and a keen sense of direction that far surpassed Jeong-soon's. Observing Soo-jeong, Jeong-soon marveled, 'I didn't know a girl could be this strong and quick,' and became acutely aware of her own ignorance and incompetence.

During the war, nearly all women who walked the streets were at risk of rape or death at the hands of the People's Army. In times of national turmoil, women's bodies and dignity were the first to be violated.

Yongam-ri, however, was a safe haven for Soo-jeong, her childhood home nestled deep in the mountains. In this remote village, Soo-jeong and Jeong-soon gathered the local girls after dinner, teaching them songs and *Hangul* (the Korean alphabet). Isolated and surrounded by mountains, Yongam-ri saw little traffic. Yet, the villagers remained uneasy, listening to the scratchy radio broadcasts each day. The countryside was so remote that no sounds of gunfire reached them.

Occasionally, people who had fled returned to the village, recounting the horrors of war. As Jeong-soon listened to these tales and the radio reports, she became more immersed in village life. Each night, after dinner and chores, the girls would sneak out to Soo-jeong's grandmother's house to spend time together.

In every home, including Soo-jeong's, windows and entrances were covered with blankets or straw bags to conceal even the faintest light from kerosene lamps. Even the faintest flicker of an oil lamp could catch someone's eye. Huddled together with their feet tucked under a large quilt spread out on the floor, eight or nine of them sang softly. Jeong-soon marveled at how a simple verse could forge such a powerful bond among them and the village girls.

During the day, they taught *Hangul* to the girls who had never learned it. Whenever they were able to find a novel, Jeong-soon and Soo-jeong would take turns reading it aloud.

Over the course of three months, Jeong-soon discovered "A Sense of Reward and Happiness" she had never known before. She felt deeply grateful to Soo-jeong. When the war ended, Jeong-soon resolved to return to Seoul, determined to find work and fulfill her dream of becoming a teacher. But Sancheong was not where she belonged. It was a place she shouldn't return to.

Until now, Jeong-soon had relied solely on the money sent by Hong-seon. She felt painfully dependent compared to Soo-jeong. She realized that financial independence had to come first. Until she could secure a proper teaching position in Seoul, she resolved to teach the local children at a night school.

Upon hearing that the South Korean military had recaptured Seoul, Jeong-soon returned with Soo-jeong. Seoul was in ruins, a chaotic landscape of destruction where no place was left untouched. The streets teemed with orphans, and desperate, hungry people wandered in search of food. Soon, Seoul was again occupied by Chinese and North Korean forces. During this turmoil, Jeong-soon's trust in Soo-jeong deepened, and she relied on her more than ever.

Soo-jeong and Jeong-soon found refuge among members of Soo-jeong's church and lived with them. Churches and cathedrals overflowed with orphans and people seeking food. Relief supplies from the United States and other countries began to arrive. From dawn until late at night, Jeong-soon and Soo-jeong worked tirelessly, running through the streets to distribute food and supplies.

Despite the ongoing war, several universities in Seoul temporarily relocated to Busan starting on January 4, 1951[51], forming what was known as the Wartime United University. Though Jeong-soon had already graduated, she frequently shuttled between her former university boarding house and the hospital, assisting Soo-jeong with her duties. She kept a firm grip on the money she had saved from what her father, Hong-seon, had sent.

It was difficult for the female students at S Women's University near her boarding house, as well as other female university students, to focus solely on their studies. Although they attended classes, Jeong-soon often overheard them complaining about the hardships they faced. Instead of reading books, they were burdened with procuring supplies for the wounded patients from the war hospitals.

The hospital work was relentless, with constant tasks of boiling and wrapping bloodstained bandages and linens from the injured. Jeong-soon and Soo-jeong were also involved in caring for orphans, providing meals at the church, and laundering and disinfecting bloodstained clothing and blankets from patients at the hospital. After their hospital duties, they would head to the orphanage, where there was an unending pile of diapers and children's clothes to wash. Gradually, Jeong-soon felt her strength waning.

Jeong-soon sighed, reflecting on how she had once been a shy, naïve girl from the countryside, utterly clueless about the ways of the world. Yet, by following the resilient Soo-jeong, she found it impossible to ignore the harsh realities of life in Seoul, no matter how arduous they became. She felt compelled to trail behind Soo-jeong, unable to extricate herself.

---

51) United College of War: Classes at the university, after its relocation to Busan, began on February 18, 1951. On May 4, 1951, the Special Wartime Measures for University Education was announced. Other Wartime United Universities were established in Daejeon, Jeonbuk, and Gwangju. Although plans were made to dissolve these wartime universities starting in March 1952, some students had yet to return to Seoul by March 1953. Reference: Naver Contemporary History, by the author.

In contrast, Soo-jeong navigated each day with confidence and an affable demeanor, making friends wherever she went. Jeong-soon lowered her head, acknowledging the stark differences between them. From the very beginning, it was clear that Soo-jeong possessed strength and capability far beyond her own.

Soo-jeong, who grew up without a mother, moved to Seoul when her father remarried. She possessed superior social and practical skills than Jeong-soon. Soo-jeong never seemed to pay heed to other people's opinions. Even if she had a quarrel with her stepmother, she never appeared depressed. Soo-jeong had a remarkable ability to quickly brush everything off.

It had already been more than a year since Jeong-soon had been living, moving between the church and the hospital with Soo-jeong. Over time, the daily routine began to shape her worldview. Jeong-soon came to believe that caring for orphans was a worthier endeavor than becoming a teacher. She even nurtured a new hope that, by returning to her hometown of Sancheong and seeking help from Hong-seon, she could establish a place for orphans there. She realized that Hong-seon's presence was a profound force, a guiding shadow in her once naïve thoughts.

However, this was merely her own wishful thinking.

Jeong-soon began to feel her physical and mental strength gradually diminishing due to the demanding work at the hospital. Moreover, she was exhausted by the loneliness of life in Seoul, where she was unknown and buried in work. Soo-jeong became increasingly busy with other matters, leaving her with progressively less time to spend with Jeong-soon. Eventually, Soo-jeong moved into her stepmother's house.

When Jeong-soon first arrived in Seoul to study, she found solace in the anonymity of the city, where no one knew her background nor cared about it. But as time passed, she realized that people, no matter where they live, can be selfish. The people she met in this unfamiliar city were no different except in name from those in Sancheong.

She longed for rest and comfort. Yet where could she find it? To whom could she turn?

Jeong-soon sent a letter to Ki-soon's boarding house address in Japan. However, no reply came. She speculated that Ki-soon might be trapped in the memories of her "failed marriage," or perhaps Ki-soon had moved on, forgetting the past and focusing solely on her studies and future.

The path to happiness seems difficult to find, but in reality, can I really find it in a life of struggle, where I become entangled with others for a simple purpose? Is that true?

Shall I stay in Seoul? Shall I go to Sancheong? Jeong-soon spent her days in anguish over these thoughts. One day, she bought a bottle of milk from the hospital store and drank it because she was too hungry to wait for a proper meal. Perhaps that was the cause of the sudden illness. She developed a high fever and collapsed on the hospital floor, suffering from severe diarrhea.

Her fellow church members, who were working late at the hospital, carried Jeong-soon to a hospital room. She writhed in pain throughout the night, her intestines twisting in pain, and she vomited frequently. Even in a hospital, all she had was a thin, stained blanket on the cold cement floor. As she lay there, clutching her stomach to endure the pain, she overheard people exclaiming, "*Hoyeolza*! It's *Hoyeolza*! (Cholera, as pronounced in Chinese characters). Quickly, send her to a quarantine ward outside the main hospital room!"

In the ensuing commotion, Jeong-soon was moved to a warehouse-like room designated for charity patients outside the main ward. As she lay on the cold floor, Jeong-soon's thoughts drifted to Sancheong and her mother. She remembered her mother's flushed eyes and slightly trembling hands on the day Jeong-soon packed to go to middle school in Jinju. Regardless of the reason for her studies, Jeong-soon always felt that *going to Jinju was an act of abandoning her mother. As a child and a daughter, leaving for Jinju meant leaving her mother alone to face the cold stares of those in the Big House.*

But Jeong-soon was young and longed for a brief moment of comfort. That's why she chose to go to Jinju. The same was true for Ki-soon and Joon-seop. Yet, Jeong-soon could never shake off the guilt, always wondering if she had been the greatest burden to her mother. As she struggled with persistent, severe diarrhea and a high fever, Jeong-soon found it difficult to breathe. She fainted, and when she opened her eyes, all she could see was her mother's smiling face before it faded away.

She wanted to get up from the cold hospital floor, where only a single, thin blanket lay, but she couldn't.

After Jeong-soon's death, Soo-jeong learned the news from the church members and rushed to the hospital. Although Soo-jeong and Jeong-soon had been together for several years since their first year of college, Soo-jeong knew very little about Jeong-soon's personal life. Soo-jeong hurried to the boarding house near the school where they had once stayed together.

To her relief, the door to Jeong-soon's room was locked, and no one else had moved in. The people in the adjacent room told Soo-jeong that Jeong-soon had returned just ten days ago and had slept for a while. The desk and the small closet remained untouched. The rooms that had not been destroyed by the war were now occupied by people Soo-jeong had never seen before, likely a family that had evacuated from another area. Using Jeong-soon's room key, Soo-jeong unlocked the door, entered the room, and began searching the desk drawers and looking under the closet.

Fortunately, at the bottom of the closet, Soo-jeong found two letters with addresses written on the envelopes. From their contents, it was clear they were from Jeong-soon's mother.

To my daughter,

Jeong-soon,

It's been a while since I last called your name. It has been over seven years since you left to study in another province. I remember you in your sailor suit, leaving for Jinju to attend middle and high school. Your school uniform was dark blue, tailored larger so you could wear it for several years. It feels like just yesterday that you walked out the gate with your new school bag, pouting, your big eyes ready to cry... Time flies so quickly.

Your father decided that you should stop learning the piano because he wanted your future as a woman to be smooth and stable. Please don't resent him for it. The piano is something you've been familiar with since you were young, so there will always be an opportunity for you to learn it again someday.

As soon as Ki-soon arrived in Japan, she wrote that she had found a teacher to resume her violin lessons. She mentioned that the atmosphere in Japan, defeated in the war, was very harsh for Koreans. I worry about whether she will finish her medical studies, but I pray every day that she will succeed.

Regarding the money, your father sends much more to Ki-soon than he does to you. This time, he sent you only a small amount again. Still, finding a small house on the outskirts of Seoul for you and Joon-seop to live in until he graduates doesn't seem like a bad idea... It feels like a dream. As time passes, I remember how your aunt always took such good care of you during your middle and high school years, which brought great comfort to my heart.

Jeong-soon, my second daughter, your mother, living in the countryside, doesn't know much about what Seoul is like. I want you to finish your studies in *Seoul* as soon as possible and return to *Sancheong*. I'm not sure why you took a break from school last year, but I want to trust you. However, I am very worried.

I will continue to support you until you finish school, sending money no matter what happens. I don't want anything else except for you to graduate safely, become a teacher, and be a confident woman responsible for your future in society. Please remember this always.

With love,
Your mother

October 1948

To my dear Jeong-soon,

Jeong-soon,

It has been almost three years since I last heard from you, and I worry about your prolonged stay in Seoul. However, as long as you are safe, I can endure and wait patiently.

Jeong-soon,

A few days ago, we held a funeral. Two years ago, Joon-seop passed away right in front of our house, but we were unable to find his body. Some time afterward, we found a torn piece of fabric from the clothes he had been wearing when discovered in the ashes. With that, we laid out two of Joon-seop's garments, a single shoe, and a book before holding the funeral. After postponing it again and again, we decided to finally hold it this year, fearing the sorrow would deepen if we let it pass once more. We held the ceremony after discussing it with the extended family.

However, there is something I have not yet told you, and I feel that writing it down may bring me some peace. What I am about to say might shock you. Both you and I are faithful believers in the Lord. I did it to ease the pain of remembering Joon-seop and to find some solace in my sorrow.

And, there is something I have not yet told you, and I feel that writing it down may bring me some peace. What I am about to say might shock you. Both you and I are faithful believers in the Lord. As I have mentioned several times before, I did it to ease the pain of remembering Joon-seop and to find some solace in my sorrow.

Before Joon-seop passed away, before he came to Sancheong, he met a woman he had traveled with on a truck for two days, who lived in Chahwang. We held the funeral with her, and we performed a "Soul Wedding" for them. Last winter, she passed away after the death of her mother, who had raised her alone. Although Joon-seop and the woman had not promised to marry, her maternal uncle agreed to the ceremony. Even as souls, they can meet in peace again. This was for the living, after all.

After that, I felt more at ease.

Above all, your father, Hong-seon, seems to be struggling lately. Joon-seop's death has caused him a great deal of pain. That is why we held the "Soul Wedding," yet Hong-seon didn't say anything to me.

Jeong-soon,

Why do I feel so frustrated and resentful? Who was this war for? The war broke out and took the lives of so many young people. Am I the only mother tormented every night by the memory of her son's face? Time will once again reduce their memory to a single commemorative day. We will rebuild on the land that absorbed the blood of their youth, and we will pave new paths, walking them with smiles on our faces.

Joon-seop, who vanished in his youth, will forever remain a young man in my mind. His face is eternally etched in my memory, just as it was the day he disappeared from my sight. Jeong-soon, do not worry about Sancheong. Yeong-soon is doing well, although she is not very active. Above all, take care of your health, and be sure to return to your boarding house early, before dark. Take good care of yourself.

Thinking of you always,
Your mother.

On a spring day in March of 1952.

The first letter was from several years ago when Jeong-soon was still in school. The paper had turned yellow with age, suggesting it was written before the war. The second letter seemed to have been written after the war began, during a time when Jeong-soon and Soo-jeong were spending time together. Soo-jeong, thinking about Jeong-soon's mother in Sancheong, who had already lost her son Joon-seop, was overwhelmed with emotion at the idea of her receiving the news of Jeong-soon's death as well.

However, the police insisted that the body be removed immediately from the hospital, where she had no relatives. Soo-jeong realized that it was crucial to send a telegram immediately before the body deteriorated further. Fortunately, she managed to send a telegram to the address listed in the letter just in time.

Soo-jeong was troubled by the mention of the "Soul Wedding" in Jeong-soon's mother's letter. No matter how much she thought about it, Jeong-soon had no intended partner for such a ritual.

Soo-jeong pondered, 'Soul wedding? Do souls exist? So many people have died in this war. Are their souls really wandering around here? Really? The world is so complicated. What I can see isn't everything... Yes, it's fortunate I'm a Christian who believes in God. But why did the dead have a soul wedding?'

For Soo-jeong, it was something beyond comprehension. To be alive is to breathe, and to be dead is to no longer breathe. The body of the deceased decomposes, is absorbed into the earth, and is carried away by the wind. But the idea of the dead marrying each other? The only benefit from this would be for those conducting the rituals to make money and to bring some comfort to the living.

Soo-jeong reflected on all the knowledge she had gained up to this point. Even if the body decays and disappears after death, does the spirit, the soul, continue to wander until it finds a new body to inhabit?

Soo-jeong returned to her house, wanting to forget about church and hospital work if only for a moment. Her small room felt especially cramped and stuffy that day. She lay awake for days, staring at the ceiling. The yellowish stains from rain, a cloth pendant with a pattern of white dots on black fabric, and small glass lamps dangling from the ceiling filled her vision. Soo-jeong thought of her friend, Jeong-soon.

'Was Choi Jeong-soon ever truly alive in this world?' she wondered. 'Are the ceiling and light bulbs in this room the only proof of the times Jeong-soon and I spent together, talking and smiling? Even that exists only in my memory?'

The thought weighed heavily on her mind.

15
Ki-soon's Return to Hometown
June 1952: Tokyo and Sancheong
—The Fading Memories

Rumors spread through the ravaged landscape that an armistice might soon bring an end to the relentless war. Perhaps it was the sight of so many fallen lives that spurred people into haste, marrying quickly and haphazardly amidst the ruins. In the chaos, it seemed almost rational, as if each marriage were a desperate act of defiance against their suffering.

Children born in these tumultuous times faced severe deprivation, lacking food while being crammed into tight, overcrowded spaces. Providing three meals a day—breakfast, lunch, and dinner—was a monumental challenge. Adults toiled tirelessly, scrimping and saving to raise their children. Quantity took precedence over quality, but even so, few ever felt the comfort of a full stomach.

In the wake of the U.S. military's retreat on January 4, 1951, throngs of people fled southward. Refugees from Seoul crowded into Busan and the western parts of Gyeongsangnam-do. The children's faces were perpetually streaked with dirt, their hair matted and unkempt, and rarely washed. Although the children did not eat properly, their bellies were grotesquely swollen.

An American doctor visited a hospital and published photos in American newspapers of a large basin full of roundworms and other parasites that were removed from one of these children.

Children and adults alike scavenged for chocolate and tinned food distributed by American and U.N. soldiers from the backs of trucks. To those who rarely tasted meat, a can of carrots and beef was a treasure. They longed for the elusive taste, believing it was the only sustenance capable of rekindling a glimmer of vitality in their weary souls.

Like S University, Korea's esteemed institution, Y University also established a branch near Yeongdo in Busan, a haven for war refugees. People flocked there, perhaps hoping admission would be easier than at its counterpart in Seoul.

Yet, in the rugged western mountains of Gyeongnam, remnants of North Korean soldiers who had infiltrated *Jiri Mountain*—known as partisans—occasionally surfaced in private homes. These phantom figures appeared sporadically, hiding like specters, awaiting rescue by the North Korean People's Army. Starved, they would descend upon private homes under the cover of night, stealing to survive. The locals clucked their tongues, commenting that they could only imagine how difficult their lives must have been, fighting hunger while chasing their ideology. Though the war was not yet over, people began fighting each other again, gradually being swallowed by the swamp of ideology.

As time passed, they started to defend and glorify the very instigators of the Korean War that had destroyed everyone's lives. Where there were wounds, they should have stitched up and mended the torn and broken places, but had the job been left unfinished? They tried to patch up the injuries temporarily with hasty, makeshift bandages, but this only led to a weakening of both their hearts and bodies. Outwardly, everyone seemed focused only on matters of survival.

The war was initiated by the initial invaders, driving southward from the north. Those who survived the war's onslaught turned to ideologies cloaked in seemingly appealing ideas. The North preached the unity of "one people." Yet, as these ideological garments faded, the blame shifted to the massacres of civilians during the war. The looming issue of national compensation—the South Korean government's obligation to its people—hung in the balance. How could they compensate for such unjust deaths?

The crux of the matter lay in who seized power, the ideology they championed, and the direction in which their will would steer the nation. The justice and humanity enshrined in books seemed to be turning into nothing more than useless, desiccated fossils. Hong-seon believed that the war hadn't truly ended but had merely been paused by a truce, leaving wounds to fester deeper within. The war inflicted grievous harm not only on his sons, Joon-seop and Jeong-seop, but on the essence of humanity itself. *War was a disease, an evil that corrupted the very core of true humanity.* The devastating impact was all too evident in his surroundings.

On a summer day in 1952, a telegram arrived from a Japanese university. Hong-seon realized that it was about Ki-soon.

Ki-soon, who had moved to Japan in 1947, was thriving there. She discovered that Koreans were not only viewed as former colonial subjects. She sensed that, at heart, the Japanese simply wanted to ignore and mistreat the Koreans. Her Japanese classmates seemed to scrutinize her every move, yet they never made their feelings apparent to her. Whether this was due to her living in a luxurious boarding house or her top grades in the first semester was unclear. Although some students subtly excluded her with glances, Ki-soon remained oblivious, perhaps because she paid little attention to those around her.

Ki-soon was taking violin lessons, and Masato, a chemistry major, was her fellow student. Despite sharing lessons for almost a year, Masato, the son of a local Japanese official, had never spoken to her. Their violin instructor, Professor Yonetani, taught them once a week in 40-minute sessions. Playing string instruments requires years of practice to produce a proper sound, and even after several years, progress was slow. Though tempted to quit, Ki-soon persevered with the financial support of her father, Hong-seon. Violin lessons were her only escape from academic rigor.

The first person to speak to Ki-soon was Yutaka, Professor Yonetani's son.

Yutaka, also a medical student like Ki-soon, had an older brother who had served as a Japanese fighter pilot in World War II and was now an opium addict in Hokkaido. Professor Yonetani had lost contact with his eldest son, pinning his hopes on Yutaka, whose artistic potential he believed might someday flourish despite his major in a different field.

Yutaka, however, humorously dismissed his father's aspirations. He treated Ki-soon with gentle sincerity, making her feel at ease and occasionally encouraging her to share her personal story. Yet, the responsibility that came with relationships at their age, particularly the prospect of marriage, made Ki-soon wary of Yutaka's attention.

Curious about Japanese marital customs, Ki-soon learned from her female classmates that Japanese practices were markedly different from those of *Joseon*. Japan, an island nation with relatively liberal attitudes toward sexual matters, had distinct cultural norms. For instance, due to Japan's high annual rainfall, men wore a "satba" (thigh band) to prevent their clothes from clinging to their bodies. Women, on the other hand, no longer wore underpants, instead enveloping themselves in multiple layers of cloth.

In Japan, a woman's premarital relationships were generally not scrutinized, but once married, her loyalty belonged solely to her husband. Essentially, the husband held exclusive control over both her body and mind.

This dynamic led to widespread sexual dissatisfaction among Japanese women, who typically refrained from sharing their personal grievances with others, especially with Ki-soon, a Korean international student. In this country, men held exclusive control over sexual matters. It appeared as though men only initiated intimacy with women when they themselves desired it.

As a result, women's desires were not prioritized, even if they secretly longed for intimacy. In marital relationships, it had to be the man's touch, dictated by his authority, that came first. Ki-soon overheard her female classmates confiding in one another, saying that most Japanese women found it extremely difficult to endure this waiting. Through this, she came to understand their struggle.

Ki-soon, too, was a young woman with natural desires, sometimes longing for a man's touch like other women her age. However, she did not want to pursue a relationship with a Japanese man. No matter how lonely she felt, she refused to lower her standards or engage with a man casually. She also did not wish to delve too deeply into understanding the Japanese psyche, fearing that the reality might starkly contrast with its outward appearances.

Ki-soon wanted to learn more about the institution of marriage and social customs.

Marriage, a social construct developed for the preservation of the species in a competitive society, is riddled with contradictions despite its necessity. A society's structure, shaped by its geographical conditions and resulting social climate, plays a crucial role in guiding its people. Social climate encompasses the habits and customs of individuals living in a particular land.

For instance, in regions with rugged mountains where men must hunt to sustain themselves, a husband's absence for extended periods — sometimes months—is common. In such places, the husband's relatives often step in to protect the family and may even cohabit with the wife to ensure the continuation of the family line. Here, several younger brothers might care for their elder brother's wife, treating her as part of their own household and maintaining the family lineage.

On remote islands, the climate often exerts a more profound influence than on the mainland. The island of Samoa, for instance, has historically faced frequent storms and the consequent deaths of many men. Historically, men in Samoa assumed the roles of homemakers, raising children and managing household chores, with a keen interest in their personal grooming. Conversely, women labored, harvesting seaweed from shallow waters and tending to the land. Thus, the necessity of preserving their community evolved into the institution of marriage, solidifying into a societal system.

Ki-soon immersed herself in medical texts, her primary occupation. However, her insatiable curiosity drove her to explore a wide range of books, even during her breaks. She had many questions, but it seemed a waste of time to just rest without reading a book.

One day, she stumbled upon *The Origin of the Family, Private Property, and the State*[52] by Friedrich Engels. Engels, a pivotal figure in Marxist theory, utilized extensive anthropological data from Lewis H. Morgan to examine the origins of monogamy and the oppression of women throughout human history. He divided the evolution of human history into three stages, linking the emergence of monogamous families and sexual discrimination to shifts in social production methods.

The first stage, the so-called Wildheit (primitive) era, relied on nature for economic production. The second stage, the so-called Babarei (barbarism) era, saw increased production through human efforts like farming and livestock breeding. The third stage, the so-called Zivilisation (civilization) era, experienced rapid advancements in production technology.

Through her readings, Ki-soon delved into the intricate connections among economic systems, family structures, and the societal roles of men and women, expanding her understanding far beyond the confines of her medical studies.

---

[52] Engels(Friedrich Engels, 1820-1895): One of the most influential ideologies both theoretically and practically from the late 19th to the 20th century was Marxism. Engels is considered a key figure in the theoretical systematization of this ideology. In 1845, he published *The Condition of the Working Class in England*, where he emphasized the critical role of material production in the development of history and argued, through an analysis of the capitalist economy, that class struggle is inevitable. As seen here, Engels had already independently developed the basic framework of historical materialism even before meeting Marx. In 1884, he published *The Origin of the Family, Private Property, and the State*. From the perspective of historical materialism, Engels studied primitive tribal societies to explain the transition from primitive societies to slavery. He also clarified the process of private property formation, the monogamous family structure, and the historical formation and nature of classes and the state.—This content is summarized and adapted by the author from the Naver Encyclopedia of Knowledge, Marx's The German Ideology (Commentary).

These modes of economic production gave rise to specific family structures and marriage forms essential for survival and prosperity. Engels' work outlined this evolution in four stages.

The first stage described a primitive state of Hetaerism, characterized by loosely established sexual relationships within a society focused on simple foraging. Engels referred to early forms of marriage in which unmarried men and women engaged in sexual relations. This indicated that some form of marriage had already existed, alongside the likelihood of prostitution as a means of sexual exchange outside these unions.

The second stage, characterized by the isolation of communities due to limited transportation, saw a gradual narrowing of marriage options. Consequently, incestuous relationships between parents and their children became taboo. Marriage evolved into consanguineous unions, in which sexual unions took place between biological siblings or distant cousins within the same generation.

Alternatively, punaluan marriages emerged, prohibiting sibling unions but allowing several sisters to share common husbands. In such societies, children traced their lineage exclusively through their mothers, recognizing only the maternal line.

During this era, a third form of marriage known as pairing marriages prevailed, in which a man cohabited with a woman but was allowed to have multiple partners. Women, however, were strictly monogamous during cohabitation, facing severe punishment for infidelity. Despite this, divorce was relatively uncomplicated for either party, with children and property generally inherited by the woman after divorce.

The fourth stage witnessed the privatization of property, necessitating a social structure that supported smaller family units rather than solely ethnic preservation. Monogamous marriage became predominant, granting men the right to inherit and manage property.

This period also saw the rise of pairing marriages, an intermediary form between collective marriage and monogamy, emerging alongside livestock farming and agriculture. As pairing marriages evolved, increased productivity among advanced nomadic groups led to surplus production and the formation of social classes. Men, being more active and physically stronger, dominated these surplus-producing groups, while women, constrained by pregnancy and childbirth, primarily engaged in settled agricultural production. This shift underscored the growing disparity between the genders in terms of economic and social power.

Through this exploration, Ki-soon gained insights into how economic systems and social structures shaped family and gender dynamics, broadening her understanding of the complex interplay between history, culture, and human relationships.

Accordingly, men, who accumulated surplus primarily through livestock farming, resisted the transfer of their wealth to the matriarchal clan. Previously, the surplus had been minimal and was not inherited by their direct descendants but rather by the matriarchal community. In those times, the family unit held no economic significance in terms of property transmission. The homes of women, who predominantly engaged in foraging, served as the family domicile.

However, as private property became substantial, men no longer wished to cede it to the matriarchal clan to which women belonged. They fervently desired to dissolve the communal system and pass their assets directly to their children. This shift gradually increased the demand for monogamy and led to the dissolution of clan-based communities.

Reading Engels's work, Ki-soon reflected on her hometown and the Sancheong House, her familial refuge. Memories of her father Hong-seon's home, the abode of the Choi clan of Sancheong, surfaced vividly in her mind. Regardless of Engels's assertions, if Morgan's anthropological records were not grossly distorted, they were grounded in reality, prompting Ki-soon to introspect on her own familial issues.

The book illuminated how women's status in the ruling class changed significantly with the rise of monogamy. Women could no longer enjoy equal sexual freedom with men or participate in production as community members. Their survival now hinged on giving birth to legitimate sons to inherit their husbands' property. The male ruling class exploited this dynamic, pursuing sexual freedom with enslaved women and prostitutes, a privilege denied to women.

It was crucial to note that men were not inherently stronger than women, nor were all men part of the ruling class. Strength and status varied among individuals. The generalized term "men" did not encompass all those who were characteristically strong. Ki-soon vehemently opposed the notion that even the weakest and most incompetent men should be included in the ruling class by virtue of their gender.

Through Engels's book, Ki-soon delved deeper into the historical shifts that shaped gender roles and property rights, broadening her understanding of the intricate relationship between economic systems and social structures. This knowledge further fueled her resolve to challenge the injustices entrenched in her own society.

Ki-soon returned home and opened her diary.

June 17, 1951

I, Choi Ki-soon, am the daughter of Choi Hong-seon. My biological father undeniably belonged to the male ruling class. But what did my mother, Hwang Pil-hye, mean to him? Why did she marry a man 26 years her senior, who already had Lady Kim as his mistress in the main house? Even if my mother's family's financial situation was important when she was 16, was she really trying to secure everything through marriage?

Did my mother, Hwang Pil-hye, find happiness in her marriage? Circumstances inevitably change from what they were at the beginning. But to what extent, and at what point, did my mother find happiness in her marriage?

She must have been content to see her siblings get an education.

Bok-hee *Olke* (my brother's wife) managed most of the household tasks of the main household. Since my mother didn't handle these tasks herself, she probably found no sense of fulfillment in them.

So, did my mother fail in her marriage and remain unhappy?

One day, I learned from Yoo-sang that my father gave Lady Kim the same high-quality herbal medicine twice a year as he did for my mother. Since then, could it be that my mother's feelings for my father wavered?

It is natural for the concept of marriage to change with the times. But why does my mind fear such change and struggle to fully accept it? I am definitely not the "child of a concubine," as Jong-cheol and others in the neighborhood insinuate.

Whether or not my mother is the second wife, whether Lady Kim's sons are alive or dead, I, Choi Ki-soon, have the right to live in this world with dignity. Legally, I am, of course, the legitimate daughter.

My brother Il-seop was wrong. He couldn't accept change. All he held onto was his identity as the son of Choi Hong-seon, whom I regard with pride. Regardless of how my father views me, I will study harder to exceed his expectations and surpass those he had for Il-seop.

I will become a good doctor. And I want to be happy. I want to be loved. I want to experience love. I am alive and young now.

October 6, 1951

When I realized Yutaka's sincerity toward me, I allowed myself to accept his love. This semester, I ranked first in my department. On the day the test rankings were announced, I went out with Yutaka that evening.

We visited Kanda Cathedral, which had miraculously withstood the Tokyo air raids despite being a primary target. Standing before the cathedral, I made the sign of the cross, tears streaming involuntarily down my face. Yutaka noticed this and seemed to find my Catholic faith acceptable. Yet, I couldn't shake the nagging concern that his affection for me might be influenced by my appearance.

That evening, we strolled along a narrow path beside the road, watching the trams pass by. One of the trams bore a placard that read, "Let's revive Japan's economy." Everywhere I looked, I saw women working diligently in simple outfits, commonly known as Japanese baggy pants. Their modest demeanor embodied a deep devotion to their country and families. Each day, the streets were being rebuilt from the devastation and meticulously cleaned.

In the years since World War II ended, Japan was emerging as a stronger nation. Japanese women, more diligent and resilient than the Korean women I had previously known, appeared obedient and calm on the surface. However, they were determined to instill the "right values" in their children. They made concerted efforts to remember the war and its lessons, refusing to let those memories fade easily.

Korea, formerly known as *Joseon*, seemed eager to forget many things quickly, in contrast to Japan. Even so, it appeared to cling more strongly to old customs, particularly those related to marriage. It appeared that the concept of *Jo-Gang-ji-che* (the first wife in polygamy, who endured hardship and lived with rice wine lees and rice bran, as per an anecdote from Emperor Gwangmu's era in late Han China) was still regarded as an ideal role.

I wondered how this mindset would shape Korea in the next century. How would these entrenched ideas influence the future of my society?

Ki-soon practically lived in the library, constantly envisioning the future of Korean society. She mused,

Yes, if private property inheritance is the only focus, it could become an obstacle to the broader growth of the nation's population. Only legitimate children would inherit property as recognized members of society, leaving illegitimate ones more likely to be abandoned.

Marriage often consumes people with selfish desires to secure their positions and interests. If they create insular worlds, the overall population could gradually decline. Whether children are born in or out of wedlock, such distinctions remain significant.

However, as Koreans, we must recognize the value of every life. Providing all young people born in Korea with education and vocational training opportunities could help Korean society grow stronger than others...

As Ki-soon pondered these thoughts, a sudden, inexplicable pain made her dizzy, and she collapsed onto the desk in the library. She woke up late at night in the library and headed home.

The next morning, Ki-soon woke up feeling groggy and in severe pain, as if she hadn't slept at all. She bought painkillers for her headache from a nearby pharmacy and took them throughout the day, yet her head and eyes grew dimmer, and the pain persisted. She vaguely remembered Yutaka suggesting a trip to the beach, but she couldn't recall if it was for this weekend or the following one. If Yutaka noticed her condition, he might think something was wrong with her. This worried her greatly.

She reassured herself, 'I won't let myself end up like before, spending the entire night slumped over a desk in the library.' The school exams were approaching, and the pressure was mounting. No matter what Ki-soon was doing—reading a book or walking somewhere—she couldn't shake the feeling that someone was constantly watching her. At lunch yesterday, she saw a male student approaching her from the end of the school cafeteria hallway, and it seemed as though he was charging at her with a knife.

In a panic, she pushed him away with all her strength. To her horror, she realized that the boy she had pushed so forcefully was actually a senior from her department, merely carrying a tray. Ki-soon couldn't understand why these incidents were happening to her.

With the exams over, a long vacation was approaching. Even so, she didn't want to return to Sancheong. Even with the news of Joon-seop's death and her mother's illness, Ki-soon used her exams as an excuse to avoid going. Recently, no matter how hard she tried to focus on her studies, she couldn't concentrate. Joon-seop's pained face disappearing in a flash of flame, Il-seop's angry expression, and the agonized, twisted look on his face as he took his last breath haunted her thoughts.

Why had she been at the scene of Il-seop's death that evening? Why had she witnessed his last performance, something she had no desire to see? That harrowing image lingered in her mind, haunting her at unexpected moments.

Ki-soon returned to her boarding house room and picked up her violin, playing Hong Nan-pa's *Balsam Flowers Under the Fence* over and over again.

Particularly in the second verse—'Somehow, summer has gone, and the autumn wind blows, harshly invading the beautiful blossoms, leaving them to fall. You have grown old! You look so forlorn!'—while playing this part, she felt a stinging pain, as though thick, stagnant blood were seeping out from somewhere within her shoulder.

As she had done for some time, after playing the violin, Ki-soon would listen to the records her mother had sent from Korea. One of them was Yoon Sim-deok's *Praise of Death*, which featured Korean lyrics set to Johann Strauss's *Waves of the Danube*, a haunting and melancholic song that had resonated with young people from 1926 through the 1950s, reflecting the somber mood of the post-war era.

But at that moment, without even realizing it, Ki-soon, who had hardly ever sung before, began to sing along loudly. The melody flowed naturally from her.

The real circumstances of Yoon Sim-deok, the Korean singer, and her lover, Kim Woo-jin, didn't matter at all. What lingered in Ki-soon's heart was a sense of envy toward their decision to end their lives on the same day, at the same time. She admired their boldness, their courage to live and die on their own terms.

Listening to Yoon Sim-deok's record, Ki-soon found herself singing loudly, as if she had become Yoon Sim-deok. She couldn't control herself. Her voice was so loud that the girl in the neighboring room peeked through the crack of her door in surprise. Soon, everyone in the boarding house gathered outside Ki-soon's room.

She collapsed onto the floor, her face pressed against the ground, muttering the lyrics.

Suicide requires courage, but on the other hand, it's a very selfish choice, Ki-soon mused while lying in the hospital room. At times, she simply wanted to know if her presence in this world was wanted. What a childish and naive thought!

Whenever she dwelt on this, tears flowed freely, day and night. She recalled a night in 1947, just before leaving Sancheong, when she had asked her mother, Hwang, a poignant question.

Ki-soon:

"Mother, if I go to Japan, I might not be able to come back for years. Even then, please don't blame me. I want to finish my studies."

Mother (Lady Hwang):

"My dear, whether you never return or cannot make it back halfway, this mother believes it is your destiny. But the life you have been given ... once you are in this world, be sure to question yourself and reflect upon it. If you have come into this world, live as you wish, and return to God's arms ... this mother has no greater wish. You are precious. Blood is blood, and bone is bone! They say that when the skin is cut, blood flows, but it is the bone that truly aches."

Ki-soon was always struck by her mother's words about blood and bone. When people speak of family or lineage, they typically refer to blood —its flow and continuity. But what did her mother mean by the connection between blood and bone?

Her mother's words about blood and bone lingered in her mind, a riddle she couldn't solve. Blood is visible; it flows, it spills when the skin is cut. But bone—bone is hidden beneath; it supports, it endures the pain.

What did her mother mean by this connection? As Ki-soon pondered these questions, she grappled with her place in the world and the deep-seated pain within her.

These days, Ki-soon often found herself standing in front of people, rambling incoherently as if lost in her own thoughts. At times, she realized that she had no recollection of what she had been talking about.

Ki-soon was discharged from the hospital and returned to the boarding house. Her brother, Jeong-seop, visited her there, much to her surprise.

Jeong-seop:

"Dear sister, we must head to Shimonoseki soon and catch a boat to Busan. Let's start packing."

Ki-soon:

"Brother, do we have to leave for Sancheong right after you arrive? I've been feeling a bit unwell lately ... I would like to inform my professors of my situation and say goodbye to them first."

Jeong-seop:

"Sister, there's no need. Your department at school sent a telegram to Korea. Stepmother asked me to come here to bring you back. You can go to Sancheong first, regain your health, and then return to continue your studies. Nihon Medical School values you, even though you are a female student from *Joseon*..." Jeong-seop trailed off.

The hospital had diagnosed Ki-soon with severe anxiety. She had sensed something was wrong and hadn't inquired about the specifics of her condition.

Now, looking at Jeong-seop, she felt a deep longing to go home. Whether it was Sancheong or anywhere else, she needed rest. It was ironic that the Sancheong house, the place she had wanted to avoid, was now the place she longed for... Ki-soon nodded to Jeong-seop, indicating her understanding. *But what about Yutaka? I promised to meet him,* she thought, shaking her head to clear her thoughts. Her memories felt as if they had vanished.

The next morning, she took Jeong-seop's hand, left the boarding house, and followed him.

As the ship sailed through the current, Ki-soon watched the white foam trailing behind.

If time flows like that and reaches its end, where will I be? she wondered, yearning to know her final destination.

Jeong-seop:

"Jeong-soon passed away in a hospital about two months ago after contracting *Hoyeolja* (cholera). I went to Seoul with Uncle Hong-man to bring her body back. Stepmother asked that we keep it a secret from you."

Ki-soon listened to Jeong-seop, struggling to comprehend. The only thing that resonated was her younger sister Jeong-soon's name. It felt as though a long time had passed since they had boarded the ship.

In a low voice, Ki-soon murmured,

"What am I seeking to reclaim by returning to the Sancheong home I abandoned? What remains of me now?"

But Ki-soon felt powerless. Her mouth refused to open; her teeth chattered, and her hands clenched involuntarily. She collapsed on the wind-swept deck of the bow.

Jeong-seop found her, gently lifting her onto his back. He carried her to the lower deck of the boat and laid her down carefully.

16
Freeloading

Autumn 1952: Busan and Sancheong
—The Family of Min-ja

Standing in Front of the Gate (Crayon Art on Kent paper, 364x515m)

In the late summer of 1950, after that day, the Saemmy House vanished without a trace. When Min-ja's home was reduced to ashes, her family was left without a place to stay. For a while, Jeong-seop stayed at the Big House, but he knew he couldn't stay there forever. During his time there, he ended up bearing Nam-gil's debts without justification. Determined, he decided to take his wife and children to his in-laws' home.

The war was still raging, and he couldn't continue relying on Hong-seon. Moreover, after Il-seop's untimely death, facing Hong-seon had become unbearably difficult. Although Hong-seon had never once blamed Jeong-seop for Il-seop's death or uttered a single reproach, the weight of unspoken sorrow hung heavily between them.

Surely, Hong-seon knew what had transpired between Jeong-seop, Il-seop, and Hong-man. Jeong-seop had never intended to push Il-seop away; he understood how much Hong-seon cherished Il-seop, perhaps even more than he cherished Jeong-seop.

The question tormented Jeong-seop: did he truly bear significant responsibility for Il-seop's tragic end? Undoubtedly, he was not entirely blameless. The shock of Il-seop's death left a deep scar on him. They were brothers, after all. He often lamented, "I shouldn't have thrown that punch at Il-seop that day." But regrets couldn't undo what had happened, especially not for someone who was already gone.

Even after Il-seop's death, Hong-seon continued to support Jeong-seop, covering his children's tuition and living expenses. During the off-season for farming, with no harvest to rely on, this support was crucial. Yet, staying in Sancheong became unbearable. With their home gone and no foreseeable income, selling land in the midst of war would only fetch a meager price, something he despised.

And another thing, Jeong-seop's wife, Kang Eun-ok, was an elite graduate of Ilshin Girls' High School[53] in Jinju, a prestigious local school. Bok-hee, Il-seop's wife, had studied the old classics at the village school. She managed the care of their seven children, the household servants, and even provided the thrice-daily meals for Hong-seon.

In contrast, Eun-ok lived a life of ease, visibly more comfortable than Bok-hee by all accounts. Everyone knew that Eun-ok contributed less to the Choi family than Bok-hee. Despite this, Eun-ok's superior education meant Jeong-seop had to be considerate of her feelings. He realized that a woman's education wasn't necessarily helpful in household management, but he feared it might become a burden on her husband. It was unlikely she respected a husband who appeared incompetent. "Character is more important than academic background," Jeong-seop mused.

Jeong-seop longed to present himself to his father, Hong-seon, not merely as a son, but as the proud head of his own household. Yet, he had never been able to do so, and it seemed increasingly unlikely that he ever would. Now, with their home reduced to ashes, he realized that he would no longer be able to see even the fleeting image of his birth mother, Lady Han, who had remarried.

Some bowls may not shatter when dropped on a rough stone floor; they may sustain only a flaw or minor scratch. Yet others break with the slightest touch. It amazed Jeong-seop that the Big House remained unscathed amid the chaos. Until now, he had been living in the house built by Hong-seon, but it was destroyed by a bombing. He could never bring himself to say, "Father, please help me find another house." Just as one

---

53) The Ilshin Girls' School that Eun-ok attended was the same school that Ki-soon, Jeong-soon, and Young-soon attended later on. During the Japanese colonial period, the Ilshin Foundation established Ilshin Girls' School, which later became Jinju Ilshin Women's High School (1925) and Jinju Public Women's High School (1939). Afterward, it was renamed Jinju Public Girls' Middle School (1946) and was divided into a 3-year junior course and a 3-year senior course. In 1950, it became Jinju Middle School (a 6-year program), and in 1951, it was split and reorganized into Jinju Girls' High School. —This information has been summarized by the author with reference to Naver sources.

replaces a broken bowl, Jeong-seop resolved to find a new home for his family, even if it meant enduring hardship.

Jeong-seop muttered in a low voice,

"In this war, few people my age have survived; most were taken to fight. I didn't perish, leaving not even a handful of ashes, like Joon-seop in the New House. Nor was I forcibly conscripted into the People's Army. How fortunate am I to have survived so safely, along with Ki-hoon of the Big House and Hong-seon, the Esteemed Elder? None of my children have died yet... So it seems life follows the will of heaven.

Despite what anyone says, this is all thanks to Hong-seon, my father, the Great Elder. There is no other reason. So, first, I must find a house on my own... The war isn't completely over. Both the Big House and the New House face equal difficulties.

With nearly twenty family members, even the Big House will be complicated, if not as much as before. Recently, Bok-hee has struggled greatly in dealing with North Korean soldiers. Bok-hee, my younger brother's wife, never has a moment's rest, tending to her family, the workers' meals, and farm work daily. It's growing even worse."

With a myriad of thoughts swirling in his mind, Jeong-seop decided to take his children down to Busan, where his in-laws resided. At that time, the only members of the Saemmy House remaining with Jeong-seop and his wife were Min-ja, nicknamed "Black Young Master Min" for her unusually freckled face and boyish appearance, and her younger brother, Choi Ki-woong.

As they moved to Busan, Jeong-seop arranged small boarding rooms for his two unmarried daughters. His wife, Eun-ok, adored their youngest, Ki-woong, with all her heart. Eun-ok was robust and had a strong constitution. She was a woman of decisive action, clear in her intentions and resolutions.

It was Eun-ok who had once told Jeong-seop's mother, Lady Han, "It's not good for my children if others see you, so please don't come to our house anymore." Eun-ok was quite different from Jeong-seop, who couldn't bring himself to utter a word that might hurt anyone, even slightly.

Lady Han, Jeong-seop's mother, longed to see her son and grandsons, yet whenever she visited, she could never muster the courage to step proudly through the gate of the Saemmy House. Seeing her in such a pitiful state, Jeong-seop began avoiding her. He would hide, and after Lady Han had left, he would be tormented by his own cowardice and the guilt of his actions.

Although Jeong-seop had prepared himself for this, the mere thought of Lady Han still weighed heavily on his heart. He muttered to himself. 'If only that damned Sancheong Elementary School wasn't directly across from our house, or rather, if it hadn't been the headquarters of the North Korean People's Army...'

He despised his inability to move past what had already transpired. Life had no room for hypothetical scenarios. The harsh reality was something he found difficult to accept. To Jeong-seop, his mother, Lady Han, the dignified madam of the main room, existed only in the distant memories of his childhood.

A few years ago, Eun-ok's family moved from Jinju to Busan. She took her husband, Jeong-seop, and their children to a place called Togok (Togok Hill) in Busan. Togok was a relatively secluded area. From there, one had to cross a small hill and a wide stream to reach Dongnae Market.

Dongnae, meaning "East Comes," was Busan's most historically rich district, bearing the marks of many eras. The market there, renowned since the *Joseon* Dynasty and through the Japanese occupation, was expansive and vibrant. It boasted an array of clothing, accessories, fabrics, bedding, shoes, and a wide variety of food stalls, capturing the essence of a bustling, timeless marketplace.

Eun-ok set aside her pride and squeezed through the crowded back alleys of the Dongnae market, finding a spot among the throng of vendors. Her "stall" was merely a small plank on which she placed an assortment of goods she had managed to procure—mostly discarded cans and second-hand clothes that had trickled down from the U.S. military bases. This makeshift display was all she had to offer. The residents of Dongnae were generally well-off and highly valued education. Min-ja would spend her time taking Ki-woong to a tiny temporary elementary school near Togok and then return home.

In this way, amidst the turmoil and upheaval, Jeong-seop and his family struggled to find a semblance of normalcy and stability, anchored by the faint hope of a better future. Eun-ok became intertwined with the new wave of refugees pouring into Dongnae Market, striving to maintain her place amid the bustling crowds. At times, she ran small errands to support her family.

Busan thrummed with noise and smoke that lingered after the war. Not only Jagalchi near the beach but also Kukje Market and every corner of the city were teeming with people. Refugees from various regions found shelter not only along the coast and flatlands but also on the hills. Busan transformed into a hive of activity, a bustling settlement, with makeshift shacks and huts made of flimsy tents stretching as far as the eye could see.

About eight months later, Eun-ok managed to secure a store with the money she had saved from her business at Dongnae Market. With her brother's help, she ventured to Gupo Market in Busan. There, meat and intestines flowed from the slaughterhouses through a drainage outlet. Near Gupo, numerous slaughterhouses processed various animals—cows, dogs, chickens, and goats. In Gupo Market, many stalls dealt in meat by-products from the slaughterhouses.

Eun-ok initially sold the meat but soon decided to change her approach. Rather than selling the meat as it was, she started selling rice with meat soup, boiling and mixing the better cuts. Her family moved from Togok-dong to a shabby room near the bank of Gupo.

Every night, as Jeong-seop closed his eyes, visions of his bombed and burning house haunted him. He saw Lady Han, his mother, watching the house from afar and then hiding whenever she encountered someone. These images were a blend of the past and the harsh reality of their present, as they struggled to find stability in the aftermath of war. They were desperately seeking a semblance of peace in a city overflowing with displaced refugees. Whether he was living in reality or a dream, Jeong-seop found it difficult to discern.

He took on any task that came his way and fulfilled every request from Eun-ok. One day, following Eun-ok's instructions, Jeong-seop carried pork, various meat by-products, and ingredients such as onions to her restaurant, only to find his wife absent. A woman from the neighboring restaurant informed him, "A while ago, the children's mother suddenly collapsed, saying she felt dizzy, and was taken to a nearby hospital."

His wife, burning with a high fever, succumbed within two days. She hadn't even received proper medical treatment and passed away in agony. The so-called hospital was a makeshift facility that also served as an animal clinic near Gupo Station, where animals and humans shared the same space and received injections from the same limited supply of medicine. On the cold cement floor of that hospital, his wife never regained consciousness.

Jeong-seop, who had never borrowed a penny from others, now faced the grim task of arranging Eun-ok's funeral and paying the rent with the remaining money. Soon, he was left with almost nothing. Thus ended the chapter of Jeong-seop and Eun-ok's lives in Busan. Lost and aimless, he didn't know where to go with Min-ja and Ki-woong.

With Eun-ok gone, there was no longer any reason to stay in Busan, a city where he had no ties left. He lacked the strength to endure any more in a place where he had no roots. He had never considered working in the kitchen or greeting guests, and now, devoid of courage, he spent his days sighing, once again left without a place to call home.

Since his youth, Jeong-seop had only done what his father,

Hong-seon, desired. He followed Hong-seon's instructions. He had even earned a silver medal as a national table tennis player while representing Japan's team at that time, during his years at Busan Commercial High School. Table tennis, a sport he had trained in, and his proficiency with an abacus were skills he mastered from an early age. But beyond these, he knew little else. After his marriage, he never sought other work, as the tasks assigned by Hong-seon, combined with the inheritance he provided, were enough to provide for their needs. Socially inept, he found himself incapable of considering any trade or way to survive in the unfamiliar city of Busan.

In this moment of despair, Jeong-seop grappled with the harsh reality of his situation while the dreams of the past remained trapped in the uncertainty of the future. Jeong-seop stood by the Nakdong River, gazing at the waters where Eun-ok's ashes had been scattered. As he stared blankly at the setting sun, something touched his hand. It was his fourth daughter, Min-ja, who had gently grasped his trembling hand, her eyes filled with concern. To Jeong-seop, it felt as if all paths had been blocked. At that moment, Min-ja turned to him and said, "Father, let's go to Sancheong now." Her words resonated with him as if they were destiny.

Yet, Jeong-seop had no idea where to go in Sancheong.

As they hastily packed their belongings, preparing to leave the one-room home on the banks of the Gupo River where they had been living, a telegram arrived from Hong-seon in Sancheong. The message read, "An urgent matter has arisen at the family home. Please return immediately." When they moved to Gupo, Jeong-seop had sent a letter to Hong-seon, informing him of their whereabouts, hoping to settle there for a few years. The telegram had come to that address. With barely enough money for the fare to Sancheong, Jeong-seop saw Hong-seon's message as a beacon of hope. Breathing a sigh of relief, Jeong-seop quickly packed his belongings in Busan and made his way back to Sancheong.

Upon arriving at the Big House, he was met with unexpected news: the death of Jeong-soon, the second daughter of the New House. On a spring day like this, cholera—a disease known as *Hoyeolja*—had claimed another life, likely as a consequence of the war. Lady Hwang had once told him that Jeong-soon had dedicated herself to caring for orphans and the sick. It seemed the hard work had left Jeong-soon too weak to survive.

As soon as Jeong-seop arrived in Sancheong, he went to find his two daughters, whom he had sent ahead to secure a room before his departure. He arranged for them to go to Sacheon, where their eldest sister had lived with her husband. With the small bundle of belongings he had brought from Busan, Jeong-seop settled Min-ja and Ki-woong into the rented room that his two daughters had previously occupied.

Just ten days after living with the children, Jeong-seop received a message from his second daughter, who revealed that she had been secretly seeing a career soldier and wanted to marry him. Jeong-seop immediately gave his blessing for the marriage.

Determined to make a fresh start, Jeong-seop promised to take on accounting work at a law office run by a high school friend. He planned to stay in Sancheong for a while, looking after Min-ja and his son, Ki-woong. However, the small rented room that his daughters had lived in proved to be extremely cramped and uncomfortable for the three of them.

But moving into the Big House or asking Hong-seon for accommodation was unthinkable. Silently bearing his burdens, he focused on fulfilling the tasks assigned by Hong-seon and his stepmother, Lady Hwang. With Jeong-soon having died of cholera, there were numerous legal matters to address. He had her body cremated at a crematorium near Seoul, as instructed by Hong-seon, and placed her ashes in an urn, which he brought back to the New House.

The next fifteen days were a whirlwind of activity. Amid this chaos, a telegram arrived from the office of Nihon Medical School, where Ki-soon was studying, stating, "The student Choi Ki-soon has been hospitalized.

Please take her home to her country."

Once again, following Hong-seon's instructions, Jeong-seop prepared everything and traveled to Japan to bring Ki-soon back to the Sancheong house, using trains, boats, and buses. As the saying goes, '*A tree with many branches never has a day without wind,*' Jeong-seop found himself constantly moving, without a moment to rest. Consequently, he could no longer continue his work at his friend's law office.

Thus, Jeong-seop's days were filled with relentless duties and constant movement, and he had to bear the weight of the Choi family's sorrows and the responsibilities demanded of him. After bringing Ki-soon back to Sancheong, Principal Hwang, Lady Hwang's younger sister, visited Jeong-seop at his residence.

Aunt of Ki-soon (Principal Hwang):

"Look here, Jeong-seop, rather than staying in this cramped rented room, why don't you take care of Lady Hwang, my elder sister, and my niece, Ki-soon, who just returned from Japan? And while you're at it, how about moving into the New House and living there for a few years?"

Principal Hwang was the first to bring up the idea. Although Jeong-seop was far from being in a position to rebuild his burned-down house or afford a new place, he couldn't immediately accept the offer. However, after receiving another request from Lady Hwang, Jeong-seop made up his mind and decided to move into the New House.

The reason Jeong-seop initially refused the offer was that he feared relying on others might eventually lead him to settle there, and he felt ashamed in front of Hong-seon. Eventually, considering his dire situation, especially for the sake of his remaining children, he could not afford to let pride stand in the way.

This was how Jeong-seop ended up bringing Min-ja and Ki-woong into the upper room of the main house, and how his family came to live together as boarders in the New House. Though they were living as boarders, in this return, Jeong-seop reflected on the intertwined fates of himself and his stepmother, Lady Hwang. He might also have been seeking the strength to rise again amidst their shared sorrow, in the indelible shadows of past loss and the unending waves of recovery.

Lady Hwang, having lost two children within the span of a couple of years, had retreated into a shell of domestic tasks, spending her days sewing, ironing, and darning. She sympathized with Jeong-seop over the loss of his wife, Eun-ok, who had died from overwork in Busan.

"It's a little late, but here's something to help you build a new house in the future," she said, handing him a substantial sum of money she had managed to save.

The changes in Lady Hwang's appearance were minimal, aside from her slightly more gaunt face. Her unusually large, clear eyes now sparkled with a darker hue. The eyes of an aging woman couldn't have grown larger; rather, they only seemed that way because they were constantly brimming with tears.

Lady Hwang was only a year younger than Jeong-seop, and as he looked at her face, he couldn't help but reflect on his own aging visage. She refrained from speaking about her children's deaths, Ki-soon's mental disorder, and the abnormal symptoms afflicting her youngest daughter, Young-soon. Until then, according to the Japanese doctor, Jeong-seop had to consider Ki-soon's condition a "mental disorder of unknown cause." Despite Hong-seon's efforts to treat her with herbal medicine, Ki-soon's condition had shown no signs of improvement. She would vomit everything she ingested after taking the herbal concoctions.

From today's perspective, it seems that missing the early intervention window for schizophrenia allowed Ki-soon's illness to progress unchecked. Another factor was the lack of effective medication for such disorders at the time.

Nearly every night, Ki-soon would flee her room, screaming,

"Someone's coming to catch me! They're trying to kill me! Look at them!" She was tormented by chronic auditory and visual hallucinations. In these moments, the house would become filled with an eerie tension, and the shadows cast by Ki-soon's suffering stretched long and dark along the walls. Her sobs occasionally echoed across the wooden floor of the central hall, audible to everyone living in the house.

There was no other choice but to silently witness the frailty of the human mind and the inexorable progression of an untreated illness. As the family struggled to cope with her condition, they were weighed down by the collective burden of sorrow and helplessness, which gradually ate away at their lives and changed them in ways they could barely comprehend.

Living in someone else's house inevitably brought a sense of unease that had not existed before. This discomfort was likely felt more intensely by the young children than by the adults. Even the simple act of eating at a table that was not their own made their situation even harder.

For the adults, it was merely a matter of two families sharing one house, but for the children, it was an immediate reality they had to confront. The intrusion of unfamiliar routines and environments weighed heavily on everyone, but for the children, the strangeness was especially profound. Each meal eaten under another's roof served as a reminder of their dislocation, a symbol of their dependence on others.

This subtle sense of displacement might linger in the children's memories even as they grow into adulthood, shaping their understanding of home and belonging.

In the summer of 1952, Lady Hwang lived in the main room of the main building of the New House. Facing this room were two other rooms, separated by the central *daecheong-maru*. It was decided that the last room, which had originally belonged to Joon-seop, would be used by Min-ja's family. Thus, Jeong-seop, Min-ja, and her younger brother, Ki-woong, moved in.

Given the circumstances, the inner quarters of the New House, where Min-ja's family stayed, had a room at the far end opposite the main room, right next to Ki-soon's sister, Young-soon. Because of this proximity, Min-ja and Young-soon often saw each other first thing in the morning.

Although Young-soon was a year older than Min-ja, Min-ja found her exceptionally immature. Every time Young-soon saw Min-ja and Ki-woong, she never greeted them kindly with her large, beautiful eyes. Instead, she would always glare at them with disdain, her lips pouting in displeasure. These encounters troubled Min-ja, but she couldn't bring herself to tell her father, Jeong-seop, who often sought rest in the *sarang-chae* of the Big House.

Young-soon's face was undeniably pretty and lovely, no matter where she was seen. In contrast to Min-ja's small, slightly slanted eyes, wider nose, and darker complexion, Young-soon's delicate features seemed at odds with her spiteful behavior. However, those who knew her were aware that Young-soon, like Ki-soon, was already ailing. For Min-ja, encountering one sickly child after another was more than disheartening—it was cruel. And inevitably, it was Min-ja who bore the brunt of criticism.

Now, in the 2020s, the condition is known as schizophrenia, formerly called split personality disorder. Back then, there was no precise diagnosis for Ki-soon and Young-soon's condition. They were simply deemed "Mad" or described as having "Lost their minds."

Even in her current state of madness, people in the neighborhood remarked that Ki-soon's large, clear, double-lidded eyes and her delicately shaped, slightly prominent nose closely resembled those of her mother, Lady Hwang. If Ki-soon remained still, without suddenly banging on the walls or muttering strange things, one might never guess that she was ill.

This made Min-ja all the more curious about her aunt Ki-soon's mental condition. 'Can a person change like that? Maybe she's doing those weird things on purpose, cursing or laughing to herself?' Min-ja pondered this time and again.

That day, after school, Min-ja peeked toward Ki-soon's room from the yard of the main building of the New House. Ki-hoon's wife, Jong-hee, had brought Jeom-rye from Jinju to Sancheong when she got married, and Jeom-rye seemed to be around the same age as Min-ja. She had only completed up to the fourth grade of elementary school before coming to live there.

As Min-ja entered after school with her bag of books, Jeom-rye quickly glanced at her. Then, after roughly finishing her work, she spoke to Min-ja.

Jeom-rye:

"Well, the Big Mistress (Ki-soon) got caught in the rain not long ago and has been barely lying there ever since. You can go in... I have to get back to work at the Big House. Got it?"

With that, she left Ki-soon alone in the room and walked back toward the *Jangdok-gan* wall near the Big House. Hearing this, Min-ja thought, 'Then, Aunt Ki-soon must be alone in the room now,' and her face brightened with anticipation. She picked up the basin that Jeom-rye had left on the floor in the kitchen of the New House and added warm water from the pot hanging over the wood-burning stove. With the basin in her hands, she prepared to enter Ki-soon's room.

Since Min-ja was in her final year of elementary school, she had already lost interest in her studies and found them dull. The destruction of her home in the bombing had disrupted her education, making school feel fragmented and unimportant. She was far more curious about what her aunt Ki-soon was up to, so as soon as school ended, Min-ja ran straight home. For Min-ja, learning about her aunt, who had just returned from Japan, was far more interesting than schoolwork.

'Beautiful and elegant, a person who would readily answer anything if I asked her. Just a little over a decade ago, the entire neighborhood used to say,—The precious and pretty lady of the Choi household,— but now she's confined indoors as a madwoman... It's absurd. I need to take a closer look. I can't believe Aunt Ki-soon, so smart and well-educated, has truly lost her mind. Maybe she's only pretending.'

This was likely what Min-ja truly felt. Her curiosity intensified, her thoughts swirling with the enigma of Ki-soon's transformation. Determined to uncover the truth behind her aunt's drastic change, she wondered whether such intelligence could truly succumb to madness or if there was more to the story.

With each step toward Ki-soon's room, Min-ja's mind raced, searching for answers to the questions that lingered in the shadows of the New House. As she approached the door, the weight of her thoughts pressed down on her small shoulders. The air was thick with the scent of rain and the unspoken fears that haunted the house. Steeling herself, Min-ja reached for the door, driven by the hope that understanding her aunt's plight might somehow bring light to the dark corners of her own life.

That day, Min-ja felt an even stronger desire to find answers to her lingering questions. She was someone who believed only what she saw with her own eyes and heard with her own ears. Like many others, Min-ja was no different. But is everything we see and hear truly real?

Min-ja, the youngest daughter of Jeong-seop of Saemmyjip, was, in other words, Ki-soon's niece. They were half-aunt and half-niece. It had been almost two months since Min-ja had moved into the room at the far end of Ki-soon's New House. Min-ja muttered to herself,

'My house was right across from the elementary school, so it got bombed! How on earth could there have been a North Korean military base in an elementary school? Kicking out those snot-nosed brats was bad luck from the start, wasn't it?'

She wiped her nose with the back of her hand. The collapsed remnants of Saemmy House lay in ruins, reduced to rubble and debris. Nothing of value remained—not even a single intact photograph.

Min-ja stopped her monologue and, carrying a basin of warm water, quietly entered Ki-soon's room. Just then, Ki-soon, who was lying on the floor, locked eyes with Min-ja as she looked down at her. In that instant, Ki-soon's expression shifted to one of profound shyness. Gone was the angry visage that had once pounded the wall with an open palm; now, she smiled bashfully like a child and began to speak with a gentle timidity.

Ki-soon:

"Oh, it's a cute black parakeet! How did you end up in my room like this? Did I fall down again?"

Without a word, Min-ja nodded, and Ki-soon, as if in surrender, turned over and lay limp on the floor. But soon, she unconsciously clenched her fists and summoned all her strength to rise.

Quickly, Min-ja set the basin of water down on the floor. She had done this a few times before. Before Ki-soon could fully rise, Min-ja swiftly knelt and wrapped her arms around her. Like a child, Ki-soon nestled into Min-ja's embrace. Min-ja believed that holding her troubled aunt with her small frame might help Ki-soon regain her composure.

Like a fledgling bird, Ki-soon gently buried her face in Min-ja's chest, finding solace in her young niece's arms.

Min-ja:

"Big Aunt, that's right. I heard you fell. When I came back from school, you were out in the yard for a while and got caught in the rain... That's why you need to lie down and rest. No matter where you go, please always wear your *beoseon*. They say people stay healthy when their feet are warm."

Hearing this, Ki-soon relaxed once more, her face drawing close to Min-ja's as if to share a secret. In a very small voice, she whispered near Min-ja's nose. Min-ja held her breath, feeling the weight of her aunt's fragile state. The scent of rain and the faint aroma of herbal medicine lingered in the air.

Despite her disheveled appearance, Ki-soon still possessed the elegance that the villagers often spoke of. Min-ja's heart ached under the weight of her aunt's reality.

Ki-soon:

"Min-ja, you're so kind. You remind me of your mother."

The words were soft, barely audible, but Min-ja hugged Ki-soon tighter.

Ki-soon:

"Parakeet! I'm a virgin! Do you know what a virgin is?"

Min-ja:

"Yes, I know everything. And you, Big Aunt, are still a virgin. And how beautiful you are. Very, very..."

Ki-soon:

"Hey, Parakeet! Then ... I still don't look that ugly? I'm always stuck in my room. I just stare at the ceiling ... and suddenly, I get scared. Even when I'm completely still, the fear creeps in. I'm really afraid the madmen will come looking for me again. I'm terrified. They'll find me again, all of a sudden, and lock me in a well or something, won't they?

I'm most afraid of being trapped! There's no light! The light..."

Min-ja nodded, having heard enough from Jeong-seop to understand what Ki-soon was murmuring about. She gently patted Ki-soon's chest, trying to comfort her like a child. But Ki-soon couldn't stay still. Her thoughts flew around at an uncontrollable speed.

Ki-soon:

"Oh ... why is my heart beating so fast? It feels like my whole body is on fire!"

Min-ja, still so young, didn't know what to do. She thought about running to the Big House to call Uncle Yoo-sang or at least Jeom-rye, but Ki-soon was clinging to her so tightly that she couldn't move.

Ki-soon:

"Parakeet, I feel like there's a heavy rock on my chest! My heart feels like it's going to explode. It's like fire is breaking out inside me, or something is pressing down on me! Oh, what should I do? Min-ja, help me ... help me! I think those people are trying to throw me in the well again."

Suddenly, Ki-soon pushed Min-ja away and ran toward the opposite wall of the room. She began banging her head against the wall. Min-ja, a strong little girl, used all her might to pull Ki-soon away from the wall and shouted loudly.

Min-ja:

"Yoo-sang *Aje*! Jeom-rye! Come here! I'm in trouble. Help me!"

After a while, Yoo-sang arrived, panting. When he saw Ki-soon in Min-ja's arms, he rushed over. He grabbed Ki-soon by the waist and pulled her away from the wall. Her forehead already bore a bluish bruise. Ki-soon struggled violently but soon collapsed, unconscious, in Yoo-sang's arms.

Min-ja thought she should have called someone from the Big House from the beginning. She had tried to handle it herself and now feared she might be scolded for it. Even though she hadn't done anything wrong, her heart pounded nervously. She glanced at Yoo-sang's face, hoping he wouldn't notice her anxiety. Yoo-sang said nothing to Min-ja. He laid Ki-soon gently on the bed, then looked into Min-ja's eyes. His expression seemed to silently implore her to keep quiet.

Min-ja had always noticed a certain reverence in Yoo-sang's demeanor toward her aunt Ki-soon whenever they interacted. Yoo-sang was, without a doubt, the man who maintained discipline in the household after Grandfather Hong-seon—except that he was merely the butler of the Big House. This, of course, excluded Big Brother Ki-hoon. Yoo-sang was consulted by Bok-hee and Lady Hwang alike, and even Jeom-rye would defer to him with a smile. He knew everything about the household.

It was said that he had quietly buried his wife's body by the bank of the *Gyeongho River* after she was shot by the People's Army and brutally trampled. There were no children between Yoo-sang and his wife. He had refused to wear the red armband—the mark of an informant for the

People's Army—and instead, he devoted himself to Hong-seon, caring for his children as best as he could. The elders in the neighborhood regarded Yoo-sang as "Hong-seon's man," someone who truly believed in and followed him. He was seen as a paragon of loyalty and consideration.

Yoo-sang looked at Ki-soon, who lay still on the floor, and motioned for silence as he left the room.

Ki-soon's accent was very different from Min-ja's. She had lived in Jinju since middle school, spent nearly a year in Seoul, and then lived in Japan for about five years. As a result, her speech bore little trace of the Sancheong dialect, making it difficult for the locals to place her origins. Only Min-ja understood her well, having grown familiar with the mix of Seoul, Japanese, and Gyeongsang-do accents.

Min-ja sang softly, her voice low, as she gently patted her aunt Ki-soon's chest. Ki-soon had fainted like a child, her eyes closed.

With her short bob haircut, straight bangs that made her look like a tomboy, and sun-darkened skin, no one would have expected Min-ja to sing so tenderly—nor would they have cared. She was merely imitating what she had heard from old Lady Hwang. She had no idea where Ki-soon's mind was wandering now, but as Min-ja's small, dark hands patted her like a child, Ki-soon remained still and quiet.

Min-ja:

"There's smoke when coal and white coal burn, but there's no smoke when my heart burns... Oh, is this the *Song of White Coal* that adults often sing? But why do I cry for no reason when I listen to this song? Why?"

Tears fell from Min-ja's eyes. She and her family were now living in the New House, but not long ago, her mother had fainted and never woken up. Min-ja recited the sorrowful lines, devoid of rhythm, and thought, 'Now, I will stop acting pitiful. Is there anything that might make Aunt Ki-soon happy, even a little?'

She decided to sing a different song, one she had learned from listening to Ki-young and Ki-ok of the Big House. Min-ja hummed softly.

"When I go over the rock hill alone,
I cry because I miss you.
I've been waiting for you, hiding above the hill,
I miss you, I miss you, I cry.
When I go over the rock hill alone,
I miss you, I miss you so much.
I've been working as a farmhand for about a decade,
I cry while hugging the azalea flower."

She lay on her side next to the sleeping Ki-soon, resting one arm beneath her head as she gazed at her aunt's profile. Then, she muttered as if talking to herself.

Min-ja:

"Auntie always says, 'Parakeet! I'm a virgin!' whenever she sees me. But if she's ever going to get married, she should at least meet someone. Yet, she stays cooped up in the house all day long. And it seems like no one even sees her as someone normal enough to get married. Poor Aunt Ki-soon..."

17
Salpuri[54] — Exorcism
Winter 1952: The Gyeongho River
―Plunging

---

54) Salpuri : *Salpuri* refers to the act of dispelling or unraveling *sal*, which means to kill, bind, or suppress. Thus, it also signifies the release of *aek*, which refers to disasters, misfortunes, burdens, or ill fate.―Referenced from Naver Korean Dictionary by the author.
This word means exorcism. Exorcism (noun) ― A ritual or spiritual practice aimed at driving out an evil spirit from a person or location. ― *Definition adapted from ChatGPT.*

The Choi family harbored doubts when they received a telegram from a Japanese school requesting Ki-soon's presence. This incident occurred a few days after Min-ja's family had settled into the New House.

One starry night, Ki-soon suddenly screamed and dashed out of her room. Lady Hwang, Jeong-seop, Min-ja, Ki-woong, and Young-soon watched in shock as she ran naked through the yard, her voice filled with anguish. Ki-soon cried out,

"Everyone, look at me! I am still pure, and I am not insane! I am the legitimate daughter of the Choi family. I was not born out of wedlock!

I can still marry a man who truly loves me.

Yutaka, I am worthy of becoming your family's daughter-in-law.

That wedding was a sham! Anyone who says otherwise is ignorant!

Yutaka, don't go! I will follow you.

Please, take me with you, Yutaka!"

Though Ki-soon's mind was troubled, her desperate cries were revealing the source of her suffering. Neighbors, awakened by her midnight outburst, gathered around the yard, listening with pity and shaking their heads in sympathy. Young-soon, who had been watching in her pajamas, suddenly shouted at Ki-soon.

"Elder sister! I know the ones who tormented you! I'll kill them all! Will that make things right? Tell me, yes or no?"

As soon as she finished speaking, Young-soon dashed into the farm equipment warehouse next to the storehouse and ran back into the yard, wielding a sickle. The so-called farm equipment warehouse was a small, dilapidated structure, crudely rebuilt after being bombed by the U.S. military. Only a few farming tools were hanging on its walls.

With a wild glint in her eyes, Young-soon raised the sickle to strike at Ki-soon, who stood trembling in the yard. Panic-stricken, everyone retreated to the farthest corners of the yard, their voices rising in alarm.

At that critical moment, Yoo-sang leaped forward and snatched the sickle from Young-soon's grip. How someone as young as Young-soon could possess such strength was a mystery, but Yoo-sang's breath grew labored, his face turning red from the struggle to wrest the sickle from her. This harrowing incident made it clear to everyone that Ki-soon had completely lost her mind, and that Young-soon was also deeply disturbed —a realization that quickly spread through the New House, the Big House, and the neighboring homes.

Lady Hwang, a devout Catholic, came to realize that the prayers of priests and nuns alone could not heal the madness that had gripped her family. Desperate to find a solution, she begged Jeong-seop to do something. Having no other choice, Jeong-seop sought assistance from neighbors and relatives, desperate for a solution.

Jeong-seop arranged for the most renowned fortune teller in both Sancheong and Jinju, known for summoning the spirits of the deceased, to come to their home. The entire neighborhood was unexpectedly drawn to an exorcism ceremony, or *gutpan*, where spirits were summoned in the courtyard of the Choi family house. The townsfolk believed, as the old saying went, that even the closest of kin and siblings could lose their sanity due to the lingering presence of the dead.

It was a superstitious ritual, believed to be necessary to remove the potent and harmful *sal*, or negative energy, left behind by the dead, which had ensnared the living. And so, they turned to this ritual, hoping to dispel the malevolent spirits.

That day, people gathered in the yard of the New House, eager to witness the fortune teller call forth *Honbaek*, the soul of the deceased.

Paksu Mudang Kim, the male shaman, raised his voice:

"Oh, so many young souls have perished in this house. Their restless spirits, heavy with resentment, cannot ascend to the heavens and instead roam aimlessly. Spirits! Reveal yourselves and speak!

First ... Choi Jeong-soon, born in 1926, departed in 1952. Step forward!"

The shaman stood tall, shaking a bamboo branch and muttering to himself. Then, suddenly, he spoke in a loud voice.

Paksu Mudang:

"What? You cry out in injustice? What wrong haunts you? How did you meet your end?"

At first, the onlookers dismissed *Paksu Mudang*'s summoning as mere theatrics, but soon, they began to watch intently. Among them was Ki-hwi, the second son of the Big House, who scoffed at the proceedings instead of attending school.

Ki-hwi:

"That short, unimpressive man, he's supposed to be a great shaman? Let's see what nonsense he spews today!"

But when the shaman declared he would summon Jeong-soon's spirit, no one had expected the spectacle that followed. Sensing the crowd's skepticism, the shaman chose to unveil something truly astonishing.

Paksu Mudang spoke:

"Yes, it's tragic that you left this world with unfulfilled desires, but when the time is right, you must move on. Since no one here can see what you look like, could you show yourself, even just a little? Where do you wish to go?"

The shaman pointed with his bamboo stick toward an empty *jangdok* sitting in the corner of the *jangdok-dae* in the New House. The crowd's eyes followed his gesture. What happened next left everyone in awe. As the shaman murmured incantations, the jar began to levitate, rising nearly three meters off the ground before gently descending. The clay jar rose once more, then settled softly on the ground without a single crack.

This incredible sight repeated itself twice, leaving the witnesses stunned and terrified. Many ran away, screaming, while a few remained, gazing at *Paksu Mudang* with newfound respect. *Paksu Mudang* spent over two hours summoning the spirits of Joon-seop and Jeong-soon, mimicking their voices as they had sounded in life during the ceremony. However, whether this ritual would bring clarity to Ki-soon and Young-soon remained uncertain. Only time would tell.

Someone in the crowd murmured, "Joon-seop even had a soul wedding. Does this shaman know about that? Why don't you say something? What kind of state is Joon-seop's spirit in now?"

When the exorcism concluded, Hong-seon and Lady Hwang invited *Paksu Mudang* into the house, followed by Jeong-seop. The shaman bowed deeply to Hong-seon and Lady Hwang and then spoke.

Paksu Mudang:

"Big Elder and Lady Hwang, beyond the souls we summoned today, five more spirits still linger in this house. Therefore, restoring Mistress Ki-soon and Young-soon to their senses immediately will be extremely difficult.

In a week, I will return with three monks, and together we will perform a ritual for these two daughters by the *Gyeongho River*. Repeating this ritual multiple times may help them regain their senses, but I cannot promise a full recovery through my power alone.

The roots of their affliction run deep and have been festering for a long time. I will do my utmost. Please prepare yourselves. I will inform Jeong-seop of the exact time and place before I leave."

Hong-seon and Lady Hwang bowed respectfully to the shaman. Hong-seon instructed Jeong-seop to fetch the prepared offering, which he placed in a small wooden box, along with two boxes of ginseng and three bottles of honey, before handing it over.

As Min-ja entered the room, she recalled the sight of the jar rising high above the *jangdok-dae*. Ki-woong cried out in fear.

Ki-woong:

"Wow! There really is a ghost! I'm scared, Noona. Do you think Mom died and is now wandering around?"

He crawled under Min-ja's blanket, seeking comfort.

After the exorcism, *Paksu Mudang* left the New House and handed a note to Jeong-seop as he departed.

The note read:

In one week, from around 1 a.m. to 3:30 a.m., we will conduct the ceremony at a deep section in the middle of the *Gyeongho River*. Three monks will accompany me. Food and travel expenses will not be required.

I have heard that Lady Hwang is a Catholic, but that is of no concern. Whether it involves the dead or the living, there is nothing we can change through our own will alone. We can only wait for a moment of equalization, brought about by a powerful, absolute force. Our role is merely to help bring that moment closer.

What we see is not all there is, and what we hear is not the whole truth.

I will see you in a week.

Sincerely,

Kakje, *Paksu* Kim

That was the essence of his message. Kakje was another name for the shaman, and it was later discovered that his family name was Kim. The shamans and monks likely considered the time of deep darkness, which ordinary people fear, to be the hour when spirits are most active, though the exact reason remained unclear. They performed the ritual from around 1 a.m. until the first light of dawn.

They used a form of shock therapy, undressing Ki-soon and Young-soon, forcing their heads underwater before pulling them back up. The exact nature of their affliction remained unknown, but it was widely believed that their condition was triggered by a traumatic event. Jeong-seop thought the intent was to reset their minds through yet another powerful shock.

At first, in order to submerge Ki-soon's head in the river, two monks grabbed her feet and held her body upside down. As they dipped her head into the water, many people initially gathered to watch. But toward the final stage of the ceremony, only a few remained. On that cold winter day, each time Ki-soon and Young-soon, wearing nothing but underwear, had their heads forced underwater, Ki-soon's anguished cries echoed along the riverside, piercing the hearts of those who listened. Her cries seemed to linger painfully in the air. For after hearing Ki-soon's harrowing cries of pain, anyone would find themselves haunted by them for a long time. About two months passed as they endured multiple such rituals.

In this context, *Salpuri* might be interpreted as a ritual dance performed to expel evil spirits. However, Jeong-seop had never heard of such a *Salpuri* performed by *Paksu Mudang* at that time. It was meant to purify the souls of Jeong-soon and Joon-seop, who were said to have died young and unjustly, unable to live their lives as they wished.

In Jeong-seop's view, the shaman, like most others, wore an outer garment woven from layers of colorful fabric and held a long pole. Yet, it was unclear whether the shaman's movements were deliberate gestures or simply erratic motions—sitting, running, or standing. Instead, the shaman held an object that appeared to be a book in his hand. He opened it and read from it under the flickering glow of a dim candle.

While the shaman and one monk chanted in unison, the other two monks repeatedly plunged Ki-soon's and Young-soon's heads into the river and pulled them back up. Observers noticed that the shaman and monk held Buddhist scriptures, which they carefully followed as they chanted. Jeong-seop alone was convinced that the true power of the ritual lay in these sacred texts.

The effectiveness of the ritual remained uncertain. However, following the ceremony, Ki-soon's episodes of running naked and crying out had significantly lessened. In moments of lucidity, Ki-soon became eerily calm, endlessly reading and re-reading a particular book. Reading had always been a solace for her, but in her current state, it had become her sole activity, an obsessive refuge.

Following the ceremony, Lady Hwang generously rewarded *Paksu Mudang* and the monks with money and food. Even amid the lingering hardships of war, she devoted all her resources to the ritual.

Min-ja frequently visited Ki-soon, who seemed to be slowly recovering, engaging her in conversations and asking for help with her studies. Aside from reading, Ki-soon seldom left her room. She often assumed a peculiar posture—bending forward with her head between her legs, her hips resting flat on the floor, and her face pressed downward. She would remain in this position, staring at the floor, for an hour or more.

To divert Ki-soon's attention, Min-ja would bring her books from her own room and offer them to her. They were English and math textbooks from middle and high school. Min-ja would place the books on a low desk designed for floor seating.

Until a few months ago, some pinwheel materials Ki-soon had crafted to keep herself occupied still lay scattered beneath the desk. Whenever Min-ja noticed them, she absentmindedly swept them aside, tucking them further under the desk to keep them hidden. Then, she would open a textbook for Ki-soon to study. As Ki-soon focused on the book, she would sometimes glance up at Min-ja with a faint, curious smile.

One day, while studying a geometry problem, Ki-soon read the question, her face lighting up with a trace of happiness. Without hesitation, she drew the figure and began explaining the formula and solution to Min-ja, step by step. She sketched the figure with remarkable precision, without using a ruler or compass. Min-ja watched her delicate, pale wrists and nimble fingers moving with ease, though she struggled to follow Ki-soon's explanation. Min-ja muttered to herself:

'Ugh, studying takes a certain kind of mind. And I don't think I have it. How am I supposed to move on to a higher school and handle something this tough? Just thinking about it makes my head hurt. Maybe I should study something else ... but what?'

As if sensing her thoughts, Ki-soon replied:

"Parakeet, even the hardest geometry problem, or any tough problem, becomes easy if you start with the simplest shape, the easiest figure to draw, and gradually build it into something more complex. The same goes for applying mathematical formulas. If you don't grasp these basics, you won't do well in higher school or get into college...

Let's go over English grammar next. I find foreign languages the most fascinating.

I hate this country. I'm so drained. ... Living here is just too hard for me."

After taking a short break from studying math, Min-ja returned to the room with a basic English grammar book titled *The Trinity*. Back then, this book was a staple for all middle and high school students. The book's original author was believed to be Japanese, but rumors suggested that it had actually been written by an Englishman. Either way, it was a well-known book, ubiquitous in Korea. It had most likely belonged to her aunt Jeong-soon and uncle Joon-seop of the New House.

Nothing could be salvaged from Min-ja's burnt-down home. By now, whose book it was no longer mattered. The quality of the book was also of no concern to Min-ja. Her only concern was finding something to capture her aunt Ki-soon's attention.

Ki-soon focused intently on the English book and began explaining the first part—the part Min-ja could grasp most easily: the indefinite and definite articles. Someone had written on the cover, "He who wants to wear the crown must bear its weight." On the back cover, it was written, "No pain, no gain"—"Nothing is gained without pain."

Even as she stared at the cover, Min-ja couldn't decipher the meaning. The words blurred together, their meaning elusive.

Ki-soon then turned to Min-ja and asked:

"Parakeet, why are you here with me? Go back to your house. Isn't this my room? Where am I supposed to be? Why don't I see Joon-seop, who used to be in the room across from mine?"

Min-ja was startled by Ki-soon's questions. She thought, *Oh, right. Auntie is still unwell. She has always been frail. Even after undergoing several rituals by the shaman and monks, she still seemed trapped between the past and the present.* Yet what pierced Min-ja's heart was Ki-soon's question: "Why are you here in my house when you don't have a home?" It was a phrase she had heard nearly every day from Young-soon.

Even though she is older than me, Young-soon, that Gasina[55]*, who was held back from starting middle school for a year due to her mental condition, disgusts me. Ki-woong suffers the most because of her cruel words ... that horrible Gasina.* Min-ja snapped back to reality at that thought.

Ki-woong, Min-ja's timid and reserved younger brother, struggled to find his place in a household ruled by older sisters. After much persuasion from Min-ja, he started calling her "*Nuna*," the term younger brothers use for an elder sister in Korean. Before that, he had always called her "*Eonni*," often saying, "*Eonni*! I need to pee. Shh!" Min-ja would take him to the outdoor lavatory.

Lately, their father had become the central figure in their struggles. A widower left without a partner, a middle-aged man without a home to shelter his children—this was Choi Jeong-seop.

When these thoughts crossed her mind, Min-ja muttered absentmindedly, *Venomous bitch, Young-soon bitch. She's only one year older than me, but she doesn't resemble her benevolent Big Aunt, Ki-soon, at all.* Instead, the image of Young-soon's face, lounging lazily in the adjoining room, flashed through her mind.

---

55) Gasina: A dialect term from Gyeongnam province for a young girl, or wench.

Then, the thought struck her—if she continued this pointless studying, Young-soon might barge in and gobble up the meal she had prepared for her family. As urgency gripped Min-ja's heart, her face flushed unknowingly, making her dark complexion appear even darker. She slowly got up, and Ki-soon looked at her, puzzled.

Min-ja:

"Big Auntie, studying English or these indecipherable letters—that's enough for now. I'll go to the kitchen, make dinner, and be back soon. Why isn't Lady Hwang, New Grandmother, back yet? She went to my great-aunt's house in Jinju and won't be back for a while.

Anyway ... Big Auntie, that's enough studying for now. I'll bring dinner. Just stay here and sit still in this room, okay? It'll take me a little while to clean the table and set it up. Just wait a moment, okay?"

Like a child, Ki-soon nodded softly at Min-ja's words. She calmly returned to the low desk, idly playing with the glue box and scraps of paper for pinwheel-making that Min-ja had pushed aside. After a while, she lay on the floor, gazing at the ceiling.

Min-ja worried that Ki-soon might act out if she didn't make her promise more firmly. She knew Ki-soon could be unpredictable—if she remembered something or was triggered, she might suddenly start slapping the wall with her palms until they turned red. Other times, she would mutter endlessly, as if speaking to someone unseen, sometimes even spitting.

The thought sent chills down Min-ja's spine, and she glanced at Ki-soon again, searching her eyes. At that moment, Ki-soon, locking eyes with Min-ja, whispered in a hushed voice.

Ki-soon:

"Parakeet, I'm hungry. When will we eat? I don't like radish rice. Sweet potato rice tastes better."

Min-ja thought to herself, *That's a relief. Rice, precious rice —Bab* (cooked rice, a staple food for Koreans), *is so hard to come by these days.*

Since rice is so scarce, we add radish and cut sweet potatoes to stretch the supply. And yet, Big Auntie wants sweet potato rice.

Bab is life itself! Nothing is harder than hunger!

Thinking this, she quickly entered the kitchen.

She looked around, but there was no rice in sight. Instead, on the wood-burning stove, she found a rice pot layered with barley at the bottom, millet and rice in the middle, and radish on top. "Jeom-rye, she runs the kitchen in this New House. I thank her. Looks like I won't have to cook after all," she said joyfully.

Usually, a bit of sesame oil, soy sauce, or salt was mixed with the radish on top, and it was eaten like a simple vegetable rice dish. Sesame oil was a rare luxury, but in the kitchen of this New House, there was an entire bottle. In the household, including both workers and family members, women mainly ate the radishes and barley, while rice and millet were reserved for the elders' table.

Min-ja half-filled a bowl with a mix of rice and millet. She poured hot water over the rice to soften it, then mixed in soy sauce and sesame oil. She hurried to Ki-soon's room with the bowl in hand. There was nothing else to go with it.

Min-ja hurried back, but by the time she returned, Ki-soon had already fallen asleep, leaning against the wall. She laid a small blanket on the floor and gently placed Ki-soon on it. Ki-soon's frail frame looked even more delicate. Her closed eyes glistened with tears, like those of a helpless baby animal.

As Min-ja looked at the sleeping Ki-soon, she noticed a wet spot spreading beneath the little blanket. Ki-soon had wet herself. "Oops... yellow water," Min-ja murmured softly. She replaced the damp blanket with a cushion from the floor, placed it down again, and gently repositioned Ki-soon. Aunt Ki-soon's present state was a stark contrast to the woman she used to be. At times, for fleeting moments, she seemed to return to her former self, only to slip back into the depths of her madness.

Tears and urine—both were simply *water*.

"The human body is mostly water," Jeong-seop had once told Min-ja. "It hides within us as blood, urine, sweat, and tears, eventually finding its way out." He had said this around the time of Eun-ok's passing, Min-ja's mother.

Jeom-rye had shared something with Min-ja a while ago, and Min-ja did not doubt her words. Jeom-rye had witnessed it by chance: Ki-soon, who had been napping on the *daecheong-maru* after a long time, suddenly woke up, sat next to an empty water bowl, urinated into it, and then drank from it. After that, Jeom-rye replaced the wide-mouthed bowl with a kettle that had a narrow opening. Since the kettle required opening the lid to urinate into, Ki-soon avoided using it, finding it too troublesome.

Ki-soon had developed *a fear of water*. Though she had to drink when thirsty, she avoided stagnant water and refused to bathe. According to Jeong-seop, "To Big Aunt Ki-soon, water didn't seem like something to drink but rather a source of torment that consumed her." He explained that it was because Jong-cheol had once captured Ki-soon and confined her in the well beside the Big House's *Jangdok-gan*. Jong-cheol had taken advantage of the absence of the household's men.

But why had it been the well of the Big House and not the New House's?

The old Korean saying, '*Ten guards cannot thwart a single determined thief,*' proved true. The house had a vulnerability, and malicious gangsters had taken advantage of it, wrapping a rope around Ki-soon's body and suspending her in the middle of the well. As expected, they had struck when no male adults were at home. This was before they had filed a lawsuit. Jeong-seop said Ki-soon had struggled, but her mouth had already been gagged with a towel.

Min-ja simply remembered what Jeong-seop had said.

Jeong-seop, the father, often remarked to himself that nothing possessed as much power as human memory. Some said that a certain man, after being widowed just 22 months into his marriage, had lived his entire life haunted by the memory and ghost of his wife. *The shadow cast by past memories could make life painful or, conversely, impossible to give up hope.*

Min-ja was merely gathering Jeong-seop's words, lost in contemplation. After all, she was still just an elementary school student.

These days, Ki-soon often flailed her arms and legs while sleeping, as if she were swimming. Min-ja had mentioned seeing Ki-soon like that to Jeong-seop. Upon hearing this, Jeong-seop had said to Min-ja, "Aunt Ki-soon is probably swimming desperately to escape from the water in her dreams because she is so terrified of it." At the time, Ki-soon spoke to no one except Min-ja and Jeong-seop, but she had seemed relatively at ease. However, whatever it was that frightened her, she never took a step outside —not only beyond her room but also beyond the gate of the New House.

But Min-ja's thoughts often drifted into her own imaginative realm, different from that of her father, Jeong-seop. *Eldest Aunt Ki-soon sometimes smiled in her sleep, her hands flailing in the air. Perhaps in her dreams, she saw a man named Yutaka. He approached like a great wave, attempting to embrace the small boat where Ki-soon sat. She felt the gentle ripple of water and the salty taste softly touching her lips. She might have awakened then, still sensing Yutaka's smiling face quietly gazing at her and the warmth of his soft, gentle hand resting on her knee. Ki-soon would have called out... "Yutaka!"* Min-ja always tried to discern Ki-soon's thoughts as she sat beside her.

In fact, until Min-ja had moved into the New House, she and her Big Aunt, Ki-soon, had rarely interacted. Although they were aunt and niece by blood, the age gap was nearly 17 years. The neighborhood children envied Ki-soon as much as they did Ki-hoon. To Min-ja, Ki-soon had been one of those lofty figures, seemingly beyond reach.

The first time Min-ja had seen Ki-soon was probably when she was three years old, so she had no memory of it. She had heard the story so often that she had nearly memorized it, making it her own. According to Bok-hee *Olke* (sister-in-law) of the Big House, it had been a rumbustious wedding ceremony that had captivated the entire neighborhood. Ki-soon's wedding had been a joyous occasion that had drawn many people together. At that time, Ki-soon had looked like a Japanese actress on the cover of a so-called Japanese book, and she had been universally acknowledged for her stunning beauty. Min-ja had been present on that wedding day, holding her mother Eun-ok's hand.

As briefly mentioned earlier in this book, Min-ja was a little country girl with a darker complexion and more freckles than most children. It's a harsh way to describe a face, but she was far from beautiful.

Just a few months earlier, when Min-ja had entered the New House holding Ki-woong's hand, the Eldest Aunt of the New House, whom Min-ja had only heard rumors about, had smiled at her and opened her arms. When Ki-soon had hugged her, Min-ja had even shed tears. Ki-soon had welcomed her warmly. Ki-soon had exclaimed,

"Min-ja! You are that little Min-ja. You're like a little parakeet! Parakeet!"

Min-ja had clung to her, exclaiming, "Wow! Big Auntie, how did you know I was Min-ja?" as she reached out and clung to Ki-soon's waist.

Perhaps this behavior had irritated Young-soon. She had shot a glare at Min-ja and said, "Don't go near my eldest sister! She is my elder sister! *Mundee Gasina*![56)"] Her lips had twitched with effort as she had tried to pull Min-ja away from Ki-soon. This had been the first meeting among Min-ja, Ki-soon, and Young-soon in this house.

---

56) Please refer to the content regarding the words *mundi* and *gasina(e)* on pages 262 and 346 of this book.

18
Blood and Bone I

1954: The New House
—Degeneration

The official armistice was signed in July 1953, bringing the Korean War to a ceasefire and dividing the Korean Peninsula into North and South. By early summer 1954, a new sentiment was taking hold: Since things had turned out this way, let's live even better than before the war.

Two years earlier, when Min-ja had first arrived at the New House, Ki-soon had exclaimed, "Parakeet!" the moment she saw her. Not knowing it was the name of a bird, Min-ja widened her eyes in surprise. "Hey, yellow-winged little parakeet!" Ki-soon had once said, gripping Min-ja's wrist. Despite the rumors, Ki-soon did not seem like a madwoman to Min-ja. She wore a sky-blue linen dress and a headband adorned with yellow flowers against a black background.

At some point, Ki-soon began working at a small desk, diligently engaging in various crafts. Sometimes, she drew pictures that Min-ja didn't understand, mostly of birds. Min-ja often found torn pieces of these unfinished bird paintings in the trash.

She wondered, What kind of bird is this? Why do its wings look so different? Until then, Min-ja had thought all birds were more or less the same—just variations in feather color, wing size, and calls. There were mother birds and their chicks, but nothing seemed fundamentally different. Her curiosity deepened. She was certain there had to be a book or a notebook filled with rough sketches of these birds somewhere in her aunt's room. 'Yes, a sketchbook or study notes—something like that must be in my aunt's room. I really want to see it with my own eyes,' Min-ja's desire grew steadily.

Min-ja was fascinated by Ki-soon, who could draw precise shapes without a compass or ruler. Her work was impeccable—even the smallest three-dimensional paper models were flawless. She even crafted a tiny twenty-sided paper ball to perfection. When Min-ja looked at such a model, she hoped that Ki-soon's spirit had returned to normal. Yet, no one but Min-ja seemed to notice Ki-soon.

The war had ended, and Min-ja had heard about the Armistice Line[57] somewhere, preventing people from traveling between the North and the South. Although Min-ja had only recently graduated from elementary school, she was precocious and burdened with many worries.

She also overheard a neighbor say that her father, who lived alone, might soon remarry. Her mind became increasingly troubled. Perhaps not immediately, but if she wished to take care of her brother and father, she never even considered the possibility of marriage. Above all, she vowed to become wiser for the sake of her younger brother, Ki-woong.

Min-ja first noticed Sang-sik in the second grade while at a neighbor's house. Having moved to Busan and only recently returned, she saw him again and found him reliable. However, she still wasn't sure if Sang-sik was as dependable as her father, Jeong-seop. Sang-sik was the first boy to ever catch Min-ja's interest. Once, instead of entering the main gate of the New House directly, she took a detour to the Big House. From near the bathroom wall of the Big House, she could see Sang-sik's house if she stood on tiptoes and craned her neck.

Some time ago, Jeom-rye caught her peeking into that boy's house. If others had seen her, there might have been rumors that the little dark-skinned girl had feelings for the boy.

Jeom-rye taunted her.

"Eoleri, kkoleri, Eoleri kkoleri!" Jeom-rye teased. "Min *Do-ryeong* (a

---

[57] Armistice Line: The military demarcation line established across the center of the Korean Peninsula at 22:00 on July 27, 1953, marking the ceasefire of the Korean War.

The 38th parallel is often confused with the Armistice Line, but they are fundamentally different. However, for foreigners unfamiliar with the detailed history of Korea and the Korean War, the 38th parallel is far more recognizable than the more technical term "Military Demarcation Line." Recognizing this, foreign media often refer to the Armistice Line as the 38th parallel, even though they know it is a misnomer.—The above is a summary of the contents from Naver Namu Wiki by the author.

sarcastic title for the boyish Min-ja) likes Sang-sik, the boy next door. Isn't Min *Do-ryeong* a *Mersmae*[58]? You, with a dark face and small eyes, like a boy as beautiful as Sang-sik. I saw everything! And this is the second time! So, do you like Sang-sik? He's the same age as you, isn't he?

If you're thinking of getting married, I'll marry first, because you're still just a little kid."

Ki-hwi, with his usual stylish air, sauntered into the yard, whistling. With a swift flick of his knuckles, he playfully tapped the two girls on the head. Ki-hwi was soon to start teaching at a middle school in Sacheon. His hair, slicked back with pomade, gleamed under the sunlight.

He scolded them, "You wet-behind-the-ears kids, always counting your chickens before they hatch. You two ugly brats are doing well... Jeom-rye, get to the kitchen and cook rice. And you, Min-ja *Gasina*, at least open a book and read a page. You barely keep up with your studies, yet you waste so many days doing useless things ... tsk tsk..."

Min-ja felt a surge of indignation. *That elder brother Ki-hwi always acts so dismissively,* she thought angrily. However, his words made her more anxious about her future than her encounter with Sang-sik had. She was uneasy about her father's plans to remarry, which would leave her and her younger brother alone. While she understood he was a widower, she couldn't help but resent it. *Is it because my father is a man? Look at Big Aunt Ki-soon, managing so well on her own...*

If only she had someone to talk to about her worries. *Can I get any hints or guidance about my future from that smart Big Aunt?* she wondered, holding onto a vague hope. She believed that Ki-soon, when in her right mind, might offer some help. This thought led to another: *If I find a note or text that Aunt Ki-soon had written before, when she was in a clearer state of mind, would it help me in my future life? What was Ki-soon thinking when she started middle school and left for Jinju, just as I am*

---

58) Mersmae: A local dialect term for a boy in Gyeongnam province.

about to? Min-ja's eyes sparkled with curiosity as she began searching for Ki-soon's notes. She scrutinized every corner of the New House, every small hidden space she could find. However, it wasn't her house, so she couldn't search freely. She was also uncertain whether her curiosity was good or bad. Despite her efforts, no such note appeared, saying, "Here I am, a note." It became clear that the only people genuinely interested in Ki-soon's every little act were probably the new grandmother, Lady Hwang, and Min-ja herself.

Neighbors found it odd that Young-soon, 16 years younger than Ki-soon, exhibited such strange symptoms. While Ki-soon had her peculiarities, various speculations had circulated about Young-soon's behavior since she was young.

The rumor that Young-soon had once stormed through her yard at night, brandishing a sickle at Ki-soon, had not yet reached Min-ja's ears. Instead, the village whispers were filled with tales about the women of Choi's New House.

In Min-ja's opinion, there was something strange about Young-soon too. Though often motionless, Young-soon would glare and curse at Min-ja whenever she saw her. At the same time, she showed no interest in her eldest sister, Ki-soon. Sometimes, Young-soon would laugh softly and brightly, or she would lie down all day, idly fiddling with her hands and staring at the ceiling.

Young-soon showed no interest in anyone from Min-ja's family, not even in Ki-soon or her mother, Lady Hwang. Whenever the villagers mentioned, "Min-ja's mother tried so hard to survive with her children, but she died of hunger and exhaustion," or "Lady Hwang of the New House suffered a stroke," Young-soon would simply dismiss it with a disinterested, 'Tch, that's their problem. Why should I care?' She showed not the slightest interest in such matters and offered no comment or reaction. Regardless, Min-ja couldn't shake the feeling that something was off about Young-soon.

Young-soon seemed oblivious to the people living in her house, never questioning their presence or absence. For instance, she might briefly wonder why Jeong-soon and Joon-seop were there one moment and gone the next, but she showed no real interest. She would simply acknowledge, "The eldest sister is my elder sister," with a dismissive glance, but as soon as she turned around, it seemed as if she had forgotten Ki-soon entirely.

Though Min-ja tried to avoid thinking about Young-soon, her feelings of animosity only grew. "A mean and terrible girl, a *Gasina* with no feelings," Min-ja muttered to herself. It was evident that Young-soon regarded only Min-ja, who was almost her peer, and Ki-woong, Min-ja's younger brother, with hostility. It seemed as if she thought, 'No matter who they are, they're bad people trying to take our house.'

Why else would Young-soon glare at Min-ja and Ki-woong every day, whether she was eating or resting?

Min-ja and Ki-woong often refrained from touching the side dishes in front of Young-soon and ate plain rice instead. On days when Jeong-seop wasn't at the table, Min-ja would set up a small table for herself and Ki-woong so they could eat separately. However, whenever the three of them sat down to eat in their room, Ki-soon always appeared.

Jeong-seop felt a deep sense of responsibility for his younger sister, Ki-soon, who was 19 years younger than he was, almost like a daughter to him. Jeong-seop would say, "Baby, why don't you come here and sit on your brother's lap? Come here." And Ki-soon, in her childlike state, would obediently climb onto his lap. During these moments, he would often remark, "It seems she still craves blood. No matter how lost she is, she knows I'm her brother."

Min-ja felt uneasy whenever Jeong-seop said, "Young-soon and I have a relationship that's worse than most ... let alone any craving for each other's blood." She disliked witnessing Young-soon's erratic behavior and yearned to leave the house as soon as possible. However, the thought of leaving Ki-soon alone in the New House weighed on her mind.

In her unstable state, Young-soon showed no concern for others, and Min-ja believed that the family members of the Big House were no different. When neighbors expressed concern about Ki-soon's madness or Young-soon's strange mutterings and prolonged eyelid-flipping episodes, the Big House residents next door remained indifferent. It was clear that they deliberately chose to ignore it.

Min-ja couldn't help but think, *It's probably because the family members of the Big House look down on those of the New House and our family as 'offspring of a concubine.'*

It wasn't a pleasant thought, but if they didn't feel that way, they must be devoid of empathy. The children in the Big House always seemed to put on airs. Although their family register was supposedly listed under Lady Hwang, the new grandmother in the New House, they didn't seem to acknowledge it.

The family members of the Big House made remarks about Ki-soon, saying, "When they found out that Ki-soon had been married once, the family of the male student in Japan sent her back to Korea to separate her from their son." Or, "No matter how well she did in her studies, Ki-soon tried to hide the fact that she was illegitimate, which caused her deep resentment and eventual madness." Or, "Although nothing had happened on her wedding night and she was still a virgin, the mere worry and unfairness drove her mad."

Some of these stories might have held some truth, or perhaps they all did. Min-ja, one of the closest observers of Ki-soon, knew that until then, she hadn't needed to know everything that the family members of the Big House knew. Nonetheless, Min-ja accepted that her eldest aunt, Ki-soon, was still peculiar. Even so, she desperately wanted to see Ki-soon's written notes or anything similar with her own eyes.

It is unclear how effective the *Salpuri* ritual was, but Young-soon had entered middle school a few months ago. Min-ja assumed that Young-soon was adjusting to school life in Jinju, as there were no further mentions of her odd behavior. Ki-soon still experienced both silent and furious episodes, but they were less severe than before the ceremony.

Amid everything happening with Ki-soon and Young-soon, Min-ja felt a sense of pride in her own resilience. She had neither a home nor a mother, but she remained healthy. She wrote in detail about everything that happened in the New House to her second sister in Sacheon through letters. However, her eldest sister was already married with a child, and her second sister was preoccupied with her newlywed life, leaving little time to respond to Min-ja's letters from Sancheong.

For all of them, getting through each day without missing a meal was crucial. Survival left little room for concern about anyone else's struggles. Instead of following the typical path to a general middle school, Min-ja resolved to attend a nursing middle and high school to support her family and care for her younger brother. At that time, nursing schools were relatively easy to enter, given the aftermath of the war lingering and the persistent shortage of medical personnel.

One cold winter evening, as the first snow fell and a biting wind began to blow, Min-ja returned home after playing outside with the children. She immediately went into Ki-soon's room to keep her company, knowing that Ki-soon would be alone. She planned to bring her eldest aunt to their room when her father, Jeong-seop, came home for dinner. Whenever Ki-soon sat next to Jeong-seop and ate modestly, she would regress to the behavior of a two-year-old. Otherwise, she would squat in the corner of the room, peeking through the slightly open door.

That day, Min-ja found Ki-soon curled up like a shrimp, clutching something in her sleep. It seemed to be one of the notes Min-ja had been so desperate to find. Her heart pounding with excitement, she opened the note. The ink had yellowed with age.

September 28, 1952

All I have are my five senses. But I always feel that you are beside me. What operates beyond the five senses? Deep in my consciousness, is what they call the unconscious at play? Is it something I possessed even before I was born as Choi Ki-soon? Or is it the consciousness staring at me from the repository of past memories, from a previous life—memories I can no longer access but that have only brushed past me? Is this the Eighth Consciousness[59]—the layer at the very bottom of human awareness, as described in Buddhism?

Is that all I can perceive? Can I know it only if I hear it with my own ears? Can I understand whether you are warm or cold only if I touch you with my hands?

You were alive within me, in my consciousness, as the warmth in my hand, as the tremor of my pulse, as the sound of my breath, as the throbbing of my heart. Even now, you live within me as you always have.

I feel you. Or am I merely convincing myself that I do?

They say I'm going crazy. That can't be true.

No, maybe it is possible. Every time I reach out to feel you, I tremble with fear. For some time, dark and frightening shadow figures have been slowly emerging from the darkness, surrounding me. They strangle me and muffle my

---

59) Eighth Consciousness: In Buddhism, the deepest layer of human consciousness—the unconscious—is referred to as the eighth consciousness, known in Sanskrit as ālaya-vijñāna. In Chinese characters, it is called (ālāyashí). According to the Yogācāra school of Buddhist thought, which analyzes the human mind into eight stages, the Eighth Consciousness corresponds to the final stage. It is the subconscious, hidden beneath the surface, functioning as the repository of all potential experiences and memories.

Also known as ālayavijñāna or storehouse consciousness, it is sometimes referred to as the repository, the storehouse consciousness, or the habitual store. If the Seventh Consciousness consists of the memories and experiences that people consciously recall and retain, the Eighth Consciousness acts as the mechanism that stores these memories and experiences and brings them to the surface when needed, influencing habitual and reflexive actions and speech.—The author's summary based on the Encyclopedia of Korean Culture.

voice so you can't hear how anxiously I call for you. No matter how much I call out, you can't hear me. They must have been watching us all along.

Wherever I go, I constantly hear the sound of their eyes rolling. They are shadow beings, but when they roll their eyes, it always makes a "rattling and rolling" sound. That rattling and rolling sound—shush, they're watching us, so I can't get close to you.

"Ki-soon, you carry the scent of roses. Come to me. If you hold my hand tightly, I know I can persuade my entire family. I'll never see you as less than anyone else. I know your noble character well. Every fine strand of your hair brings me to life. I'll be waiting for you for the rest of my life."

I have never forgotten what you said on that day. When Yutaka spoke those words, his eyes seemed to shine brighter than anything in the world. I could clearly see a halo of light around his face, glowing with myriad lights.

December 4, 1952

That rattling and rolling sound—I can hear them rolling their eyes. I will live my life by marrying you and taking pride in my work. They look at me and say, "Dirty Koreans"—Chosŏn'in. Do they think we look dirty because many Koreans live in poverty and struggle to find enough to eat?

We, too, have warm blood running through us and bone that ache when they collide.

You and I are both trapped in social traditions that separate us. Can't we cross this divide?

One day, you asked me this, didn't you? You heard from a relative who was sent to Chosun (*Joseon*) that I was once married and that my mother was not a lawful wife.

But I am still a virgin who has never spent a night with anyone. My mother is the second wife, but she is legally recognized as the first wife. Would your parents be satisfied if I told them so?

I am the same as I was at birth—a human being made of blood and bone.

Shouldn't traditions evolve? I thought that an enlightened Japan would be different from Chosun. The important thing is that nothing else matters.

"The blood of the Korean people is dirty, and their bone is not pure"—this perception remains deeply rooted in Japanese society. To them, appearance and outcome matter above all else.

That rattling and rolling sound—I'm the coward ... the one who has already killed you! I can't cross that symbolic river that stands between us!

The river is filled with our blood and strewn with countless skulls and bones. If I cross the bridge, what will remain of my family and myself?

Yet, blood remains blood, and bone remains bone.

February 1953

Don't open your mouth!
Every time you speak, a stench taints the air.
Your stench,
My stench,
Each word you utter,
Each time I try to speak.
It's not just your mouth that stirs.
It's the fragments of your memory, constantly churning.
The stench of corruption rising from unfulfilled greed and remorse.

Everything that lives rots.
But only humans emit the vile stench bred by greed and stupidity.

They are nothing but the saliva and sweat that seep from deep within you. Byproducts of your tears and the hormones you suppress to maintain control. They mix with your epidermal cells, becoming sticky — tangled in every breath, mingling with the bitter sighs of watching those beneath you thrive.

You secretly envy the success of those you deem less capable.

Thus, each exhale of frustration and bitterness
becomes further entangled in every breath,
hardening even more.
The essence and oils once formed a thin film of tiny, soft grains.
Over time, your unfulfilled desires and stupidity merge,
hardening into an unyielding mass.

These remnants harden into habits,
etched into your body and mind.
The deep-seated roots of sighs, blood, sweat, tears, and resentment.
We remain carriers of our own inherent stench.

A vast sea of habit!
It's hard to shake off personal habits.
Harder still is escaping the sea of convention forged by the collective.

And so, we are trapped.
We live, rooted in the soil of our habits.
Inhabitants! A bound collective of dwellers!

Three families under one father — all of us, his children.
But each family lives beneath the care of its own mother,
In a separate house.
Yet to outsiders, we seem as one.
I am a descendant of the Choi clan,
dwelling in Sancheong, Gyeongnam, Chosun!
We are bound tightly as one.
My father distributed rice paddies and fields equally,
provided similar houses,
and planted a pagoda tree in each garden as a lasting emblem.

Only the earth understands
and endures the foul stench of our lives.

Don't pollute the soil beneath my feet
by moving your tongue thoughtlessly.

A mouth,
a gateway where the wind flows in and out.
When the wind speaks, do not let it ignite your rage.
If anyone asks what you heard, repeat only what was spoken.
The wind turned into fire and devoured my being.
Your loose tongue, in the end, became the noose of convention
that stole my life away.

Min-ja had read up to this point when Ki-soon stirred, her eyes moving beneath her lids. Min-ja hurriedly closed the note and tucked it back into Ki-soon's arms. At that moment, Ki-soon rose quietly from where she lay. She opened the door and slipped out of the room, her beoseon feet silent on the floor.

Min-ja called softly, "Big Aunt Ki-soon!" but Ki-soon, without acknowledging her, stepped out of the room and began to mutter.

Ki-soon:
"Oh! Scarecrow swaying in the wind,
deluding yourself into believing you're alive!
Do not devolve into a human being!
Do not thoughtlessly spread
the whispers of the wind to others for your own gain!
Your lies destroy the lives of others."

At that moment, Min-ja felt as though someone were following Ki-soon, a tall shadow looming behind her. Had Aunt Ki-soon truly gone mad? Afraid that she might lose her mind alongside her aunt, Min-ja quickly ran to the *Jangdok-gan* of the Big House and called urgently, "Jeom-rye! Jeom-rye!"

19
Blood and Bone II
1955: The Big House and the New House
—Instinct and Habit

The cease-fire announcement washed over the people like a soothing, albeit deceptive, balm, whispering false promises that the war had truly ended. It was merely a cease-fire, not a true end to hostilities.

Yet, many convinced themselves that as long as bullets no longer whizzed past their ears, the tense standoff between the South and the North would settle into a prolonged, uneasy peace. A collective sigh of relief echoed through the populace.

The fallen soldiers, those who perished in the chaos, were consigned to the recesses of memory. Life carried on, adapting to the new norm wherever survival was possible. Improvements to daily life were slow in coming. The survivors, in their pragmatism, pushed away troubling thoughts to ensure their own survival and that of their families.

Everyday life was filled with a flurry of activity, marked by weddings and funerals. In the meantime, they dined with a sense of momentary comfort, applauding politely before scanning the horizon for the next occasion of joy or grief.

Emotions were expended with careless abandon, draining them further with each instance of use. Tears and confrontations became commonplace. In this cacophony, the loudest voice often emerged victorious, but nothing was ever truly resolved. Justifications were offered as needed. Hollow words became the currency of deceit, masking lies with an air of plausibility.

Below the belt, faces ceased to matter. When he encountered a woman of notable beauty, he would approach her without hesitation, sometimes even whistling. If she yielded, a night of fleeting pleasure was his reward; if she responded with cold indifference, he accepted dismissal without regret. When the required men and women appeared, they were paired off like pawns in a game. He believed that life was made easier by such pragmatism, ignoring the struggles of others as inconsequential.

A growing number of people were pursuing only their own interests and immediate comfort. Perhaps it was the war that twisted their minds so. Among these opportunists was Hong-man, the younger brother of Hong-seon. And no one embodied this lifestyle more than Hong-man. He squandered his life, indulging in the wealth provided by his elder brother. His contributions were minimal: Overseeing the grocery store established by Hong-seon and occasionally offering advice in person when summoned.

His greatest asset was his sharp tongue. When asked about someone, he would instinctively highlight their faults, regardless of how well he knew them. He always positioned himself as the foremost authority on any given matter. With a facade of profound contemplation, he would deliver critiques and praise with such sharp precision that his words seemed to leap from his mouth.

However, it was impossible to take his words at face value. Hong-man was far from impartial. His perspective was invariably skewed by his own interests, twisting reality to suit his needs. If something even slightly benefited him, it was white; if it did not align with his interests, it was entirely black.

Despite being aware of this, Hong-seon often sought Hong-man's counsel. Most decisions were made with Hong-man's input, reinforced by their bond as brothers. After the death of Il-seop, the son he had cherished most, and the subsequent losses of Jeong-soon and Joon-seop during the war, Hong-seon began to meet with Hong-man more frequently. In those times of immense loss, Hong-seon, with his rigidly principled nature, desperately needed someone to lean on—a presence like Hong-man's.

Therefore, Yoo-sang couldn't help but realize that Hong-seon's upright character also needed a pillar of support.

Hong-man would say,

"Don't fret too much, *Hyeong-nim* (elder brother). You still own vast lands and considerable property. Jeong-soon succumbed to a *Hoyeolja*, busy with her studies or church work while in Seoul. As for Joon-seop, his short life remained uncertain.

Frankly, it was a grim blessing that Jeong-soon died as she did, rather than suffering some unspeakable fate at the hands of men, only to meet a crueler end. Who can say if she was treated well in an unfamiliar city during the war, or if she died in agony?

And Ki-soon, despite her mental troubles, remained at home, sheltered. In times when women were scarce and precious, who knows? A girl as lovely as she was rare. Families unfamiliar with Ki-soon might even consider her for marriage, dazzled by her beauty, especially during a meeting with a prospective suitor."

Hong-seon:

"Goodness! *Dongsaeng* (younger brother), what are you saying? Don't dwell on the foolishness of the past ... I called you today because of Jeong-seop. Did you know that his house was burned down and his family has nowhere to go, now taking refuge in the New House?"

Hong-man:

"*Hyeong-nim*, no matter how angry you are, I have to speak my mind... It's a mistake to send a girl to an unfamiliar place like Seoul or Japan. What can a girl truly achieve through study?

What's the point of spending a fortune just to become a pompous doctor or secure a public office? Wasn't I, honestly, right about that? Isn't it best for all girls to get married and devote themselves to their husbands?

But let's get back to the point ... are you planning to build another house for Jeong-seop?"

Hong-seon surmised that Jeong-seop could no longer remain trapped in grief over his deceased wife. He needed to find a new partner and remarry, especially since Jeong-seop had an unmarried daughter, Min-ja, and a young son. Recently, Hong-seon had heard through Yoo-sang that Lady Hwang was looking for a suitable match for Jeong-seop.

Thus, he thought Jeong-seop would also require a new residence, perhaps in the Saemmy House, though it wouldn't be the same as before. Jeong-seop and his future wife would need a home with rooms for Ki-woong and Min-ja, a room for the newlyweds, and space for any future children. With this in mind, Hong-seon decided to build a house for Jeong-seop. He asked Hong-man to sell some land and secure the funds for this new house.

As usual, Hong-man, with his thin, unusually red lips and long eyelashes, which lent him a girlish appearance, was quick to speak.

Hong-man:

"*Hyeong-nim,* I'm not trying to stop you from building a house for Jeong-seop, but I have genuine concerns. Do you remember what happened with Il-seop? Looking back now ... I didn't do much. The biggest issue was that Jeong-seop, being a year older than Il-seop, struck him hard several times. Yes, that's right! After hitting the proud Il-seop in the face, do you think hot-tempered Il-seop, who couldn't stand losing to others, would just let it go without retaliation?

And now ... you're going to build a house for Jeong-seop, who treated him that way... If Il-seop, now deceased, could hear this, wouldn't he feel a bit disappointed? And perhaps even his wife, Bok-hee, would feel somewhat let down?"

Hong-seon cut him off, covering his mouth.

Hong-seon:

"Oh! Enough with these old stories. I've made up my mind not to blame anyone or anything anymore. What good will resentment do now? Do you know what's really important, brother? Tell me, do you?"

Hong-man, seeing the anguish etched on Hong-seon's face, gave a quick nod. He pocketed the memo, which contained the address of the land to be sold, prepared by Hong-seon, and left the main room of the *sarang-chae*.

Hong-seon, left alone in the room, only then did he notice the relentless sound of pouring rain. It had been pouring for some time. He looked out of the room. The rain seeped deep into the ground, each drop a persistent reminder of his grief. As he stared at the relentless downpour, a heavy, tar-like pain settled heavily in his chest. He sank to the floor, clutching his chest, his forehead pressing against the cold, hard surface as he cried out in agony.

Hong-seon:

"Il-seop! You left this world in such a senseless way. You fool! How can I forgive you? Did you do this to show me the weight of this punishment, just to make yourself feel better?

You're the biggest fool under the heavens! You tore a gaping hole in your father's heart, and now you rest peacefully in the cold earth.

You selfish child! I don't want to forgive you! If you had ever thought of me, you wouldn't have done something so foolish...

No, that's not it. I really miss you!

I think of the days after setting up the Hwashin general store in Jinju, wandering around joyfully. I wish I could see you riding that big horse like a carefree child. You foolish child!

You shattered me, and yet I miss you so much..."

No one heard his words. Only a hoarse cry blended into the heavy rain, like the wail of a wild goose. From outside the room, it must have sounded like the sobbing of a great beast. People said that the Hadong-ddigi family next door, and the family living right beside them, heard an indistinct hoarse cry, interwoven with the rain, for a long time that day.

When a man tries too hard, does he only make things worse?

Who bears the blame for that?

How closely did Hong-seon watch over Il-seop, careful not to make any mistakes, because he had more children than anyone else? All Hong-seon wanted was to help him become a good father. Jeong-seop slapped Il-seop, and it wasn't Hong-man, acting as the uncle, who orchestrated the meeting to bring him under control. But things quickly spiraled out of control. Before anyone could stop him, Il-seop couldn't bear the humiliation and took his own life a week later.

Hong-seon rushed into the rain as it fell incessantly. How wonderful it would be to wash away his guilt over Il-seop with the rain. Sometimes Hong-seon wondered if he had noticed what Il-seop was thinking a little sooner and stopped him, whether Il-seop would have changed his mind.

No, even if Il-seop had survived but never walked again after that day, confined to this room in the *sarang-chae*, merely staying alive ... he had once entertained such a delusion.

What had Hong-seon expected from Il-seop?

"I want to live. Father, please save me..."

It had been a faint murmur just before Il-seop died. Those had been his final words to Hong-seon, as Hong-seon watched his son's face turn blue, his mouth foaming. His words were barely louder than the hum of a mosquito. The hour was late, and the poison, with its high alcohol content, had already spread swiftly through his body. Any hope of saving him through gastric cleansing was already gone.

After Hong-man left, Hong-seon stood in the yard, drenched in the relentless downpour for nearly an hour, before finally collapsing in exhaustion in front of the main room door where Lady Hwang sat inside.

Lady Hwang was busy inside when she saw a large, dark figure slump to the ground outside. With all her strength, she forced the door open and found Hong-seon lying there. She hurriedly called for Jeom-rye and Yoo-sang to help move him into her room.

Lady Hwang observed Hong-seon as he slept fitfully. His body was drenched in rain, his lips had turned a chilling shade of blue, and his body shivered uncontrollably—a stranger, a man in his seventies. This was the man she had relied on since she had been sixteen. This was her husband. The man he truly was. In his prime, constantly traveling for work, she had never imagined he would end up this way.

Given his state at that moment, the old man lying there was someone desperately in need of help. He had always cared for his family and had done little for his own well-being.

Yet ... being human, there were times when he tried to care for himself as well.

In the eyes of others, it seemed as if he had two wives—or, if you count the one he had separated from after a few years, three. Did he have three wives solely for his own benefit? Some might have seen it that way. But to Lady Hwang, the Hong-seon he had known was more than that.

He had devoted his life to educating and raising his children, supporting many lives under the name of family. But as time passed, more children were born, and not everything turned out as Hong-seon had hoped. Still, he devoted himself to his family. His life was always frugal, in everything from food to clothing. Still, he strove to educate and provide for the children until his final days—land, resources, and guidance. The children he had raised gradually grew up and drifted apart. Even so, he never gave up and kept caring for them.

Lady Hwang's gaze wavered as she looked at Hong-seon. What had she done for him, who had hoped for so much?

She glimpsed herself in the mirror on the dressing stand. Who was this woman with sagging skin, wrinkled cheeks, and deep furrows?

Lady Hwang thought, 'What would I do if there were no one around me, if no one were left? How badly have I lived? Is it better to die before him? And if so, when? No, Ki-soon and Young-soon are still alive... What am I supposed to do? Is all of this my fault?'

As Hwang looked at Hong-seon, she suddenly recalled the song she had heard playing from the phonograph when she had briefly visited Ki-soon's room not long ago. It was *Hymn of Death* by Yoon Shim-deok. At some point in the past, she had bought that record and sent it to Ki-soon, but no matter how much she thought about it, she couldn't recall why she had done it.

From Hwang's perspective, there were fleeting moments when Ki-soon seemed to be in her right mind. Yet, those moments were brief, often giving way to confusion all over again. Whenever Ki-soon's eyes were lucid, Hwang was gripped with fear, dreading the inevitable moment when she would lose her grip on reality once more. Hwang avoided meeting her gaze directly, instead averting her eyes. The uncertainty of whether Ki-soon would ever return to normal weighed heavily on her, filling her with deep frustration.

> A life running in the vast wilderness
> Where are you going?
> In the rough, lonely, and bitter human world
> What are you looking for?

This song had remained popular even after the war. Only yesterday, Jeom-rye had been humming it as she moved in and out of the kitchen. At first, Lady Hwang dismissed it as just another popular song, without giving much thought to the lyrics. But now, much like the first line of the song, she often found herself wondering where she was going and what she was looking for.

Just then, Hong-seon stirred.

Lady Hwang took the warm red ginseng tea that Jeom-rye had left on the side table and sipped it. It was still warm enough to drink. She propped Hong-seon up, lifting his head onto her lap, and gently spooned the tea into his mouth, hoping he would wake. The tea trickled down his wrinkled throat. He tried to raise his head to swallow more easily. Lady Hwang placed two more pillows behind him, helping him sit upright against the wall.

Despite his age, Hong-seon's health had always seemed robust. The sound of tea trickling down his sturdy throat was quiet but steady. After feeding him the tea, Lady Hwang laid him down on the bedding.

She then opened a small box wrapped in a cloth near the foot of the room. Inside lay garments made of white silk—shrouds. The garments meant for the afterlife, prepared for both herself and Hong-seon. She knew Hong-seon's measurements by heart, her hands having long mastered the task.

Why had she started sewing these shrouds three years after marrying Hong-seon? If someone asked, she would say it had begun as a simple pastime. It had started when her eldest daughter Ki-soon was born and she was pregnant with Jeong-soon. It had begun during those weeks when she was nearly faint from severe morning sickness, unable to eat. She was almost six months pregnant when the Eastern medicine doctor checked her pulse, shook his head, and signaled bad news.

How much time had passed?

Lady Hwang, lying down, felt a pang of hunger and tried to rise, but dizziness overwhelmed her, and she sank back to the floor. She heard the sound of overlapping footsteps outside her room and the whispers. Lady Hwang didn't want to listen, yet she couldn't help overhearing.

Il-seop:

"Yoo-sang, what did Dr. Shim say about that woman in the room? I'm telling you this while Father is away, so pay close attention. Hwang from the New House—if anything bad happens during childbirth, I refuse to allow her to be buried in our *Seonsan* (family's ancestral burial ground).

As long as I'm alive, with my eyes open, that woman is never to be accepted."

Yoo-sang:

"Yes, yes, Master Il-seop, I understand. Besides, she is still very young, so nothing will happen anytime soon. Of course, this is what you want. If the Elder Master comes, I'll discuss it with him when he arrives.

Wouldn't it be more practical to decide then?"

Il-seop:

"Oh! Yoo-sang, if someone else heard, they might think I'm asking you to prepare for her death. That's not what I mean, and I don't mean right now. But still ... how can we ever know the ways of life? There is an order to birth, but none to death. Even someone as young as me, pregnant and unable to eat properly ... just imagine how bad her state of mind must be.

Isn't she a woman who married into the Choi family even though the family already had a wife? It's upsetting enough that she's in the family register, but I ... I will never allow her to be buried in our family tomb, even if it causes me great distress!

I will bring this up with Father next time. Just remember what I said. *There is no order to death.* When it happens, it happens!"

Yoo-sang:

"Oh, Master Il-seop! Yes, yes, I will remember your words for as long as I serve in this house. And death ... isn't it just a matter of misfortune?"

It was a conversation between Il-seop and Yoo-sang that day.

From that moment on, Lady Hwang resolved to change her ways. She made a vow to survive, no matter what. Even when she had no appetite, she forced herself to eat. Even when she didn't want to work, she continued managing the household. She decided to bear as many children as possible and keep on living.

As Il-seop had said, one could never truly know what the future held, and thus she found herself cursing the frailty of the heart she had been born with. Long before her eventual death, she decided to make her own shroud for that day. Since she was sewing one for herself, she made one for Hong-seon as well. No one ever knows when it will be needed. Only God knows and prepares for that day, she chose to believe.

She told those around her that she wished to be cremated and have her ashes scattered in the *Gyeongho River*, and she prayed for her wish to be granted.

When Ki-soon returned to her home in Sancheong from Japan, she was astonished to see how drastically the household had shrunk in number. The once bustling Big House, once filled with the noise and presence of her half-brothers, numerous servants, and the familiar neighborhood women who helped with the housework, was now eerily quiet.

There was something she had heard while she was in Japan. She had been told that when Japan was on the verge of collapse after its defeat in World War II, the outbreak of the Korean War had come just in time, allowing Japan's economy to recover instead.

That seemed to be true. Korea had become overrun with beggars and starving people. The streets were crowded with disabled soldiers. Many orphans who had lost their parents flocked to busy areas to shine shoes for a living. They scavenged for cans left behind by military bases, filled them with *jjambap* (military rations), and ate whatever they could find.

Ki-soon realized that almost everything the Japanese had said had been accurate. Korea, despite the circumstances, had to persevere, with some of its youth perishing and others struggling to rebuild their lives. The nation needed time to regain its strength.

More than a year after Ki-soon returned to Sancheong, she noticed that rice and salty fish began to appear occasionally on Min-ja's family's table. To block out the haunting hallucinations and phantom sounds of the night, Ki-soon would cover her ears and burrow under her blanket. Her memory of when she last had a proper night's sleep was fading. The arrival of morning was signaled by the loud shouting of Hong-seon calling for his youngest granddaughter, Ki-seon, from the *sarang-chae*.

Hong-seon:

"Ki-seon! Come and clean my chamber pot!"

When Hong-seon called out from the *sarang-bang* of the New House, Ki-seon, his granddaughter from the Big House, would rub her eyes and open the door to the *sarang-bang*. Despite having been partially destroyed by bombings during the Korean War, the remaining sections of the *sarang-chae* had been repaired. Ki-seon glanced toward Ki-soon's door as she carried out Hong-seon's spittoon and chamber pot. She slightly cracked the door open, perhaps wanting to gauge Ki-soon's expression, and peeked inside. Bok-hee proudly told Lady Hwang that Ki-seon, a diligent and obedient elementary school student who often ran errands for her grandfather Hong-seon, had been awarded as a model student at her school.

Young-soon, having enrolled late in Jinju Girls' Middle School, was no longer at home, as she had moved to Jinju the previous year. Now, only Lady Hwang and Ki-soon remained in the New House. A few days ago, Min-ja's stepmother, who was six years younger than Jeong-seop, had visited Lady Hwang to pay her respects. After she had left, Lady Hwang called Ki-soon into her room.

Lady Hwang:

"Ki-soon, how are you feeling today? I'll prepare your favorite pine nut porridge for dinner. Even if you don't feel like eating, please try to eat a little. With Jeong-seop's marriage, new children will be born, and your father's burdens will increase. In a few months, when the new Saemmy House has been built, Min-ja and Ki-woong will move there. After that, we won't see them as often. For now, Min-ja's family is still with us, and our home feels full and lively. Soon, it will be just you, me, and of course, your father."

Ki-soon:

"Mother, the blood of Jeong-seop's new wife will mix with the bone of this house, and new Choi children will emerge. What is it in my blood that drives me mad?"

Lady Hwang was taken aback by Ki-soon's words. Ki-soon had never before acknowledged her condition so plainly. Lady Hwang had always suspected that schizophrenia came from her side of the family, and she recalled her own aunt's similar fate. Her aunt, after marrying and having three children, was tormented by auditory hallucinations and delusions and spent the rest of her life in her parental home.

But no one outside the family knew this, as far as Lady Hwang knew.

The Choi family members, both from the Big House and the extended family, seemed to believe that Ki-soon and Young-soon's afflictions were due to some misfortune brought upon by Lady Hwang. But they whispered amongst themselves, "Oh, how fitting. A young girl married a man almost 30 years her senior in a house where he already had a wife, and now all her children are ill. Isn't that heaven's punishment?"

No. Perhaps they didn't say it to my face, but they might know, Lady Hwang thought anxiously. It was said that the disease had a genetic predisposition and was triggered by psychological stress and aging.

One day, Hong-man spoke in a way that seemed intended for Lady Hwang to hear. Hong-man:

"To put it bluntly, there was no such disease in our family that caused people to go mad like Ki-soon or Young-soon. Maybe some bad blood entered the family. Don't you think so, *Hyeong-nim*?"

Hong-seon:

"No! You're a terrible person! What kind of nonsense are you talking about? In any household, worries never cease, and all blood is precious. Blood must unite with bones to sustain life. Is there truly good or bad blood? Ordinary people like us don't know. They're simply unlucky that something bad afflicted them. No one knows why. From now on, don't say such things anywhere else!"

Hong-man left the room, pouting and stroking his chin. After that, Lady Hwang returned to her room, trying to calm herself. Hong-seon seemed completely unaware.

Lady Hwang quietly spoke to Ki-soon, who, for the first time in a long while, sat calmly. Lady Hwang:

"I think your father was right. No matter what anyone says, Hong-seon is your father, the one who gave you life, your blood, and bones. The label of illegitimacy is not the fault of blood and bones, it's a construct made by people. Your blood comes from me, and perhaps even the illness did too.

Blood and bone may be forcibly separated, but life arises from their harmony. Imposing a status of illegitimacy within the same family, labeling one's blood as "dirty"... such divisive notions are likely exclusive to humans. Uncle Hong-man, who had subtly insinuated that I am impure, is truly despicable. I cannot help but loathe him."

Ki-soon looked at her mother, but without truly hearing her, she became lost in her own thoughts.

'People often say, −That person comes from a distinguished family. Does this refer solely to the father's lineage that passed down the family name? Is it because fathers traditionally pass down social status to their children?

Then, what is lineage? Lineage, at its core, means the inheritance of blood. Blood is inseparable from bone. Blood courses around a framework of bone, infusing life into delicate blood vessels.

Consider Shakespeare's *The Merchant of Venice*. Human flesh is intertwined with blood, and without bone, the flesh and blood would dry up, becoming nothing more than a dry, lifeless husk.'

As Ki-soon was lost in these thoughts, she suddenly felt something tightening around her neck and collapsed forward. At that moment, it became clear that Ki-soon was strangling herself with her own hands.

Lady Hwang quickly grasped Ki-soon's hands, prying them away from her neck. She gasped and cried out to Ki-soon,

"Ki-soon! Don't forget to breathe. Don't forget to breathe. Breathe..."

Witnessing Ki-soon's strange behavior, Hwang pondered what kind of unknown, mysterious force could be at work within her mind, compelling her to strangle herself. Once her hands were pried away from her neck, Ki-soon muttered to herself.

"Could it be said that blood is the womb and bone is the father's affection? Blood and bone intertwine, forming the body and governing the mind, maintaining what is known as *Sa-nyeom-cheo*.[60]

Yet, despite sharing the same bones, some feel superior as legitimate offspring, using their status to humiliate and control the illegitimate. What cowardly and despicable behavior!

Labeled as the child of the second wife, you must never show subservience or submission to the people of the first wife's household in the Big House. The discrimination between legitimate and illegitimate children is not a matter of blood and bone but of tradition and custom.

It's the simple habits, the ingrained behaviors of those within their social environment. Inertia, those tendencies absorbed from the environment since childhood, should not be tolerated. The notion that Young-soon and I inherited a genetic predisposition for madness, as they claim, is far from certain.

Nothing is definite. It's all a matter of probability."

Ki-soon shook off Hwang's hand and returned to her room, hastily jotting down her thoughts in a notebook. She feared the strange twists her mind might take and was terrified most of losing control over herself.

September 1955

What certainty can we place on what we see with our eyes, hear with our ears, and feel with our bodies?

Perception varies from person to person, and even within the same individual, behavior and emotions shift with each passing moment. We know that significant decisions can be influenced by fleeting glances and subtle gestures. In a brief, seemingly trivial moment, a person may make choices that shape their destiny.

---

60) The Four Foundations of Mindfulness (Buddhist philosophy): Body, feelings, mind, and phenomena—focusing on these to cultivate self-awareness and regulate oneself. (Author's interpretation.)

Why did I make that choice? Why did I agree to marry a man like Jong-cheol, whom my parents described as worse than a beast?

Could such a marriage have occurred without my implicit consent?

Let's set aside Jong-cheol's gluttony and thoughtless speech.

But when he sneered, "just a dirty concubine's child..." would I have stayed in that marriage if he hadn't uttered those words?

Yutaka and his family claimed they had someone investigate me and my family. But why? Because they didn't trust me?

And why did the investigator meet Hong-man of all people?

Would his family have reached the same conclusion about me if they had met someone other than Hong-man?

What if they had accepted me? If Yutaka and I had married, would I have been able to adapt to that married life?

A union of different blood and bone, between different races?

This was where it all ended. As Ki-soon scribbled down her thoughts in her notebook, she sensed a faint rustling outside her room. Who could it be? She tried to open the door, but it remained stubbornly shut. Then, without warning, she felt a tumultuous wave crash against her, submerging her entire body. The frigid seawater clutched at her legs, freezing them in place. Desperately, she curled up her legs and clamped her hands over her ears. Her earlobes swelled, a burning red, as if they might burst, and her head felt feverish and heavy. Her teeth grated together, producing a harsh, grinding sound.

She withdrew beneath the thick blankets, retreating into the depths of her own long, dark tunnel...

20
The Child in Silk Beoseon

1960: The Big House
—A Web of Thoughts Weighing on the Scale of Time

Silk Beoseons (Crayon Art on Kent paper, 364x515m)

Hong-seon laid Lady Hwang flat on his lap after she had collapsed to the floor, clutching her chest. He gently massaged her chest in circular motions and rubbed her arms and legs, all while ensuring her body remained still.

He then waited anxiously for the arrival of the new doctor who had opened a clinic near the Sancheong market just a few days earlier.

Doctors were a rare sight in Sancheong. Most of the oriental medicine practitioners who had once settled there later moved to urban areas due to poor business prospects. During the war, both Western and oriental medicine doctors who had come down from North Korea had settled in various places across South Korea. There were many rumors that some of them, once they had accumulated enough wealth, had planned to emigrate to the United States or Brazil. People who heard these rumors understood that it was likely because they had not wanted their children to experience ideological conflicts any longer.

The doctor Hong-seon had been waiting for was born in Pyongyang and had arrived in Sancheong-eup from Geoje Island with the help of his cousin. The villagers were skeptical of the new doctor. His credentials were uncertain, and his unusually small stature only deepened their doubts. They kept their distance, mistrusting his appearance. "How can such a weak-looking man treat anyone's illness? He looks like he might collapse before his patients do," they would murmur among themselves.

The doctor's name was Ryu Jin-hwan. His relative, who had helped him move to Sancheong, was an acquaintance of the photographer Cheol-jin. When neighbors inquired about Dr. Ryu, Cheol-jin would reply,

"Oh, don't be so prejudiced. Prejudice is the most useless thing, isn't it? This doctor who has just arrived in Sancheong is highly competent, he graduated from a medical college in Japan. His father was a leading figure at the hospital in the Heungnam fertilizer factory in the North.

After his father perished in the war, he managed to escape with his five-year-old son during the January 4 Retreat[61]. He had likely endured great hardships, and his appearance had suffered from surviving severe gastroenteritis three times. His relative told me that he once had a straight, well-proportioned physique.

Trust me, the crucial point is that the doctor is skilled at treating illnesses. What else matters?"

Hong-seon chose to trust the doctor, as Cheol-jin often vouched for him. He then asked Yoo-sang to summon Dr. Ryu. Dr. Ryu arrived at the main house of the New House and began examining Lady Hwang.

Dr. Ryu said,

"Big Elder, it appears your wife has suffered a myocardial infarction. Even if she regains consciousness soon, it would be best to take her to a large hospital in Jinju. As you know, the medical facilities here are quite inadequate."

Following Dr. Ryu's recommendation, Hong-seon began making preparations and instructed Yoo-sang and Jeong-seop to transport Lady Hwang to Jinju. However, Lady Hwang had her own wishes.

Lady Hwang said slowly and clearly,

"*Yeobo*, please don't do anything to me. Instead, let me stay with Ki-soon in her room from now on." Having no other choice, Hong-seon replied, "I will do as you say."

As soon as Lady Hwang regained some of her strength, she moved from the main room to Ki-soon's room, determined to spend all her time with her. From then on, they ate and slept together. Meanwhile, Hong-seon relocated to the *sarang-chae* of the Big House, where Bok-hee resided.

Nearly 900 *pyeong* of the New House lay in desolation. Few people came or went. Hong-seon inspected the New House about twice a day, his

---

61) The term "1·4 Retreat" refers to the UN forces' withdrawal from Seoul on January 4, 1951 marking a retreat from the North Korean offensive.
　—Source: Naver, Doosan Encyclopedia, summarized by the author.

eyes scanning the quiet, empty spaces. Lady Hwang seldom left Ki-soon's room. Filled with curiosity and anxiety that something might be wrong, Hong-seon felt on edge. However, going in and out of the room where his wife and daughter stayed was different from entering and leaving the room where Lady Hwang lived alone.

During this time, the tightness in Hong-seon's chest gradually eased, but he became acutely aware that his physical strength was waning. Eight years after Il-seop's death, Hong-seon allocated more land to Bok-hee in preparation for the future marriages of children or other significant family events.

In 1960, he added 15 *majigi* to the remaining land and gave it to Bok-hee. He also allocated an additional 10 *majigi* to Young-soon, Hwang's youngest daughter, who had been staying at home since graduating from high school that year.

Throughout his life, Hong-seon had worked tirelessly to distribute the wealth he had inherited from his mother and expanded, ensuring it was done fairly. "Share fairly," he reminded himself, striving to uphold this principle to the very end. The misfortune of unfairness was one of the things he despised most.

But what is fairness—something universally fair to everyone?

Some say it is like the light of the sun, just like air and water. Yet even the sun's light is not distributed evenly; it varies depending on where it shines. In a forest of tall trees, small trees struggle to grow, overshadowed and deprived of light. The same applies to houses where people live. Basements receive little sunlight, making semi-basement homes prone to mold and bacteria, which are unhealthy for habitation. Conversely, too much sunlight brings heat, thirst, and discomfort, affecting health and comfort.

What, then, do all living people enjoy equally? It seemed to

Hong-seon that air and another element shared this universal fairness. But what was this "It" that Hong-seon pondered?

For Hong-seon, the fairest thing in the world was "Time." He believed that wasting time was the greatest sin. "Save time, a fair asset given by the Absolute," he would say. In his youth, he despised gambling, whoring, and stealing—*misdeeds carried out by hand and a waste of time.* To Hong-seon, moving, breathing, working, and thinking with the right mindset within the time given to each person was the most important and sacred duty to the Absolute.

So, what can we say about "Time"?

Time can be perceived through sight and touch, but our perception of it is never the same for everyone. For example, when you suddenly look at the clock while doing something and think, "Ah! An hour has passed!" you consciously acknowledge it by visually confirming the movement of the clock's second, minute, and hour hands. At that moment, you are recognizing time.

However, depending on the situation, even one minute of the same duration can feel different. A single minute can seem extremely long in a desperate moment but incredibly short when you are relaxed. In such cases, a desperate second feels unbearably long, while a moment of happiness, when you are indifferent to your surroundings, feels fleeting. At that moment, it is not just perception but also a state of consciousness and the flow of consciousness that makes you aware of time.

Therefore, *time is both perceived and experienced through consciousness.* But no one has ever truly seen time. It exists in the mind and can only be felt by those who are alive. Even patients in a coma, sustained by an oxygen respirator, are affected by time. Thus, Hong-seon believed that the most equally given thing to all living beings in this world is "Time."

Additionally, time is a rule created by the rotational and orbital movements of the sun and the Earth; it is a concept born from these movements. From the moment a person is born on Earth, *time* becomes the *most honest* and *equally distributed personal asset one can have*. It is the *only element of true equality*, just like the gravity felt on Earth.

Could the existence of God—the deity his wife, Hwang, believes in and prays to every morning and evening—be the most equitable element given to all humans? Who has ever seen that deity with their own eyes? Does God exist whether we, the living, believe in Him or not, sharing His grace equally with all who are alive?

Ultimately, who was it that brought the regularity of movement created by the sun and the Earth, known as "Time," into the rules and systems shaped by human perception and consciousness?

Whoever named it, *it was a human*. Time is a human-made framework, and the dead are merely actors who have exited its stage. *Humans continue to believe in and rely on the unseen force of time, recording its passage in the annals of history.*

Does the "Existence of God" fit into the rules and systems created by humans, like "The Existence of Time"? Probably not. While God, like time, distributes His grace and blessings equally, He should not exist within the confines of human-made institutions and regulations. At the very least, if a person comes to realize even a little of the futility and vanity they experience within the flow of time throughout their life, they will understand that nothing they achieve is accomplished solely by their own strength.

"*Nemo Deum vidit*"—"No one has ever seen God" (John 1:18). Can it be said that those who believe in unseen time yet deny the existence of an unseen God are acting in a more human way?

Whether people acknowledge time or not, both the dead who have left the stage and the living who remain accept time's dynamism in their minds. Similarly, one does not often consider the existence of God when life proceeds smoothly (when everything goes according to plan), just as one does not always perceive the passage of time in daily life. But in moments of true desperation, people inevitably recall the existence of God, the Absolute, and place their trust in Him—whatever name they give to Him.

For a condemned prisoner who must die tomorrow, today's time becomes the God he most wants to believe in and follow, transcending the present. In the prisoner's mind, the concept of "Tomorrow" remains alive until the very moment his life is extinguished. *It is in moments of utmost desperation that a person seeks to find and confirm the reality of time, life, God, and even their own existence.*

No one has ever seen God. No one has ever seen time. Just as one believes in the existence of time, one must believe in the existence of God. It matters not whether this belief profits or costs you—it exists simply by being, accompanied by the condition of free will, as an Absolute being both within and beyond memory.

Someone once said that everyone is born free, yet ensnared by the fetters of social convention. But were we truly born free? The greatest impediment to that freedom is societal convention.

Convention is a vast sea formed by the small and trivial habits that you and I create. It becomes a swamp, difficult to escape once fallen into. These habits, along with the repetitive actions and reactions they generate, function like the springs of a clock that keep turning. This swamp and sea transform into the social interactions we take for granted, becoming tools with which we tame one another. Initially unfamiliar conventions are gradually accepted over time, solidifying into the framework of our lives.

Hong-seon reflected on the conventional fetters that had bound his life. *Conventions must also change with the passage of time...* Unconsciously, he took a deep breath and gazed out from his *sarang-bang*.

Hong-seon:

"This was my universe. No matter how grandly we glorify or expand it, everything humans create is nothing more than a swamp and a bubble. After I die, how will my children and their children live? Was my life merely an endless effort to pass on my genes?

Buddha taught that the universe is composed of Six Paths (the Six Realms of Existence)[62], and it is difficult to be reborn as a human after passing through them...

As I recall, many people I've encountered have been reluctant to share anything they possess with others... Such selfishness leads to a lack of mutual aid, ultimately resulting in the self-destruction of our race. Was it a futile dream of mine to hope that my descendants would share their lives fairly for the preservation of their species, as other animals do? At the very least, it should have been so for my descendants in this small land of Sancheong..."

Reflecting on his life, Hong-seon realized he had not acted because someone told him to. He simply liked people, regardless of their social status, and considered those from his household—whether Choi family members or those related to the Choi family—as belonging to him. Thus, whether they were servants or his own children, he had always tried to help them in whatever way he could. The living continue to live, and the dead remain silent, but Hong-seon had always tried to share with them as much as possible. Perhaps *the Fairness* he envisioned existed only within his own mind.

As Hong-seon lay lost in thought in the *sarang-bang*, a figure appeared. It was You Nam-gil, Lee-seop's wife.

---

62) The Six Paths: The worlds of heaven, humans, asuras (Buddhist demons), animals, hungry ghosts, and hell. Heaven, or the heavenly world, is where all desires are fulfilled and pleasures abound. Yet, it remains part of the cycle of reincarnation, existing one level below the ultimate goal of Buddhism—paradise or nirvana.

The human world, where we reside, is more painful than the heavenly world. However, it is also a place where freedom can be experienced, and the ability to actively respond to karma is most evident. Thus, Buddhism regards it as the most suitable realm for practicing its teachings.

—The above summary is based on information from Naver Knowledge Encyclopedia, summarized by the author.

Nam-gil spoke,

"Father, are you there? It's Nam-gil, your second daughter-in-law. I've been too busy living in Seoul to visit you. Today, I had some business in Sancheong and decided to stop by. I have something to discuss with you."

Hong-seon pushed open the *sarang-bang* door, inviting Nam-gil inside. She looked worn and had gained weight, appearing as an ordinary middle-aged woman. What was the point of dredging up past grievances now?

Hong-seon said,

"So, you've been living in Seoul? What brought you there? And are all the children doing well?"

Nam-gil:

"No, I didn't have any connections, but if I'm willing to live anywhere... Anyway, I married off my eldest daughter, Jin-young, to a doctor. My second and third daughters are also doing well. The second daughter finished nursing high school, and I'm trying to have the third daughter take the exam to become a school teacher.

Is everything all right in Sancheong?"

In truth, Nam-gil had received a considerable sum of money from Hong-seon on her last day in Sancheong, a fact she had kept secret from others. Regardless of her circumstances at the time, she spoke as if she and her children were now well settled in Seoul. Hong-seon recalled hearing from Bok-hee that her eldest daughter's husband was an elderly doctor from North Korea.

Nam-gil continued,

"Father, I heard you recently gave some land to Young-soon. How about arranging a marriage for her? I know a suitable man from North Korea."

Hong-seon said,

"She has just graduated from high school, but nowadays, would a girl really want to get married so quickly?"

Nam-gil replied,

"Well, I'm not sure about other girls, but as for the young ladies in the New House, it's a bit awkward to say, but ... there are already rumors about some health issues. Because of that, Young-soon wouldn't be able to introduce herself to respectable families in our neighborhood or nearby areas. If it's a family from another region who knows nothing about us, maybe it could work... But, as it happens, I met a young man from the North while I was staying in Seoul. That's why I'm bringing this up to you first, Father."

Hong-seon couldn't answer that question. It was already widely known that Yeong-soon, like her older sister Ki-soon, was not mentally healthy. Just a few days ago, despite Bok-hee from the main house trying to stop her, Young-soon had suddenly run into the kitchen and started pinching and arguing with one of the working girls. Unlike Ki-soon, who preferred to stay silent and alone, Young-soon, though older in age, had the mind and behavior of a third grader. She wasn't malicious or wicked at all, but she would often bicker and play with children much younger than herself.

Yet, with her large, expressive eyes and gentle demeanor, and the dimples that appeared when she smiled, Young-soon undeniably resembled Lady Hwang. She looked endearingly cute and innocent, like a child. Especially striking were the large, double-lidded, deep brown eyes shared among the women in the family—beautiful by anyone's standards. Without the support of her aunt, Lady Hwang's sister and the principal of a high school, Young-soon might never have completed her high school education —let alone at the prestigious Jinju Girls' High School.

When Hong-seon hesitated to respond favorably to Nam-gil's suggestion, Nam-gil laughed loudly and spoke with conviction.

Nam-gil said,

"Father, I'm determined to see Sister-in-law Young-soon married to the northern man I mentioned. If you don't approve of him, there's another man I know in Seoul. It would be beneficial for the Choi family to arrange her marriage now. However ... I will need some money to prepare for the wedding."

Hong-seon didn't entirely trust Nam-gil, but he understood that arranging Young-soon's marriage was one of his life's responsibilities. His decision was swift. After a moment's thought, he retrieved money from the closet and handed it to Nam-gil.

Nam-gil immediately began making arrangements, visiting Lady Hwang in the New House to prepare for Young-soon's marriage.

Lady Hwang asked,

"Thank you for finding a match for my daughter, but how far did he go in school?"

Nam-gil replied,

"Stepmother, considering the turmoil of the war, does it really matter how far he went in school? He's a carpenter by trade, capable of building houses and working on construction sites. Most importantly, he will cherish Young-soon. What more could we ask for? Just allow me to introduce him to her."

Indeed, Young-soon's prospective groom had no formal education. As Nam-gil had suggested, Lady Hwang accepted that, in these times, survival itself was a blessing—perhaps even a divine choice. Countless lives had been lost in the war; soldiers from America, Turkey, France, and many other countries had died for Korea under the United Nations' banner.

Lady Hwang asked Nam-gil to discreetly observe the young man from a distance. His overall appearance did not suggest a rough or unkind nature. Upon closer inspection, although his inability to keep his gaze steady and his habit of nervously glancing around were less than ideal, he did not seem to possess a fundamentally bad character. It seemed likely that he would keep his promise to Nam-gil to treat Young-soon kindly, as one would a child, for a considerable period.

His name was Kim Dal-soo.

Young-soon's wedding was planned as a quiet, simple affair in Busan, not Sancheong. They rented a small wedding hall, and only close relatives traveled by bus to attend. The bride and groom were set to return to Sancheong about a year after the ceremony. In the meantime, Hong-seon prepared two small rooms for their newlywed life in Busan. The following year, they would naturally settle into the main building of the New House in Sancheong.

The hurried arrangement of Young-soon's marriage was intended to preempt any neighborhood gossip about her health. It was timed perfectly, taking advantage of a period when everyone was preoccupied with their own livelihoods. If they're already married and bring household goods into the house, who will nitpick and ask questions? Lady Hwang despised gossip more than anything. Thus, Young-soon's marriage was concluded. Ki-hoon's wife, Jong-hee, remarked to Lady Hwang, "I'm saddened that my Youngest Aunt, a blind little girl, got married so hastily, like raising her hair on a dark night."

After the wedding, Hong-seon felt uneasy about the newlyweds' room. He and Lady Hwang took a bus back to Sancheong, leaving Yeong-soon to settle in Busan. That night, with Yeong-soon gone, Hong-seon and Hwang silently wiped their tears in separate rooms, not even turning on the lights.

After Nam-gil arranged Young-soon's marriage and left Sancheong, a major issue arose in the town. The money Nam-gil had received from Hong-seon had been spent somewhere. This time, she borrowed money from members of the main house's family and fled. Among those who had lent her money was Bok-hee's eldest son-in-law.

The story of Bok-hee's eldest daughter, Ki-jeong, and her son-in-law goes like this:

Ki-jeong fell in love with her sixth-grade homeroom teacher and insisted on marrying him. Despite her kind heart, Ki-jeong was incredibly stubborn. "Mother, I won't marry anyone but that teacher. It has to be him," she had declared vehemently. Though Ki-jeong wasn't academically inclined, she excelled in sewing due to her dexterity. She was the least attractive of her sisters—short in stature—but kind and gentle at heart.

Her homeroom teacher's name was Kim Byeong-jin. He had been the top student at Jinju Normal School and a standout soccer player for the school team. However, at the prime age of 20, he had contracted severe pulmonary tuberculosis, which left him weakened and limited his career to being an elementary school teacher. The intelligent bachelor from Jinju Normal School was the most popular and talented male teacher at Sancheong Elementary School.

Bok-hee's eldest daughter, Ki-jeong, would ask her mother to bring warm lunches and snacks to the school every day. Bok-hee gladly complied, not just out of duty but because she greatly admired the young, handsome teacher and saw him as an ideal son-in-law. This devotion sparked a rumor in the neighborhood that "Hyori-ddigi was crazy about a young teacher."

Eventually, Ki-jeong finished middle school and stayed at home until she married Byeong-jin. In 1954, they had their first daughter, and Byeong-jin continued working as an elementary school teacher in Sacheon. Bok-hee's eldest son-in-law was saving money to attend university because he wanted to become a middle school teacher rather than an elementary school teacher. This was due to the gradual reorganization of Korea's education system after the war, which required a four-year bachelor's degree to qualify as a middle or high school teacher.

Nam-gil didn't stop there; she also used Bok-hee's eldest son-in-law's name to borrow more money from two teachers she knew. The total amount was quite substantial. With the borrowed money and the debts incurred by his colleagues, chaos erupted in Bok-hee's eldest daughter's household. Ki-jeong's husband, distraught and refusing to eat, turned his back on the world, leaving Ki-jeong no choice but to seek help from her family in Sancheong, tearfully pleading with Bok-hee.

With no other option, Bok-hee sold part of her land and, along with the money her eldest son, Ki-hoon, had provided, gave it to Ki-jeong to settle her husband's debts.

At that time, Jeong-seop had recently remarried and had two sons with his new wife. Unfortunately, his new wife was so dull and naive that she became the subject of ridicule in the town. It wasn't that she was bad; she was just frequently teased for her actions. She couldn't take proper care of Jeong-seop, who, unlike before, now always wore dirty, stained clothes. The house was constantly untidy, and their young children cried incessantly due to a lack of care.

Min-ja, Jeong-seop's daughter, felt sorry for her father, her younger brother, and her two half-brothers. While attending nursing high school, she saved money by working nights at Sancheong Health Center during vacations, contributing almost all of it to the household. Her two younger half-brothers, Choi Ki-cheol (born in 1957) and Choi Ki-jin (born in 1959), added to the financial strain, causing Jeong-seop's wealth to dwindle even further.

Although they received aid from Hong-seon and Lady Hwang, the house that had burned down could not be rebuilt as it once was. The funds Hong-seon had provided mysteriously vanished, and the need to repay others' debts reduced their land to a mere hundred *pyeong*. Consequently, the house itself shrank to just three rooms. Min-ja's family used the remaining part of the original *haengnang-chae*.

Young-soon harbored an intense dislike for Min-ja, but Min-ja did not envy Young-soon for marrying before her. It was revealed that Nam-gil, who had returned to Sancheong to arrange Young-soon's marriage, had also borrowed money from Min-ja's older sisters. She had even borrowed the savings that Min-ja's third eldest sister, who worked at the Sacheon Public Health Center, had set aside for her own wedding.

When Min-ja heard about Nam-gil's actions, she was bewildered. Unlike Young-soon, she couldn't even dream of getting married within the next two to three years. Min-ja had to care for her younger siblings, who were still barely taking their first steps. Her father, who struggled after remarrying a woman who lacked sense, relied heavily on Min-ja. The situation was difficult, but Min-ja couldn't express her feelings openly. Yet, as a woman, she felt a deep sense of longing and distance from the life she wished for.

However, when Min-ja visited the New House and saw her Big Aunt Ki-soon, she realized she was in a better position. Since Min-ja's family had left the New House, Ki-soon had been living in a small room next to the main room, receiving little attention. Ki-soon remained isolated, meeting no one.

Lady Hwang had briefly stayed in Big Aunt Ki-soon's room but moved back to the main room as preparations for Young-soon's wedding continued. On the day Young-soon's bridal belongings were sent to Busan, Ki-soon lay in her room, staring blankly at the ceiling. Occasionally, she would wander out onto the wooden porch and, as if reaching for an invisible string hanging from the beam, she would raise her hand and make futile grasps at the air.

Lady Hwang had been almost paralyzed on one side since she had collapsed a year ago, making it difficult for her to care for Ki-soon. Yet, she stubbornly remained by Ki-soon's side. With her left hand and leg paralyzed, Lady Hwang could barely stand or sit properly, as only one side of her body was functional.

To help with the chores, Hong-seon found a 12-year-old girl named Ok-ja to run errands around the New House, especially after Yeong-soon got married. Ok-ja helped Lady Hwang and Ki-soon, serving as a link between them and the Big House. Jeom-rye had entered a nunnery a few years earlier.

Summer arrived, and the people were busy with farming. Hong-seon, suffering from a summer cold that even animals avoided, struggled as his phlegm worsened. Bok-hee instructed Ok-ja to empty his chamber pot and clean the room diligently. The youngest daughter, Ki-seon, was not at home, as she was attending high school at her eldest brother Ki-hoon's house along with her older sister Ki-ok.

That day, Bok-hee prepared grilled salted herring and abalone rice porridge for lunch for Hong-seon, who had lost his appetite and had been skipping meals, and brought it to his room.

Hong-seon said,

"Sori-ddigi, you've done well cooking and enduring the heat on such a hot day. Look ... it's not much, but always keep it under your pillow. Take it."

He handed her a small gold statue of Buddha, wrapped in a silk bundle, which had been hidden under his pillow.

Bok-hee couldn't hide her surprised expression and said.

"Father, this precious item... You've always kept it with you. Can you really give it to me?"

Hong-seon replied,

"Sori-ddigi, I may have property, but it is that of a rural farmer. I know how hard you've worked. I know your habit of saving even small things and gathering them in advance. Aren't you the one who cuts an onion only as much as needed? The side dish you made is especially delicious today. You've done an excellent job.

Sori-ddigi, if it weren't for you, even after Il-seop left, there wouldn't have been a chance with the property I gave him. There are still a couple of houses and rich paddy fields left, so look after the rest of your children well. When girls get married ... they can sometimes be driven out due to circumstances or need to live there for the rest of their lives. If a woman marries without any family support, her life can be very pitiful.

You have four daughters, and there will always be times when you need them. That's why I instructed Yoo-sang to add 15 *majigi* under your name. Keep it well; the time will come when you need it. Thank you, Sori-ddigi. As the eldest daughter-in-law of this house, you have done everything your husband should have done."

Bok-hee couldn't hide her surprised expression and said,

"Father, what are you saying? If you, my father, hadn't been here since Il-seop passed, I might have already collapsed. Please stay strong. I think you're feeling weak this evening, so I'll cook *samgye* porridge (porridge with ginseng and chicken). I'll kill the chicken in the yard, braise it, and bring it to you with glutinous rice and ginseng."

As Bok-hee spoke in front of Hong-seon's table, they heard Yoo-sang's voice outside.

Yoo-sang called out,

"Big Elder, Madam Hyori, your nephew has arrived from your parents' house. He just came from Masan."

Bok-hee opened the door to the *sarang-chae* with a glad heart. Outside stood a man with well-defined and neat features, dressed in a fine suit. He appeared to be in his thirties and held a boy, about two years old, whom she assumed was his son.

Bok-hee said,

"Oh, it's been a while. Come on in. Soo-gon, is this your son, Yo-han? Let me give him a hug."

Hong-seon said,

"Yeah? Is that the son of Sori-ddigi's second elder brother? You're a high school teacher now?"

Soo-gon replied,

"Yes, I had business at the school here and thought to visit since I haven't seen you in a while. I brought my son to say hello. Big Elder-in-law, have you been well?"

Bok-hee decided to prepare an extra meal for them to dine with

Hong-seon. The man was Jeong Soo-gon, the only son of Bok-hee's second brother. His father had been a policeman during the Japanese colonial period but had soon left the job due to his upright and gentle nature. His family had embraced Christianity after the August 15 Liberation.

Hye-young, Soo-gon's wife, was the daughter of a renowned Christian minister from the North who had built a small church in Masan. Hye-young, an elementary school teacher, was his only daughter. Soo-gon had met Hye-young during his college years in Masan and had married her the year he graduated.

Hong-seon smiled and asked Soo-gon,

"Soo-gon, since you married into a very devout Christian family, do you not perform the ancestral rites?"

Soo-gon replied,

"Yes, my wife and I are happiest taking our children to church every week. During the *Joseon* era, Confucian-style ancestral rites were inevitable due to national policy. Now, many people have converted to Christianity or Catholicism... Serving ancestors is akin to serving people..."

Hong-seon didn't ask Soo-gon any more questions, for he knew a bit about Soo-gon's background. He understood that, for Soo-gon, the concept of an ancestor meant something different. He also knew that Soo-gon had a birth mother, which complicated the typical parent-child relationship.

Hong-seon remained silent and shared the meal with Soo-gon. After eating, Soo-gon went to greet the New House and Jeong-seop's house.

Hong-seon then asked Bok-hee,

"Hey, Sori-ddigi, is Soo-gon the child who just came to greet us wearing silk socks?"

Bok-hee replied,

"Yes, Father, that's the child who entered my elder brother's house wearing silk *beoseon*."

Bok-hee returned to the kitchen, and Hong-seon opened the door of the *sarang-bang*. It had been raining for some time. Hong-seon muttered, "Soo-gon and his son shouldn't have been caught in the rain..." Even though it was early July, the rain was unusually heavy, more so than during the typical monsoon season.

He closed his eyes and reminisced about his younger days when he would journey to the market, leading a horse laden with goods. The steep, winding mountain paths he had traversed came to mind. The small package on his back had contained cash earned from trading and precious ornaments for the market. Among those items was the Japanese gold Buddha statue he had recently given to Bok-hee.

He had always traveled with three or four young, energetic men, but few could keep up with him. In those days, Hong-seon's face had shone with vitality, his body had been strong and muscular, and his eyes had been clear and sharp. He had moved quickly and efficiently, fulfilling his duties despite the arranged marriage to Lady Kim, as orchestrated by his mother, Lady Cho.

He thought of Lady Han, Jeong-seop's birth mother, who had given him his first son, Jeong-seop. He remembered holding Il-seop and the pretty face of the young and beautiful Lady Hwang... The memories of Il-seop's death and Joon-seop's face flooded back to him.

Hong-seon said,

"Oh, my God! I never intended to harm anyone, and I never wasted time unfairly. Why do I feel so sad and frustrated?"

That evening, Bok-hee prepared *samgye* porridge and was about to take it to the *sarang-chae* when the rain started pouring heavily again. She went back to the kitchen, found a hemp towel to cover the food, and noticed that the door to the *sarang-bang* was wide open.

Bok-hee muttered to herself,

"Why isn't Father closing the door when it's raining cats and dogs?"

She put the table back on the stove and went to the *sarang-chae*.

There, she found Hong-seon motionless, his eyes closed, hands folded on his stomach.

The rain poured relentlessly for three days, creating a large hole in the yard from the water running off the tiled roof. The flag on the prepared white flower bier became soaked and tattered. The bier carriers transported it, the flag flapping in the wind. Ki-hoon, the chief mourner, walked in front with a photo of Hong-seon, holding the fallen flag.

When they arrived at the mountain, the rain stopped, and the weather cleared. Despite the heat, a five-day funeral was held.

Ki-hoon's son, Se-joon, stood out among the mourners. Ki-hoon's colleagues and university students, Ki-hwi with his daughter from Busan, Bok-hee's married daughters, Jeong-seop and his family, and Bok-hee's relatives from Hamyang and nearby areas attended. Nam-gil, who was in Seoul, could not be reached. In total, about 250 people, including relatives and locals, attended, as Yoo-sang had informed Ki-hoon.

Bok-hee prepared hot beef soup, rice, and vegetables for the mourners at *Seonsan*, the family gravesite. Despite the funeral, relatives crowded the *sarang-chae* and *an-chae* of the Big House for about ten days, eating and sleeping there.

Since Hong-seon had passed away at the age of 79, people said, "The death of the Big Elder is a propitious mourning."

However, Jeong-seop wept bitterly. "He came into this world and returned to the ground ... it doesn't make sense to call it propitious mourning!" The neighbors, seeing Jeong-seop's grief, said, "Jeong-seop's wail is the most heartfelt ... perhaps it's hardest for him these days."

It is often true that those who cry the most at a death are the ones struggling the most.

Soo-gon and Yo-han, who had come to greet Hong-seon's family, were stranded due to the unexpected funeral. Only after the ritual was completed could they return to Masan. On the bus to Masan, Soo-gon's mind was filled with the words of the Big Elder.

Mr. Jeong, do you know the recent circumstances of your birth mother? I don't know if I'm saying this because I lost my son, but seek out your birth mother. The affection of a person, when longed for deeply, can become an emotional sediment, even a grudge. Be sure to find your birth mother and say hello. A mother can live on her son's sweet voice for the rest of her life, Hong-seon had said, holding Soo-gon's hand.

On the bus, Soo-gon held Yo-han's little fist as the boy slept. He whispered, "Yo-han, I'll protect you. You are the eldest son of the Hadong clan Jeong family."

Soo-gon was still uncertain. The fear that he might lose everything he had cherished in his daily life if he acknowledged the woman as his *biological mother* lingered within him. Quietly, he closed his eyes and offered a prayer to his God, seeking solace and guidance.

21
The Shadow of the Past

1961: The New House
—The Wind of Convention

Hong-seon was interred in the earth, wrapped in a shroud lovingly crafted by Lady Hwang. Crafting the shroud had provided her with a distraction from the bitter truth that she was merely the second wife of the Choi family.

When she had first entered the marriage at the tender age of sixteen, she had naively believed that her status would be legitimized once she was listed as the formal wife in the family register. The neighbors, who regularly came and went, addressed her with respect, calling her "The Madam of the main room in Choi's house." Yet, in times of urgency, they would invariably say, "We must inform the Big Madam, Lady Kim, first," and would promptly head toward the Big House.

Then one day, Il-seop barged into Lady Hwang's main room, where she was alone with young Ki-soon and baby Jeong-soon. On that unforgettable day, without even removing his shoes, Il-seop had struck the large central pillar of the main building with a heavy stone from the yard.

No one had come to Lady Hwang's aid. Although Bok-hee and other servants had been present in the Big House, they had not approached the New House. The absence of Hong-seon and Yoo-sang was most keenly felt. The neighbors, drawn by the commotion, had merely peeked over the fence.

Some might have feigned ignorance, wary of becoming entangled in the ensuing drama. Others, perhaps sensing an impending eruption, had chosen to distance themselves. Only after the incident did they cautiously whisper to Hwang, "We always suspected Il-seop might do something drastic. His eyes were always so intense, it felt like we were walking on thin ice."

Whenever Hong-seon left to attend to business or household duties, Lady Hwang would anxiously lock the door of the main room, her fingers trembling. She remained ever vigilant, attuned to the sounds and atmosphere emanating from the Big House.

The hope that each day would pass safely and without incident, along with the underlying anxiety, drove Lady Hwang to immerse herself in sewing. It was, in fact, Il-seop's ominous words—"That woman should never be buried in my family's *Seonsan* ... there is no order to death; it can come suddenly."—that compelled her to keep a needle and thimble perpetually in hand.

She crafted numerous pieces, including *hanbok* for Hong-seon and the children, as well as blankets and mattresses. Delicate peony blossoms adorned the silk-covered cushions and fancy mattresses where Hong-seon would sit. On the 100th day after the birth of their youngest daughter, Young-soon—born when Hong-seon was sixty—Lady Hwang created a white baby cape and garments using Japanese knitting thread and a crochet hook. Dressed in her handmade creations, Young-soon nestled in Hong-seon's arms. His face, radiant with affection, softened as he held her close. Young-soon wore a yellow and red *hanbok*, a *jokduri*, and the white knitted cape.

Witnessing this tender scene, Hong-man approached Hong-seon, his voice low as if speaking in passing.

Hong-man said,

"Oh my! Brother, what's so special about such a little girl? I have two daughters myself, and all I foresee are the troubles they will bring to me and the household. If you were anyone else, you'd be thrilled to have a daughter at an age when you could be a grandfather. As for Ki-soon, rather than pushing her toward studies and a teaching career, wouldn't it be more practical to marry her into a good family?"

But Hong-seon seemed not to hear Hong-man. His only wish was for his children to live rich, stable, and happy lives. Regardless of whether it was Il-seop or Jeong-seop, he had always imparted the same wisdom: "Live doing what you most desire, with honesty and diligence."

Yet, after Il-seop's death, had Hong-seon finally come to accept the changing times?

Lady Hwang was the first to notice this shift as she listened to him address the gathered relatives.

Hong-seon said,

"My grandson Ki-hoon, with his brilliance, should become a judge wearing a gold-trimmed robe, for the sake of our country and family, don't you think? Why did I ever believe that wealth alone was enough? I was blind to the world's potential. I wasn't as perceptive as I should have been."

This realization struck Lady Hwang deeply, making her recognize the regret she would feel if she continued to sit idly by.

She reflected, *As a wife, I believed I should trust and follow my husband in everything ... I expected too much from him. While it's important to have a strong son for the family, I can't force Joon-seop, who is gentle by nature. What more can I do as a woman of the Choi family?*

A sense of resignation had crept upon her unnoticed. Now, hearing such words, she felt powerless. Even her sewing, once a refuge from her worries, seemed inadequate.

Hong-man, always eager for praise and recognition from his elder brother Hong-seon, believed that by pleasing him, he could secure more wealth and land. He thought nothing could harm him as long as he remained in Hong-seon's good graces. This was evident in his involvement in Ki-soon's marriage.

Hong-man said,

"Elder Brother, even in *Joseon*-era Korea, a daughter could sometimes surpass a son in usefulness. A son could never become king without avoiding conspiracy, but if a daughter were raised well, she could become a queen. They say everything is decided by the pillow, don't they? So, instead of keeping your pretty and intelligent daughter, like Ki-soon, focused on her studies, I think it would be better to marry her to the son of a government official to secure the family's future."

Hong-seon responded, "That's possible," but his tone was unenthusiastic, merely acknowledging the idea. He seemed disinterested in everything. However, Hong-man seized this moment of indecision to further his own agenda. Hong-man, as if seizing the opportunity, spoke eagerly, his eyes gleaming as he wetted his lips.

"Elder Brother, I will take it upon myself to find a suitable man for Ki-soon and bring him to you. Just wait. If anything, it will help you, not be a loss. You'll see, I guarantee it. And ... as it happens, there is already someone who took a liking to Ki-soon after seeing her from afar."

Hong-seon, with a weary nod, seemed to concede, allowing Hong-man to take the reins.

As it turned out, Ki-soon's groom, Jong-cheol, had not been found merely through a search. Hong-man had orchestrated the match, first gauging the interest of the family members and then receiving money from them. This fact naturally came to light during Ki-soon's legal proceedings.

How had Hong-man planned and executed such a scheme with such composure?

Lady Hwang and Hong-seon proceeded with the marriage to Jo Jong-cheol, trusting Hong-man's assurances. Of course, Ki-soon was completely unaware of these dealings. As mentioned earlier, Jong-cheol was the son of the governor of Sacheon-gun, and his tall, fair-skinned appearance made him relatively handsome. However, had Hong-man been more forthright, Jong-cheol would never have been considered a suitable match for Ki-soon. The breakup revealed his true character—a man who spent much of his time in the *gisaeng-bangs* and had a propensity for gambling.

How much had Hong-man truly known about Jong-cheol, and how would they have discovered the truth without the lawsuit? Until the lawsuit arose, Lady Hwang had no concrete evidence of how Hong-man had arranged the marriage. Although the lawsuit files submitted by Governor Jo clearly stated that money had been given to Hong-man in advance, Hong-man insisted to Hong-seon and Lady Hwang that it was merely "money borrowed from Governor Jo."

After Ki-soon's marriage fell apart, Hwang's maternal uncle, who lived in Sacheon, lamented, "Niece Pil-hye, had you asked me about Jong-cheol's behavior, this unfortunate event could have been avoided..." Despite this, the damage had already been done. Hwang now realized more clearly that Hong-man harbored a black heart, incapable of tolerating even a cousin's success. Though Hong-man and Hong-seon were brothers, the locals often wondered whom they truly resembled among their parents.

Hong-man was a slender, small man with a beautiful, almost feminine face, double eyelids, and long eyelashes. He was known for his high-pitched voice and his skill at whispering sweetly. In stark contrast, Hong-seon was straight-laced, kind-hearted, and incapable of deceit. The two brothers could not have been more different, leading many to doubt their familial connection.

Hong-man had a fairly large store in the heart of Sancheong-eup, a business that Hong-seon had helped establish for him throughout his life. The grandchildren of the Big House affectionately called him "The Little Grandfather of the Store." He relied heavily on Hong-seon for almost everything and never worked hard. Instead, he excelled at socializing, had a wide circle of acquaintances, and was skilled in small tricks and manipulation.

He had two daughters and a son. His daughters attended the same S Women's University in Seoul as Ki-soon, but both dropped out and got married, settling in Masan and Jinju. The eldest daughter married a man who ran a lumber mill in Masan. Though less educated than his wife, he was a genial, easygoing man. The second daughter married a man who owned a bowl shop and lived a wealthy life in Jinju.

His eldest son graduated from medical school, completed his service as an army doctor and opened a small hospital in Choryang, Busan, the same year Hong-seon passed away. The hospital, primarily treating patients with industrial injuries, was located near Busan Train Station—the bustling center of the city—and thrived under his management.

Despite his children's settled lives, Hong-man would often tell them, "If your partners make you uncomfortable, don't endure it—separate from them. You all have good appearances and can hold your heads high wherever you go." This was one of his frequent sayings.

There was also an incident that illustrated Hong-man's character.

After his wife's death, Hong-man lived with a middle-aged woman with a round, cute face, affectionately called "Geochang-ddigi." People might try to conceal their past lives, but cohabitation often reveals true natures. With his probing nature, Hong-man discovered that she had originally been a *gisaeng* from Jinju. After returning to Sancheong, he begged her to stay with him, and she eventually did.

Though he was initially thrilled with the arrangement, Hong-man soon began to torment Geochang-ddigi with harsh words. She always wore a smile but was not one to chat or nag like most women. Their relationship had begun with the sentiment, "What does it matter to others if we like each other, regardless of whether you were a *gisaeng* or not?" However, as their relationship stabilized, Geochang-ddigi started to see Hong-man as her husband. This newfound dynamic led him to hurt her with offhand, cutting remarks.

Hong-man said,

"Darling, no matter how much I think about it, you said you were a *gisaeng* in Jinju, but it turns out you went to Manchuria during the Japanese colonial period and ended up selling your body. How many times a day did you offer yourself? What a waste for me! I can't believe I'm living with such a low-quality woman like you. So ... did you make a lot of money? Does making money mean you permitted your body carelessly? I shouldn't say this, it puts me in a bad mood..."

At first, when Geochang-ddigi heard such words, her face turned red with shame, and she gnashed her teeth in anger. However, when she realized that Hong-man was using her past to taunt her, deliberately bringing up painful memories, she was deeply hurt.

When she had married Hong-man, she had some land from her mother, who was living in Geochang. Her reason for leaving her parental home had been the failure of her first marriage.

Unable to endure Hong-man's torment any longer, she changed her mind. After several years with him, she left and disappeared into the mountains one day. Bok-hee recalled Geochang-ddigi's complaints before she left Hong-man and comforted her, blaming Hong-man's cruel personality. Lady Hwang also heard about this from Bok-hee and came to understand the extent of Hong-man's vile behavior.

Lady Hwang regretted not realizing sooner what kind of person Hong-man truly was. She should not have rushed Ki-soon's marriage based solely on his words. But when Ki-soon went to Japan to study, Lady Hwang reflected, *Was everything that happened to my daughter simply Ki-soon's fate? The world has changed now, and I've heard that if women study well, they can secure good jobs and build careers. That is the path my daughter Ki-soon should take,* she reassured herself.

As people grow older, they are more often haunted by memories of the past. Lady Hwang developed a habit of clutching her chest, feeling that she was to blame for everything that had happened to Ki-soon and her other children.

To Lady Hwang, Hong-seon was someone she believed in and followed as if he were her heaven. He had kindly taken care of everything, as if he were her father. He was the most special person in her world.

The one thing she could never tell Hong-seon was that Ki-soon and

Yeong-soon's illnesses had originated from her own family.

She struggled with a guilty conscience, believing that she, as their mother, was the cause of Ki-soon and Young-soon's suffering. Somewhere in the depths of her mind, she believed that she had wronged Hong-seon's original wife, Lady Kim, and that her children were now suffering as a consequence of that sin.

The secondary mental illness caused by an ill-fated marriage was not just a legal issue—it seemed to stem from the whispers of neighbors who, without the children's knowledge, referred to them as "the second wife's child" or "the child of a concubine." When she expressed these feelings to Hong-seon, he embraced her and said, "Honey, no matter what anyone says, you are my rightful wife. It's all my fault for not shielding you from this." He sought to comfort her in her distress.

How powerful is the force of convention? What use are man-made laws in the face of it? *Convention precedes law*, exerting an even greater influence on the inhabitants of the land.

Hong-seon did not choose Lady Hwang as a mere mistress while abandoning his first wife, Lady Kim. He chose Lady Hwang fully aware of the responsibility of enduring all the judgment and resentment from Lady Kim's children. Such an act required considerable courage. It was not legally sanctioned, and Hong-seon understood the additional pain imposed by societal convention. But in his youth, he was steadfast and resolute.

On the day Hong-seon first met Lady Hwang, he spoke before her parents:

"Father, Mother, I am older than Pil-hye and have children, but I will take full responsibility for everything that happens in this household. I have ensured that Pil-hye will not face any social stigma by properly organizing the family registers. Therefore, please allow me to marry Pil-hye."

Hong-seon was strong, but the winds of convention were too fierce for Lady Hwang and her children to withstand. On the surface, he appeared more resilient and unwavering than anyone else. However, after Il-seop's death, he gradually weakened.

Lady Hwang often felt the weight of being the cause of the family's troubles, whether sitting or standing. More than anything, determining the root cause of Ki-soon and Young-soon's mental illnesses was even more challenging. No one knew for certain. Had they been predisposed due to innate factors, or had their conditions been facilitated by their family environment?

If Joon-seop had lived, would he have succumbed to the same illnesses as Ki-soon?

After Hong-seon passed away, Hwang found herself trapped in a state of delusion and pain.

In the meantime, her younger sister, Pil-yeon, came to visit.

Pil-yeon (Supervisor of Education at the time) said,

"*Eonni*, now that Brother-in-law is gone, what are your plans? Aside from Young-soon, who is married, would you and Ki-soon consider living with me or perhaps moving somewhere quiet?"

Lady Hwang replied,

"Pil-yeon, I understand your concern. But I can't decide. There are moments when Ki-soon doesn't seem entirely lost in madness ... times when she appears normal when she's with me. Of course, I can't predict how she will change over time, but leaving this house because of my situation would mean severing all ties with the Choi family and my identity within it. Moreover, it is impossible for me to leave with Ki-soon in her current state.

The Choi family only accepted me out of obligation when I married into it. Although I am the second wife of the Big Elder, if I leave this house, I will never regain this position.

Above all, I am the legitimate wife of the Choi family. Soon, Yeong-soon will return to this house in a few months. After that, Ki-soon and I can live here with her, even if it is difficult. I am not in a position to leave freely as if I were alone. My daughters and I must remain part of this house, the Choi family."

Pil-yeon said,

"*Eonni*, is it because of the property here? I can take care of you and Ki-soon."

Lady Hwang replied,

"No. Regardless of what anyone says, I am the legitimate wife of this house. I never dreamed that the descendants of this grand house would perform ancestral rites for me after I die ... but what does it matter what happens after my death? Even when Joon-seop was alive, my feelings were the same.

Pil-yeon, do you know that my husband, Hong-seon, supported your education and the youngest's? That he purchased the house where our parents lived and the adjoining farmland?

Young-soon, the youngest, will return soon with her husband. How can I possibly leave now? I will remain here. Your care and concern for me are debts I carry in my heart."

While talking with Pil-yeon, Hwang's memories somehow drifted back to the past.

She clearly remembered what Hong-seon had said to her on their first night together as he gently removed her *jokduri*. At sixteen, Pil-hye had never forgotten the way Hong-seon spoke with a trembling voice, like a nervous boy, while holding her hand.

Hong-seon said,

"Darling, may I call you that? Despite our age difference, I am your husband. The family register is just a formality ... it's already settled, and all the children in the Choi household are listed under you and me.

Lady Kim, my first wife, was never an evil or bad person, but she wasn't right for me. From the beginning, my mother and I saw things differently.

I have three sons, as you know, but they are grown now. They are precious to me, but I need to live my own life as well. Love for a child and love for a wife are different things. In our lives, even if the children cause us distress, let's discuss it honestly and resolve it together.

I'm sorry. I was born before you, and I might leave this world sooner. Even if one of us passes away first, let's both stay in this house until the end. I will be your strength. You are the Mistress of the main room in this Choi household."

As Hwang thought back to what Hong-seon had said, for the first time since living in this house, Lady Kim's sorrowful face suddenly came to mind.

That's right. Had Lady Hwang ever truly felt sorry—even for a moment—toward Lady Kim in all these years? She had simply accepted everything Hong-seon told her as the truth. But was it really true?

Even though he had said so, before the bitter cold of winter arrived or when the crisp days of spring came, Hong-seon always made sure to brew medicinal herbs for Lady Kim to take.

At first, Lady Hwang believed she was the only one receiving the herbal medicine. Then one day, when Ki-soon was in the fourth grade, she mentioned that the same medicinal scent was wafting from the kitchen yard of the Big House. This realization unsettled Lady Hwang.

She then recalled the mischievous pranks that the grandchildren of the Big House played on their aunt, Ki-soon, and Jeong-soon. Though she never complained or mentioned these incidents to Hong-seon, she had felt disappointed on several occasions.

Moreover, Lady Hwang had always strived to maintain the dignity of a legitimate wife—perhaps even more so than Lady Kim. The idea, as Pil-yeon had suggested, that she stayed because of the property was deeply unpleasant to her.

No one in the neighborhood or the Big House could question Lady Hwang's dignity. She was extremely cautious with her words and actions, always mindful of her role as the legitimate wife. Even when something unpleasant happened, she never displayed her anger.

What was more humane? Lady Hwang wondered. *For a young girl like me ... it was not easy to treat a boy of the same age or just a year older as a son when I married at sixteen. How much did Hong-seon truly accept my thoughts and behaviors?*

Lady Hwang shook her head, trying to dispel the past that kept resurfacing. When she reflected on it, she realized that Hong-seon had accepted almost everything she said. He had been delighted to have two daughters and had treated Lady Hwang with kindness. Their marital affection had remained unchanged.

However, she could never bring herself to speak about Il-seop, who had been the most defiant toward Hong-seon. She had witnessed the profound sense of loss that Hong-seon felt after Il-seop's death — because she had seen that loss in every detail.

And the series of tragedies involving their children — the turmoil caused by Ki-soon's broken marriage with Jong-cheol, the deaths of Jeong-soon and Joon-seop, Ki-soon's schizophrenia after returning from Japan, and the struggles of their youngest daughter, Young-soon — all cast a shadow over Hong-seon, leaving him feeling abandoned by hope and expectation.

When Joon-seop and Jeong-soon died, it was clear that Hong-seon had been deeply afraid. The memories of the children who had left before their father, particularly Il-seop's death, caused him immense pain...

How much had he once enjoyed mingling with the local children, earning the nickname "Jayu"? Since Il-seop's death, Hong-seon had rarely played with children. The days of holding Joon-seop's hand, catching locusts and sparrows in the autumn, were gone forever.

Although Hong-seon still liked children, his expectations for each one varied. The fervor he had once held for Il-seop was not the same for the others. Was he losing faith in himself?

When Ki-soon returned from Japan, several exorcisms were performed in an attempt to treat her schizophrenia, and through it all, Hong-seon remained calm. Of course, he never said anything hurtful to Lady Hwang about Ki-soon or Young-soon. She gradually realized that Hong-seon had long since looked at their children without any expectation. It was clear that he, a broken man, had resigned himself to silently accepting all the disappointments, weighed down by the guilty conscience of feeling like an unworthy father.

His once-formidable presence could no longer be measured by Lady Hwang's standards. At some point, she simply stopped thinking about him.

With these thoughts, Lady Hwang sat next to Pil-yeon for hours in silence. When Pil-yeon saw that Lady Hwang had not spoken a word, she quietly stood up, gave up waiting for an answer, and left for Jinju without having dinner.

After Pil-yeon had gone, Hwang, with great effort, pressed her body to the floor, wiped it clean with her functioning hand, and laid out her bedding. She was already paralyzed in one hand and foot. As she lay in bed, she thought to herself:

I boasted to my younger sister that I was the legitimate wife, but can the future of my children, who remain in the Choi house, truly be bright?

Did marrying an older man with a wife, for the sake of supporting my family and sisters, lead to this punishment upon my children by the hatred of some higher being, of God?

Even so, if I were to take Ki-soon—who, as Pil-yeon says, is mentally unstable and unwell—and encourage Young-soon and her husband to leave, completely emptying this house, then what?

Would that erase all traces of my marriage to Choi Hong-seon?

Where is my place to stay forever?

If I leave this house, I might be able to stay here and there for a few days, but would it ever compare to the home my husband, Hong-seon, built for me? No, Ki-soon will only become even more desolate in the future... Should I just disappear somewhere with that child?

I appreciate Pil-yeon's words and thank her for coming to see me often... but how should my daughters and I live in the future?

These thoughts came one after another, and Lady Hwang couldn't sleep, tossing and turning endlessly. The shadow of Hong-seon rose like a haze above her head and then disappeared.

Recently, Ki-soon had been increasingly losing control over her bowels. Not only did she urinate uncontrollably, but sometimes she would mumble incoherently, throw her feces at the walls, or smear it. The children running errands in the house would scream and look at Ki-soon as if she were an insect. Neither the errand girl nor the older women could restrain Ki-soon's erratic behavior.

After a few days, they all left. Min-ja's family departed, and after Hong-seon's death, Ki-soon's condition worsened significantly. She lay in her room all day without speaking, staring at the ceiling, murmuring, laughing, or crying.

While Bok-hee continued to observe the situation, Lady Hwang of the New House had not left her room since her sister, Pil-yeon, had visited. Had something happened between her and Ki-soon during that week?

Choon-ja, who had been running small errands in the New House, had been cleaning up Ki-soon's messes and washing her with hot water. Bok-hee decided to prepare some delicious food and visit Lady Hwang the next day.

However, that evening, Choon-ja knocked on the door of the main room in the Big House, where Bok-hee was staying.

Choon-ja said,

"Hyori-ddigi Little Madam, the New House grandmother has collapsed on the floor and can't move. Please come quickly. I don't know if she has fallen asleep or lost consciousness."

Bok-hee hurriedly dressed and rushed over to the New House. Choon-ja explained,

"Little Madam, the New House grandmother, despite her discomfort, has been cleaning Aunt Ki-soon's room about three times a week. Even though Lady Hwang skipped meals this morning, she insisted on cleaning up the feces herself and asked me to bring more rags. So, I did..."

The floor of the *Hanok*, a traditional Korean tile-roofed house, was covered with thick yellow paper treated with soybean oil to prevent dirt buildup and maintain a glossy finish.

Lady Hwang tried to stand up on her weak left foot, unaware that Ki-soon's urine had seeped into the floor. As she moved, both feet slipped into the feces that had already been there, causing her legs to twist and slide. She injured her right ankle in the accident and was left lying helplessly beside Ki-soon.

When Young-soon heard about her mother's accident, she arrived at the house in Sancheong earlier than planned, coming from Busan. Her husband, Dal-soo, didn't dislike his wife, but having to adjust to an unfamiliar Busan right after marriage—and now dealing with his mother-in-law's ankle injury—left him burdened with all the housework.

His face was flushed with anger as he entered the house, perhaps due to the unpleasant situation. He always looked unhappy. However, with his hometown in the north, he had no other place to go except this house. He couldn't voice all his grievances, so he took on the responsibilities of the New House family with a bitter expression, his mouth perpetually in a pout.

When Min-ja from the Saemmyjip occasionally stopped by to check on her Big Aunt Ki-soon and said something to him, Dal-soo would curtly respond, "I don't know. I don't know anything."

To Lady Hwang, the only person in the family without any physical defect seemed to be Young-soon, but even she had to consider her husband, Dal-soo. Dal-soo's thoughts often turned presumptuous.

Dal-soo said,

"Hey, honey. Now that Father-in-law Hong-seon is gone, we could tear down all the *sarang-chae* and the warehouse in this house and turn it into a block factory. That way, I wouldn't have to travel far."

Soon after, the yard's structure was renovated. At that time, the Korean government was promoting a policy to improve rural housing. As a result, there was a growing demand to tear down old thatched houses and replace them with western-style houses built from concrete blocks.

Dal-soo's block factory managed to operate on the surface, but despite its appearance, it barely sustained itself. Thanks to him, it seemed to help them get by for quite some time, but the household expenses repeatedly came out of Lady Hwang's pocket. Dal-soo soon started talking about having a child, wondering if making blocks would help him save enough money.

"How nice would it be to have children while we're married?" he would say to Young-soon.

Dal-soo spent a lot of time socializing with people who came to work at the block factory, often at a local coffee shop. No matter how naïve Young-soon was, she couldn't help but notice her husband Dal-soo's behavior.

Lady Hwang thought, "Even if a child were to come into this world and die young like my son, how wonderful would it be if Young-soon had children now?" Then she scolded herself, "Hwang Pil-hye, you're so hopeless. Do you really want a grandson now?" She felt a pang of guilt for such thoughts. However, the more Lady Hwang thought about her youngest daughter, Young-soon, the deeper her sorrow grew. Her heart ached at the thought of Young-soon spending years in sadness because of Dal-soo, especially if she remained childless.

So she sent word through Choon-ja, asking a nun she knew well to visit her home. When the nun arrived, Hwang made a request:

"If there is a baby abandoned by their parents who cannot be raised, please ensure that my daughter Young-soon can raise the child."

At that time, there were not only war orphans but also many abandoned children. After the war, people across the country were working hard to improve their lives. However, not everyone's circumstances improved so quickly.

Perhaps that's why daughters of poor families, who had given birth without proper knowledge of contraception, were sent to other people's homes to work as maids. Sons were sent elsewhere to labor. Since food was precious, some parents, unable to support their children, abandoned them. "You have to do anything if you are just fed. A farmhand, a kitchen maid, a factory job where you eat and sleep—you should do it if you're told," these parents would say, closing their eyes as they left their children behind.

Lady Hwang reached out to people everywhere, seeking help. However, for some reason, there was no response from the nuns or from those she had contacted through her younger sister, Pil-yeon, who lived in Jinju. Lady Hwang speculated that perhaps the rumors about Young-soon's unstable mind had discouraged people from responding, even if a child had been found.

Despite her physical discomfort, Lady Hwang forced herself to move. She had carefully folded the shroud she had made for herself and Hong-seon, placing it in a thin wooden box in front of her closet—easily accessible for anyone who might need to find it.

These days, whenever Lady Hwang closed her eyes, memories of her time with Hong-seon flashed before her.

She vividly recalled the time Hong-seon took her and a group of people on a tour of *Geumgang Mountain*[63]. Hong-seon had visited *Geumgang Mountain* six times in his life. About three months after Lady Hwang gave birth to their eldest daughter, Ki-soon—two years into their marriage—he gathered a group for another tour.

Leaving Ki-soon with a nanny, he took Lady Hwang and Jeong-seop, while Il-seop refused to join, and Hong-man was reluctantly brought along.

Their tour of Geumgang Mountain included the upper stream of Bukhan Mountain leading to *Nae-geumgang*, where the rivers had relatively gentle slopes, and *Oi-geumgang*, known for its short, steep rivers and rough terrain. For Lady Hwang's sake, Hong-seon stayed longer at *Nae-geumgang*, where they could enjoy the scenery.

They planned their trip for late summer, before the first frost, which typically fell in early October. Their journey took them as far as Jangjeon Port, where they spent the first night at an inn. Lady Hwang fondly recalled the cozy night she spent in Hong-seon's arms. From the next day, they explored the strange rocky cliffs, which resembled towering folding screens both from a distance and up close. The rock formations were identified by names such as vertical joints, sheeting joints, and dip joints, depending on their shapes.

Even if she returned to Geumgang Mountain, where she had spent ten days eating and staying, she wouldn't know how to find those exact spots

---

[63] Geumgang Mountain spans the regions of Hoeyang County, Tongcheon County, and Goseong County in Gangwon Province. Its highest peak, Birobong, reaches 1,638 meters, with a circumference of about 80 km and a total area of approximately 160 km². The name Geumgang originates from the Buddhist scripture *Avatamsaka Sutra*, which mentions "Geumgangsan, where a Bodhisattva resides in Haedong."The mountain is known by different names depending on the season: In spring, it is called Geumgang because it is covered with fresh sprouts and flowers. In summer, it is referred to as *Bongrae* due to the lush greenery covering its peaks and valleys. In autumn, it is called *Pungak,* as its 12,000 peaks are beautifully colored with autumn leaves. In winter, it is known as *Gaegol,* when the leaves have fallen, leaving only the exposed rocky landscape. The geological structure of Geumgang Mountain was formed by inclined and bent movements that occurred during the Paleocene epoch of the Tertiary period in the Mesozoic era.—Based on information from Naver Encyclopedia, summarized by the author.

again. However, as she thought of Hong-seon, Lady Hwang felt as if, by simply closing her eyes, she could see him greeting her happily on the mountain.

When she was young, she had believed that as long as she was by Hong-seon's side, everything would be fine. She had felt like the happiest woman in the world. At the bottom of the box containing the shroud lay several photographs of her and Hong-seon. There were moments when she would lose herself in thought, close her eyes, and wish never to open them again.

As Hwang surrendered herself to these thoughts, a loud noise erupted outside her room.

"Grandma Ki-soon is missing!"

It was the voice of a boy—Se-joon, the eldest great-grandson of the Big House. Se-joon was the older brother of Jae-joon, a child who had been raised in Sancheong for five to six years before moving to Busan under Bok-hee's care. While Bok-hee's more well-known grandson was Jae-joon, Se-joon, the eldest, had also come to Sancheong, following his father, Ki-hoon.

When the children visited, Lady Hwang would give them rice cakes, *yugwa* (deep-fried sweet rice cakes), and sometimes fairy tale books. Because of this, Se-joon's voice was familiar to her. Now an elementary school student, it seemed he had come with his parents to visit Bok-hee.

Lady Hwang spoke in a voice filled with surprise and joy.

"Huh? What do you mean? Se-joon, you came all the way to my house. Who did you come with from Busan? Oh ... is no one out there? Young-soon, Young-soon! Oh no. Se-joon, can you find Grandma Young-soon? Tell her to come to me."

Lady Hwang relayed the message to Se-joon and called out louder for Choon-ja and Young-soon from her room. *Where did Ki-soon go? Just an hour ago, she was lying in the next room, staring at the ceiling and muttering to herself. I must have missed her when I came into this room,* she murmured to herself.

A few hours later, Lady Hwang received a call from the Sancheong Police Station. Even an elderly person in Sancheong-eup would have been aware of the situation regarding Choi's eldest daughter, Choi Ki-soon, at that time.

That day, it was reported that Ki-soon had deliberately dressed as if she were going somewhere. She had put on her clothes and sat on a chair at the Sancheong bus stop for more than two hours, silently watching people pass by. Her appearance was so unusual that a bus ticket saleswoman called the police substation. Since the ticket saleswoman was from another area and not a local of Sancheong, she didn't know anything about Ki-soon.

Naturally, how could anyone in the neighborhood—who thought they knew Ki-soon from the past—recognize a woman who had been secluded at home for ten years?

Ki-soon was no longer the pretty, bright young girl she once had been. At forty, she had become a middle-aged woman—thin, with hazy eyes. It would have been difficult for anyone to recognize her.

Yoo-sang received the call and went to the police substation to bring her back. Ki-soon didn't utter a word to the police officers but hugged Yoo-sang tightly as soon as he entered the station. "*Aje*, why are you here now?" she said, surprising the policemen around her.

Yoo-sang, nearly sixty and looking his age, had been a widower since his wife's death. Living alone, he was thin, and his legs were weak. He felt deep sorrow and pity for the childlike Ki-soon, who obediently followed him, clutching his wrist.

For Yoo-sang, the New House and the Big House, despite their physical proximity, felt worlds apart. The Big House, where he stayed, and the New House had always been distant in spirit. This gap only widened after Hong-seon's death, as the servants of the Big House and the residents of the New House no longer visited one another. Yet, Yoo-sang remained responsible for all the work at the Choi house alongside Bok-hee, making him the only person who moved between the two houses. No matter how busy he was, Yoo-sang would return to his room in the Big House after making a couple of rounds around the main building of the New House, where Ki-soon and Lady Hwang lay.

Despite the changes in the world and the absence of Hong-seon, Yoo-sang remained the faithful servant of the house. If anyone found it odd that a servant was emotionally invested in the well-being of a lady from a prestigious family, they would scoff.

Yet, in his heart, Ki-soon was always the lady of the New House. No matter how much she lost her mind or smeared feces on the walls, Yoo-sang rejoiced whenever she seemed to regain her senses. "Oh, Ki-soon, the Big Mistress must have come to her senses. Finally, the day when she becomes a normal person is coming soon," he would exclaim—only to be disappointed when she exhibited strange behavior again two nights later.

Her once youthful, firm skin was gradually withering.

After Young-soon and Dal-soo moved into the Sancheong house, it became increasingly difficult for Yoo-sang to enter Ki-soon's room in the New House. Dal-soo often gave Yoo-sang sidelong glances, as if scrutinizing him. 'Why is he glaring at me like that?' Yoo-sang wondered. But he decided not to let a meaningless dispute with a much younger man tarnish his character. He had to be mindful of how others perceived him.

They said the distinction between master and servant had vanished, that all social ranks had been abolished. But Yoo-sang knew that as long as he remained within the confines of the Choi household, the vestiges of those divisions would persist—etched indelibly in the hearts of those who lived there.

Dal-soo seemed to know only *Hangul*. Yet, Yoo-sang had seen him a few times with Miss Kim from Star Coffee Shop, near Grandpa

Hong-man's house at the intersection. Whenever Yoo-sang went to the market alone, he would notice Dal-soo sitting there, chatting with her and fumbling with his hands. Yoo-sang thought to himself, 'This guy doesn't suit the pure and pretty lady, Young-soon.'

Dal-soo, for his part, had his own reasons for disliking Yoo-sang. There was something about him that he just couldn't stand. What also weighed on his mind was that he had locked eyes with Hong-man several times at the coffee shop near the corner store by Hong-man's house. However, Hong-man always pretended not to recognize him. Dal-soo was convinced that Hong-man would never mention him to Lady Hwang, his mother-in-law.

To Dal-soo, it was amusing that Hong-man, despite being almost eighty years old, still visited the coffee shop and treated the young waitresses to a cup of *ssanghwacha* (black herbal tea), cracking jokes as he did so. 'It seems like some part of him still feels alive as a man,' Dal-soo thought to himself, letting out a derisive chuckle.

On the other hand, Yoo-sang neither smoked nor drank. Instead, he spent his entire day following Bok-hee, focusing solely on housework. When Dal-soo saw such dedication, he thought to himself,

'That's why you can't abandon the spirit of a servant. Now that Father in law Hong-seon is gone, you could work and live in another house. But whether he's here or not, you just keep doing this. Fine, then ... die a servant! Hey, man!' Dal-soo cursed under his breath.

However, more than anything, what Dal-soo hated most was the way Yoo-sang looked at Ki-soon. He felt there was a certain emotion in his gaze that made him uneasy. Muttering in a low voice, Dal-soo said to himself,

"I'm sure he has my sister-in-law on his mind. Why does he look around the room every night before going back to his own, as if checking where my sister-in-law and mother-in-law are staying? Yeah, I'm going to have to block the wall next to the *Jangdok-gan*. That way, he won't be able to enter this house anymore. This is my house now. I have my block workshop. The newlywed room is decorated in a cozy way in the detached house. I won't let anyone else peek into this house ... never again."

Dal-soo pondered this for a few days. About a month after Ki-soon had returned home from the police substation, he blocked the wall next to the *Jangdok-gan*, which connected the Big House and the New House, using blocks and finishing it with cement. Then, he spoke to Yeong-soon.

Dal-soo:

"Dear, now that Father-in-law is no longer with us, I feel uneasy about the Big House and this house being connected. What do you think? We happen to have plenty of leftover blocks, so I think using them to close off the wall by the *Jangdok-gan* area would be perfect."

Young-soon:

"... I'm not going to oppose what you do. But I... if there's something I don't know, I run to Sister Bok-hee and ask. And when the grandchildren of the Big House come, I talk to them... During vacation, Se-joon and Jae-joon, the eldest grandchildren, are here. Why do you want to build a wall? I think they're cute, they keep me company, and they listen to everything I say."

Dal-soo:

"Well, you're still their great-aunt, but people say you're immature because you spend time with elementary school kids like that. Now, don't talk to such young children. How dare they call their great-aunt over to talk and play with them? If others find out, they'll speak ill of you. Besides, this house is now mine and yours, so no one should interfere."

Young-soon thought, 'But Mother will need to discuss things with Sister Bok-hee and Uncle Yoo-sang. What should I do if something happens? And what about *Eonni* Ki-soon?' She murmured these words to herself.

After the wall was blocked, she expressed her concerns to Bok-hee. Upon hearing this, Bok-hee said, "So, this happened because of Uncle Dal-soo. Not long ago, you, Aunt Yeong-soon, had a miscarriage and went through a hard time... You worry about Big Aunt Ki-soon, and now you're an adult." For the first time, Bok-hee looked at Young-soon with a gentle smile and a steady gaze.

But Lady Hwang grew anxious when she heard about Dal-soo blocking off the Big House from the New House. *I am the legitimate wife of this house, and even though my husband has passed, Dal-soo should have asked for my permission first. I need to discuss house matters with Bok-hee. I'm concerned about my future.*

I don't know what Dal-soo was up to in the North, but did he marry Young-soon with an eye on this house's property? The person who introduced him to us was Nam-gil. How spiteful and selfish she was! Though it's unknown whether her husband is alive or dead, her children depended on her, and she received the same property as Il-seop, yet she lost it all to other men...

What am I going to do about this?

Darling! What do you want me to do? Please take me with you. I don't want to be alone in this world. I'm afraid every day. How did Bok-hee, who became a widow at thirty-five, survive for so long?

She truly longed to return to the wind, to the earth. The mother she called out to was Mary, the mother of Jesus. She wound a wooden rosary with a small rose-shaped ornament around her hand and placed her hands together over her chest.

22

The Death of the Lady Hwang

1963: The New House
—The Edge of Time

How many hours do I spend awake each day, subtracting the hours of sleep from the total twenty-four? Out of those waking hours, how much time do I spend with a clear mind? Furthermore, how much time is dedicated to the basic necessities of relieving myself and eating with my own hands?

Lady Hwang learned through Japan's NHK radio broadcast that the Japanese had been conducting a large-scale "National Life Time Survey"[64] for several years to analyze how people spent their daily time. The meticulous nature of the Japanese people was evident in this effort. Perhaps their goal was to enhance the lives of their citizens by examining the minutiae of daily activities.

Lady Hwang was amazed at the level of detail considered by those who orchestrated such an extensive study. In contrast, she had never encountered such a thorough investigation in her own country, *Joseon*, Korea. She marveled at the Japanese precision. The survey not only measured the time spent on various activities but also tracked the materials used for each basic action, including per capita consumption of water and electricity — meticulously recorded by time of day.

Since Choon-ja, who had once run errands between the Big House and the New House, had left, there was no one nearby to handle trivial tasks for Lady Hwang. Young-soon, burdened by her own struggles, was unable to assist either her mother or Ki-soon. Moreover, after suffering two miscarriages, she remained depressed and listless.

Lady Hwang often lamented, *Why do I live like this? Pil-hye, let's go. To my husband, Hong-seon...* She found herself sinking deeper into despair

---

[64] National Time Survey: In 1960, NHK's Broadcasting Culture Research Institute initiated this National Life Time Survey to gather essential data for broadcast programming. — This content is from Park Byung-jeon, *Housing Studies* published by Kimundang in 1985, p. 32 —Requoted by the author.

with each passing day. Hwang learned from Young-soon that, although Dal-soo's block factory was flourishing, he brought no money home. As a result, Hwang was forced to sell the remaining farmland and jewelry, distributing the proceeds to Young-soon as monthly living expenses.

Additionally, Lady Hwang asked Young-soon to find a new household helper to assist with small errands for her and Ki-soon. Young-soon relayed the message to Bok-hee, who then informed Yoo-sang:

"Lady Hwang of the New House wishes to discuss something with you. Please come to the New House."

Ever since Dal-soo had blocked the passage connecting the right yard wall of the New House to the side of the *Jangdok-gan* in the Big House, reaching the New House had become a time-consuming process. Lady Hwang muttered, "If only he hadn't taken down the *Jangdok-gan* wall, this wouldn't take so long. This is all Dal-soo's doing. What a frustrating person!"

A few days later, the errand girl arrived at the New House. Her name was Soon-joo, and she was about thirteen years old. A distant relative who had introduced her mentioned her circumstances. Living in such difficult times, Soon-joo's face was dotted with freckles, and dry patches appeared on her scalp. Her hair was unkempt. Despite her appearance, she took on the unpleasant tasks assigned by Lady Hwang and Ki-soon without complaint and performed them quite well.

During the time it took to liquidate Lady Hwang's farmland and jewelry, Yoo-sang and Dal-soo frequently came and went. The funds from Lady Hwang brought new energy into the household, and before long, Dal-soo began staying out late. Young-soon, sniffling, lamented, "I guess Dal-soo is wandering outside more because I haven't been able to bear a child, even after three years of marriage." And she added.

Young-soon:

"Mother, he always comes home late these days, spending all his time making blocks. ... Wouldn't it be better if we had a child? Why haven't we received any news from the places you asked about, Mother? My heart feels even emptier since the granddaughters and grandsons of the Big House came to Sancheong and left.

Perhaps I'm foolish, but wouldn't Dal-soo be more devoted to our home if we had a child together? Mother?"

Lady Hwang asked Soon-joo once again to relay a message to the nuns or relatives. This meant enduring the same lengthy process to convey her words to Yoo-sang. However, she couldn't rely solely on them. Knowing that Young-soon was still young, Lady Hwang also asked, through Soon-joo, for Bok-hee to take Young-soon to a reputable herbal medicine shop for a diagnosis.

Following this request, Bok-hee had a few words for Young-soon.

Bok-hee:

"Lady Young-soon, even if your mother lies facing the wall, she is still alive and worried. Please take good care of her."

Feeling accused, Young-soon retorted sharply said.

"*Olke* Bok-hee, why do you say that? Are you suggesting I'm not taking good care of my mother? Dal-soo and I do everything we can. You don't even know how much effort we put in..." She pouted as she spoke.

As Bok-hee left the main room of the New House, she muttered to herself, 'Lady Yeong-soon is still so immature despite being married. It's frustrating. Just the other day, she seemed concerned about Aunt Ki-soon, and I thought she was improving. But alas...' The news of Young-soon's pregnancy was scarce. Despite living next door, Bok-hee rarely saw Young-soon unless Lady Hwang insisted on sharing updates.

Lady Hwang pondered as she stared at the wall, much like Ki-soon often did. *How much time is granted to assert one's existence in the world as a living person, to say, "This is me!"? If I subtract eight hours of sleep, the time spent eating and washing, and the hours spent moving purposefully through the streets, that leaves roughly fourteen hours. Yet, I've never had a moment truly to myself,* she sighed.

After a long time, Lady Hwang lay beside Ki-soon in her room, holding her hand. Since Soon-joo's arrival, Lady Hwang had occasionally returned to her own room, often out of sheer exhaustion. These moments became more frequent when Ki-soon, in her fits of rage, punched the wall and cursed.

Observing Ki-soon's harsh behavior, Lady Hwang muttered,

"My daughter Choi Ki-soon is truly herself only when she acts like this. Is this the only time she asserts her existence?"

As Ki-soon's mother, Lady Hwang reflected on her past. Two years after marrying Hong-seon, she had become pregnant, and Ki-soon was born. *When is the time to live solely for myself? Was there ever a moment for me, from being born a daughter, marrying into another family, to living as a wife, daughter-in-law, and mother? Did I ever have that kind of time?*

I'm fifty-five years old now. What harsher trials must I endure before this life ends? I can't bear it any longer. Truly... Lady Hwang continued to sigh while facing the wall.

Nowadays, Lady Hwang whispered desperate prayers, hoping that Ki-soon would pass away before her. However, this wish had yet to be fulfilled.
A few days ago, Ki-soon woke up, approached Lady Hwang, and said,

"Mother, what should we do today? Should I just study math and English books? That's the easiest thing..."

As she observed Ki-soon—who, after speaking, would soon lapse into a blank state—her resolve gradually solidified. She fervently wished for her desperate prayer to be answered: an unrefined plea that Ki-soon's life would end naturally before her own breath ceased. She despised herself for waiting endlessly. It was painfully clear that dying before Ki-soon would inflict even greater suffering and hardship on Young-soon.

No matter how much Lady Hwang tried to move her hands and feet, she had to rely almost entirely on Soon-joo, as one side of her body was paralyzed. Like domestic livestock, she was fed and washed by the young girl's hands. Ki-soon was in a similar state. Although she was not paralyzed, her body seemed to be gradually stiffening from spending nearly every day lying down.

When Soon-joo brought the table, Ki-soon would overturn the rice bowl, throwing it onto the floor, or play with the grains of cooked rice with her hands. She would then pick up the grains, eat them, crush them with her fingers, and smear them on the wall. The room where Ki-soon lived became increasingly filthy and malodorous. Except for Soon-joo, no one would enter. Young-soon rarely came by.

Lady Hwang asked Soon-joo to move her sleeping quarters back to the main room. As she left the room, she thought,

Oh, Ki-soon and I are living in hell. This is hell...

She prayed incessantly.

Mother, Mother of Jesus, St. Mary,
Those who suffer in poverty
Pray to be freed from it.

Like worms crawling on the ground in search of food,
Those who have fallen to the bottom, ridiculed and scorned,
Eat rice mixed with tears and dust.
A lump of cold rice sustains the life
You have predetermined.

No matter how much I eat,
No matter when I eat,
My worries and pain remain unsatisfied —
They torment me.

The struggle is not only hunger or injury,
But the loss of freedom from myself.

Mother, those who are sick and cannot walk,
Those who can barely breathe, pray.
We long to go where we wish, to walk on our own feet,
To move our bodies by our own will,
To stand and think freely.

We wish to go to the bathroom when we need,
To cleanse our itchy hair, to rid ourselves
Of the smell of sweat and urine,
To gently stroke our own hair with our own hands.

Mother, the physical father and mother who bore us,
Those who hate and curse each other within the family, pray.
In the name of family,
We suffered as much as we craved each other's love.
We were abandoned as much as we longed to lean on them.
We resent it.

Is it so?

In truth,
Deep in their hearts, too desperately,
Don't they still hope for each other's happiness?

Like no one knows the beginning,
It is hard to know the end.
Expectation turns into resentment,
Into hatred...
Knowing the end,

I pray for peace,
For the strength to calm my heart.

Mother,
Those who know they have been ignored
And alienated by others pray to you.
They pray to be part of a group,
To breathe and feel together,
To cry and laugh as one.
But,
To belong—gradually,
At times,
They must turn a blind eye to others' hardships,
Harm others for their own gain,
And completely forget what shame is,
This causes them great pain.

Even if it is the path of evil,
Some may not hesitate.
The allure of that sugary evil
Constantly pulls them in,
Even as they recognize
The endless depths of its darkness.

One day, trapped,
Becoming prey to a venomous spider,
If they realize their fate,
They will pray to you again—
To grant them freedom…
Even if it means living alone
And dying in solitude.

A human being, hollow as a shell,
The mind tangled within,
Worse than a beast begging for food in the streets,
Living only by the care of others—
One who sees and lives with this every day prays,
To go somewhere from which she would never return,
Believing it would bring happiness...

Lady Hwang called for Soon-joo. Lady Hwang:

"Soon-joo, I need to ask you something. These days, Great-Aunt Ki-soon (Soon-joo had learned to always refer to Ki-soon as Great-Aunt) doesn't even try to eat and often overturns all the rice, right?"

Soon-joo nodded in affirmation. Lady Hwang:

"That's why I'm saying this ... I'm going to use some medicine to help Ki-soon eat better. You mustn't show or tell anyone about this medicine. It's a secret just between you and me.

This white powder contains a lot of healthy "nutritional supplements," and if you mix it into your Great-Aunt's rice, she will likely eat well and improve. This way, you won't have to clean up after her every day. Things will get better. So, will you make sure to add this medicine to her rice tomorrow morning, just as I instructed?"

Soon-joo nodded again, indicating she understood.

"Yes, Grand Madam, I'll do that," she replied and took the medicine. After handing it over, Lady Hwang sighed with relief, drank a bowl of water, and felt her entire body tremble unknowingly.

About two or three hours after Soon-joo left, Lady Hwang, who had been lying down, suddenly sat up. She wanted to check her shroud in the closet. There was no particular reason—she simply felt compelled to inspect the clothes she had sewn, to see if anything was amiss. At that moment, her paralysis and ankle pain were forgotten, driven by her restless mind.

But suddenly, Lady Hwang could no longer stand. A sharp pain squeezed her chest. As time passed, it tightened further, and the severe pain persisted, making her feel nauseous and weak. Breathing became increasingly difficult. She tried to call for Soon-joo or Young-soon, but no sound came out. Her voice failed her. She collapsed onto the floor, grasping the edge of the blanket with one hand while clutching her aching chest with the other, as if trying to tear the pain away.

That evening, despite her youth, Soon-joo—who had spent half a year living in another household—had already gained considerable wisdom. When given instructions by her superiors, she often hesitated, torn between complying immediately or consulting other family members.

Lady Hwang's request earlier that day had clearly troubled her. She had noticed the tremor in Grand Hwang's hand and the pallor of her face. She considered showing the white powder—what Lady Hwang had called "nutritional medicine"—to Madam Bok-hee for advice. However, she knew how perpetually busy Bok-hee was and feared being scolded for causing unnecessary worry.

Deciding to confirm the medicine with Lady Hwang once more, Soon-joo approached the door of the main room where Lady Hwang slept. Remembering Grand Hwang's words, "Before you stand before adults and speak, you must first clear your throat," she cleared her throat softly. But as she did, a chill suddenly emanated from the room, sending a shiver down her spine.

Was it her experience from moving between households, or merely instinct? *Death* can arrive in an instant, without scent or sound, yet in the end, it is simply *the passage of breath—a fleeting wind.*

Soon-joo sensed a certain shift in vitality, a life force that had slipped away. When she opened the door, she found Lady Hwang lying face down on the floor, curled like a shrimp, clutching her chest. Nearby, the chamber pot lay overturned. Shocked, Soon-joo leaped over the *Jangdok-gan* wall leading to the Big House and ran, calling out for Bok-hee and Yoo-sang as she searched for them.

Those who arrived at the New House later confirmed, "Lady Hwang had already passed away before Soon-joo found her." Realizing that only Dal-soo had been present at the New House, Bok-hee quickly contacted the other relatives. As the eldest, Jeong-seop took charge of the funeral arrangements. In accordance with her wishes, Lady Hwang's body was cremated, and her ashes were scattered over the *Gyeongho River* in Sancheong by her younger sister, Educational Supervisor Hwang.

> No one else has the right to do so.
> I pray because I know that only You hold that power.
>
> Life arrives like the wind and departs just the same,
> Each breath opening and closing the door to existence.
> The life You lent us for but a fleeting moment —
> Even if we spend our remaining days in tears,
> In the twilight of her journey.
>
> A life crafted from mere drops of oil and water,
> May we witness her anew in another realm.

The chief nun concluded Lady Hwang's farewell with words of peace and rest. Although uninvited, two monks who had previously assisted with Ki-soon and Young-soon's exorcism ceremony appeared, offering to chant a Buddhist prayer. Dal-soo muttered, "Aren't those monks just here to chant for money?" but Young-soon quickly silenced him. The Catholic nuns, however, showed respect for Lady Hwang by exchanging a few words with the monks. Lady Hwang was 56 years old. The monks chanted Sutras for about thirty minutes before leaving the house. They did not ask for any compensation.

As the funeral concluded, the family and relatives swiftly returned to their homes, unlike the extended stay following Hong-seon's funeral. Young-soon found herself alone. When Dal-soo returned home, he changed his clothes without a word and left again. Seeing this, Young-soon sighed, "Why is he always like this? Always thinking of leaving the house." Ki-soon remained unchanged. While the family attended the funeral, only Soon-joo had stayed behind to watch over her.

Late that night, Dal-soo returned unexpectedly and moved the heavy wooden rice chest from the *daecheong-maru* into Ki-soon's room. Then, with a strong rope he had evidently prepared in advance, he tied one of the chest's legs to Ki-soon's foot.

From that day on, Ki-soon was confined, able to move only within the one-meter length of the rope. Following Lady Hwang's funeral, Ki-soon was bound to the heavy rice chest, marking the beginning of her confinement—trapped within the walls of her room, unable to move freely.

23
Ki-soon, Flying as a Bird

1968: The New House
—Shards of a Mirror

Ki-soon, Flying as a Bird (Oil Painting on Canvas, No. 100)

Ki-hoon's children, who lived in Busan, arrived in Sancheong for vacation. Ki-hoon, the eldest grandson of the Choi family—always dependable and proud—had traveled abroad for an academic conference, prompting Bok-hee's grandchildren to visit Sancheong.

Although Bok-hee did not dislike her grandchildren, she soon realized Ki-hoon's true intention—to give his frail wife, Jong-hee, some much-needed rest. Nevertheless, she was pleased that her favorite, the second grandson, Jae-joon, had come. Eager to prepare meals suited to his taste, she busied herself in the kitchen.

Se-joon and Jae-joon went out to play in the rice paddies with their uncles, Ki-cheol and Ki-jin, the sons born to Jeong-seop of Saemmy House from his second marriage.

Meanwhile, Jong-hee entered Lady Kim's modest room, gazing at her portrait as she paid silent tribute—a respectful greeting to the deceased. Lady Kim had passed away three years earlier. The small, empty room contained only a pair of yellow sedge baskets, neatly arranged by size, which Lady Kim had cherished.

Her portrait rested behind an incense burner, encased in a simple photo frame atop a small tray. Kneeling before it, Jong-hee greeted the picture and lit incense, offering a quiet moment of reverence.

Five years earlier, in the year of Lady Hwang's passing, there was a fact known only to Dal-soo, the son-in-law of the New House—one that he had quietly chosen to overlook. Dal-soo had discovered it when he went to report Lady Hwang's death: her name was missing from the family register.

This omission was the result of Ki-hoon's actions. After the passing of his grandfather, Hong-seon, Ki-hoon had promptly returned to Sancheong and reorganized the family register, erasing all traces of Lady Hwang. In other words, she had been expunged. As a result, Ki-soon and Young-soon were listed as Il-seop's younger sisters, officially recorded as the children of Lady Kim and Hong-seon.

Lady Hwang likely had no knowledge of this. When Dal-soo learned of the fact while reporting her death, he chose not to inform Young-soon. There was nothing that could be done, even if he had told her. In effect, Lady Kim had once again regained her position as Hong-seon's legal wife.

From what Jong-hee could discern, Ki-hoon had been waiting for the right moment to take such action for a long time. She, too, happened to learn the truth when she stopped by the district office to obtain a family registry for Se-joon. At that time, organizing family records was far less complicated than it is today. Moreover, due to the aftermath of the Korean War, many households needed to amend and reorganize various documents, such as adjusting a person's age or modifying family registries.

For the time being, Jong-hee decided to put thoughts of Lady Hwang aside and instead recalled the last time she had seen Lady Kim.

Lady Kim lamented,

"Children, prod my back with a stick. It's been over a week since my last venture, and my belly feels as though it's about to burst."

Upon hearing this, the woman next door, along with Bok-hee, fetched a bottle of flaxseed oil from the kitchen, measuring out several spoonfuls into a bowl and bringing it to Lady Kim. Bok-hee's daughters arrived, smiling gently.

"Grandmother, you've been eating just half a bowl of rice for lunch every day and replacing the rest of your meals with half a kettle of *makgeolli* for decades. No wonder you're having trouble now. You should have eaten more rice, he-he..." They spoke in a half-joking, half-playful tone.

Whether she had somehow caught that faint remark, Lady Kim responded sharply.

"What are you implying, you young ones? My belly is ablaze, an unending torment. Do you think I can just swallow down rice when it feels like this? No, it's the liquor that soothes me ... it slips down easily, that's what keeps me clinging to life. You spout such naïve nonsense, thoughtless in your youth, don't you?"

As Lady Kim's plight became the talk of the neighborhood, local children often parroted her words in jest. They'd scamper through the alleys, playacting her distress with exaggerated fervor, shouting, "Dig behind me! My stomach is in knots. How many days has it been?" Their laughter echoed behind them, a mocking mimicry of her pained exclamations.

And then, when it came to Lady Kim, there was one phrase that Jong-hee remembered most clearly. It was shortly before Lady Kim passed away when Jong-hee happened to visit Sancheong from Busan. She bowed deeply at the *gol-bang*'s door, and although Lady Kim did not smile, she responded with gentle words.

Jong-hee had heard from Bok-hee that, in her younger days, Lady Kim's tone of speech often led to disagreements between her and Hong-seon. However, in her later years, her tone had softened considerably. There were many possible reasons for this, and Jong-hee believed that the deaths of her husband, Hong-seon, and Lady Hwang were among them.

Lady Kim said,

"My dear granddaughter-in-law, Jong-hee! Was the journey to Sancheong too arduous for you? How burdensome it must be, with such delicate skin and frailty. Above all, take care of yourself. Let neither household chores nor concerns for your children and husband's affairs weigh you down. You must rest. It's a rare visit to Sancheong, after all."

These words, particularly the mention of "delicate skin," secretly pleased Jong-hee. It felt like a compliment on her fair complexion—a stark contrast to her mother-in-law Bok-hee's usual critique: "Her skin is so fair, she hardly seems suited for outdoor labor." This unexpected praise filled Jong-hee with a quiet sense of pride in her appearance. As Lady Kim brought her hand to her mouth, she seemed to recall distant memories.

Lady Kim said,

"Jong-hee, your mother-in-law bore four daughters, and you have two brothers-in-law. The burden on your shoulders, to see them all well-married, must be profound. I often wonder why she chose to fill her home with so many souls. While a crowded hearth brings warmth, it also brings burdens. You've done well, ensuring your sisters-in-law not only completed their schooling in Busan but also entered into good marriages. I also remember the silk and beautiful *hanboks* you brought as a bride. ... All passed down to your sisters-in-law while you made do with plain black cotton through all seasons. Your resilience and grace under such trials did not go unnoticed. I know everything."

Her voice softened as she spoke, offering words of consolation that acknowledged the unseen struggles woven through Jong-hee's daily life.

Looking back, Jong-hee's visits to Lady Kim had been infrequent—countable on her fingers—especially after moving to Busan with her husband. When Grandfather Hong-seon passed away, Lady Kim confined herself to her room for nearly a month. Eventually, she emerged, leaning heavily on her cane, to take a solitary walk around the inner courtyard before retreating back to her secluded chamber. Later, she began venturing out twice a week, walking the courtyard before returning to her quarters. Jong-hee had learned about this routine from her youngest sister-in-law.

Then one day, Bok-hee pleaded with Lady Kim, "Why don't you move to the room across from mine—the one I use as the main room? There's no one else in the house." However, Lady Kim insisted on staying in her small room (*gol-bang*). That tiny space, about one and a half *pyeong*, had been her home ever since her son Il-seop and Bok-hee got married. Claiming that her legs hurt, she never joined them on a trip to Geumgang Mountain, even when Hong-seon was still alive. She lived in that small room like a ghost and passed away five years after Hong-seon's death, having long suffered from chronic constipation.

As Jong-hee sat in the *gol-bang*, lost in thoughts of her grandmother-in-law, Lady Kim, she suddenly heard Bok-hee calling from outside. Bok-hee frowned as if annoyed and said.

"My dear, Se-joon's mother, just wait until tomorrow before heading up. I'm feeling a bit fatigued, and every joint aches with pain. The annual task of preserving persimmons, along with the endless duties of managing this large household, has taken its toll. The doctors say it's severe arthritis from years of hard work. The medication makes me bloated, leaving my face round like the moon.

I'm not sure exactly when Se-joon's father will return from his overseas training and come to Busan, but take the children and leave as soon as tomorrow. Or, if you'd rather, stay a few more days and then take me up to Busan with you. I'd like to stay at your house and eat the food you cook. I'm tired of my own cooking—I want to eat something prepared by someone else."

As he entered the yard, Jae-joon overheard the conversation and said,

"Grandma, are you feeling unwell? Is it arthritis? What will I do if you're in pain? I worry about you more than I worry about Mom."

Hearing this, Jong-hee made up her mind.

"Yes, understood. Then we'll have breakfast tomorrow, get ready, and take you up to Busan."

The conversation set in motion a flurry of preparations. Despite her pains, Bok-hee busied herself with sending provisions to her youngest daughter, Ki-seon, who had married a few years earlier and had since settled in Sancheong. Ki-seon's husband had been running a night school in Sancheong for quite some time, dedicating himself to educating rural youths. At that time, he was serving as the education officer for the newly formed *Saemaul Undong* Council.

During this period, Korea was in the midst of the *Saemaul Undong* movement, which aimed to help villages recover from the scars of the Korean War. Dal-soo's block factory also thrived within this context. Additionally, old and worn-out surroundings were gradually transformed into cleaner environments, and people were encouraged to plant trees on April 5th, traveling from mountain to mountain.

Middle school students across the country participated in caterpillar hunting during the summer and rat hunting in the fall. As a result, even in rural villages, narrow and congested roads were widened to allow for easier car access. Night schools were established in various locations, providing educational opportunities for youths who had been unable to study due to financial difficulties.

It was a busy evening when Jong-hee, after arriving in Busan with Se-joon and Jae-joon, was preparing dinner alongside Bok-hee. Suddenly, the sharp ring of the telephone pierced the air, carrying an urgent voice. Yoo-sang's words, heavy with concern, echoed through the receiver:

"Little Madam in Busan! Ki-soon, the Big Aunt of the New House, has vanished. I've already alerted the police and will update you as soon as I hear anything. For now, please inform the Elder Madam in Sancheong."

With that, the line went dead.

Jong-hee immediately relayed the troubling news to Bok-hee, whose expression darkened upon hearing it. Irritation flickered across her face as she lamented the burden Yoo-sang had to bear, particularly because of Dal-soo's irresponsibility.

Bok-hee sighed in frustration.

"After making the long trip to Busan, now I have to turn around and head back to Sancheong again. I might as well just wait for a phone call — someone will probably bring Aunt Ki-soon back, just like last time. But honestly, what is Dal-soo doing? He leaves everything to Yoo-sang, even matters concerning his own sister-in-law. How can he make an elderly man like Yoo-sang handle all his family affairs? Tsk, tsk ... I really can't stand him.

... How can he be away from home so often?"

Two days later, the phone shattered the silence once again with grim finality. "Mistress Ki-soon has been found deceased on the mountain. It's best that you come to the New House immediately," Yoo-sang conveyed solemnly. With Ki-hoon away on business, Jong-hee and her sons prepared for their somber return to Sancheong. Bok-hee had already departed a day earlier, ensuring that everything was in place to receive the mourners — a testament to her swift and capable handling of family matters. In the midst of preparations, Young-soon clung to her, her silent tears a tribute to the tragedy.

Jong-hee marveled, 'My mother-in-law is truly quick-handed. How did she manage to prepare everything for the funeral in just one day?' The police gathered the family in the yard and delivered the stark reality: "Ki-soon lost her way on a mountain trail in the early summer heat and succumbed to the elements without food or water."

The funeral was held promptly upon Jong-hee's arrival, primarily arranged by Young-soon and Dal-soo. Had Bok-hee not rushed over, Dal-soo would likely have insisted on taking Ki-soon's body directly from the police station to the crematorium. As the diligent daughter-in-law of the Head Family, Bok-hee fulfilled all her duties to the very end.

As Jong-hee stepped into the New House, memories of the past flashed through her mind. When she first married into the Head Family, she had gone one morning to greet Lady Hwang, her grandmother-in-law. At that time, Lady Hwang had said to her, "A rare beauty has entered this household." These words had become a great source of strength for Jong-hee.

In Jong-hee's eyes, Lady Hwang had been an exceptionally striking woman, and she had felt happy that such a beautiful person had recognized her own appearance. According to the whispered legends of old, '*A writer pledges loyalty to the one who cherishes their words, and a woman, her fidelity to the one who admires her beauty.*' Such sayings drifted through the air, deceptively sweet, ensnaring many in a web of self-deception.

Like many women, Jong-hee lived within her own illusions. She often heard people around her say, "Could there be someone as beautiful as her? Will she also grow old?" These remarks had fueled her pride, and she took particular satisfaction in the admiration of others. Each time whispers of her beauty reached her ears, Jong-hee's heart would swell with pride, as if aging itself could be held at bay by the marvel of those who beheld her.

Ki-soon, in Jong-hee's eyes, had once been a beacon of beauty, a mirror reflection of her mother, Lady Hwang. But time spares no one; Ki-soon had now become nothing more than a memory, her existence reduced to mere ashes.

Gazing into the old mirror in the *daecheong-maru* of the New House, Jong-hee traced the contours of her own face with her fingers, pondering the fleeting nature of beauty and the solitude of a house now haunted by echoes of the past. Then, she noticed Young-soon sitting absentmindedly on the wooden veranda of the main house.

Who remains in the New House now? Jong-hee knew well that only Young-soon, with her childlike mind, was still living there. Tears welled up in Jong-hee's eyes for no apparent reason. She realized she was comforting herself by thinking, *Though Aunt Young-soon has the mind of a child, this house will remain hers, and she has inherited land too. Just that much makes her better off than me. It's a small relief.*

Jong-hee's reflections drifted to darker times, to when her once-affluent family had been undone by deceit and familial greed—a tale as old as the *Joseon* dynasty itself. Without realizing it, she let out a deep sigh.

The ancient codes—the *Chilgeojiak*[65], with its seven damning acts,

---

[65] Chilgeojiak: The seven evils that granted a husband the right to expel his wife. These seven

and the *Sambulgeo*⁶⁶⁾, the three exceptions—were relics of a feudal era, echoes of a harsh societal order that no longer held relevance in the modern world. Yet, despite the rigid dictates of the past, Jong-hee found herself paradoxically taking solace in the very structures that had granted her a place in the Choi family as Ki-hoon's wife.

For a fleeting moment, she considered that Confucian education might still have its uses. She even wondered if Young-soon, her husband's aunt—who at least had her own home to return to—might be in a better situation than she was. Jong-hee, after all, had been left with nothing after her father's passing.

Ki-soon had vanished without a trace. The paths leading to the New House had become overgrown, further sealing it off after Dal-soo built a wall around the *Jangdok-gan*, isolating it completely. Elder Hong-seon, aware of his own mortality, had once entrusted Yoo-sang with a solemn duty: Hong-seon said,

"Yoo-sang, the day will come when I am no longer here. Look after the women of the New House ... those souls with nowhere else to turn. Lady Hwang's parents are long gone, and her youngest sibling never even had the chance to marry. As you may have heard, it is Young-soon's eldest aunt, Principal Hwang, who has taken it upon herself to care for that

---

evils are: ① Failing to properly serve one's parents-in-law ② Failing to bear a son ③ Engaging in adulterous behavior ④ Displaying jealousy ⑤ Suffering from an inheritable disease such as leprosy or epilepsy ⑥ Being excessively talkative ⑦ Committing theft Among these, ③ and ⑦ were recognized as legal offenses by general societal standards, while ① through ⑥ stemmed from the inevitable demands of the feudal family system.
—From the Encyclopedia of Korean Folk Culture. Recited from Naver by the author.

66) Sambulgeo: In Confucianism, the three conditions under which a wife could not be expelled, even if she had committed one of the seven evils (*Chilgeojiak*). These conditions were:①If she had observed the three-year mourning period for her parents-in-law ②If her husband had become wealthy after marrying her when he was poor ③If she had no place to return to or no one to rely on—Requoted by the author from Naver.

sibling. ... I trust you to look after them well."

The few who gathered at the New House for Ki-soon's modest memorial soon departed, leaving behind only whispers of her name. Despite his deepest contemplation, Yoo-sang could not understand why Mistress Ki-soon had left the house. The mystery of her tragic demise haunted him. The lingering doubts over her pitiable end and his inability to fulfill Hong-seon's final request weighed heavily on his heart, casting an even darker shadow over his spirit.

Had it been about four months since Ki-soon's departure?

In the early dawn, as the autumn wind blew refreshingly crisp, Yoo-sang was mending the handle of an axe, preparing to gather firewood from the *Jangdok-gan* of the Big House to store in the kitchen. It was then that he noticed Soon-joo, the errand girl from the New House, hurling a black cotton bundle into the vacant lot behind the block factory.

After Hong-seon's passing, Lady Hwang had sold the land where the main gate once stood—damaged by bombing during the Korean War. Dal-soo, after moving in, left the remaining land untouched, not even bothering to put up a gate. The block factory, which had taken over the area where the *sarang-chae* and warehouse had once stood, gradually encroached toward the main building. Dal-soo sustained himself by selling off most of the land.

Blocks were stacked and stored in and around the factory. Part of the remaining vacant lot was used as a garbage burning site, with large iron plates set up as walls for incinerating household trash. Yoo-sang left the main gate of the Big House, made his way toward the incineration site, and then crossed over to the shabby New House, which had even lost its small gate. He quickly retrieved the black cloth bundle, which had been left for burning, and carried it back to the Big House.

Taking the bundle to his room in the *haengnang-chae*, Yoo-sang carefully unwrapped it. As he had suspected, it contained items belonging to the late Mistress Ki-soon. Inside were small Japanese porcelain toys she had played with as a child, a woolen hat adorned with white feathers on one side, and crumpled Japanese poplin handkerchiefs embroidered with yellow violets. There were also *beoseons*, along with a few notebooks and books.

Among them, he found a pair of Ki-soon's beoseons—exceptionally small and delicate for her age, made of white cotton. Holding them close to his chest, he felt the weight of the memories they carried. Though he never fully understood why, Yoo-sang often reflected on how delicate and beautiful his late wife's feet had been before she perished in the war. Unlike the feet of other women who worked the fields—feet that grew large and calloused from labor—his wife's remained small, smooth, and almost glossy, as if always anointed with oil. Ki-soon's feet, too, had been notably small and delicate.

He recalled a time long ago when he had carried her after she fell into the pond in the yard. As he lifted her, he had tightly grasped her petite and graceful feet with both hands. Even though she was wearing wet *beoseon*, he could still feel her plump, pretty toes—perfectly sized to fit in his palm.

Ki-soon, once vibrant and lovely, had descended into madness, her psyche scarred by the waters that had nearly claimed her. Over time, however, she even began to touch, immerse herself in, and play with that very '*water*'—the same element that had once evoked such terror, all because of Jong-cheol's cruelty and the misfortunes of a misguided marriage. Had Ki-soon, who had once submerged herself in the pond, truly overcome her *fear of water*?

Whenever Yoo-sang thought about those days, his heart would race involuntarily, clinging to the hope that she might return to normal once again. 'But now, the spirit that once danced like light upon the water had been stilled, overshadowed by the trials she had endured...' he mumbled.

Within the bundle, he found a diary adorned with lilies, its pages serving as a sanctuary for her thoughts.

September 22, 1953

What, then, is a family? Is it merely a group of people who share features and habits, who, by breaking bread together daily, unknowingly come to mirror each other's gestures and expressions? *Is family a breeding ground for self-replication, or is it a flashpoint for social conflict?*

As people grow, their hearts gradually fill with sharp fragments of broken mirrors. Each time their existence is denied in some way, the once-whole mirror shatters further into smaller, sharper pieces. In such moments, familiarity does more than just breed resemblance—it forms a mosaic of the soul, where each shard of the mirror reflects and magnifies even the smallest details, until personal boundaries blur and identities intertwine. Gazing into that fractured mirror, where fragments of each other remain, they may catch glimpses of themselves.

Yet, as the mirror continues to break, it transforms into a weapon. When they wound and attack each other with it, the pain cuts even deeper. In the corridors of the heart, these mirrors splinter under the weight of unmet expectations, their jagged edges turned into blades that inflict the cruelest wounds—because they are wielded by familiar hands. What we see in one another becomes a tableau of both suffering and self-preservation, a reflection of our deepest wounds and our fiercest defenses.

The concept of "family" extends beyond blood and lineage, eagerly adopted by nations, political parties, corporations—any entity seeking to sanctify its assembly through a shared bond. Beneath the facade of familial norms, humans boldly replicate themselves, even as they inflict harm on others. A species that reproduces itself with unrestrained audacity, even while wounding those around them—humankind, in all its variations.

Under the banner of "family," the convergence of intertwined fates—our karma—clashes and coalesces, shaping destinies bound together, whether in harmony or discord.

Yesterday, Yutaka didn't come to see me again. I waited for him so desperately, yet he is not here with me now. The idea of "our family" will never exist for me. I will never be able to create it. If Yutaka and I had built a family together, could we have lived happily? What about the children we might have had?

A week ago, when Yutaka came to see me, I reached out to touch his face —but the moment I did, he disappeared, leaving me behind. Is my inability to create my own family also part of my karma?

The dreams we once shared for the future now seem as distant as the stars —unreachable, inscrutable. If karma is a form of energy, then it acts as a force shaping every land we inhabit. Even if I were to meet Yutaka again, I might no longer be able to embrace him as the secret fiancé he once was. Because Yutaka and I have been transformed into new forms of energy, shaped by the karmic forces we each carry. And when these karmic forces intertwine, no one can predict which aspects will manifest or what form our relationship will take, moment by moment.

Had he stayed, would our home have echoed with laughter, or would the inevitable strains of our entwined karmas have created rifts too wide to bridge?

In this dance of fate, where karma flows like an unseen current, our paths may never realign as they once did. Changed by time and trials, Yutaka and I might meet again as strangers, our past intimacy buried beneath the currents of a newly forged energy—unpredictable and profound.

Yet, how well did I truly know him? Between the conflicting narratives of nations—Japan's claim of civilizing a backward land and Korea's mourning of cultural erasure—the truth of Yutaka, like the truth of every personal connection, remains veiled. As I search for understanding, I find myself grasping at shadows, realizing that perhaps I never knew him at all. Our shared history is a story told in two irreconcilable languages.

In the stillness of those moments, history unwound itself like the threads of a silken tapestry, revealing the tangled interplay of duty and exploitation between two lands. The notion of help, cloaked in the guise of benevolence, often concealed ambitions not of uplift but of dominion, transforming assistance into subjugation. Japan and *Joseon*, despite their long entanglement, remained strangers to each other—brothers by circumstance rather than choice—bound together by unspoken truths and unseen depths, as vast and unknowable as the ocean.

If Yutaka and I were to cross paths once more, in this ever-shifting kaleidoscope of fate, we might find ourselves as strangers beneath a familiar veneer. Love and death, those mercurial forces, hold the power to transform us in ways unforeseeable to the human heart—until the very moment of reunion.

January 6, 1954

Amid the vast tapestry of existence,
I am but a mote of dust, spiraling in the silent ballet of decay.
From the remnants of my being—skin, hair, the detritus of daily life—
I am swept into the endless molecular dance of existence.

Yutaka and I, particles adrift in the cosmic web,
find each other only to lose ourselves again—
in the spaces between moments,
in the hollow chambers where love once dwelled.

A wave, colossal in its indifference,
has severed the ties that once bound us,
leaving me a spectral voyager upon the shores of convention,
unable to cross the river that both sustains and divides.

April, 1954

F-a-t-h-e-r!
The earth endures wind and dust,
Absorbing blood and bone,
Only to release the waters.

Blood becomes fire,
Water becomes blood again.
Bones turn to dust,
Scattering into the wind.

The seed bears seed,
And through death, life continues.

Inhabitants!
Within this endless cycle,
Fathers and sons stand as trees,
Daughters become leaves—
And with time, they fall.
Bye.

As he was reading, Yoo-sang suddenly felt a sharp gust of wind whistling through the air. He opened the door of the servant's quarters and stepped outside to look around, but nothing was visible. Closing the notebook, he placed it back into the bundle that held Ki-soon's belongings. Carefully, he wrapped the bundle once more and tucked it inside the wooden box beside his bed.

Spreading out his bedding, Yoo-sang lay down, trying to sleep. But just as he was about to drift off, he thought he heard the sound of footsteps somewhere nearby. The moment he turned off the light, the footsteps came to a halt at the entrance of his room. Yoo-sang called out, "Is that you, Lady Ki-soon?" and flung the door wide open.

At that instant, a bird with large wings appeared in his sight, flapping powerfully before perching on a thick branch of the pagoda tree just outside. It was a white bird, its feathers and body as pure as freshly fallen snow. Even against the pitch-black curtain of the night, its immaculate form stood out clearly.

Yoo-sang called again, "Lady!"

The bird stretched its wings as if awakening from a deep slumber, then gave a powerful flap and soared from the tree. Higher and higher it rose, circling the pagoda tree once before vanishing into the darkness.

Only a faint whisper lingered in his ears:

"The ones you should fear

Are the masses trapped in convention! Shh..."

24

Bok-hee's 60th Birthday Party

1970: The House of Ki-hoon in Busan
—Blessing and Ill Fate

Bok-hee decided to spend a month at the home of her eldest son, Ki-hoon, located at Mt. 83 Beonji in Beomjeon-dong, Busan. The occasion was her 60th birthday, a milestone she wished to celebrate surrounded by her family. All her sons, except for the third, had settled in Busan. Ki-hoon was a professor at Pusan National University, while her second son, Ki-hwi, worked as a public official at Busan City Hall.

Her eldest daughter's husband, Mr. Kim, was a middle school teacher. The second daughter, having divorced due to infertility, lived alone. The third daughter had met her husband during her college years—a professor—and had left school to marry him. Her youngest daughter had recently moved to Gaegeum-dong, Busan, following her husband, who had resigned from his position in Saemaul Education in Sancheong. He was now establishing a new school, Citizens' Night High School, where he served as principal. Despite the challenges, the couple managed their household with a sense of pride.

As for her third son, he was a skilled engineer and researcher working between Daejeon and Seoul, contributing to national projects. Whenever Bok-hee thought of her children, she was filled with warmth and pride.

At the funeral of her mother-in-law, Lady Kim, as well as her aunt Ki-soon's funeral, Bok-hee's sister-in-law, Nam-gil, was notably absent. Instead, she sent a message through another relative, saying, "I'll come down to Busan when I have time." This time, she initially gave the impression that she might attend, but as Bok-hee's celebration drew closer, she sent word that she would not be able to come after all.

All she shared was a brief update—that her third daughter was working as a middle school teacher and that her youngest son had recently been promoted to section chief at Cheil Jedang.

Among the relatives, some lingering debts that Nam-gil had left unsettled still remained. Bok-hee suspected that Nam-gil was deliberately avoiding the gathering, fearing that if they met in person, tensions would rise, voices would be raised, and old grievances would inevitably resurface.

Bok-hee pondered over Nam-gil's actions. "How could she, who was always called 'little mother' by my children and who placed everyone she was close to in debt, dare to show her face? Does she have no sense of shame?" she muttered to herself.

Despite these thoughts, on the day of her birthday, Bok-hee decided to invite Yoo-sang and Seok Sen, who had been her lifelong companions and helpers during her years in Sancheong. For Bok-hee's 60th birthday, the family prepared a lavish feast. Alongside three or four racks of pork ribs, they added two racks of beef ribs, fish, various fried pancakes, an assortment of alcohol, rice cakes, several types of kimchi, a variety of snacks, fruits, cinnamon punch, and sweet rice drink. On that special day, her sons, daughters, sons-in-law, and grandchildren all gathered at Ki-hoon's house.

The grandchildren filled the home with laughter and chaos, running through the rooms and yard, rolling, tumbling, and playing games throughout the day.

For nearly ten days leading up to the celebration, Jong-hee had worked tirelessly alongside a kitchen maid to prepare everything. Yet, despite Jong-hee's earnest efforts, nothing seemed to satisfy Bok-hee. To her, Jong-hee was nothing but a thorn in her side—someone she found utterly detestable and difficult to warm to. It was hard to tell whether Bok-hee had always been this way or if she simply adored her son Ki-hoon so much that no woman would ever seem worthy enough to be his wife.

The 60th birthday, marking six decades of life, was a momentous occasion in Korea, and everyone dressed appropriately for the celebration. The guests donned beautiful *hanbok*, with even the children wearing their finest attire. They gathered before the grand table, laden with carefully prepared dishes, and bowed deeply to Bok-hee before capturing the moment in a commemorative photograph. Then, they indulged in the feast.

After lunch, people gathered on the *daecheong-maru* (wooden floor). The family began playing *Yut*, a traditional game in which four sticks are thrown, determining how game pieces advance. The competition quickly became lively, with the winning and losing teams taking turns singing and dancing, much to the children's delight. As the merriment grew, the yard was transformed into a dance floor, where Bok-hee's sons, sons-in-law, and daughters swayed to the music playing from an old record player.

Toward the end of the celebration, Bok-hee's youngest son-in-law, Principal Kim, offered a drink to Yoo-sang. A man who enjoyed drinking and had many friends among writers, he struck up a quiet conversation with Yoo-sang and then posed a thoughtful question.

Principal Kim said,

"Whether a person is young or old, they see the world clearly when their mind is in the right place, don't you think?

But do you have any idea why Aunt Ki-soon ended up the way she did? Who on earth could have driven her to such a fate? There were times when she seemed lost, out of her senses, but to find her dead in the mountains, so far from home...

Surely, someone else must have had a hand in it, don't you think?"

At Principal Kim's words, Yoo-sang simply stared at the liquor table before him, his gaze fixed and his lips sealed in silence. He looked straight ahead, lost in thought. After a moment, he rose to bid farewell to Bok-hee and the other family members, preparing to return to Sancheong. As he was about to leave, he leaned in close to Principal Kim and whispered softly in his ear.

Yoo-sang murmured,

"Principal Kim, now that you've made your debut as a poet of Korean verse, you must see the world through a different lens. Lady Ki-soon... she had such a deep love for birds. Perhaps that's why she wandered off—to the mountains, to the fields ... chasing after them. She was always captivated by the flutter of their wings and the sweetness of their song. She was a woman with such a tender, lovely spirit."

Principal Kim, already well into his cups, absorbed Yoo-sang's words only half-heartedly. He waved his hand in a vague gesture of understanding and then, with a sigh, remarked,

"It's all in the past now. The time of suffering is over. Let's believe that."

How many hours had passed in the company of loved ones? How had they spent them? Could such moments ever truly capture the depth of human connection?

Bok-hee pondered these questions as she sat alone in a quiet room after the party. She wondered how much Il-seop, her late husband, would have enjoyed the gathering if he were still alive. Since his passing, Bok-hee had spent countless years running from place to place, raising their children on her own. Those days now felt distant, as if they belonged to another lifetime. She knew she could never relive such times again. Her age weighed heavily upon her, and she marveled at the strength she had once possessed.

I can hardly believe I've raised my children alone for nearly 25 years after my husband's death... Bok-hee reflected with a sense of pride.

Each of her children was precious to her, and the thought of losing even one of them filled her with pain. Yet, if she had to choose the one who had suffered the most, it would be her second daughter, Ki-young. As mentioned earlier in this story, during the war, Ki-young had been caught in a bombing while running an errand for her eldest brother, Ki-hoon. A bullet fragment had lodged itself in her eye, leaving her blind in one eye.

Ki-hoon had been devastated, overwhelmed with guilt that his sister had been injured while helping him. In an effort to make amends, he arranged for two surgeries to fit her with an artificial eye. But the physical damage was only part of Ki-young's suffering. As a woman, she bore even deeper scars.

Fragments from the bomb had embedded themselves within her body, leading to bacterial infections in her organs. In her youth, her robust health had been enough to keep the infections at bay. But as the years passed and her strength declined, her body began to betray her.

Her first husband, a career soldier stationed in Sacheon, had been unable to father children with her, so they adopted a girl named Eun-sook. Ki-young had heard that Aunt Young-soon of Sancheong had also adopted a child, which influenced her decision.

Eun-sook cherished Ki-young as if she were her own biological mother. However, despite living together for several years, Ki-young ultimately gave up on the adoption. She cited the child's mischievous behavior and habit of stealing as the reasons, but the truth ran deeper.

The real cause was the devastating revelation that Ki-young was permanently infertile. Her husband, realizing that Eun-sook, who did not share a drop of their blood, could never bridge the emotional gap between them, saw no reason to continue their marriage. He began preparing for a new life with another woman, declaring that his union with Ki-young had lost all meaning. In response, Ki-young quietly accepted the divorce without a single word of protest.

Afterward, Ki-young set up a small canteen at the school run by her youngest sister Ki-seon's husband and lived alone. Lacking specialized skills, she found it difficult to pursue other work, so she simply made do with what she had. Although the institution was called a school, it was actually a Citizens' Night High School, catering to students from challenging family backgrounds who could only attend classes after finishing their shifts at nearby factories. These students sought out affordable snacks like donuts and fries at Ki-young's canteen.

She spent her Sundays at church, lived in a small room adjoining the canteen, and devoted herself to caring for Ki-seon's children, knitting quietly in her spare time.

Ki-seon, the youngest sibling, was another source of heartache for Bok-hee. Being a posthumous child, born after Il-seop's death, Ki-seon held a special and poignant place in Bok-hee's heart. Ki-seon was eleven years younger than her husband, Principal Kim.

She was strikingly beautiful—tall enough to turn heads wherever she went in Korea. Standing at 170 centimeters, with double eyelids and a high-bridged nose, Ki-seon possessed features that were rare and captivating for a Korean woman of her time. Yet, perhaps it was that very high nose that led to her downfall at beauty contest.

After graduating from high school in Busan, she moved to Sancheong, where her mother was living, and volunteered as a teacher at a night school. Had she not taken this path, she might never have met her future husband, Principal Kim, who was then overseeing education at the *Saemaul* School in Sancheong while also running a night school.

And Bok-hee was never satisfied with Principal Kim. He came from a poor family, was short in stature, and lacked the charm that might have compensated for his modest appearance. Moreover, the significant age gap between him and Ki-seon would have given any mother reason to object. Their marriage took place despite Bok-hee's strong opposition, and it wasn't long before Ki-seon's health problems began.

Her first pregnancy resulted in an ectopic pregnancy, leading to the removal of one of her ovaries—a devastating blow to both her health and her hopes for the future. The attending doctor had warned, "It may be impossible for her to conceive in the future." Yet, against all odds, Ki-seon bore five children after the operation, with scarcely a year between each birth. Principal Kim, who had initially been disheartened by the prospect of his wife's near-infertility, often felt pangs of envy whenever he passed homes where children's diapers hung from clotheslines. But a decade later, he found himself the father of five.

Ki-hwi, Bok-hee's second son, had been a troublemaker since childhood. His mischievous pranks often targeted Ki-soon and Jeong-soon of the New House, especially their uncle, Joon-seop.

One of his more infamous tricks involved defecating in a corner of the yard, extracting a roundworm from the stool with a stick, and then scattering it around the New House yard. When Joon-seop, mistaking the worm for an earthworm, attempted to clean it up, he was met with a foul stench that revealed its true source.

On another occasion, Ki-hwi dirtied freshly laundered clothes by hurling mud at them as they hung on the clothesline. Among the soiled laundry were group gym uniforms that all students were required to wear the next day. Although Joon-seop was older than Ki-hwi, he never reacted with anger nor informed the rest of the family, not wanting to cause his mother, Lady Hwang, any distress. Bok-hee eventually learned of these incidents from the kitchen maid.

After graduating from J Agricultural University, Ki-hwi secured a position as a math teacher at Sacheon Middle School, where he met his future wife. She was well-known for her beauty in the neighborhood, yet she concealed her family's struggles by borrowing clothes from friends during their courtship. By then, rumors had already circulated at the school that Ki-hwi was the grandson of a wealthy family in Sancheong, making him a subject of interest among the female students.

Eventually, Ki-hwi and the woman grew close, leading to marriage. However, her family's financial situation was dire. She had younger siblings, and her mother—once from a relatively affluent background—had graduated from Dongnae Girls' High School in Busan during the Japanese colonial period. However, her mother had separated from her husband and was raising three children on her own.

She felt the pressure to marry quickly, Ki-hwi's wife sought stability, as she needed to support her mother and siblings. For some, marriage is a means to secure a stable life. Although Ki-hoon, Ki-hwi's elder brother, and Bok-hee strongly opposed the union, the situation had already been decided—Ki-hwi's wife was pregnant, leaving them no choice but to accept the marriage.

After getting married, Ki-hwi abandoned his teaching career and moved to Busan, securing a position as a city hall official through an introduction. At that time, connections and recommendations from influential people were essential for obtaining such jobs. However, this new employment did not last long. Ki-hwi's wife was dissatisfied with the modest salary of a civil servant.

Wherever they moved, she borrowed money from neighbors, yet her inability to manage finances led to inevitable failure. She decorated their home to appear wealthy, but after living extravagantly on borrowed money from acquaintances, she fled twice in the dead of night—escaping their debts in Busan.

Above Ki-seon, Bok-hee's youngest daughter, was Ki-ok, who was just a year older. Ki-ok was skilled at playing the piano and possessed a sharp wit and wisdom in her own way. Both Ki-seon and Ki-ok had entered the Miss Korea Busan Competition three times when they were around nineteen years old, but they failed each time. They were not the petite, delicate figures that were favored by the public at the time.

Standing at 168 and 170 centimeters tall, with high nose bridges and prominent double eyelids, they were striking but did not fit the conventional beauty standards sought by the Miss Korea judges. After their repeated attempts, they decided:

"Let's stop here. Entering these contests requires money and diligence, and we're just not cut out for it. Other girls dream of becoming celebrities or movie stars through these competitions, but that's not for us."

They shared their conclusion with Jong-hee, their elder sister-in-law. Observing the two of them, Jong-hee privately thought, *Miss Korea should embody the "petite and delicate Korean beauty," and my two sisters-in-law are not quite suited for that.*

Among the two, the younger Ki-seon had a powerful voice and rich emotional depth, making her an excellent singer. People around her often suggested that she should pursue a singing career, but by then, she was already married to Principal Kim, and her musical aspirations remained nothing more than a distant dream.

Meanwhile, Bok-hee's eldest son, Ki-hoon, and her third son were excelling in their respective fields, both known for their sharp intellects. Whenever Bok-hee thought of them, her heart swelled with pride.

Before moving to Beomjeon-dong, Ki-hoon had lived in a spacious home in Dongnae Oncheonjang. In those days, before the daughters and the third son were married, the entire family enjoyed living together in that large house near the entrance of Geumgang Park, a place filled with laughter and warmth. After dinner time, they would sing in the high areas of the park, share joyful moments, and return home late at night.

After his sisters married and his younger brother moved to Seoul, Ki-hoon's family relocated to Mt. 83 Beonji in Beomjeon-dong. The new house was a handsome tile-roofed home, covering approximately 80 *pyeong*. While Bok-hee had cherished their old home near Geumgang Park in Oncheonjang, she eventually came to appreciate their new residence in her own way.

More importantly, this was a house that Ki-hoon had secured on his own, without depleting the family's property in Sancheong — a fact that Bok-hee deeply respected.

By the evening of Bok-hee's sixtieth birthday, the celebration was winding down. Young-soon arrived late, well after dinner, accompanied by a young girl she was raising at the time. When they entered Ki-hoon's house, Bok-hee's family greeted them, but the reception was lukewarm—little more than a nod of acknowledgment.

Jong-hee didn't like the way her in-law relatives treated Young-soon, but she had no choice but to watch in silence. She escorted them to Se-joon's room, where she served snacks and food on a small table for Young-soon and her daughter to share. The girl's name was Gyeong-mi. As Jong-hee watched Young-soon care for Gyeong-mi—feeding her and ensuring she ate well—she found herself observing the warmth and tenderness in their interaction.

Later, Jong-hee retrieved a pair of leather gloves and a wool muffler embroidered with delicate flowers from the main room. These had been gifts from one of Ki-hoon's female students. She placed them in a small paper box and handed it to Gyeong-mi. Though Young-soon wasn't engaged in hard labor, her hands were rough and calloused. Gyeong-mi's short bobbed hair made her look cold and vulnerable. The two stayed the night at Ki-hoon's house. The next morning, Gyeong-mi wrapped the muffler around her neck, and Young-soon donned the gloves as they set out early to catch the bus back to Sancheong.

Of course, among the members of Min-ja's family from Saemmy House, Ki-woong, who had recently married, came to greet them with his wife. Ki-woong had become a police officer, and according to Min-ja, he had married his wife just a month after receiving his new post. Min-ja lamented that, until now, she had been the one taking care of the family on her own and had only recently married herself. The money she had earned and saved had been spent on supporting her younger brothers and stepmother.

Since she had also supported her younger brother, Ki-woong, she had hoped that once he secured a job, he might repay her in some way for all the sacrifices she had made over the years. However, on the very day Ki-woong started his job, a matchmaker visited him and arranged a marriage with her friend's daughter, quickly setting the wedding date. In the end, Min-ja married him off without ever receiving any financial support from him. Later, she confided in Jong-hee, sharing the emptiness she felt and her disappointment in how things had unfolded.

Min-ja and Ki-woong rarely missed family gatherings at the Big House, and for Bok-hee's 60th birthday, they arrived bearing a basket of fruit to pay their respects. When Jong-hee saw Min-ja and Ki-woong, she couldn't help but think of Jeong-seop. During the most difficult and painful periods of his life, Jeong-seop would occasionally visit her in Busan, staying for a couple of days before returning to Sancheong. Though she couldn't fully articulate why, Jong-hee always felt a deep sense of sympathy for Min-ja's family—the Saemmy House household in Sancheong.

Unlike Ki-hoon, who rarely displayed much emotion when Jeong-seop visited, Jong-hee always made a point to welcome him warmly. She carefully prepared meals for him during his stay, mended any missing buttons or torn parts of his clothes, and discreetly slipped some travel money into his hand before he left. Whenever possible, she would accompany him to the bus terminal, seeing him off on his journey back to Sancheong.

For many people from Sancheong, Ki-hoon's house in Busan served as a kind of refuge—a rest stop where they could share their troubles and seek assistance. Jong-hee often thought to herself that *"The Head Family" was meant to be this kind of place—a pillar of support for all the relatives.*

But as time passed, fewer and fewer relatives visited, and the younger generation of the Sancheong family grew increasingly detached from the Head Family. Their interactions with Ki-hoon dwindled, reduced to twice-yearly requests for donations under the guise of the "Hometown Clan Association." Even the ancestral rites, or *sisa*, held twice a year, saw diminishing attendance.

Eventually, the gatherings shrank to include only the immediate family—namely, Hong-seon's direct descendants. The wider Choi family stopped attending, leaving the Head Family's role diminished in all but name, with only Hong-seon's descendants maintaining what few connections remained.

Bok-hee's nephews from Masan traveled to attend her 60th birthday celebration. She had four brothers. Her eldest brother had a son and a daughter, but, as a staunch socialist who openly praised North Korea, he eventually defected to the North alone and disappeared from their lives. Left behind, his son and daughter were raised almost entirely under Bok-hee's care. After moving between various relatives' homes, they eventually lived in Ki-hoon's house in Busan for several years. The son worked in a laboratory at P University Hospital for nearly three years, while the daughter lived with their uncle, Bok-hee's second eldest brother, for nearly a decade.

Bok-hee's third and fourth brothers had both passed away recently, succumbing to old age. However, it was Ki-hoon who secured jobs for nearly all of their sons. They relocated to Busan, where they found employment in affiliated organizations, thanks to Ki-hoon's connections. The burden of supporting his extended family was a constant weight on his shoulders. This responsibility extended not only to the Choi family but also to the Jeong family, his mother's side. *Throughout his life, Ki-hoon remained a steadfast pillar, carrying the burdens of his relatives.*

Jong-hee, too, bore her share of the family's responsibilities. At just 30 years old, she inherited all the family rituals from Bok-hee. Each year, she was responsible for 14 memorial services for the deceased family members (*gi-jesa*), along with two seasonal rites for the ancestors from the fifth generation and beyond (*si-jesa*) in spring and autumn, as well as two holiday rituals. This meant that ancestral rites took place nearly two or three times a month.

For Jong-hee, who had only recently married and was still struggling to adjust to rural life due to her frail health, it was an overwhelming responsibility. However, she persevered, knowing that *performing these rituals was an unavoidable duty as the eldest daughter-in-law.*

Among Bok-hee's nephews who attended her 60th birthday, the one she held in the highest regard was Soo-gon, the son of her second eldest brother. He had come to Sancheong to pay his respects to Hong-seon on the final day of his life and had remained through the funeral. At that time, Soo-gon was still living in Masan, and for Bok-hee's 60th birthday celebration, he arrived with his two daughters and son.

Mi-jin, his eldest daughter, was attending a nursing high school at the time. She was the same age as Ki-hoon's eldest son, Se-joon, both born in 1953. His second daughter, Mi-young, was born in 1960. Although he had a third daughter, Mi-soon, she did not accompany them.

Soo-gon's greatest pride was his son, Yo-han (John), born in 1958, who had placed first in the first-year middle school mock exam in Masan. Yo-han bore a striking resemblance to his mother, as did his younger sister, Mi-young. Both children had round faces and were perpetually cheerful, always greeting those around them with warm smiles.

Yo-han was recognized for his intelligence wherever he went, earning the admiration of nearly all his peers in Masan. His name, John (Yo-han in Korean), carried a distinct Christian influence, and Bok-hee's eldest brother's daughter proudly told those gathered that Yo-han was not only popular among his friends but also well-liked by all the teachers at his school.

Though Yo-han mostly took after his mother's side of the family, his eyes bore a striking resemblance to his father's, with long eyelashes and large, expressive pupils. Soo-gon adored his son, especially since they shared this distinctive feature. Mi-young, Yo-han's younger sister, had charming, petite eyes like their mother's. Yet, what truly stood out about the siblings were their eyebrows, which were bold and unmistakable. Both Yo-han and Mi-young had crescent-shaped, smiling eyebrows that drew attention wherever they went. Anyone who noticed their matching brows would smile and say, "Oh, they have the same smiling half-moon eyebrows."

As Bok-hee's 60th birthday celebration drew to a close, those who remained gathered once more on the floor for another commemorative photo. It was then that Se-joon, Ki-hoon's eldest son, suddenly stepped forward and offered to read a poem he had written. The room fell silent as everyone listened, particularly Principal Kim, Ki-seon's husband, who, as a poet of Korean verse, paid special attention to Se-joon's words.

Se-joon had recently participated in the Gaecheon Art Festival in Jinju, where he had left school early to attend and won an Excellence Award. Ki-hoon had initially wanted to scold Se-joon for skipping school, but he knew his son possessed a remarkable talent for writing—something evident from an early age. So, in the end, he chose to let it go.

In Ki-hoon's mind, his eldest son, Se-joon, should strive to become a doctor. Though entering medical school required immense effort, the profession itself also came with its own set of challenges and hardships. On the day Se-joon decided to pursue medicine, he approached his father with a thoughtful reflection.

Se-joon said,

"Father, I've realized how difficult life would be if I became a doctor. The same applies to the years of study required. To endure the grueling and monotonous nature of medical school, I feel I need something else to focus on. That's why I'm going to keep writing."

Hearing this, Ki-hoon, who had already gained insight into the pressures of the medical profession through conversations with his doctor friends, nodded in agreement. He understood that while it would be ideal for Se-joon to become a doctor, it was just as important to allow him to pursue his passion for writing. For Se-joon, writing and reading were his only means of escaping a world that often felt painful and overwhelming.

Ki-hoon encouraged his son to consider the practical benefits of a medical career, given the realities of life in Korea, but he also recognized the importance of nurturing Se-joon's literary aspirations.

After dinner, with several relatives gathered around, Se-joon read aloud a poem he had written, sharing a piece of his soul with those who listened.

Dream

In my hometown,
The land of *Hwajeon-ri, Sancheong-gun, Gyeongnam,*
A summer night, restless beneath the glow of mosquito fires,
To the very edge of the sky,
A cascade of calves tumbled down.
They kept descending, endlessly,
Yet, I gathered them all—
The painful darkness as vast as the blue sky,
Only the dawn's sweat, soaking the hemp,
Stained my chest like blood.
In moments more precious than life,
A great nail
Has driven itself deep.

Law of Love · 3

How agonizing it must be to behold,
Can I ever glimpse my mother's land?
In the darkness, filled only with dreams,
A clear blade of grass sways with dizzying grace,
The land of a transparent heart,
Like a single drop of water in the universe,
Swaying in white silk,
Somewhere in the river of the sky.

How softly must I sing

To reach your distant, unfamiliar island?
The lights flicker low on the horizon,
My voice grows hoarse, evading sorrow.

An empty sea of darkness,
A popular song, scattered like mist by the wind,
Drifting around the corner of the dock.
How long must I wait?
One man's two hands
Wet the deep sea of a woman's heart.
Could I conjure rain from a mother's love?

And yet,
Our emptiness, harmonized with wet lips,
Exists only for a future that remains uncertain,
A star waiting in the depths of dreams.
In the night sea, we two,
I hurl my freedom with all my might
Into the unknown.

The others listened to Se-joon's poem with little more than polite interest, offering words of encouragement that felt rehearsed. Soon after, they drifted away to resume their game of *Hwatu*[67]—the Korean card game they had started before dinner—gathering around a blanket in the small room adjacent to the dining area. Their *Hwatu* match was merely an excuse to assign playful penalties that involved singing and dancing among the family. Had Ki-hoon been present, the younger siblings' families likely wouldn't have even considered playing such a game. Like Hong-seon, Ki-hoon would never have allowed *Hwatu* to be played in the household.

---

67) Hwatu is a Korean card game often played during holidays with family, using a colorful deck known as "flower cards." It is derived from Japanese Hanafuda and is commonly enjoyed both recreationally and as a gambling game. (Author's note.)

Amidst the noise, Se-joon noticed his mother, Jong-hee, sitting quietly, resting without a smile in the midst of the crowd.

To Se-joon, his mother had always been a central figure in his life—not just as a parent, but as someone he deeply cared for and worried about. Jong-hee, perhaps, went through life unaware of how profoundly her son saw and understood her burdens. From an early age, Se-joon had decided that caregiving was not solely a parent's role; rather, it was also his duty to look after his mother, to carry the weight of her worries on his own shoulders.

Jong-hee, constantly pursued by the unending demands of household duties, often sought refuge from her mother-in-law Bok-hee's ever-watchful eyes—a woman renowned for her flawless domestic skills. And it was Se-joon, her son, who knew and understood this struggle best. Frail from birth, Se-joon had been sent to live with Jong-hee's mother for a time, growing up away from the family home. Upon his return, he carried the weight of being the eldest son, enduring both the scrutinizing gazes of others and the burden of expectations placed upon him.

As Bok-hee's 60th birthday celebration wound down at Ki-hoon's house, the guests who had traveled from other regions began to disperse, heading back to Masan, Hamyang, and Sacheon after three days of festivities. Soo-gon's mother, Jin-ok, who was also Bok-hee's second eldest sister-in-law, ensured that Soo-gon and her grandchildren, Yo-han and Mi-young, returned home that evening, while she herself stayed on for three more days.

Jin-ok was a kind and graceful woman, someone Se-joon deeply admired. Whenever she encountered Se-joon and Jong-hee in the house, she would look at them with warm, affectionate eyes, gently patting them on the back. Se-joon felt a stronger bond with Jin-ok than with his own grandmother, Bok-hee. Jin-ok, with her ever-gentle smile, never smiled too broadly; her kindness was always expressed in the subtlest of gestures.

Jin-ok said softly,

"Se-joon, you share a special bond with your mother. Don't worry too much, there is an unbreakable thread between a mother and her child that no one can sever."

She spoke with tenderness, but Bok-hee, who had been listening nearby, couldn't hide the change in her expression. Her face darkened at the exchange. With a sharp tone, she interjected,

"Oh my, if anyone else heard what *Olke* says, they might think your son, Soo-gon, has another mother entirely. But let's be clear, no matter what anyone says, you are his true mother. It's been said since ancient times that the bond with the mother who raises a child is deeper than with the one who gave birth. Of course!"

Upon hearing those words, Jin-ok's earlobes turned red, and her face flushed. Se-joon noticed the sadness and astonishment in the old grandmother's eyes.

Later, Se-joon retreated to his room, his mind swirling with thoughts, and began to write.

Lost Child

A dead end is turning.
All day long, dry tears,
I can't go any further.
Through this sorrowful face,
The wind twists like a snail's shell.

If I take a step forward, paths multiply,
The maze becomes even more disorienting,
The evening sunlight scatters like a kaleidoscope.
The child leans against a stone wall,

Escaped from the alley,
Drunk on the last rays of sun.

The tag game has ended,
Everyone has returned home,
Leaving behind only a terrible darkness.
Screaming and shouting alone,
A winter evening from my childhood.

Oh, the day it rained on New Year's Eve,
You, on the immigrant ship,
On the night I left, at the street corner,
I saw it clearly.
That which never emerged from the mud,
Never escaped from there—
Your "White Nose Rubber Shoe,"
Just one.

Bok-hee retired to bed after her relatives had left. She could see that most of them were doing well, yet her thoughts lingered on her second daughter, Ki-young, whose vision had deteriorated. Not long ago, when Bok-hee learned that Ki-young had applied for a medical examination to check for any physical abnormalities, she let out a deep sigh.

Ki-young, divorced and childless, lived alone, and Bok-hee's heart ached for her. How painful life must be with the loss of one eye. Recently, Bok-hee heard that small lumps had appeared around Ki-young's forehead and eyes for no apparent reason and that she was undergoing a biopsy. Bok-hee silently prayed, *Please, let there be no more bad news...*

Ki-young wasn't just caring for the children at the home of her youngest sister, Ki-seon. Bok-hee disapproved of the way her other daughters relied on Ki-young to watch their children and prepare side dishes. Both the eldest and third daughters were guilty of this. Although Bok-hee sometimes vented her frustration to her daughter-in-law, Jong-hee, she could never bring herself to express such displeasure toward her own sons and daughters. *I, as their mother, must never say anything that could hurt these children who lost their father so early. They must never feel diminished by the fact that they were raised by a widow! Yes, that's right,* she reassured herself.

Bok-hee had always held fast to this belief. She felt deep sorrow for Ki-young, but she never voiced her disapproval to her other daughters, who often left their household duties in Ki-young's hands. Yet, it was unlikely that any of them truly understood the depth of her feelings.

After all the guests had departed, Bok-hee called Jong-hee to her.

"Jong-hee, you worked hard preparing for my feast this time. But you know, don't you, that most of the dishes on that table were made by my own hands? I don't know how much longer I'll be around, but from now on, you'll be the one in charge of hosting and handling every aspect of these gatherings. I'm stepping away from food preparation. Do you understand?"

"Yes," Jong-hee replied quietly before leaving the room. As she watched Jong-hee's retreating figure, Bok-hee clicked her tongue in disapproval, narrowing her eyes with a hint of malice. "Something's lacking. There's nothing about her that pleases me. It's like I've poked out my own eyes. Tsk, tsk..." Bok-hee muttered, just loud enough for Jong-hee to hear.

From that moment on, the food served to guests during holidays or on Ki-hoon's birthday was prepared solely by Jong-hee. Having taken more than three years of cooking classes, she managed well. Her desserts—such as apple pie and red bean paste made with chestnuts and beans—along with her water kimchi, cucumber kimchi, and white kimchi, earned praise from Ki-hoon's friends and fellow professors. However, when it came to Korean lettuce wraps, refined rice wine, and traditional snacks, Jong-hee's skills could never quite match Bok-hee's expertise.

In those days, a household's culinary reputation rested on the abilities of its women. It was a time when dining out at famous restaurants was rare. Even Se-joon and Jae-joon's friends often came over, two or three at a time, to savor the leftovers from Bok-hee's 60th birthday feast. Se-joon's friends, who had tasted Jong-hee's cooking back then, continued to enjoy her meals even as college students.

Whenever Jong-hee prepared something particularly delicious, Ki-hoon would always say, "*Yeobo*, today's meal was excellent. Thank you." Sometimes, Jong-hee would fondly recall the times when he had left her a note with those same words.

25
The Eldest Grandson of the Family, Bone or Entrusted ?

Since 1971: *Busan*
—The Sons of Ki-hoon

Se-joon had set his sights on K High School, a prestigious institution in Busan, but when he failed to pass the entrance exam, he ended up at D High School instead, a school that had only begun accepting second-round applicants that year. D High School was no stranger to Se-joon's family—his grandfather, Choi Il-seop, had once walked its halls.

Motivated by the sight of his peers growing stronger and more confident, Se-joon decided to embark on a journey of self-improvement from his very first year. He dedicated himself to both physical and mental discipline, training rigorously at a Japanese karate dojo in Dongnae.

Se-joon was a remarkable student, excelling in all subjects, but he truly stood out in Korean language, ranking at the top of his entire grade. By 1971, his final year of high school, he was on the brink of entering university. His homeroom teacher, Mr. Han Jin-bae, a distinguished graduate of S University, held a particular fondness for Se-joon.

Mr. Han, who had majored in Biology, was highly admired by the students. He was intelligent, handsome, competent, and brave—qualities that commanded respect. Few students dared to lie in his presence.

When it came time to fill out college applications, Mr. Han often said to him,

"Se-joon, you're a talented writer, and you have a remarkable nose. In all my life, I've never seen a more handsome nose on a Korean. But tell me, Se-joon, is college really that important to you?

Does your major truly matter?"

Mr. Han's words carried a deeper meaning—a question that lingered in the minds of his students: Is college more important, or is your major more important?

At that time, students typically chose their universities based on their test scores rather than their true interests or aptitudes. If a university's social reputation mattered most, they would often opt for any department within that prestigious institution, even if their grades were insufficient or the subject didn't align with their true calling. But if passion and aptitude were the priority, students would focus on choosing a major that matched their interests, regardless of the university's prestige.

It became a running joke among the students, a question they would playfully throw at one another with a laugh:

"Hey, is college more important, or is aptitude more important?

That's the real dilemma!"

Se-joon said,

"Teacher, the department is what truly matters to me."

Mr. Han replied,

"Is that so? With your grades, you could easily be admitted to the Dental College at Y University in Seoul or the Medical School at P University in Busan. But as for S University, even the College of Pharmacy might be out of reach."

Se-joon responded,

"I don't have a strong desire to become a doctor. That's more my father's dream than mine. Even if I become a dentist, as long as I can still enjoy music and write the poems I love, that would be enough for me. Please give me a little more time to decide."

Mr. Han said,

"Really? I understand. I'll give you more time.

Come see me in three days."

In truth, Se-joon's heart was set on studying Korean literature. But ever since his second year of high school, he had found himself at a crossroads—a choice between the humanities and the natural sciences, a decision forced upon students in Korea.

His father, Ki-hoon, a man who had witnessed the brutal clash of ideologies during the Korean War, had forbidden him from pursuing the humanities. In his father's mind, a career in the natural sciences—

engineering or medicine—was the only sensible choice, a path that promised practical skills and stability. Ki-hoon was deeply aware that, under socialism, art and literature were often twisted to serve the regime, stripped of their purity and purpose. His convictions were not born merely of theory but of experience.

In the late 1960s, Ki-hoon spent three months in West Germany—an experience that profoundly affected him, though he never spoke of it to anyone. Upon his return, he narrowed his academic focus to legal philosophy and maritime law within the realm of international law, a decision that seemed to signify his resolve to distance himself from ideological conflicts and embrace a more pragmatic worldview.

One day, Ki-hoon spoke to Se-joon, his voice tinged with the weight of his convictions.

Ki-hoon said,

"Se-joon! If I had pursued a different career, I would have wanted to be a diplomat, traveling around the world. But I learned that the life of a diplomat comes with its own challenges, especially the frequent relocations that make social adaptation difficult for their families.

We must always have a clear understanding of the political situation in Korea. If we're not careful, we could lose people. Not long ago, I lost a good friend who was a diplomat."

Ki-hoon also tried to firmly assert his thoughts in this way:

"It's almost impossible to truly understand what goes on in another person's mind. Perhaps it's better to take things at face value. If you choose to study the natural sciences, a field where decisions are clear-cut and straightforward, you'll be better equipped to take control of your life in this country, divided as it is by ideology.

As your father, this is the least I can do ... steer you toward a profession that will secure your future."

But for Se-joon, writing was a passion that refused to be extinguished. He even considered secretly applying to the Korean literature department without his father's knowledge. Yet, he couldn't bring himself to fully betray his father's strict expectations. The weight of his dilemma grew heavier as the college entrance exams drew near.

Se-joon began spending nights studying in a reading room near Seomyeon, rarely coming home. The strain of his internal conflict became evident in his absence.

Sensing the turmoil that had enveloped her son, Jong-hee decided to take matters into her own hands. She had heard whispers from other mothers about a fortune-teller renowned for predicting which universities students would be accepted into. Convinced that a glimpse into her son's future might offer some solace, she resolved to visit this fortune-teller.

One day, Jong-hee set aside time to make the journey with her sister-in-law, Ki-young, to the place where the mothers of high school seniors sought answers, hoping to find some clarity amid uncertainty.

Ki-young and Jong-hee made their way through the narrow alleyways of Choryang, eventually arriving at the fortune-teller's house. After receiving their number ticket, they joined the crowded waiting area. The place was bustling, as it was the end of the year—a time when many sought guidance ahead of entrance exams or career changes.

Finally, their turn came, and they entered the dimly lit room where the fortune-teller, Master Kim, awaited them.

Master Kim (fortune-teller) said,

"Ah, Choi Ki-young and Choi Se-joon. So, you're the student's mother, aren't you? You're not here for your own fortune?

It's 30,000 won per person. I can only tell you as much as the money covers. If you want more, you'll need to pay extra or return another time.

Ah, yes, let's take a look at the Four Pillars—year, month, day, and hour of birth—written on this paper.

Ah, that's right. Mother of the student, take a look as well. What's written on this paper represents the Four Pillars of Destiny for the individuals in question, correct?"

Ki-young and Jong-hee exchanged a glance, leaning in closer to hear what Master Kim had to say. Master Kim said,

"Choi Ki-young, what should I tell you? Are you feeling unwell? A time is coming when you will have to travel far. You should visit the hospital and consult with the doctors. Your husband and you were separated too soon."

Jong-hee replied,

"Well, Choi Ki-young is my children's aunt, and she hasn't been feeling well lately. She's undergoing treatment at the hospital, but...

What do you think? Do you see any plan or direction for her?"

Master Kim said,

"I was born into the Gwangsan Kim clan, destined to study divination and assist others. I do this because it is my calling. But the fate of a person's lifeline is beyond my control.

Take her husband, for example, he cared for his sick ex-wife for eight years. In the end, it was his fate to lose all the wealth he had accumulated because every wife he married fell ill. So, how many years have you been married to him?"

In a barely audible voice, Ki-young responded,

"A little over two years."

Master Kim didn't press further about Ki-young's situation. Instead, his gaze shifted to Jong-hee, who sat with her hands clasped tightly together, looking disheartened. Master Kim continued,

"Lady Kim Jong-hee, people might say you married a husband who is more than you bargained for, isn't that right? Your husband is known for his intelligence and good nature, but... In truth, all that your husband possesses was brought into the family by your fortune.

You were a Minister's wife in your previous life, and you will be a Minister's wife in this life, too. However, I must tell you that your lifeline has already begun to crack. It's not very long.

And... I'm sorry to say this, but you have two sons. The younger one, though not born as the eldest, will eventually have to take on the role of the firstborn, the Head of the Family as the eldest grandson."

He paused, as if to let the words sink in, then added,

"Oh, by the way, are you here about your first son's education? He'll follow the path he desires, for now. His grandmother's hidden prayers are with him—your mother, with her prayer beads, prays for her first grandson every day. But that's all I can tell you. You should go now. Ha-ha..."

Ki-young and Jong-hee felt that the session had passed too quickly. Jong-hee wasn't sure whether to believe Master Kim's words, but something about them resonated—an air of approximate truth. She relinquished her seat to the next customer, reflecting on the fortune-teller's parting words as she left the house.

"The Born Eldest Grandson and the Entrusted Eldest Grandson of the Family," Jong-hee murmured to herself, contemplating their meaning.

As they stepped outside, Ki-young's expression darkened, troubled by Master Kim's words. She turned to Jong-hee and spoke with a furrowed brow. Ki-young said,

"Sister, I find it hard to believe that my eldest brother isn't blessed with good fortune while you are. Yet, everyone says Master Kim is so accomplished ... but what does he really know? And what am I supposed to do about my own situation? It seems my days are numbered."

As she spoke, Ki-young's fingers gently traced the small lumps protruding from her face. Jong-hee, aware of the biopsy results, knew the truth behind those growths, particularly the ones on Ki-young's forehead.

The silent distress etched on Ki-young's face spoke volumes, though she said nothing more. The cause of Ki-young's infertility had been uncovered long ago, a revelation that led her to accept her divorce with resigned grace. But life had dealt her another cruel blow—two decades after sustaining injuries in the war, small lumps began to appear on her face. A recent biopsy had revealed the presence of Mycobacterium tuberculosis within the lumps.

In other words, it was unclear whether the loss of one eye during the Korean War—which had never received proper treatment and had only healed on the surface—was the cause. Doctors believed that tuberculosis bacteria had settled in her body during that time due to the untreated conditions.

In her early twenties, Ki-young had suffered an ectopic pregnancy with her former husband. Even then, during the examination, tuberculosis bacteria had been found in her ovarian tissue. The initial diagnosis had led to the removal of both ovaries, but the surgeon at the time, mindful of her youth, had decided to spare one.

"Removing both ovaries at such a young age would drastically reduce your quality of life," he had said. "I'll leave one side intact."

But in retrospect, this decision seemed to have sown the seeds of her current suffering. The cancer that now ravaged her body had likely originated from the ovary that had been left behind. And now, it was the same doctor from P University Hospital, who had treated her ovarian condition years ago, that was overseeing her cancer treatment.

Next week, Ki-young was scheduled to undergo a new experimental treatment—a trial for a newly developed drug. It was, in essence, a human experiment, but Ki-young had agreed to it, hoping to alleviate the financial burden on her newlywed husband.

As they walked side by side, Jong-hee couldn't help but glance at Ki-young, her face filled with worry and concern.

Ki-young said,

"*Eonni*, what went so wrong with my life? I lost an eye to a bomb, was abandoned by my husband, and now, after nearly 20 years of living alone, I finally remarry, only to face saying goodbye once more. I've drained all the savings my new husband had...

Was I destined to live like this?"

Jong-hee had no words to offer, so she walked silently, her eyes fixed on the ground. After a while, Ki-young broke the silence, saying she had something to do, and boarded a bus alone.

The bus stopped in front of the Shinil Theater in Beomil-dong. As Ki-young disembarked, she was suddenly overwhelmed with longing for Prince Lee, the man she had once met every night, almost every day.

Before she remarried two years ago, she and Prince Lee had often danced at the cabaret near *Chobang* (the abbreviation for "Chosun Textile" in Beomil-dong, Busan). She had never asked for his real name; perhaps both she and Prince Lee had understood that theirs was a fleeting connection—a life lived day by day without the promise of tomorrow.

How deeply had Ki-young's ex-husband, a career soldier, once loved her? Yet, when the doctor had told him she couldn't have children, he had insisted, "I don't need an adopted child; I need one of my own blood." With that, he had asked her for a divorce, and Ki-young had quietly complied.

She had to send Eun-sook, whom she had adopted, back to the orphanage, and she had felt truly sorry toward both the orphanage and Eun-sook. But alone, without a husband, she had seen no future in raising a child. As she walked, she thought to herself, *How much longer do I have, as Master Kim suggested? And why am I suddenly longing for Prince Lee? He's known as a Casanova, a dancer, and, in the end, a scoundrel in Busan... But still, he treated me with respect and was always willing to be by my side whenever we met.*

Only her younger sister, Ki-seon, and her sister-in-law, Jong-hee, knew about the secrets she had shared with Prince Lee.

As she stepped off the bus, Ki-young found herself drawn to the entrance of the theater, hoping to learn something about him. Dusk had settled in, and the theater's caretaker was sitting by the ticket booth, having just set out a chair.

Ki-young said,

"Excuse me, sir. Can I ask you something?

Is Prince Lee still around these days?"

The theater keeper responded bluntly: Theater keeper said,

"Oh, that dancer? He's washed up. His face is completely dark, like he's been struck by some terrible illness, and he's in debt up to his neck. Women come looking for him all the time, trying to find out where he's gone. Not too long ago, the police were even after him for something.

But I don't know any more than that. Why are you looking for him? What's your business with him?"

Ki-young snapped,

"Why are you running your mouth? What do you even know about him? Do you have any idea how kind-hearted he is?"

Theater keeper shrugged,

"Yeah, I've heard a thing or two. He's the type who doesn't chase after the girls who leave and doesn't hold back the ones who come. That's who he is.

He's been obsessed with social dance—Cha-Cha, Jitterbug, you name it—all his life, and he lost everything because of it. How much money did he spend like some millionaire's son?

He'd wear white pants and white shoes, living it up, only to end up broke after lending money to the wrong women.

This world is full of cheats and swindlers. You don't seem like the type to be caught up in that...

But, yeah, women are impossible to figure out."

Ki-young couldn't hide her frustration, regretting that she had asked such an insensitive person. She stood silently in front of the theater for another ten minutes, lost in thought, before catching a bus toward the Nakdong River.

The bus took her close to the riverbanks at Gupo. As it crossed Gupo

Bridge, the calm waves of the Nakdong River, shimmering under the setting sun, caught her eye. Tears began to fall beneath her glasses—the tinted lenses she always wore to conceal her artificial eye.

The sunlight reflecting off the water seemed to draw out her tears, and she dabbed at them with a handkerchief from her bag, sniffling quietly. Noticing her distress, a young woman sitting in front of her kindly offered her seat.

Ki-young was set to spend a week in the hospital after receiving a cancer treatment injection the following Monday. When she returned home, she knew her husband would bring her a freshly caught carp from the Nakdong River, lovingly prepared and simmered until tender.

Her husband doted on her, perhaps driven by the memory of losing his first wife to illness. It was Ki-young who had helped his eldest daughter—who had been on the brink of losing her way—return home, refocus on her studies, and rebuild her life. It was also Ki-young who had pooled her savings with his to buy their current small apartment, moving them out of the cramped rental they had previously shared.

Yet, in her mind, Ki-young found herself drifting back to memories of dancing with Prince Lee on the slippery cabaret floor. In his arms, she had discovered, for the first time, how warm and expansive a man's chest could be.

That day, she had worn white shoes with eight-centimeter heels and a delicate, flowing white silk skirt that brushed just below her knees.

Meanwhile, only after leaving the fortune-teller's house did Jong-hee realize that she had forgotten to ask whether Se-joon would pass his exams. "For now, he will do what he wants to do," Master Kim had said. Did that mean he would pass soon? She pondered, unsure.

Se-joon had been spending most nights at a reading room near Seomyeon, rarely coming home to sleep. He didn't return that night either.

Jong-hee longed for a good night's sleep before her husband, Ki-hoon, came home. But her thoughts kept returning to the way Ki-young had reacted when Master Kim had said, "This is the face of a Minister's wife, and your husband thrives because of your fortune."

Her mother-in-law and sisters-in-law had always looked down on her. "She's not good enough for my son. My brother deserves better!"— Jong-hee had endured those withering looks year after year. They were never satisfied with her.

Yet, when they needed something, they never hesitated to ask for her help. Ki-jeong, the eldest sister-in-law, lived close by and would often come to borrow money when her children's tuition or living expenses ran short. The youngest, Ki-seon, also turned to Jong-hee whenever she needed money, whether for her many children or some other issue.

As for Ki-hwi's wife, her sister-in-law by marriage, Jong-hee hadn't seen her since she fled to Seoul recently, overwhelmed by her extravagant spending habits. But before she left, she would often say, "If I were the daughter-in-law of this house, I wouldn't just do housework. I'd go out and start a big business," always ending with a request for money.

None of them ever repaid the money they had borrowed from Jong-hee. The funds she lent out were often part of the living expenses she received from Ki-hoon, their eldest brother. They had no idea how much Jong-hee had saved and collected over the years, nor did they know that she had secretly taken on side jobs to supplement her income without Ki-hoon's knowledge.

Jong-hee would embroider silk cloth to make beautiful quilt covers, which she then sold to her cousin, who ran a quilting business. She never spoke of these efforts to her sisters-in-law or her sister-in-law by marriage. This was, at the very least, her pride as the superior wife. Jong-hee didn't begrudge the money she had given to her sisters-in-law and sister-in-law by marriage. She saw it as her duty, a responsibility that came with being the daughter-in-law of the Head Family.

Ki-hoon lived on a modest professor's salary, and during particularly tough times, he sometimes sold off land in Sancheong to make ends meet. Yet, he never handed over the proceeds from selling the farmland to Jong-hee. She managed the household on the modest sums she received, quietly and without complaint. She conducted numerous ancestral rites and entertained guests with whatever resources she had. This had been her way of life since the beginning of their marriage.

While she was lost in these thoughts, she heard someone at the front gate. Just then, she noticed Se-joon, whom she hadn't expected to return that night, opening the gate and stepping inside. She said nothing about her visit to the fortune-teller earlier in the day. Instead, she simply told him, "Se-joon, if you study as hard as you can, you'll pass," the words escaping her lips almost automatically.

As he disappeared into his room, she murmured to herself, *Yes, no matter what anyone says, this family won't be able to ignore me anymore. Soon, I'll be the wife of a Minister, and...*

In 1972, Se-joon entered the pre-medical course at Pusan National University (PNU). During his first summer vacation, he embarked on a daring adventure known as a Penniless Journey with his high school friends.

For a month, the six of them roamed from place to place, surviving on whatever work or manual labor they could find, earning just enough to cover their meals. They began their journey in Busan, trekked to the summit of Seorak Mountain in Gangwon Province, and eventually made their way back home.

When Se-joon returned, his face bore the marks of a month spent outdoors—weathered and darkened, his frame reduced to little more than skin and bones. He resembled a ghost of his former self, much like the friends who had accompanied him on this grueling journey.

Yet, neither Jong-hee nor anyone else in the family seemed overly concerned about Se-joon's haggard appearance. Only his younger brother, Jae-joon, expressed worry, saying, "Brother, you look terrible. You need to take care of yourself. Are you sure you're not sick? I'll never go on a penniless journey, even if I do get into college." Bok-hee and Jong-hee dismissed his concern as a joke, laughing it off.

Se-joon's friends, noticing his deteriorated condition, marveled at his endurance. "Those who've worked hard since childhood might manage, but for someone who's only ever studied to endure such hunger and hardship—you're truly tough!" Se-joon shrugged it off with a wry smile, saying, "They say '*it's good to face challenges when you're young*,' even if you have to seek them out. I hadn't really seen the world before, but I had gotten a good taste of it this time."

As Se-joon finished his first year in the premedical department, troubling news began to circulate among his relatives: His aunt, Ki-young, had become so gravely ill that she could no longer move.

Her abdomen was swollen with fluid, making it impossible for her to lie down or even sit comfortably; she could only sleep propped up against the wall. Eating and sleeping had become arduous tasks. While the rest of the family slowly grew accustomed to Ki-young's frail and deteriorating state, Se-joon found himself deeply troubled by her suffering. He often brooded over how he might alleviate even a small part of her pain.

When students were admitted to the pre-med program, they didn't go to Ami-dong, where the medical university hospital was located, for their classes. Instead, they studied general education courses at the Jangjeon-dong campus. During this period, Se-joon became close to a young philosophy professor who was popular with the students and made a wide circle of friends.

Se-joon's talent for writing shone through when one of his poems was published in the *Pusan National University Student Newspaper*. Later, as he advanced to the medical department, he took on the role of chief editor for both the university's newspaper and the medical school's magazine.

However, Se-joon faced his greatest challenge with the anatomy dissection course, a core subject in his medical studies. The mere scent of blood made him nauseous, and he often had to leave the room to vomit.

He studied just enough to pass his exams, spending the rest of his time immersed in the arts. He spent countless nights with theater groups, music majors, and friends who played various instruments, losing himself in their company. His classmates often joked,

"Hey, Choi Se-joon, you must be a genius. You barely show up, but you still manage to pass everything, even when you only cram at the last minute!"

Se-joon gradually became acquainted with the theatrical circles in Busan and Gyeongnam.

The money he received from Ki-hoon for his textbooks often ended up supporting struggling artists in the theater community. As his popularity grew, particularly among female students, he found himself spending more and more nights engaged in lively discussions over drinks. Perhaps it was this immersion in the complexities of human behavior that led him to develop a deep interest in psychiatry, the branch of medicine he felt most drawn to.

Jae-joon, his younger brother, suspected that Se-joon's preference might also stem from the fact that psychiatry was the one medical field where he wouldn't have to endure the sight or smell of blood.

Whenever Jong-hee observed Se-joon and Jae-joon together, she couldn't help but recall Master Kim's words: "The born eldest grandson and the entrusted eldest grandson of the family."

Though Jae-joon was her son, Jong-hee bore a hidden wound—a distance between them that pained her deeply. Unlike Se-joon, who was always warm and affectionate toward his mother, Jae-joon felt distant.

Perhaps it was because he had been raised by her mother-in-law, Bok-hee, in Sancheong until he was five, only coming to live with Jong-hee in Busan later on.

Jae-joon seemed to take his mother's presence for granted, disregarding her in a way that often left her wondering. Jong-hee often asked herself if his attitude had been shaped by the way his grandmother openly dismissed and disrespected her. Perhaps, as a young child, Jae-joon had absorbed these behaviors, seeing his mother through the lens of his grandmother's disdain. Or perhaps there was something about herself—something she couldn't quite define—that Jae-joon found lacking.

Yet, despite the emotional distance, Jae-joon was still her son—the child she had brought into the world through the pains of childbirth. Even so, she couldn't help but feel the sting of his unfavorable view of her, accepting it as an inevitable part of their relationship.

Since childhood, Jae-joon had gained a reputation in the neighborhood as a mischievous troublemaker. People would often remark, "The second son of Professor Choi's family is so different from the first—he must be a half-brother." Jong-hee heard such comments frequently, and they weighed heavily on her heart.

It wasn't just his attitude. When Jae-joon was at home, he often caused chaos, dismantling and reassembling small machines. Then, one day, he took apart both of the Sony radios that Ki-hoon treasured, leaving them completely unusable. Yet, Ki-hoon didn't scold him at all.

Whenever Jae-joon went outside, he acted like the boss of all the neighborhood kids, often returning home after beating them up just for fun.

When Jae-joon was in the fourth grade, Jong-hee was bedridden with severe stomach cramps. As she lay in agony, Jae-joon walked into the room and asked, with little concern, "What are you doing? Are you still in pain?" His indifference angered Jong-hee, and she reached for a small cane, determined to correct her son's attitude once and for all.

"Roll up your pants," she demanded, her voice trembling with both pain and frustration.

After that day ... the distance between Jong-hee and her son only deepened.

When she had tried to discipline him, Jae-joon had snatched the cane from her and, in a shocking act of defiance, struck her legs and thighs with all his might. Jong-hee was left speechless—more stunned by his words than the pain. "Who do you think you are? If you think you can hit me just because you're my mother, you're wrong. You deserve a beating instead," he had said, lashing out at her without hesitation.

Who could Jong-hee turn to with such a painful and humiliating secret? Certainly not her husband, nor anyone else. For a long time, she hid her bruised and battered legs beneath long skirts, ashamed and unable to comprehend why her own son would treat her so cruelly. How could anyone imagine a son doing such a thing to his own mother?

Se-joon, ever perceptive, was the first to notice that something was amiss. He observed that his mother limped slightly when she walked. One day, while Jong-hee was napping, Se-joon gently lifted the hem of her long skirt and was horrified to see her legs, covered in bruises—the marks of a thick cane snaking across her skin. As he stared at the injuries, Jong-hee awoke, and upon seeing his expression, she began to cry.

"Se-joon, please, pretend you didn't see these marks. Don't tell anyone about this. I'm so ashamed of myself, as your mother. Don't ask me anything."

Se-joon nodded as if he understood, but in his heart, he wrongly assumed that it was his father, Ki-hoon, who had caused the injuries. At that time, Se-joon made up his mind that on the day he received news of his acceptance to medical school, he would kneel before Ki-hoon and ask about the scar on Jong-hee's leg.

At last, that day had come. On the very evening he received news of his acceptance into medical school, after dinner, Se-joon knelt down, just as he had imagined, ready to confront the issue that had haunted him for so long. Se-joon said,

"Father, I entered medical school to fulfill my duty as your son, to honor your wishes. My heart was set on studying Korean literature, but I chose medicine for you. I struggled with my studies, but by some fortune, I passed.

But there's something I've never been able to forget. When I was in K Middle School ... why did you hit Mother with a cane? That image has never left my mind. Please, tell me why."

Ki-hoon, startled, replied,

"What? What are you talking about? You think I hit your mother? I married her without ever meeting her before our wedding day, but I have never once laid a hand on her in violence. What? When was this? When did you ever see such a wound on your mother?"

Se-joon insisted,

"Yes, I saw it clearly, and Mother asked me to keep it a secret. I've never spoken of it to anyone until now. Are you sure you don't remember? Don't lie to me. No matter the reason, a lie is never justified. I think..."

Ki-hoon tried to act as if he knew nothing, but he had already seen the wound on Jong-hee's leg and was exhausted from trying to control Jae-joon. Frustrated, he smoked three cigarettes in a row. Watching this, Se-joon spoke again.

"Father, I've followed the path you set for me, studying as you wished. But I am also the child of a mother who was beaten by her own husband. From now on, I will live as the child of that 'ugly' mother."

Ki-hoon replied,

"What? Se-joon, you're precious to me, as valuable as a piece of *Koryo* celadon. But do you think you've become an adult just because you've entered university? You think you understand everything, but you don't know the full story. Do you even realize who could have done something like this in our house? You're a bright child, but..."

Ki-hoon's gaze fell to the yellowed paper on the floor, his mind sifting through memories he had never truly forgotten.

After a moment, Ki-hoon murmured,

"Yes, there was a time like that, wasn't there? She kept her distance from me, hiding beneath her long skirt, making sure no one in the family noticed.

Se-joon, you are a son who tries to understand and listen to me. But there is another child—one whose world I cannot comprehend, despite being his father. He's out of control. You know who I'm talking about..."

In the next room, Jong-hee had been listening quietly. With a heavy heart, she made up her mind and entered.

Jong-hee spoke,

"*Yeobo*, and Se-joon, the truth is ... it was Jae-joon who caused that wound. I couldn't bring myself to tell you because I blamed him.

I had intended to discipline him with that wooden cane, but instead, he turned it on me, hitting me as hard as he could. No matter how much I tried to convince myself that Jae-joon was just a child who didn't know any better, it was hard to get close to him after that.

It's strange ... Se-joon, please don't misunderstand. This is all because of your 'ugly' mother."

When Se-joon confronted Ki-hoon and Jong-hee with these painful truths, Jae-joon was a freshman in high school. Though he managed to study, he often got into trouble at school, spending two weeks writing daily letters of apology. Jae-joon was fiercely loyal to his friends, but that loyalty often bordered on stubbornness.

At that time, he was punished for something he hadn't done, choosing to remain silent to protect a friend who was guilty. Because of this, he became the target of disdain from all the teachers in the staff room.

Recalling the injury on Jong-hee's leg, Ki-hoon let out a deep sigh and spoke. Ki-hoon said,

"Yes, Jae-joon is clever, but he's always been difficult to manage. Since he was a child, my mother coddled him, saying he resembled my father, and she never allowed anyone to discipline him. And so, things have turned out this way. He's too much for me to handle."

As Se-joon listened to Ki-hoon, he began to understand, but he could also see the deep pain his mother, Jong-hee, carried—a pain that had been slowly crushing her spirit. A sense of guilt washed over Se-joon, making him wonder, 'Isn't it my responsibility, as her eldest son, to protect her?' He felt an unspoken shame for not having acted sooner.

Despite his indifference toward his medical studies, Se-joon channeled his energy into establishing the first theater group within his medical school. He wrote the scripts and directed the plays himself.

His friends later speculated that this endeavor was deeply connected to his emerging passion for making psychotherapy more accessible to the general public. This creative process seemed to be his way of escaping the traditional path of medicine that he was expected to follow. Ultimately, this passion laid the foundation for his decision to pursue a residency in psychiatry at the National Psychiatric Hospital.

Among Se-joon's belongings was a small notebook with the name "Choi Ki-soon" inscribed on the cover. Yoo-sang of Sancheong had given it to him on the occasion of Bok-hee's 60th birthday. Unfortunately, Yoo-sang passed away the following year.

One evening, after coming home drunk, Se-joon took out the old notebook he had received from Yoo-sang and added the following words, continuing from the last part written by Ki-soon.

About the Dream

I think of the sea in this silent night,
Something stirs,
In the solitude of time,

And in this freedom, my unconscious self dances.
The fog unfurls from the darkness,
Deepening toward death,
Drawing nearer,
It drifts into sleep.

Without form or sound,
It brushes the grass by the river's edge,
Takes one step into my slumber by the sea,
And then, deeper still,
Gently at first,
It awakens the spirit from its sleep.

—White flowers bloom on an old tree, a woman weeps within a man,
Woman and man entwined, souls adrift in the sea,
In the sea of blue-red puppets that fly through the sky,
The funeral bier departs—

Oh! The sea of tangled unconsciousness.

Suddenly, an animal stands on a distant cliff,
The wind's force pushes hard,
A shadow falls into the sea—fear!

The fog still lingers outside the window,
When eyes open from half-death,
It's 2 AM, a state of semi-consciousness,
Sleep continues once more.

26
Missing of the Mi-young
1975: Masan, Busan, and Sancheong
—Soo-gon and Hye-young's Hardships

In the early summer of 1975, Bok-hee packed a small bag and set out from Sancheong to visit Ki-hoon's house in Busan. The thought of not seeing Young-soon for a whole month weighed on her, so she decided to stop by the New House before leaving. It was not a short walk—just a turn around the alley from the Big House—but the route was frustratingly roundabout.

Bok-hee muttered to herself,

"That damn man, Dal-soo. Even though I live right next door, I have to take such a roundabout way, how inconvenient and ridiculous. On the land he sold, several unfamiliar families have already moved in, and they've even built fancy houses ... tsk tsk..."

Last winter, Young-soon had given birth to a son, and Dal-soo couldn't contain his joy whenever he gazed at little Won-je. Their foster daughter, Gyeong-mi, now in elementary school, had taken on her small duties with surprising skill. Young-soon seemed content, at peace with her life. She had the son she had longed for, and even the bright young girl they had taken in was flourishing.

When Young-soon saw Bok-hee, she welcomed her with the exuberance of a child, her eyes sparkling with joy. Young-soon said,

"*Olke*, can you believe it? I have a son. Sometimes I wonder if this is all a dream. People used to say I'd never even lay eyes on a child, but now, those very words have been swallowed back into their mouths. It's been over a year since he was born, and with each passing day, he grows stronger and healthier.

Dal-soo is absolutely smitten with him. Ho ho... Although it's only been about seven months since his birth, according to his Korean age, he's nearly a year old. Korean age can be so strange sometimes, but when you think about the time a baby spends in the womb, it's not entirely unreasonable.

Sometimes, it feels like Won-je recognizes my face—his mother's face. If this keeps up, by the time he turns one, he might just say, 'Sir, come and eat my first birthday rice cake.' When I mentioned this, Mrs. Heo, who lives right behind me, said, 'Then Won-je will be an extraordinary child.' Ho ho..."

Bok-hee replied,

"My dear, it seems the shadows that once lingered in your household are finally lifting, and good fortune is finding its way in. But remember, a child speaking early isn't always a sign of brilliance.

Did you hear about the photographer's grandson across the bridge? They boasted about how quickly he learned to speak, but that poor boy was struck by a terrible illness that left him unable to straighten his back, paralyzed his limbs, and silenced his mouth.

Won-je is a child you've longed for, so it's only natural to want the best for him. But in the old days, when a child was especially precious, parents were careful with their words and raised them with a certain restraint.

Anyway, I'm heading down to Ki-hoon's house in Busan tomorrow. Is there anything you need me to take care of while I'm there? Also, I wanted to ask if you could keep an eye on the Big House while I'm away. These days, I'm left to tend to it alone... There was a time when the house was bustling with family members, but now, with even Yoo-sang gone, it's hard to find a man around the place.

If I need help with something strenuous, I have to ask someone, and finding anyone to do labor is becoming more difficult since no one farms anymore. So, I've taken it upon myself to keep the Big House clean, but I haven't touched the *sarang-chae* in years.

When I return from Busan, I think I'll rent out the empty *sarang-chae*, just for a bit of extra money."

Young-soon replied,

"*Eonni*, is that why you sold off the *haengrang-chae* and the mill? But still, can't the new owners take care of it? When I passed by, I noticed they had put something strange on the roof and made a mess of the place. It really left a bad taste in my mouth."

Bok-hee said,

"No, if you're going to put it that way, you should have sold off the *sarang-chae* and the warehouse for a bargain long ago... Oh, but that's not what I meant to say.

I'm just asking if you could look in on the Big House now and then. If the neighborhood kids think it's empty, they'll sneak in to play and cause a ruckus. If they leave the lights on for days, it'll rack up quite the electricity bill... That's why I came to see you."

"Okay," Young-soon replied, but her voice was distant, her gaze fixed on her sleeping son, Won-je, lying on the floor. As Bok-hee left the house, a sense of unease settled over her.

She thought to herself,

'It's a blessing that she has her son in her arms. God rewarded her for all the love and care she poured into raising Gyeong-mi.

If Ki-hwi hadn't pressured me so much, I never would have handed the *haengrang-chae* over to him... Oh, how unfortunate. These days, our family is so small, but who tends to everything when the house is so large?

In a way, it's a good thing. I wonder if Ki-hwi, who fled to Seoul after squandering money on his debt party, ever managed to pay off what he owed...'

When Bok-hee arrived in Busan, she was disappointed not to find Jae-joon at home—the one she had missed so dearly. Bok-hee assumed that Jae-joon had returned home because he was in the midst of midterms and had some free time after finishing his exams.

She laid out bundles of seaweed crisps and perilla seed flower chips on the living room floor—treats she had painstakingly made in Sancheong.

These were Jae-joon's favorite side dishes.

Bok-hee sat on the floor, watching the kitchen maid go about her work, her eyes drifting to the dogs wandering the yard. She had heard that they were English Pointers, a breed favored by Ki-hoon. The two Pointers, with their brown coats speckled with white, roamed alongside two Korean Jindo dogs.

Ki-hoon had moved to this large house last spring, a place sprawling over more than 200 *pyeong*. He had built enclosures for small animals along the wall—a chicken coop, homes for *Joseon*'s native Silkie chickens, large peacocks, and even several rabbits in the last compartment.

Despite being hounds, the dogs had grown up alongside these animals and showed little interest in them, lounging in the yard with bones in their mouths.

Then, the phone rang. Jong-hee quickly handed the receiver to Bok-hee.

"Mother, it's a call from Uncle Soo-gon's mother in Masan. You should take it right away," she urged.

Bok-hee said,

"Hello! Yes, I'm here. What? *Eonni*, what are you saying? I can't believe... Mi-young has disappeared. What on earth happened? I'll come down there to hear the whole story, and once Ki-hoon comes home, I'll ask him to contact some police officers he knows in the Busan area to look into it. I'll head down there right away.

What? You say there's no need for me to come? Well ... in any case, let's wait a bit longer. I'll make sure to tell Ki-hoon to be careful. You and my brother should stay strong."

As Bok-hee placed the receiver back in its cradle, a trace of worry crossed her face, which did not escape Jong-hee's notice.

Soo-gon, with his striking beauty and large, expressive eyes, had always been a presence in their lives. During holidays, he would visit Ki-hoon's house to pay his respects and often expressed concern for

Jong-hee's well-being. Soo-gon would say with genuine care.

Soo-gon said,

"Ma'am, you never seem to get a moment's rest with so many people coming and going. Please, take a break. Go into your room and relax. You don't need to overextend yourself. The food you've prepared is more than enough; let them help themselves.

If you keep tending to everyone day after day, it will take a toll on you. Your face will show it."

These words of kindness were something Jong-hee had never heard from her own brothers-in-law. To them, it seemed only natural that she, as the eldest sister-in-law, should shoulder the burden of household duties. Ki-hwi, in particular, was the most indifferent, caring only for his own affairs. Even on the day of memorial services at Ki-hoon's house, he wouldn't permit his wife to be summoned, leaving all family responsibilities to Jong-hee. Se-joon's aunts came over but only chattered among themselves.

To Jong-hee, Soo-gon, with his gentle nature, stood in stark contrast to her other brothers-in-law. 'A devout Christian, he seemed to embody the spirit of compassion. Why, then, had such misfortune befallen him?'

Jong-hee had also heard about that family. It was said to be a household where the father-in-law, a devout Christian, and Soo-gon's wife, his only daughter, brought harmony and joy. Even Soo-gon's father had converted to Christianity, and the family was always described as a home filled with laughter and warmth.

Worry gnawed at Bok-hee after the phone call, leaving her both concerned and curious. In the back of her mind, she decided to rush to her second brother's house in Masan early the next morning to hear more details from Soo-gon's wife. As she pondered the situation, a memory surfaced — of the silk socks Soo-gon had worn when he first entered their home, a gift from his birth mother.

In those days, it was an extremely rare luxury for a family to make even socks out of silk. Soo-gon's birth mother had torn apart a *hanbok jeogori* she cherished and, with her own hands, carefully stitched those silk socks, one stitch at a time, sending Soo-gon off wearing them.

Soo-gon's birth mother was a *gisaeng* from Jinju. This young *gisaeng*, who had entered the *gisaeng-bang* for the first time at the tender age of 14, had caught the eye of Bok-hee's second elder brother. At just 15, she had *raised her hair* for him—a phrase in Korea that signifies the moment when a maiden, transitioning into adulthood, first loosens her braided hair to wear an ornamental hairpin, symbolizing *her first night spent with a man.* This was how she had formed a bond with Bok-hee's second brother.

Bok-hee's second brother had served as a policeman during the Japanese colonial period. He was a tall, strikingly handsome man, with a quick and agile frame. But after only a few years in the force, he resigned. The burden of his role, which often required him to act against his fellow Koreans, weighed heavily on his conscience, and he could no longer continue.

He had been married to Jin-ok, Bok-hee's sister-in-law, for several years, but during that time, they had not yet had any children. Jin-ok suffered daily, her pain compounded by the judgmental glances of her husband's family. When she learned that her husband had fathered a child with a young *gisaeng*, she sought out the woman and made a tearful plea.

Even from her perspective, the *gisaeng*, who had entered the *gisaeng-bang* at a tender age, understood all too well the difficulties of raising a child in such an environment. Though her circumstances were challenging, she still hoped to raise her child herself when the time came. Sending her firstborn away was an agonizing decision, especially since her husband had been the first man she had truly loved.

But Jin-ok's earnestness and kindness touched the *gisaeng*. After much deliberation, she entrusted the child to Jin-ok, regardless of whether it was a boy or a girl.

When the baby was born, it was a stunningly handsome boy — Soo-gon. His unique beauty was immediately apparent. When the child reached 100 days old, healthy and thriving, he was given to Jin-ok. As a final gesture, the *gisaeng* tore apart the *hanbok jeogori* she had received from Bok-hee's second brother and fashioned a pair of silk socks (*beoseon*) for the child. Along with these, she included two extra pairs and a *hanbok* for the boy's first birthday.

This was how Soo-gon came to live with Jin-ok.

Upon hearing news of his daughter Mi-young, Soo-gon sat on the wooden platform in the yard, lost in thought.

He did not know whether his birth mother had ever come to see him when he was still an infant. What remained in his memory was that around the time he turned five, a woman had come to visit the main room of the house.

As soon as the woman entered, she kept looking around as if searching for someone. Although it was the first time Soo-gon had seen her, she didn't feel unfamiliar, as though he had seen her somewhere before. Dressed in a beautiful jade-colored *hanbok*, she said to Soo-gon, "Come here, sweet boy. My pretty little gentleman," as she opened her arms to embrace him.

He took one step after another toward her, ready to be held by that young woman. However, Soo-gon suddenly realized that, for some reason, his mother, Jin-ok, was nowhere to be seen. He stopped walking toward the young woman and stepped up onto the wooden floor of the main room, where Jin-ok would usually be. Then, he cried out, "Mother, where are you?" and burst into tears.

Jin-ok had purposely hidden herself deep in the kitchen. She had a strong desire to let Soo-gon meet his birth mother, even just once. Yet, at the same time... Soo-gon, on his way to the young woman, stopped. Without letting her embrace him, he kept calling out, "Mother, Mother," searching only for Jin-ok.

Having no choice, Jin-ok emerged from the kitchen. As she wiped the tears streaming down Soo-gon's face, she said.

Jin-ok:

"My dear, why are you crying so sorrowfully? This mother isn't going anywhere. Now, go to that aunt over there, quickly."

She spoke gently, urging Soo-gon toward the young woman—his birth mother. But even as she gently pushed him forward, her hands trembled. Soo-gon, though only five years old, could sense the deep unease in his mother's touch. Instead of moving toward the woman who had given him life, he turned and ran back to Jin-ok, clinging to her as he cried out, "Mother, I'm your son. I love you the most."

This brief, almost theatrical moment unfolded between Soo-gon and Jin-ok, leaving an indelible mark on both. Soo-gon remembered that his birth mother had come to visit him about three more times after that.

By the time Soo-gon reached the third grade, he had begun to piece together the truth about his origins. In a family, secrets—especially those concerning one's birth—rarely stay hidden for long. It's as if there's an unspoken understanding between parent and child, a connection that reveals truths even when words go unsaid.

For example, Soo-gon often wondered why Jin-ok, his mother, treated him with such delicate care, as if he were a fragile glass bowl. Even when he misbehaved, as all mischievous boys do, she never scolded him harshly. Instead, she would grow silent, her face clouded with worry. He rarely saw her laugh or take joy in anything.

Over time, the tension in the household led Soo-gon to realize that something was being kept from him. Was this, then, the sensitivity a son nurtures toward his mother—the unspoken awareness that grows within him?

As Soo-gon grew older, the more he came to know and understand Jin-ok, his mother, the more he began to grasp the nature of compassion toward others. Of course, Soo-gon also went through adolescence, but out of consideration for Jin-ok, he endured that time quietly and painfully.

The woman in the beautiful *hanbok* who had visited the house was his birth mother, while Jin-ok, who had always cared for him, was the mother who raised him. He knew that if he ever showed any sign of longing for or searching for his birth mother, Jin-ok would be deeply hurt. More than anything, he feared that all the stability he had enjoyed up until then could collapse in an instant. That was his greatest fear.

So, Soo-gon decided to rely more on his Christian faith, which emphasized valuing the present life, rather than on outdated concepts like blood ties and natural bonds.

When Soo-gon heard the news that Mi-young was missing, he had no idea what his wife and other children were thinking. But one face clearly came to mind—his biological mother's face.

The sound of Jin-ok's phone conversation with Bok-hee echoed unusually loudly. She was exchanging words with Aunt Bok-hee.

Bok-hee said,

"Yes, yes, so the last time you saw Mi-young was when she went to the theater to watch a group movie. Mi-young is in her first year of high school. How old is she now? Oh, that's right, she's 15 years old. And none of the other kids saw or bumped into her? Where could she have vanished in that theater?"

Jin-ok, who had been unable to eat for over a week, grew visibly weaker as she spoke with her sister-in-law. Eventually, she lay down on a blanket in the room, her strength waning. Soo-gon's father sat alone, reading the Bible, while the rest of the family huddled around the phone, waiting anxiously for news, staying up all night.

Soo-gon returned to the school where he worked, only to find himself bombarded with questions about Mi-young. People expressed their concerns, but to Soo-gon, their words felt more like prying into his private life. It was as if they were whispering behind his back, questioning the integrity of his family.

Yes, but ... how proudly he proclaimed his home as a Christian household, yet now a healthy young girl has vanished from such a place. What could be wrong? Do they have some dark secret? Something hidden that we don't know about?

These thoughts haunted Soo-gon, and he couldn't tell if they were real whispers or merely auditory hallucinations born from his heightened sensitivity. Everywhere he went, it seemed as if people were exchanging similar words, and this relentless torment weighed heavily on his mind.

Hye-young, Soo-gon's wife, also endured the agony of overhearing her colleagues—the elementary school teachers she worked with— murmuring about her.

Soo-gon and Hye-young lived each day as if needles were constantly piercing their bodies, the pain unrelenting, day and night. In his suffering, Soo-gon often wished to end it all by drowning himself in the salty sea. But his thoughts always returned to Hye-young and the unbearable pain she must have been enduring.

After leaving work, Soo-gon wandered through the night, eventually finding himself at the edge of the sea in Masan. He had walked and run aimlessly, driven by despair, until he stood motionless at the water's edge. With no clear intention, he waded into the shallow water. As it reached his waist, he plunged his tormented head into the salty depths, hoping to drown his anguish.

But instinctively, he raised his face to the surface, gasping for air. The natural will to survive took over, yet the more he struggled against it, the deeper his mind sank into despair. He thought about his family—what would happen to them if he ended his life? These thoughts haunted him as he stumbled onto the sea breakwater, collapsing with a vacant, unfocused gaze. Soon, he became aware of the sound of footsteps gathering around him.

In the early dawn, a man had walked into the sea fully clothed, repeatedly submerging his head beneath the water. People who witnessed this gathered around Soo-gon. As they looked into his glazed eyes, they saw the shadow of death and felt a slight chill. His eyes even seemed to flash with the madness of a deranged person. Then, he stood up again and, with hollow, lifeless eyes, slowly began to walk deeper into the water. Each time he submerged his head, the icy seawater filled his nose, further disconnecting him from reality. The men nearby, alarmed by the sight, called for help and eventually led him to the police station.

Soo-gon spent the rest of the dawn hours there, his mind a blur of pain and confusion, before finally returning home by taxi in the early morning.

At Mi-young's house, her family continued to hold out hope that she would return one day. It wasn't until ten days after her disappearance that Soo-gon officially reported her missing, even offering a reward for information. Months passed, and with them, the thin thread of hope began to fray. The news of Mi-young gradually faded from everyone's minds.

The following year, Jin-ok mentioned to Bok-hee that they should consider moving from their old, uncomfortable detached house to a new apartment. Yet, Bok-hee's second brother and Jin-ok decided to remain in the old house, where they would continue waiting for Mi-young. They even requested that the telephone office keep their old single-digit phone number instead of assigning them a newer two-digit one, clinging to the past as time quietly passed.

Se-joon felt a deep sorrow upon hearing of Mi-young's disappearance. The memory of Mi-young, whom he had last seen at Bok-hee's 60th birthday celebration, lingered in his mind—a girl with short hair, smiling half-moon eyebrows, and a charming, round nose.

In recent days, Se-joon had been pouring his energy into studying playwriting and production, surrounding himself with a group of theater enthusiasts. Yet Ki-hoon, oblivious to Se-joon's true passions, remained unaware of his pursuits.

Ki-hoon, assuming that Se-joon would use any money given to him wisely, had handed him funds for English textbooks. The cost of medical school textbooks was no small sum, especially in those days when photocopying technology was just emerging and pirated versions were beginning to circulate. English medical textbooks were particularly expensive.

However, the money Se-joon received from Ki-hoon often ended up in the hands of struggling artists within his circle. In essence, the funds intended for Se-joon's medical education became his tuition for the study of art. He kept only a small portion for himself, borrowing textbooks from friends to continue his medical studies.

Despite his unconventional approach, Se-joon managed to balance his medical studies with his passion for theater, maintaining his grades just well enough to pass. His friends teasingly called him a "genius of memory," but Se-joon could not escape the gloom that settled upon him after hearing about Mi-young.

He was the kind of person whose heart ached when others suffered—exceptionally sensitive and deeply empathetic. Se-joon also had a tendency to let his thoughts spiral into dark extremes. As soon as he heard of Mi-young's disappearance, he couldn't help but imagine the worst—that she had met a tragic end.

The thought of the young and pretty Mi-young being lost in some unknown place tormented him, driving him to drink alone in despair. No one questioned why he was so deeply affected, and Se-joon left his pain and sorrow etched only in his writings.

Missing

She returned as a cold body,
Lying still, facing the ceiling.
She doesn't know why she died.

No words, no trace—
Only the God who gave her breath knows.
Essence and form,
Death and the dead,
Blood and bones,
Camel and the desert,
Wine and water.

No one is praying.
Those who pray are mocked and crushed.
They come under a yoke and drift across the sea.
Deformed reason and shattered pride—
You are the one at the edge of protection,
The one suspended from grace.
God is no longer needed in this complex system.

The lies you and I spoke,
The arrowhead with a purpose,
Aphasia and amnesia.

The scarf with red dots
Wrapped around your neck.
That day, you went
To a place even you didn't know,
Step by step.

Se-joon's concern for Mi-young was not just as Yo-han's younger sister but as one of the many girls he had known. Se-joon, who was surrounded by a wide circle of friends, also found himself the object of affection for many young women who were drawn to the artistic crowd he moved in. Eager to catch his attention, these girls sought him out, hoping for a chance to spend time with him.

In those days, many Korean teenagers spent their high school years focused solely on studying, with little time for anything else. College life, especially in cocducational settings, was envied as a kind of "love heaven." Se-joon, like many young men his age, drank with these girls and didn't shy away from opportunities to sleep with them if they arose. He was fearless in his youth.

Yet, if Se-joon had ever been truly loyal and serious about any of the women he encountered, there was only one among them who might have claimed his heart above all others.

Se-joon's first girlfriend was a fellow student at the same university, a domestic college within PNU. Her name was Yoon Hye-jeong. Together, they listened to American pop songs and attended rare opera performances. They spent nights talking passionately about plays and novels while listening to arias. However, their relationship was short-lived.

One reason was that Se-joon had many friends involved in theater, writing, and music. The other was the strict educational rules imposed by Hye-jeong's family.

Hye-jeong couldn't wait for a medical student who had little time to spare, and the thought of waiting for him to complete his internship and residency—years of uncertainty—was unbearable. Her parents, firm in their traditional views, were adamant that she marry before graduating from college. Even in those days, when female students were making strides in education, the mindset hadn't changed much since the 1940s.

The idea that women should marry quickly, often in their second year of college, was still deeply ingrained. Despite their academic pursuits and the rigor of college entrance exams, many female students still saw higher education as a path to marriage. The notion of pursuing a career or further training after graduation was not yet widely accepted.

Ultimately, Se-joon and Hye-jeong parted ways. She became engaged to an older man—seven years her senior—who worked for a company and had been introduced to her by her brother-in-law.

After the breakup, Se-joon resolved not to let himself be swayed by any woman again. He dismissed the idea of eternal love or romantic ideals, deciding instead that men should avoid being trapped by the consequences of fleeting relationships. He believed it was better to maintain a casual demeanor, pretending to believe in what women said just enough to avoid harsh criticism. With this in mind, Se-joon tried to immerse himself in a persona of masculinity and strength.

Occasionally, when a woman attempted to hold on to him after a one-night stand, he would jokingly wave a model of flippers in the air, declaring his farewell with a laugh. He convinced himself that he was more at ease with the casual, half-hearted nature of relationships. Over time, Se-joon became someone who placed little importance on love between men and women, a decision he seemed to have made deliberately.

Yet, when Se-joon found himself drunk and spending the night with a stranger, he would scrutinize her face, searching for a resemblance to Mi-young—a woman with half-moon eyebrows, fine teeth, and a small round nose. He treated these encounters with an unusual sincerity, refusing to see these women as mere fleeting companions. However, he never sought them out again.

After making love to these women, he sometimes contracted gonorrhea but never blamed them. Instead, he blamed his own carelessness and the alcohol. Despite being a medical student, he failed to grasp the sensitivity of the human body and the long-term consequences of his promiscuous actions. The price of his reckless behavior would come back to haunt him.

Burial of the Living with the Dead · 1

Drink pure water beside the lifeless body.
Still in the dry wooden coffin,
Your sensual beauty remains uncorrupted,
Knocking on the walls of life, heavy with bones and flesh.

Resilient tears fall,
Touching the soul that has not yet escaped.
In the dry chest, more than mere wet love,
Returning to the drops of the universe,
Until dawn turns into an empty jar,
Just endless waiting,
Drinking only pure water again.

I am alive,
You are in the afterlife.
In this lonely time,
Azalea flowers, far away, sadly
Drenched in the rain...

I did not die for you.
Only the dry wind shakes the saint's band of my love,
Licking the dew that rises from the weeds.
It only wounds the pure heart.

This poem had once been published in *Modern Literature*, a prestigious literary magazine in Korea. Se-joon often reflected with deep regret on his choice to pursue medicine rather than following his true passion for literature. He was one of those who, in a vague but profound way, understood that the future of medicine lay not just in treating the human body but in healing the mind.

One decision, however, was clear in his mind: he would become a psychiatrist. Moreover, although medicine was not his true calling, Se-joon found solace during his university years in the company of friends who lived and breathed the world of art. Amidst them, he managed to carve out a space where he could endure, even if his studies did not ignite his passion.

27
An Unreachable Hand

Since 1978: Busan and Seoul
—First Love

Se-joon during his final year at medical school

If medicine spares one from pain,
Great art frees thousands from grief.
If life is precious beyond all,
Then death is nobler than most.
—Ah, all is a battle—
Waves, sea, wind...
A struggle against nature's will.
A lone droplet in the boundless void,
This tiny seed of chaos—
An endless war between me and the self I might become.

—Se-joon's farewell message in his yearbook.

Soo-gon's son, Yo-han, came to greet Ki-hoon after being admitted to the law school at SNU. Soo-gon, who accompanied him, looked indescribably haggard and somber. From his appearance, it was clear that there was still no news about Mi-young.

Sensing this, Ki-hoon excused himself, murmuring, "I have some work to attend to," before hastily departing. It was his habit to avoid lingering when relatives or other visitors came by. Despite Soo-gon being a maternal cousin, Ki-hoon saw the faces of the Soodong family from Hamyang only a handful of times each year.

Soo-gon never asked Ki-hoon for anything. However, perhaps due to the many trivial requests from other cousins, Ki-hoon often kept his interactions brief and distant. When he did encounter them at home, he offered a quick greeting and then promptly made his exit. As always, it was Jong-hee who took on the burden of hosting.

After Ki-hoon left the house, Jong-hee served tea and snacks to Soo-gon and Yo-han, gently urging Soo-gon to try the *yugwa*[68] she had prepared. Jong-hee said,

"Soo-gon *Aje*, are you eating properly? Now that Yo-han has entered Korea's top law school, you must gather your strength and think of your other children. Mother will be coming up from Sancheong in a few days. She found a child to help her with chores—someone to keep her company so she won't be so lonely. She'll bring the child with her.

Soon the weather will warm, and the people in Sancheong will be busy foraging for wild greens. If work overwhelms them, it may be difficult for her to visit... Spring has already arrived."

---

68) Yugwa: A traditional Korean rice puff snack made from glutinous rice dough that is pounded, shaped into thin pieces, dried, and deep-fried. After frying, it is coated with honey or syrup and sprinkled with puffed rice or other toppings. (By the author's interpretation.)

Soo-gon could not bring himself to meet Jong-hee's gaze—a father weighed down by the loss of his child. He could not lift his eyes to face those around him. No matter how much he steeled himself, his resolve crumbled again and again.

After a while, Se-joon, on the brink of his college graduation, entered the room. He greeted Soo-gon briefly before leading Yo-han out of the main room. Soo-gon spoke softly, almost hesitantly,

"Ma'am, *Hyeong-nim* Ki-hoon is always so busy. It's hard for someone like me to visit this house often unless you make me feel welcome. To be honest, I'm a bit afraid of *Hyeong-nim*.

And ... actually, something strange happened a few days ago. You know that my mother and father still live in that old house, right?

It happened the day my wife, Hye-young, brought them some side dishes. She was tidying up before heading back to our apartment when my mother called her urgently. So, when my wife quickly picked up the phone ... there was silence. No words..."

Summarizing Soo-gon's words, the call had been eerie—when Hye-young answered, there was no response from the other side, only the sound of someone quietly sobbing. After a few moments, there was a strange, dull noise, and then the line went dead.

Soo-gon continued, his voice trembling slightly,

"I don't know if I converted to Christianity because I couldn't bear hearing talk of rituals like the ancestral rites performed after one's parents pass away or terms like 'past lives' and 'karma.' Up until then, I was doing well ... until my daughter, Mi-young, disappeared like that.

How could I not think of my birth mother? First and foremost, I feel most ashamed to face my wife, Hye-young, as if I've done something terribly wrong in my life. No matter how hard I try, I can't seem to find the root of this pain except in the way I've turned my back on my birth mother.

When Hye-young finally fell ill, she said, 'A mother can't just lie down like this,' and then she began searching everywhere again, saying she was looking for Mi-young... Fortunately, Yo-han was able to take the entrance exam for S University this time, and I owe it all to Hye-young's perseverance."

Jong-hee, with gentle concern in her voice, asked,

"*Aje*, as I mentioned last time, have you tried to see your birth mother?"

Soo-gon nodded slowly.

"Yes, though it was difficult. No matter how much my mother wept, holding the silk socks (*beoseon*) my birth mother sent with me when she gave me away, I didn't want to face it. Why does my mother still keep those silk socks, hidden away for over ... fifty years? But I gathered my courage and went to find my birth mother. I wanted to hear her out, but I only met her nephew. I learned how she's been living.

After sending me to my current mother, she worked in a *gisaeng* house for five or six more years and then moved to a relative's home. Since then, she has drifted from place to place, and now she stays at her nephew's house—the one I met. It's in a poor village, high up in the mountains. I wandered around before finally finding her. I knocked on the door, and her nephew came out. He went back inside, and when he returned, he told me, 'She doesn't want to see your face.'"

Jong-hee sighed.

"If she's lived such a transient life without a place to call home, her sorrow must be immense. But surely, she has missed her son ... terribly. Sometimes, it seems that fate can be incredibly cruel. *Once a person's heart closes, it's almost impossible to open it again.*"

Soo-gon's voice grew even more forlorn.

"The second time I visited her, her nephew told me, 'Does he have any proof that he is my son?' So I placed the silk socks on the floor and turned away.

Those silk socks—so deeply cherished by my current mother, never forgotten by my birth mother—what are they, really? My birth mother placed my umbilical cord inside one of the socks and sent it to the mother who raised me. One sock was put on my foot, and the other held my umbilical cord...

They are both my mothers, yet why have I spent so long pretending not to know my birth mother? I don't even want to think about how indifferent I've been. I can't bear to look at myself. It's even more painful because I can't speak freely about this to ... Hye-young."

Jong-hee observed his weary face.

"*Aje*, I can tell you've been drinking more than usual, even though you don't normally drink. Your face is rough ... but the living must carry on. In time, her heart may soften, and you shouldn't think that Mi-young's disappearance is some twisted result of your relationship with your birth mother. We only know what we see and hear, nothing more. I hope you find the strength to regain your former self—your clean, beautiful face."

Soo-gon's face tightened into a frown, an old habit resurfacing as he caught a word from Jong-hee that grated on his nerves: "a beautiful face." It was the phrase he had despised most during his school years.

From a young age, the neighborhood kids and his middle and high school friends would taunt him, saying,

"Hey, Jeong Soo-gon, you pretty boy, looking like a *gisaeng-orabi*—why are your hands so pale, your face so delicate and beautiful? Why are you so fair?"

The term "*gisaeng-orabi*," traditionally referring to a man who was as delicately featured as a *gisaeng* or one who lived a life of leisure, focusing on appearances rather than work, had always struck a nerve with Soo-gon.

Though, in this context, the word might have been used by his friends to describe his unusually fair complexion, pretty eyes, and dark eyebrows—traits that, by all accounts, were compliments—Soo-gon couldn't stand it. The phrase "You look like a *gisaeng-orabi*" carried with it a stigma, one that hinted at idleness and insincerity rather than genuine admiration for his looks. It was a label that implied weakness and vanity, something far removed from being considered handsome.

Perhaps Soo-gon's sensitivity to the word also stemmed from the fact that his birth mother had been a *gisaeng*, a connection that only deepened his aversion to the term. Whenever he heard it, his expression would immediately harden, and he would always end up in a fight with the boy who uttered it.

These brawls were often intense, leaving both sides bloodied, particularly around the mouth and nose. The fight would only end once enough blood had been spilled, and even then, it wasn't truly over for Soo-gon until he had extracted an apology from the offender. At least, that was how it had to be in Soo-gon's world.

Se-joon offered Yo-han a cigarette, and without a word, Yo-han took it and placed it between his lips.

Lighting his own, Se-joon asked,

"Yo-han, does your father know you smoke?"

Yo-han exhaled slowly, the smoke curling around him like a veil.

"No, he probably doesn't. Cigarettes are a personal choice, but I don't see why only adults should have that freedom. I drink too—not just for my father's sake, but because I can handle it.

You know, I didn't take the college entrance exam two years ago. After that, it was like our family lost its voice—no one spoke. I started smoking when Mi-young disappeared. I guess I felt guilty, like I wasn't enough of a brother to protect her. If only I'd known more about what she was doing, what she was interested in ... I've thought about that a lot. I still don't know.

So, where are you planning to do your internship next year?"

Se-joon flicked ash from his cigarette, a wry smile playing on his lips.

"My alma mater, P University Hospital, turned me down, so I'll be heading to Seoul. I guess professors don't take too kindly to students who don't toe the line. It's probably for the best.

And Yo-han ... it's not anyone's fault that Mi-young is gone. Don't let other people's idle talk weigh on you too much. Your family has always lived with such faith—so much stronger and more diligent than most.

No one knows your family's story in detail; they're not interested. They just see a family that seemed to live happily, without any misfortune, and when tragedy strikes, they think, 'Ah, see? You can't live without some problem. Let's see how much pain you can endure.' But that's all it is, people's misguided thoughts.

Now that you're in law school, are you planning to follow our great-grandfather Hong-seon's wish and become a judge?"

Yo-han turned his head and spoke indifferently, as if his voice carried barely a trace of emotion.

"No, I don't have any plans yet. This might sound like an excuse, but since Mi-young disappeared, all my plans for the future seem to have vanished too. The plans are mine, but whether they come to pass is up to the Lord above. I didn't even want to go to college. My mother wanted it so badly ... and when I passed the exam, everyone congratulated me.

Hyeong[69], before Mi-young's disappearance, I thought my father was the best. Other kids might have admired powerful and famous people, but to me, my father—faithful to his family and always by my side—was the greatest. Who do you respect the most?"

Se-joon paused for a moment, showing a faint smile, and then replied a few minutes later. As he often did when talking with his friends, he made his characteristic expression: widening only his right eye, which had a distinct double eyelid, while slightly pulling down one side of his mouth. Like Hong-seon, Se-joon had a double eyelid on only one side.

"You might find my response surprising, Yo-han. You, with your

---

69) Women use *Eonni* for an older sister figure, while men use *Hyung* or *Hyung-nim* for an older brother figure. (Author's interpretation.)

brilliant mind, might not expect this, but ... I respect 'Jesus, the human.' Jesus was just like you and me—not merely human in appearance, but the most human of us all. He felt the pain and tears of others as his own.

When we pray, it's a private meeting between me and the God within me. It's a time when I am alone with the Absolute—Jesus. You know this better than anyone, having grown up in a Christian family.

And ... before this private meeting, I believe only the truth can see Jesus clearly.

Yo-han, the truth is invisible. People call it an abstract noun. Most things we can see with our eyes are general nouns. But ... but the things you can't see, those you can feel, are often abstract nouns...

What abstract nouns come to mind for you, Yo-han?

What's easiest to grasp?"

Yo-han exhaled a cloud of smoke, deep in thought.

"Abstract nouns? Brother, beyond all that—feelings, acceptance, the senses—eyes, ears, nose, mouth ... and our conscious world? If I die, will there be no consciousness?"

Se-joon nodded slowly.

"Abstract nouns are usually ideologies, formed from our perceptions and consciousness. Things we can't put into words, things we can't write down—these belong to the world of consciousness.

Is consciousness only for the living? If God, the Lord, exists only within your consciousness, then yes, He would disappear when you die. But is that really the case?

When people speak of the unconscious, the collective unconscious, the personal unconscious, they're clinging to the world of consciousness. But does it only exist if you're alive to feel it? Or is it all just imagination?

Ha ha ... Yo-han, anyway, I think you need to move beyond one level and ascend to another. People often compare Jesus with Buddha, but such comparisons are beyond our grasp. You might not have been interested until now, but I'd recommend studying Buddha deeply. Sakyamuni's 'emptiness' isn't merely void or meaningless. It's in the *Banyabaramilda*, the heart of the most revered sutra, the *Banyabaramil Sutra*.

If we confine everything to the consciousness system, we remain trapped in what we call the mind or heart. When Jesus said, 'Always be awake,' perhaps he was urging us to embrace emptiness within our consciousness.

And our basic feeling, I think, should be to look directly at the five aggregates[70], Panca Khandha, in Buddhism. But most ordinary people, like me, believe that 'looking straight' is about the eyes, so we focus all our energy on them. When that energy becomes overwhelming, we close our eyes. It's fascinating to think that you can see more clearly with your eyes closed.

Yo-han, I think you should take a better look at your parents. Mi-young's disappearance might have clouded all of their perceptions. If we're not careful, we might end up searching for God only within the

---

[70] Panca Khandha (Five Aggregates): In Buddhism, this term refers to the combination of the material element, rūpa (form), and the four mental elements, collectively known as the Five Aggregates. In older translations, it is also referred to as the *Five Skandhas* or *Five Heaps*. The term khandha means an aggregate or a constituent element, and the Five Aggregates are rūpa (form), vedanā (feeling), saññā (perception), saṅkhāra (mental formations), and viññāṇa (consciousness). Initially, the concept of the Five Aggregates was used to describe the components that constitute a human being, but it later evolved to encompass the entire phenomenal world.

When the Five Aggregates are viewed as the components of a human being, rūpa refers to the physical body as the material element; vedanā pertains to the sensory experience of pleasure and pain, including emotional responses; saññā involves the cognitive process of identifying and conceptualizing objects; saṅkhāra represents all mental activities other than sensation, perception, and consciousness, particularly the functions of will and latent tendencies; and viññāṇa is the process of cognition or subjective consciousness.

The philosophical significance of the theory of the Five Aggregates lies in its explanation that all human existence is compounded, impermanent, and empty, devoid of any substantial self. This doctrine teaches that one should not cling to these aggregates, as they are ultimately empty and without intrinsic essence. This is captured in the phrases pañca-khandha-upādāna (the Five Aggregates as grasping) and pañca-khandha-sūnyatā (the Five Aggregates as emptiness).

—— This summary is adapted from the Naver and Doosan Encyclopedia by the author.

confines of our own ideas and be deceived by the sediment of those thoughts. But anyway ... I'll stop here with my thoughts for today. Once we both move to Seoul, we'll have more chances to talk.

Don't become too obsessed with Mi-young, but don't give up on her entirely either. I only saw her twice, but her image is still vividly etched in my mind. Once, when I was a child and happened to visit Sancheong, and the other time on our grandmother's 60th birthday. It's as if her image has been indelibly imprinted somewhere deep in my memory.

If her memory is that strong for me, you can only imagine how much more intense and overwhelming the pain must be for you.

Yo-han, stay strong. You're the eldest son now, and with that comes many responsibilities. Remember, the world is vast, and there's so much ahead of you."

Yo-han smiled and shook his head at Se-joon's lengthy musings. When the two stepped out onto the floor, Soo-gon also emerged, seemingly ready to depart for Masan.

As soon as Soo-gon saw Yo-han, shivering slightly from the cold, he instinctively clasped the back of Yo-han's hand with both of his and gently rubbed it to warm him. In that moment, Yo-han noticed—perhaps for the first time—the deep lines etched into his father's face, wrinkles that spoke of sorrow and years that had passed unnoticed. It struck Yo-han as something new, though those wrinkles had been there for some time. He realized that it had been a while since he had truly looked into his father's face.

The two remained silent on the bus ride down to Masan. When they arrived at the station, they would return to the old detached house. His grandparents had slowly transformed into figures of sorrow—backs hunched, laughter faded, and only pain remaining. The smiles they had once shared with Yo-han during his childhood had long disappeared.

Those joyous, carefree days seemed like a lifetime ago, as if all the laughter had been used up. Now, it felt as though such vibrant, hearty laughter would never return—not for him or his family.

After sending Yo-han home, Soo-gon walked out of the house alone. Perhaps tonight, Yo-han would be packing his bags with his wife, preparing to leave for Seoul. Meanwhile, Soo-gon entered the church, knelt down, and clasped his hands together in prayer.

> Day unto day utters speech,
> And night unto night reveals knowledge. (Psalms 19:2)
> There is no speech nor language
> Where their voice is not heard. (Psalms 19:3)
>
> The wind in my heart echoes
> With the trembling sound of the weather strip,
> Even the feathers that fall from the wings of a bird in flight —
> Perhaps they will carry news of my child's whereabouts.
> Hopelessly, I've been wandering in the forest after dark all day.
>
> The quiver slung across my back is full of arrows,
> But the true target eludes the passage of time.
>
> There is a karma from which one cannot escape,
> No matter how one tries.
> The weight of this karma dangles upside down from a tree,
> And the tightening rope squeezes the blood,
> As if it were flowing backward.
> Until when, until when,
> How much must the yellow earth be soaked to reveal it?
>
> In a body entwined with blood and flesh,
> The day all the water is drained away,
> If my exhausted karma drifts to the great sea,
> If only I could escape from its grasp once more,

I would return to the womb.
But everything returns to the beginning.
I will become you, and you will become me again.
The pomegranate buds of karma bloom, each one red as blood —
Bite into them,
Chew and swallow,
And I will lick your torn and broken wounds.

Two years later, a letter arrived for Soo-gon—a message that bore the weight of finality. It informed him that his birth mother had passed away. The letter read: "Hello, my aunt asked me not to inform anyone of her death, but I am reaching out to you now. I believe you should know."

The words were simple, yet they left Soo-gon in a state of uncertainty —was she truly gone, or was this her way of ensuring he would no longer attempt to see her? At the end of the letter, the nephew wrote, "My aunt, at a tender age, sacrificed herself to become a *gisaeng* in order to provide for her family, and throughout her life, she saw only your father as the man she loved."

Soo-gon's thoughts spiraled as he reflected on the loss of his own daughter, Mi-young, at the tender age of fifteen. Had his birth mother's parents felt a similar agony when they lost her to the world of the *gisaeng*? A deep longing for forgiveness swelled within him—forgiveness for the immature deeds of his past—but the opportunity for reconciliation had vanished. She had left this world, returning to the earth.

Had his birth mother been pulled back into the order of time once again?

Soo-gon shook his head, resolving to visit her grave as soon as dawn broke.

Back home, he lay down to sleep, but his mind remained sharp, refusing the embrace of slumber. Hye-young and Soo-gon had been sleeping in separate rooms since last year. Restless, Soo-gon returned to the dark streets and walked, and walked, until he realized—only at 2 a.m.—that he hadn't eaten since the previous day. A gnawing heartburn reminded him of his hunger.

Glancing around, he noticed a lone cart bar still lit in the empty space near the apartment. The cart likely wouldn't close until four in the morning.

As Soo-gon stepped inside, he was surprised to find several elderly men and women gathered around a table. "Ma'am, please make me a bowl of noodles. And two fishcake skewers, please," he said, casting a glance at another table. There sat members of his own church.

The tables, crudely assembled from plywood, were few in number—just three. When they noticed Soo-gon, they stood and nodded in acknowledgment, to which Soo-gon quickly responded with a nod of his own. Though they tried to appear indifferent, Soo-gon felt their silent judgment, as if they could read the turmoil in his heart.

I am such a wretched man. I am ... I am ... too weak, he thought, as hunger gnawed at him while he awaited his noodles.

The church members, familiar with Soo-gon's usual abstinence from alcohol, seemed taken aback by his presence at the cart bar in the early hours of the morning. Their surprise deepened when they saw him order a bottle of *soju* and drink it. Soo-gon, who had once openly declared, "Alcohol clouds the mind, so you must never drink," had said it to his fellow churchgoers more times than he could count.

But now, alcohol seemed necessary. Necessary for those who suffered. Yet he knew, deep down, that alcohol could not soothe the pain. It was merely an excuse, a hollow pretext.

In the past, Soo-gon had been the first to criticize drinkers, to find fault with them. Now, the men at the table rose before Soo-gon and quietly left the cart, the flap of the entrance rustling as they exited.

Lately, Soo-gon had discovered in himself a troubling need to drink until he was nearly drunk, as if only then could he find sleep. And at the same time, he prayed that he would not be consumed by alcohol, that it wouldn't devour him whole. Soo-gon fell silent, deep in thought.

'What was truly most precious to me? Did it really matter if others knew the circumstances of my birth?

This life—this fleeting stopover on the journey—why had I feared it so much?

When my birth mother smiled at me and said, "Come here, my child, quickly now," what if I had just followed my heart in that moment?

What might have happened then? Would she have accepted me when I first sought her out, when I finally went to the house where she lived? Could I have found forgiveness in her eyes?

And now, after all these years of taking pride in living a Christian life, I find myself easily accepting terms like—this life and karma. Where am I really heading now?'

Soo-gon's thoughts drifted back to that unforgettable face from his youth. He had once told his mother, Jin-ok, "I hardly remember anything from my childhood," truly believing he had forgotten.

But now, Soo-gon's mind drifted back to when he was about five years old, when a young woman had visited their home, smiling warmly at him as he played in the yard. Startled, little Soo-gon quickly buried himself in Jin-ok's skirt.

Soo-gon:

"Mother, who is that? Why is she smiling at me, calling me 'baby'?

I don't feel well. Please, tell her to go home quickly. Hurry!"

Even as he said this, Soo-gon felt an overwhelming desire to run to the young woman, to be embraced by her. Yet, the stronger that desire grew, the more he resisted. As young Soo-gon tried to push the woman from his heart, Jin-ok, with a gentle smile, said softly:

"Boy, that's the one who loves you most in the world. You should reach out to her, give her a hug. I'm fine.

I'm nothing to you. Of course, of course."

Jin-ok's words wounded Soo-gon, leaving him with the vague sense that Jin-ok was, in fact, the person he needed most. Just a boy of five, yet...

'Lord, I should have been truthful back then, in the time You gave me,' Soo-gon prayed.

No matter what he did, no matter where he went, it wasn't that Soo-gon *couldn't* remember, as he had told Jin-ok. Rather, he had never forgotten the time when a young woman, dressed beautifully in *hanbok*, had tried to hold his hand, and he had longed to be in her arms.

'Lord, punish me for not being truthful in that moment. I deserve to be punished.'

Before leaving for Seoul, Se-joon decided to call the girl who had first made him aware of his own manhood when he was a college freshman. He made the call from a phone booth at Busan Train Station.

The first voice he heard was that of an older person—likely one of her parents. Startled, Se-joon quickly hung up. He stepped outside the booth, lit a cigarette, and smoked several in succession. After a moment's hesitation, he dialed again.

This time, she answered.

Hye-jeong:

"Hello? Se-joon? It's Se-joon, right? Please, say something. I was just wondering when I saw the phone hang up without a word. It's Hye-jeong. Go ahead."

Se-joon:

"Hye-jeong, I just ... I just wanted to hear your voice. I'm sorry. I hope your parents aren't worried..."

Hye-jeong:

"What are you sorry for? That doesn't sound like you, Se-joon.

I'm fine. You don't need to be sorry."

Se-joon:

"No, I really am sorry. I don't think I was as sincere with you as I should have been. I was too focused on myself..."

Hye-jeong:

"Se-joon, when we were together, we gave everything we had. That's what matters most. Sometimes, when I think of how much I gave to you, I wonder if I'll ever be that sincere with anyone else. I'm more sorry for that.

I heard from a friend that you're going to Seoul. Take care of yourself. I'm getting married soon."

As she spoke, the soft strains of Don McLean's *Vincent* played faintly over the phone. It had been their song, the one Se-joon and Hye-jeong had cherished together. But now, with the news of her impending marriage, was it time to sever all the emotions and memories that lingered between them? Was this truly the end?

Se-joon thought it might be—out of respect for the man Hye-jeong would soon marry. He believed it was his duty to let her go, to ensure she could move on without the shadow of an old love hanging over her.

It was, at the very least, Se-joon's way of showing courtesy to Hye-jeong.

First love ... why does it hurt so deeply?

Se-joon reflected that perhaps it was because, *during that time, both of them had been their most faithful, their most sincere. Whether it was unrequited or not, whether or not they had shared a physical relationship, what mattered was the purity of their feelings.*

It was because, during that time, the intense longing and yearning for the other person had been utterly genuine.

For Se-joon, Hye-jeong had been his first love.

Later, he heard that Hye-jeong had married the man her brother-in-law had introduced to her. Se-joon thought of the letters she had written, the small treasure box she had kept hidden away since childhood. When she met Se-joon in college, she had given him something that was uniquely hers.

Se-joon decided that the next time he went down to his home in Busan, he would burn everything, including that necklace. The necklace was a pendant made of silver-coated shapes of stars, the moon, and rings connected together. Whenever Se-joon got drunk, he would detach the star and moon from the necklace, put them in his pocket, and carry them around, often touching them.

He had been doing that ever since he had received the breakup letter from Hye-jeong. Perhaps *it was because her hands were now unreachable, and he wanted to hold on even more.*

By 1978, Se-joon was working tirelessly as an intern, running through the hospital corridors each day, barely finding time to sleep. The demands were constant—he was called to patient rooms at all hours from his quarters. The place once known as Seoul Municipal Hospital had been renamed National Medical Center.

One day, an elderly patient approached Se-joon, the novice doctor, and asked, "Doctor, let me ask you something. Can you tell where I'm hurting just by looking at me? After all the years you've studied, shouldn't you be able to see the source of my pain?"

Se-joon was taken aback by the question but managed to smile and respond:

"Mom, the human body is so intricate and complex that we can't diagnose everything based on just one symptom. Where do you feel the most discomfort, Mother? You can be completely honest with me; you don't need to hide anything. Once you tell me, I can relay it to the other doctors. After all, who else can you trust to brag about your ailments? Ha ha."

In Seoul, Se-joon met many poets he had long admired while working on a medical journal and the university newspaper at P University, where he had also served as an editor during his student years. For him, poetry was like a surgical procedure—a way to heal the most desperate and wounded parts of the human psyche using the scalpel of language.

He found himself more drawn to the path of an artist than that of a doctor. In his medical school yearbook, he left this reflection:

"If medicine saves one person from suffering, great art liberates thousands from sorrow."

Touch-me-not·I

Please, do not touch my body.
Pain surges through every joint in my hand,
Flesh clings to flesh,
Bones collide with bones,
And they sit back, weeping.

Please, let the wind pass by.
In the cold light of a winter operating room,
Tearing through the darkness,
The emptiness flees,
And red petals fall upon the snow.

Please, do not awaken my soul.
Throughout the long night,
I give a name to every nerve,
Leaving dreams as mere dreams.

With eyes wide open,
I see the windowpane,
Frost-covered and white.

The leaves, their hair loosened and weeping,
Wet with the darkness—
The hair of the rain.

Modern Literature

Revival
—For the Thirsty Sheep

When I open my eyes anew,
The lambs, trembling with fear,
Shed their purest tears,
Cautiously observing one another.

In the western sky,
The last rays of sunlight slowly, slowly,
Retreat from the field.
The wind, silencing the grasses,
Grinds its lips against a distant stone.

The horses, their brown manes flying,
Fall under the weight of sadness,
Galloping across the snow-covered field.
In the dawns where I wept in hiding,
The bruised rivers, abandoned by the darkness,
Leave behind only faded footsteps,
Scattered in the whirlwind.

Amidst the meetings and partings,
In the field of sorrow,
What do we come to understand, little by little?

Those who depart leave with nothing.

In the winter sea,
No one remains—
Only the tattered fragments of time flutter in the wind.
Let those who must depart, depart,
Like a camel chasing a mirage,
Let us begin anew,
With an empty heart,
Its beak crashing against the sky,
Like a crow that has perished

With our right hand trembling,
Unaware of the left,
Let us remember the cries of the departing horses.
The wind, fickle and false,
The blades of grass, swaying insincerely,
Words, spoken without truth—
Wipe away the tears of the last language...
And for a long time,
Fall into a dream from which we shall not wake.

When we open our eyes anew,
The poor, frightened lambs,
Even in their fear,
Search for the roots of pure water.
Closer. Closer,
They begin their journey anew.

Doctor's Newspaper

28
Those Who Erect Their Own Tombstones
1979−1981: Seoul, Busan, and Masan
—Ignition of Desire

Yo-han had come to visit Se-joon. As he entered the coffee shop, he was accompanied by a friend, and it was clear from their demeanor that they were being pursued by something ominous. The tension between them was palpable, and Se-joon could not help but notice the charged atmosphere they brought with them.

With a half-smile, Yo-han introduced his companion.

"Se-joon *Hyeong*, let me briefly introduce this friend of mine. Last year, he won an award in the creative writing category for college students nationwide. It was in the field of literary criticism. But this friend of mine, after skillfully critiquing literature, turned his sharp pen against the government and became somewhat of a dangerous figure. Ha-ha... Now, he's on the run. As you can see, it's a bit of a mess.

I don't think he's quite as gifted in literature as you are, though. When the police took him in, he couldn't even grasp their lofty jokes or find his tongue to respond. He understood their questions well enough, but they were so far removed from his own thoughts that he sat there, silent as a stone. Somehow, he was released last night, but now he has nowhere to go.

The police are swarming all over Seoul Station. I was wondering if you might let him stay at your place tonight, just for a night, but please, don't feel ... pressured. I'm sorry to impose like this."

Se-joon lived in a small rented room in a place called Hwagok-dong, quite a distance from the National Medical Center where he worked. The area was filled with old detached houses and shacks that had been retrofitted with slate roofs and rented out for a monthly fee. His room was in one of those tightly packed houses, divided into a single room with a small kitchen. The room itself was decent enough, but the kitchen, layered with white dust, showed no signs of ever having been used.

The friend Yo-han had brought along was named Hyeon Jong-seok.

He was a second-year philosophy student at SNU. His father, a minister from the North, worked as a chaplain at a middle school in Busan.

Se-joon turned to Jong-seok and asked quietly, "Jong-seok, you're studying philosophy at S University. Does your father know what's happening to you now?"

Jong-seok spoke softly, his voice carrying a hint of resigned bitterness. "My father ... he takes pride in his poverty as a pastor, holding fast to his moral compass, unwavering in his devotion to God."

With these words, Jong-seok painted a picture of his father—a man of steadfast principles. Both Yo-han and Se-joon couldn't help but chuckle at the irony in his tone, and for the first time in what felt like ages, laughter touched Jong-seok's weary face. Yet beneath the brief moment of levity, it was clear just how drained he was.

It was October 13 when they met Se-joon. Jong-seok, now marked as a student with "dangerous thoughts," was under investigation. The atmosphere was tense, filled with uncertainty, and it was unclear why the authorities had chosen to release him temporarily. There was no assurance that he wouldn't be summoned again at any moment.

During the reign of President Park Chung-hee, anti-communist ideology dominated the political landscape. Any student, whether from S University or another institution, who was suspected of left-wing activism risked having their life upended. The fate of such individuals was often grim: an inevitable trip to the police station, followed by a potential prison sentence that would rob them of their youth.

Few truly understood the intricacies of socialism, and many were simply swept up in the tide, following the lead of their seniors without fully grasping the consequences. In those days, even an innocent explanation of a concept to a tutoring student could result in someone being branded a leftist sympathizer. All it took was a suspicious father's accusation to bring down the full weight of the state's paranoia.

In a country divided between North and South, opportunists thrived, exploiting the situation to serve their own interests. Meanwhile, those who had witnessed the might of socialism firsthand were haunted by its ruthless power. The majority chose silence, believing that ignorance and inaction were the safest courses.

That day in Hwagok-dong, as the three of them conversed, Yo-han attempted to steer the discussion toward the emerging class of the "new rich"—a group rapidly rising in prominence.

By the time law students reached their second year, they were forced to choose their specialty. Therefore, most students said they started focusing on the bar exam early on, even from the beginning of their first year. The new rich fueled this competitive atmosphere, driven not just by a hunger for wealth but for the influence they lacked. It became common practice to seek out young law graduates, groom them into judges and prosecutors, and secure them as sons-in-law.

Korea, even now in the 2020s, remains relentless.

—There's no room for mercy. Let's climb to the top. By any means necessary, let's get into prestigious universities, build a respectable social reputation, and bask in economic prosperity. Let's send most of our children to study in the United States or abroad. What else? Yes, if circumstances allow, let's buy houses overseas and secure permanent residency. And what of money? Power? Of course, true power. It was the kind of political and legal clout that forced others to submit—men and women, children and the elderly alike, all eager to wedge themselves into that hierarchy.

Their eyes searched only for this, their gaze roving, gleaming with the intent to seize any opportunity, growing more cunning, more ruthless, and even brutal in their pursuit.

One thing was true then, as it is now: nothing had truly changed. Each person was intent on crafting their own legacy, as if building their own tombstone with their own hands. Wealth was the ultimate necessity—the key to living a life of respect and ensuring that their children could rise to greater heights than they themselves had achieved.

They believed that only those who ruled over others could lead lives of true splendor.

Don't you think so?

Those who sought to carve their own epitaphs were, day by day, staining the minds of others with a dull, murky hue—from Seoul to Gyeonggi-do and Jeju Island. People swayed back and forth, driven by the lure of immediate gains before their eyes.

The thought of these people, so eager to build their own monuments before death, sent a shiver through Yo-han. The main preoccupation of many students at S University had become the bar exam—an obsession that eclipsed their chosen fields of study. From the moment they set foot on campus, their energies were wholly consumed by it.

Yo-han, too, feared that a country boy like himself, naïve to the world's cruelty, might be ensnared in their machinations. Yet, Yo-han had chosen a different path. He had dedicated himself to something else.

Back then, students entered university under a general quota, regardless of their intended major, and only selected their specific field in their second year. Though his academic standing had been more than sufficient to secure a place in the law department, Yo-han had instead chosen to major in political science and diplomacy—departing from the path that most high-achieving students pursued.

Se-joon listened in silence as Yo-han recounted his decision.

Jong-seok listened too, though their talk of the new rich held little interest for him. He had already heard too much of it while living in Seoul. Instead, his thoughts drifted to his father, Pastor Hyeon.

It had been two years since he had last spoken with his father, and he hadn't returned to Busan since starting university. His father's voice echoed in his mind—words spoken with the weight of experience from a man who had survived the Korean War.

Pastor Hyeon had said:

"Jong-seok, do you know what the scariest thing in the world is? It's a human being. When you're out on a remote mountain path at dusk and hear a sound, you won't be afraid if you know it's an animal. But if you realize it's a human, that's when fear grips you.

And the next thing to fear is hunger. You know, I was taken to South Korea as a prisoner of war, still wearing the uniform of the North Korean People's Army. If I had known the way south earlier, I would have come on my own. But as a prisoner on Geoje Island, it was so cold—colder than anything back home. It's nothing compared to the weather where I lived, but still, it was just cold. Yet the cold wasn't the worst part; it was the hunger. Every time I opened my eyes, the hunger gnawed at me.

At night, the hunger was unbearable. I would think of home, of my mother, and it drove me mad with longing. No American beef could ever taste as good as the rice cakes my mother used to make. One day, a middle-aged woman who had come down from the North brought rice cakes in a basin to sell near our camp. We were desperate, scrambling to get even a small piece. But we had no money. So we stripped off our underwear and tossed it to her in exchange for the rice cakes. She took our clothes and threw the rice cakes over the barbed-wire fence. Even though we shivered through the night until we received new underwear, the taste of those rice cakes—of home—was worth it.

South Korea was warmer, less cold than the North. Just between us, the clothes we gave up were 100% wool, as they say these days. Even though they were marked with 'P.W.' for prisoner of war, somehow she must have removed the lettering. She sold the clothes to civilians, made money to feed her grandchildren, and sent them to school. After all that, I am grateful to live in South Korea, having renounced my former ideology.

I always tell you this: I didn't become a soldier in the People's Army by choice. I was swept up in their hands and sent to the battlefield. Decades have passed since the war ended, and sometimes it feels like I've forgotten the horrors of that time. The people here have changed, growing more confident, more arrogant. But above all, freedom is the most precious thing, the highest good.

Whatever you do, I trust you. Do as you see fit, as long as it doesn't infringe on others' freedom. I believe everything we live through is by God's will. Just trust, follow, and wait. I mean it."

Jong-seok could never bring himself to tell his father, Pastor Hyeon, that he had been detained by the police as a student spreading "dangerous leftist ideas." The thought of being a burden to his father weighed heavily on him. But as he resolved to visit home in Busan, to see his father again, his determination hardened. Se-joon and Yo-han noticed the sudden steely resolve in his eyes as they continued their conversation.

It was said that Jong-seok spent his nights teaching at a school in a remote mountain village when he wasn't attending his college classes. The books he introduced to his students, though often enlightening, were occasionally found among those the government had deemed subversive. The police grew suspicious of Jong-seok, believing he had incited the night school students to rebellion. Hiding someone like Jong-seok, whose name had been inscribed on the list of dangerous thinkers, was itself considered a violation of the National Security Law.

Unlike Yo-han, who bore the weight of his family's expectations without it manifesting in nightmares, Jong-seok had no such solace. Pastor Hyeon had never dictated his future, instead urging him, "Find the path that God has laid out for you." But try as he might, Jong-seok couldn't find that path. And so, he too was tormented by insomnia, wrestling with his thoughts each sleepless night.

That evening, they spent the night at Se-joon's modest home, planning to catch an early intercity bus to Busan the next morning. As they spoke about their impending journey, a sudden longing to see Jong-hee welled up in Se-joon. However, the demands of his work at the hospital weighed on him, and the thought of the added burden convinced him to postpone the visit. Instead, he handed Yo-han a slip of paper with the phone numbers of a few juniors at PNU.

Busan, where Jong-seok and Yo-han arrived, was still a city simmering with unrest. Just two days after their arrival, on October 15, 1979, the so-called Buma Struggle—a wave of protests led by students and citizens in Busan and Masan—erupted. This uprising served as a prelude to what would soon become a historic turning point, occurring just before the assassination of President Park Chung-hee.

On that fateful October 15, students from PNU gathered in protest, with their rally centered on Korea's economic and political situation. However, beneath the surface, the protest's true focus was opposition to President Park Chung-hee's *Yushin* Constitution—a system designed to further entrench his power after more than 18 years of rule. The unrest grew so severe that it compelled President Park to declare partial martial law in the region. Then, on October 26, 1979, President Park Chung-hee was assassinated.

He was the man who had steered Korea through countless political and economic crises, laying the solid foundations that transformed a war-ravaged nation into a burgeoning powerhouse. But after 18 years of his unrelenting grip on power, deep-seated resentment had festered among those around him. It was this tension within the ranks that led to his assassination at the hands of Kim Jae-gyu, one of his most trusted confidants—a man whose motives were rooted in the fierce power struggles of the time.

Reports suggested that Kim Jae-gyu, then director of the Central Intelligence Agency, had meticulously planned the assassination because he could no longer tolerate being slighted by Cha Ji-cheol, the head of the security service. The stagnant waters of power, which inevitably fester when left unchecked, had culminated in this terrifying climax against the nation's supreme authority.

When the long-standing pillar of power was finally struck down, the very people who had once placed their unwavering faith in President Park were gripped by anxiety, fearing the chaos that might now engulf the country.

As Jong-seok and Yo-han traveled back and forth between Busan and Masan, time was already on the verge of slipping into another year. Everywhere they went, whether in Busan or elsewhere in Korea, the atmosphere felt overwhelmingly grim.

The news Se-joon received about Jong-seok revealed that, at some point during that period, Jong-seok had returned to his father's house in Busan, his spine severely damaged from brutal torture and beatings at the hands of a government agency. However, it remained unclear whether it was the police or the National Security Agency that had been responsible. Meanwhile, Yo-han continued his studies in the department of political science and diplomacy without incident.

There was one thing Yo-han confided only to Se-joon and not to his father, Soo-gon: during his undergraduate years, Yo-han had taken the bar exam. However, he had failed the final interview, an assessment that bordered on an ideological interrogation. At first, he didn't understand why, but eventually, he realized it was because of his great-uncle.

Yo-han's elder grandfather (the elder brother of Yo-han's grandfather) had been a well-known socialist who had openly praised North Korea and had even voluntarily defected there—a fact that was no secret in their community.

In the end, Yo-han resolved to complete his studies and pursue a career in mass media, a field more suited to his natural inclination for engaging with people. There was still no word about Mi-young. Then, Soo-gon's father passed away, leaving Jin-ok alone. She spent her days at their former detached house and returned to the apartment at night, where Soo-gon and Hye-young now lived.

Hye-young's desire to see Yo-han's youngest sister married as soon as possible grew stronger. She fervently wished for Mi-soon, her youngest daughter, to marry while still in college. Mi-soon, in turn, accepted her mother's wishes and agreed to marry after completing her second year of college. Having entered E Women's University in Seoul, Mi-soon carried the weight of Hye-young's aspirations in her heart.

By the early 1980s, several Korean newspapers frequently reported on the growing power of the new rich, whose fortunes had soared with the sudden surge in land prices in Seoul. These were tales of people who had stumbled upon vast wealth as cheap rice paddies and abandoned fields were transformed into expensive urban developments. But alongside this sudden wealth came the rise of large-scale fraud, veiled in the guise of power, as unscrupulous individuals sought to plunder the pockets of these newly wealthy.

These so-called "big-mouthed frogs with big hands" were said to be people who didn't truly understand the value of their wealth. Their riches hadn't been earned through hard work or careful saving, and they were seen as shallow thinkers who believed that money could accomplish anything, while those without it were not even worthy of being considered human. Such superficial thinking made it easy for them to be deceived by those who flattered them with promises of even greater power.

As previously mentioned, the new rich were eager to forge connections through marriage with individuals from the legal and medical fields—people who, though not wealthy, were intelligent and had attained respectable positions through hard work. To achieve this, they had to immerse themselves in a culture of appearances, even ordering books with expensive leather covers solely for display.

They adorned their homes with world-renowned luxury items. When decorating the interior, they meticulously arranged their living rooms with famous, costly artworks and artifacts from both the East and West, ensuring that their newfound affluence was apparent from the very entrance of the foyer.

The study was designed to reflect the elegance of a family that had long upheld the traditions of refined education, a lineage rich with history. Shelves were lined with an impressive array of literature and philosophical works, including Machiavelli's *The Prince*. Though most reading was now done online, there was a sense of formality in maintaining a collection of ongoing subscriptions to *The New York Times* and *Newsweek*, carefully preserved in their physical form. The room also boasted an exquisite set of golf clubs, alongside a wardrobe filled with luxury clothing and shoes.

Such a setting surely suggested that the owner was a person of considerable learning and social insight, well-versed in the art of society. The living room, too, was a testament to their taste, with bookshelves and a home bar stocked with expensive liquors and crystal glasses, all prepared to welcome guests, along with an assortment of imported cigarettes.

Se-joon, however, felt distinctly uneasy around those who had suddenly come into wealth. In contrast to the decorative books and American periodicals found in other homes, Ki-hoon's study was filled with well-worn foreign legal and philosophical texts, as well as the latest international journals covering a wide array of subjects.

Of course, Ki-hoon's tastes extended to expensive pipe tobacco, thick foreign cigars, and high-quality whiskey. Yet, even these small indulgences would not have pleased Se-joon's great-grandfather, Hong-seon, had he been alive. As for Se-joon himself, he had little interest in Ki-hoon's displays of affluence.

Se-joon reflected that within each person who yearns for material wealth, there exists a seductive whisper of temptation. It is like a vast reservoir of greed, buried deep within the heart—much like oil hidden beneath the earth. He often wondered what would happen when this longing to appear brilliant and impressive was ignited by the spark of temptation. He mused whether many in this land, after having tasted the sweet nectar of abundance following years of bitter poverty, might end up like insects—unaware that their wings were being singed as they dove headlong into the flames. Like moths drawn to a fire, they remained heedless of the dangers lurking in the swamp of desire.

However, there was one aspect of Ki-hoon's study that Se-joon did appreciate—its vastness. During his medical school years, he had even installed a high-quality sound system in the study so that he and his brother, Jae-joon, could enjoy Western classical music in all its richness. Se-joon covered the cost of materials, while a friend from the engineering college contributed the technical expertise to complete the setup. Above all, Se-joon wanted to share the beauty of Western classical music with Jae-joon. Whenever he had the time, he would select traditional literary works or the latest movie scripts to introduce to his younger brother.

However, Jae-joon's tastes leaned more toward Korean *pansori*—a traditional form of musical storytelling. The expensive Western classical LPs that Se-joon had bought for him rarely saw the turntable, spinning only a few times before being set aside. Instead, Jae-joon spent his pocket money on records of traditional Korean music.

Ki-hoon, for his part, looked on with disapproval at his sons for spending money on anything other than books. To Ki-hoon, music was a frivolous luxury; only books held true value. This marked not only a generational divide between father and son but also a difference in taste between brothers.

Unlike the newly wealthy, Se-joon had no desire to amass art or flaunt it before others. He wasn't interested in collecting music and literary works just for the sake of ownership; he wanted to experience them firsthand—to see with his own eyes and hear with his own ears.

Gradually, he began to feel the need for a companion—someone who could understand these works alongside him, someone with whom he could share and communicate his emotions. Over time, Se-joon decided to seek out such a partner and turned to a renowned matchmaker known as "*Madam*

Tu" (Madam Matchmaker of Seoul). Se-joon, too, wanted to marry.

Se-joon began his residency at the National Mental Hospital, where he met several remarkable doctors who inspired him to strive for excellence as a physician. The National Mental Hospital, where Se-joon was a resident, had established a daytime ward in 1976, marking a new chapter in psychiatric rehabilitation treatment. Notably, the hospital had introduced psychodrama therapy in 1975 at the suggestion of the esteemed psychiatrist Dr. Kim You-kwang.

The psychodrama sessions at the National Mental Hospital, which first took place at 3 p.m. on Thursday, July 5, 1975, were an innovative fusion of psychological therapy and theatrical performance, involving both professional actors and patients with mental illnesses. This groundbreaking approach created a significant stir in society. By 1979, the hospital experienced a marked increase in patient numbers, prompting the construction of a new outpatient clinic. In 1981, the establishment of a training center for mental health nursing assistants within the National Mental Hospital marked a major step forward in overseeing medical care, research, and education.

From that point on, the National Mental Hospital evolved into the country's foremost institution for training medical professionals in the field of mental health. Specialized wards for senior citizens and patients struggling with alcoholism were also established, ushering in an era of specialization and national focus on mental health care.

Se-joon thrived in this environment, immersing himself in his studies at the National Mental Hospital, where he found both fulfillment and a deep sense of purpose in his work in medicine and psychiatry.

Flammability

In the darkness,
Someone strikes a match.

My damp chest,
Where pain lingers,
Feels the wind blow.

An ancient tree is embraced,
Lips grind against the ashen whetstone
Until they crack.
The sky above
Whimpers.

Birds with broken beaks
Faint among the blades of grass.
Nameless tombstones
Stand askew in scattered disarray.

Amid the rain of anguish,
I cool the feverish blaze,
Spending only
The solitary hours of resilience.

All night long, the white blades of grass
That trembled in the darkness
Shed their skin,
And fleeing flower snakes
Are chased by naked children.

Mad fireflies,
Drifting like corpses,
Tumble and writhe.
Inside granite tombs,
Like the hardened dead
Who turned their backs,

Coal soaks in the rain.
Choosing the deepest wound in the darkness,
In the hollow seat of desire,
Someone strikes a match
At the edge of the sky.

29
The Man and the Woman
1980−1982: Busan and Seoul
—False Expectations

At Jong-seok's house, where he lay confined to his bed, the conversation had meandered through various topics. Then, whether Yo-han was listening or not, Jong-seok began to speak.

Jong-seok said,

"Ideology is never a simple matter. Once ideology takes hold of something, it shapes and molds every facet of reality, bending all phenomena to fit its form. After the Korean War, when the nation was split in two, the possibility of reconciliation between the opposing sides was lost. This ideological divide is not merely political—it runs deeper than the physical separation of North and South Korea. It fractures every soul on this land, reducing everything to stark contrasts of black and white.

We become trapped in an 'us-versus-them' mentality, where the middle ground dissolves into an indistinct blur, barely perceptible. Everyone is drawn into the vortex of this ideological struggle, where the world is painted in the harsh, unforgiving strokes of binary opposition.

Take heed—if someone claims neutrality yet subtly harms one side through their words or actions, they cannot truly be called neutral. They are either black or white, merely masquerading as something in between. In such times, outcomes matter more than intentions. No matter how fair one claims to be, if you are not on their side, you are automatically against them—a villain, a deceiver. How can anyone see the truth clearly under such conditions?

The Korean War, which erupted in 1950, may one day be retold in myriad ways through the pages of textbooks—its facts reshaped, its history glorified or obscured, all depending on who holds the reins of power. Yet one truth remains clear: North Korea was the first to invade the South. Still, there are those who incessantly revisit the events leading up to the war, scrutinizing them in search of a thread that might support their cause.

Before the war, those who fled North Korea spoke of a land where freedom of religion and art was merely a facade, tools for political expression, while personal desires were dismissed as extravagant and unnecessary. The North Korean Communist Party held absolute dominance.

Does anyone still believe in God there? Kim Il-sung took the place of divinity himself, replacing Christianity's 'Our Father in Heaven' with the 'Father Leader' of his regime."

Yo-han:

"How could anyone call you a leftist provocateur with such thoughts? When did these ideas come to you?"

As the conversation continued, Jong-seok turned to Yo-han with a somber expression, the weight of shared past experiences hanging in the air. Jong-seok:

"Yo-han, my friend. Didn't you suffer as I did last year? Tortured, though perhaps not as severely as I was. I heard a little about it, but we haven't really seen each other since then. Ha ha..."

Yo-han:

"Really? Is that so? I didn't even tell my father, but I injured my leg a little at the time. It troubled me for about a month. But anyway, let me be clear, I'm not someone who stands by and advocates for North Korean ideology. I was just trying to express my thoughts, that's all...

For example, what truly worries me is that our fellow countrymen, those living under North Korean rule, are utterly cut off from the rest of the world. There are people there who not only deceive others but also deceive themselves, living in fleeting luxury. I've heard that beneath the surface of so-called equality, the gap between the rich and the poor is even more severe.

Moreover, most people in North Korea are trapped within their society, constantly indoctrinated with the idea that capitalist labor is dangerous and evil. They harshly criticize themselves, just as the Party instructs them to do, and through relentless ideological education, they spend each day tearing down the so-called formidable capitalist ideology in their minds. And isn't it true that they are forced to live each day by suppressing such thoughts? Even basic human needs and freedoms are devoured by the Party, which preys on the lives of ordinary people under the guise of ideology.

On the other hand, here in South Korea, we fail to teach students — or anyone, for that matter, what ideology truly is. Depending on who holds power, political opportunists in South Korea simply drift back and forth, thinking only of filling their bellies. It's crucial for the younger generation to be taught and to understand the difference between ideologies.

Yet people here grow increasingly indifferent, unwilling to think deeply about ideology itself. The more indifferent they become, the more ignorant and dull they grow. As we know, ignorance is the most dangerous thing. Meanwhile, in North Korea, the Party is held above all else, and nothing matters except the Party. So what happens? Their greed knows no bounds, and they seek to twist every situation to their advantage.

The influence of ideology runs deep, profoundly shaping an individual's sense of humanity. We all value ourselves, for without self-regard, it is difficult to endure even a single day. But even if I act out of a sense of self-importance, I must not cross a certain line. We must ask ourselves whether we will merely chase the immediate benefits before us or consider how these temporary gains might affect others. If my actions harm others, then it is right to stop.

So, if there exists even the slightest intention, by any means, to set a limit on how evil one can become in the name of humanity and to uphold that boundary, then at least it would not be a complete betrayal of the land one lives on.

To accomplish this, we require the name of a god with absolute power, no matter what that god may be called. If we can sense, even faintly, the presence of that Being, who was imprinted in our hearts long before we came into existence ... we can find our place anywhere. To me, that Being is God, the absolute divine.

Some might say, 'God exists everywhere,' but must God and religion always be clothed in the same ideological garments? I believe that questions such as whether one believes in religion, why they believe, and how they believe should begin with the issue of the essence (Essen, Wesen) and form or shape (Eidos or Form) of faith. The color of the clothing pertains to form, while the essence remains unrelated to that color. The essence does not change according to the ideological clothing it wears. The existence of an absolute God is certain because the existence of God is the truth, at least for me.

Saying that my God is right because He brings me prosperity, or that my God is wrong because He brings me poverty and sorrow, or denying God's existence altogether in the face of the endlessly expanding universe theory, is ignorance. Instead of chasing only selfish interests, one must seek what is true and discover the essence."

Jong-seok:

"Yo-han, what confuses so many people today isn't the nature of religion or belief. I think it's that people's perspectives are buried in form and methodology rather than in essence. For example, whether you follow Hinduism, Islam, Protestant Christianity, or, like that girlfriend of yours, choose Catholicism, the essence remains the same, the differences lie only in form and practice. Or, at its very core, it might just be a game of territorial gain...

Even though people perceive the nature of religion as the same, it is something that can't be fully captured in words or imperfect writing. So perhaps people have forgotten its essence, choosing not to understand it. I believe the focus has shifted from the essence to the names of gods and the forms in which they are worshiped."

Yo-han:

"Oh! That reminds me, your younger sister, Joon-mi, is Catholic, unlike you. Since when?"

Jong-seok:

"Oh, Joon-mi? She attended a Catholic mission school in high school, so it must have been around that time. I heard she's coming down from Seoul this week. You'll be seeing her, right? You two have met up in both Seoul and Busan before. Now that you're in Busan, I'm sure she's even more eager to visit."

Yo-han:

"Yes, I know her well. Even if she weren't your sister, she's a delight to be around, she always carries such a bright spirit. I rarely meet girls as sweet and patient as Joon-mi. She has cared for you and your father, Pastor Hyeon, in place of your mother since high school. She's truly thoughtful."

Jong-seok:

"Wow, Yo-han, you sly fox. So that's why you've been visiting my house so often! What a crafty fellow! But you know what? You're welcome to stay here until Joon-mi arrives. Consider it a holiday of sorts. I'll even absolve you of all your sins! Both of you, in fact! I'm serious!"

Yo-han:

"Thank you. You've always treated me like family.

But, Jong-seok, imagine someone coming to you and saying,

'Let me see God right before my eyes, and then I'll believe in Him! I'll convert on the spot!'

How would you go about proving the existence of the God you believe in?"

Jong-seok:

"Yo-han, let's approach this carefully — this isn't just wordplay. Many people demand, 'Show me God right now! Then I'll believe, and I promise I'll devote my life to Him.' They seem so sure of themselves.

Now, let's say we have Proposition A: *God exists*, and Proposition Not-A: *God does not exist*. Have you ever seen the God you believe in? May I ask you that first?"

Yo-han:

"I can't say with certainty. But my father and mother, as well as my grandmother, all speak fervently with God every morning and evening, in the form of prayer. Could this form of prayer be the 'essence of religion' you're talking about? I pray, too. While praying, did I see God?"

Jong-seok:

"Exactly. Is there anything as certain as prayer? When you pray, you align yourself with the belief in your God, in His existence.

Now, regarding the proposition I mentioned — whether it's Proposition A **or** not A — this alone doesn't lead to a definitive answer. But if we reframe it as A **and** not A — *God exists* **and** *God does not exist*, we can consider it from another perspective.

Take Proposition A: *There exists a man who is 250 cm tall* versus Not-A: *No man of 250 cm exists in the world.*

So far, none of us has encountered a person that tall. But if someone happens to see a person who is exactly 250 cm tall, or even taller at 260 cm, then it would mean that a person of 250 cm height does indeed exist. So if you believe that someone has seen such a tall person, even if you haven't seen him with your own eyes, then a person of 250 cm height does exist.

So to sum it up, in the statement '*A* **and** *not A*,' a person who is 260cm tall would essentially serve as a negation of *not A*. If one of us has seen such a person, then it would mean that *not A* is being negated — so wouldn't it be fair to call this the proposition of '*A* **and** negation of *not A*'?

Similarly, people believe that the Bible teaches humanity to have absolute faith in God, much like believing in something extraordinary, even without direct evidence."

Jong-seok smiled, releasing a long breath after finishing his thought. Then, with a reflective gaze, he continued.

Jong-seok:

"So you could say, *A* is the truth, and *not A* is also the truth. The middle ground is 'silence.' And silence, it seems, carries a positive weight. I am one who believes in the 'and.'

God ... I am certain He exists. But, Yo-han, listen to what I think.

Doubt!

The more deeply you doubt, the more the existence of God, the absolute deity, is proven. What reason is there to doubt something that does not exist? *It is because you feel His presence but do not want to acknowledge that powerful feeling, so you doubt and deny even more.* But only those who traverse the mountain of doubt will truly see!

Do not deny the land you live on and the time that is now. And do not deny your God. Even though He may not appear before your eyes at this moment, and even though you have not directly heard His voice..."

Hearing this, Yo-han leaned in closer to Jong-seok, a hint of sarcasm on his face.

Yo-han:

"Let me see God's face right here, right now. Then I will bow down as His devout servant. But if He doesn't appear, I'll become a fervent atheist and willfully deny both you and the God you speak of for the rest of my life!

I haven't found Mi-young yet, and my God hasn't shown Himself to me. I think I'll live like the other smart, modern people, relishing the confusion as a cool atheist!

Jong-seok, I get where you're coming from, to some extent. But with how advanced science is today... could the person saying this actually be the ignorant one? Or is it simply because we are still young that we talk this way?"

Jong-seok:

"Hey! Yo-han, Jeong Yo-han, God isn't something we can define with words as we're doing now. And science ... science doesn't create something from nothing. It creates something from something, born out of probability and built upon the achievements of countless people.

And isn't that something humanity has debated for a long time? If everything had been accomplished by human effort alone, why would this debate have continued for so long?

Human power can't do everything.

All we can do is try ... effort, effort."

Yo-han:

"Yeah, you're right. But people spend their entire lives clinging only to what they can see, even though they live seeking and trying to prove God. They do this because it makes them seem greater or better than others.

Of course, sometimes it becomes an obsession with a single belief. In many cases, that obsession and the views one holds become obstacles that blind them to the truth. Whether it's Islam, Catholicism, Christianity, Buddhism, or any other religion, people often don't even try to understand other faiths. They only look at and think about their own, and somehow, not clearly stating one's beliefs has become a virtue. Yet, they still insist on their own religion!

You're one of them! Mr. Hyeon Jong-seok! Ha-ha...

But seriously, Jong-seok, I've been learning a bit about Sakyamuni lately. Sakyamuni never claimed to be a god. The way I see it, he radiated a brilliant light, a light for all to see. And he existed in silence ... that's how I would describe it."

Then, Jong-seok asked Yo-han.

"Yo-han, did your interest in Buddhist scriptures spark after meeting that guy, Se-joon, in Seoul? You come from a Christian family, just like me. I'd like to study Buddhist scriptures too."

Yo-han:

"Yes, that's right. But actually, I've been interested in Buddhist scriptures for a while now. I've always had this lingering thought that my current life is somehow influenced by a life I lived before, a previous life, if you will.

As you know, there's no such thing as a life without pain or a family without worries. However, I think that certain kinds of pain, like losing a younger sibling as we did in our family, are among the hardest to overcome. I couldn't help but feel that way.

Se-joon once said, 'I love Jesus of Nazareth so much. Love your neighbor as yourself! How moving is that? It means to share in others' pain and walk with them. Just that alone ... Jesus taught a great deal of mercy to those consumed by vengeance. He practiced what He preached. I believe He truly is the Son of God. There's no doubt about that.'

I think I'm studying because I want to uncover a deeper wisdom that I have yet to understand, and I believe Buddhist scriptures might hold some of those answers."

Jong-seok:

"The conversation between us, Yo-han, is not unlike Galileo's proclamation that 'The earth is rotating.'

In other words, there's Set 1: *God exists*, and Set 0: *No God*. If someone has seen God, felt His presence, or heard His voice, that experience becomes a *subset* of Set 1: *God exists*. The existence of that *subset*, I believe, confirms that the existence of God is real, as it forms part of the overarching nature of Set 1.

People can only perceive, feel, and contemplate the world within the limits of their own understanding, and anything beyond their mental framework cannot be spoken of with certainty.

Of course, the existence of God transcends ordinary probability. If a coin is flipped 100 times and lands on heads 46 times, with tails showing 54 times, that's merely a calculation based on the assumption of randomness. The existence of God, however, lies beyond such probabilities; it belongs to a realm outside human thought. And in that realm ... continuous effort, the pursuit of truth ... must exist."

Yo-han found himself contemplating this. It had been almost two years since he had last engaged in such a conversation with Jong-seok. Now, as he stood reading *The 1982 Corporate Open Recruitment Announcement* on the school bulletin board, memories of those youthful days flooded back — days when he and Jong-seok had dreamed of something truly idealistic.

But with his spine severely injured, Yo-han found little left to discuss with Jong-seok, who remained bedridden, seemingly preoccupied with that singular issue.

As Jong-seok had suggested, did every issue that lay beyond the reach of an ordinary person's mental capacity belong to the domain of God? This was something Yo-han had never considered—until the day his younger sister, Mi-young, suddenly vanished without a trace.

Just because we've never thought of something doesn't mean it won't happen.

"Yes, God lives everywhere," Yo-han muttered under his breath.

Meanwhile, Se-joon had decided to pursue marriage. He had spent time with various women, shared meals, and enjoyed their company, but now he longed for stability—a warm, cozy home where two people could sit face to face and share their lives.

A call came from Busan. Jong-hee had found a potential match through Busan's matchmakers and urged him to come down and meet her. The woman was the daughter of a wealthy family from Daeyeon-dong, Busan, and a graduate of E Women's University in Seoul.

Se-joon traveled to Busan to meet her. She had a round, soft face that exuded a gentle charm. She was petite, with a meticulous demeanor. They agreed to a second meeting, this time in Seoul, where Se-joon resided. But every time they met, an emergency at the hospital arose, almost as if fate itself were intervening. As a result, most of their meetings were brief encounters in front of the hospital, hastily concluded before Se-joon had to rush back to work.

Despite these fleeting interactions, their families arranged an engagement within a month of their first meeting. Se-joon, weary from his life away from home, felt mounting pressure as he watched his colleagues settle down, the urgency to start a family growing within him.

But was this hasty decision destined to lead to problems?

Up until then, Se-joon had lived in the bustling, unfamiliar city of Seoul, working as an intern and resident. He had enjoyed the freedom of casual relationships, meeting different women without the burden of commitment.

However, the woman he had agreed to marry could not understand why Se-joon had become so distant and indifferent whenever she visited the hospital. From afar, she would see him chatting warmly with another woman, his smile easy and relaxed. But when she approached, his expression hardened, and he grew less talkative.

She shared her concerns with her father. As her doubts grew, she confided in her parents once more, expressing her suspicion that Se-joon might have agreed to marry her for the sake of her family's wealth.

After some hesitation, she informed Se-joon that she was breaking off the engagement.

Once again, Se-joon found himself alone, left in a state of bewildered solitude.

Se-joon was deeply shaken by the rejection he had faced from the woman. The experience left him confused, and in its aftermath, he resolved to postpone thoughts of marriage and instead focus on his studies.

During his residency, he authored several papers at the National Mental Hospital, which were published in reputable journals. He found solace in his academic pursuits. Moreover, his interactions with various poets in Seoul proved to be another significant achievement. As a poet, Se-joon realized his long-held dream of making his literary debut in the esteemed magazine *Modern Literature*.

Se-joon felt a sense of relief, distancing himself from the enormous burden of being the eldest son of his father, Ki-hoon, and from the pressures of living in Seoul. In Se-joon's eyes, it was clear that Ki-hoon regarded him, both publicly and privately, as "Someone who couldn't even secure a place at S University's medical school." To Ki-hoon, Se-joon seemed an inferior being, a second-rate individual who had failed to achieve the excellence of first place.

Though these thoughts were never spoken aloud, Se-joon could feel the disdain in the stern, cold gaze that pierced through Ki-hoon's glasses.

One day, Ki-hoon remarked, as if intending for Se-joon to hear, "I've had no luck with my children. Not a single son of mine entered S University."

With those words, Se-joon's worst suspicions were confirmed—he was seen as a deficient and weak second-class player in his father's eyes.

Despite the enjoyment he found as a trainee doctor and in his studies at the National Mental Hospital, Se-joon couldn't shake the feeling that marriage might fill a void within him. Only a few months had passed since his engagement had been called off, but he decided to re-enter the marriage market, hoping to resolve the issue of marriage once and for all.

Life in Seoul was growing increasingly difficult by the day, and Se-joon found himself running from one hotel coffee shop to another, meeting new women every Sunday morning. Eventually, these efforts bore some fruit.

At their second meeting, one woman remarked to Se-joon, "Dr. Choi, you're cool," before she vanished from his face. Most of the women he met were younger than him and undeniably charming. Yet Se-joon often confided in his friends, saying, "I prefer women who are a few years older than me, who are reliable, like an older sister. I think I could marry someone like that."

He yearned for a companion who could provide him with emotional support—a woman who could be a partner in conversation, someone dependable, someone to whom he could turn in times of difficulty. The woman who left him with the words, "You're cool," was named Jeon Hwa-young.

The very idea of finding genuine comfort and being comforted in a relationship between a man and a woman—that was, in fact, what had narrowed Se-joon's perspective. When Se-joon looked at women, he had already placed a distorted and flawed ruler before his eyes, one twisted by his preconceived notions.

In doing so, he had ensnared himself in a web of illusions of his own making—a web woven from the idealized notion that a relationship between a man and a woman should involve mutual comfort, enduring sacrifices, and unwavering truthfulness.

It seemed that Se-joon had fallen victim to his own imagined trap.

Three months after meeting Hwa-young, Se-joon resolved to marry her. Despite advice from those around him to learn more about her, Se-joon was captivated by her confident speech and bold, fearless demeanor.

The man promised to marry the woman.

In April 1980, they were wed in a ceremony held at a wedding hall in Busan, followed by a honeymoon on Jeju Island. However, the wedding day was not without its troubles.

Jong-hee, Se-joon's mother, was deeply upset. The issue arose from the marriage gifts—items traditionally sent by the bride's family to the groom's house before the wedding. The gifts Hwa-young's family sent were, by all accounts, inexpensive—a far cry from what was expected.

Some time later, Lee-seop's wife, Nam-gil, the groom's younger grandmother, visited Se-joon's home in Busan. She looked over the marriage gifts with a disapproving expression, clicking her tongue in disdain. Nam-gil:

"I heard the bride's family isn't exactly poor ... that they even own a small building."

And yet ... here's our handsome Se-joon, with a respectable job, and what does she bring? Cheap trinkets from the market as her precious marriage gifts. Tut-tut... It seems this Choi household has no luck when it comes to marriage."

She continued to voice her dissatisfaction with every item.

On the bride's side, there was an expectation that the groom's family would purchase a house, but they were disgruntled when they realized they had to contribute more than half of the cost. Despite these undercurrents of dissatisfaction, both families tried to maintain a surface-level harmony.

However, the relationship between the bride and groom began to sour when Jong-hee sent the marriage gifts back to the bride's mother, demanding that they be exchanged for better items. Tensions between the two families threatened to boil over, but the bride and groom managed to endure the wedding, determined to see it through.

Their courtship had been brief, and perhaps it was natural for an arranged marriage to be influenced by economic negotiations. As a resident at a hospital, the groom's salary was modest, and his financial resources were limited. Yet, it was widely understood that the groom's future as a doctor promised considerable financial stability.

From the groom's perspective, this implicit understanding was common knowledge and factored into such transactions. Though Se-joon could have entertained offers from the nouveau riche in Seoul, he chose not to pursue marriage in that manner. Such considerations clashed with his own values, and he committed to marriage based on faith in his family and his own convictions.

Thus, Se-joon endured Hwa-young's complaints about their newlywed home. The groom had contributed nearly 40 percent toward the purchase of their house—the most he could manage.

In hindsight, it could be said that Ki-hoon, Se-joon's father, understood the situation to some extent and contributed accordingly to help buy the newlywed home, mindful of his son's position. The bride's father, who was also involved in a field related to the university, likely saw this as reasonable, given that Se-joon's father was a professor.

But truth be told, Se-joon's marriage was somewhat shaky from the start.

In the same month that Se-joon married, Korea was politically unstable. The New Military, which had seized power after the December 12 Incident in 1979, declared national martial law in April 1980. Protests erupted around university districts, and large-scale democratization movements, especially in Gwangju from May 18 to 27, escalated. These movements, later known as the 5·18 Democratization Movement.[71]

Se-joon and Hwa-young began their married life in a small apartment in Seoul, where housing prices were steep. Se-joon thought to himself that if they lived frugally, they wouldn't be too hard-pressed for money.

But this was only Se-joon's idea.

The bold, generous personality that had once seemed so embracing turned out to be quite different in reality. Barely a week into their honeymoon, Hwa-young began to complain incessantly, saying, "We're short on money."

At that time, as now, a modest honeymoon life, funded by the meager resources provided by parents, was inevitably short on cash.

Although Hwa-young was employed as a part-time lecturer at a university, teaching mainly liberal arts, her job provided only a small income. And in those early days, regardless of the couple's professions, economic hardships were inevitable as they started their household from

---

71) 5·18 Democratization Movement(1980): Initially referred to by the media as the Gwangju Uprising and the Gwangju Turmoil, but officially recognized after 1988 as the Gwangju Democratization Movement—culminated in a tragic event that claimed the lives of many citizens opposing the New Military.—This content is a summary by the author based on information from Naver Namu Wiki.

scratch. Even doctors had to be prepared for such financial struggles.

As a young, impoverished doctor, Se-joon would often try to soothe Hwa-young's complaints with lighthearted jokes, attempting to warm her cold heart whenever he returned home.

While preparing for his specialist exam, Se-joon took it upon himself to pack his own lunch in the name of saving money. But his lunch box was almost always filled with barley rice, accompanied by a single fried egg and a bottle of spoiled kimchi.

Once, when Jong-hee visited her son's home, she opened the lid of his lunch box. Tears welled up as soon as she saw the contents, and she quickly closed the lid again. She also noticed that Se-joon packed two lunch boxes because he had to work from morning until late at night, studying at the hospital. To any observer, Se-joon's meals appeared woefully deficient in nutrition.

Jong-hee hesitated to tell Ki-hoon about Se-joon's situation and to offer him some financial assistance. However, she decided to wait a little longer before bringing it up and returned to Busan. Jong-hee couldn't quite comprehend how such poor nourishment could sustain a young man who worked tirelessly day and night, especially with his naturally frail constitution.

Given her experiences with her in-laws at the Sancheong House, she felt it was her role as a mother to discuss the situation with Se-joon and devise a plan. But bringing up such matters felt like adding unnecessary worry to Ki-hoon, so she decided against it, irritated by the thought. The discontent she had caused over the marriage gifts still troubled her mind.

Hwa-young frequently frowned at Se-joon, complaining about their financial situation while at the same time purchasing relatively expensive clothes and cosmetics. She often boasted that, as a university lecturer, she needed to maintain her appearance.

Se-joon, on the other hand, had no complaints about his clothes, perhaps because he was naturally handsome. Even the old raincoat, winter coat, or suit that he had inherited from Ki-hoon and repurposed by turning them inside out was good enough for him.

Se-joon didn't bother much about his appearance, and he found Hwa-young's complaints about wanting new clothes rather endearing. The only new suit he owned was the one he had received when they got married.

Se-joon:

"Men and women are different. Women always want to show off with new clothes, but not us men, at least not me. Honey, I'm sorry I can't afford to buy you new clothes every time..."

He smiled apologetically.

Hwa-young's appearance and her true nature were worlds apart. She was neither as strong nor as mature as Se-joon had first believed. From morning to night, she seemed consumed by thoughts of how much better off her friends were, how tight their finances were, and how undignified their lives felt in comparison.

Whenever Se-joon saw her like this, he would smile and say:

Se-joon:

"Wow, what's bothering my Professor Jeon? Honey, one day, we'll look back on these days and laugh about how we used to struggle. But remember, envy won't disappear with money, so be confident.

We're not starving right now. Let's hang in there. Cheer up today, Professor Jeon?"

With these words, he would head off to catch the bus to the hospital.

At the hospital, even the other residents were busy driving and parking their own cars. But Se-joon wasn't envious of wealth or status. He admired the poet Cheon Sang-byeong, a Korean literary giant known for his innocent, pure-hearted verse. Cheon was a man who lived with childlike innocence and economic naivety, traits that Se-joon deeply respected.

Se-joon was not the type to envy the financial stability of others. He never spoke of his difficulties to anyone, focusing solely on his duties and studying for his specialist exam.

I Live as a Hunchback

I, with my back bent
In the wind of greed,
Among the dried-up trees—
Is it better not to live as bamboo?

As my spine arches
In the fiercely tearing wind,
Leaving thirsty footprints
Among skulls with eyes wide open,
Like a camel,
In pursuit of the mirage of an oasis,
Should I carry this sadness
And speak of it unjustly?

Perhaps I should go to the sea,
On a sun filled with germs,
Riding the waves of the microcosm,
Strumming a guitar with an unfamiliar scent.
Ah, near the equator, with fear and hunger,
I'll find a ghost ship laden with them,
And with eyes held wide open by starvation,
I'll search for the theory of death.

If the dryness in my throat burns my vocal cords,
Singing without sound,
My nails clashing against the waves gone mad.

Ah, to drift near the equator for a hundred days,

Falling asleep to a lullaby,
The ghost ship heavy with my grudges.
Not a single living soul aboard,
You'll find me on a broken mast, or
When my red eyes catch sight of it.

For this fragile, broken dream
That I live,
My voice is the tears
Spilled from jealousy.

As flesh departs from flesh,
Driven mad by the arrogance of betrayal
And the pallor of hypocrisy.

Under my dishonest sun,
Unfolding my bent back,
Shedding the burden of grudges.
Ah, even if death comes while absorbed in the theory of death,
I,
I'll live as a hunchback.
As a hunchback.

Pusan National University Student Newspaper

30
True Betrayal

1983: Busan, Seoul, and Masan
—Greed and Emptiness

The Windmill in My Head (Oil Painting on Canvas, No. 100)

Soo-gon had long wondered what Yo-han was truly thinking. After graduating from college, Yo-han had called his home in Masan a few times but had chosen to remain in Seoul. Soo-gon, however, never inquired. Yo-han had only informed him, "Dad, I'm working at a small magazine. Don't worry about me." That was all Soo-gon knew.

It was said that Hye-young, Soo-gon's wife, had glimpsed Yo-han's face a few times in Seoul around that time, as their youngest daughter, Mi-soon, who had married the previous year, was living there. Jin-ok was still going back and forth between new apartment and the old house in Masan.

Soo-gon had recently retired from his position as a high school teacher and was now working as a school inspector at the Office of Education. One day, on his way home, he entered a small church with a modest spire—New Church, where Hye-young's father served as the pastor. Sitting on a wooden pew, Soo-gon quietly meditated and then opened the Bible before him.

Psalms 10:4
In the pride of his countenance the wicked
does not seek him;
all his thoughts are, "There is no God."

Psalms 39:1
I said, "I will guard my ways, that I may not sin with my tongue;
I will bridle my mouth, so long as the wicked are in my presence."

Psalms 39:5
Behold, you have made my days a few handbreadths,
and my lifetime is as nothing in your sight.
Surely every man stands as a mere breath!

Psalms 39:6

Surely man goes about as a shadow!

Surely for nought are they in turmoil;

man heaps up, and knows not who will gather!

Psalms 39:8-13

Deliver me from all my transgressions.

Make me not the scorn of the fool!

I am silent, I do not open my mouth;

for it is you who have done it.

Remove your stroke from me;

I am spent by the blows of your hand.

When you chasten man with rebukes for sin,

you consume like a moth what is dear to him;

surely every man is a mere breath!

Hear my prayer, O LORD, and give ear to my cry;

hold not your peace at my tears!

For I am your passing guest,

a sojourner, like all my fathers.

Look away from me, that I may know gladness,

before I depart and be no more!

Psalms 22:6-8

But I am a worm, and no man;

scorned by men, and despised by the people.

All who see me mock at me,

they make mouths at me, they wag their heads;

He committed his cause to the LORD; let him deliver him,

let him rescue him, for he delights in him!

As Soo-gon reflected on these verses, Hong-seon's words suddenly echoed in his mind: "*Don't deny your roots.*" A decision crystallized within him—he would finally share with Yo-han and his youngest daughter the story of his own birth mother.

It had been eight years since Mi-young had disappeared. Concealing from Soo-gon the fact that he had a biological mother besides Jin-ok would never help in finding news of Mi-young, who had gone missing.

Soo-gon realized that his remaining children had a right to know their father's true origins, just as they needed to understand that Mi-young's disappearance was tied to the gravest sin of his life. He knew how deeply Yo-han, Mi-jin, and Mi-soon had grieved over Mi-young's absence, each in their own way—none more so than his wife, Hye-young.

Thus, he resolved to confess everything to Pastor Gil, Hye-young's father. Soo-gon was haunted by shame for his past decision to hide his roots, as though denying them could erase them.

It was all in the past, and whether he spoke of it or kept silent, the truth of where Soo-gon's roots lay was unalterable. No one could change that, and the sorrow Jin-ok would inevitably endure because of it was beyond his control.

After all, no matter what anyone said, she was Soo-gon's mother. The shame he felt now, for believing that he could simply close his eyes and turn away, thinking nothing would come of it, was overwhelming.

He was most ashamed before the God he believed in. He had betrayed himself, and in doing so, he felt he had denied his faith.

Se-joon had just passed the specialist examination. At that time, the field of Neurological Psychiatry was bifurcated into two distinct specialties: Neurology and Psychiatry. With relentless dedication, Se-joon succeeded in both, immersing himself so completely in his studies that he momentarily abandoned his college passion for art.

With his studies completed, he was now bound, like many young men in Korea, to fulfill his military service. Those who had studied medicine underwent basic military training for about three months in Yeongcheon, Gyeongsangbuk-do. At the end of their training, they were assigned to either the Ministry of National Defense or the Ministry of Health and Social Affairs.

When Se-joon's training came to an end, his family made the long journey to Yeongcheon to visit him. Jong-hee, Jae-joon, and Bok-hee took the bus to the training center, laden with an abundance of meat for grilling and carefully prepared side dishes. The families of the other trainees also gathered, filling the air with lively conversations and laughter.

Since his marriage, Se-joon's body had begun to swell, and it appeared as though he had gained weight. His relatives, seeing how hard he studied and worked, attributed his weight gain to the food he ate to sustain himself through sleepless nights. However, in hindsight, it seemed likely that his swelling was not a result of overindulgence but rather a sign of declining health.

During his time in Seoul, Se-joon's body remained swollen, and his face had grown unnaturally pale, as white as a sheet of paper. Colleagues at the hospital would often comment, "Is Dr. Choi in good health? Or is he gravely ill? When Dr. Choi walks down the hall, his face has this ghostly, whitish hue. What could it be?"

Yet no one, including his wife, Hwa-young, paid much attention to these remarks. She showed little concern for Se-joon's health, attributing his weight gain to the food she prepared, remarking, "Of course, it's because he's eating my cooking." But as previously mentioned, Se-joon had survived on just two lunch boxes a day, prepared by Hwa-young, for over a year.

When Se-joon finally emerged to greet Jae-joon and Jong-hee, they were shocked by his appearance. The rigorous training had left him gaunt and sunburned. Jong-hee, upon seeing her son, now unrecognizably thin and tanned, could not hold back her tears. She embraced him tightly, her heart breaking at the sight of his transformation.

Despite his weight loss and darkened skin, Se-joon's eyes shone brightly, revealing a newfound sharpness.

As Jong-hee busied herself preparing the food, Se-joon turned to Jae-joon and Bok-hee, his voice tinged with a mix of curiosity and concern.

Se-joon:

"Grandmother, Mother, and Jae-joon! Thank you for coming all this way. I've lost a lot of weight, haven't I? But tell me, have you heard anything from my wife?"

His words hung in the air, and when Jong-hee remained silent, Se-joon offered a sheepish smile and pressed further.

Se-joon:

"Mother, you might be wondering why I'm asking about Hwa-young first. The truth is... she hasn't sent me a single letter since I started training here in Yeongcheon. How could that be? I can't help but wonder if something has happened, something I don't know about.

Well, usually, after going through such grueling training, the only comfort and joy we have is receiving letters of encouragement. Hwa-young knows how much I love receiving letters. She's seen me pore over movie scripts for two years instead of watching the films themselves. She knows this about me, yet even after I wrote to her first, there was no reply.

Soon, my training will come to an end, and I'll be assigned somewhere new. But ... when I was living with Hwa-young, I never realized it, but being away from her here has given me time to reflect, and I've started to notice some troubling things.

At times, the thoughts are almost unbearable, and I find myself horrified by the limits of what a person can be.

Perhaps I've made a terrible mistake in choosing my partner. I'll tell you more about what I plan to do when I come home.

Everyone here receives letters from their loved ones, except me. I wrote to her, I called, but there's been no response. Three months is a long time... but even a few words from her, even if insincere, would have brought me some comfort. Yet, not a single letter has arrived..."

When the topic of letters came up, Jae-joon felt a pang of guilt. He hadn't written a single letter to his older brother, Se-joon. It was clear that Se-joon was probably waiting for a letter from his wife, Hwa-young, more than from anyone else.

Jong-hee was also unsettled by Se-joon's words because there were aspects of her daughter-in-law, Hwa-young, that she didn't like. Still, she made an effort to avoid acting like an overbearing mother-in-law toward Hwa-young as much as possible.

Jong-hee herself had endured a difficult married life in her mother-in-law's house, unbeknownst to others, under Bok-hee. As she quietly listened to Se-joon speak about Hwa-young, a sense of frustration welled up inside her, as if all her efforts had been in vain.

She couldn't shake the discomfort gnawing at her, thinking, *I should have played the role of mother-in-law more properly...*

The sudden anxiety that seized Jong-hee's heart was palpable. Se-joon, who had always been gentle and without complaint, now voiced concerns she had never imagined would come from him.

As they left the training ground, Jae-joon remarked, "Well, I suppose it's possible. Maybe sister-in-law has been very busy... But not even a single letter? I'm his brother, and she's his beloved wife. Why would she do that to him?"

Bok-hee and Jong-hee exchanged glances but remained silent, their minds clouded with unspoken worries. For once, they were at a loss for words.

After completing his training, Se-joon was unexpectedly assigned to a branch of the Uiryeong public health center. For someone with his qualifications, this was an ill-fitting placement, as such branches were typically reserved for recent medical graduates who had yet to earn their specialist credentials.

Se-joon, too, was disheartened by the situation. Yet, he was not the type to brood over such matters for long. He consoled himself, thinking, *I'll make the best of it here. At least the quiet will help my writing flow.*

Though Se-joon felt a pang of disappointment at the injustice, he decided to embrace the tranquility of rural life, seeing it as a welcome change from the chaos of Seoul. But beneath this resolve lay a deeper exhaustion—a weariness born from the unspoken tensions in his work and family life, most notably with his wife, Hwa-young.

Since Se-joon's move to Uiryeong, Hwa-young had scarcely spent more than a few days at home each week. "I'll be staying at a friend's place and going to school for lectures. You understand," she would say, remaining in Seoul.

Se-joon had no idea where she spent her nights in the city, and she visited their home in Uiryeong only once every week or two. Hwa-young taught a basic liberal arts subject at the university, a course typically scheduled to be taught over one or two days a week. Se-joon was well aware of her timetable, yet she seldom came home to Uiryeong, always finding an excuse to stay away.

When Se-joon was first posted to Uiryeong, he had imagined using the quiet of the countryside to clear his mind, complete his military service, and focus on his writing. Afterward, he planned to open a small private clinic in Gaegeum-dong, Busan, where Ki-hoon was making preparations for him.

However, Hwa-young's peculiar behavior began to gnaw at his peace of mind, planting seeds of doubt and unease. The wound in his heart, first opened by the absence of letters during his training in Yeongcheon, festered further when he overheard a disturbing conversation.

Once trust in a person begins to crumble, each suspicion gives birth to another, until the imagination is overwhelmed.

It all began when Se-joon first met the other men at the military training camp. As they exchanged stories, Se-joon casually mentioned to the trainee beside him, "My name is Choi Se-joon, and my wife is Jeon Hwa-young, a part-time lecturer in Biology at a university in Seoul."

One of the men, Kim, turned to him and asked,

Kim (trainee):

"Your wife, Hwa-young—did she grow up in Busan and attend a cram school in Seoul? I think I might know her."

Se-joon:

"Yes, that's possible. My wife and I are both from Busan. She graduated from B Girls' High School there and then studied at a cram school in Jongno, Seoul, before attending K University."

Kim responded with a curious smile. "What a small world," he remarked. "I never expected to hear about her here." Se-joon smiled in return, thinking, *Isn't it? Korea is such a small place.*

Two days later, as Se-joon stepped outside the training center for a drink of water, he overheard a conversation between some of the trainees. He recognized Kim's voice among them.

Kim:

"Hey, did you hear about Se-joon from Busan? I didn't want to say this in front of him, but I know Hwa-young all too well, how she used to be, at least. This place really is too small. That girl, Hwa-young ... well, to put it simply, she was quite the character. She's nothing like Se-joon, who's so serious and thoughtful. I can't imagine how those two ended up together."

At that moment, Se-joon stepped into view, and Kim, noticing him, quickly addressed him directly.

Kim:

"Se-joon, I'm sorry to bring this up, but it's all in the past now. You know what Jongno is like, right? When girls are out on their own at such a young age, away from their parents, who knows what they might get up to? But don't take this too seriously. Sometimes, when women get married, they change completely from how they were before. It's mostly for the better ... so don't misunderstand me."

Kim's words didn't carry any malice but rather an offhandedness, as if he were merely voicing a passing thought. Yet, Se-joon couldn't shake the feeling that there was a connection between Kim's words and something Hwa-young had once said.

It had been only three months into their marriage when she told him:

Hwa-young said,

"Se-joon, do you know why I chose you as my husband? You're so handsome—the kind of man who naturally attracts women. By marrying someone as good-looking as you, I can show you off, make you mine.

Besides, men who've dated many women often don't really understand women at all. I chose you because you're the kind of man who, having experienced many women, wouldn't care about his wife's past.

You know, I used to be quite the sensation. There wasn't a boy in Jongno who didn't know my name. Back then, who cared about jobs, academic backgrounds, or anything like that? When I was in the mood ... to have fun, all that mattered was that the guy was handsome and nice to me."

As she spoke, Hwa-young massaged her face with white cream, her once-flawless skin now faintly freckled, her words hanging in the air like a ghost from another time.

When Se-joon first met Hwa-young, he had noticed the dark freckles scattered across her face—marks that seemed out of place for someone her age. These blemishes gave her an appearance older than her years, but Se-joon did not let that alter his feelings. At the time, he simply assumed that the pressures of completing her two-year master's program and the challenges of living far from home had taken their toll.

Se-joon had only one brother, while Hwa-young was the only daughter among her siblings. As she had once remarked, Se-joon was popular with women, and he had indeed dated many. Yet, despite his experiences, he gradually came to realize that there were facets of women

—deep, fundamental aspects—that he had never fully understood.

After their marriage, Se-joon noticed a framed photograph of Hwa-young as a college freshman on her dressing table. In the picture, she looked bright and beautiful. He couldn't help but wonder, *When did those dark freckles begin to mar her face?*

As time passed and Hwa-young started staying out all night, rarely returning home, Se-joon's thoughts grew darker. He couldn't shake the suspicion that the freckles were not merely a natural occurrence but the result of something more troubling—perhaps the consequence of repeated physical and emotional stress.

His doubts about Hwa-young had begun to intensify from the time he was at the Yeongcheon training camp. This notion seemed to align with what he had overheard from Kim, a fellow trainee at the military training center.

Although Se-joon was reluctant to trust his own instincts—especially based on the passing words of someone he had only just met—he couldn't dismiss the feeling that Kim genuinely knew something about Hwa-young—something significant.

Se-joon had always been adept at deciphering the hidden meanings in others' words, but after that initial encounter, he avoided Kim. Despite sharing the same barracks, they didn't speak again. Se-joon feared hearing more unsettling truths about Hwa-young—truths that could deepen the already festering wounds in his heart.

Throughout the training period, there was no letter from Hwa-young. Whenever Se-joon found the time to call their home in Seoul, the house was always empty. On the rare occasion when he managed to reach her late at night, breaking the rules of the training camp, her voice on the other end was slurred and weary, betraying signs of inebriation.

Hwa-young:

"Oh, Se-joon? I wondered who it could be... Why are you calling at this hour? I'm exhausted ... I was planning to stay at a friend's house tonight, but something about her made me uneasy, so I decided to come home instead.

You know, I'm not the kind of woman who's easily swayed by intuition. Ho ho ... her husband wouldn't be able to resist me ... there's no man I can't catch.

Hey, Se-joon, if you've got nothing important to say, just hang up. I'm really tired!"

And with that, she hung up.

That was the only time he had managed to speak to her on the phone. Hwa-young neither wrote nor called, even though she could have reached out to Se-joon's family in Busan.

Gradually, Se-joon felt himself being drawn into a deep, inescapable pit of despair. During his time in Yeongcheon, his thoughts were consumed by a relentless inner monologue—a painful inquiry into the true nature of the woman he had married.

Even after being assigned to Uiryeong, Hwa-young's indifference toward him remained unchanged, compounding his sense of isolation.

By 1983, Korea was a nation in turmoil, with people whispering in hushed tones, hiding secrets from prying eyes. The new military regime that had seized power after President Park's assassination had consolidated its control, becoming the backbone of the Fifth Republic.

In mid-June of that year, Se-joon traveled to Seoul to meet his friends. He also sought to celebrate the upcoming publication of his poetry, which had been recommended by the esteemed poet Kim Yoon-sung for the July issue.

After gathering with his literary friends, Se-joon met up with his colleagues from the hospital, sharing conversations about the state of the world over drinks. Late into the night, he hailed a taxi, suddenly recalling the apartment in Jamsil where he and Hwa-young had lived for several years.

Their newlywed home had been in the Jamsil Jugong Apartments, but since Se-joon had not yet received the full deposit, a few of his belongings remained there. This time, as he was heading down to Uiryeong, he needed to collect the remaining deposit. It had been agreed between the landlord and Se-joon that all the belongings left in the apartment would be cleared out.

However, the night's heavy drinking had muddled his mind, and he mistakenly alighted from the taxi in an unfamiliar place. Whether he had given the driver the wrong destination or simply failed to remember it, he couldn't say. Sitting there in the unfamiliar surroundings, it took him a long while to regain his senses. When he finally did, he muttered to himself, "I've completely lost my bearings," and began walking aimlessly, unsure of where he was or where he was going.

Barely managing to find the bus stop, he sat down on the wooden bench and lifted his head. From somewhere, the faint light of dawn gently touched his forehead, as if offering a quiet greeting to the morning.

As Se-joon glanced at the signpost at the bus stop, the words "Garibong-dong" stood out in faded letters. His clothes were soaked with sweat and stained with dirt. Again, he muttered to himself, "Life is so hard," as a heavy weariness settled over him—a weariness that had never been there before.

As dawn began to break, casting a faint light on his shadow, Se-joon watched as tired workers and early risers gradually filled the buses. They boarded and departed for their destinations. He let several buses pass by, his thoughts heavy and slow. After a long while, he finally stood, took a heavy step forward, and boarded a bus that would take him back to the apartment in Jamsil.

7 a.m. The space where they had lived was silent, empty, void. Not a soul remained. That morning, he had resolved to meet Hwa-young at home,

intending to sort through his last belongings before leaving for Uiryeong.

Se-joon had recently noticed that whenever he drank, he would quickly succumb to a numbing haze. He waited in the vacant house, but Hwa-young never arrived. He couldn't fathom what was happening.

Eventually, he left the house and ordered a bowl of pork and rice soup, eating it in solitude. By noon, he called the assistant's office at the department where Hwa-young taught, but still, there was no word from her. He waited yet another day.

All Se-joon knew was that Hwa-young had unmistakably betrayed his heart. During the three days he spent in Seoul, Se-joon bitterly ruminated on the raw taste of betrayal, chewing over it again and again. At the same time, he tilted his head back, trying to steel himself—to become more rational, more detached.

In the end, Se-joon packed his belongings alone and went to the real estate office to inquire about the situation. The agent then asked him, "The wife came by two days ago and collected the deposit. Why? Haven't you met with her?" Se-joon was stunned. *The last vestige of hope I had clung to —that Hwa-young might still be my wife in some small way—vanished completely.*

Se-joon moved to a new environment in Uiryeong, hoping that the change might somehow bring about a change in Hwa-young's behavior. But deep down, he knew it was futile.

Looking back, ten days earlier, when Hwa-young had briefly visited Uiryeong, Se-joon had asked her about the deposit for their Seoul apartment. Se-joon:

"Honey, the lease deposit for our old apartment—if you're too busy, should I stop by and pick it up when I go to Seoul to meet my friends? Also, pack my things."

Se-joon had suggested. But Hwa-young responded with irritation.

Hwa-young:

"Se-joon, don't talk to me about the house. How much is that little money worth anyway? Hmph!"

Her words implied that it was only fair for her to handle it, given that more of the deposit had come from her family's funds. Se-joon felt a sting of anger but swallowed it. 'That money isn't what's important. I mentioned it just to try to lessen the burden a bit...'

With that thought, Se-joon simply gazed at Hwa-young's face. Silence, after all, could take on different meanings depending on who was interpreting it.

And after that, without offering any explanation, Hwa-young hastily gathered a few belongings and left their home in Uiryeong.

Se-joon had returned from Seoul to Uiryeong, and about two weeks later, on a rare Saturday evening, Hwa-young returned. When they finally faced each other again, Hwa-young unleashed yet another tirade about money. Hwa-young:

"Look, Se-joon, I'm dying inside, terrified that my friends might find out I'm stuck in this countryside. If you don't have enough money to keep up with me, don't even think about showing your face. Got it? Comparing my life to theirs is driving me mad. As long as you live like this, you're already dead to me."

Her words were cutting, merciless. It was clear that her heart had long since drifted away, beyond any hope of return. He could tell just by the feeling.

But Se-joon wanted to get his mother, Jong-hee's, consent first. At the very least, he decided to be honest with her about his relationship with Hwa-young.

Around mid-September of 1983, during *Chuseok* (Korean Harvest Festival — a major holiday in Korea, celebrated on the 15th day of the 8th month of the lunar calendar, during the full moon), Se-joon and Hwa-young both traveled to his parents' house in Busan, each coming from different places

—Hwa-young from Seoul and Se-joon from Uiryeong.

After the holiday rituals were over and only Jong-hee remained at home, Se-joon began to speak as evening approached.

"Mother, ... I think it's time for Hwa-young and me to divorce. I don't have the strength to continue living with her. There's no hope left between us, and after what happened in Yeongcheon, I can't bear the thought of staying with her. I believe Hwa-young feels the same. But I want your acceptance, Mother! Please, allow me to end this marriage."

As expected, Jong-hee reacted with fervor, her emotions boiling over. She refused to hear a single word from Se-joon, as if the proposed divorce between Se-joon and Hwa-young were her own—as if it mirrored the struggles between herself and Ki-hoon.

Since *Chuseok*, when Se-joon had first uttered the word "divorce," he had drowned himself in alcohol, day after day. He neither ate nor slept. 'Hwa-young, a woman who craved only physical pleasure, who worshipped money above all else—I could never comprehend how much wealth could possibly satisfy her insatiable desires.'

Hwa-young had done many things.

During *Chuseok*, Se-joon and Hwa-young remained at his parents' house in Busan, maintaining a veneer of normalcy. However, even though it was her in-laws' house, Hwa-young tormented Se-joon all night, barely letting him sleep. No matter how much Se-joon said he was tired, Hwa-young insisted on having her way. Se-joon, drained and desperate for rest, wished to sleep in a different room, away from Hwa-young, if only to catch a few hours of peaceful sleep.

But when he mentioned this, Jong-hee erupted in protest, preventing him from doing so. It seemed even the sanctuary of sleep was denied him in his own home. Night after night, Hwa-young, bare and unashamed, demanded that Se-joon satisfy her desires.

Se-joon became increasingly aware that, to Hwa-young, he was likely regarded merely as a sex machine and a money-providing machine.

Despite having no children, Hwa-young was still referred to as the "new bride" in Ki-hoon's household. Though three years had passed since their marriage, she was still expected to perform the role of a new bride during *Chuseok*, serving the family as a granddaughter-in-law. Upon arriving at her in-laws' house, under the watchful eyes of the elders, Hwa-young made an effort to appear helpful, bustling in and out of the kitchen, reading faces.

But by the second day, when she found herself alone while cleaning the table, her facade slipped. She tossed the dishcloth aside, her gaze drifting disdainfully from the room to the kitchen. She muttered something under her breath, smacked her lips in annoyance, and wore an expression of pure distaste.

Bok-hee, who had come to Ki-hoon's house in Busan for *Chuseok*, happened to witness this unguarded moment. Concealing her surprise, she entered the main room where Jong-hee sat alone and spoke to her.

"Jong-hee! Listen, your daughter-in-law, the one who lectures at a university—she's a different person inside and out. For all her education, she doesn't even know how to wear *beoseon* or tie the *jeogori* properly.

When I offered to help, she snapped, 'Who even wears these socks right anymore? And who in their right mind wears *hanbok* in this day and age?' She brushed me off as if it was nothing.

Let me tell you something while we're at it. No matter how much you may be Se-joon's mother, if you care for him even a little, you'd better be prepared. Stop worrying about what your daughter-in-law might think and take care of your son.

Look at him, suffering all day long, drinking just to muster the courage to get your approval. Se-joon, who was always so gentle, so obedient. Do you think he would lie there on the floor, groaning, his face unrecognizable, unless something was deeply wrong? He's drowning in his own sorrow, unable to rise above it, even with alcohol.

Don't you understand why Se-joon is acting this way? No one can predict what life has in store. No one knows. For Se-joon, who used to be so gentle, who would follow your every word without question — how bad must it be for him to lie there on the floor, his face clouded, groaning in pain?

Even though he can't handle his drink. You, of all people, should know how frail he is. You should be focused on saving your son first. A mother, of all people ... Tsk, tsk."

Jong-hee was not ignorant of these things. Yet, when it came to Se-joon's divorce, she had made a solemn vow to herself that she would never allow it. Because she saw herself as inferior to Ki-hoon, Jong-hee knew all too well how difficult her married life had been. And she knew all too well the pride-shattering and grueling ordeal it was for a woman to return to her parents' home after a failed marriage.

Jong-hee often imagined that Ki-hoon might have cast her aside long ago were it not for the weight of societal expectations, the silent pressure of '*Sambulgeo*.[72]' Remembering the harsh looks and veiled criticism from Bok-hee and her brothers-in-law, she resolved, *Never. I will not let a divorce stain this family. I've survived too much to allow that.*

To be honest, Jong-hee wasn't truly concerned about Se-joon and Hwa-young's marriage, nor was she trying to protect Hwa-young. Her real fear was that if Se-joon went through with the divorce, it would give her husband, Ki-hoon, a reason to consider divorce more acceptable — thus giving him an excuse to cast her aside.

In truth, Jong-hee was projecting the unresolved tension of her own troubled marriage onto her son, venting her frustrations with Ki-hoon by interfering in Se-joon's life.

Se-joon was a gentle son, one who had always listened to his mother with unwavering obedience, perhaps out of deep pity for her. Yet despite his kindness, Jong-hee, driven by stubborn pride, took advantage of him.

---

72) Refer to footnote 66) on page 454 of this book.

She knew all too well that Se-joon could never stand up to her. Determined not to let his resolve prevail, she made up her mind to thwart his will at any cost.

Until a child dies, do parents not realize that their child's life is irreplaceable? If the true worth of a person is only understood after they are lost, then it can be said that the parents are tragically ignorant.

No matter how much life may seem subject to God's will, a mother has no right to belittle the value of her child's existence. Once born into this world, his life belonged to no one but himself.

Hwa-young returned to Seoul on the third day after *Chuseok*. It seemed that Se-joon had resigned himself to abandonment, surrendering to despair. He scarcely touched food, and after more than fifteen days of relentless drinking, the consequences were inevitable.

Se-joon began to show signs of severe illness. By mid-October, after *Chuseok*, red abscesses erupted across his body, his temperature soared, and he was too weak to rise from his bed. Se-joon did not return to Uiryeong; instead, he continued to drown his agony in alcohol.

Jong-hee thought to herself, *It's useless to threaten me like this. Who do you think I am? No matter how much you drink, I will never grant permission for something like that. I've endured a harsh marriage and remained the wife of this house. Didn't the fortune-teller say I would someday become the wife of a Minister?*

I was determined to show him clearly that in this Choi family I married into, no man ever abandons his wife, no matter how difficult married life may be. I must make it clear that a man should never abandon his wife. Of course ... a man should never abandon a woman.

At the very least, Jong-hee should have faced the reality of what Hwa-young and Se-joon's marriage had become. It was unwise of her—a failure in her duty as a mother. She completely disregarded how much her son longed for her thoughtful and careful judgment.

Instead, she projected her own circumstances onto him, concerned only with maintaining the facade of Se-joon's marriage, as if nothing were amiss.

Ki-hoon, unable to bear Se-joon's suffering, sought an opportunity to talk to him and understand what was happening. But Ki-hoon was at a crossroads himself, his name listed as the next president of the university— a long-cherished dream.

Within days, he was appointed president, and on the day of his inauguration, the entire family gathered at the university auditorium. Ki-hoon was elated, consumed by the responsibilities and busy schedule that came with his new position. In the whirlwind of organizing his thoughts and meeting people, when Se-joon crossed his mind, he brushed it aside, thinking, *He's grown up; he'll manage.*

In the end, Se-joon, sensing his worsening condition, diagnosed himself with leukemia. It was only when Ki-hoon learned of the severity of his son's illness that he acted, sending Se-joon to a university hospital for a proper diagnosis. The doctors confirmed Se-joon's fears: acute myeloid leukemia. At the time, there was no definitive treatment.

Se-joon believed that if he stayed in a local university hospital, he might eke out another two to three years, even with his poor health.

However, Ki-hoon, perhaps feeling the weight of a father's duty even in his delayed realization, insisted on taking Se-joon to Seoul, believing that it was the least he could do for his son. He was adamant that Se-joon needed the best possible medical care, better than what was available in Busan. And so, following Ki-hoon's resolve, they decided to move Se-joon to Seoul.

This all unfolded shortly after Ki-hoon assumed the role of university president. Se-joon was diagnosed with acute myeloid leukemia. Around that time, he was admitted to Seoul St. Mary's Hospital in Gangnam, known as the first in Korea to use sterile treatment methods specifically for leukemia patients.

A facility specializing in myeloid leukemia treatment with newly introduced aseptic therapy — it was still the early days for such treatments in Korea.

Jong-hee tended to Se-joon alongside Hwa-young, but she couldn't stand the sight of her daughter-in-law. At the hospital, Hwa-young caused a commotion, weeping and clinging to the young medical staff as though Se-joon had already died. She played the role of the tragic, bereaved wife, seeking sympathy from those around her. Jong-hee, however, saw through her act, believing that Hwa-young was merely trying to garner attention from other men, exploiting Se-joon's illness. Jong-hee despised her for it.

Se-joon received the best care available at the hospital, but revealing the details of his treatment serves no purpose now.

Suffice it to say, Se-joon died on November 11, 1983, in that hospital, after enduring a series of painful procedures, including the removal of his lung, his body thoroughly ravaged. After nearly twenty days of enduring Hwa-young's presence, Jong-hee returned to Busan, her heart heavy with grief. It was the very afternoon that Se-joon had passed away.

Upon arriving home, she was met with more troubling news: Bok-hee had fallen on the porch in Sancheong, splitting her head open, and was now hospitalized at P University Hospital. Jong-hee went to visit her, only to be met with a mournful lament from Bok-hee.

"Oh, this old body should have been the one to go, yet my precious grandchild has left us first," she sighed loudly, ensuring that Jong-hee could hear her sorrowful words.

Jong-hee grew to resent Bok-hee even more for displaying such behavior. Regretting her foolishness in letting Se-joon slip away so easily, she locked herself in her room. As a mother who had lost her child, she withdrew into herself, festering in a prison of irreversible delusions, hatred, and sorrow. There was no doubt that losing her son, Se-joon, had left a profound impact on her.

Even though she had devoted her entire life to her husband, Ki-hoon, Se-joon had been her most reliable eldest son. Jae-joon had always felt distant, but not Se-joon. He was the son who understood her, who cared for her the most—the sensitive, intelligent one—and now he was gone.

She suddenly remembered the words of Master Kim, whom she had consulted when Se-joon entered college.

"This son is a Born Eldest Grandson, and the other son will be an Entrusted Eldest Grandson."

The burden one carries from birth and the one who eventually shoulders it may not be the same. Se-joon, born first, died first, leaving behind only the duty of being the Eldest Grandson.

Hwa-young, without attending Se-joon's first memorial service, gathered her belongings. She settled her finances, converting the deposit for the house in Uiryeong, as well as the ring and watch she had received during her wedding, into cash.

Up until then, she had spoken smoothly to her in-laws about resuming her abandoned plans to study in Germany—plans she had discarded even before marriage. Hwa-young said,

"Father, Mother, I've decided to go to Germany to pursue the studies I had planned before marrying Se-joon. But now, I'll be leaving alone, with a fresh start. I hope you can understand."

Fate works in mysterious ways. A brief marriage, a fleeting moment of anger and betrayal—sometimes that's all it takes. The bond between Se-joon and Hwa-young had brought him so much pain, yet in hindsight, perhaps that pain was short-lived. Was it a blessing, after all, that they never had children?

Hwa-young, on her part, seemed weighed down by the label of widowhood, her already drooping eyes perpetually cast downward, wearing a look of endless sorrow and resignation. For some reason, after Se-joon's death and before her departure to Germany, Hwa-young stayed at Ki-hoon's house in Busan. During her stay, she was often on the phone with her friends, seemingly glued to the receiver for hours on end.

Jong-hee overheard one of these conversations, where Hwa-young lamented,

"Did I really do anything so terribly wrong? If I had known things would end up like this, we should have packed our bags and gone our separate ways long ago. What a shame!"

But instead of anger at Hwa-young's words, Jong-hee felt only a growing frustration with her own situation.

"Just as that fortune-teller Kim said, I did become the wife of a National University president, in other words, the wife of a high Minister by old standards ... but now that I've lost the son who would have believed in me, my situation might become even more pitiful in the future."

She muttered to herself repeatedly.

With Se-joon, who had cared for and trusted her so deeply, now gone, Jong-hee felt a renewed sense of anxiety and fear. She feared she would remain nothing more than a wife with no worth in the eyes of Ki-hoon.

The day before Se-joon's death, he wrote with a feeble, trembling hand, struggling to hold the pen, as though he were a child once more. The letter he wrote was passed on to Jae-joon.

A Sensitive Soul

When I yearn to meet lost souls,
I become the faded purple of the rainbow,
Chasing our blue shower.
Falling naked, at least once,
As a star—neither life nor death—
I wish to meet you as an insect at the dawn of desire.

When I long to smell the living earth,
That hid millions of breaths in your letter,

I watch the sender
Or seek the worth of my name on the envelope.
With the cry of the earth's flowers at the soil's edge,
Blooming—
In the end, our sweat wets the wrist of the universe.

I long to smell it.
You, the true touch of death
Felt at the fingertips—so void and hollow!
Where is it that we now wish to meet
In a blue downpour, piercing the fiery arteries?

Even today, I summon the dead souls,
Meeting, yet not truly meeting,
Holding, yet sensing no scent—one by one.
Burning with a fever so intense it feels deadly.
My most beloved needle,
Its eye aches.

In the wake of Se-joon's death, his relatives, college friends, and medical colleagues gathered at the mortuary (*daecheong-maru* at Se-joon's house) to pay their respects. Jae-joon, unnoticed by the others, picked up one of Se-joon's old shoes, now left without an owner, and quietly tucked it away in a corner.

Se-joon was gone, and Jae-joon was now the only one left. He continued his work at the research institute of a prestigious steel company in Busan. In his quiet moments, Jae-joon found himself wondering whether Hwa-young, who had disappeared without a word, would ever return to this house after completing her studies in Germany.

Years passed without any contact from her until, one day, a letter arrived for Ki-hoon. "Please help me," she wrote. "I'm in need of financial assistance to complete my doctorate." Despite everything, Ki-hoon felt compelled to send her a substantial sum each month, driven by a lingering sense of duty and affection for his late son, Se-joon.

Though Ki-hoon's responsibilities as university president kept him busy, he found moments of solitude where he would light his pipe and lose himself in thought.

As the smoke curled around him, he pondered whether it was a blessing or a curse that Se-joon had left no children behind. Only Se-joon could have truly known how deeply Hwa-young had hurt him. Se-joon had closed his eyes forever without revealing to anyone but Jong-hee the full extent of his pain.

That secret now weighed heavily on Jong-hee — another burden she would carry alone.

31

Nemo Deum Vidit — No One Has Ever Seen God

1990–2001: Busan, Seoul, and Masan
—Hope and Conviction

Yo-han was not surprised when Soo-gon confessed about his birth mother, as though he were seeking absolution. A subtle clue had already hinted at the tension Jin-ok, his grandmother, always felt when addressing her son, Soo-gon.

To most children, a mother like Jin-ok might not have posed such a challenge. Of course, a wise mother refrains from speaking too freely in front of her child, especially as that child grows older, attains a high position in government, and is esteemed for their noble character. Yet Jin-ok's behavior toward Soo-gon was far more restrained than mere respect; it was the behavior of a mother who was constantly on edge, troubled by the fear of losing her son's affection.

After hearing his father's confession, Yo-han naturally began to talk about how he had fully decided to pursue a career in journalism and how he would never choose to take the bar exam in the future. Soo-gon, emphasizing his words, said, "I trust your decision."

This trust meant that Yo-han no longer had to prepare for the bar exam—a path he had never truly desired. He had come to understand that honesty between them was the easiest way to connect on a deeper level. From that moment forward, Yo-han resolved to be completely transparent with Soo-gon and Hye-young, sharing everything with them.

Years had passed since Yo-han had graduated from college. As he walked down the darkened street, the sound of Christmas carols floated from store to store. When he looked up at the sky, he noticed an electronic signboard through the gray clouds, announcing "Christmas Grand Festival 1990" above a department store.

Yo-han sighed unconsciously, murmuring to himself, "I should hurry up and settle down..." The sky looked as though it was about to snow, its expression furrowed in anticipation.

Yo-han sat by the bus window, flipping through a book of potential interview questions, carefully selecting those most likely to appear. Just then, a seven-seater van suddenly overtook the bus from behind, speeding past with surprising swiftness.

The bus driver, determined to catch up, blared the horn and shouted angrily, accelerating in pursuit. Yo-han closed his book and turned his attention to the van. Before long, both vehicles found themselves side by side, coming to a simultaneous halt at a red light on the wide boulevard ahead.

As the bus came to a stop, Yo-han finally allowed himself a moment of relief, shifting his gaze back to his workbook. However, a sudden and intense feeling washed over him, as if a pair of eyes were piercing through him. The gaze was sharp, cold, and unwavering, emanating from one of the women in the van.

"Oh! My sister, Mi-young!"

The realization struck him like lightning.

Without a second thought, Yo-han sprang from his seat, his voice rising in urgency. Yo-han:

"Driver, please drop me off here! Hurry, please! I'm sorry!"

he pleaded, his desperation evident.

The bus driver cast a brief glance at him and replied in a gruff tone,

Bus driver:

"What? Don't you see I could endanger all the passengers because of that car? That van driver must be on something, a real lunatic!"

That was all the driver said.

Despite his protests, Yo-han's frantic knocking on the door eventually convinced him to let him off the bus. As Yo-han disembarked, he could barely make out the van speeding away in the opposite direction.

Yo-han:

"Oh, Mi-young... That had to be Mi-young. Should I go to the police? But I don't even know the license plate number... What should I do?"

Nemo Deum Vidit — No One Has Ever Seen God · 613

He muttered to himself, panic creeping into his voice. Passersby threw curious glances at him but continued on their way, leaving him to wrestle with his dilemma alone.

A Bible verse he had read that morning suddenly flashed in his mind:

Psalms 69:8
I have become a stranger to my brethren,
an alien to my mother's children.

It could have been a trick of the light, a mere illusion. Yet, those eyes and eyebrows that had been staring intently at Yo-han—they were unmistakably Mi-young's.

How could he not recognize the face of the sister he had spent fifteen years of his life with? The smiling, half-moon eyebrows of the woman sitting in the back seat of the black van, visible through the window, bore the most striking resemblance between Yo-han and Mi-young.

He had gotten off the bus, but when he checked his watch, it was already 8:35. Even if he hurried, he knew there was no way he would make it to the interview on time. Frustrated, Yo-han called his home in Masan and then tried his father's workplace, but both lines were busy. "I really need to get a personal cell phone," he muttered to himself, realizing how rapidly communication was evolving.

He decided to send a message to Soo-gon via beeper, adapting to the changing times. Yo-han switched buses and returned to his rented room, resigning himself to attending another interview at a different newspaper in two days. It was almost 11 a.m. when Soo-gon finally called Yo-han's landlord.

Yo-han noticed that his father's voice was unusually weak—a stark contrast to his usual tone. Soo-gon:

"Yo-han! I heard you were supposed to have an interview at the broadcasting company today... What happened?

But, Yo-han ... I just received some terrible news. Your sister, Mi-soon, was in a serious car accident this morning while returning to Seoul after attending a memorial service at her in-laws' last night.

Your mother has already prepared to head to the bus station to go to Seoul, and by now, she's probably on her way there.

Yo-han, are you okay? Oh ... oh ... why did this have to happen..."

Yo-han:

"Dad, how ... an accident? Is Mi-soon okay?"

His voice trembled with fear.

Soo-gon:

"I don't know much yet ... I only got a call from the police station.

After your interview, go to the hospital where Mi-soon is as soon as your mother arrives in Seoul. I'm going to the church with your grandmother and your mother's father to pray.

Did you finish your interview already? I remember it was supposed to be at nine this morning."

Yo-han:

"No, Dad, it seems like that broadcasting company isn't the right fit for me, so I'm planning to go for interviews at other places. I've already passed the written exams.

But, Dad ... is something serious happening with Mi-soon? I ... I'm fine, really. Earlier, I just wanted to check in on how the family was doing, so I sent a beep and called you. I'll contact you again after I meet with Mom and learn more about Mi-soon's situation.

By the way, do you know which hospital Mi-soon was taken to? Oh, I guess we'll have to wait for Mom to let us know...

Dad, stay strong. I'll be in touch again soon."

Soo-gon:

"Yo-han, I think they mentioned which hospital, but I can't recall right now. The police said one person was killed and another badly injured.

Your mother will contact you once she's in Seoul. Lately, I've been forgetting things right after I hear them. Take care of yourself. I'm planning to retire soon and move back to our old house in Masan... Maybe we'll receive some news there, too."

Yo-han:

"Dad, let's not dwell on Mi-young for now. She's probably out there somewhere, just facing difficult circumstances. If she's alive, there's always a chance we'll see her again. So let's stay hopeful.

Don't move back to the old house in Masan just yet. Wait until you hear something about Mi-soon from Seoul. And don't worry, I'll get us all cell phones soon. I'll make sure you and Mom have one too.

Try not to worry too much, just hang in there."

After ending the call, Soo-gon stepped out of the building and watched a flock of birds soar across the sky. His life felt as fragile as a blade of grass drifting in the wind.

Psalms 103:15,16
As for man, his days are like grass;
he flourishes like a flower of the field;
For the wind passes over it, and it is gone,
and its place knows it no more.

As these verses ran through his mind, the ground beneath his feet seemed to soften, as if turning into a sponge. He recalled how, ever since Mi-young's disappearance, there had been no distinction between day and night for him. Soo-gon reread a passage he often turned to.

Psalms 19:2,3
Day to day pours forth speech,
and night to night declares knowledge.

There is no speech, nor are there words;
their voice is not heard.
Psalms 104:29
When you hide your face, they are dismayed;
when you take away their spirit, they die
and return to their dust.

Jong-hee received a call from Soo-gon.

Soo-gon:

"Ma'am, how have you been?" His voice cracked with emotion. For several minutes, he could do nothing but sob quietly.

Jong-hee had only returned to Korea from Japan yesterday, along with Ki-hoon. She had been delighted to speak Korean again after months of using only Japanese and had been curious about Soo-gon's situation.

After completing his term as president of PNU, Ki-hoon became a professor of law at Kyushu National University in Japan in 1988. Then, starting in 1990, he worked as a professor of law at a private university in the region, with a contract to retire there.

This private university was well known for its humanities department in Japan. Professors in its law department were eligible to obtain international lawyer certification. Ki-hoon frequently traveled between Korea and Japan, balancing his work as an international lawyer. Whenever Jong-hee stayed in Japan with Ki-hoon, she deeply missed her Korean-speaking relatives. That's why Soo-gon's call brought her even more joy.

After a few minutes, Soo-gon managed to control his sobbing and continued speaking. His voice was thick with despair.

"Ma'am, why does this keep happening to me? I just heard a few days ago that Yo-han had passed the newspaper exam. But ... this morning, Yo-han vanished in the middle of Seoul ... I'm losing my mind. I really wish I could disappear, too. I just can't handle this."

The words "Yo-han disappeared" echoed in Jong-hee's mind, but she couldn't fully grasp their meaning. It wasn't until she heard Soo-gon's continued sobbing that the gravity of the situation began to sink in.

Yo-han, who was so intelligent and sociable, had always been the one Bok-hee had pinned her hopes on to restore the Jeong family's fortunes. It had already been eighteen years since Mi-young was lost. The time lost since 1975—that stagnant clock—now pointed to 1993.

Three years ago, the youngest daughter, Mi-soon, had been in a car accident. Her mother-in-law had passed away, and Mi-soon remained in a coma. They had heard that only the baby she was holding and her husband in the driver's seat had survived unscathed.

And now, Jeong Yo-han ... Soo-gon's son, Mi-young's brother, and the bright, smiling face of hope, was dead.

What kind of cruel fate was this?

Speechless, Jong-hee simply held the phone to her ear, listening to Soo-gon's voice without uttering a word.

Soo-gon continued:

"Ma'am, Yo-han was on his way to work this morning, covering the newly elected president, when he collided with a massive oil truck in the heart of Seoul. The impact was so severe that he disintegrated completely, right there in the air.

We can't even find his body—it's all gone, consumed by flames.

In that inferno, Yo-han was burned and turned to ash in an instant. How can this be? I can't even bear to tell anyone ... I just needed to talk to you. Hye-young is out of her mind, sitting by Mi-soon's bedside in the hospital right now.

Ah! Why is this happening to my family?"

As Jong-hee listened to Soo-gon's account, an overwhelming pain coursed through her body, causing her teeth to chatter involuntarily. Her molars throbbed as if they were being ripped from her gums, and a heavy ache settled in her chest.

She clutched the phone tightly, but at some point, the line had gone dead. Yet, in that silence, the tears she thought had dried up long ago—since Se-joon's death—began to flow uncontrollably, making it hard for her to keep her eyes open.

When Ki-hoon entered the house, Jong-hee quickly relayed what had happened to Soo-gon.

Ki-hoon, the problem-solver of the family, always took charge of difficult situations—not just because he was the eldest grandson, but because it was in his nature. Yet this time, with Yo-han gone, vanished into thin air ... there was nothing anyone could do. He had no choice but to accept Jong-hee's words as the bitter truth.

Soo-gon, who had always been the apple of his mother Bok-hee's eye, had hoped for great things from his son, Yo-han, whose brilliance was undeniable.

To Ki-hoon, it was tragic that a gifted child like Yo-han had chosen a career as a newspaper reporter. In Ki-hoon's mind, if there were both journalists and judges or prosecutors, the latter held a higher status.

Ki-hoon mused aloud,

"A child enters this world through the lifeline of a parent, yet the journey to the afterlife is one that cannot be controlled by human hands.

Se-joon, Yo-han ... if only they had stayed with us longer... To a parent, a child is like a protective fence, a sanctuary. But why did these bright, gifted children leave so soon?

One barely reached thirty, and the other thirty-five, before returning to the earth. How heartless they were to leave us so early."

As Jong-hee watched Ki-hoon, she found herself grappling with the unsettling thought that sending Se-joon away had somehow been easier than facing Yo-han's sudden death.

Those days ... Jong-hee recalled the time when Se-joon lay in the hospital, groaning in pain. He had wasted away to nothing but skin and bones, unable to eat, unable to even lift a pen with his frail arms. Yet, despite his suffering, Se-joon would always gaze longingly at the manuscript paper and pen beside him.

As time passed, a thin beard began to grow on his gaunt face. Describing Se-joon's unshaven face as "dirty," Hwa-young had trimmed his beard with the small scissors she normally used to clean her nails.

The act, seemingly trivial, became catastrophic.

In Se-joon's sterile environment, where every precaution was taken to prevent infection, the bacteria introduced by those scissors caused a severe infection. Ultimately, he had to have a lung removed to drain the pus.

Every aspect of his life had to be as sterile as possible, yet she had used those same nail scissors to shave the beard of a patient confined to a sterile room...

But why, Jong-hee wondered, shaking her head as a sharp pain split through her temples, *Why am I thinking about Se-joon when I just heard about Yo-han?*

In 1988, Bok-hee closed her eyes for the last time after years of suffering from severe arthritis and other ailments of old age. At her funeral, Soo-gon and Hye-young forced smiles as they expressed their desire to see their youngest daughter, Mi-soon, married soon, so they could hold a grandchild in their arms.

'I understand their feelings,' Jong-hee thought.

'After losing a child, no pleasant thoughts or cherished memories remain. The joys of the world, the happiness ... they all disappear...

How had Hong-seon, my grandfather-in-law, endured his life?

How had Lady Kim, my grandmother-in-law, and Lady Hwang, the matriarch of the New House, spent their years after such losses?

My mother-in-law, Bok-hee, had many children, and perhaps because it was her daughter and not her son who passed first, the depth of her sorrow wasn't as visible to me.

But is there a difference between losing a daughter and losing a son? Does that sorrow manifest differently in a parent's heart?'

Jong-hee felt her thoughts, like wet paper—heavy and unable to unfold.

Soo-gon sat alone in a corner of the church, his thoughts heavy and sorrowful. *My treasure, all my hopes, my son—he was the very reason I lived. Now, at the tender age of thirty-five, he has turned into a flame, as if carried away by a fleeting wind, only to vanish in a blaze.*

Not a trace of ash remains, all of him has been scattered to the wind.

He had heard that Yo-han was on his way to work for his first official assignment when the tragedy struck. Until then, Yo-han had been just a trainee, but after years of searching for his place in the world, it seemed he had finally found his path.

Was it fate?

Soo-gon had believed that his bright, gifted son was finally ready to settle into his life's calling. Now, there was no sign left that Yo-han, his intelligent, vibrant son, had ever existed.

When was he my little boy? Soo-gon wondered, his heart aching.

When was it that he lay in my arms, smiling, reaching out to touch my bearded chin with those tiny hands?

And now, after leaving so suddenly, there's nothing left?

How am I supposed to go on living?

When Mi-young disappeared, Soo-gon, as her father, had tried to keep her memory alive, even if only as faint as a spent matchstick, no longer able to ignite.

But now, Yo-han had become the fuel for an immense fire.

The searing heat and the pain that must have been Yo-han's last sensations were now burning throughout Soo-gon's own body.

Is there nothing left for me? he asked himself, grief-stricken.

'I remember Yo-han laughing at three months old, his tiny hand tickling my palm, his laughter light and buoyant like a balloon.

Those smiling half-moon eyebrows, that joyful face...

If only, as a baby myself in silk *beoseon*, I could have held my birth mother's hand just once and brought her happiness...

Oh! Delusions, just delusions again...'

Mi-young had disappeared, but that was not the end of Soo-gon's trials. The burden of suffering seemed deeply embedded in his fate, hidden away, waiting to surface. Yes, Soo-gon had thought he had endured enough pain because of Mi-young.

But the agony that befell Soo-gon and Hye-young did not stop.

It didn't end with Mi-soon lying in a hospital bed, trapped in a coma.

And then, there was Yo-han...

Yo-han's body had disintegrated into the air, leaving nothing behind. His physical form, reduced to dust, had scattered in the wind. Soo-gon clung to his son's memory, holding a funeral with nothing but Yo-han's name.

Months had passed since Yo-han's tragic death, yet Mi-soon remained trapped in her coma. How long would it be before she returned to them — if ever?

The doctors offered little hope, something Hye-young had heard countless times over the past three years. Despite this, she continued to keep vigil by Mi-soon's bedside. Soo-gon's overwhelming sense of guilt and self-loathing gnawed at him. The thought of driving something sharp into his chest, letting the blood flow endlessly, crossed his mind again and again. Only by doing so, he believed, could he perhaps find even a sliver of forgiveness from Hye-young and Jin-ok.

Two women visited the hospital where Hye-young was tending to Mi-soon. They introduced themselves as the daughters of Nam-gil, the wife of Choi Lee-seop, who was related to Hye-young's husband's aunt, Bok-hee of Sancheong.

Living in Seoul, they said they couldn't help but visit after hearing the news about Yo-han and Mi-soon. One of the women was a middle school teacher from Busan, while the other had recently retired after a career as a nurse. They shared that Nam-gil's only son, Ki-hwan, had passed away suddenly from liver cancer the previous year. Ki-hwan, who had been a section chief at a company called Jeiljedang, had left behind a considerable fortune. However, the women told Hye-young that Ki-hwan's wife had squandered most of it through an affair.

As they prepared to leave the hospital, they offered Hye-young a few words of encouragement, saying, "Stay strong." From their conversation, Hye-young gleaned that, despite their own losses, these women had not suffered the death of their children as she had. This alone made Hye-young feel a twinge of envy.

As they exited the hospital, the two women whispered to each other.

Ho-jin (Ki-hwan's third eldest sister, the middle school teacher):

"*Eonni*, what do you think about Soo-gon's family in Masan? Why is life so hard for them?

Hye-young, who is caring for Mi-soon, and Soo-gon—they're such good people, never speaking ill of others. What's happening?

And, by the way ... which university did your eldest son graduate from? I heard your second son got into the College of Education."

Hee-jin (Ki-hwan's second eldest sister, former nurse):

"Hey, keep your voice down. We're in a hospital ... and you know how many people I know here. Let's discuss this outside."

Ho-jin:

"Relax, no one here knows us. We're in Seoul, not some small countryside town. People are too busy with their own lives to worry about others.

But really, don't you think it's easier to live with your children if you're not married? I told you not to get involved in secret, illegal marriages, didn't I?

Now, even though you've got two grown sons, and maybe you think everything's fine, the world still doesn't see it that way."

Hee-jin:

"Ho-jin, have you ever wondered what my life was like in Germany?"

Ho-jin:

"Of course, I'm grateful for the education I received thanks to the money you sent. And I wouldn't have even known you were one of the nurses dispatched to Germany[73].

Hee-jin:

"That's why I don't talk about it much, even to my own sister. You wouldn't understand what it was like to go to a foreign country and endure the hardships I faced there. Who knows the sacrifices I made during those years in Germany? The Korean government sent me there to support our family and pay for your and Ki-hwan's education.

If not for my sacrifices, would our family have relied solely on our eldest sister's help to finish college? My brother-in-law was so stingy, it was nearly impossible to get any financial support from him.

When I met my husband in Germany, I had no idea he was already married. He was exhausted and worn out, just like I was. We needed each other.

I was lonely and struggling every day... When I returned to Korea with a young baby and a five-year-old son, I tried to raise them discreetly, away from prying eyes. We shed countless tears of blood, trying to keep our heads above water.

As you mentioned, the world wasn't kind to us. But now, things have

---

[73] Nurses dispatched to Germany: Between 1966 and 1976, the Korean government sent 10,000 nurses to West Germany as part of an overseas manpower export initiative to tackle unemployment and earn foreign currency. Alongside the nurses, 18,899 miners were also sent. Many of these workers were highly educated and played a crucial role in helping Korea overcome its economic hardships. German society treated these dispatched workers exceptionally well. In 2020, a law was enacted to honor the miners, nurses, and nurse aides who had worked in Germany.—Summarized by the author based on Naver materials.

changed. My husband has finally come clean to his family, and when our second son graduates from college, he'll find a good job. As for our eldest, university wasn't the right fit for him, so he's learning to be an auto mechanic now. He's much happier with that than he was studying to be an electrician.

By the way ... Ho-jin, have you heard anything about our mother's estate since she passed? Any hidden property or anything like that?"

Ho-jin spoke with a touch of bitterness.

"Are you really asking about Mother as if you don't know? Sure, she said she put us through school, but even in her old age, she painted her lips red and spent time with old men. She borrowed money from local women and squandered it all on opening a restaurant, a meat place, I think. In the end, she left behind quite a bit of debt.

Our eldest sister somehow managed to cover it. She married a North Korean man, miserly and much older ... and endured a difficult life. But at least she didn't struggle financially like we did. I wonder how she felt inside?"

Ho-jin sighed before continuing.

"Now that I think about it, we've led quieter lives compared to some of our other cousins, haven't we? Since I came all the way to Seoul this time, you should visit Busan next. When you come, let's stop by our brother Ki-hoon's place. He's a professor at a private university in Japan, and he visits Busan from time to time before heading back.

Does that mean sister-in-law Jong-hee is lucky? No, not really! Her first son died, so I can't say she's had it easy.

Anyway, see you in Busan next time. I'm heading to Seoul Station to catch the Saemaul train. We'll be in Busan in four and a half hours. The world's really come a long way, hasn't it?

Well, I'm off."

Children are not important just because they care for their parents in old age. As Ki-hoon often said, a child is like a thread that connects a couple, serving as a protective fence around them. If it weren't for the title of daughter-in-law, Jong-hee might not have been able to care for her mother-in-law, Bok-hee, at home for so many years.

She spent nearly 40 years with Bok-hee, fulfilling her role as a daughter-in-law to the best of her ability. Jong-hee believed that simply living together and facing each day meant that older parents and their children were fulfilling their duty.

In Korea, a daughter-in-law was often referred to as a "slave without a document." Yet, Jong-hee would often remind herself, "That slave is better than a daughter, who is no longer considered family after marriage."

And she often said,

"Convention holds more power than blood."

By this, she meant that a daughter-in-law, bound by the laws of custom, cares for her mother-in-law more diligently than a daughter by blood ever would. Come to think of it, Jong-hee had become someone who deeply understood the power of social conventions.

However, when it came to parents and children, the relationship couldn't be defined by blood or law alone. Each person is born with their own fate, each following their own path from the start.

Isn't that right?

Sometimes, *as we grow older, we may wish to untangle ourselves from the relationships bound by marriage and convention.*

Jong-hee came to believe that the desire to shed the burdens of familial and social ties naturally arises with age. Whether bound by convention or blood, she found it difficult and exhausting to maintain strong, enduring relationships. Perhaps part of the reason was her own declining concentration.

She often felt that she lacked the physical and mental strength, as well as the perseverance, to keep these connections intact.

'In my younger days, the chains that bound me were strong, but as they slowly weaken like a fragile web, old age and illness will inevitably find me, and my life will flicker out.

When that time comes, even the bond between Se-joon and me, he who was my child in this life ... will truly vanish.

I am such a frail mother.'

Jong-hee sighed deeply at the thought, a habit she had developed since Se-joon's passing.

One day, Ho-jin and Hee-jin visited Jong-hee's house in Busan. As they conversed, Hee-jin began speaking about her son with a hint of pride, almost as if she were boasting. Yet, Jong-hee refrained from asking when Hee-jin had gotten married. She already knew the story from her youngest sister-in-law, Ki-seon.

For Jong-hee, what mattered more was that Hee-jin had children and had raised them well, regardless of whether the marriage had been formal or not. While the institution of marriage was significant, what truly mattered was building a family and living together. Moreover, there was no denying the profound importance children held within a marriage. Jong-hee considered it a blessing that Hee-jin had two sons.

Later, Jong-hee went out to have dinner with Hee-jin and Ho-jin, who had come to visit. These days, much like her neighbors, Jong-hee preferred not to cook at home, especially after returning from Japan. The three women chatted about people they knew from Sancheong, but soon each drifted into her own thoughts. As they walked to eat, they wandered off separately, lost in thought.

Jong-hee occasionally wondered, 'What if Se-joon had had a child?' But she had never voiced this thought to Ki-hoon. *What would remain for them as they aged, when all their children were gone and the intense passion between them as husband and wife had faded?* She couldn't help but question the nature of their relationship—had they ever truly been in love as a couple?

As she walked with Hee-jin and Ho-jin, Jong-hee murmured to herself, "In the end, I will be left alone."

The place they chose for dinner was a Chinese restaurant, where Jong-hee ordered a couple more dishes than they had initially planned. Despite their age and the inevitable bloating that came with overeating, they joked, "Can we really eat this much when our digestion isn't what it used to be?" Yet, they enjoyed the meal thoroughly.

As they left the restaurant, Jong-hee mentioned that Soo-gon's daughter had been in a car accident and was now in a coma. Since the two women had already visited the hospital, they simply clicked their tongues and remained silent on the matter.

Ho-jin sighed and remarked,

"Soo-gon and his wife were always devout believers, passionate about their faith. When they were dating in Masan, their friends would tease them, saying, 'These days, the church is just a place for young people to meet and date.' When the church bells rang to announce the start of worship, they'd joke, 'Ah, the love bells are ringing! Pretty Soo-gon and Hye-young, hurry up and get to church.'

But what does it matter? In the end, they haven't had much luck. What's the point of having children who are praised for their intelligence and academic success if life doesn't end well? A person needs to finish well."

As she spoke, Ho-jin pouted, her words echoing what she had heard from fellow teachers who had transferred from Masan. Hearing this, Jong-hee was reminded of the expression Nam-gil often wore as she observed Ho-jin's demeanor.

Hye-young prayed fervently each day in the hospital room where she kept vigil over Mi-soon. She had resolved never to give up on her daughter, no matter the circumstances.

In the car accident, Mi-soon's husband had been driving, with his mother seated in the back. His mother died instantly, while Mi-soon, seated in the front passenger seat, was trapped—her lower body crushed by the twisted metal. Her legs were paralyzed, and even if she emerged from the coma, she was certain to be paraplegic.

Their infant son, whom Mi-soon had cradled tightly in her arms, was now being raised by his grandaunt in her husband's family home. Miraculously, Mi-soon's husband escaped with only minor bruises and was otherwise unharmed.

Every day, Hye-young found it almost unbearable to see Mi-soon's husband in the hospital room. For three years, he had visited nearly every day. But Hye-young knew that, eventually, his visits would become less frequent, and in the end, it would be just Mi-soon and Hye-young left alone. Their son would be raised by his father, but Hye-young could not bring herself to tell Mi-soon's husband to stop coming. That was a decision only he could make.

Like her husband, Soo-gon, Hye-young wrestled with her faith in God, questioning what she could have done to bring such suffering upon her children. After losing Mi-young, her faith had been shaken to its core.

Thirteen years after Mi-young's disappearance, she had managed to rekindle a small flame of hope. Mi-soon had married, just as Hye-young and Soo-gon had wished, and for a time, Hye-young believed that hope had been restored.

But now, there was no Mi-young. No Yo-han.

Was Mi-soon truly still with her, simply because she wasn't dead?

Hye-young knew that as long as Soo-gon was alive, she, too, had to continue living. To give up on Mi-soon would be to give up on herself— and on her God. Though she feared that the embers of hope might soon be extinguished, she resolved to hold on with all her strength.

Hye-young murmured to herself, "Can I dare to hope again?

Psalms 39:2-3
I was mute and silent,
I held my peace to no avail;
my distress grew worse,
my heart became hot within me,
As I mused, the fire burned;
then I spoke with my tongue:

Psalms 39:7
And now, LORD, for what do I wait?
My hope is in you.

Five months after Yo-han's passing, Hye-young remained by Mi-soon's side in the hospital. One day, she received a call from a young woman. "Hello? Who is this?" Hye-young asked.

Joon-mi:

"Hello, are you Yo-han's mother? I'm not sure how to explain over the phone, but I'm planning to visit the hospital soon. I'll explain everything when I arrive."

Not long after, a young woman entered the hospital room. As soon as Hye-young saw her, she studied the woman's face closely.

Hye-young:

"Oh, you must be the girl ... I've heard about you. You're Jong-seok's sister, Yo-han's friend, aren't you?"

With a shy nod, the young woman, Joon-mi, stepped forward. She was visibly pregnant, her belly already somewhat swollen. Without realizing it, a smile spread across Hye-young's face.

"Oh, God, You've given me another chance. Thank You, God! Thank You!" she silently cried out.

It turned out that Joon-mi and Yo-han had secretly gotten engaged without their parents' knowledge. They had planned to visit their families and share the news after Yo-han received his first paycheck as an official reporter. Overcome with emotion, Hye-young fell to her knees, clasping her hands together in prayer.

Hye-young:

"Lord! It is choice, existence, feeling, and conviction. You are the first to breathe life, and even if that breath is taken away by Your hands..."

At that moment, a brilliant, golden light suddenly shone down on the spot where Hye-young knelt, and from within it came a clear voice. Overwhelmed, she found herself unable to suppress the sound that surged through her.

Voice:

"You do not know what you seek.
Can you drink the cup I offer?

As they say,
'We can do it.'

As I say,
'You will drink my cup. But to sit at my right and left is not mine to grant, but for those whom my Father has prepared.'

No one has ever seen Me (Nemo Deum Vidit)[74]*,*
But I am always with you."

Eight years later, in 2001, Mi-soon awoke from her coma. Though

---

74) The book title *Nemo Deum Vidit* is a transcription of a Latin phrase. It is originally a shortened form of *Deum Nemo Vidit Umquam*, which means "No one has ever seen God," a verse from John 1:18. The author intended to emphasize "the existence of God (or divinity)" in a paradoxical yet more affirmative sense through this passage.

confined to a wheelchair, she was able to manage most tasks at home. She was pregnant with her second child and remained married to her husband. Meanwhile, Yo-han's son grew up healthy and strong, embraced by the love of Hye-young and Soo-gon.